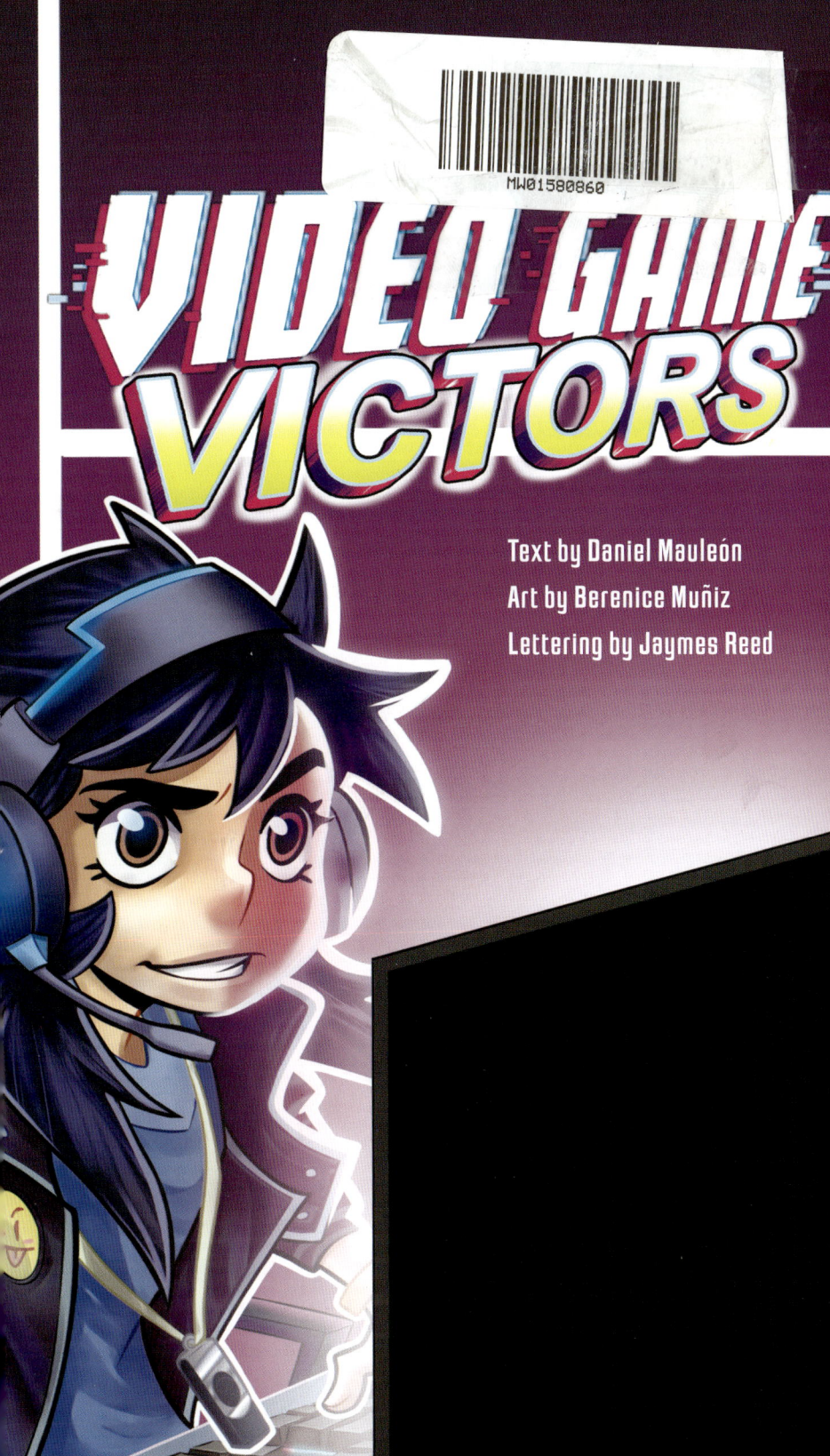

VIDEO GAME VICTORS

Text by Daniel Mauleón
Art by Berenice Muñiz
Lettering by Jaymes Reed

CHOOSE YOUR CHARACTER
DARK ELF
SPARTAN
SPELLCASTER
ROGUE
ARCHER
VALKYRIE
KNIGHT
ORC
WARRIOR CAT
BABY DRAGON
VIKING
WIZARD
HEALER
DANCER
MAGE
PRINCESS
SPELLCASTER / VALENTINA
MAGE / BENNETT

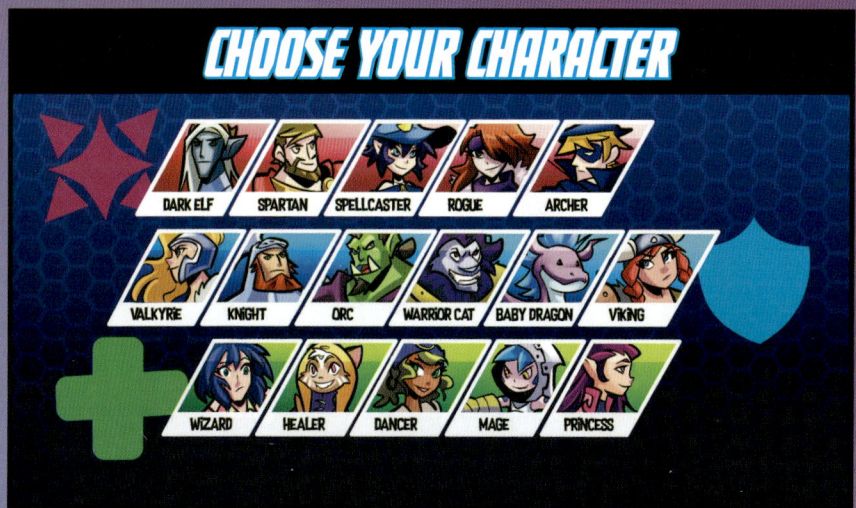

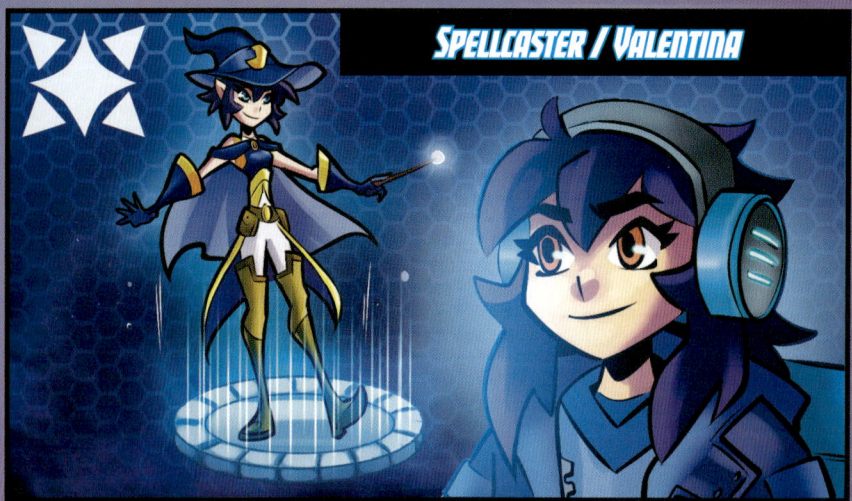

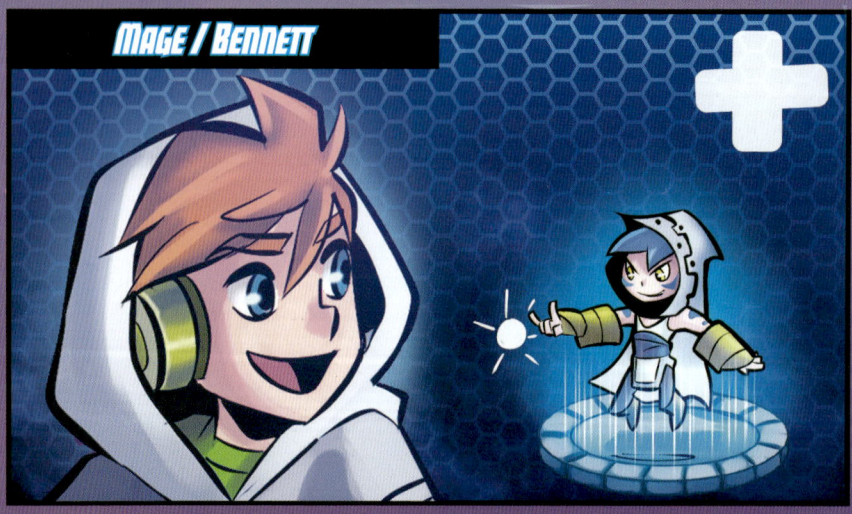

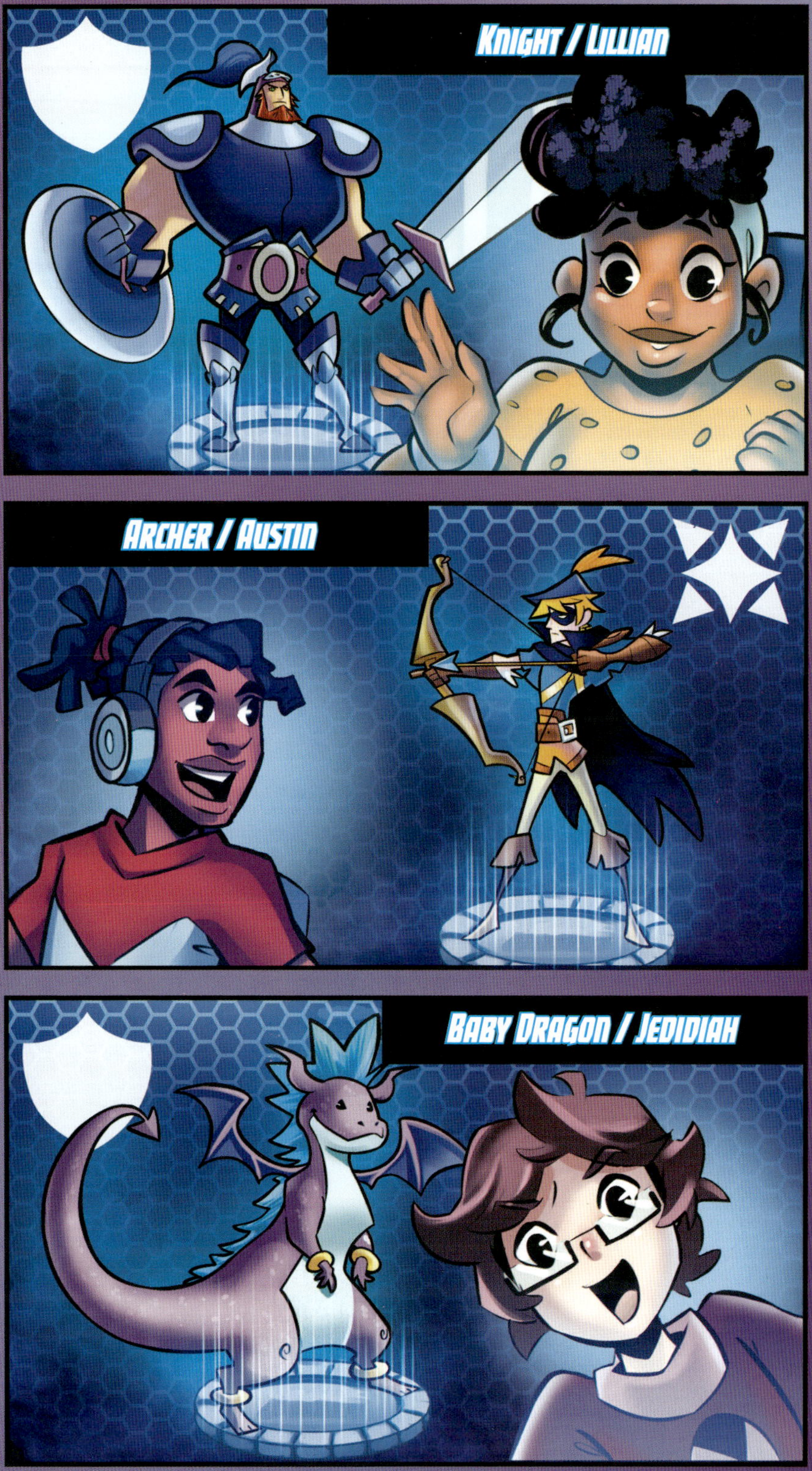
KNIGHT / LILLIAN
ARCHER / AUSTIN
BABY DRAGON / JEDIDIAH

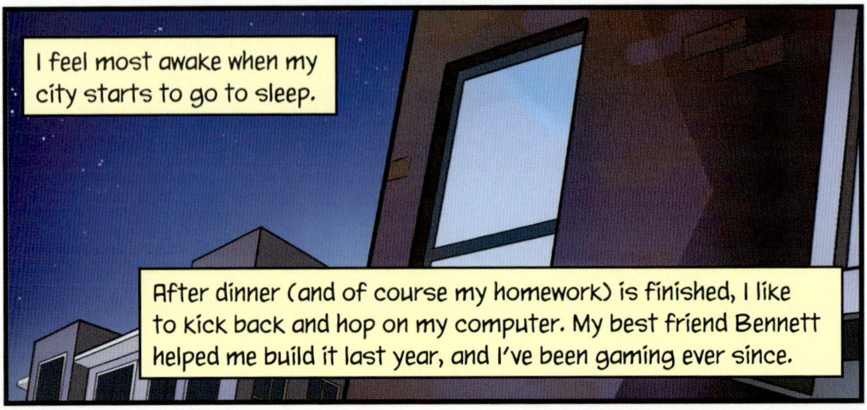
I feel most awake when my city starts to go to sleep.
After dinner (and of course my homework) is finished, I like to kick back and hop on my computer. My best friend Bennett helped me build it last year, and I've been gaming ever since.

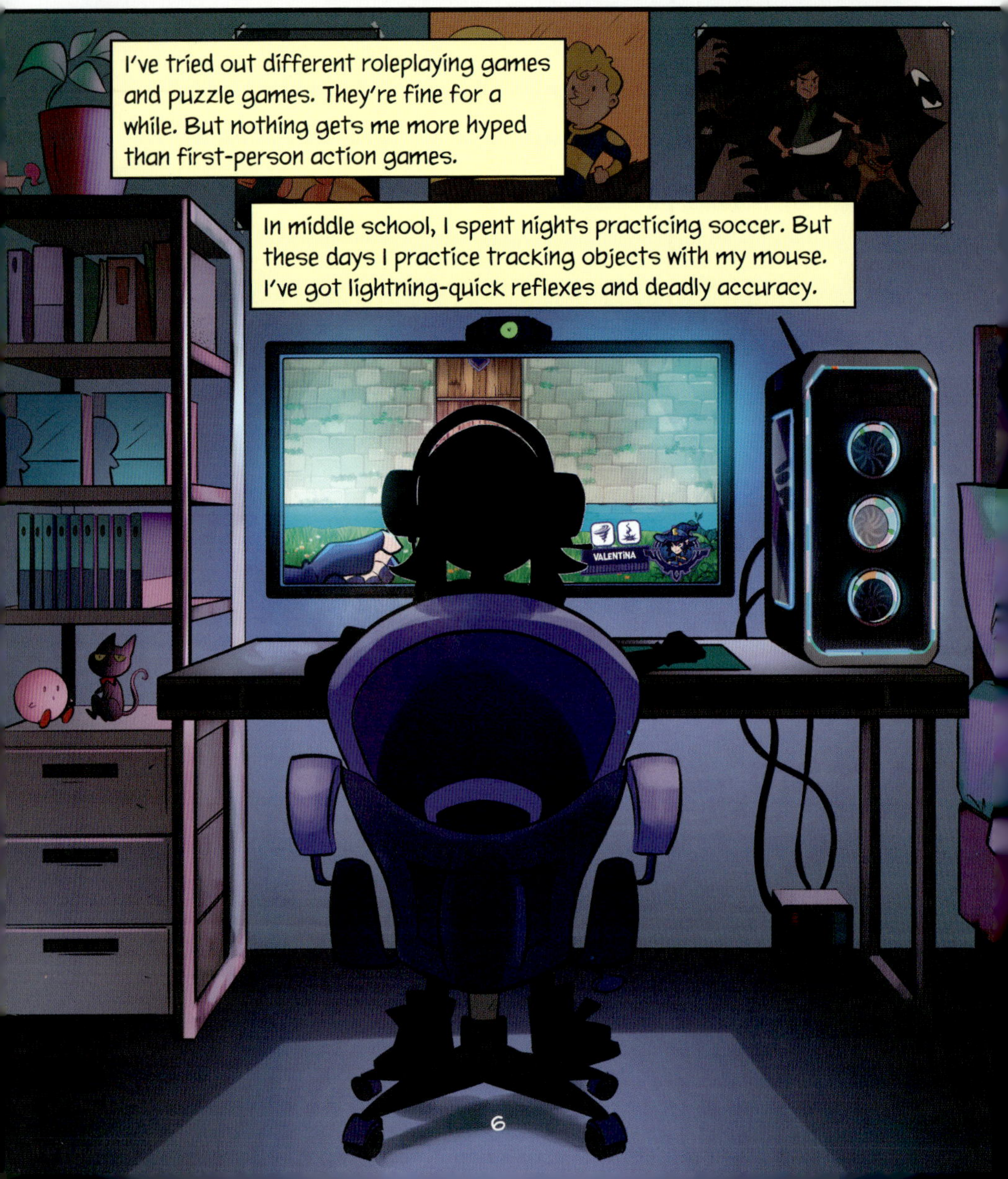
I've tried out different roleplaying games and puzzle games. They're fine for a while. But nothing gets me more hyped than first-person action games.
In middle school, I spent nights practicing soccer. But these days I practice tracking objects with my mouse. I've got lightning-quick reflexes and deadly accuracy.
VALENTINA

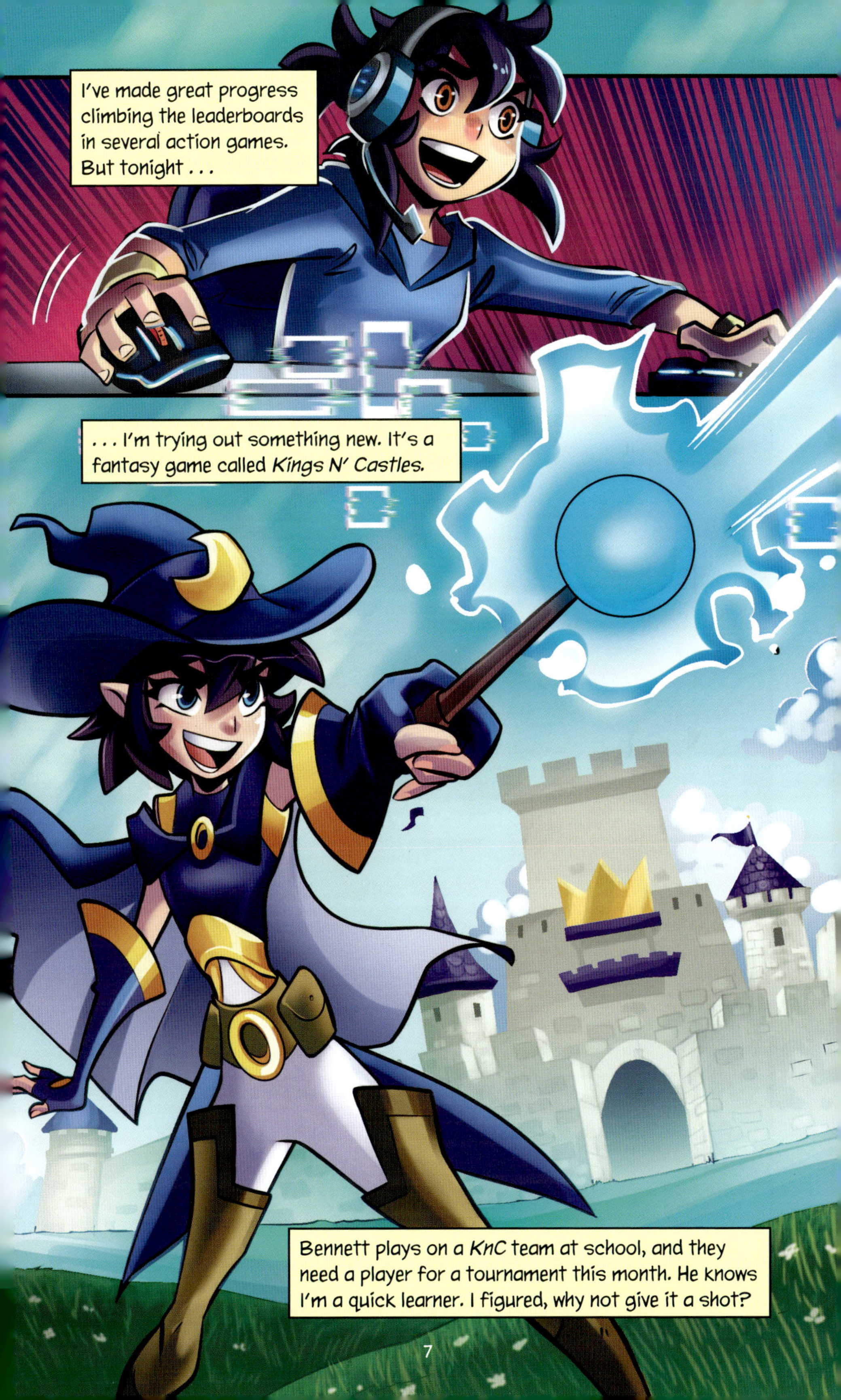
I've made great progress climbing the leaderboards in several action games. But tonight . . .
. . . I'm trying out something new. It's a fantasy game called *Kings N' Castles*.
Bennett plays on a *KnC* team at school, and they need a player for a tournament this month. He knows I'm a quick learner. I figured, why not give it a shot?

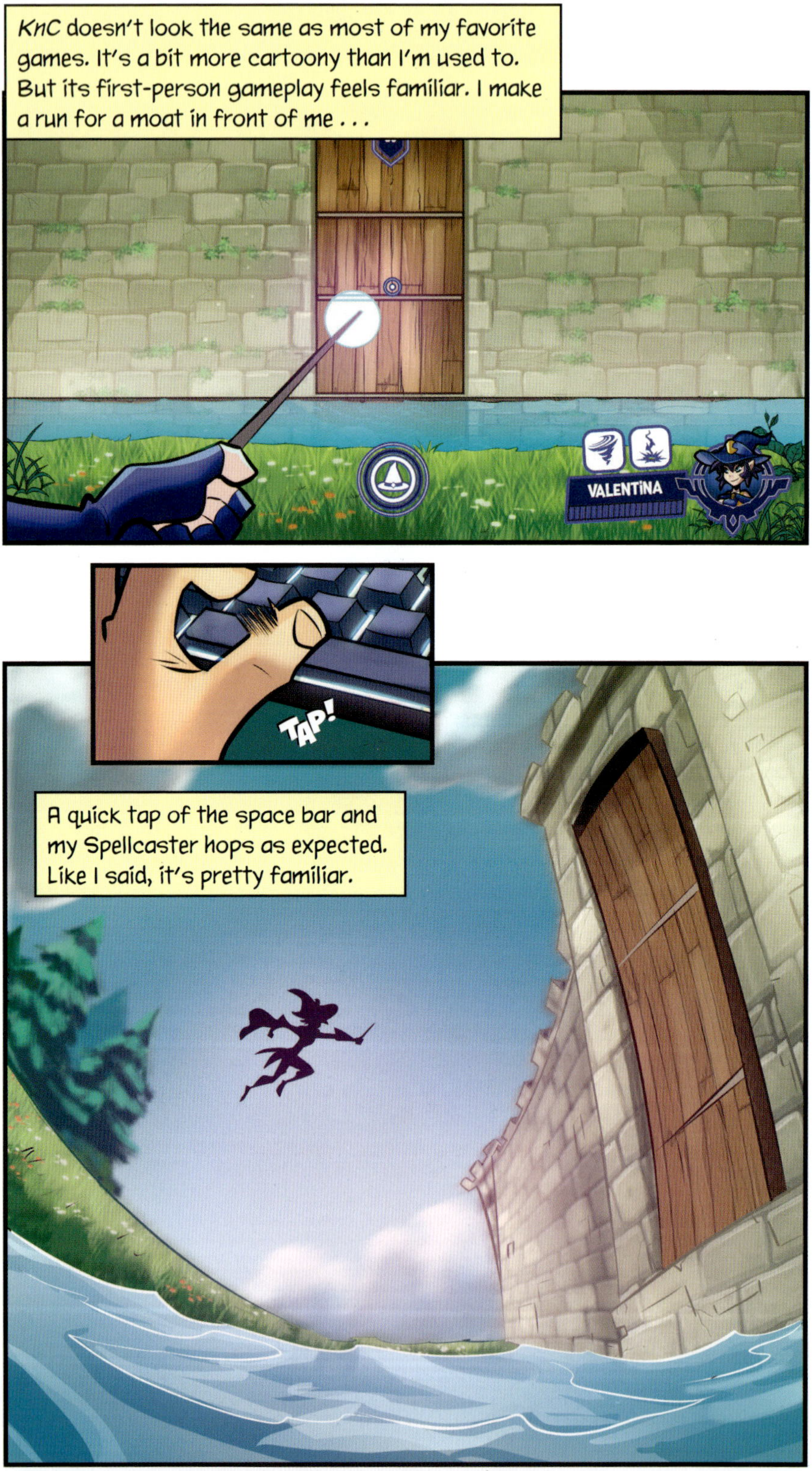
KnC doesn't look the same as most of my favorite games. It's a bit more cartoony than I'm used to. But its first-person gameplay feels familiar. I make a run for a moat in front of me . . .
VALENTINA
TAP!
A quick tap of the space bar and my Spellcaster hops as expected. Like I said, it's pretty familiar.

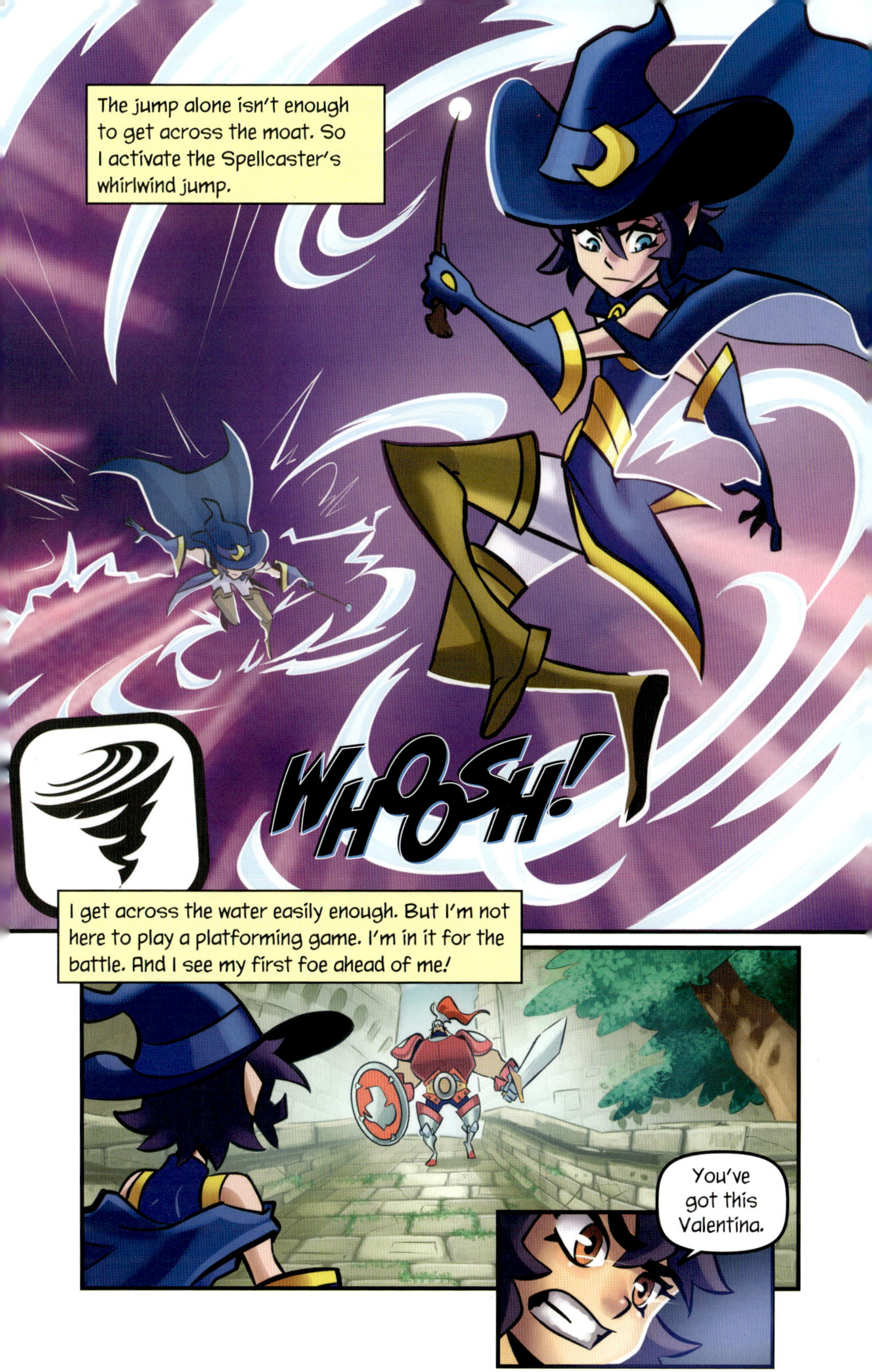
The jump alone isn't enough to get across the moat. So I activate the Spellcaster's whirlwind jump.
WHOOSH!
I get across the water easily enough. But I'm not here to play a platforming game. I'm in it for the battle. And I see my first foe ahead of me!
You've got this Valentina.

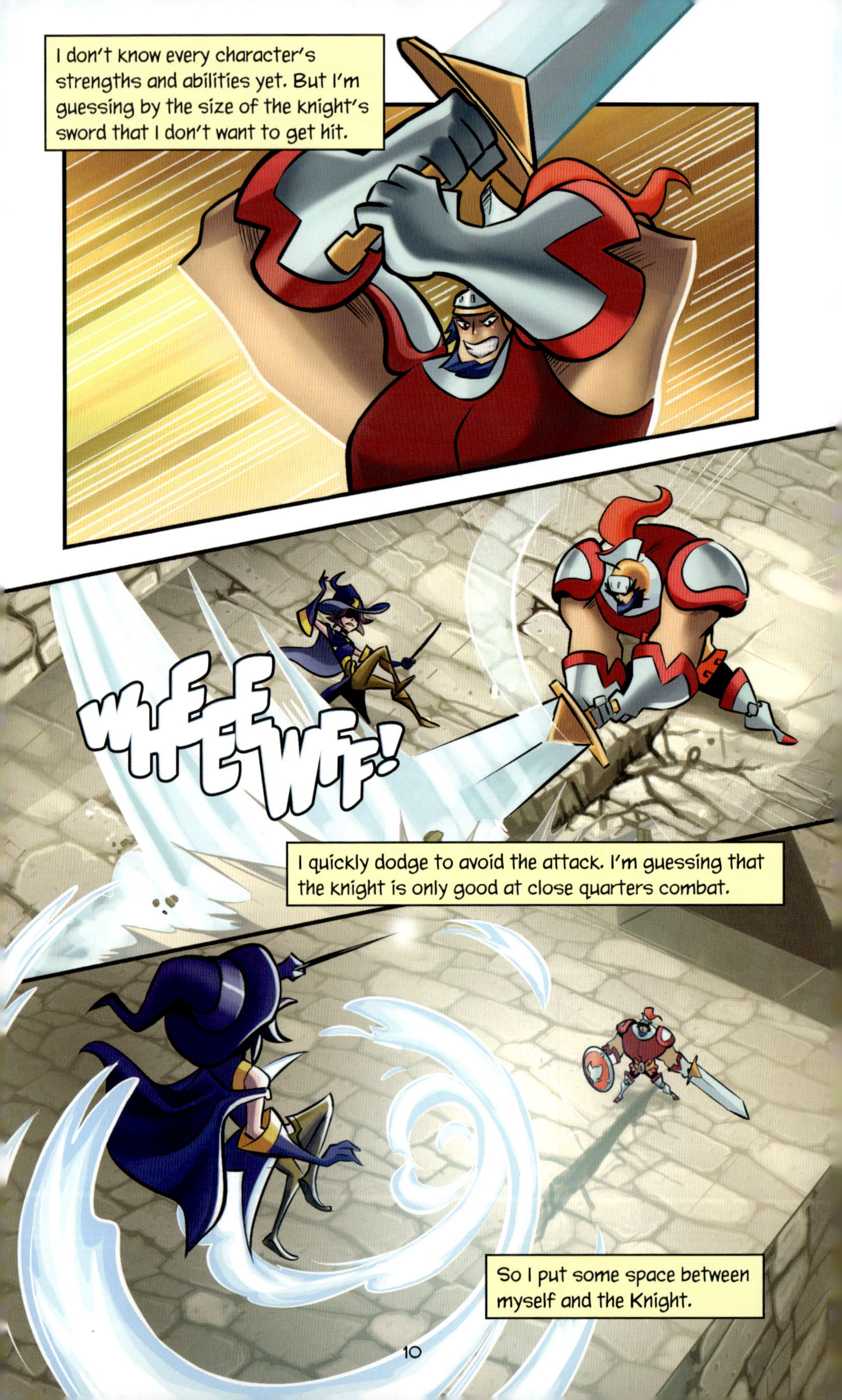
I don't know every character's strengths and abilities yet. But I'm guessing by the size of the knight's sword that I don't want to get hit.
WHEEEWFF!
I quickly dodge to avoid the attack. I'm guessing that the knight is only good at close quarters combat.
So I put some space between myself and the Knight.

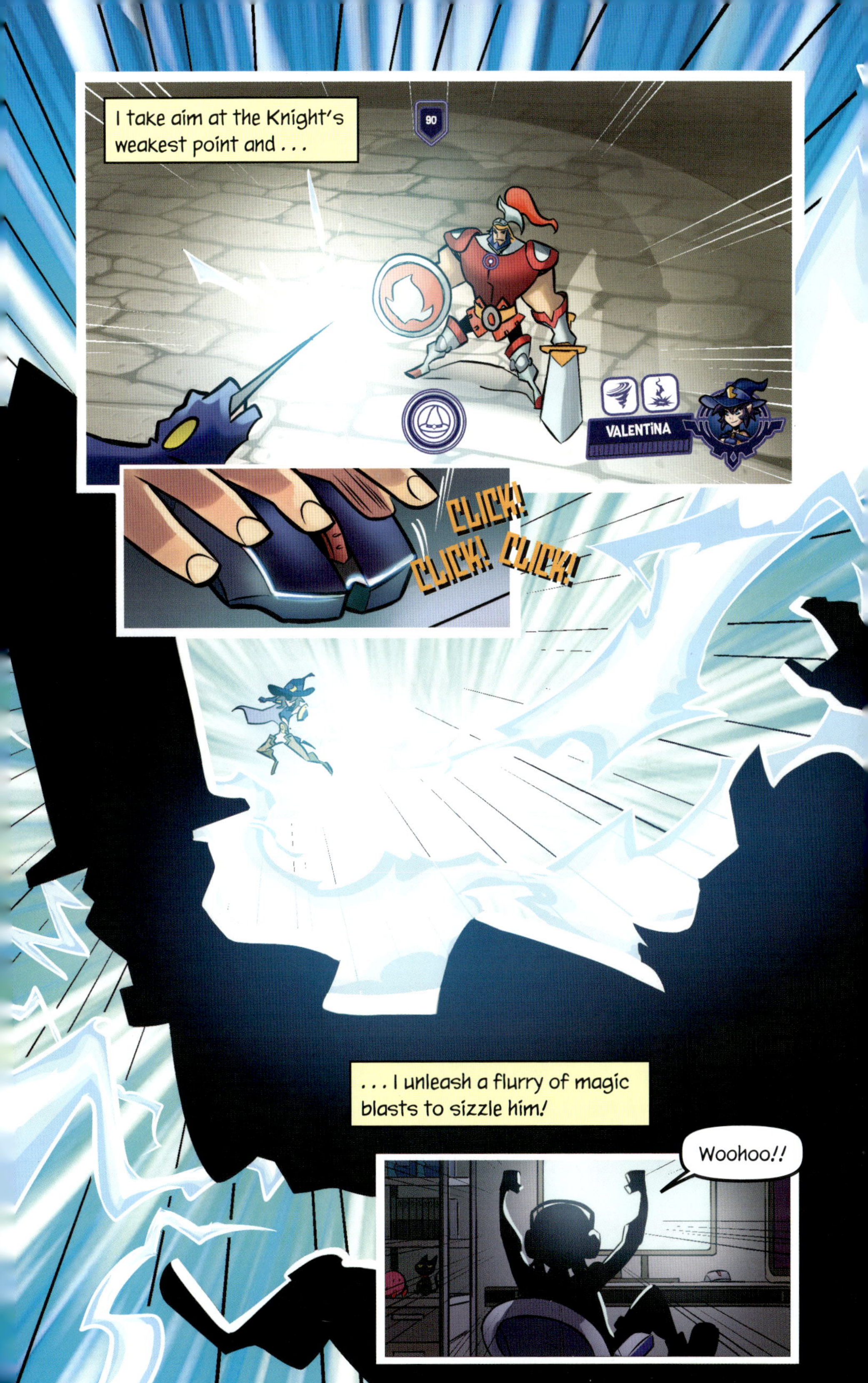

I take aim at the Knight's weakest point and . . .
90
VALENTINA
CLICK!
CLICK! CLICK!
. . . I unleash a flurry of magic blasts to sizzle him!
Woohoo!!

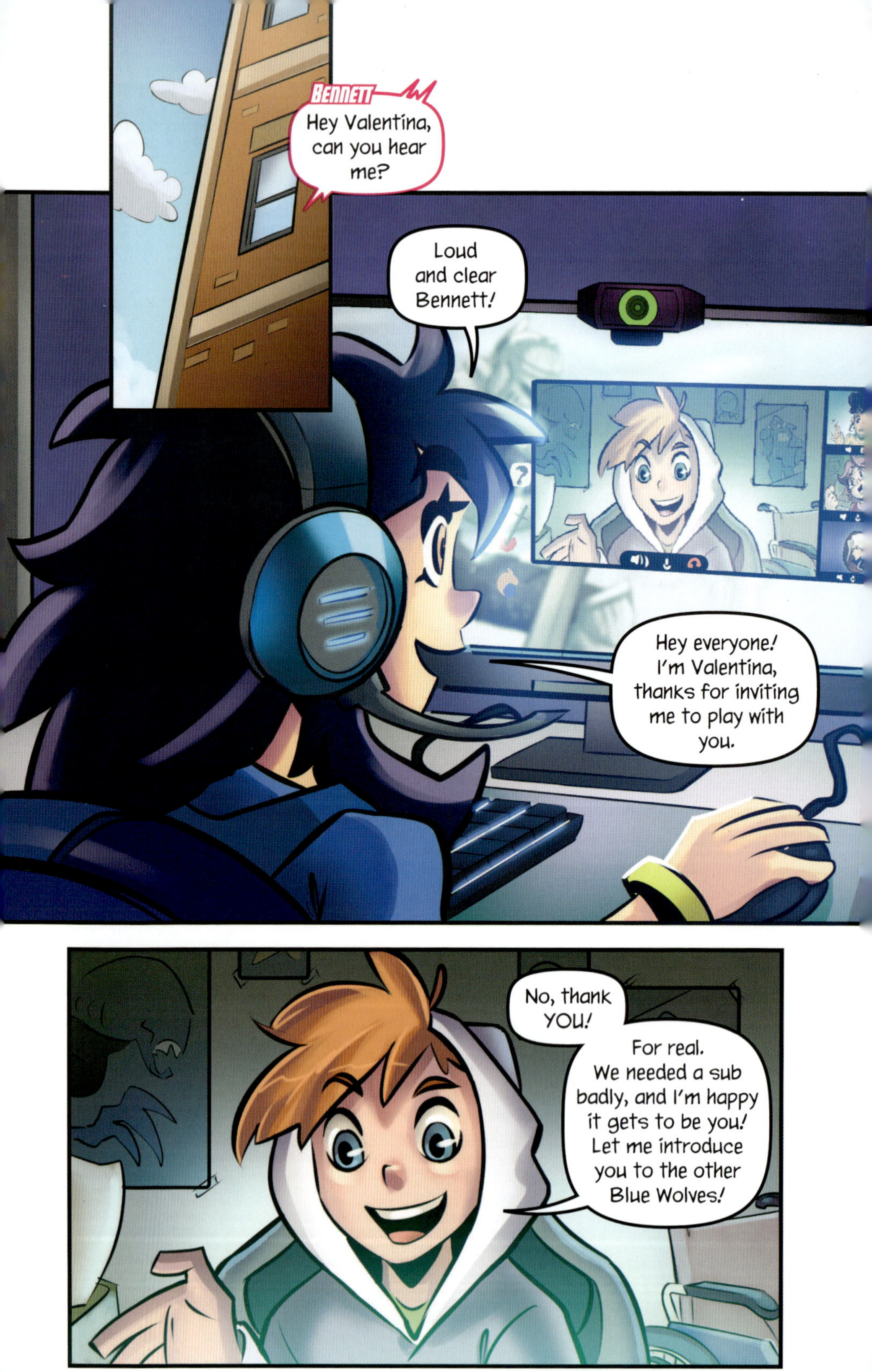
BENNETT
Hey Valentina, can you hear me?
Loud and clear Bennett!
Hey everyone! I'm Valentina, thanks for inviting me to play with you.
No, thank YOU!
For real. We needed a sub badly, and I'm happy it gets to be you! Let me introduce you to the other Blue Wolves!

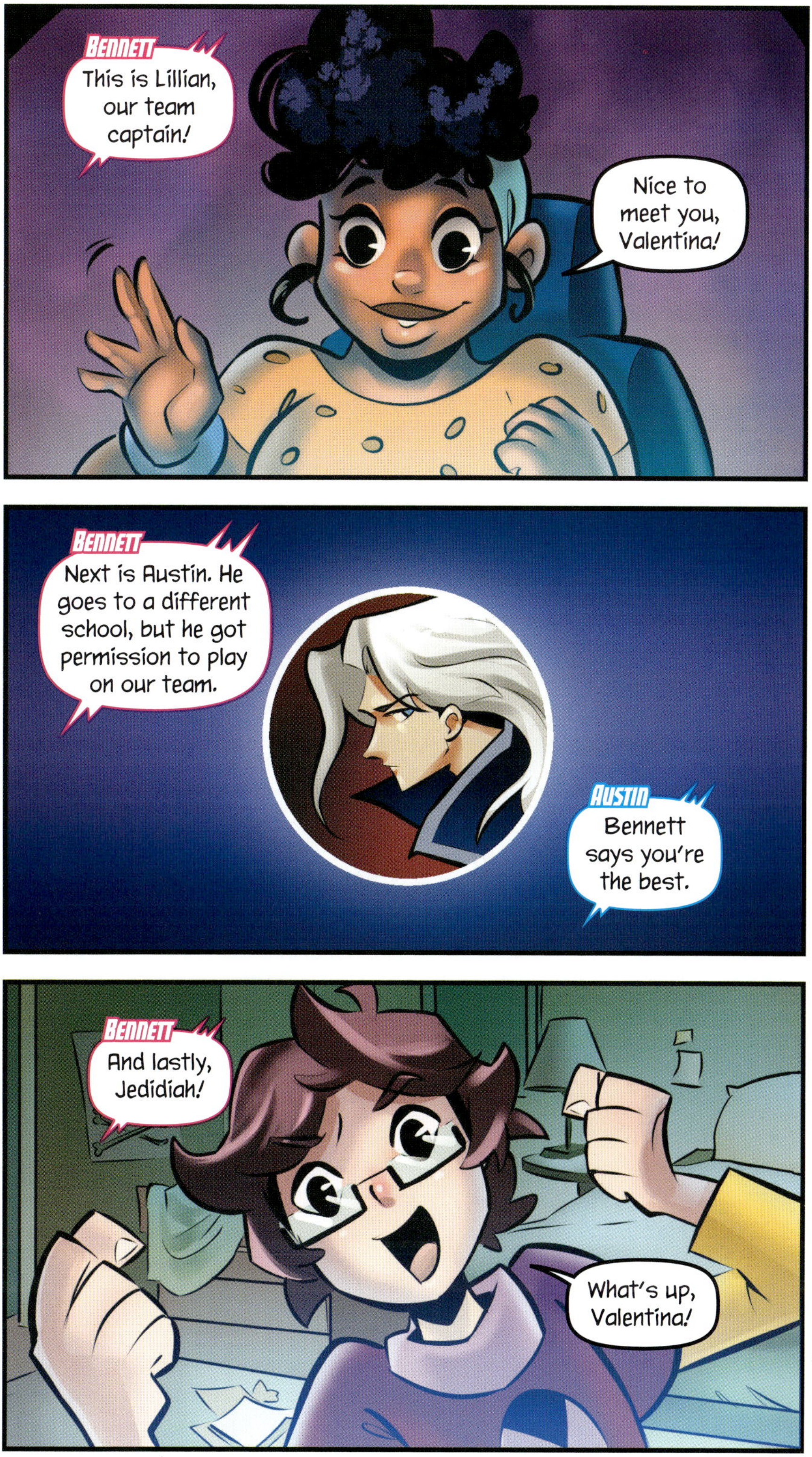
BENNETT
This is Lillian, our team captain!
Nice to meet you, Valentina!
BENNETT
Next is Austin. He goes to a different school, but he got permission to play on our team.
AUSTIN
Bennett says you're the best.
BENNETT
And lastly, Jedidiah!
What's up, Valentina!

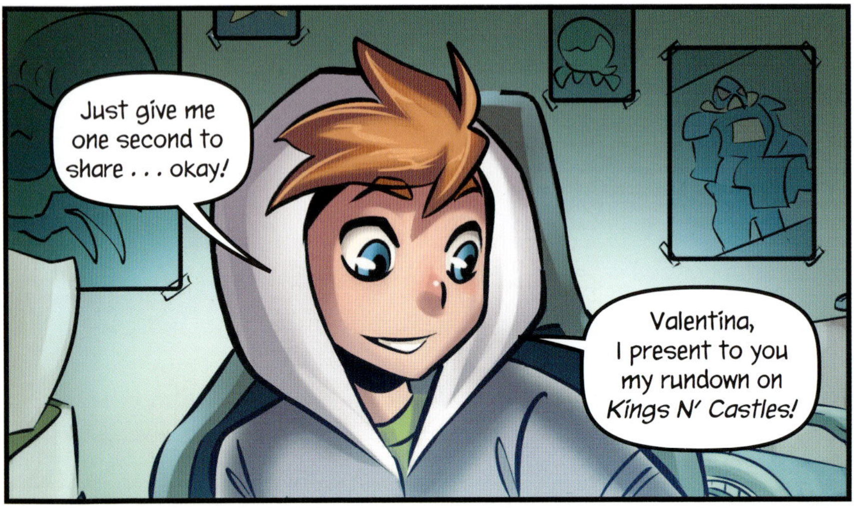
Just give me one second to share . . . okay!
Valentina, I present to you my rundown on *Kings N' Castles!*

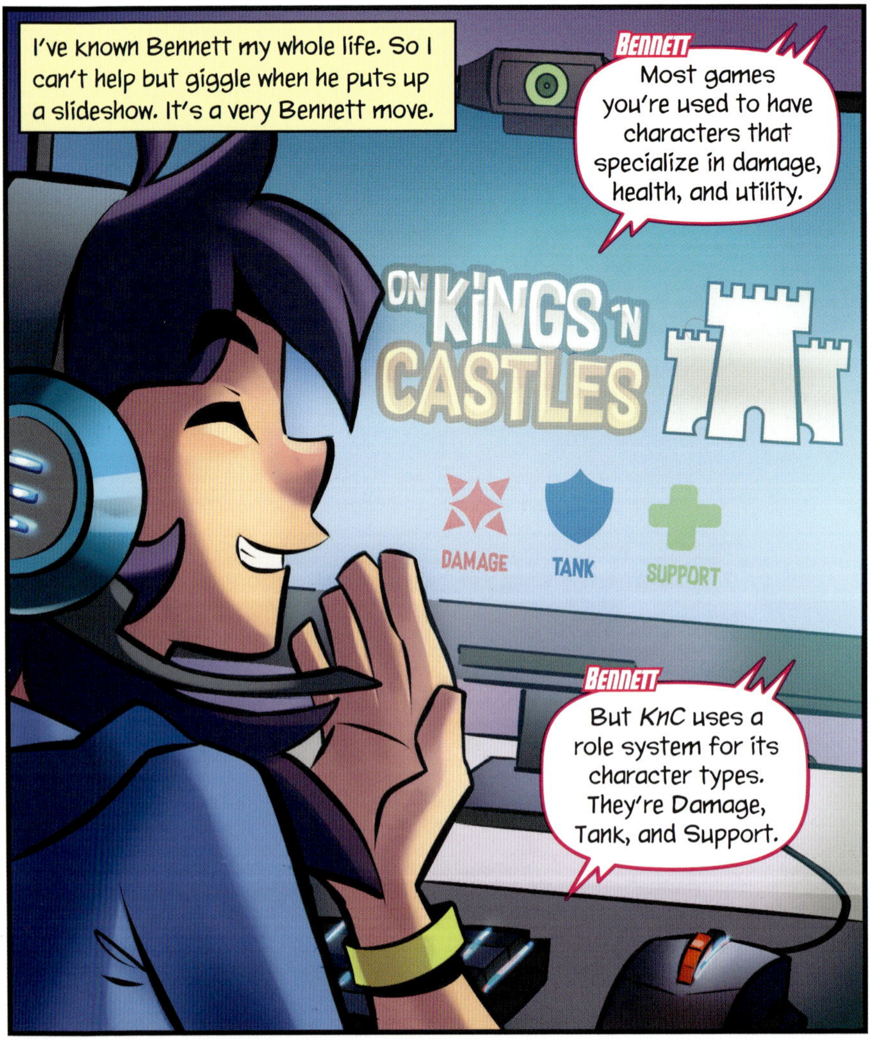
I've known Bennett my whole life. So I can't help but giggle when he puts up a slideshow. It's a very Bennett move.
BENNETT
Most games you're used to have characters that specialize in damage, health, and utility.
ON KINGS 'N CASTLES
DAMAGE
TANK
SUPPORT
BENNETT
But *KnC* uses a role system for its character types. They're Damage, Tank, and Support.

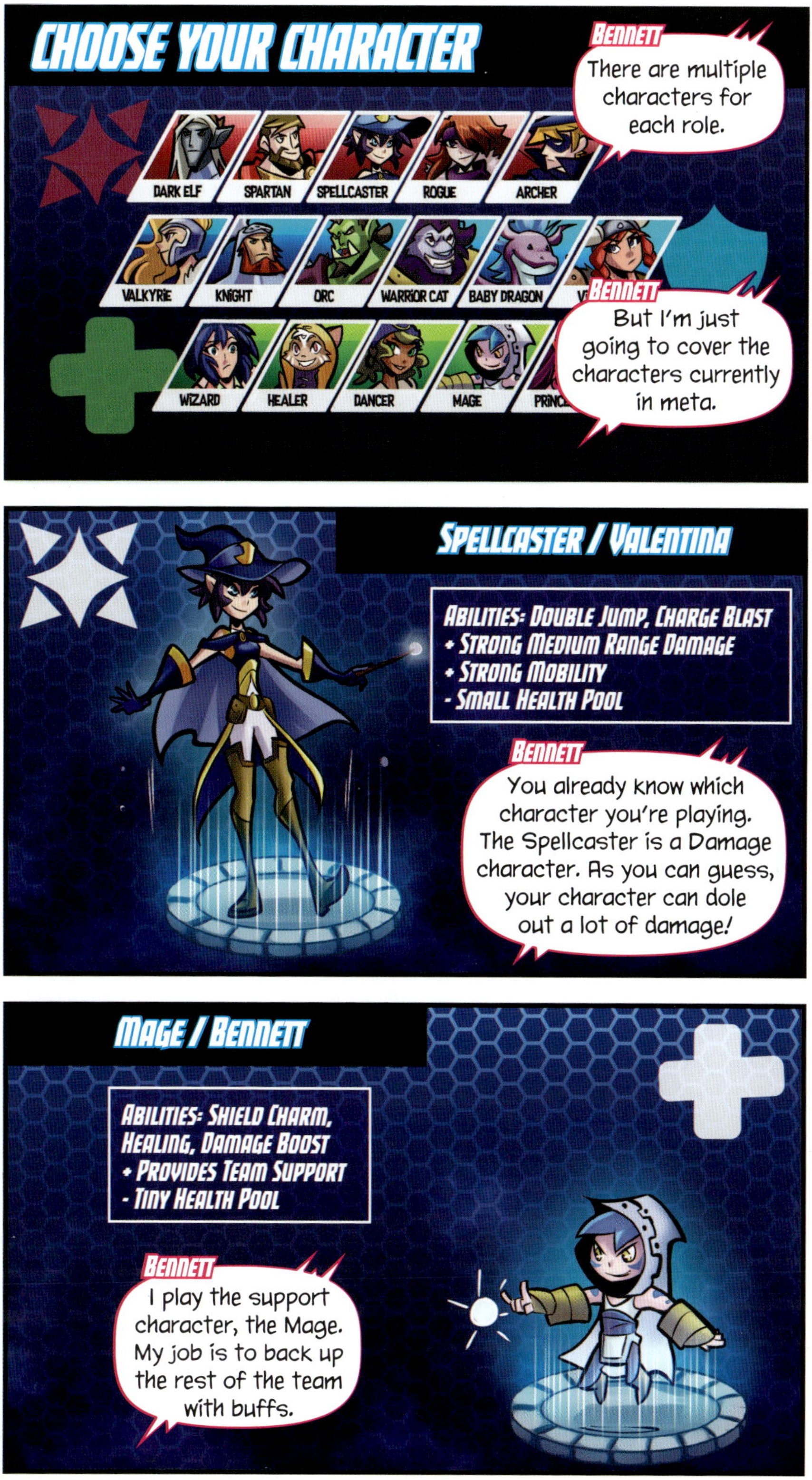

CHOOSE YOUR CHARACTER
BENNETT
There are multiple characters for each role.
DARK ELF
SPARTAN
SPELLCASTER
ROGUE
ARCHER
VALKYRIE
KNIGHT
ORC
WARRIOR CAT
BABY DRAGON
BENNETT
But I'm just going to cover the characters currently in meta.
WIZARD
HEALER
DANCER
MAGE
SPELLCASTER / VALENTINA
ABILITIES: DOUBLE JUMP, CHARGE BLAST
+ STRONG MEDIUM RANGE DAMAGE
+ STRONG MOBILITY
- SMALL HEALTH POOL
BENNETT
You already know which character you're playing. The Spellcaster is a Damage character. As you can guess, your character can dole out a lot of damage!
MAGE / BENNETT
ABILITIES: SHIELD CHARM, HEALING, DAMAGE BOOST
+ PROVIDES TEAM SUPPORT
- TINY HEALTH POOL
BENNETT
I play the support character, the Mage. My job is to back up the rest of the team with buffs.

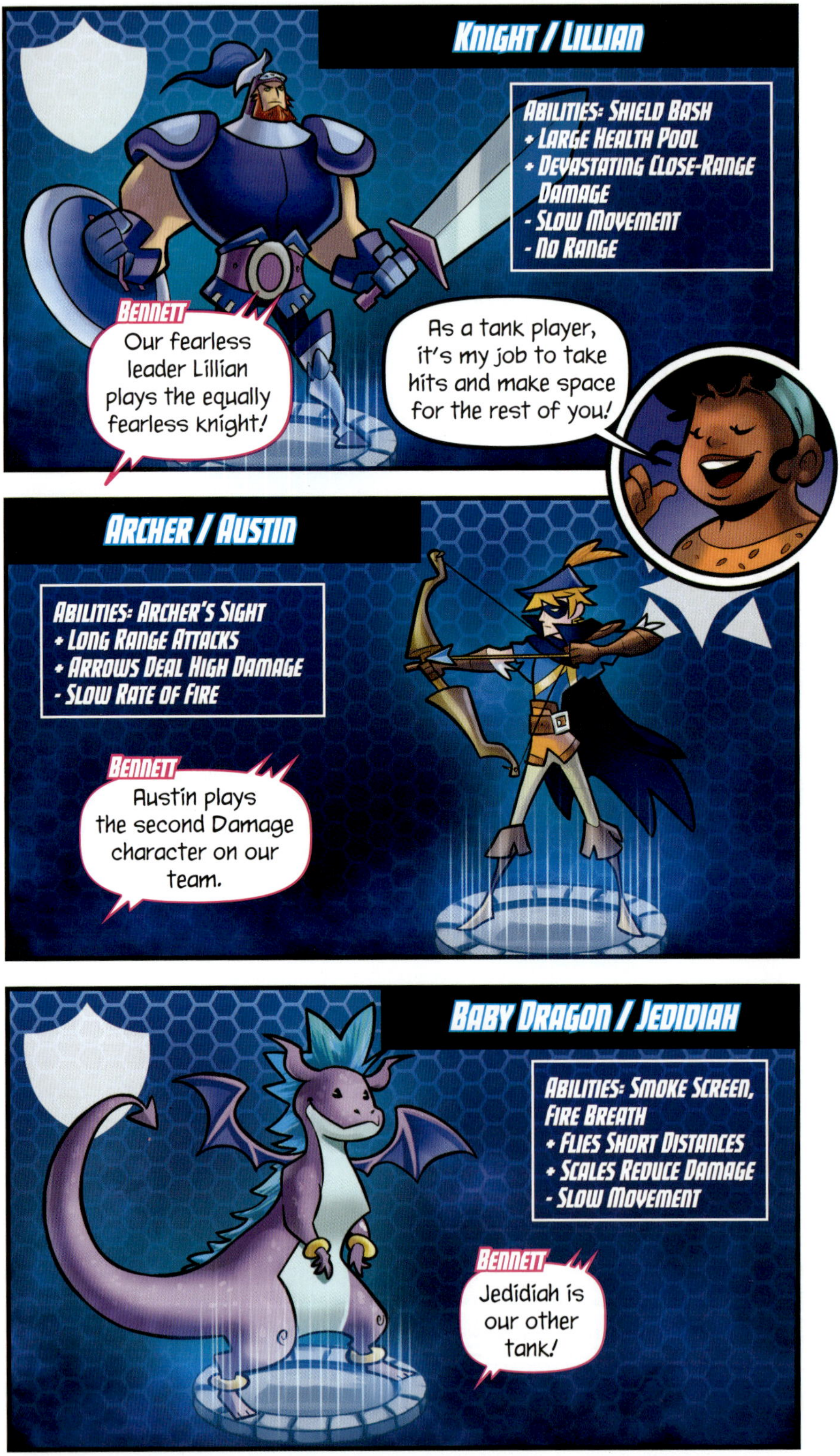

KNIGHT / LILLIAN
ABILITIES: SHIELD BASH
+ LARGE HEALTH POOL
+ DEVASTATING CLOSE-RANGE DAMAGE
- SLOW MOVEMENT
- NO RANGE
BENNETT
Our fearless leader Lillian plays the equally fearless knight!
As a tank player, it's my job to take hits and make space for the rest of you!
ARCHER / AUSTIN
ABILITIES: ARCHER'S SIGHT
+ LONG RANGE ATTACKS
+ ARROWS DEAL HIGH DAMAGE
- SLOW RATE OF FIRE
BENNETT
Austin plays the second Damage character on our team.
BABY DRAGON / JEDIDIAH
ABILITIES: SMOKE SCREEN, FIRE BREATH
+ FLIES SHORT DISTANCES
+ SCALES REDUCE DAMAGE
- SLOW MOVEMENT
BENNETT
Jedidiah is our other tank!

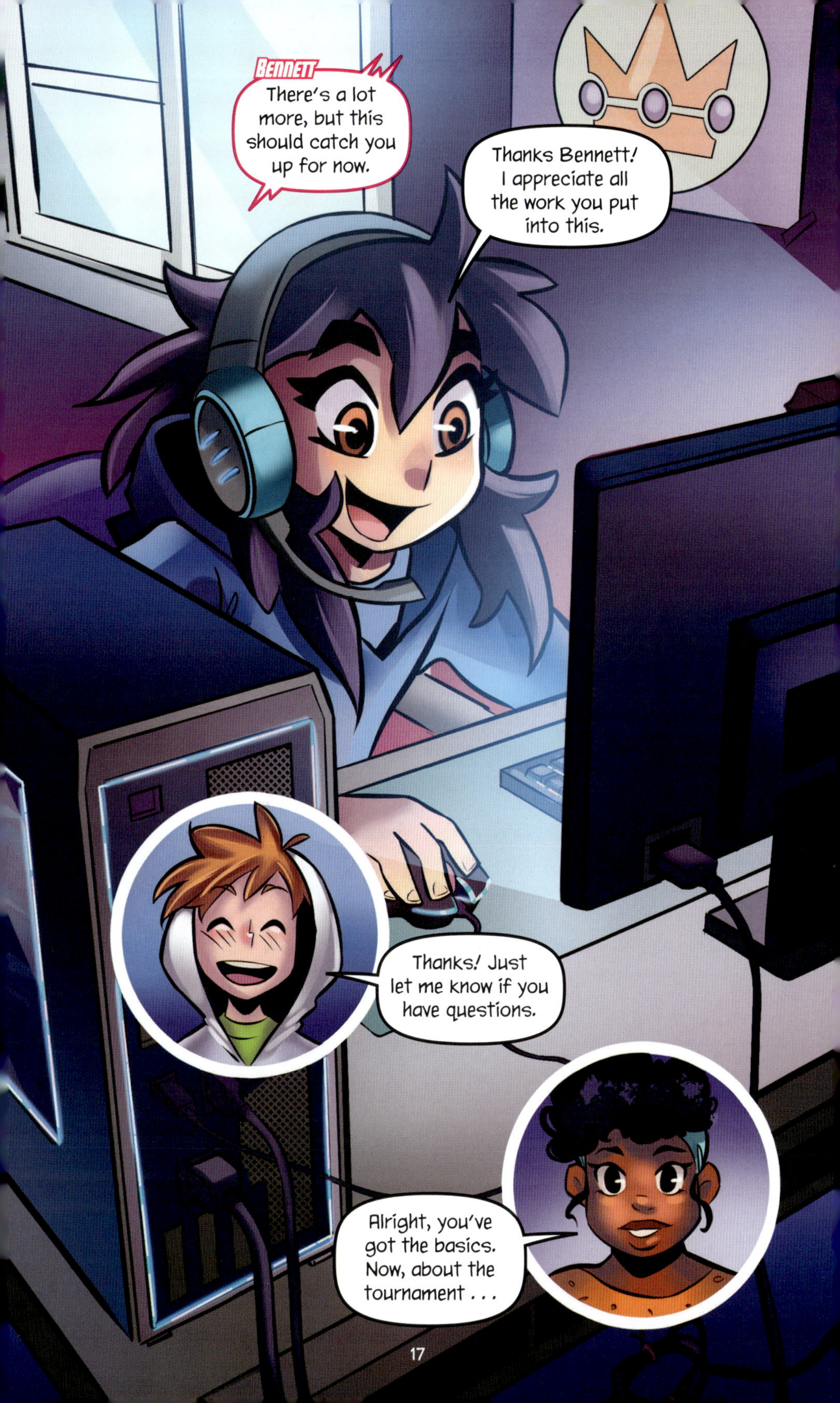
BENNETT
There's a lot more, but this should catch you up for now.
Thanks Bennett! I appreciate all the work you put into this.
Thanks! Just let me know if you have questions.
Alright, you've got the basics. Now, about the tournament . . .

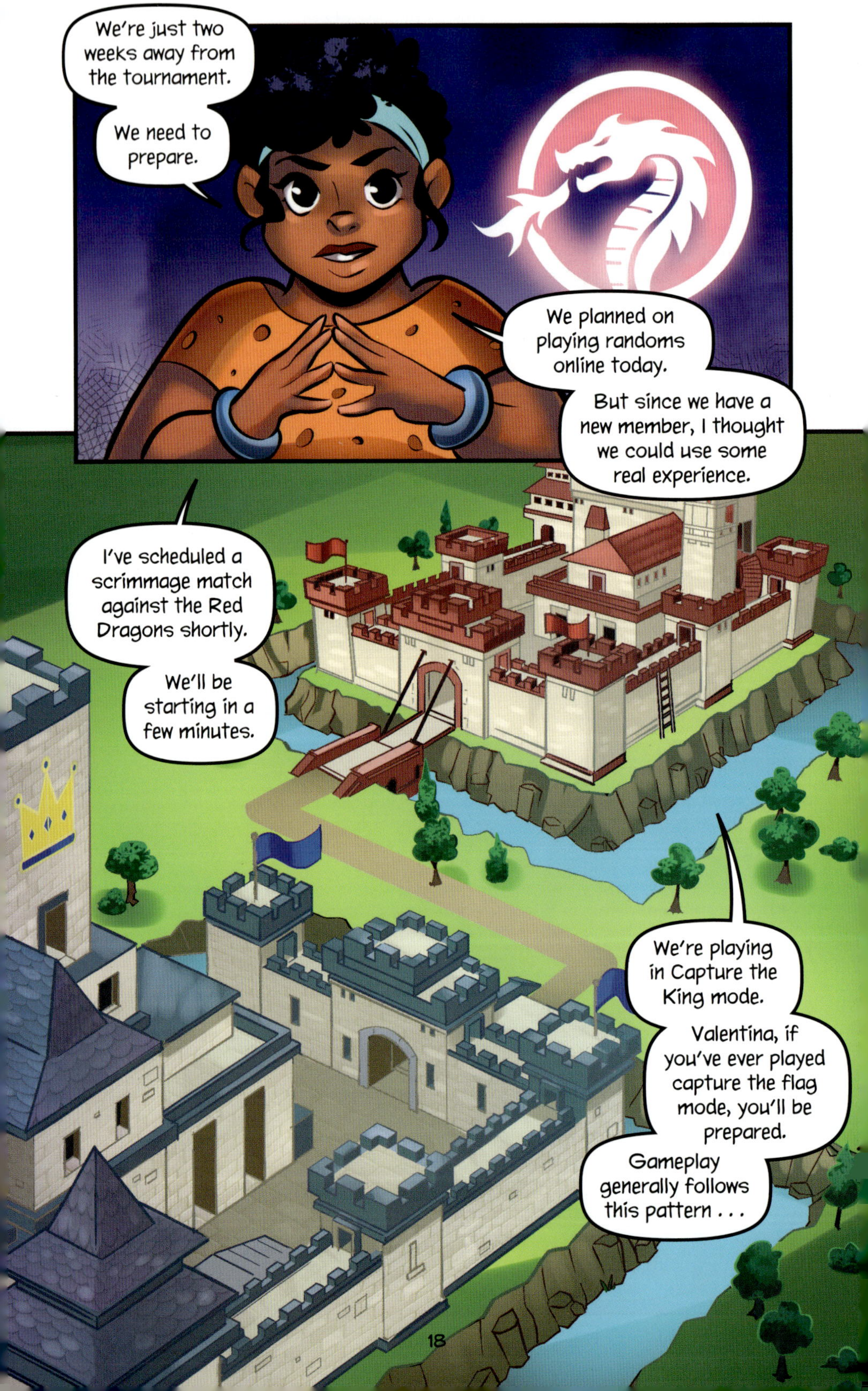

We're just two weeks away from the tournament.
We need to prepare.
We planned on playing randoms online today.
But since we have a new member, I thought we could use some real experience.
I've scheduled a scrimmage match against the Red Dragons shortly.
We'll be starting in a few minutes.
We're playing in Capture the King mode.
Valentina, if you've ever played capture the flag mode, you'll be prepared.
Gameplay generally follows this pattern . . .

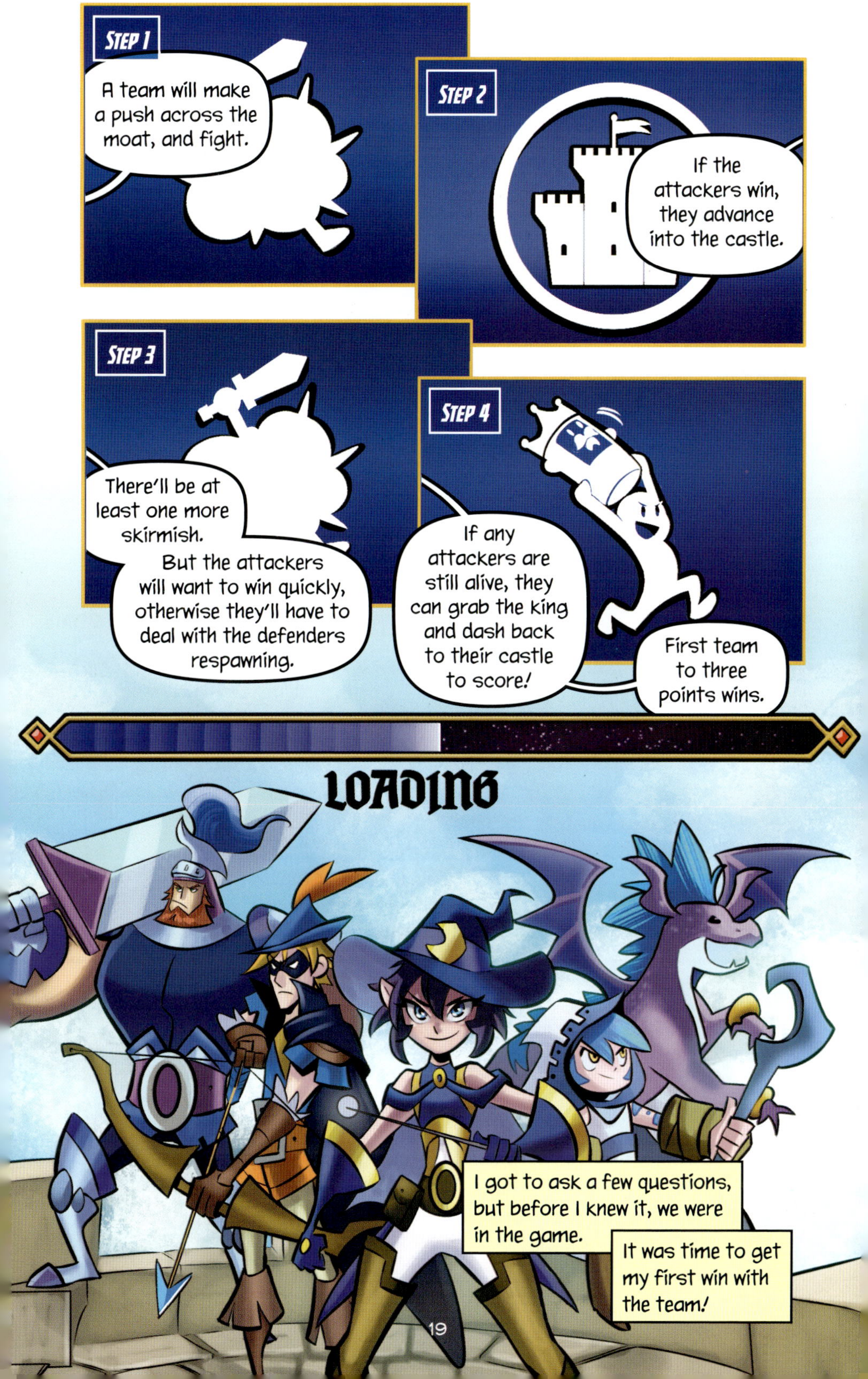
STEP 1
A team will make a push across the moat, and fight.
STEP 2
If the attackers win, they advance into the castle.
STEP 3
There'll be at least one more skirmish.
But the attackers will want to win quickly, otherwise they'll have to deal with the defenders respawning.
STEP 4
If any attackers are still alive, they can grab the king and dash back to their castle to score!
First team to three points wins.
LOADING
I got to ask a few questions, but before I knew it, we were in the game.
It was time to get my first win with the team!

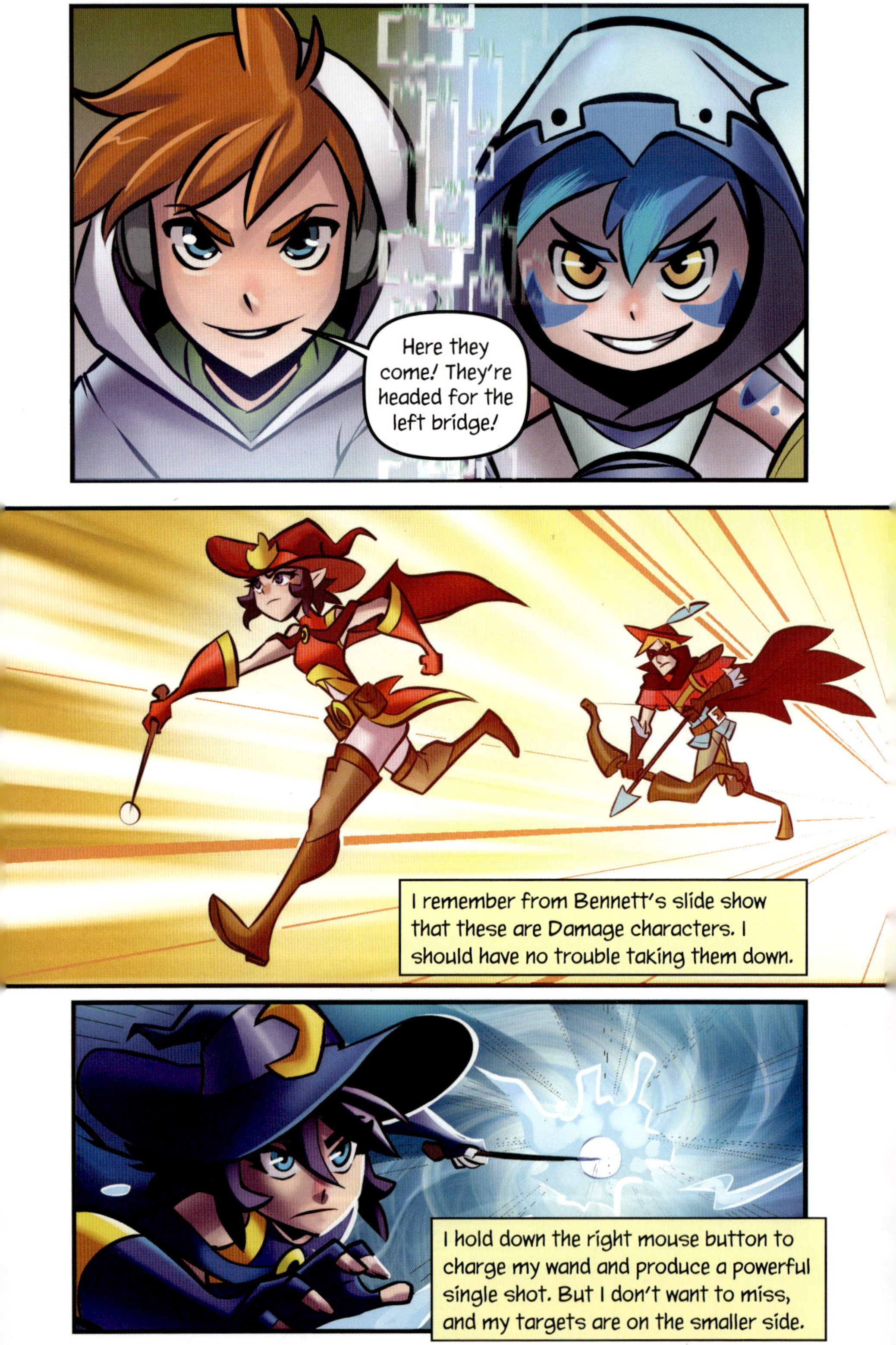
Here they come! They're headed for the left bridge!
I remember from Bennett's slide show that these are Damage characters. I should have no trouble taking them down.
I hold down the right mouse button to charge my wand and produce a powerful single shot. But I don't want to miss, and my targets are on the smaller side.

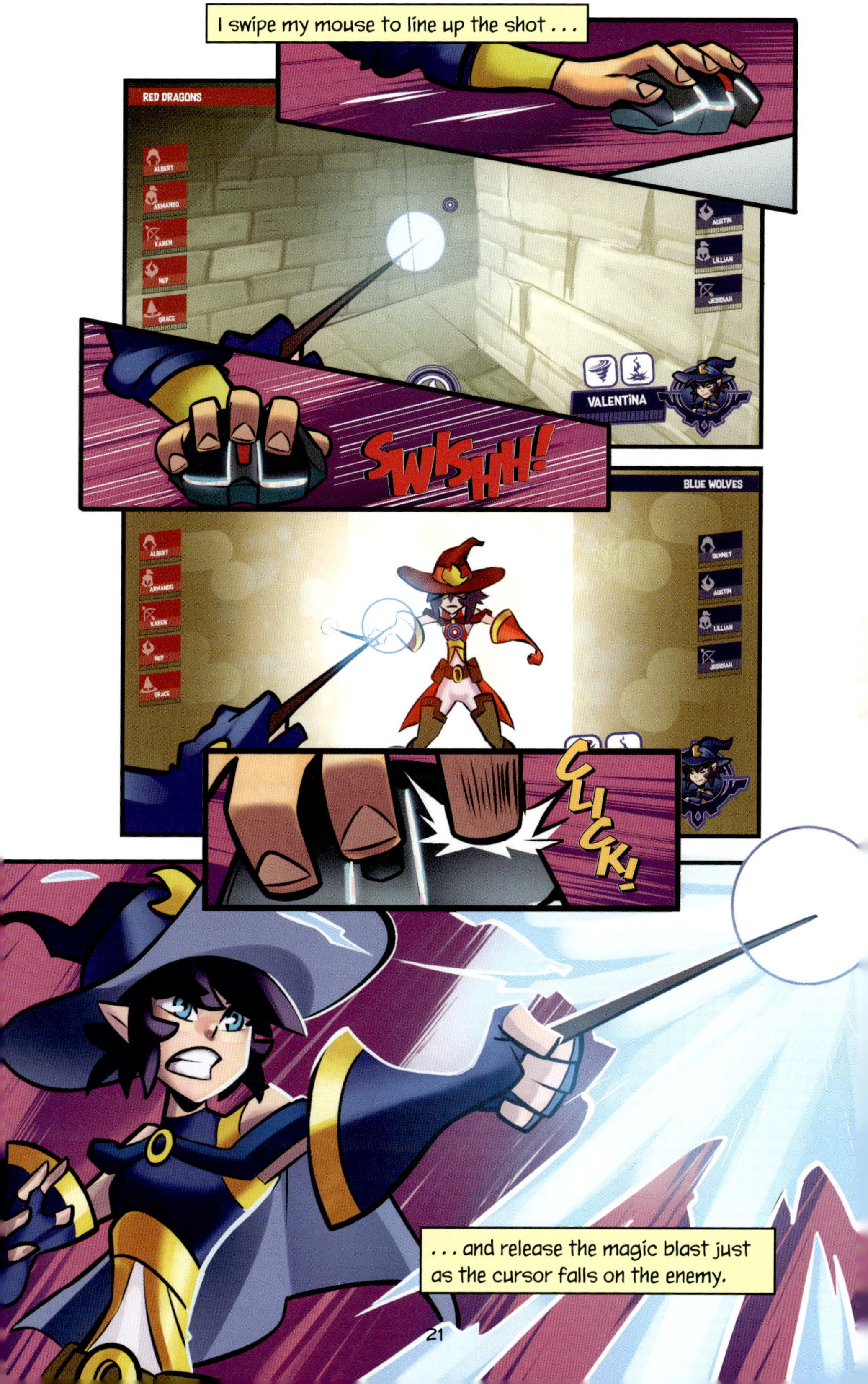

I swipe my mouse to line up the shot . . .
RED DRAGONS
ALBERT
ARMANDO
KAREN
NEP
GRACE
AUSTIN
LILLIAN
JEDIDIAH
VALENTINA
SWISHH!
BLUE WOLVES
ALBERT
ARMANDO
KAREN
NEP
GRACE
BENNET
AUSTIN
LILLIAN
JEDIDIAH
CLICK!
. . . and release the magic blast just as the cursor falls on the enemy.

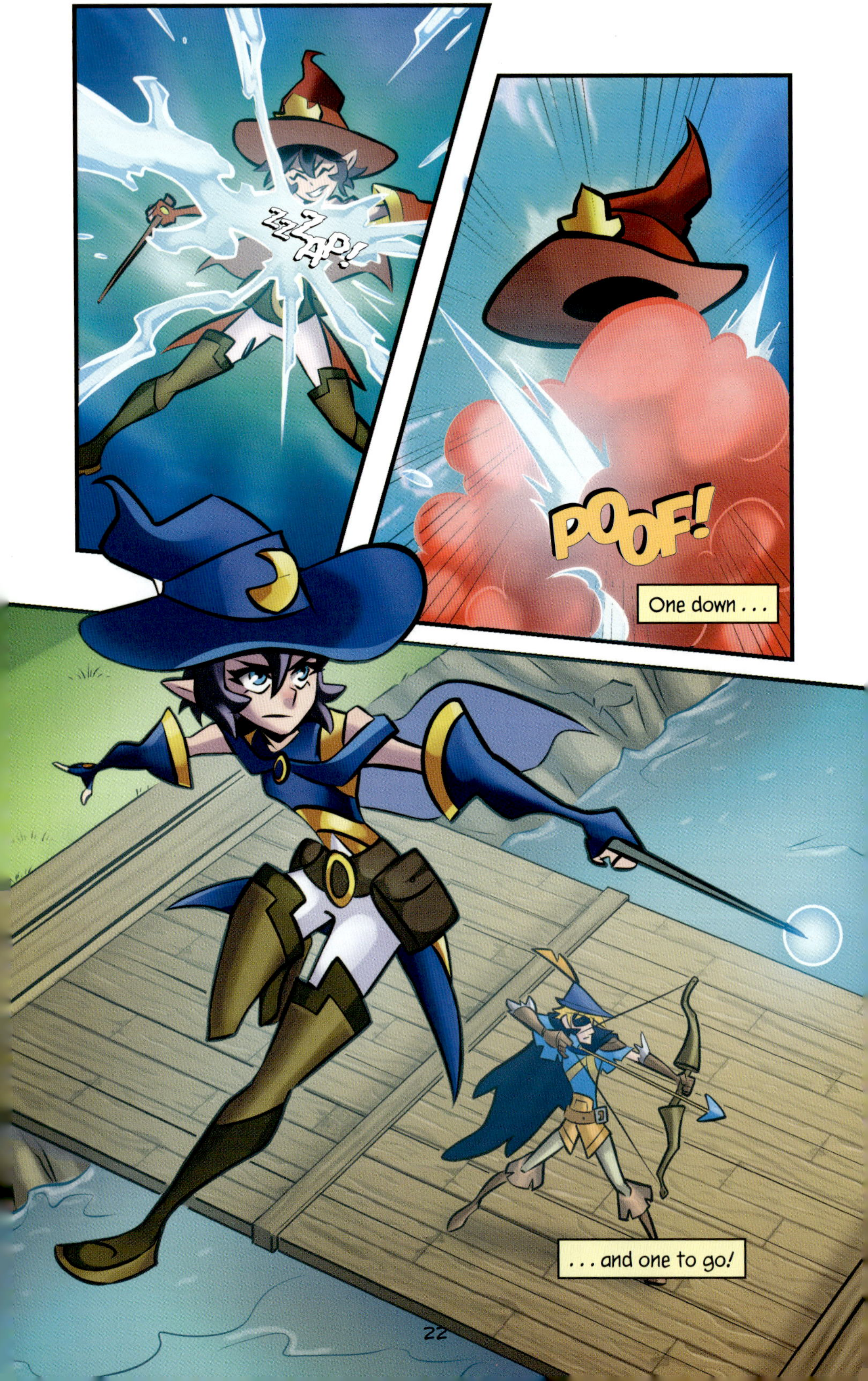
ZZZAP!
POOF!
One down . . .
. . . and one to go!

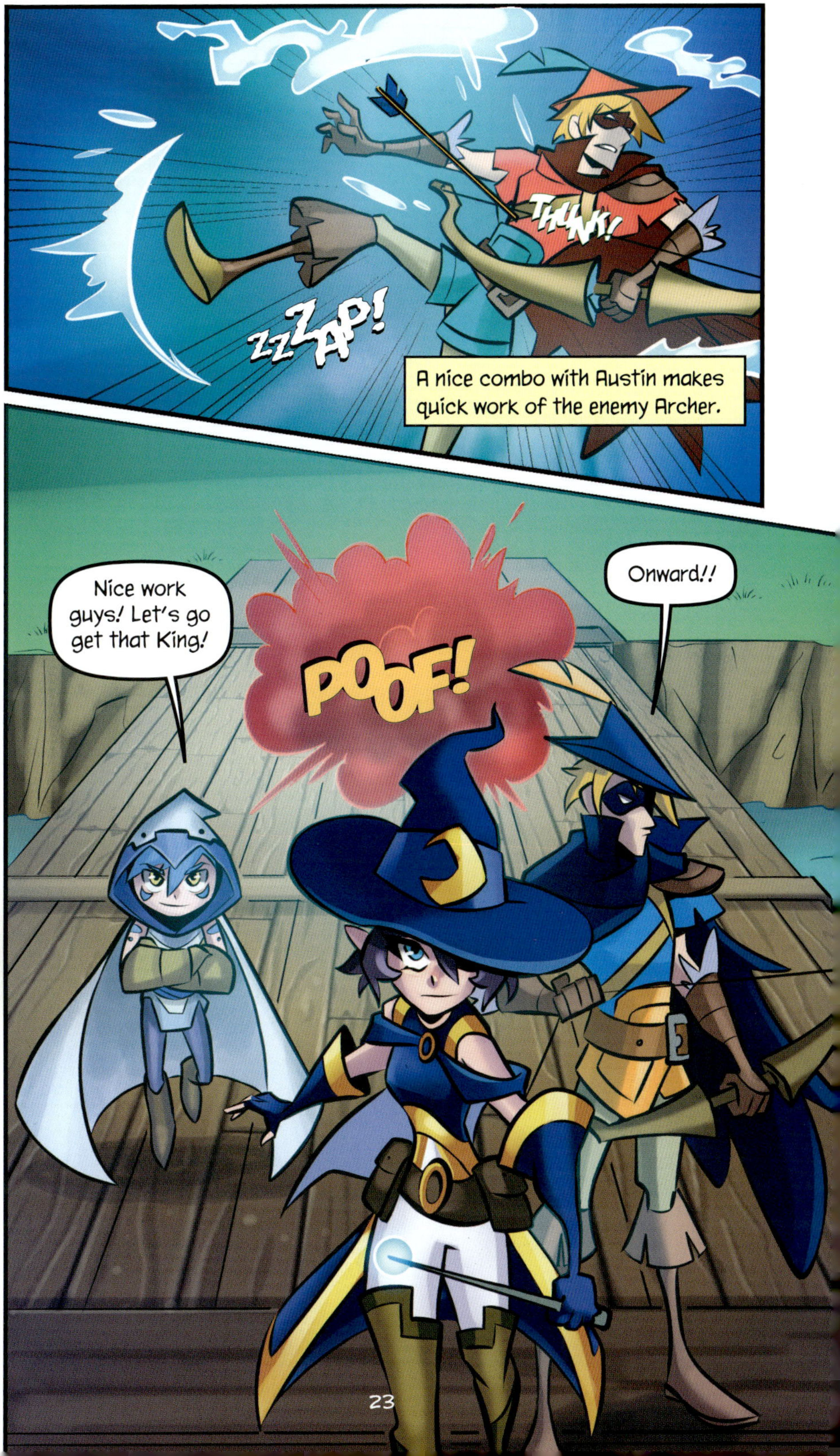
THUNK!
ZZZAP!
A nice combo with Austin makes quick work of the enemy Archer.
Nice work guys! Let's go get that King!
POOF!
Onward!!

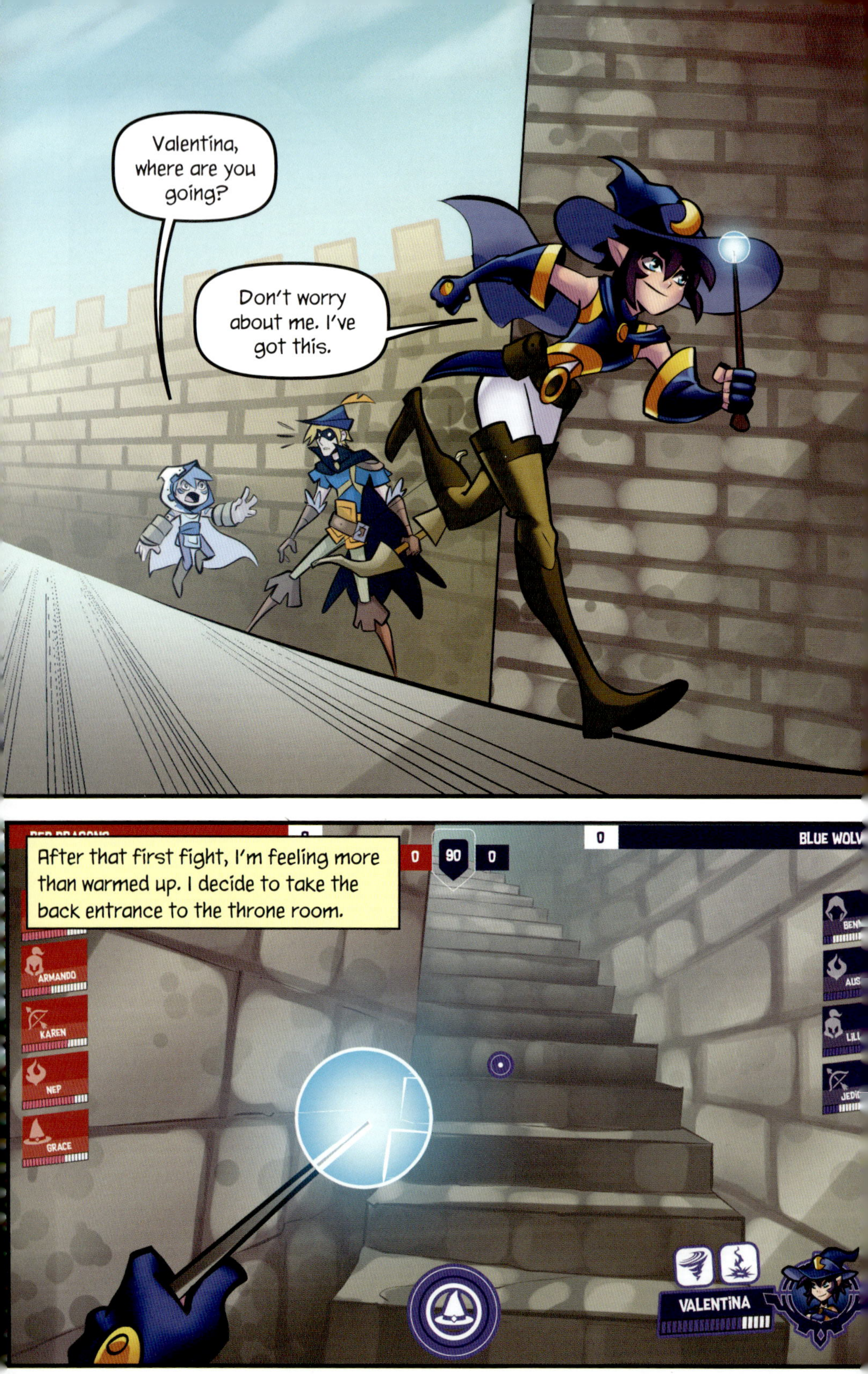
Valentina, where are you going?
Don't worry about me. I've got this.
After that first fight, I'm feeling more than warmed up. I decide to take the back entrance to the throne room.
0
90
0
0
ARMANDO
KAREN
NEP
GRACE
VALENTINA

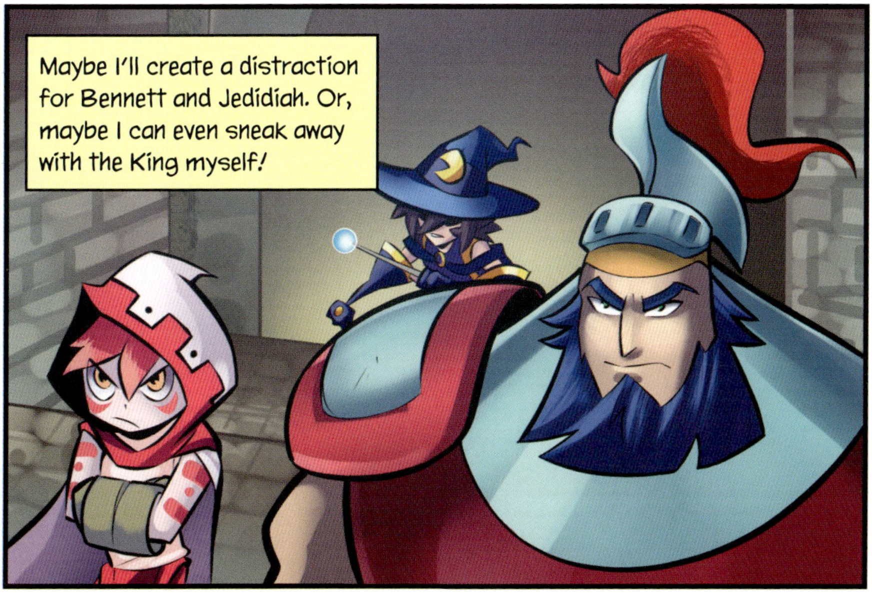
Maybe I'll create a distraction for Bennett and Jedidiah. Or, maybe I can even sneak away with the King myself!

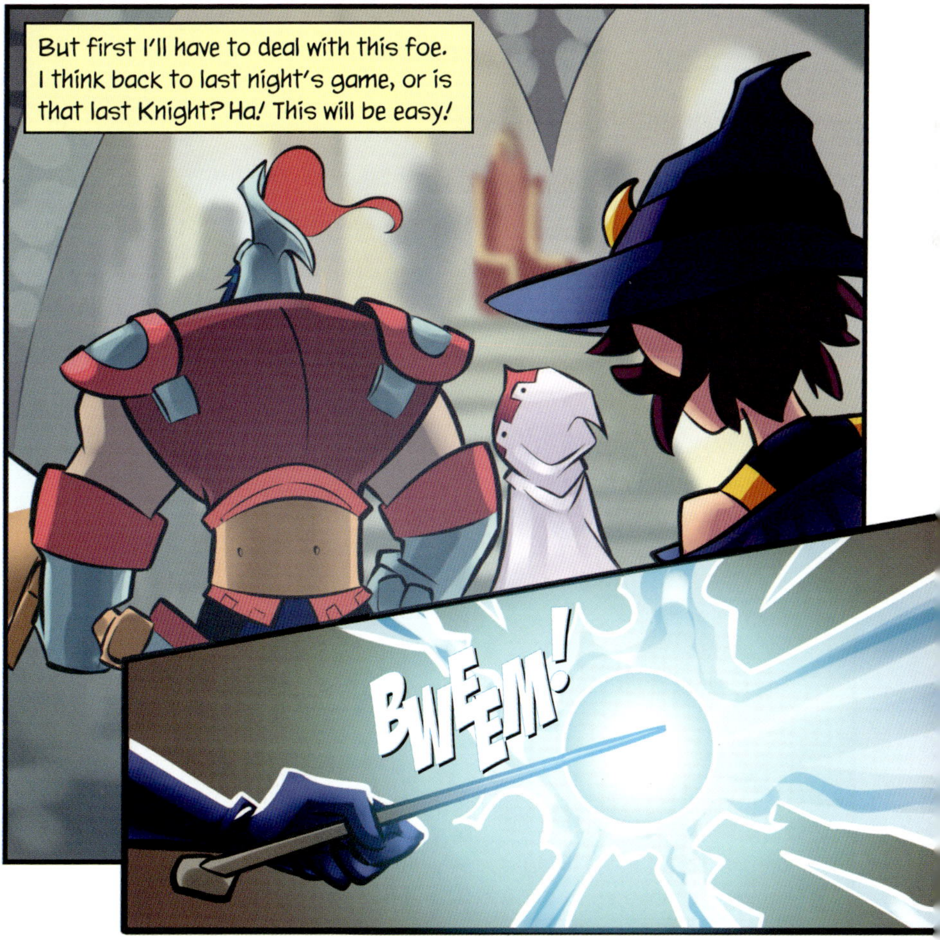
But first I'll have to deal with this foe. I think back to last night's game, or is that last Knight? Ha! This will be easy!
BWEEM!

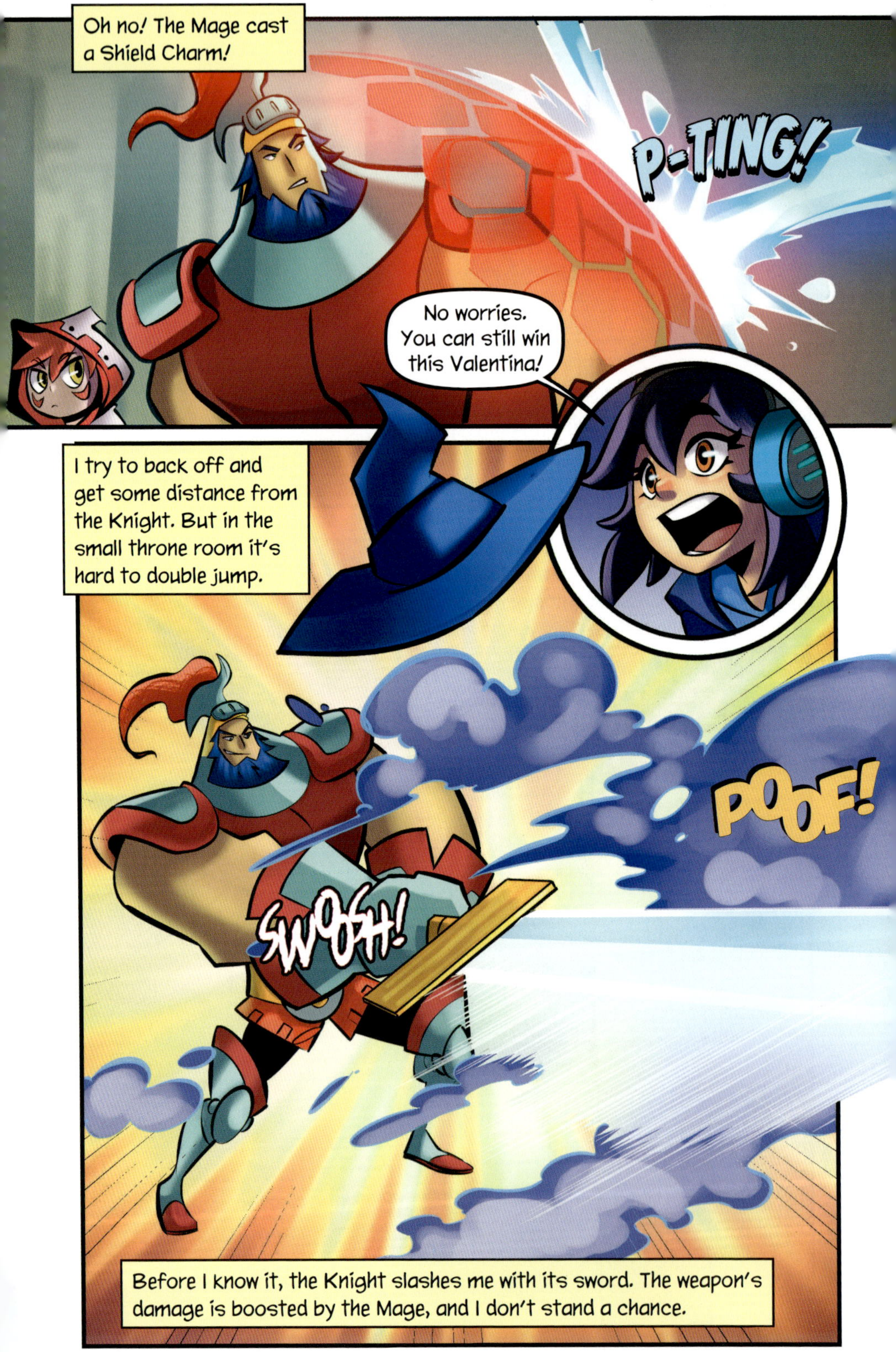
Oh no! The Mage cast a Shield Charm!
P-TING!
No worries. You can still win this Valentina!
I try to back off and get some distance from the Knight. But in the small throne room it's hard to double jump.
POOF!
SWOOSH!
Before I know it, the Knight slashes me with its sword. The weapon's damage is boosted by the Mage, and I don't stand a chance.

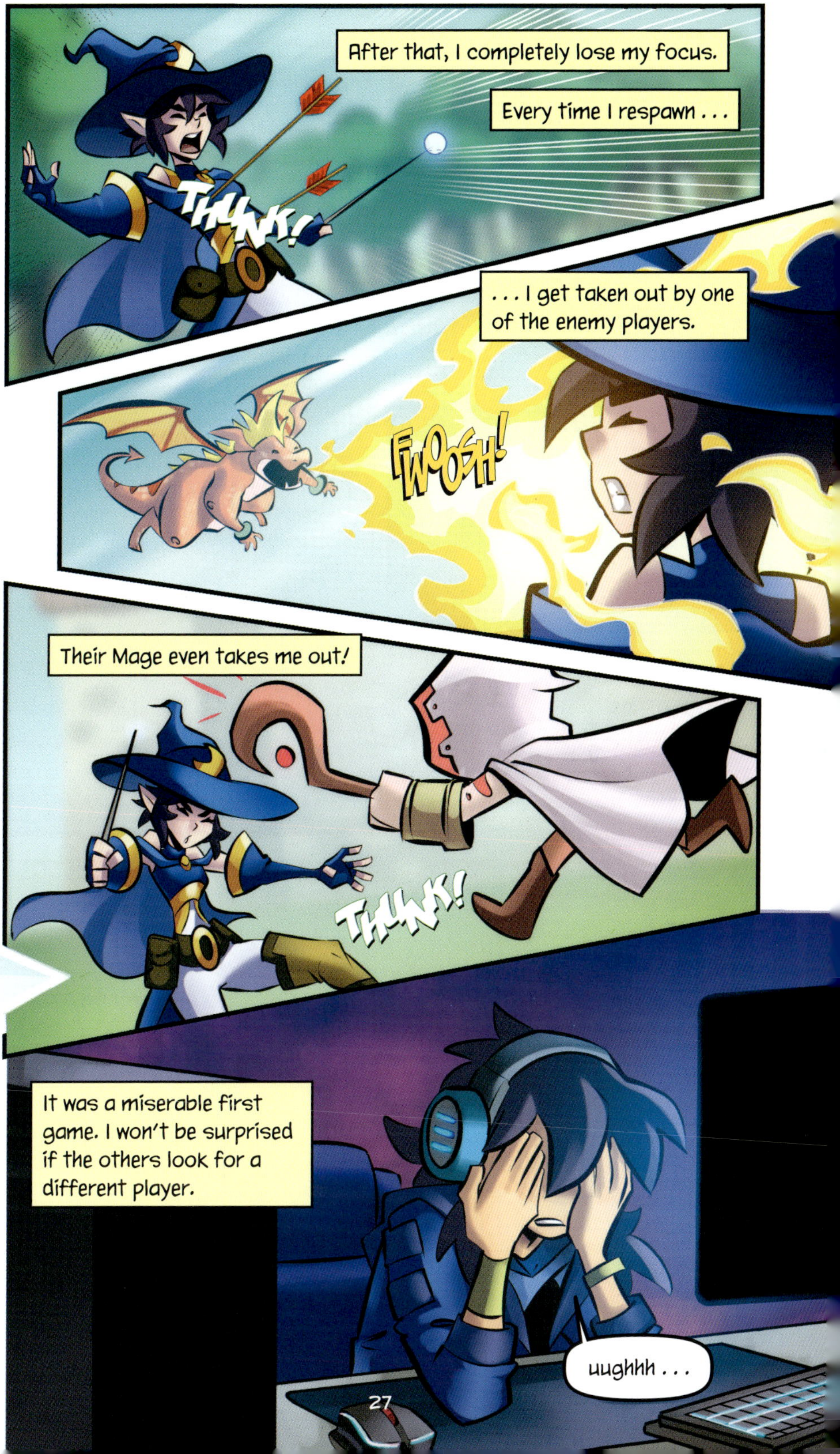
After that, I completely lose my focus.
Every time I respawn . . .
THUNK!
. . . I get taken out by one of the enemy players.
FWOOSH!
Their Mage even takes me out!
THUNK!
It was a miserable first game. I won't be surprised if the others look for a different player.
uughhh . . .

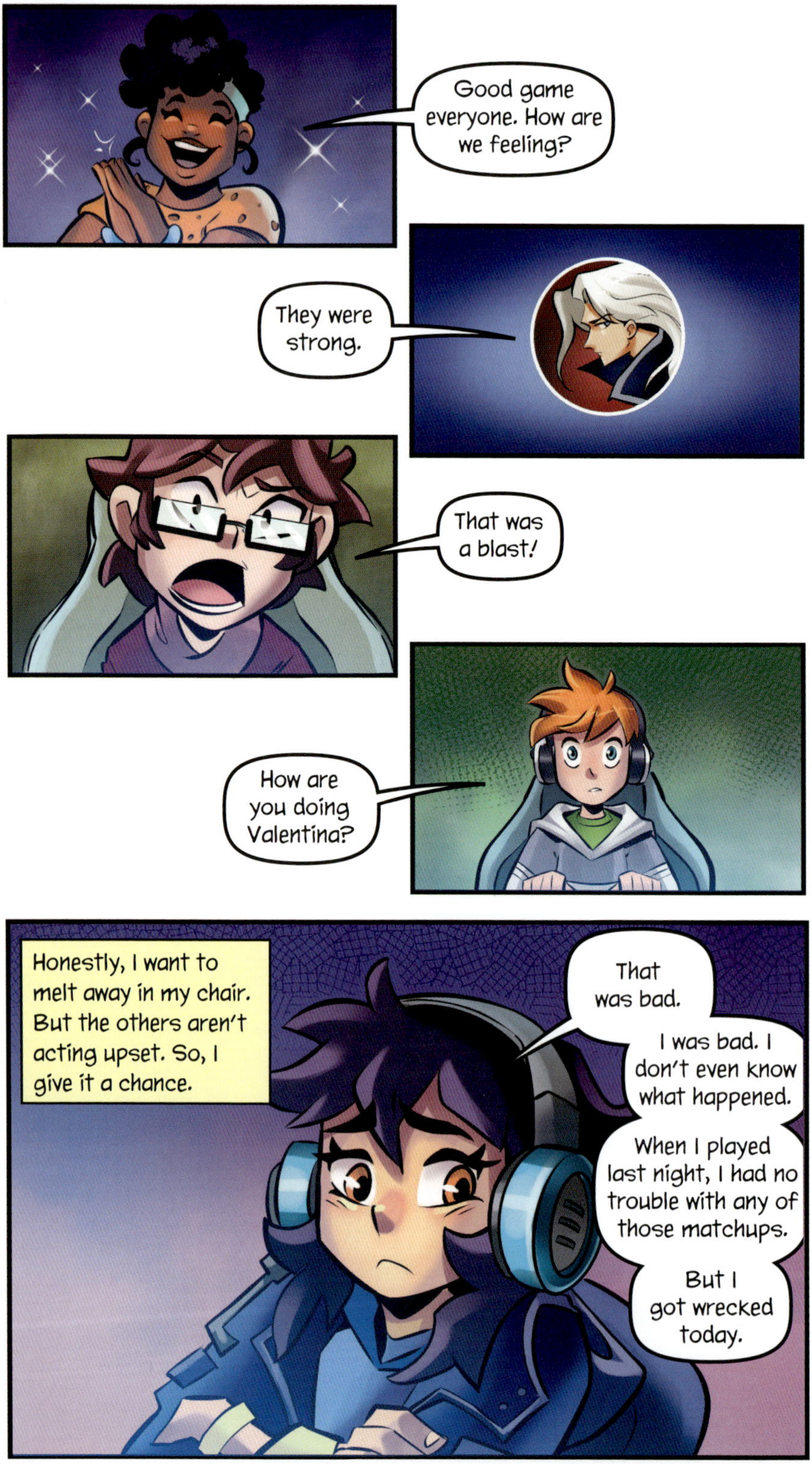
Good game everyone. How are we feeling?
They were strong.
That was a blast!
How are you doing Valentina?
Honestly, I want to melt away in my chair. But the others aren't acting upset. So, I give it a chance.
That was bad.
I was bad. I don't even know what happened.
When I played last night, I had no trouble with any of those matchups.
But I got wrecked today.

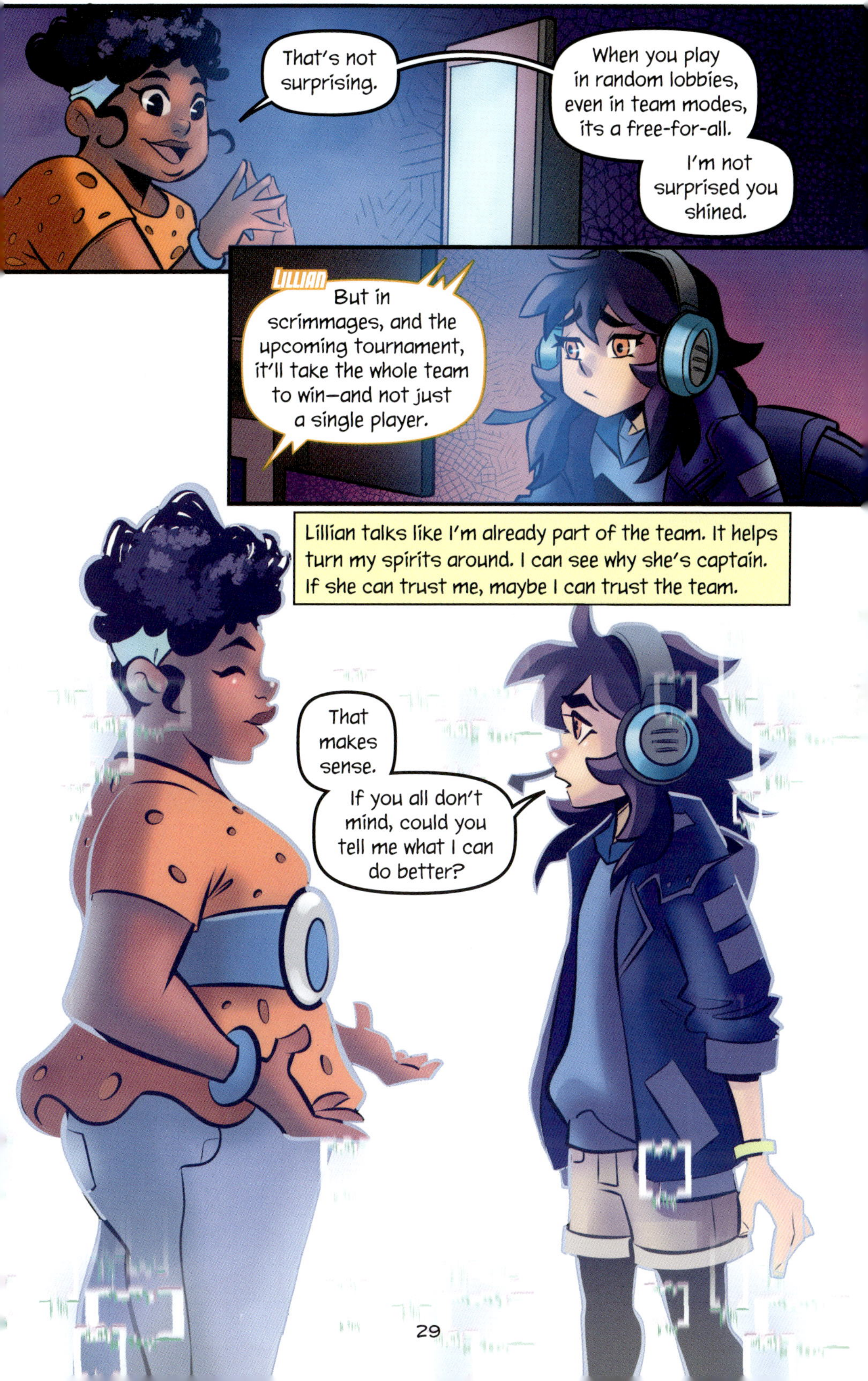

That's not surprising.
When you play in random lobbies, even in team modes, its a free-for-all.
I'm not surprised you shined.
LILLIAN
But in scrimmages, and the upcoming tournament, it'll take the whole team to win—and not just a single player.
Lillian talks like I'm already part of the team. It helps turn my spirits around. I can see why she's captain. If she can trust me, maybe I can trust the team.
That makes sense.
If you all don't mind, could you tell me what I can do better?

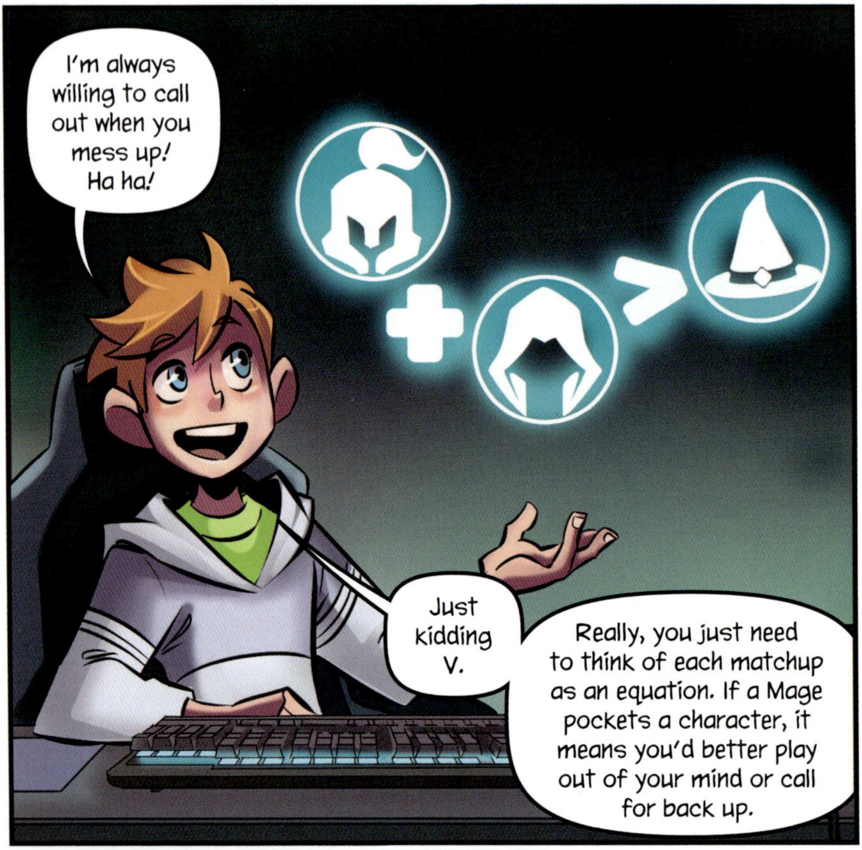
I'm always willing to call out when you mess up! Ha ha!
Just kidding V.
Really, you just need to think of each matchup as an equation. If a Mage pockets a character, it means you'd better play out of your mind or call for back up.

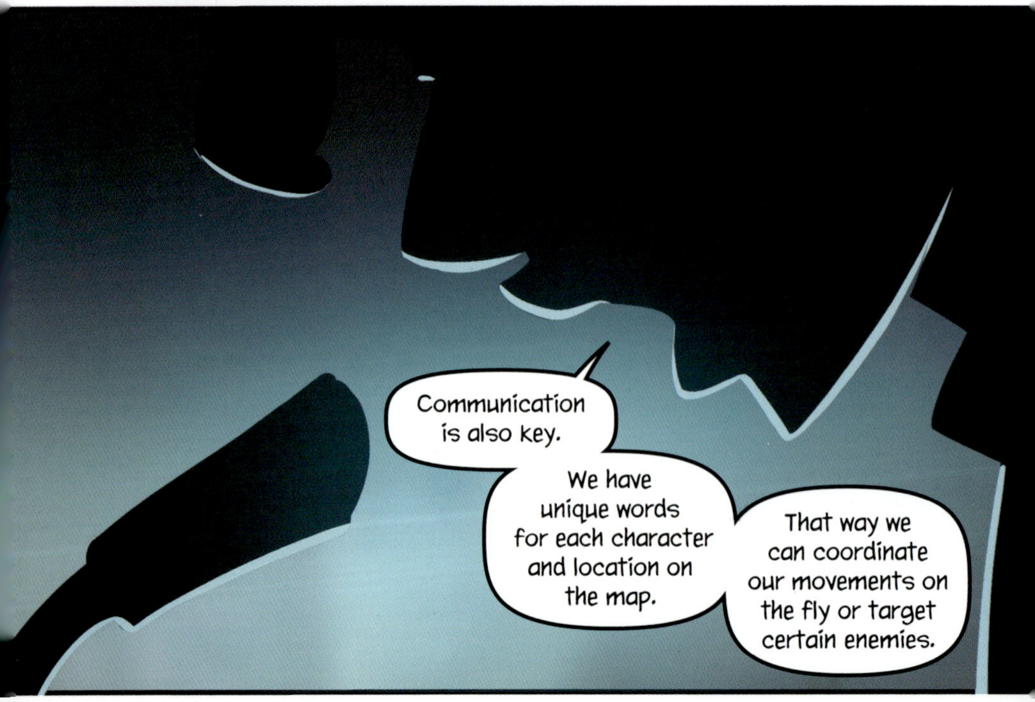
Communication is also key.
We have unique words for each character and location on the map.
That way we can coordinate our movements on the fly or target certain enemies.

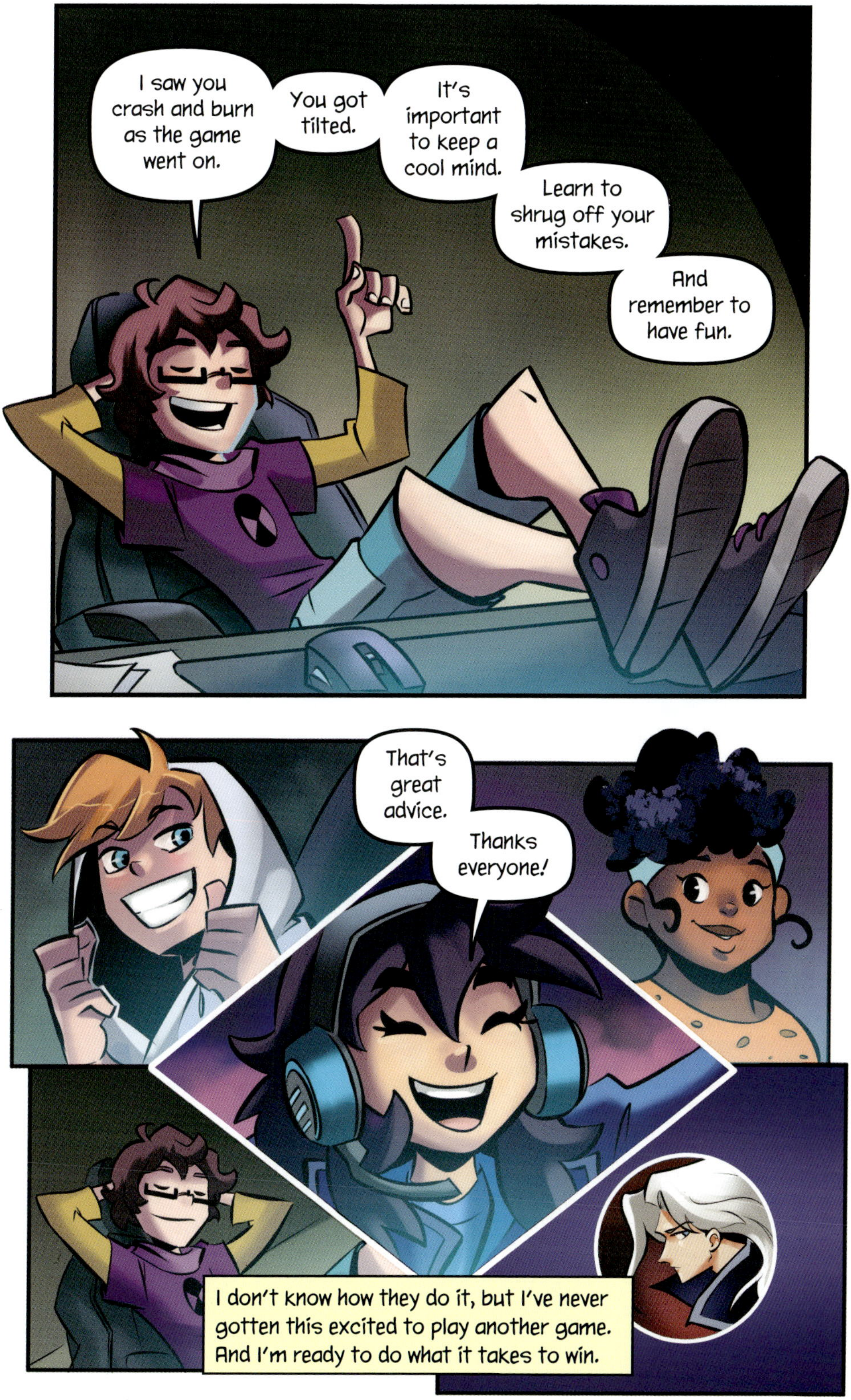
I saw you crash and burn as the game went on.
You got tilted.
It's important to keep a cool mind.
Learn to shrug off your mistakes.
And remember to have fun.
That's great advice.
Thanks everyone!
I don't know how they do it, but I've never gotten this excited to play another game. And I'm ready to do what it takes to win.

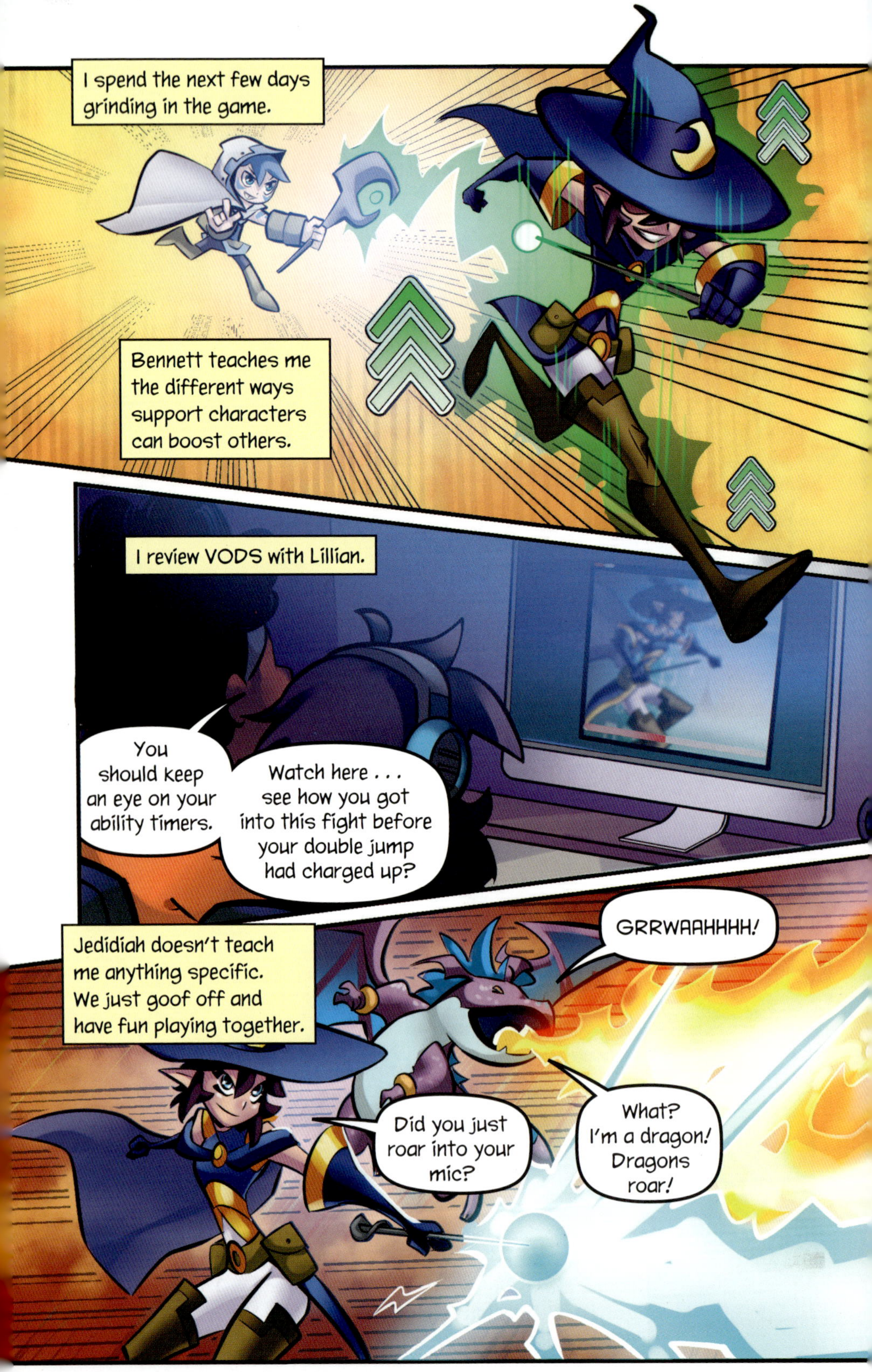

I spend the next few days grinding in the game.
Bennett teaches me the different ways support characters can boost others.
I review VODS with Lillian.
You should keep an eye on your ability timers.
Watch here . . . see how you got into this fight before your double jump had charged up?
Jedidiah doesn't teach me anything specific. We just goof off and have fun playing together.
GRRWAAHHHH!
Did you just roar into your mic?
What? I'm a dragon! Dragons roar!

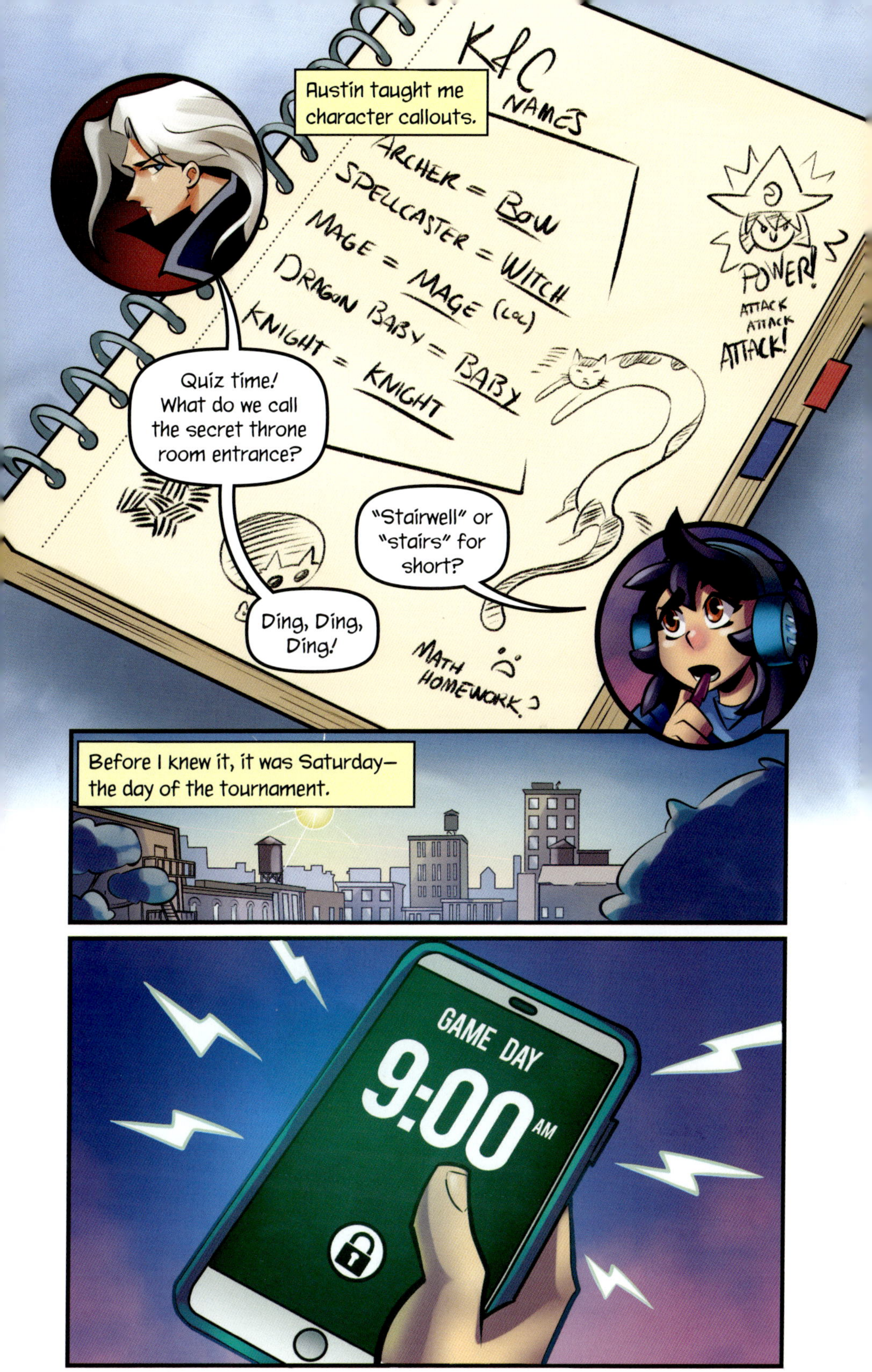
Austin taught me character callouts.
K&C NAMES
ARCHER = BOW
SPELLCASTER = WITCH
MAGE = MAGE (LOL)
DRAGON BABY = BABY
KNIGHT = KNIGHT
POWER!
ATTACK ATTACK ATTACK!
Quiz time! What do we call the secret throne room entrance?
"Stairwell" or "stairs" for short?
Ding, Ding, Ding!
MATH HOMEWORK
Before I knew it, it was Saturday—the day of the tournament.
GAME DAY
9:00 AM

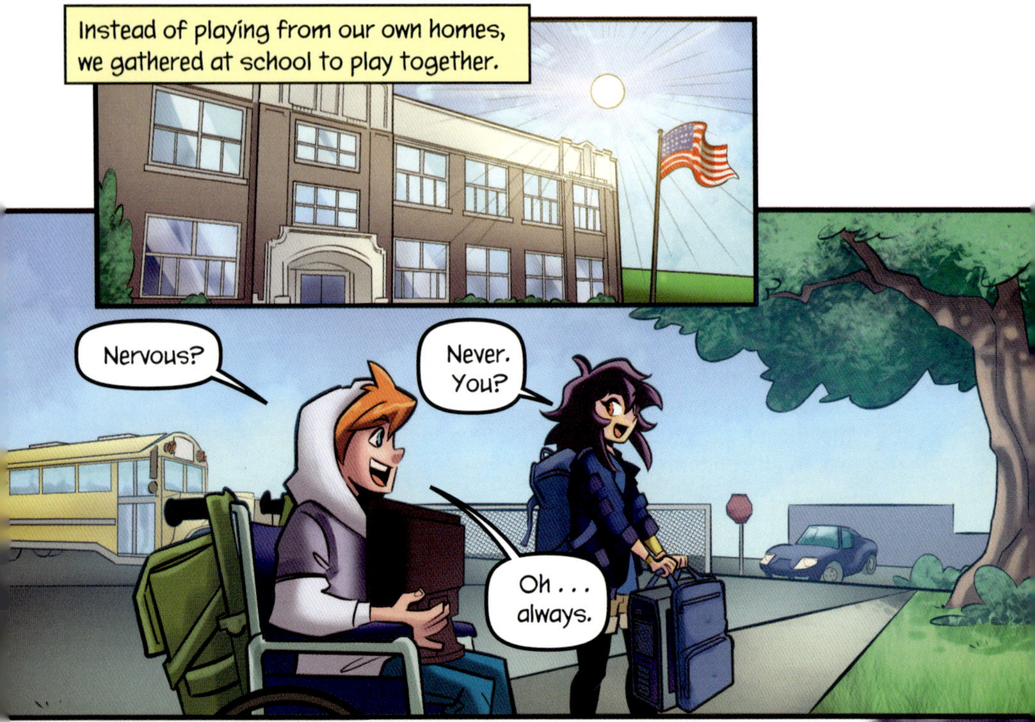
Instead of playing from our own homes, we gathered at school to play together.
Nervous?
Never. You?
Oh . . . always.

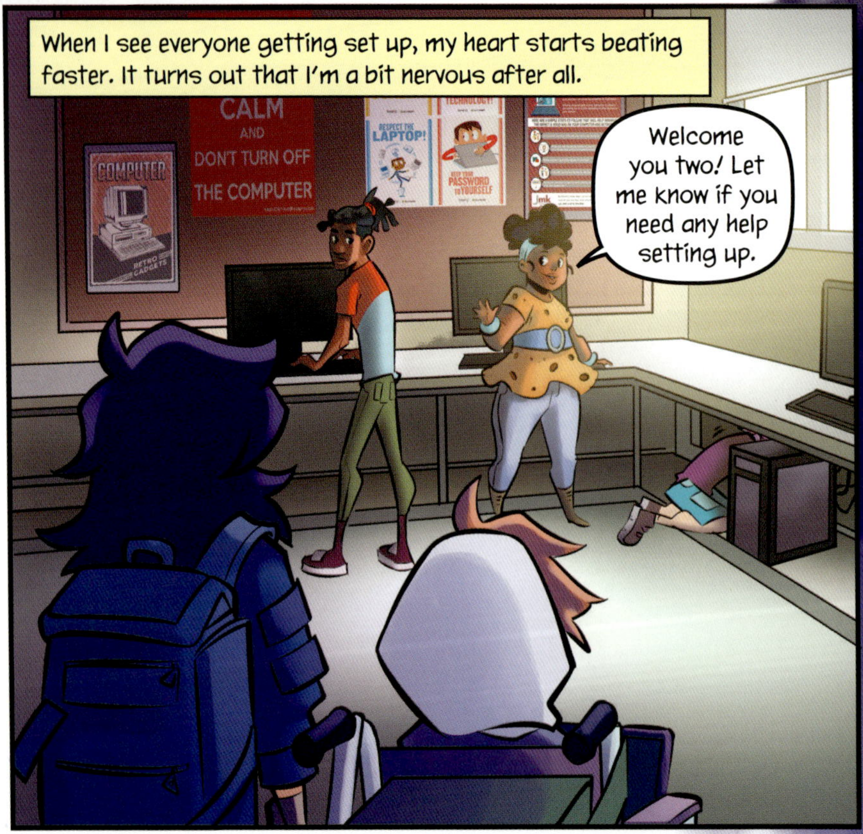
When I see everyone getting set up, my heart starts beating faster. It turns out that I'm a bit nervous after all.
COMPUTER
CALM
AND
DON'T TURN OFF
THE COMPUTER
LAPTOP!
PASSWORD
Welcome you two! Let me know if you need any help setting up.

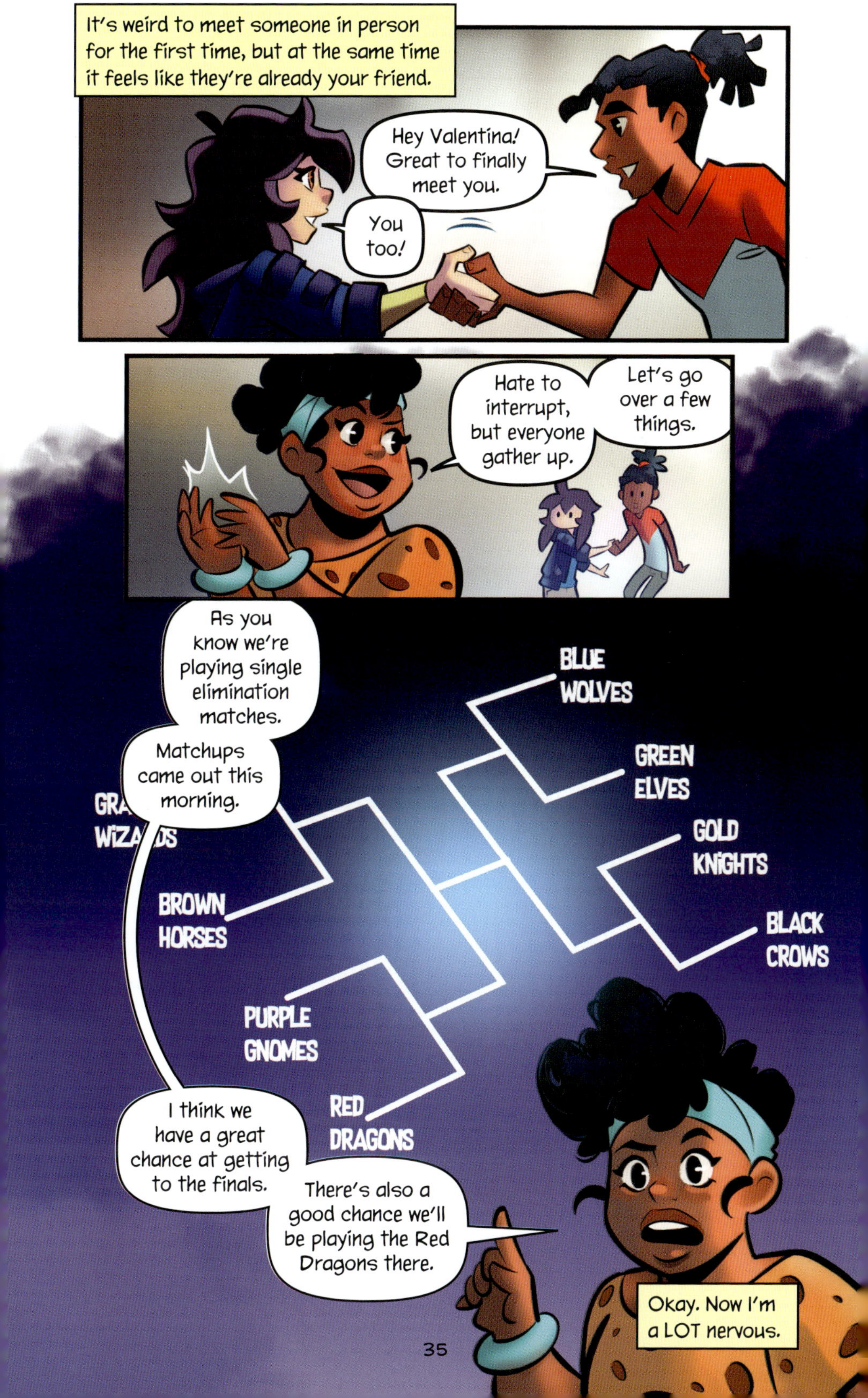

It's weird to meet someone in person for the first time, but at the same time it feels like they're already your friend.
Hey Valentina! Great to finally meet you.
You too!
Hate to interrupt, but everyone gather up.
Let's go over a few things.
As you know we're playing single elimination matches.
Matchups came out this morning.
BLUE WOLVES
GREEN ELVES
GOLD KNIGHTS
BLACK CROWS
BROWN HORSES
PURPLE GNOMES
RED DRAGONS
I think we have a great chance at getting to the finals.
There's also a good chance we'll be playing the Red Dragons there.
Okay. Now I'm a LOT nervous.

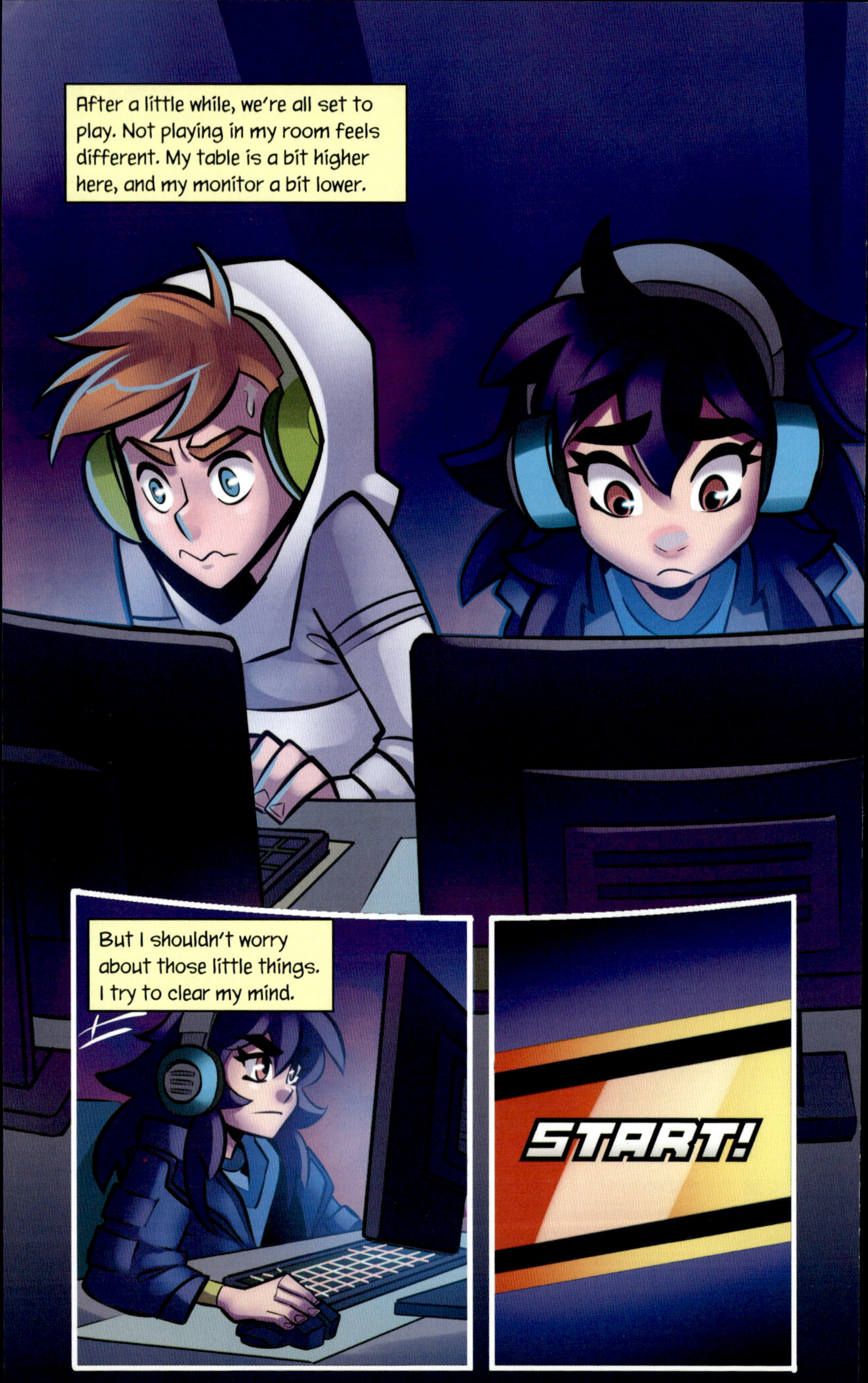
After a little while, we're all set to play. Not playing in my room feels different. My table is a bit higher here, and my monitor a bit lower.
But I shouldn't worry about those little things. I try to clear my mind.
START!

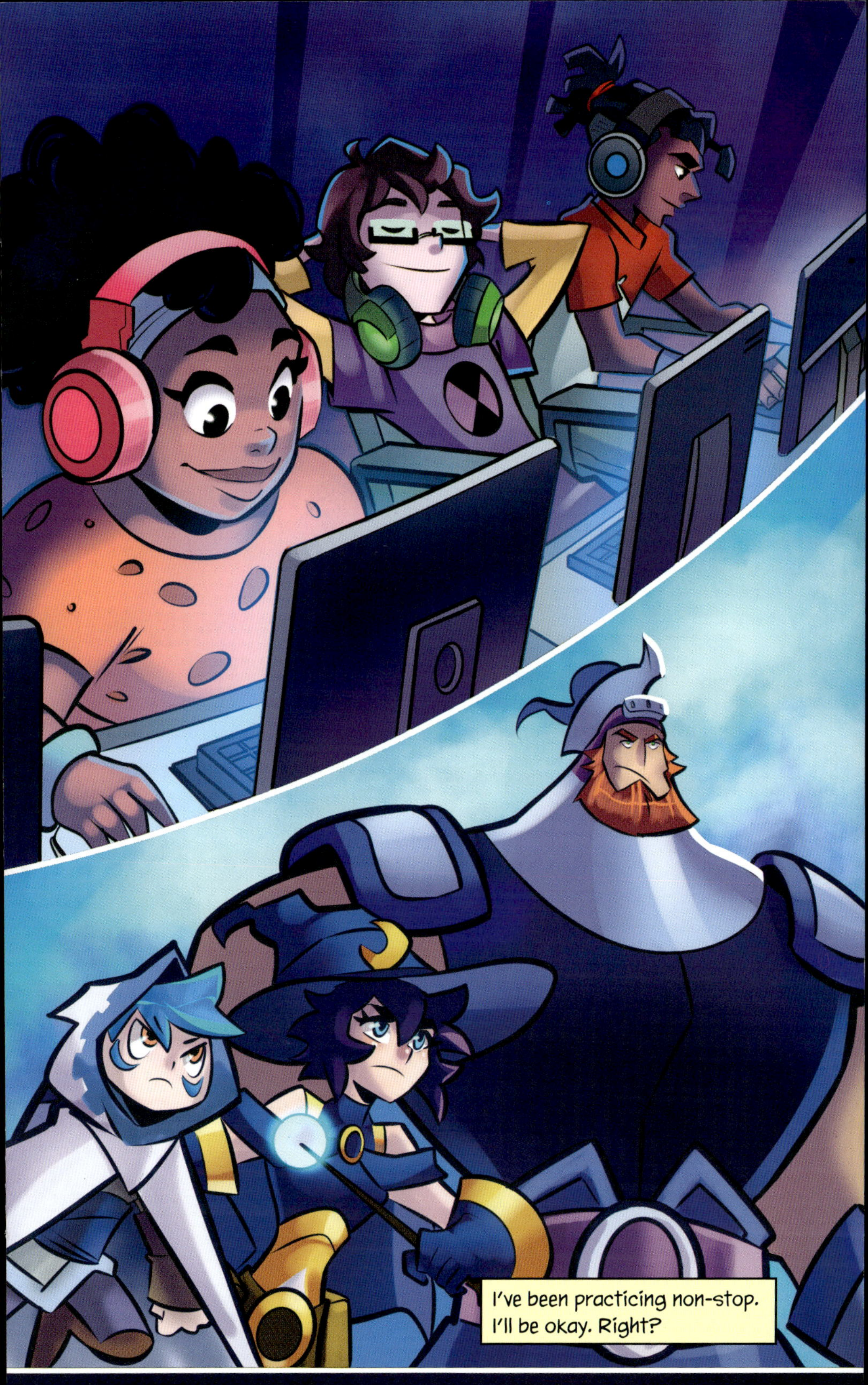
I've been practicing non-stop.
I'll be okay. Right?

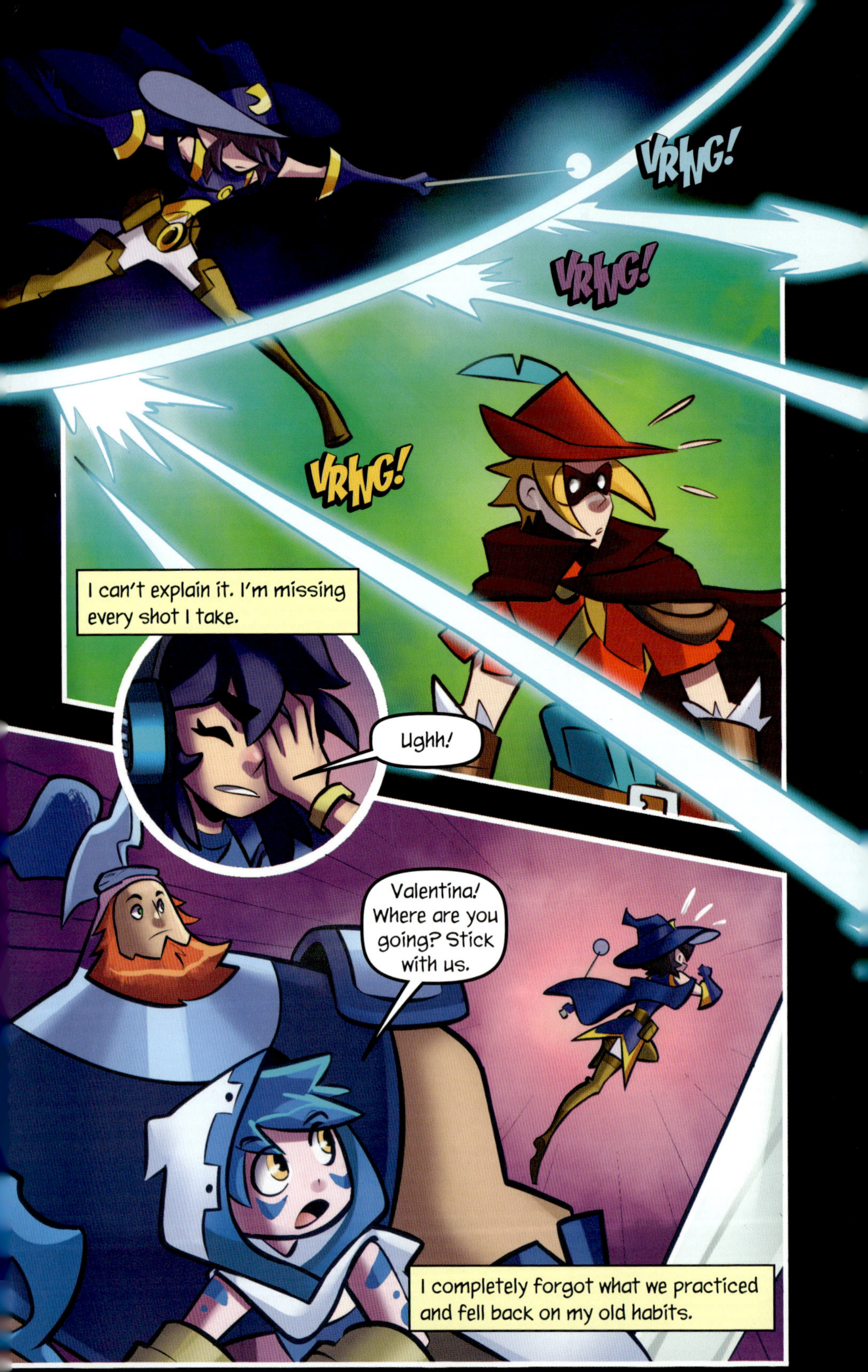

VRING!
VRING!
VRING!
I can't explain it. I'm missing every shot I take.
Ughh!
Valentina! Where are you going? Stick with us.
I completely forgot what we practiced and fell back on my old habits.

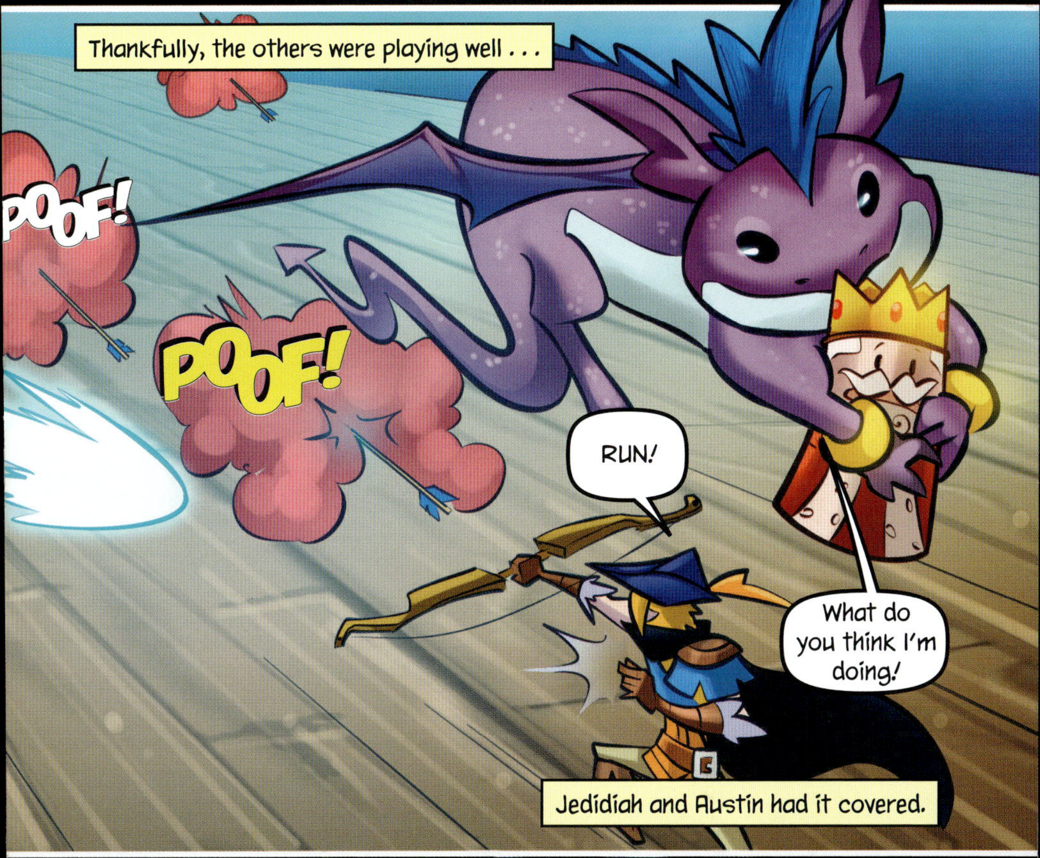
Thankfully, the others were playing well . . .
POOF!
POOF!
RUN!
What do you think I'm doing!
Jedidiah and Austin had it covered.

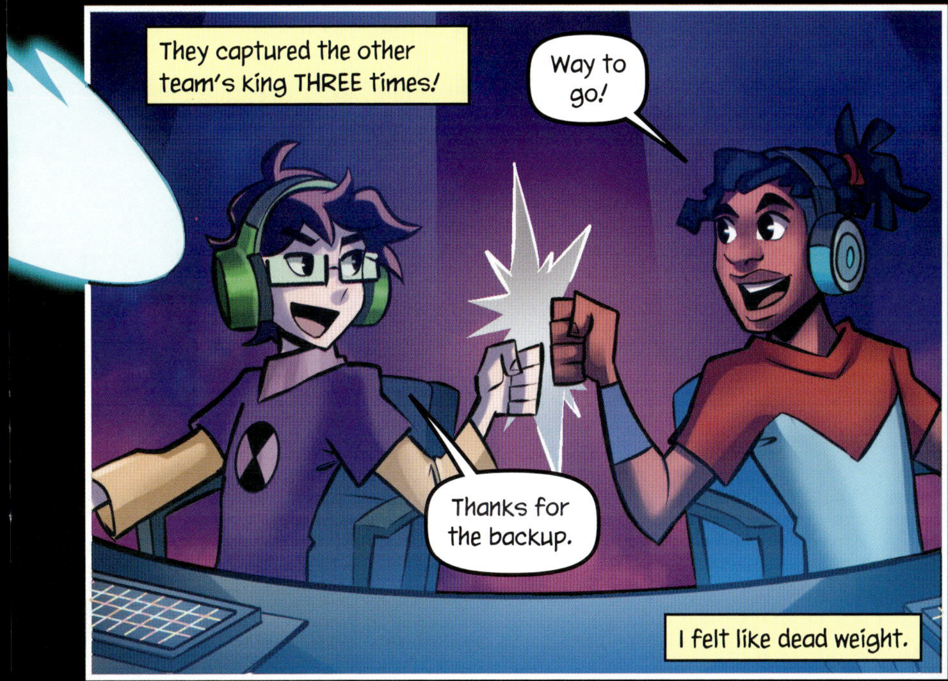
They captured the other team's king THREE times!
Way to go!
Thanks for the backup.
I felt like dead weight.

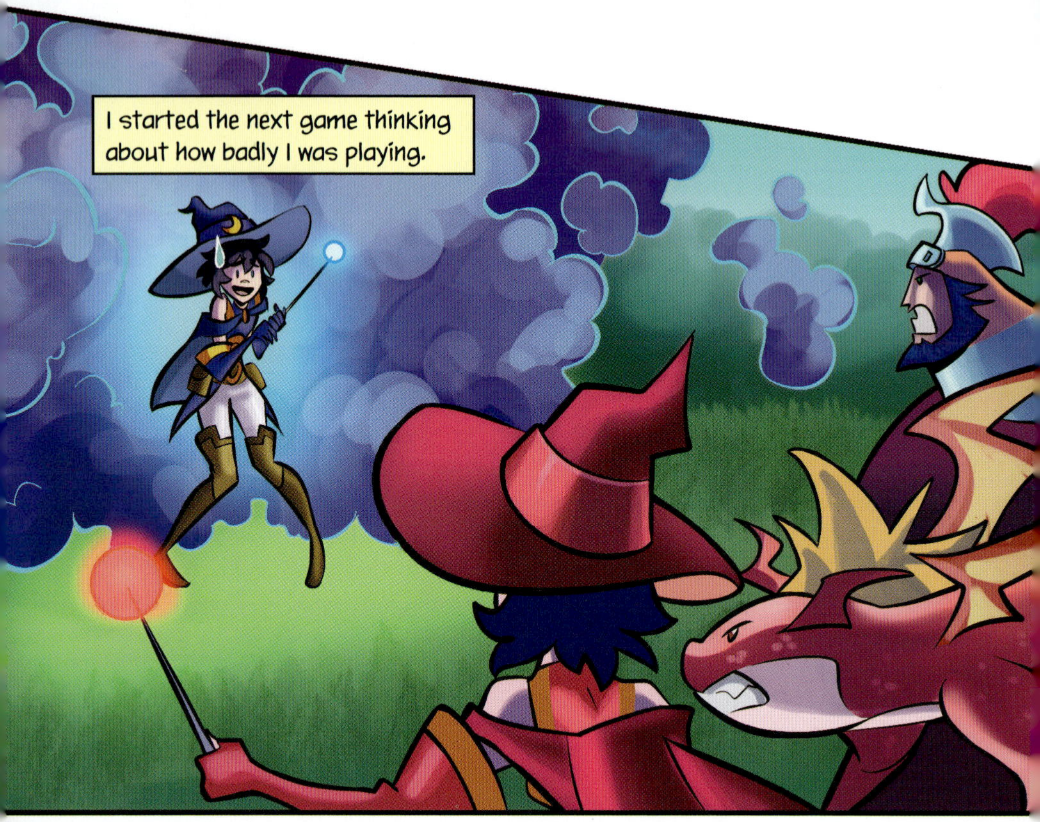
I started the next game thinking about how badly I was playing.

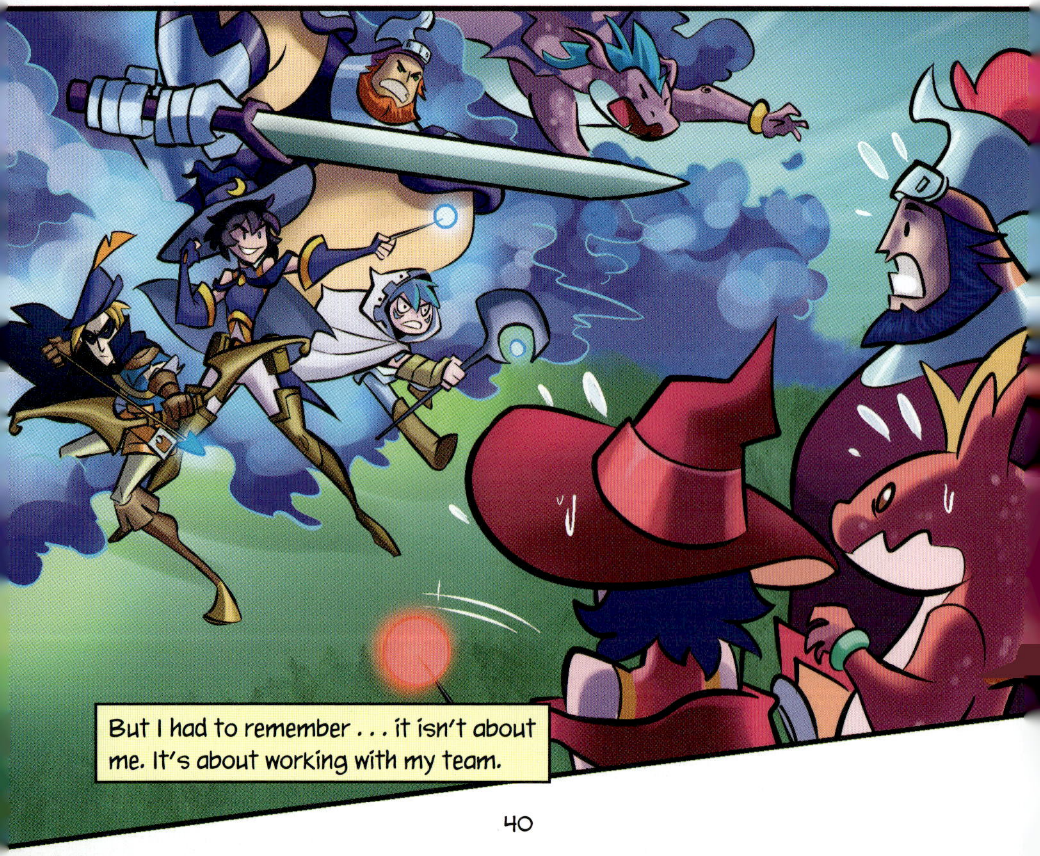
But I had to remember . . . it isn't about me. It's about working with my team.

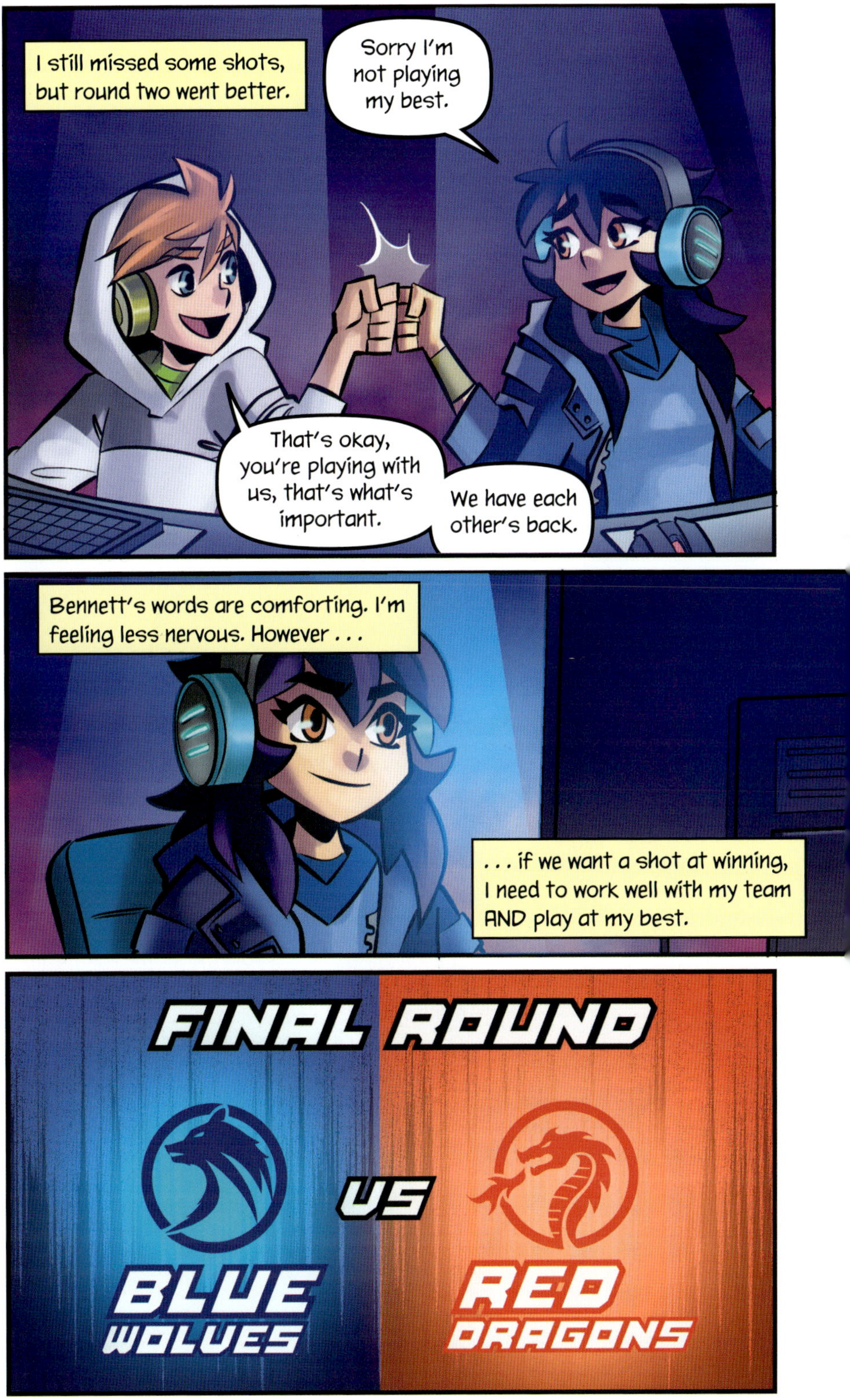
I still missed some shots, but round two went better.
Sorry I'm not playing my best.
That's okay, you're playing with us, that's what's important.
We have each other's back.
Bennett's words are comforting. I'm feeling less nervous. However . . .
. . . if we want a shot at winning, I need to work well with my team AND play at my best.
FINAL ROUND
VS
BLUE WOLVES
RED DRAGONS

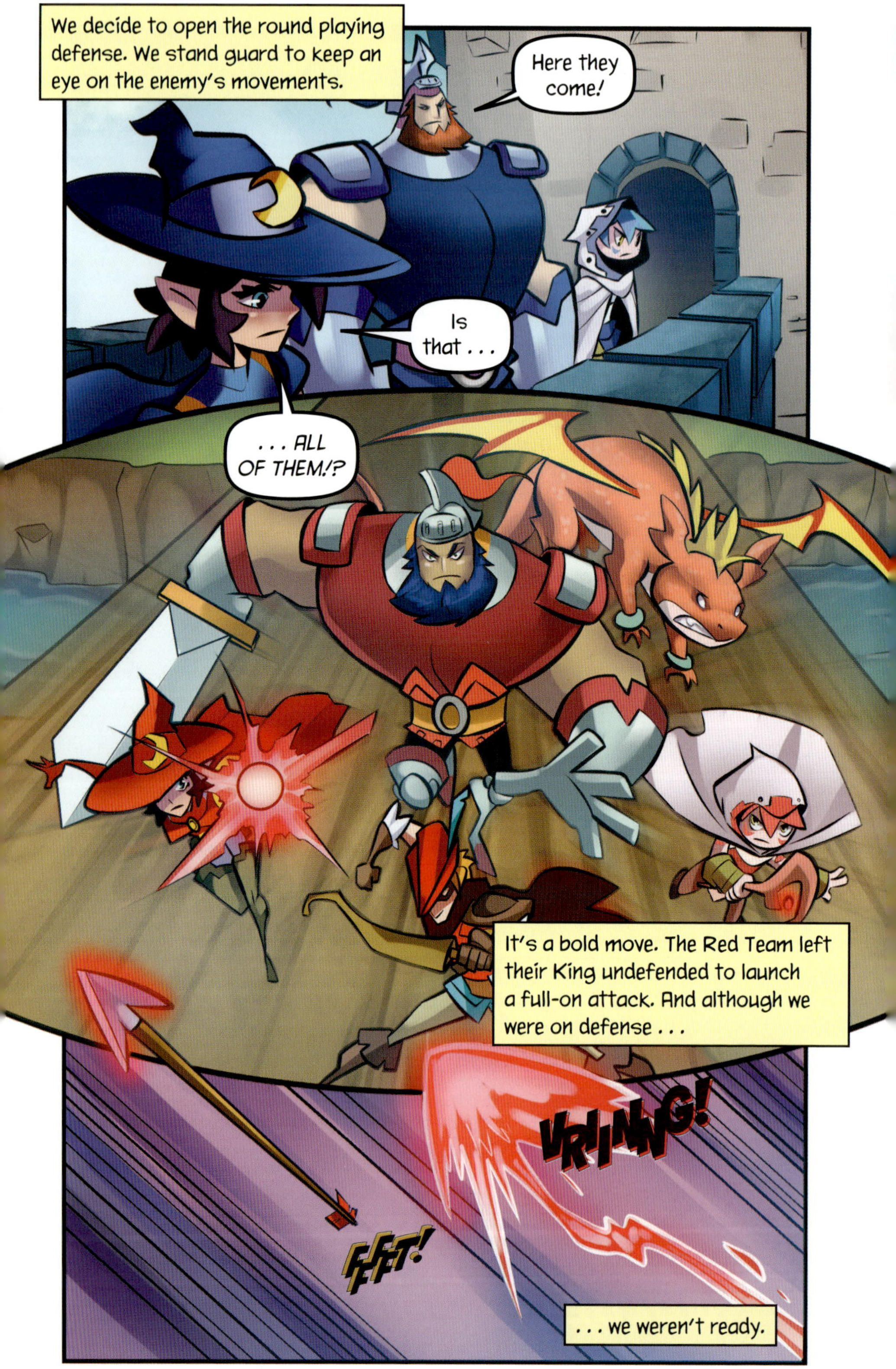
We decide to open the round playing defense. We stand guard to keep an eye on the enemy's movements.
Here they come!
Is that . . .
. . . ALL OF THEM!?
It's a bold move. The Red Team left their King undefended to launch a full-on attack. And although we were on defense . . .
VRIINNG!
FFFT!
. . . we weren't ready.

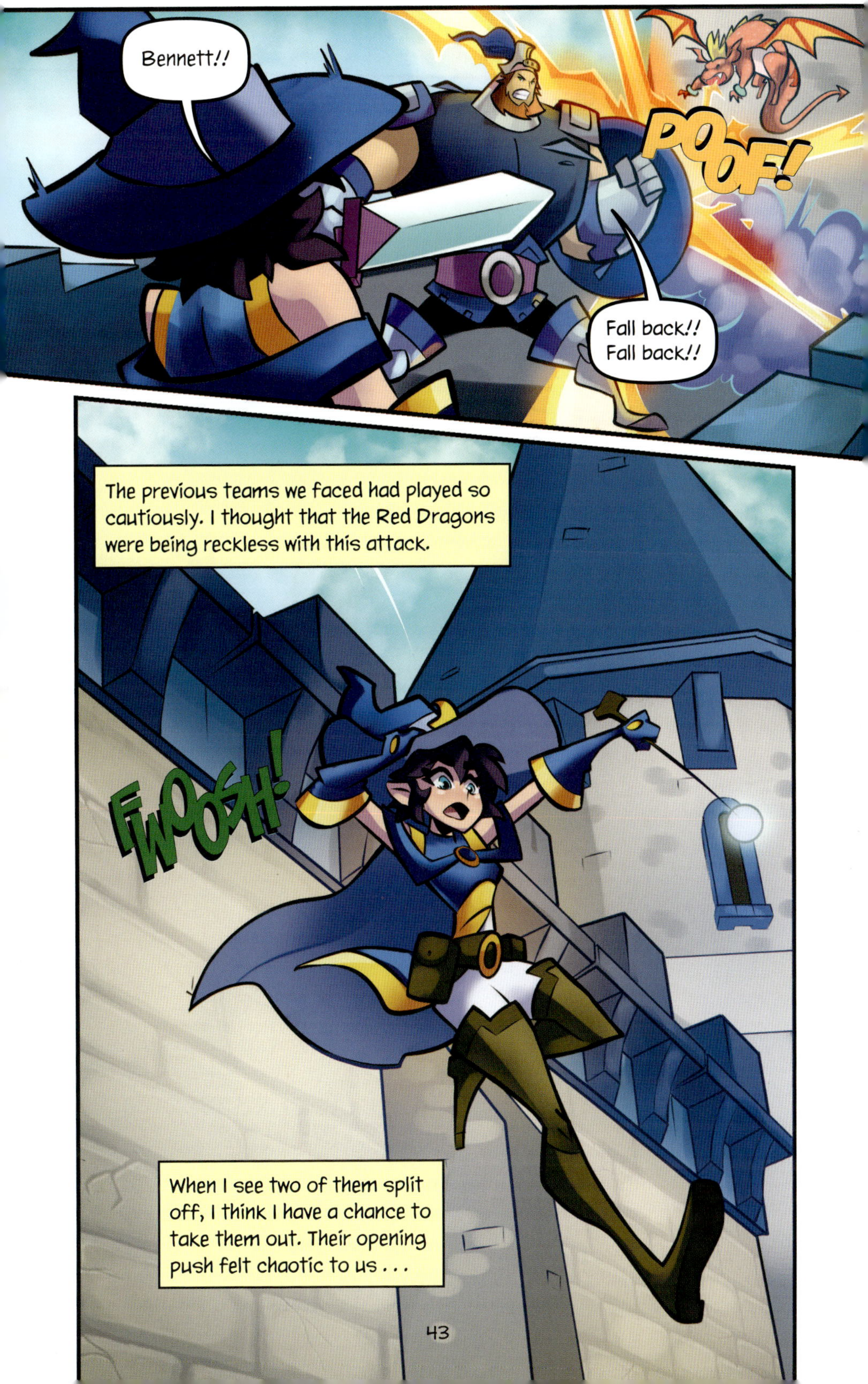

Bennett!!
POOF!
Fall back!! Fall back!!
The previous teams we faced had played so cautiously. I thought that the Red Dragons were being reckless with this attack.
FWOOSH!
When I see two of them split off, I think I have a chance to take them out. Their opening push felt chaotic to us . . .

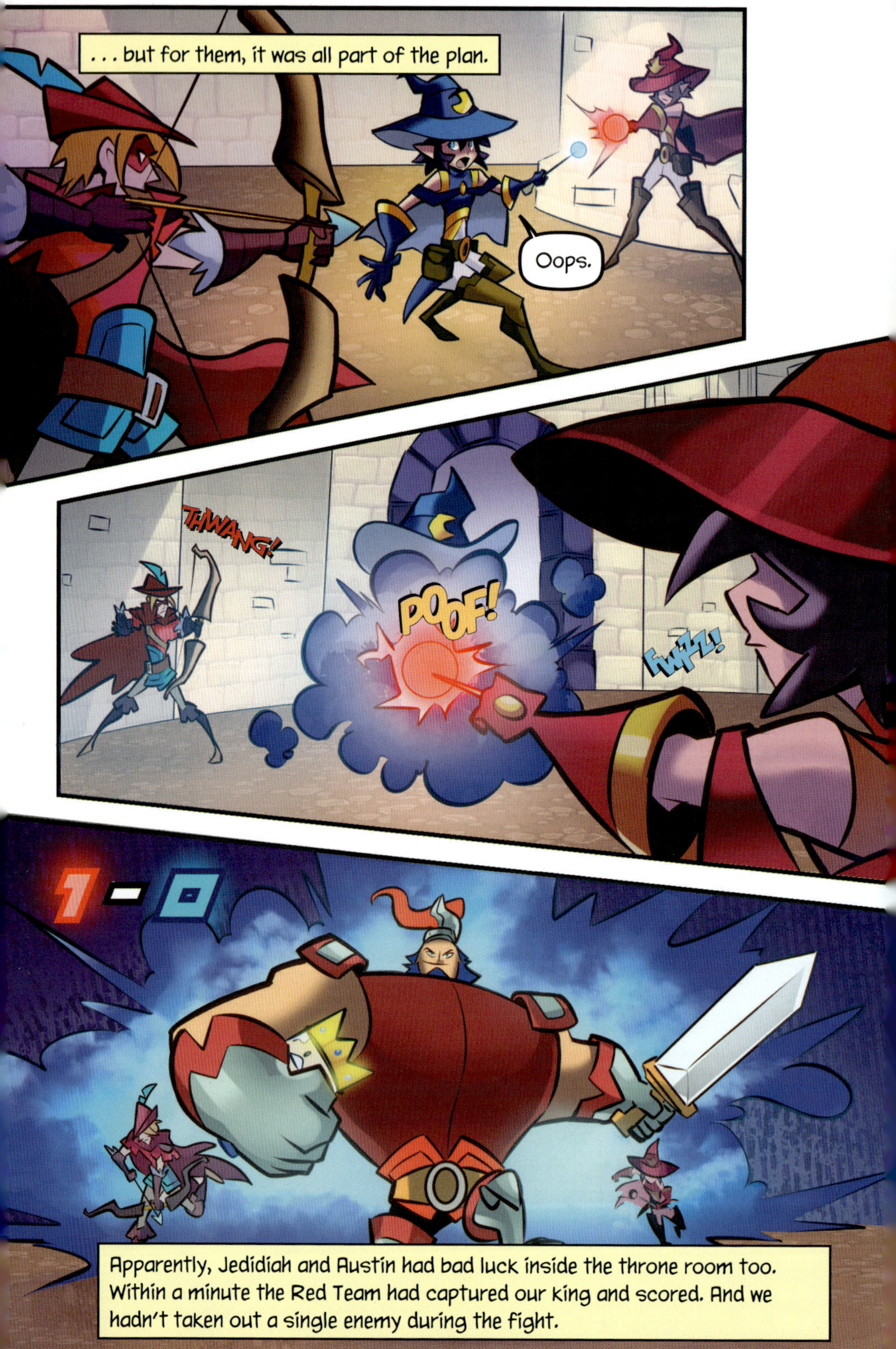
. . . but for them, it was all part of the plan.
Oops.
THWANG!
POOF!
FWIZZ!
1 - 0
Apparently, Jedidiah and Austin had bad luck inside the throne room too. Within a minute the Red Team had captured our king and scored. And we hadn't taken out a single enemy during the fight.

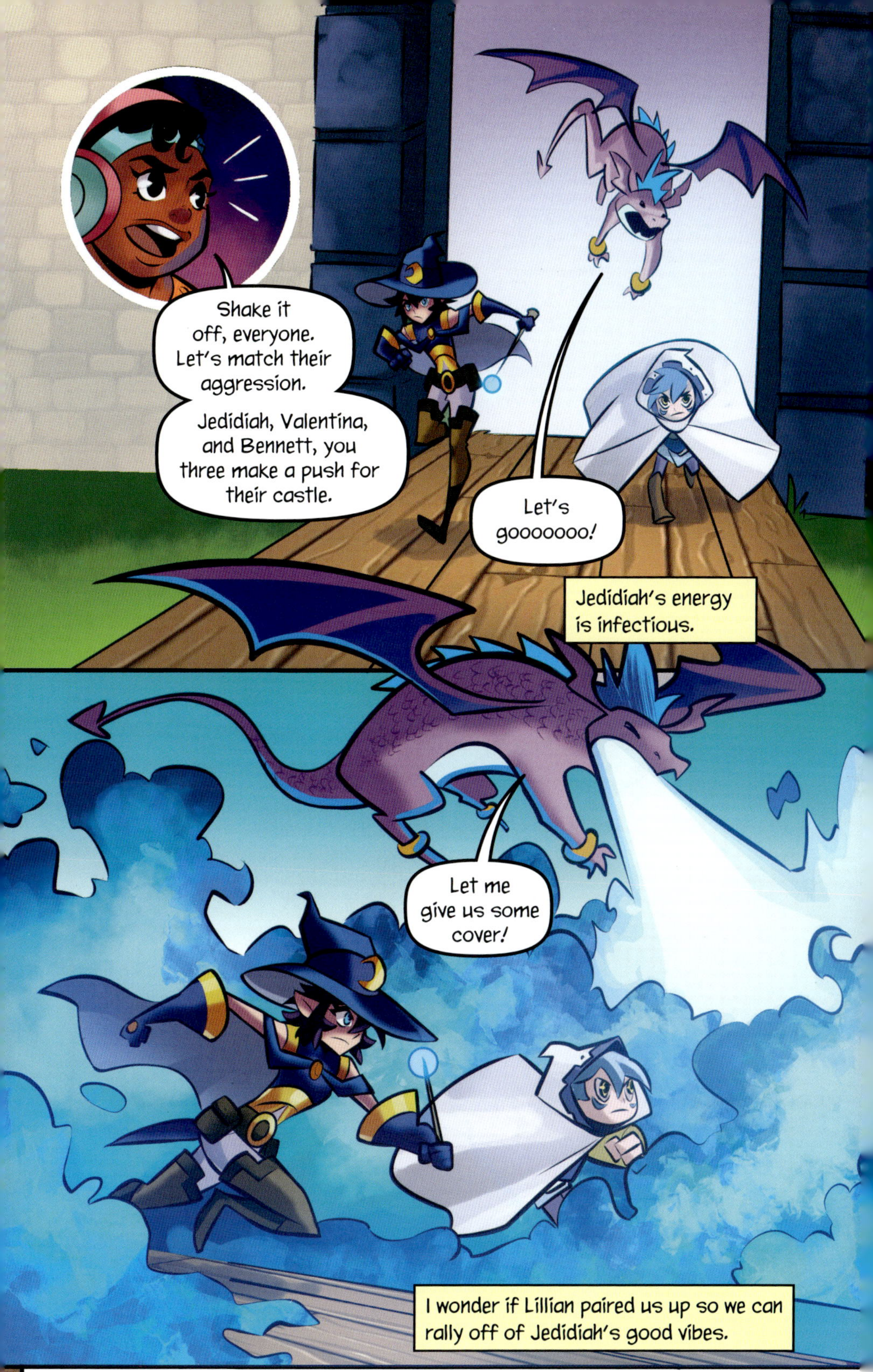
Shake it off, everyone. Let's match their aggression.
Jedidiah, Valentina, and Bennett, you three make a push for their castle.
Let's gooooooo!
Jedidiah's energy is infectious.
Let me give us some cover!
I wonder if Lillian paired us up so we can rally off of Jedidiah's good vibes.

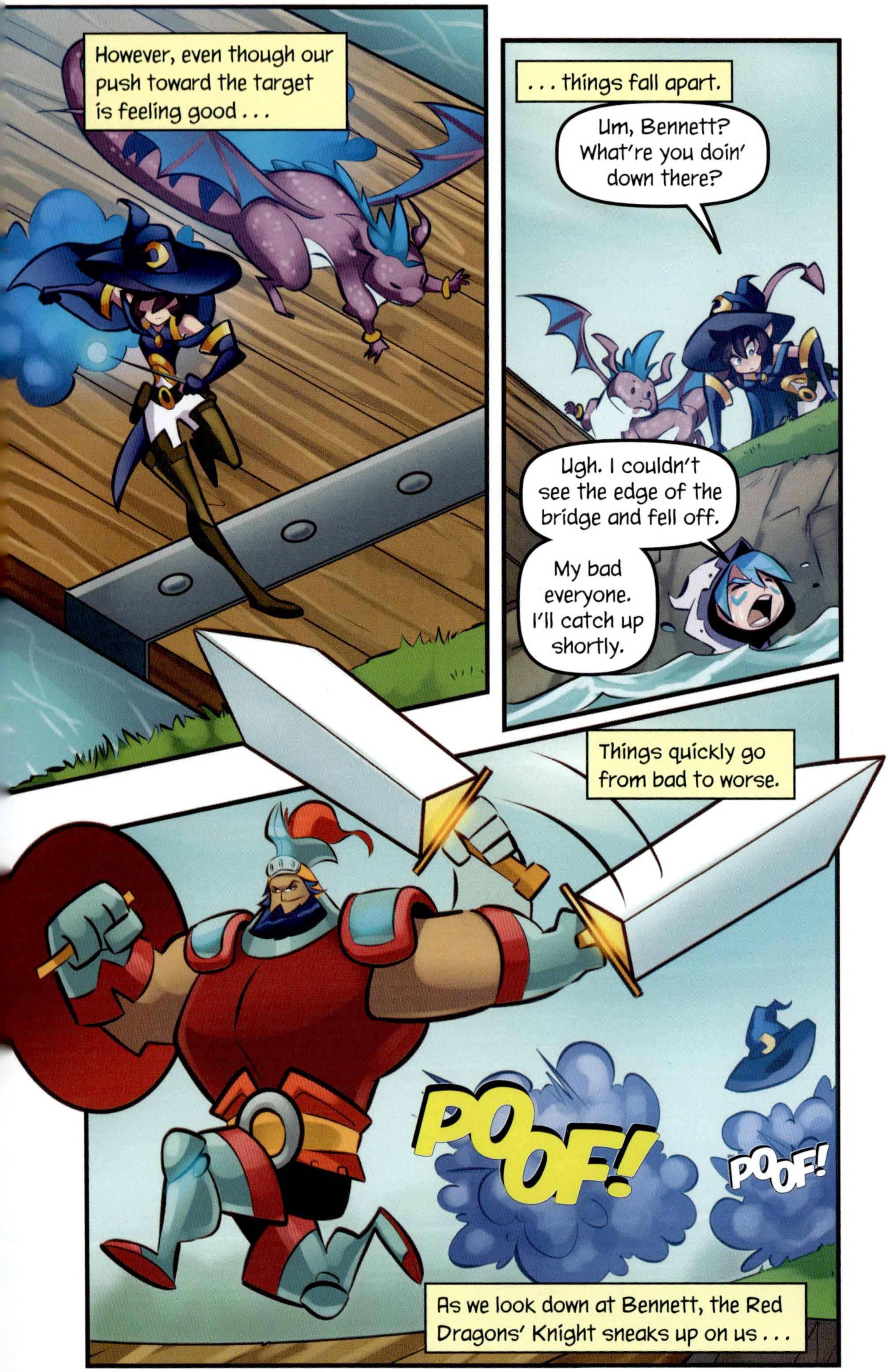
However, even though our push toward the target is feeling good . . .
. . . things fall apart.
Um, Bennett? What're you doin' down there?
Ugh. I couldn't see the edge of the bridge and fell off.
My bad everyone. I'll catch up shortly.
Things quickly go from bad to worse.
POOF!
POOF!
As we look down at Bennett, the Red Dragons' Knight sneaks up on us . . .

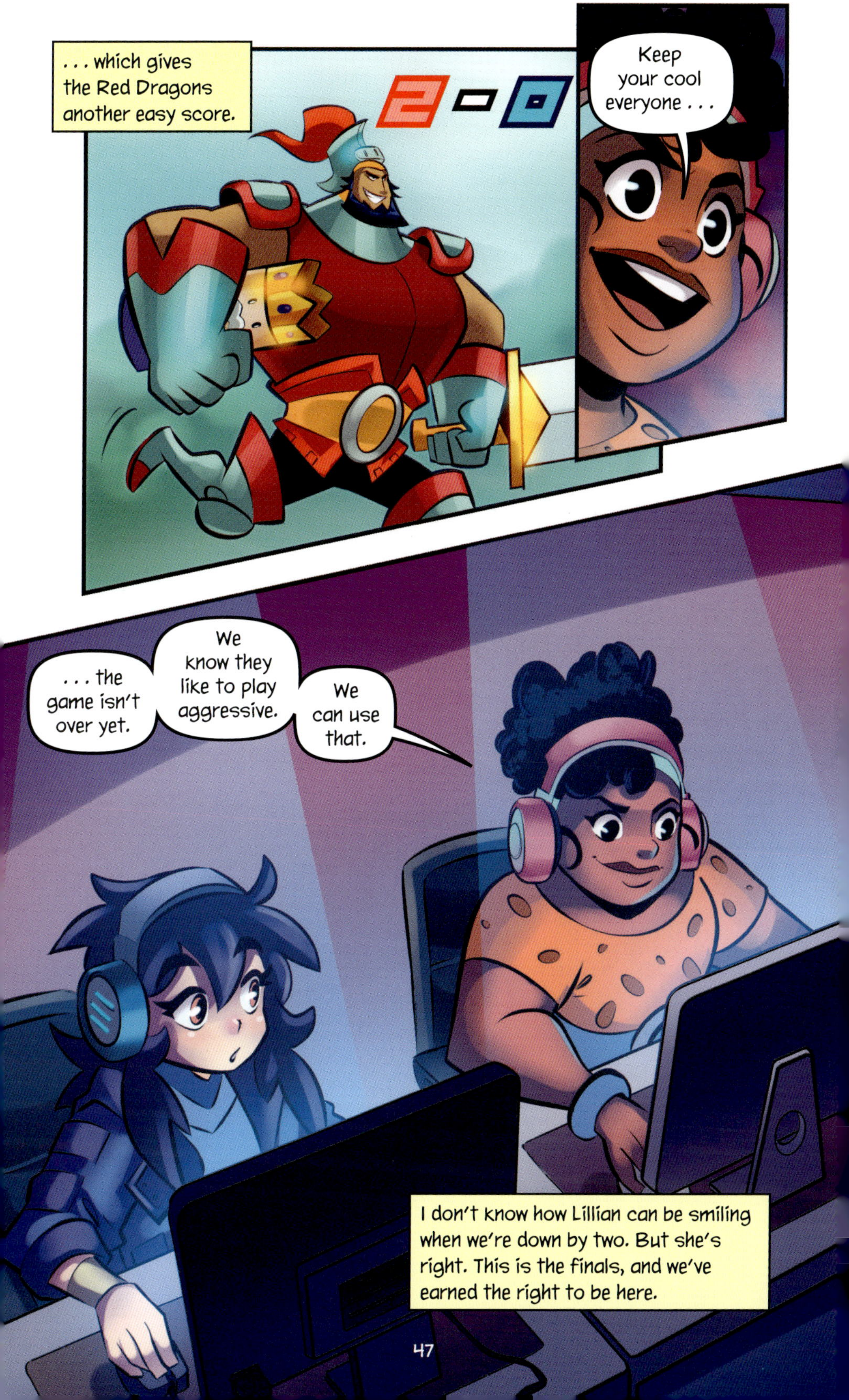
. . . which gives the Red Dragons another easy score.
2 - 0
Keep your cool everyone . . .
. . . the game isn't over yet.
We know they like to play aggressive.
We can use that.
I don't know how Lillian can be smiling when we're down by two. But she's right. This is the finals, and we've earned the right to be here.

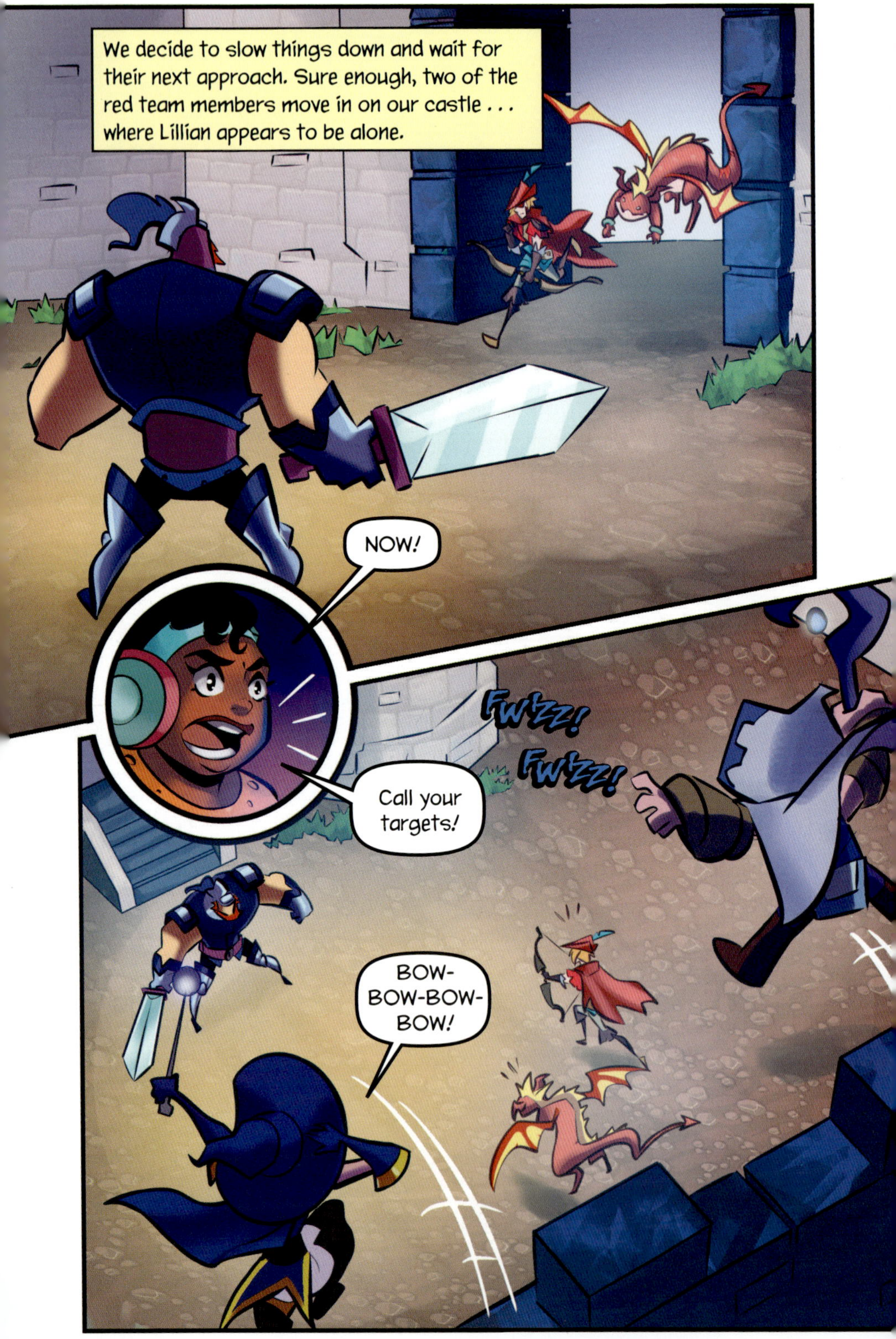
We decide to slow things down and wait for their next approach. Sure enough, two of the red team members move in on our castle . . . where Lillian appears to be alone.
NOW!
Call your targets!
FWIZZ!
FWIZZ!
BOW-BOW-BOW-BOW!

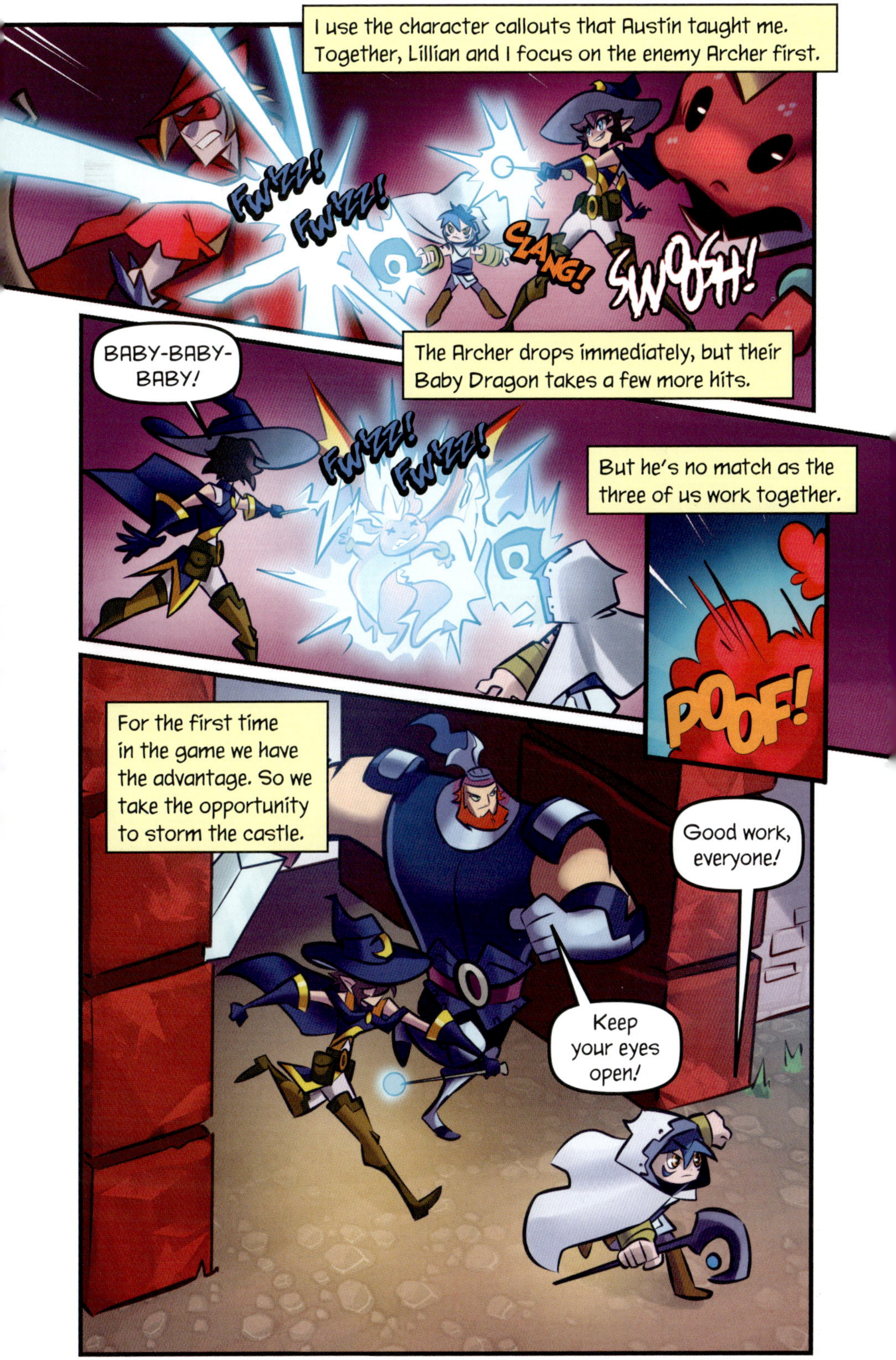
I use the character callouts that Austin taught me. Together, Lillian and I focus on the enemy Archer first.
FWZZZ! FWZZZ!
CLANG!
SWOOSH!
BABY-BABY-BABY!
The Archer drops immediately, but their Baby Dragon takes a few more hits.
FWZZZ! FWZZZ!
But he's no match as the three of us work together.
POOF!
For the first time in the game we have the advantage. So we take the opportunity to storm the castle.
Good work, everyone!
Keep your eyes open!

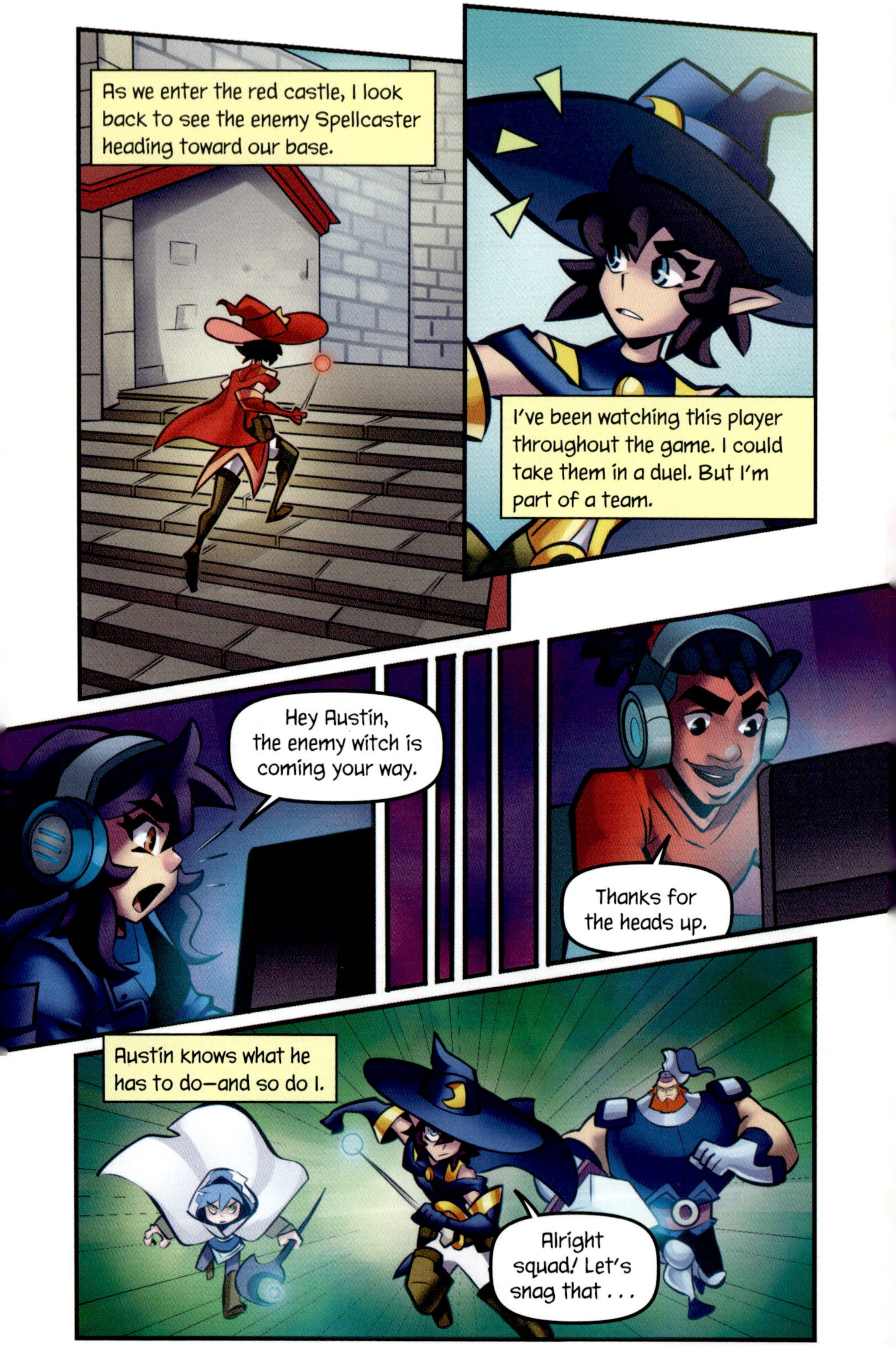
As we enter the red castle, I look back to see the enemy Spellcaster heading toward our base.
I've been watching this player throughout the game. I could take them in a duel. But I'm part of a team.
Hey Austin, the enemy witch is coming your way.
Thanks for the heads up.
Austin knows what he has to do—and so do I.
Alright squad! Let's snag that . . .

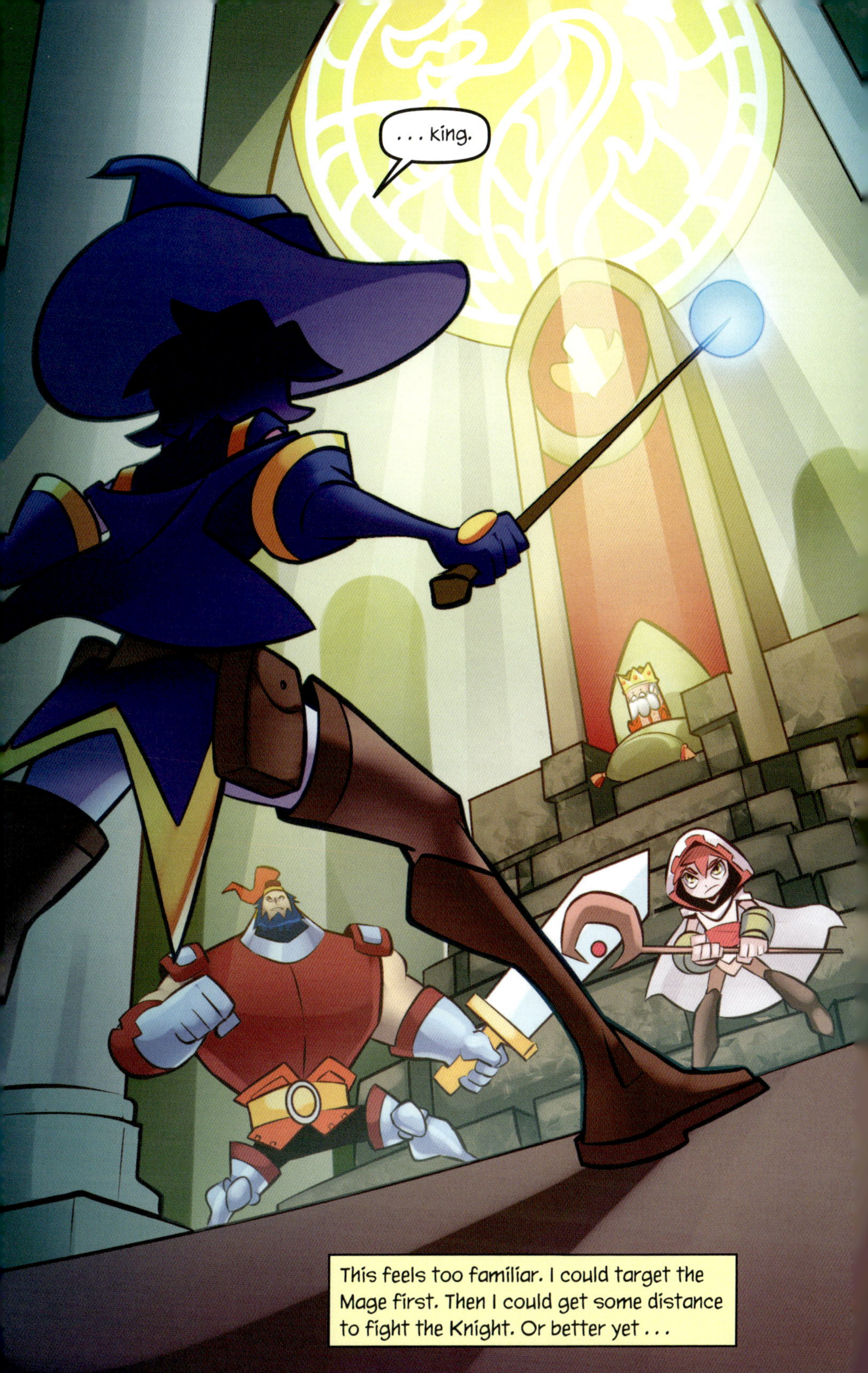

. . . king.
This feels too familiar. I could target the Mage first. Then I could get some distance to fight the Knight. Or better yet . . .

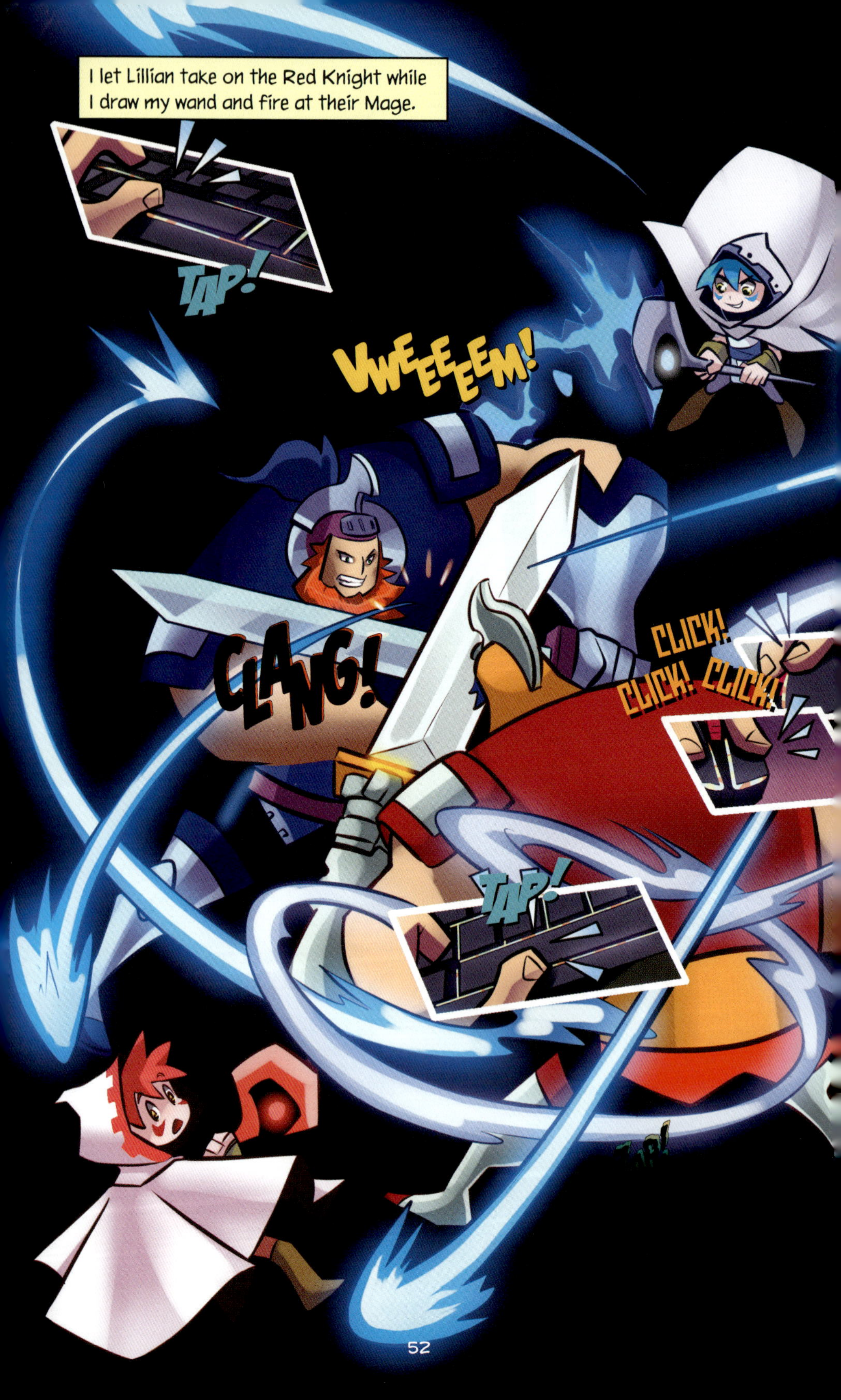
I let Lillian take on the Red Knight while
I draw my wand and fire at their Mage.
TAP!
VWEEEEEM!
CLANG!
CLICK!
CLICK! CLICK!
TAP!

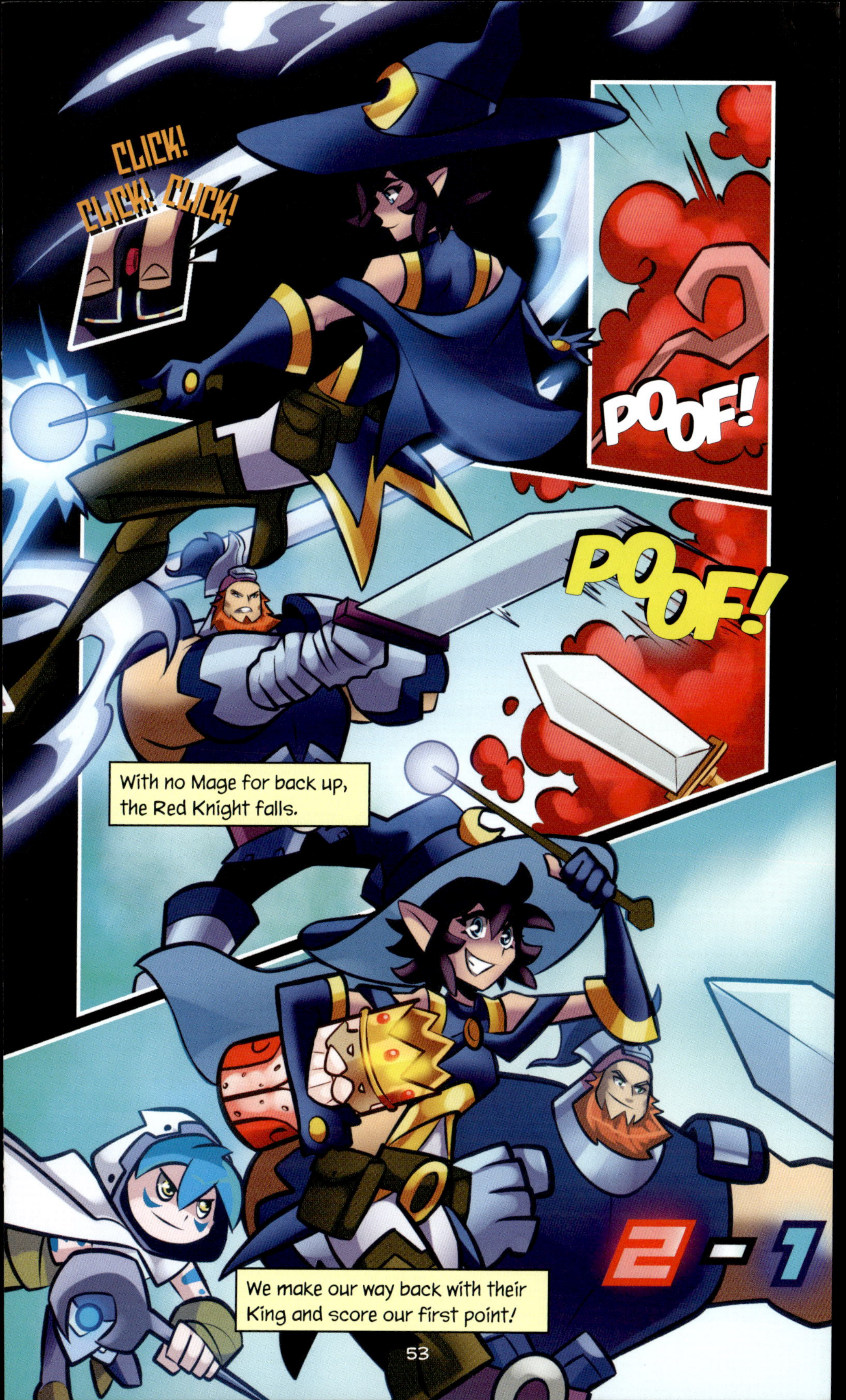
CLICK!
CLICK! CLICK!
POOF!
POOF!
With no Mage for back up, the Red Knight falls.
2 - 1
We make our way back with their King and score our first point!

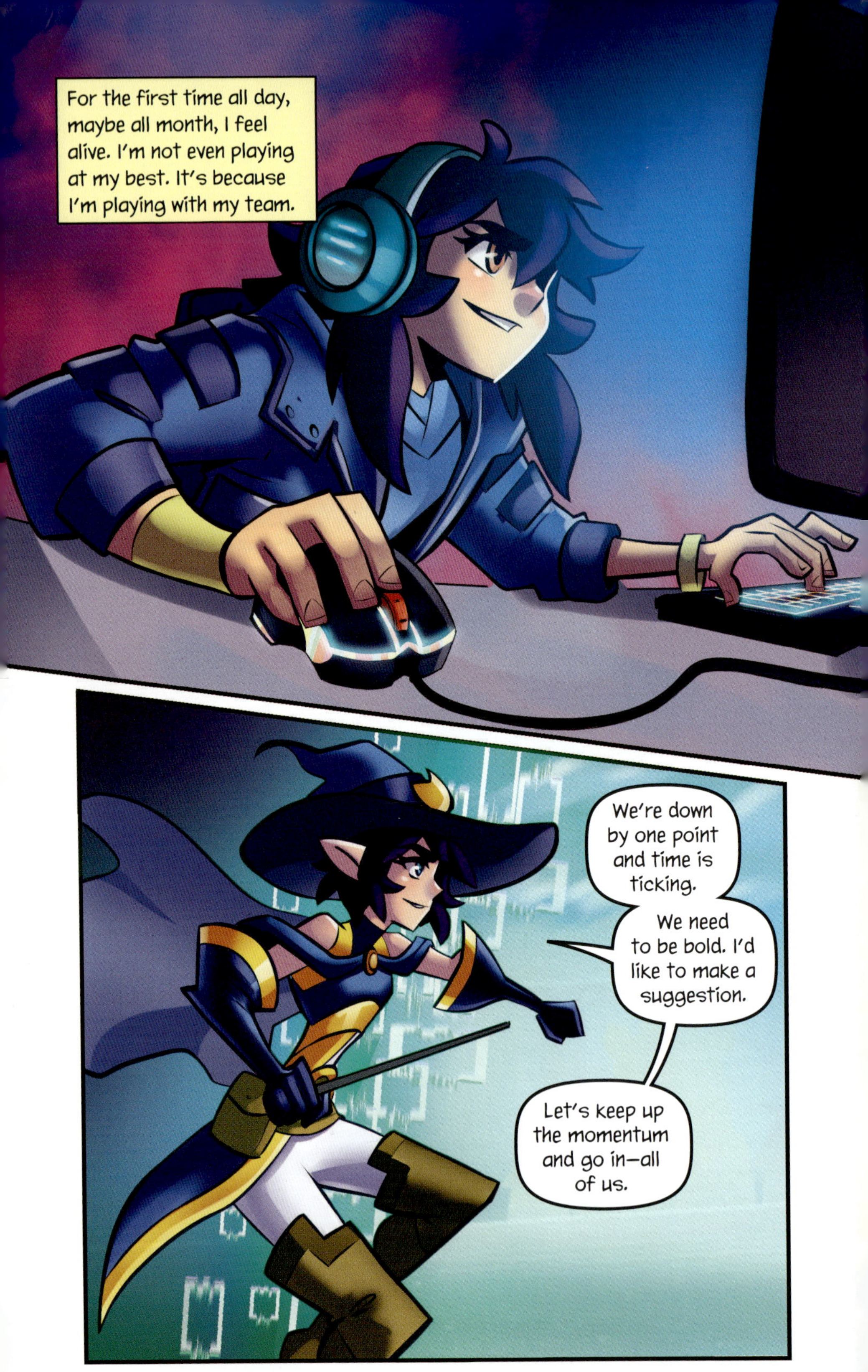
For the first time all day, maybe all month, I feel alive. I'm not even playing at my best. It's because I'm playing with my team.
We're down by one point and time is ticking.
We need to be bold. I'd like to make a suggestion.
Let's keep up the momentum and go in—all of us.

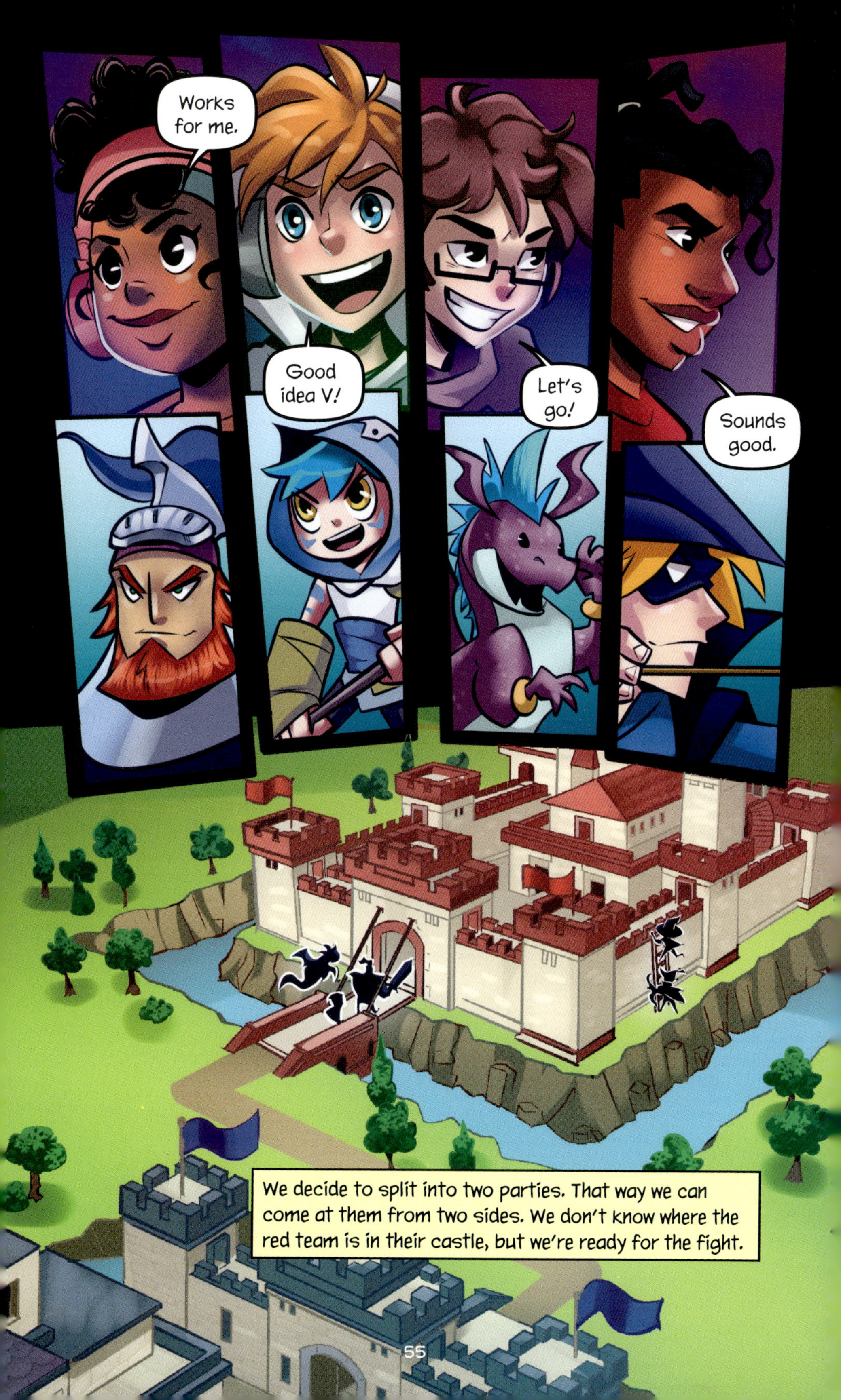
Works for me.
Good idea V!
Let's go!
Sounds good.
We decide to split into two parties. That way we can come at them from two sides. We don't know where the red team is in their castle, but we're ready for the fight.

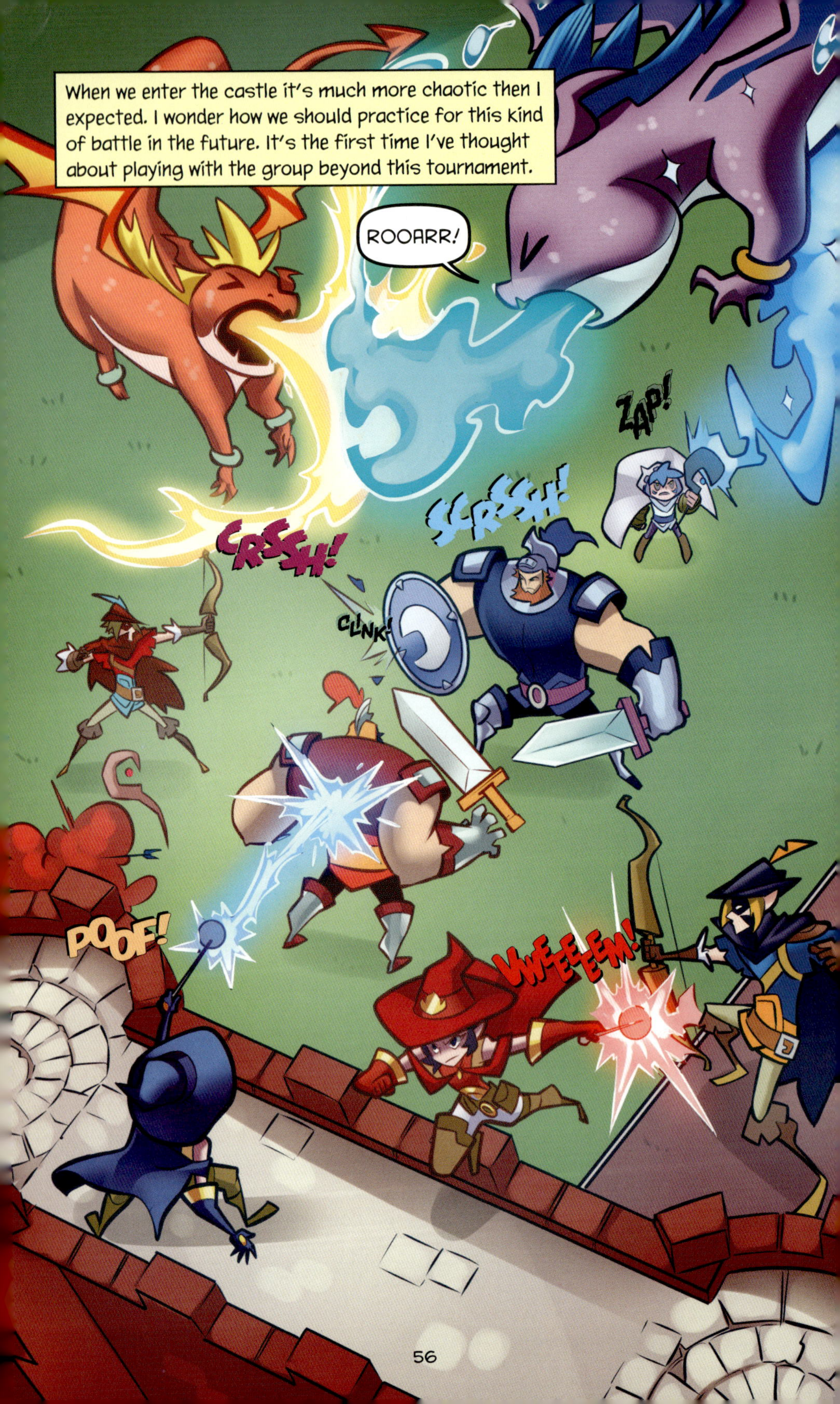
When we enter the castle it's much more chaotic then I expected. I wonder how we should practice for this kind of battle in the future. It's the first time I've thought about playing with the group beyond this tournament.
ROOARR!
ZAP!
SCRSSH!
CRSSH!
CLINK!
POOF!
WEEEEEM!

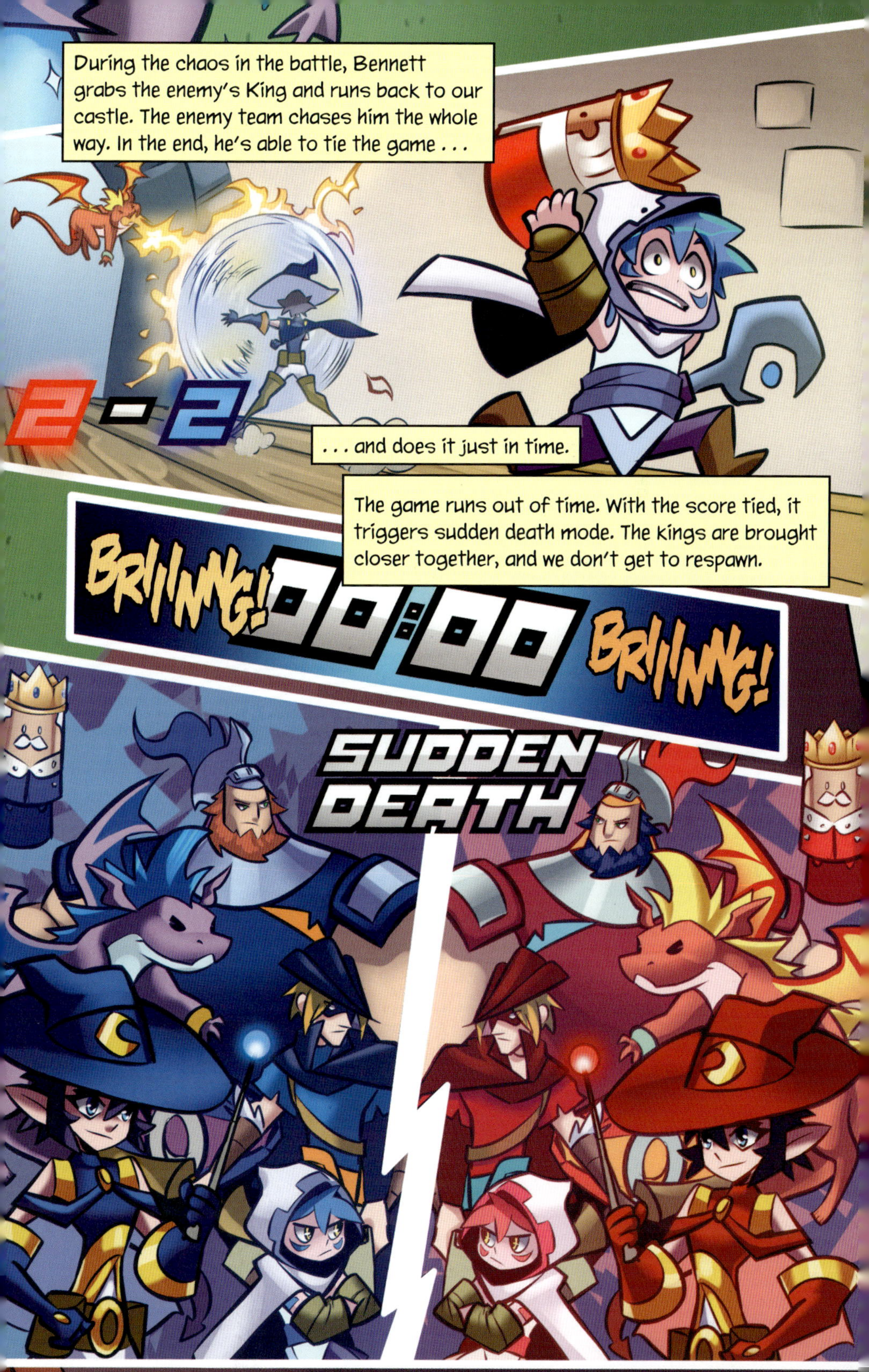
During the chaos in the battle, Bennett grabs the enemy's King and runs back to our castle. The enemy team chases him the whole way. In the end, he's able to tie the game . . .
2 - 2
. . . and does it just in time.
The game runs out of time. With the score tied, it triggers sudden death mode. The kings are brought closer together, and we don't get to respawn.
BRIIING!
00:00
BRIIING!
SUDDEN DEATH

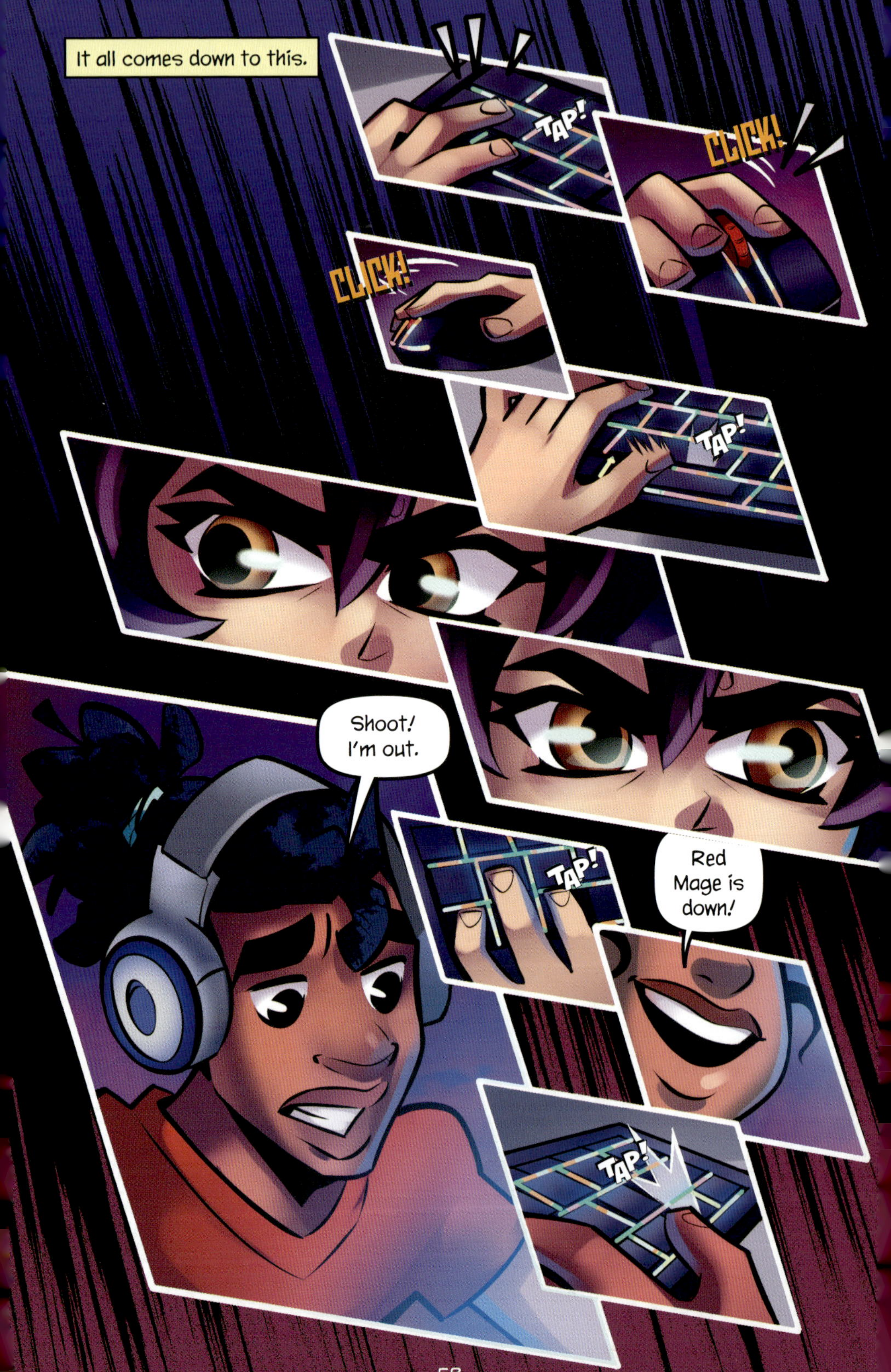
It all comes down to this.
TAP!
CLICK!
CLICK!
TAP!
Shoot! I'm out.
TAP!
Red Mage is down!
TAP!

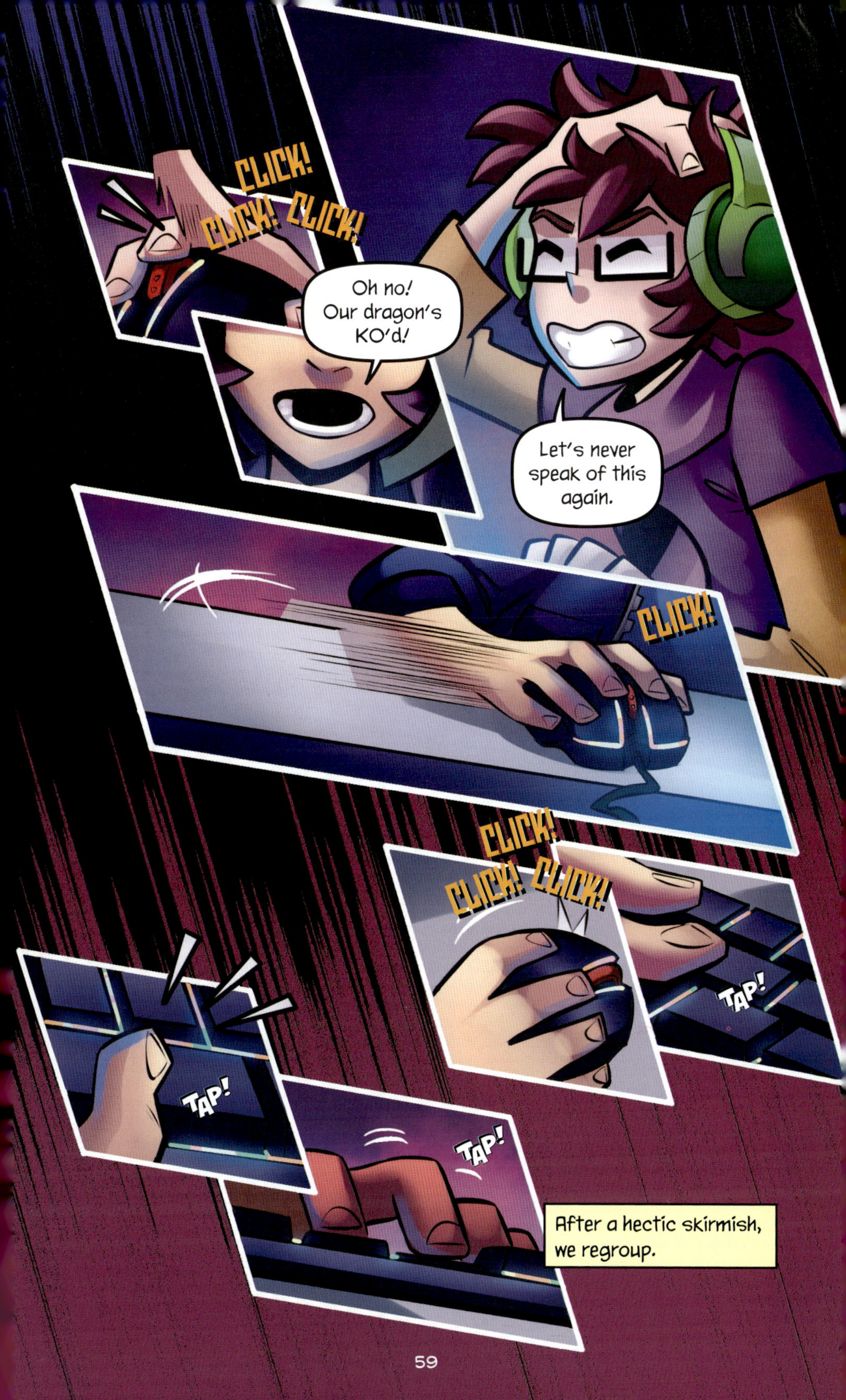
CLICK!
CLICK! CLICK!
Oh no! Our dragon's KO'd!
Let's never speak of this again.
CLICK!
CLICK!
CLICK! CLICK!
TAP!
TAP!
TAP!
After a hectic skirmish, we regroup.

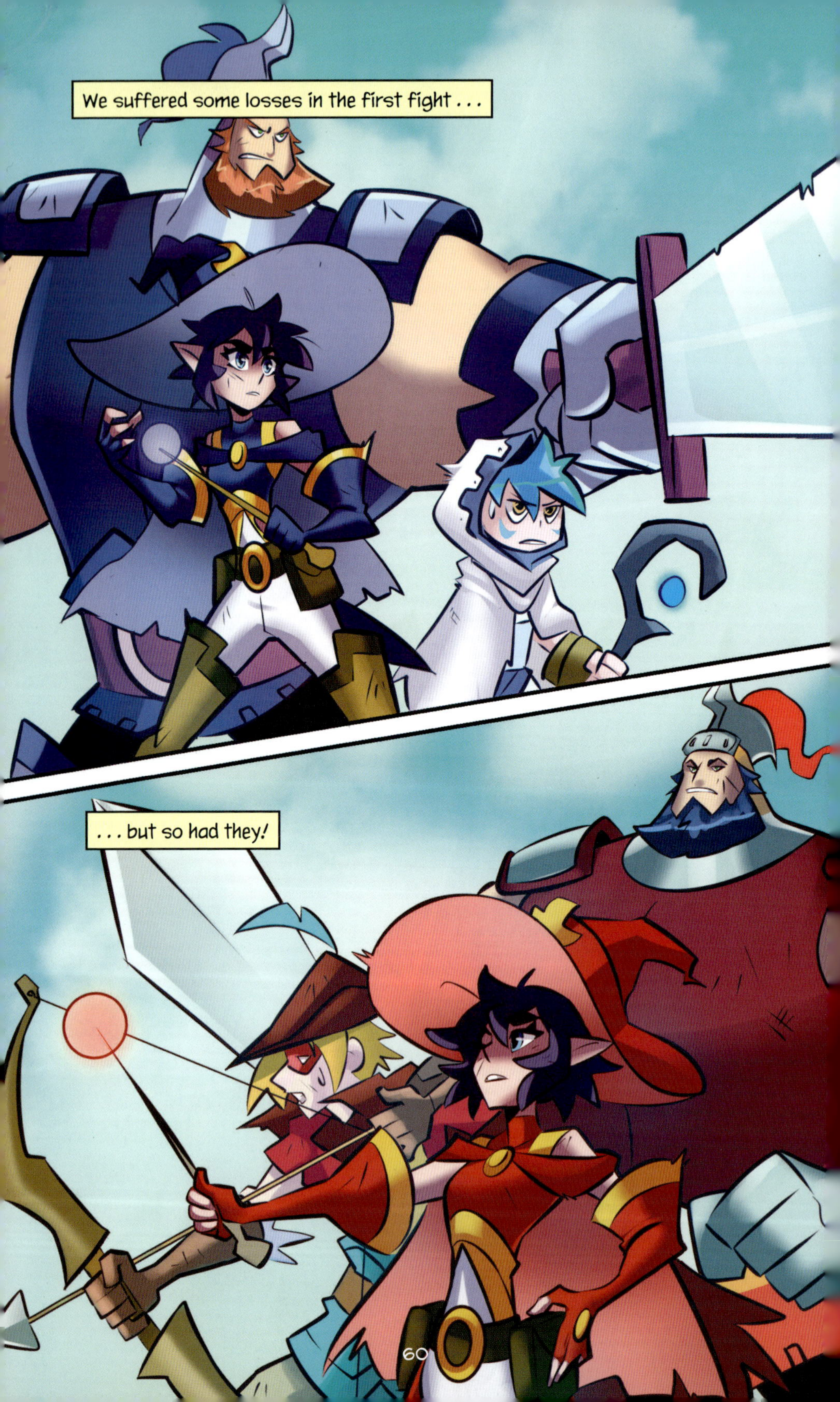
We suffered some losses in the first fight . . .
. . . but so had they!

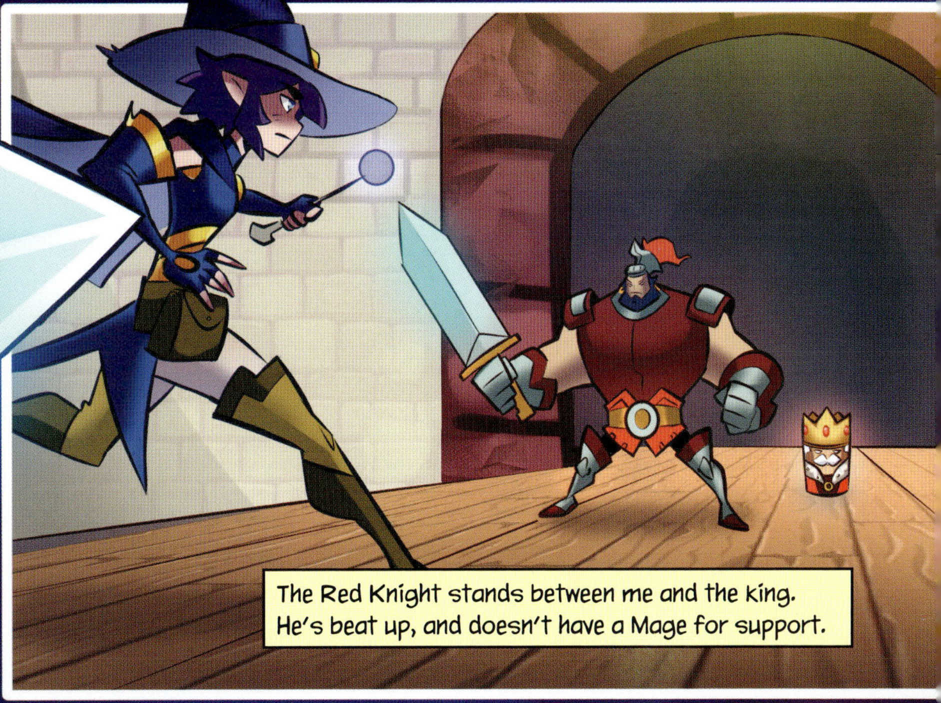
The Red Knight stands between me and the king.
He's beat up, and doesn't have a Mage for support.

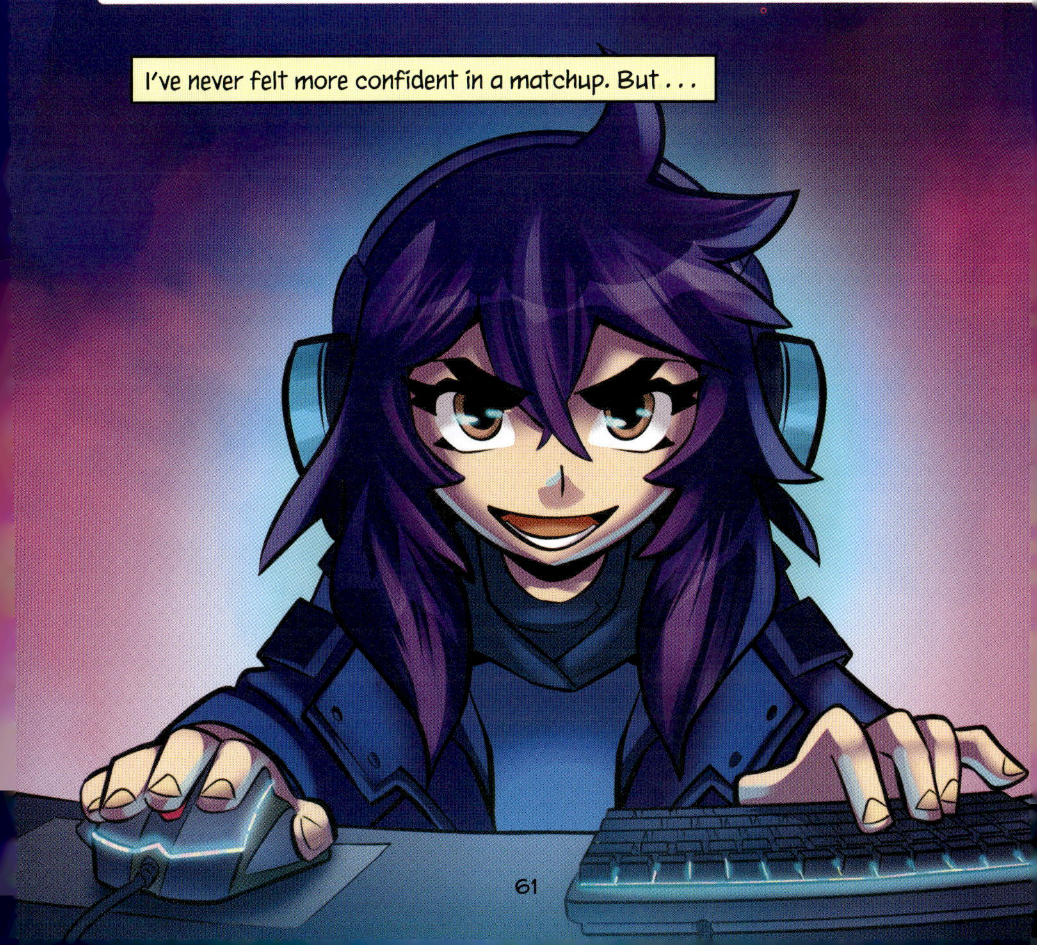
I've never felt more confident in a matchup. But . . .

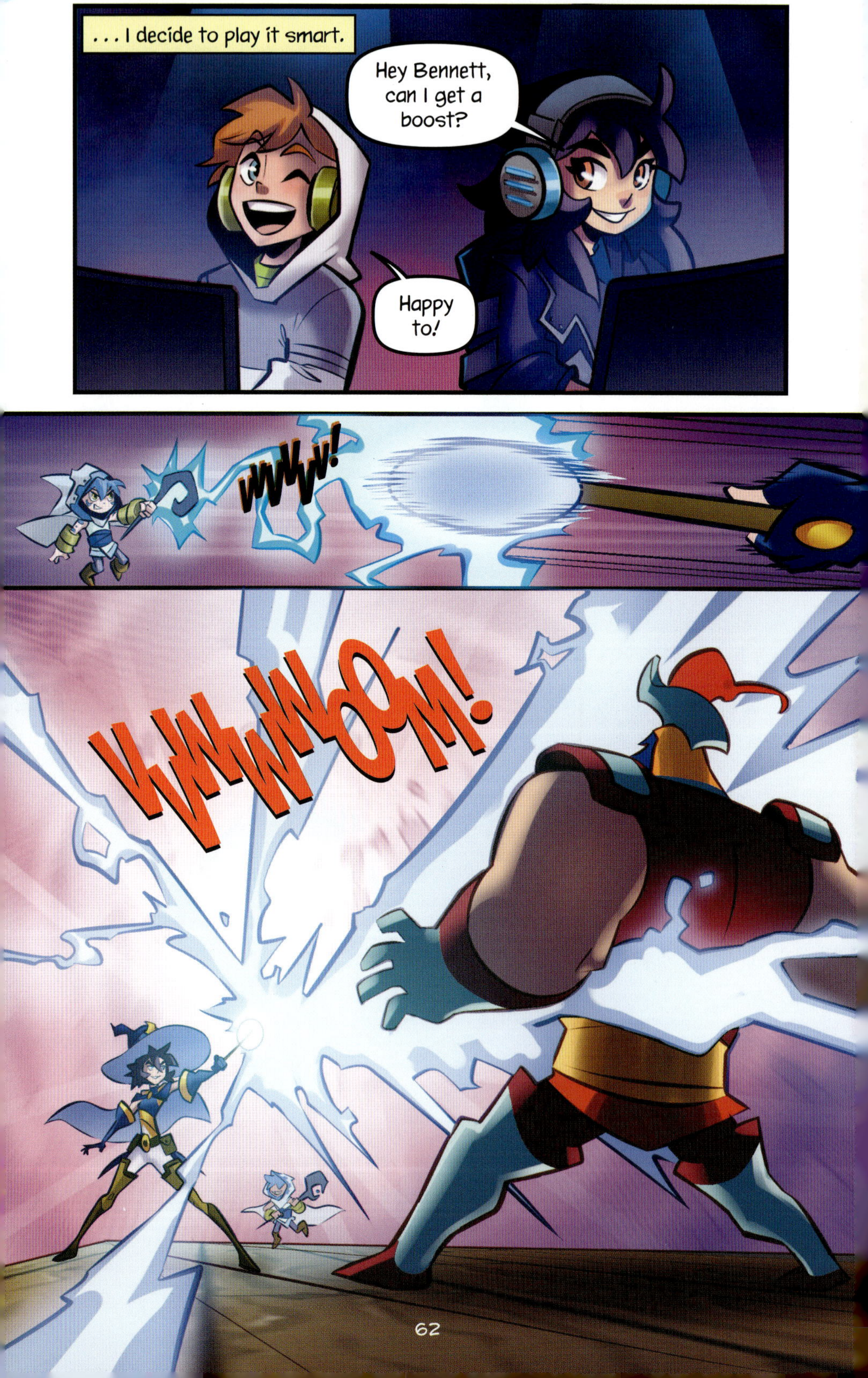
. . . I decide to play it smart.
Hey Bennett, can I get a boost?
Happy to!
WVVVV!
VWWWOOM!

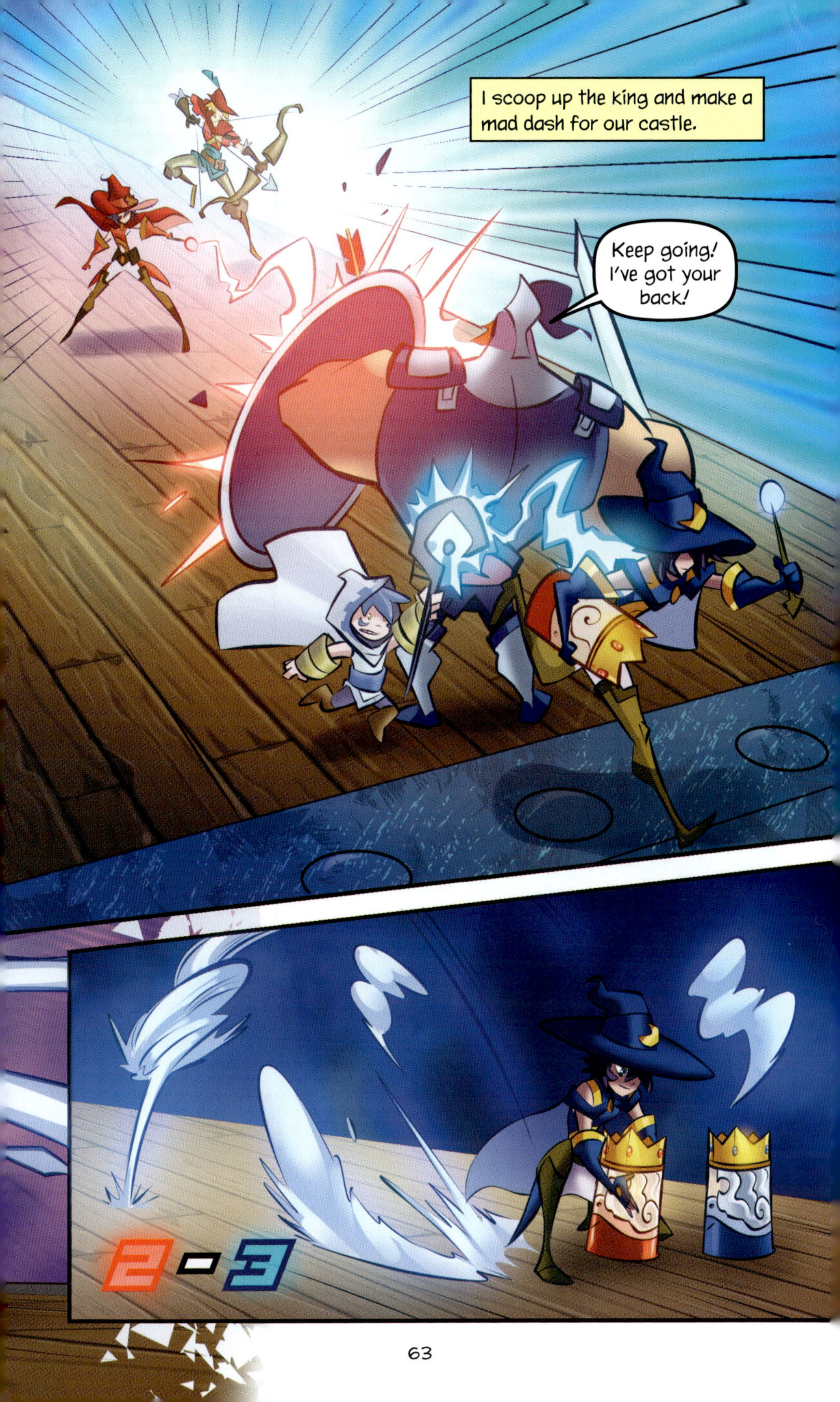
I scoop up the king and make a mad dash for our castle.
Keep going! I've got your back!
2-3

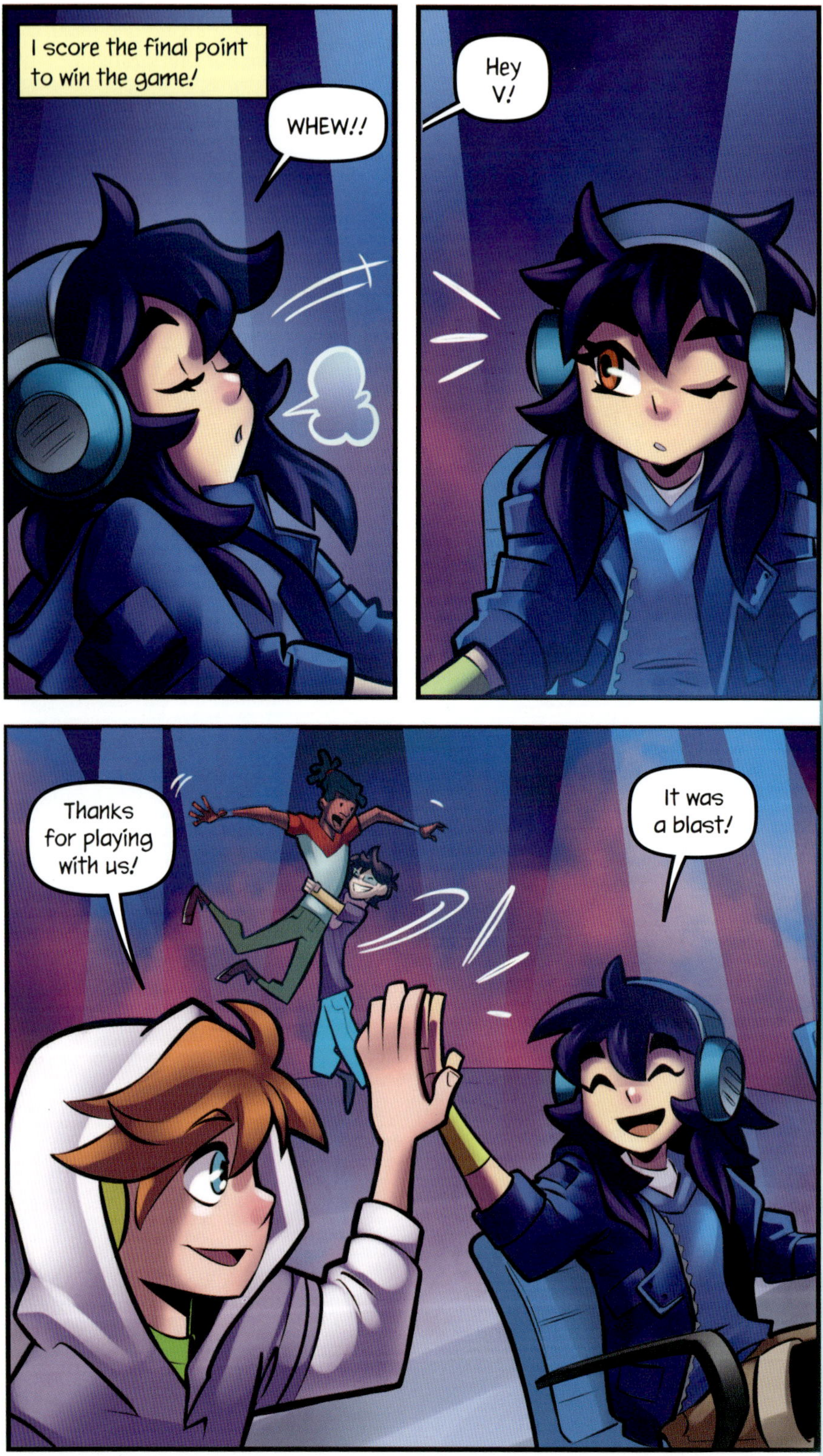
I score the final point to win the game!
WHEW!!
Hey V!
Thanks for playing with us!
It was a blast!

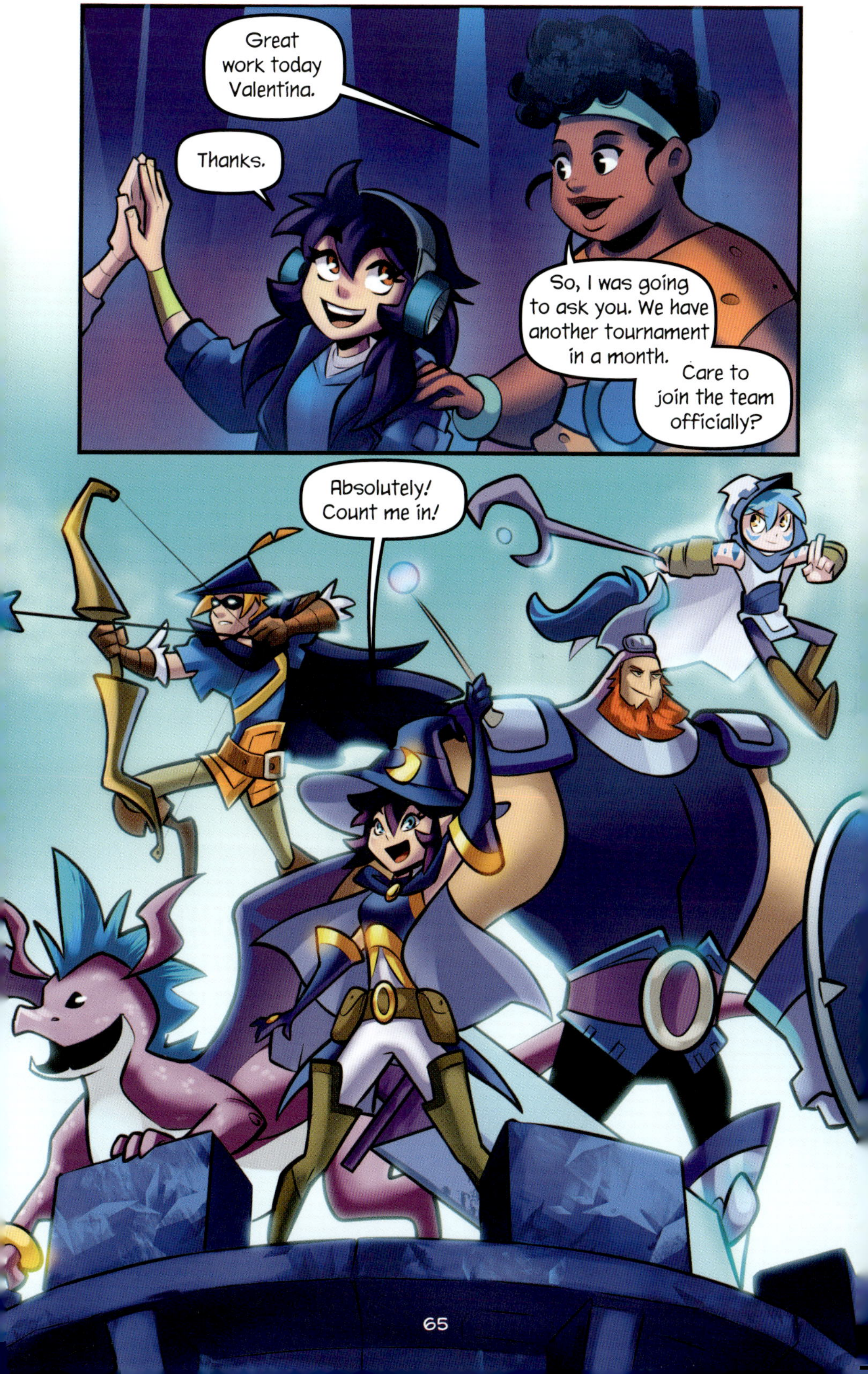
Great work today Valentina.
Thanks.
So, I was going to ask you. We have another tournament in a month.
Care to join the team officially?
Absolutely! Count me in!

VISUAL DISCUSSION QUESTIONS

1. Look at the characters above. In what ways are the story's characters similar to the characters they played in the game? In what ways are they different?

2. Look at the icon in the lower left corner of this panel. Can you tell what ability the character is using based on this symbol?

3. Graphic artists can show a lot of action in a single panel. Look at the scene to the right. Can you tell which characters are winning this intense battle?

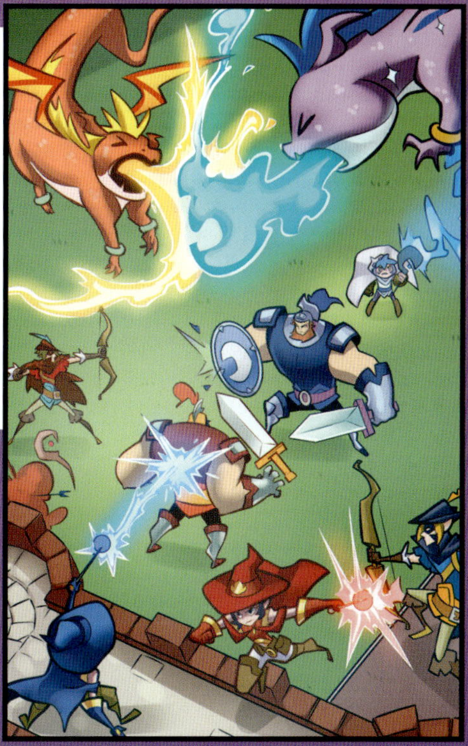

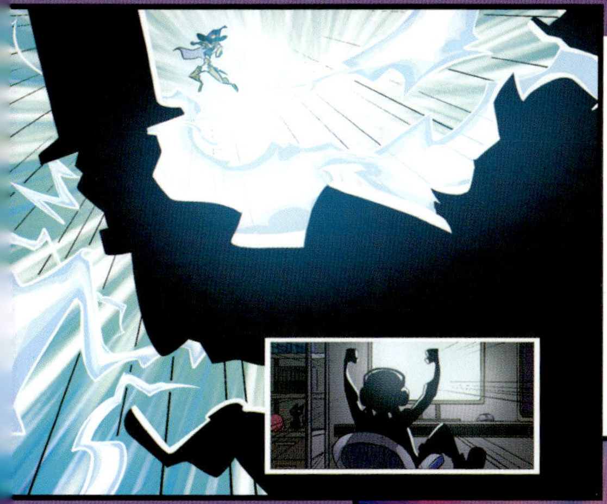

4. The way scenes are lit can help add certain moods to a story. How does the lighting in these panels help increase the action or drama in each scene?

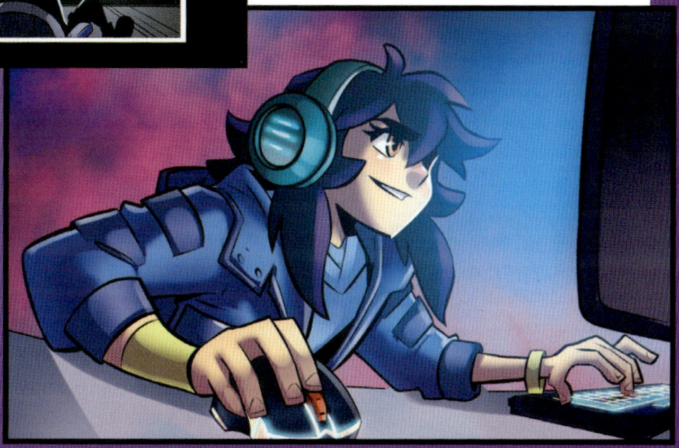

MORE ABOUT ESPORTS

The first major esports tournament was held in 1980. More than 10,000 players competed for the best score in *Space Invaders* for a spot in the finale in New York. Rebecca Ann Heineman won first place at just 16 years old!

Participating in high school esports can open the door to more opportunities. More than 170 U.S. colleges have esports programs with annual scholarships of more than $16 million.

The fictional game *Kings N' Castles* is based on team-based shooters such as *Team Fortress* and *Overwatch*. *Overwatch* has its own international league with teams from seven states and more than five countries.

When the League of Legends World Championship began in 2011, the winning team earned $50,000! The prize grew each year and peaked in 2018 at $2.4 million!

ESPORTS WORDS TO KNOW

buff—a power-up used by one player to boost another player's ability

first-person—a type of video game where players view the action through the eyes of the character they are playing

melee—low damage hand-to-hand combat performed at close range in a game; often involving handheld weapons

meta—the current set of characters or strategies that are being used by players

pocketing—when a support character is dedicated to helping another player, instead of the whole team

push—when a team moves together toward an objective

respawn—when a character reenters the game after being knocked out

skirmish—a fight between several players from both sides of a game

third-person—a type of video game where players view the action from above or behind the character they are playing

tilted—when a player is so frustrated or angry that they begin playing poorly

tracking—the ability of a player to follow targets accurately across a screen

VOD (Video-on-Demand)—recorded video of a game that players can replay to study their or their opponents' moves

GLOSSARY

advantage (ad-VAN-tij)—a condition in which a team has the edge over an opponent in a competition

close quarters combat (KLOHS KWOR-turs KOM-bat)—a fight that takes place in a small space with little room to move around

cursor (KUR-ser)—a moveable marker that indicates where a character is looking or aiming a weapon in a game

leaderboard (LEE-dur-bohrd)—a list showing the names and scores of the top players in a game

mobility (moh-BIL-uh-tee)—the ability to move quickly and easily

momentum (moh-MEN-tuhm)—a quality of a team that has confidence and is playing well together

platforming game (PLAT-form-ing GAYM)—a game in which a player controls a character to jump between levels and avoid various obstacles to achieve a goal

roleplaying game (ROHL-play-ing GAYM)—a game where players take on the roles of imaginary characters and take part in an adventure

scrimmage (SKRIM-ij)—a practice game

single elimination (SING-uhl ih-lim-uh-NAY-shuhn)—a type of tournament in which the loser of each matchup is removed from competition

tournament (TUR-nuh-muhnt)—a series of matches between several players or teams, ending in one winner

JAKE MADDOX
GRAPHIC NOVELS

SWIM TEAM TROUBLE

STONE ARCH BOOKS
a capstone imprint

JAKE MADDOX
GRAPHIC NOVELS

Published by Stone Arch Books,
an imprint of Capstone.
1710 Roe Crest Drive
North Mankato, Minnesota 56003
www.capstonepub.com

Copyright © 2021 by Capstone. All rights reserved. No part of this publication may be reproduced in whole or in part, or stored in a retrieval system, or transmitted in any form or by any means, electronic, mechanical, photocopying, recording, or otherwise, without written permission of the publisher.

Library of Congress Cataloging-in-Publication Data
Names: Schenkel, Katie, author. | Alves, Lelo, artist. | Reed, Jaymes, letterer. | Muñiz, Berenice, cover artist.
Title: Swim team trouble / text by Katie Schenkel ; art by Lelo Alves ; lettering by Jaymes Reed ; cover art by Berenice Muñiz.
Description: North Mankato : Stone Arch Books, 2021. | Series: Jake Maddox graphic novels | Audience: Ages 8–11. | Audience: Grades 4–6.
Identifiers: LCCN 2020025299 (print) | LCCN 2020025300 (ebook) | ISBN 9781515882343 (hardcover) | ISBN 9781515883432 (paperback) | ISBN 9781515892335 (ebook pdf)
Subjects: LCSH: Graphic novels. | CYAC: Graphic novels. | Swimming—Fiction. | Teamwork (Sports)—Fiction. | Friendship—Fiction.
Classification: LCC PZ7.7.S26 Swi 2021 (print) | LCC PZ7.7.S26 (ebook) | DDC 741.5/973—dc23
LC record available at https://lccn.loc.gov/2020025299
LC ebook record available at https://lccn.loc.gov/2020025300

Summary: Grace enjoys hanging out with her swimming teammates and making new friends. But when Chloe joins the relay team, she and Grace clash. Grace tries hard to be friends with Chloe but fails every time. Then at a big swim meet, Chloe blames Grace for getting disqualified. Grace can't believe it. She doesn't understand why Chloe is so hostile toward her. Will the two girls learn to look past their differences and work together for the good of the whole team?

Editor: Aaron Sautter
Designers: Brann Garvey and Heidi Thompson
Production Specialist: Tori Abraham

Printed and bound in China. PO 6096

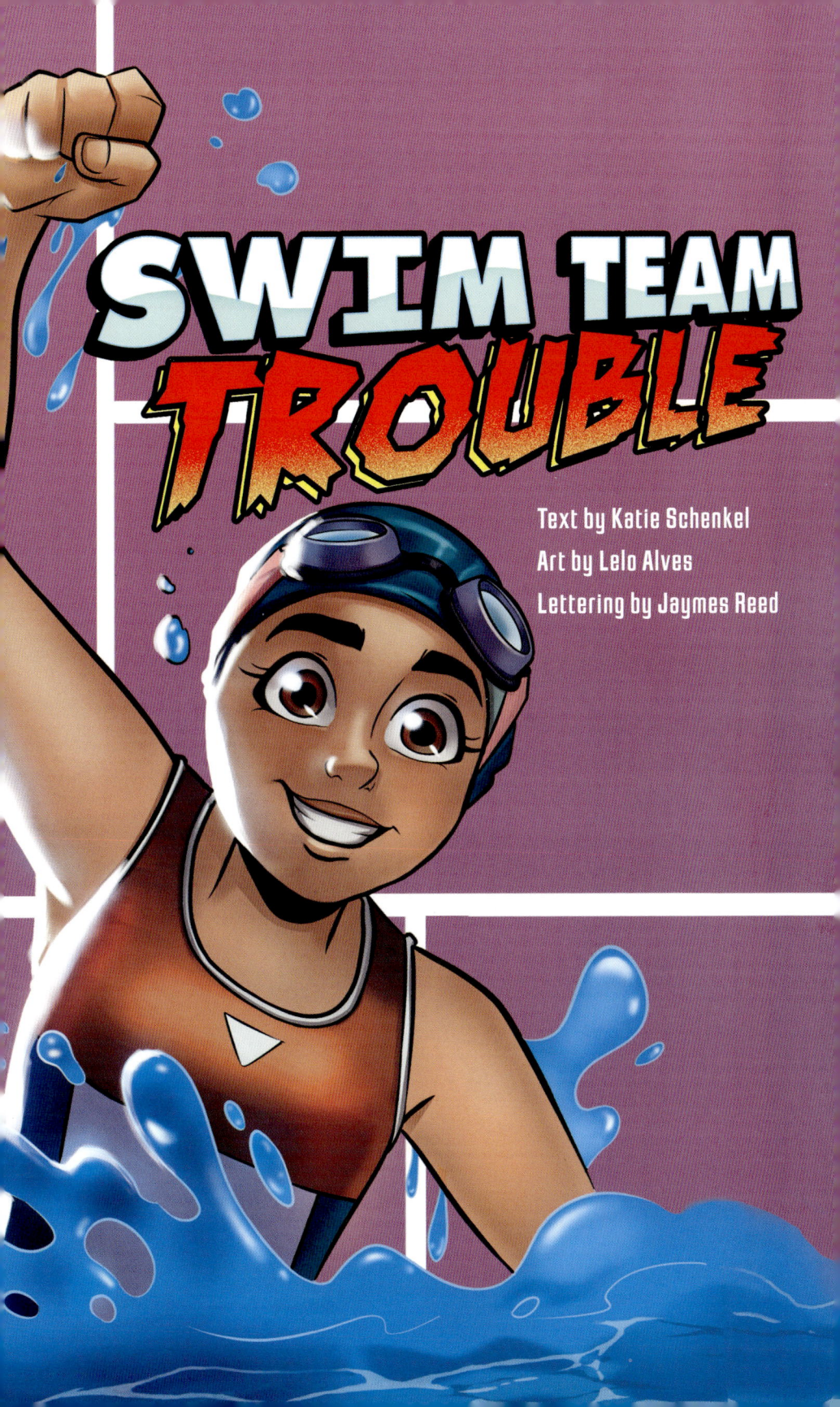

STARTING LINEUP

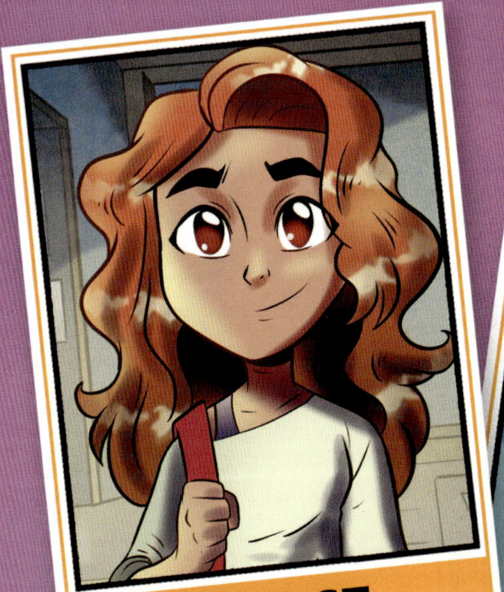
GRACE

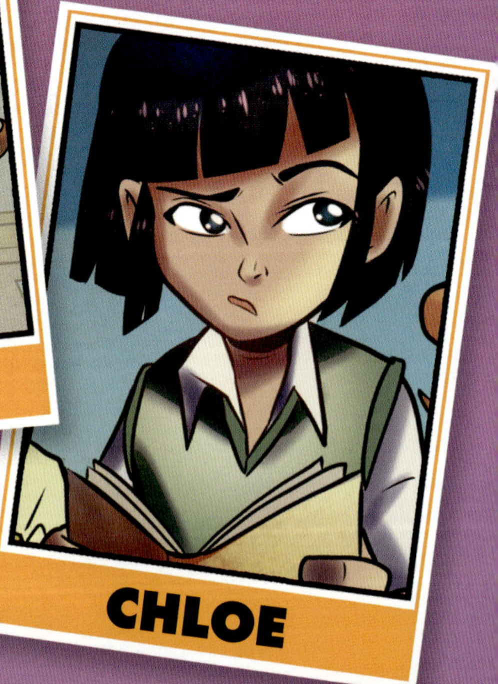
CHLOE

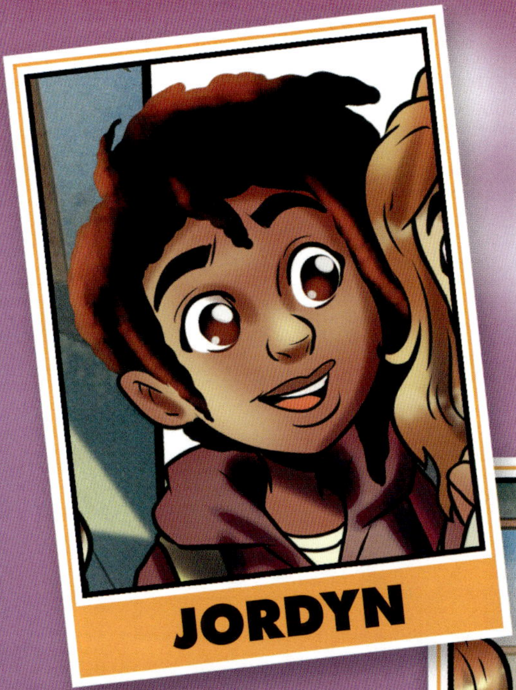
JORDYN

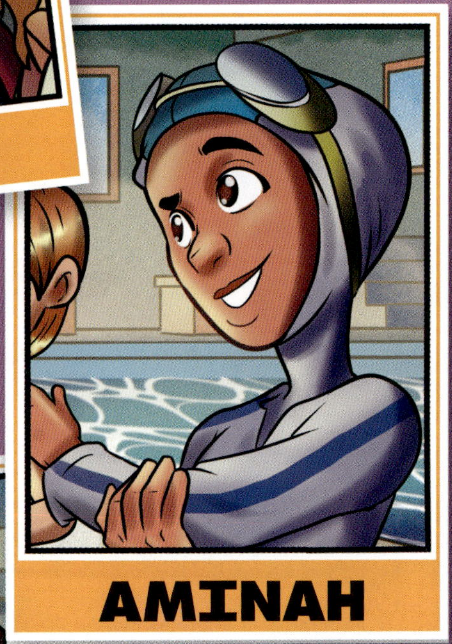
AMINAH

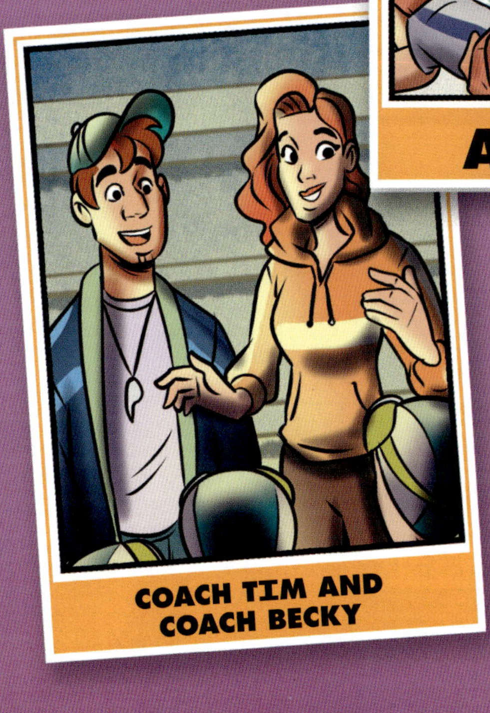
COACH TIM AND
COACH BECKY

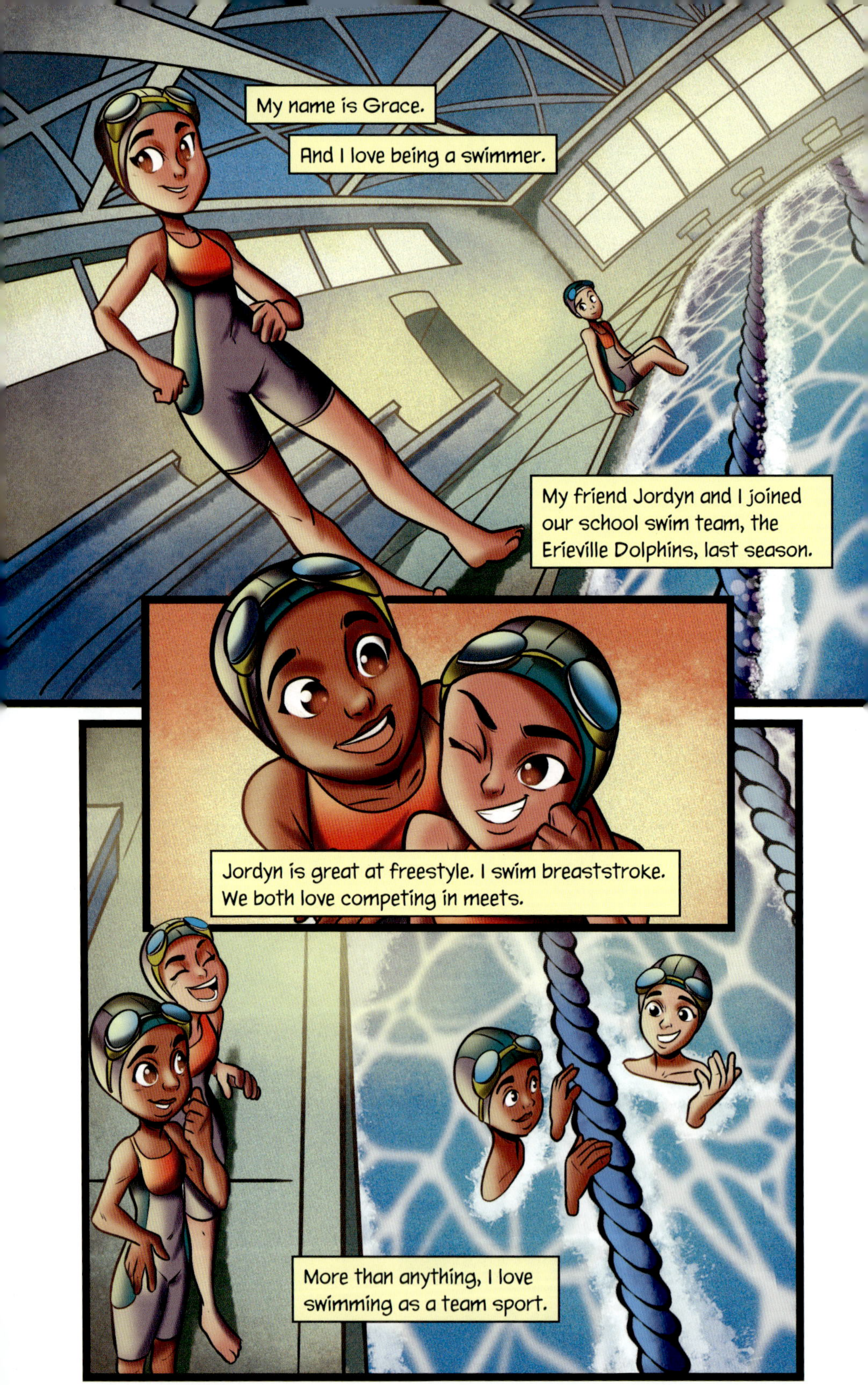
My name is Grace.
And I love being a swimmer.
My friend Jordyn and I joined our school swim team, the Erieville Dolphins, last season.
Jordyn is great at freestyle. I swim breaststroke. We both love competing in meets.
More than anything, I love swimming as a team sport.

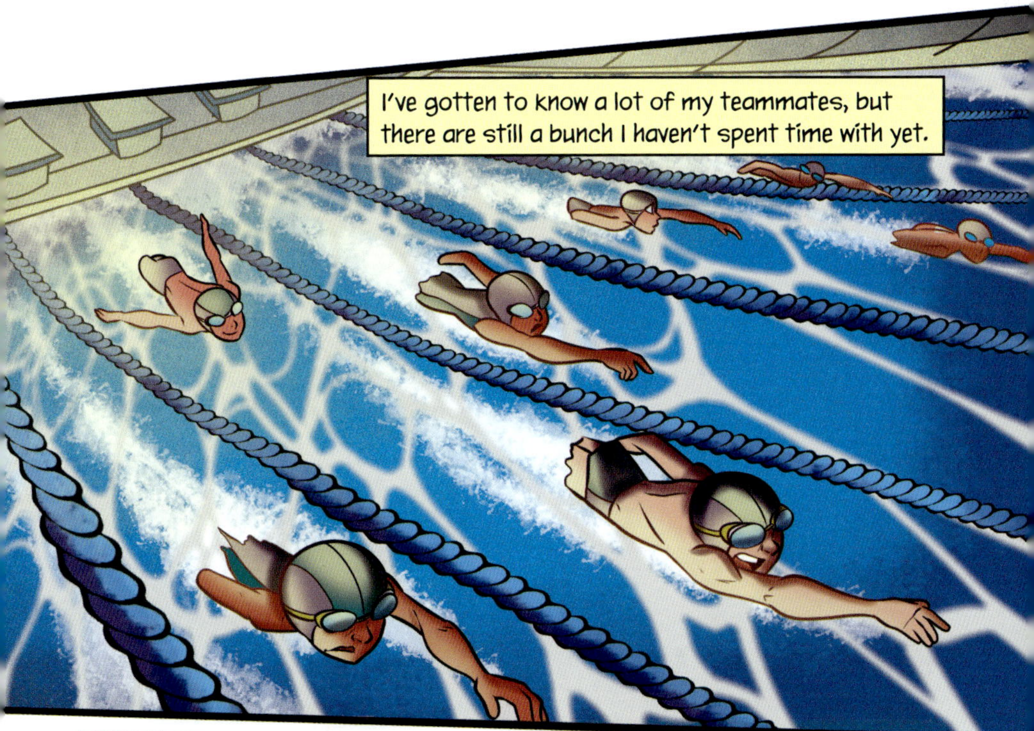
I've gotten to know a lot of my teammates, but there are still a bunch I haven't spent time with yet.

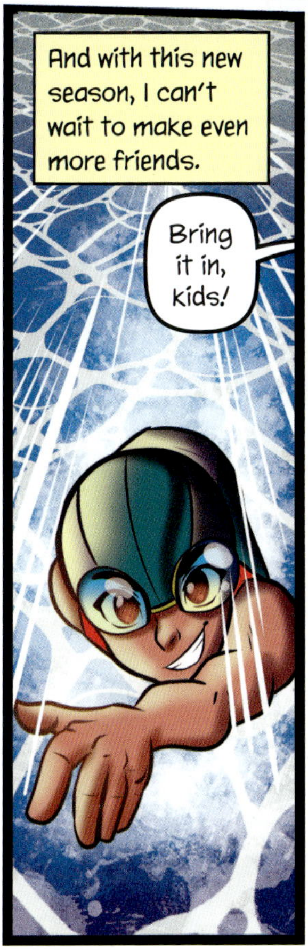
And with this new season, I can't wait to make even more friends.
Bring it in, kids!

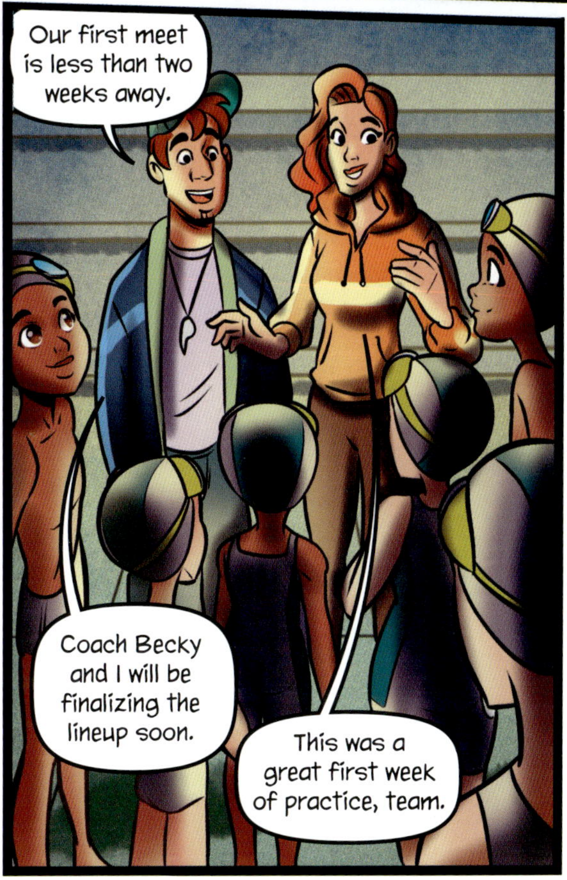
Our first meet is less than two weeks away.
Coach Becky and I will be finalizing the lineup soon.
This was a great first week of practice, team.

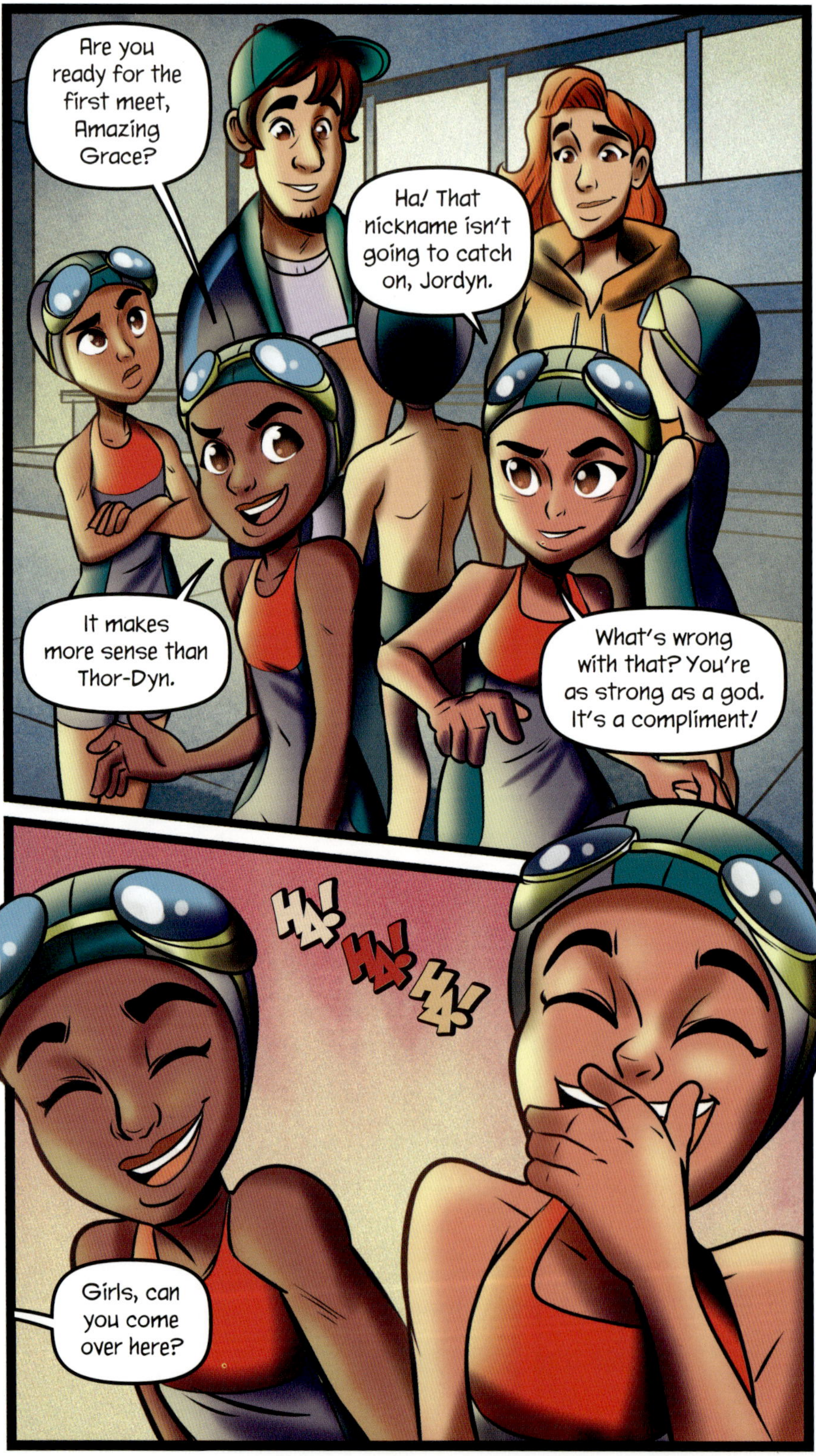
Are you ready for the first meet, Amazing Grace?
Ha! That nickname isn't going to catch on, Jordyn.
It makes more sense than Thor-Dyn.
What's wrong with that? You're as strong as a god. It's a compliment!
HA! HA! HA!
Girls, can you come over here?

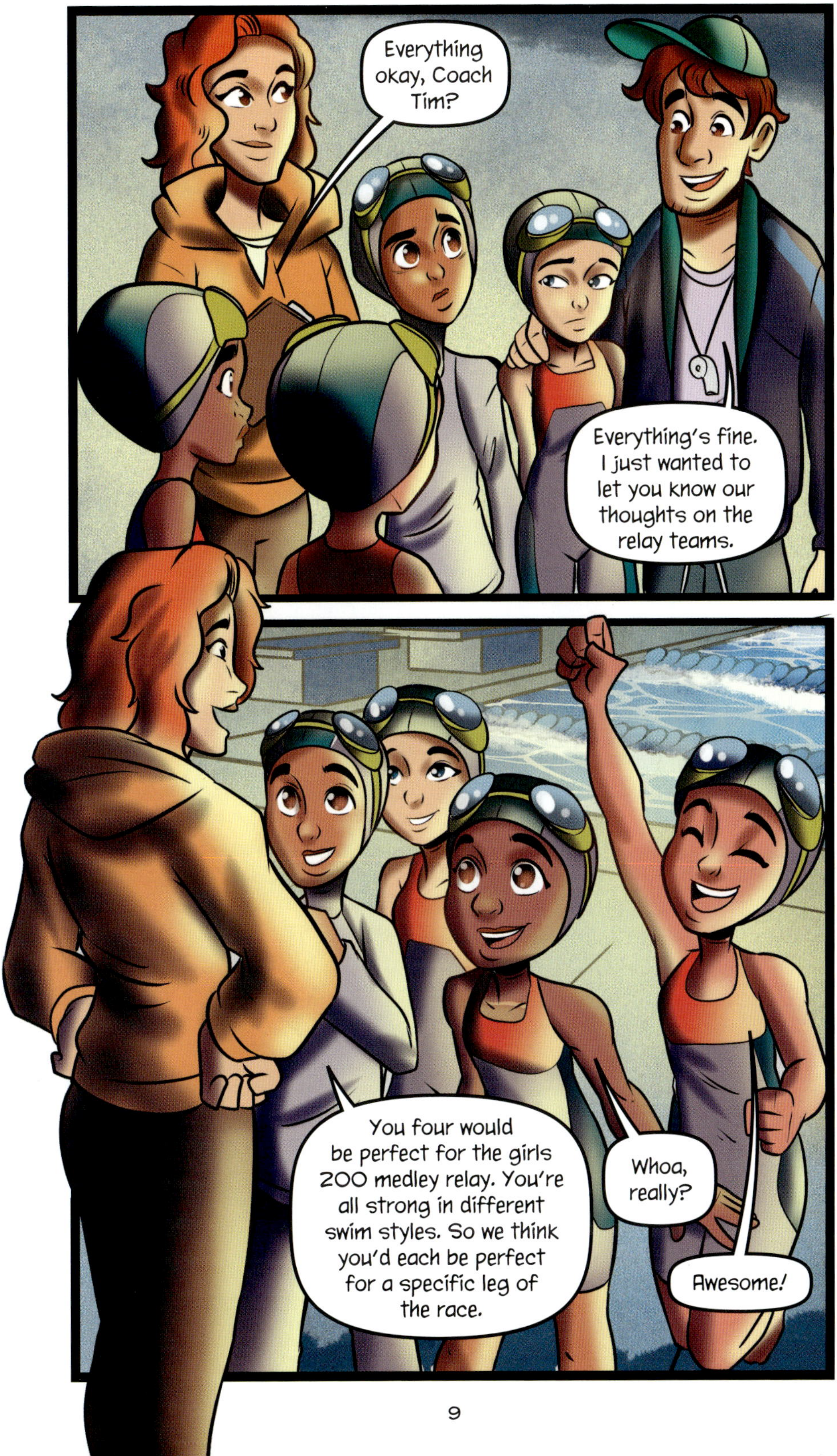
Everything okay, Coach Tim?
Everything's fine. I just wanted to let you know our thoughts on the relay teams.
You four would be perfect for the girls 200 medley relay. You're all strong in different swim styles. So we think you'd each be perfect for a specific leg of the race.
Whoa, really?
Awesome!

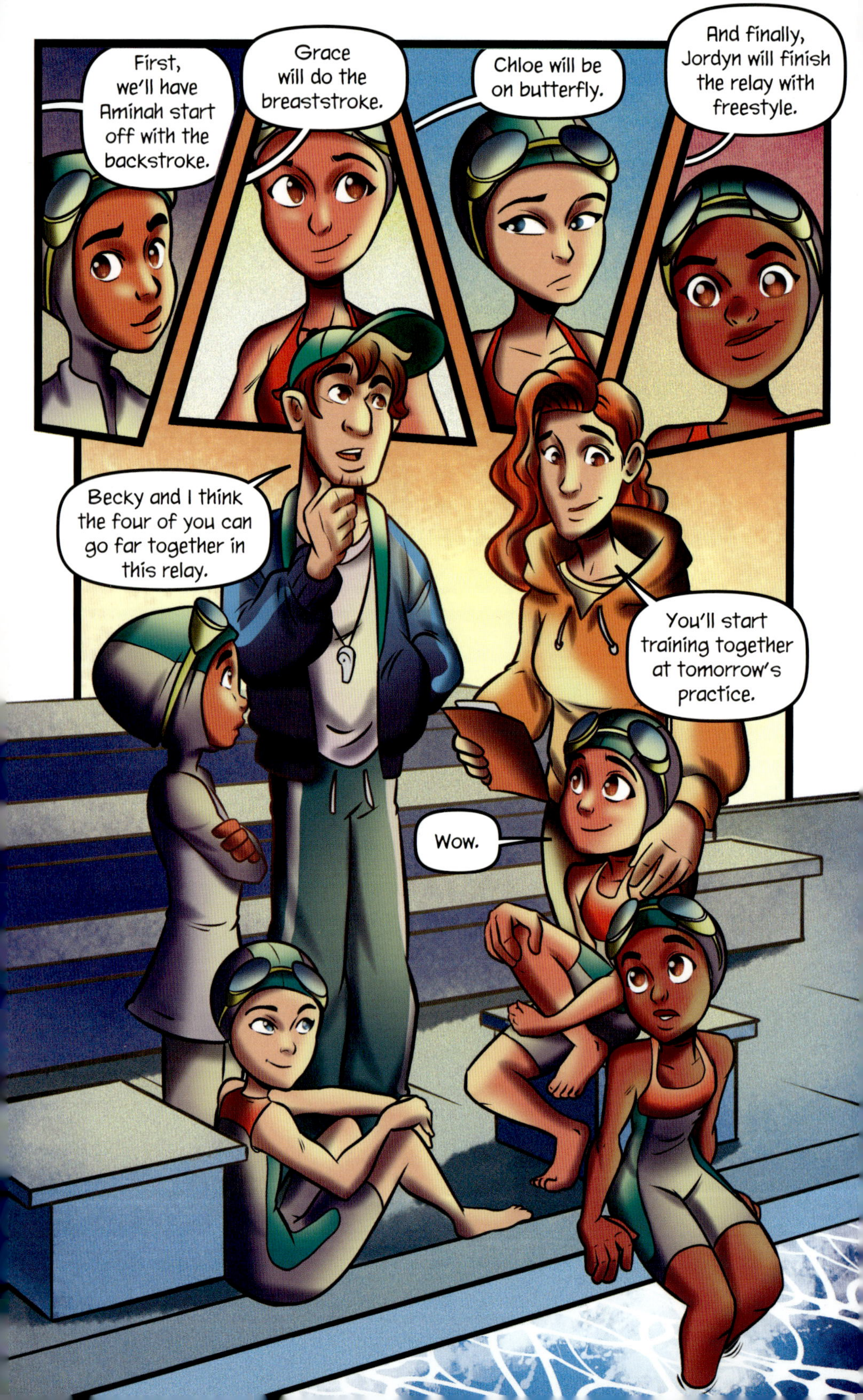
First, we'll have Aminah start off with the backstroke.
Grace will do the breaststroke.
Chloe will be on butterfly.
And finally, Jordyn will finish the relay with freestyle.
Becky and I think the four of you can go far together in this relay.
You'll start training together at tomorrow's practice.
Wow.

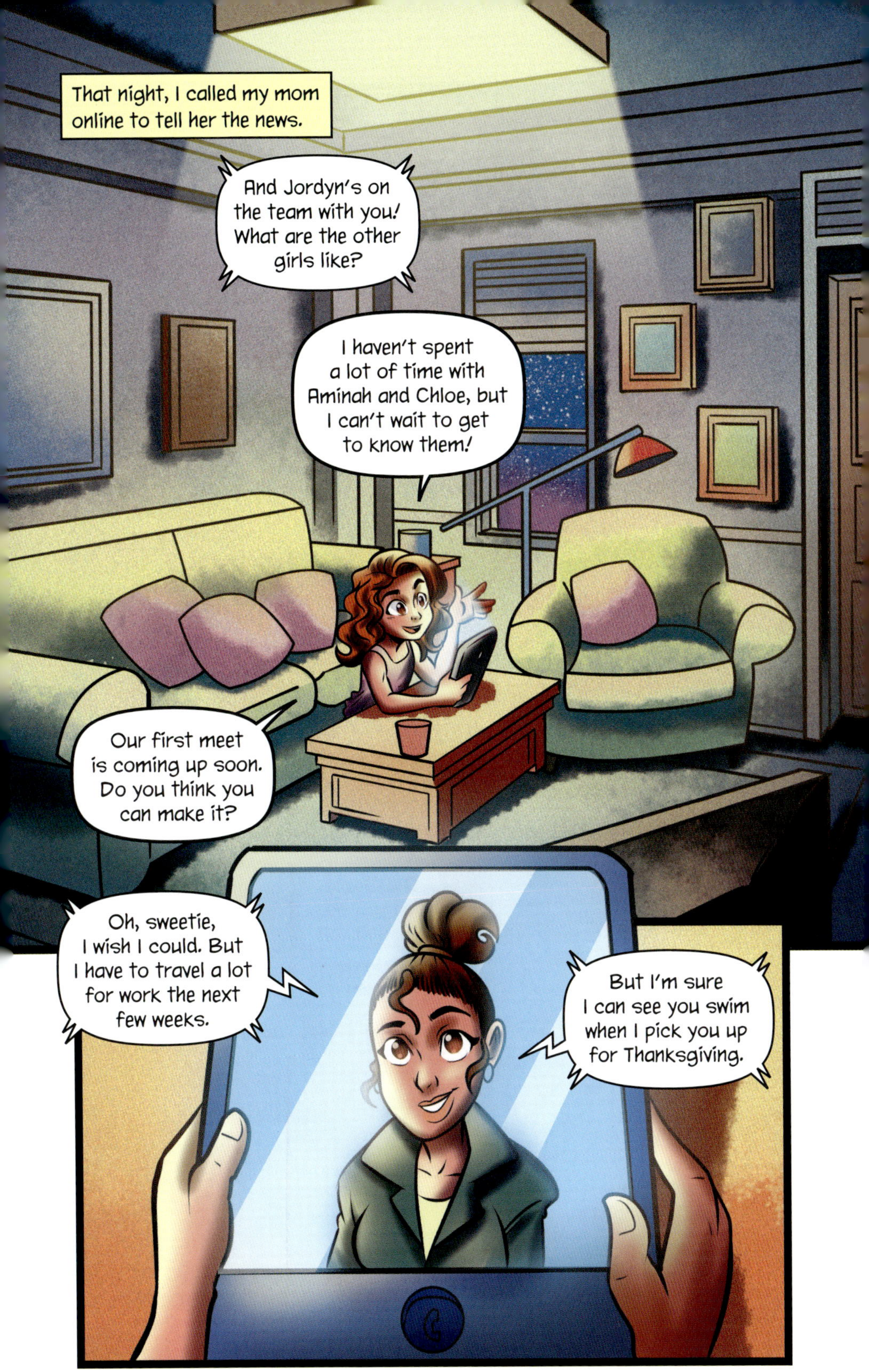
That night, I called my mom online to tell her the news.
And Jordyn's on the team with you! What are the other girls like?
I haven't spent a lot of time with Aminah and Chloe, but I can't wait to get to know them!
Our first meet is coming up soon. Do you think you can make it?
Oh, sweetie, I wish I could. But I have to travel a lot for work the next few weeks.
But I'm sure I can see you swim when I pick you up for Thanksgiving.

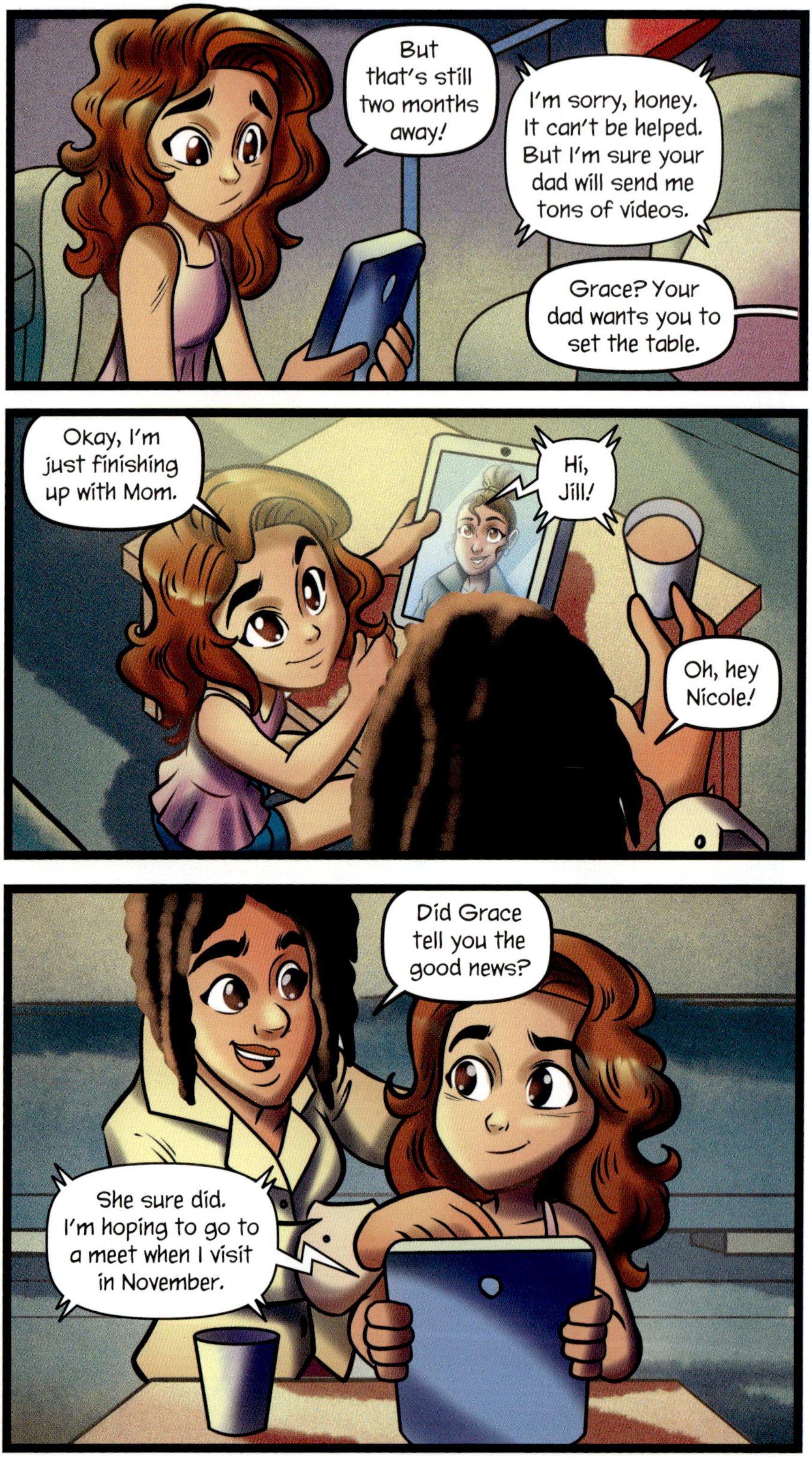
But that's still two months away!
I'm sorry, honey. It can't be helped. But I'm sure your dad will send me tons of videos.
Grace? Your dad wants you to set the table.
Okay, I'm just finishing up with Mom.
Hi, Jill!
Oh, hey Nicole!
Did Grace tell you the good news?
She sure did. I'm hoping to go to a meet when I visit in November.

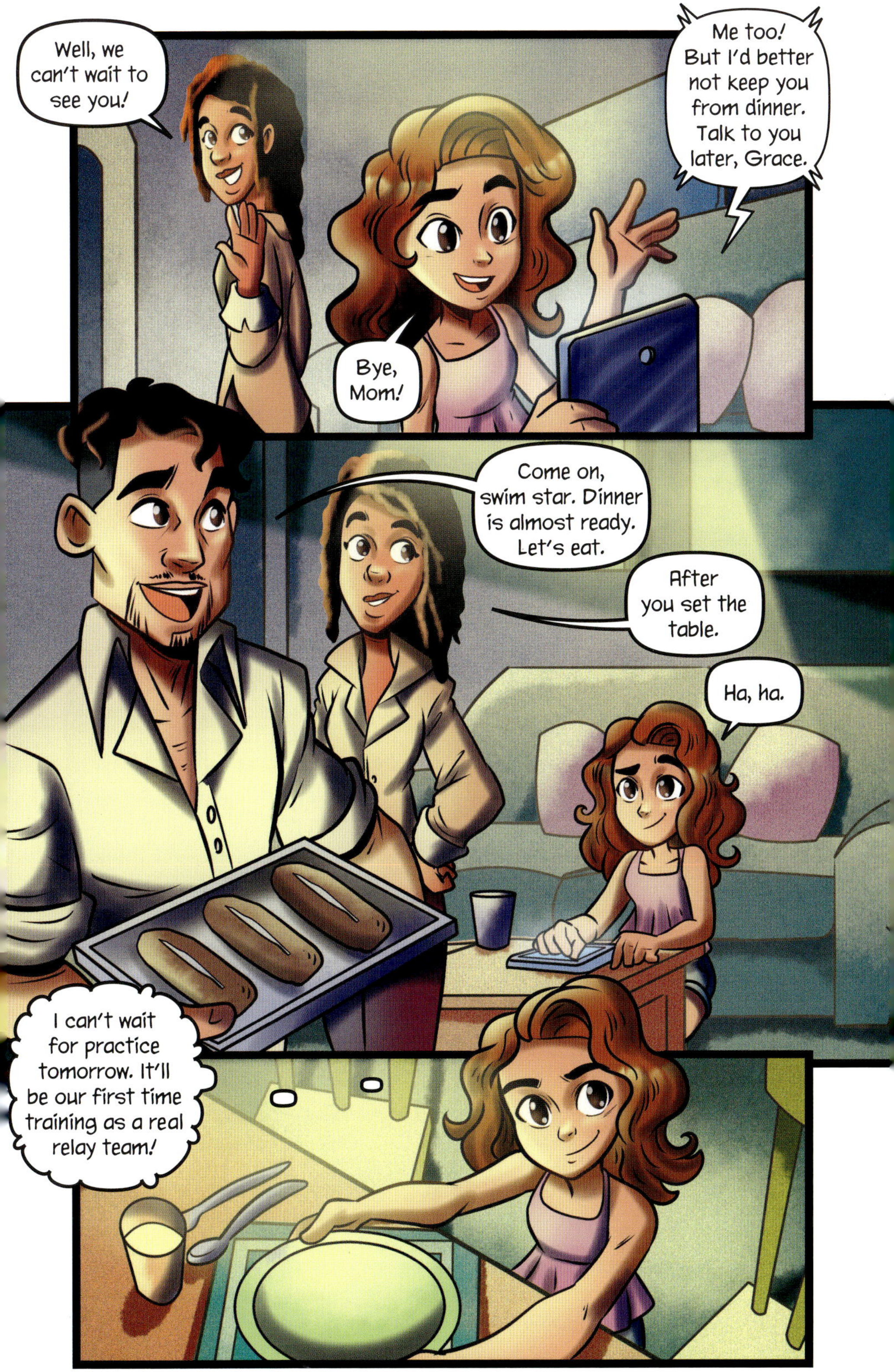
Well, we can't wait to see you!
Me too! But I'd better not keep you from dinner. Talk to you later, Grace.
Bye, Mom!
Come on, swim star. Dinner is almost ready. Let's eat.
After you set the table.
Ha, ha.
I can't wait for practice tomorrow. It'll be our first time training as a real relay team!

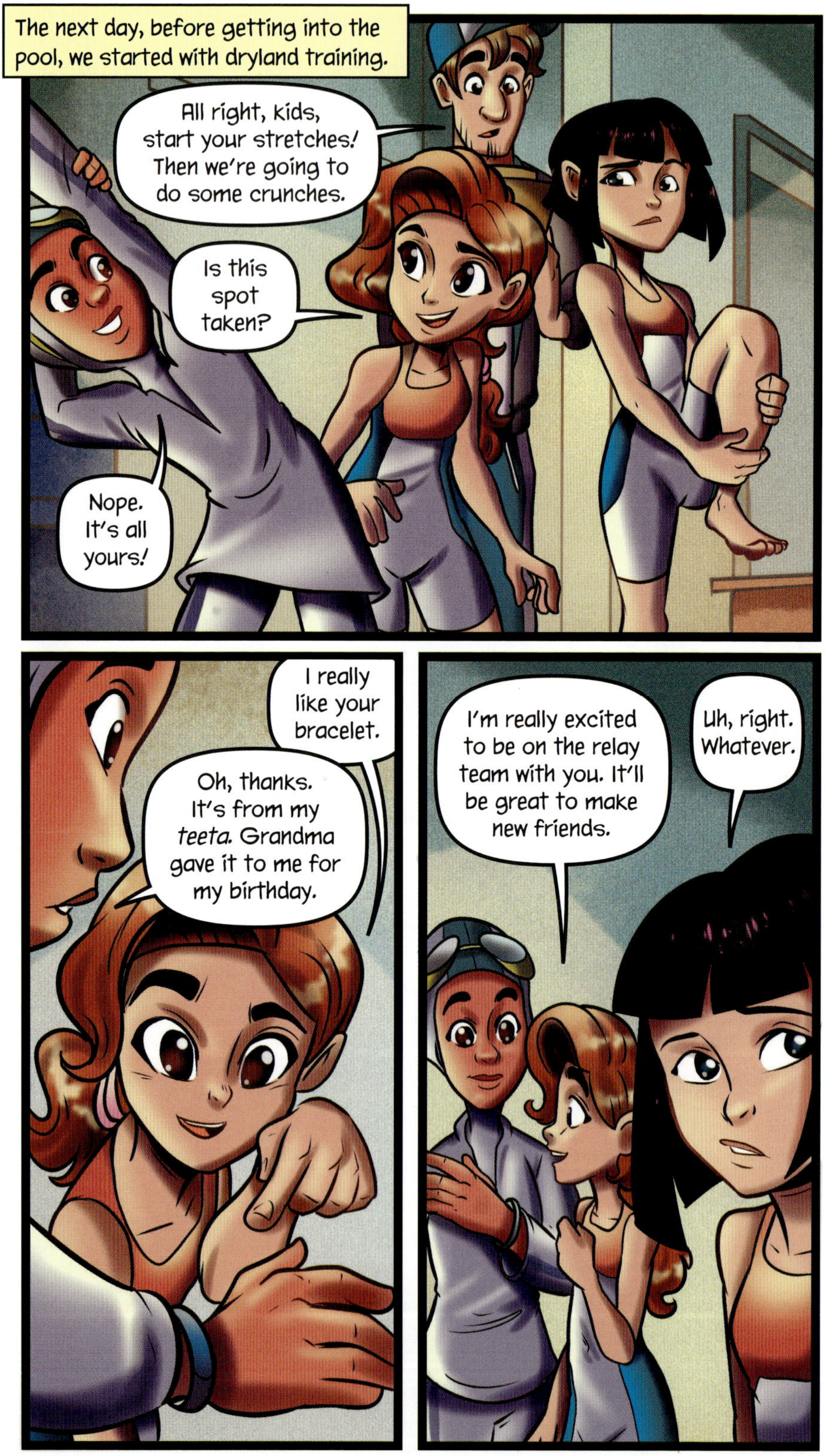

The next day, before getting into the pool, we started with dryland training.
All right, kids, start your stretches! Then we're going to do some crunches.
Is this spot taken?
Nope. It's all yours!
I really like your bracelet.
Oh, thanks. It's from my *teeta.* Grandma gave it to me for my birthday.
I'm really excited to be on the relay team with you. It'll be great to make new friends.
Uh, right. Whatever.

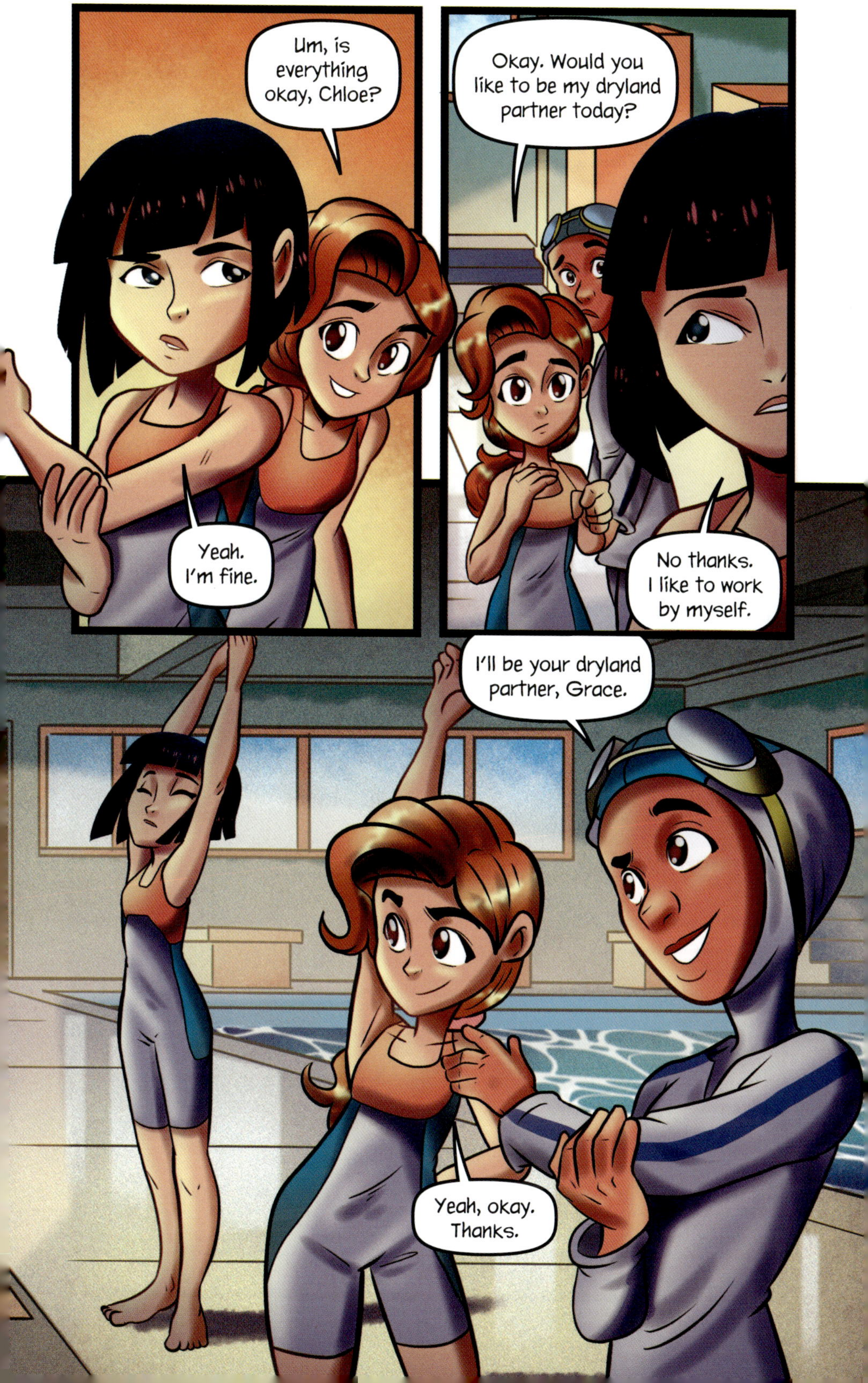
Um, is everything okay, Chloe?
Yeah. I'm fine.
Okay. Would you like to be my dryland partner today?
No thanks. I like to work by myself.
I'll be your dryland partner, Grace.
Yeah, okay. Thanks.

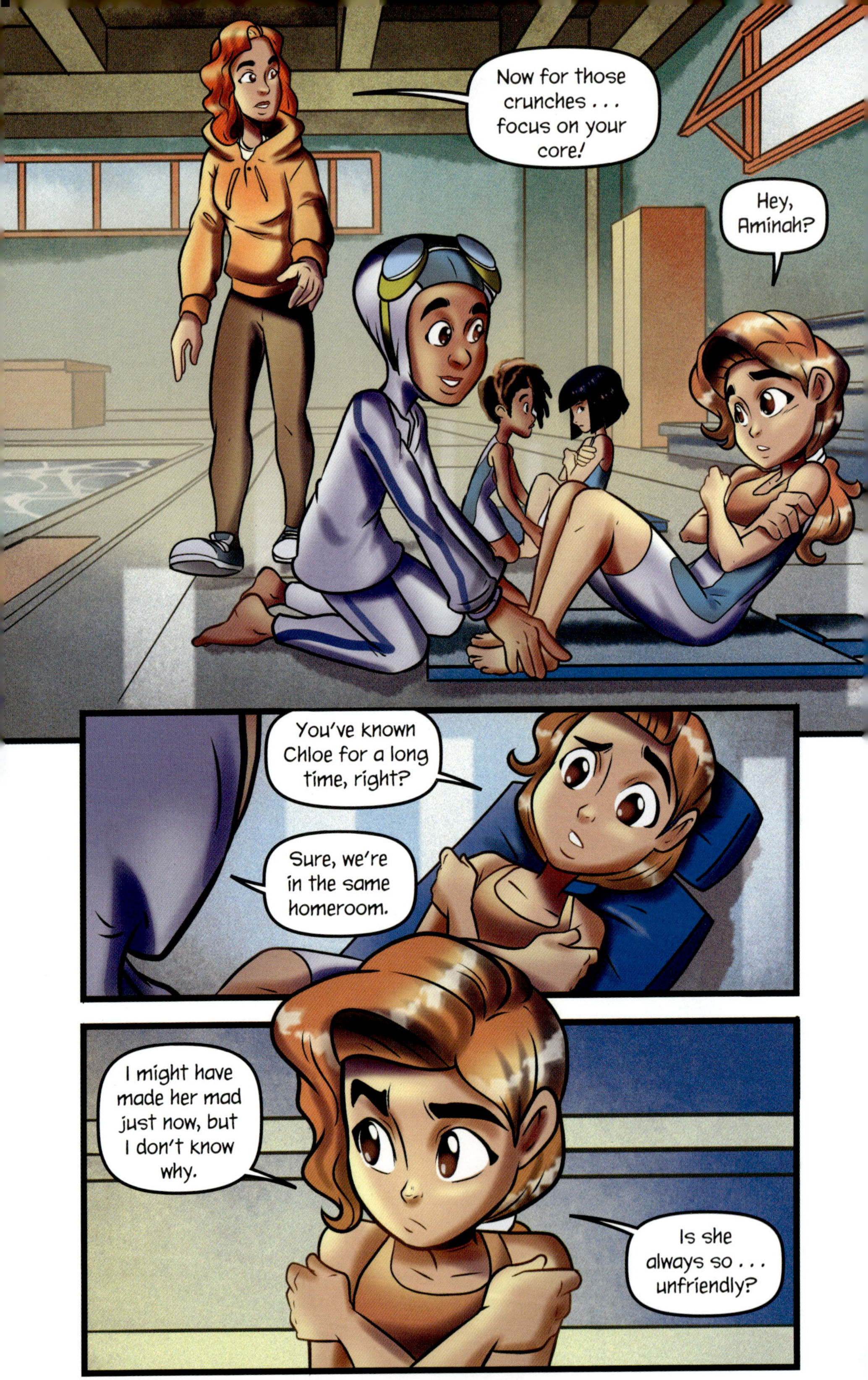
Now for those crunches . . . focus on your core!
Hey, Aminah?
You've known Chloe for a long time, right?
Sure, we're in the same homeroom.
I might have made her mad just now, but I don't know why.
Is she always so . . . unfriendly?

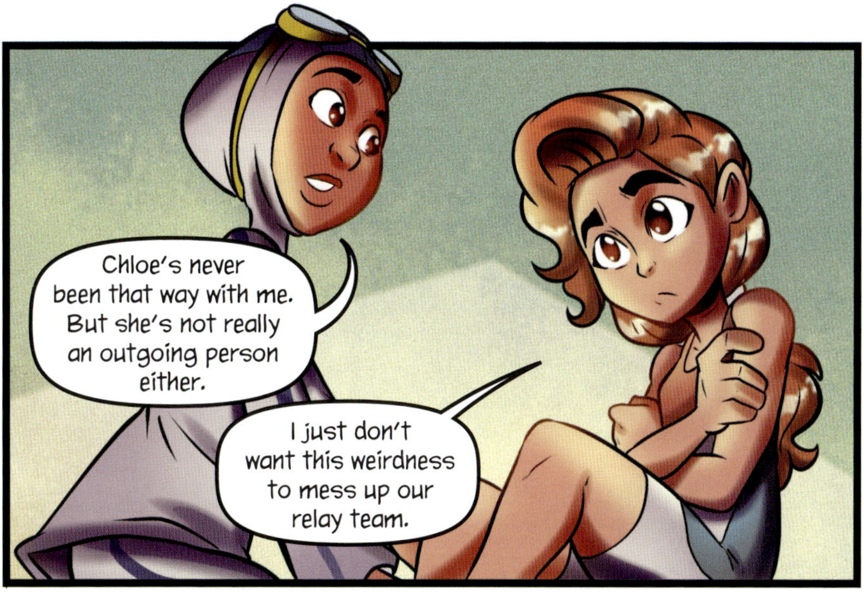
Chloe's never been that way with me. But she's not really an outgoing person either.
I just don't want this weirdness to mess up our relay team.

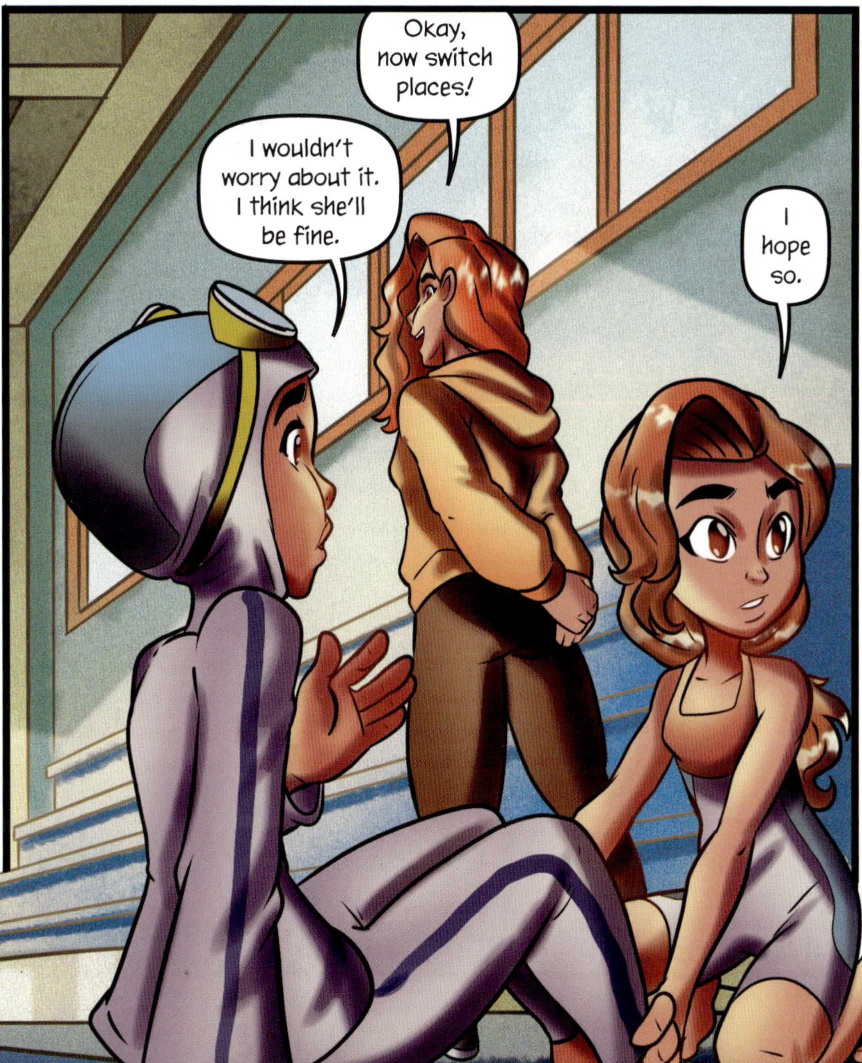
Okay, now switch places!
I wouldn't worry about it. I think she'll be fine.
I hope so.

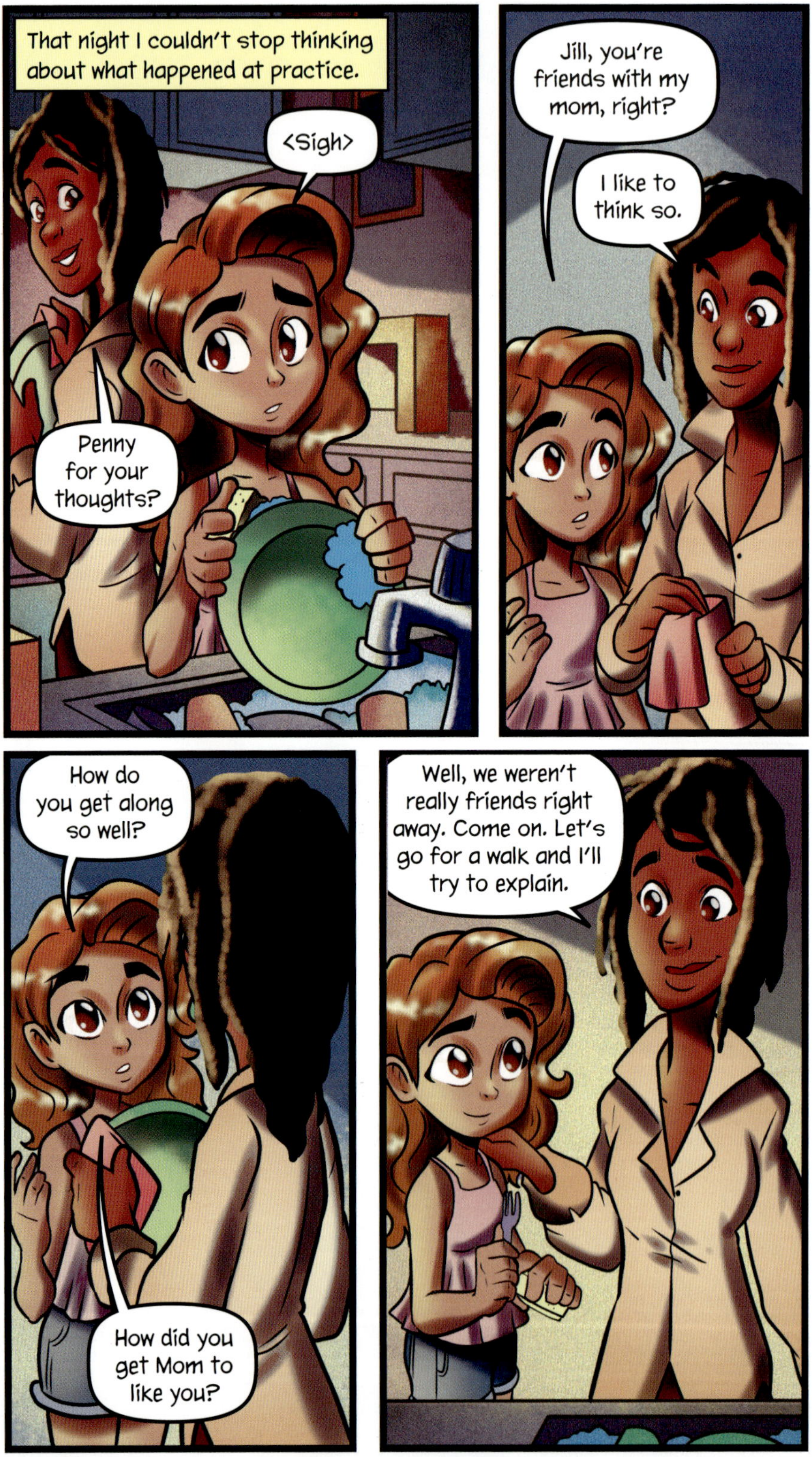
That night I couldn't stop thinking about what happened at practice.
<Sigh>
Penny for your thoughts?
Jill, you're friends with my mom, right?
I like to think so.
How do you get along so well?
How did you get Mom to like you?
Well, we weren't really friends right away. Come on. Let's go for a walk and I'll try to explain.

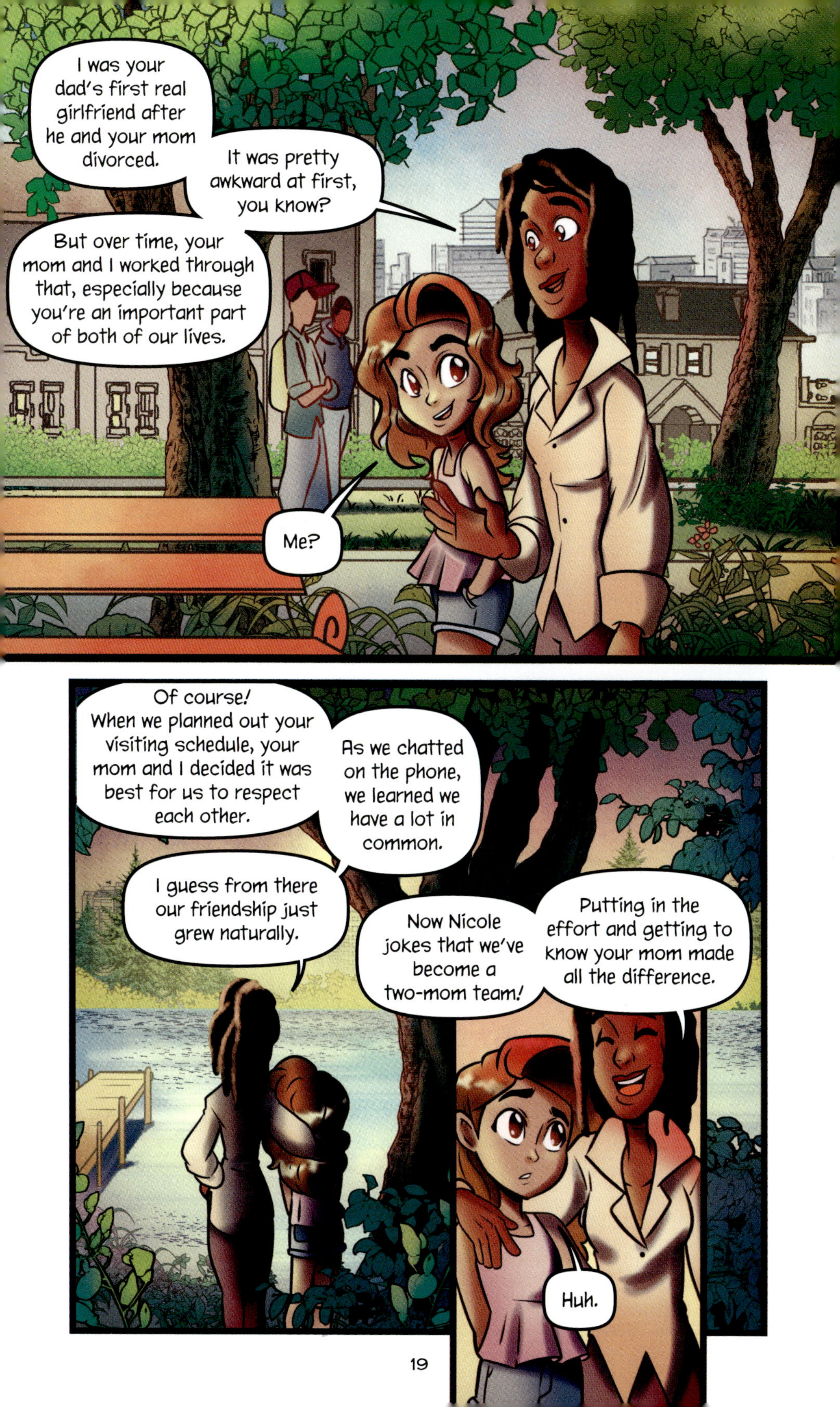
I was your dad's first real girlfriend after he and your mom divorced.
It was pretty awkward at first, you know?
But over time, your mom and I worked through that, especially because you're an important part of both of our lives.
Me?
Of course! When we planned out your visiting schedule, your mom and I decided it was best for us to respect each other.
As we chatted on the phone, we learned we have a lot in common.
I guess from there our friendship just grew naturally.
Now Nicole jokes that we've become a two-mom team!
Putting in the effort and getting to know your mom made all the difference.
Huh.

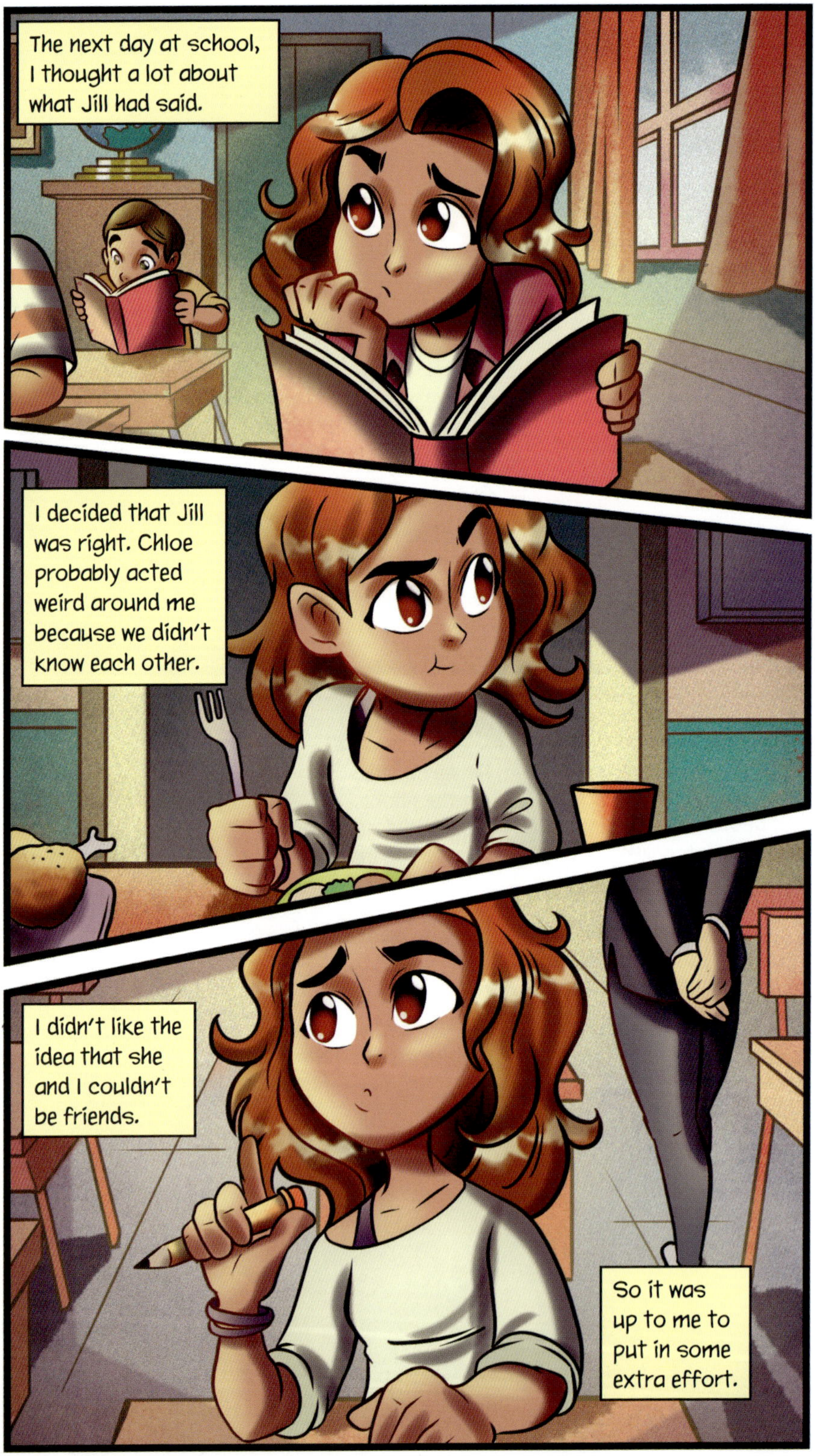
The next day at school, I thought a lot about what Jill had said.
I decided that Jill was right. Chloe probably acted weird around me because we didn't know each other.
I didn't like the idea that she and I couldn't be friends.
So it was up to me to put in some extra effort.

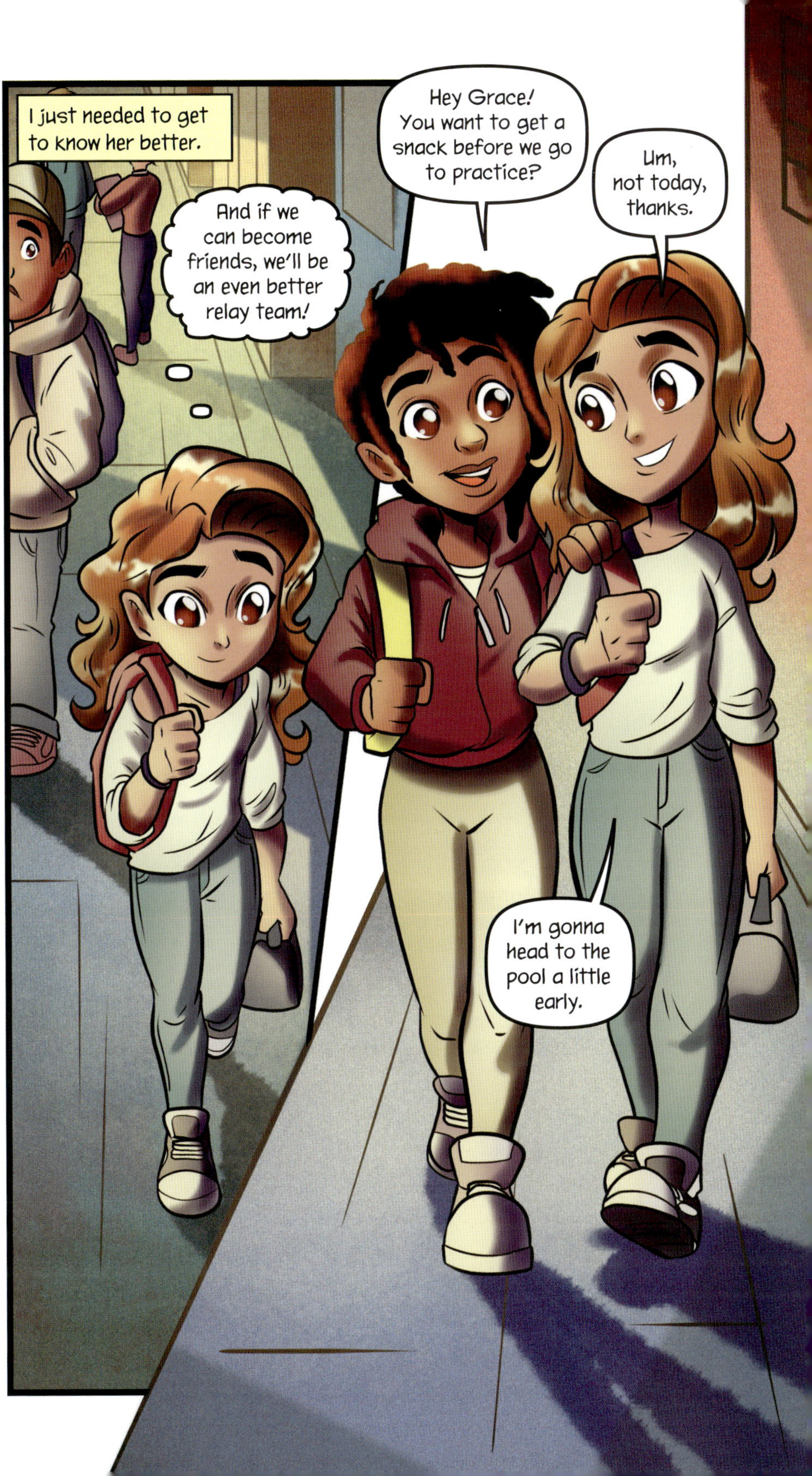
I just needed to get to know her better.
And if we can become friends, we'll be an even better relay team!
Hey Grace! You want to get a snack before we go to practice?
Um, not today, thanks.
I'm gonna head to the pool a little early.

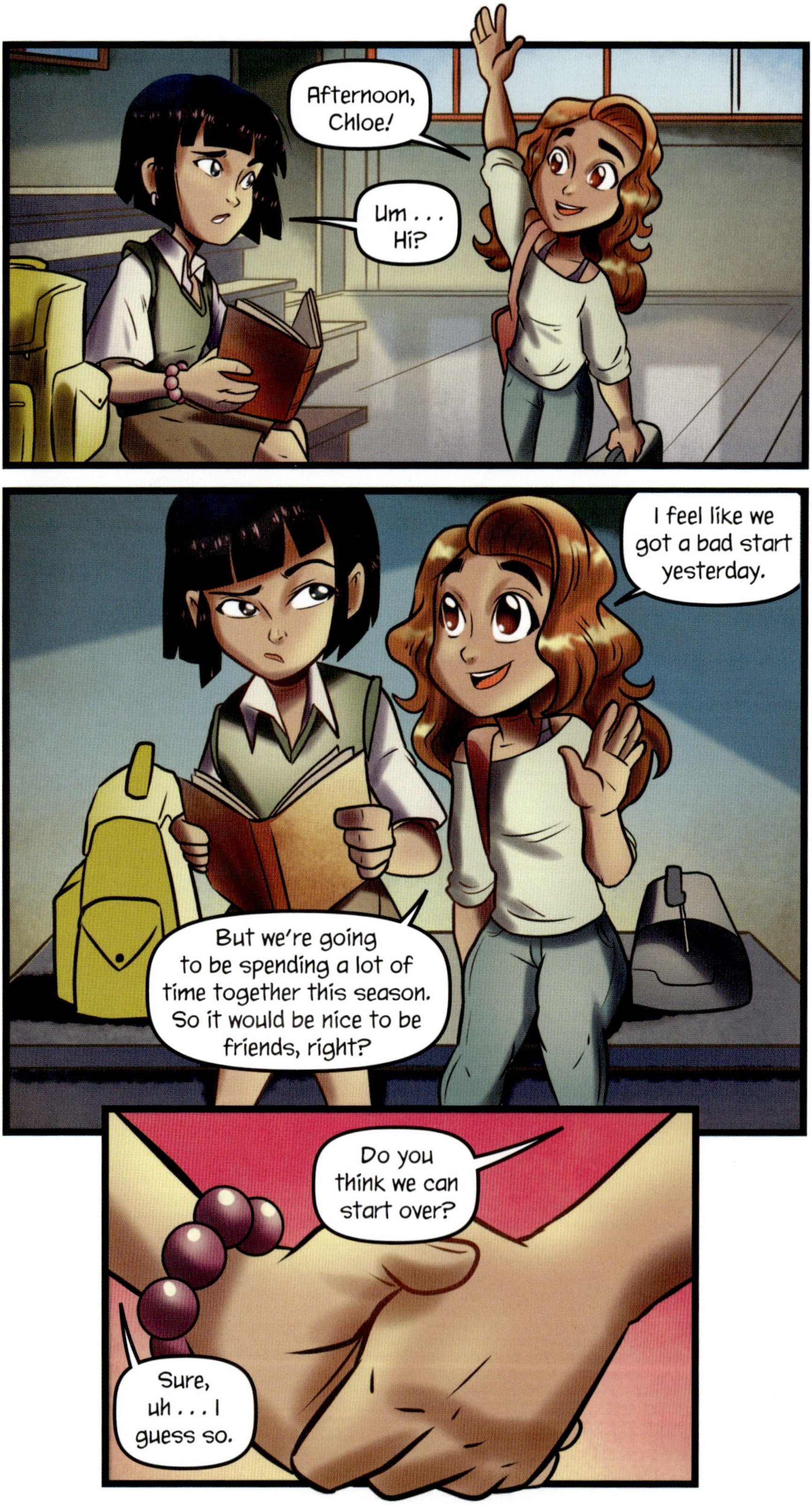
Afternoon, Chloe!
Um . . . Hi?
I feel like we got a bad start yesterday.
But we're going to be spending a lot of time together this season. So it would be nice to be friends, right?
Do you think we can start over?
Sure, uh . . . I guess so.

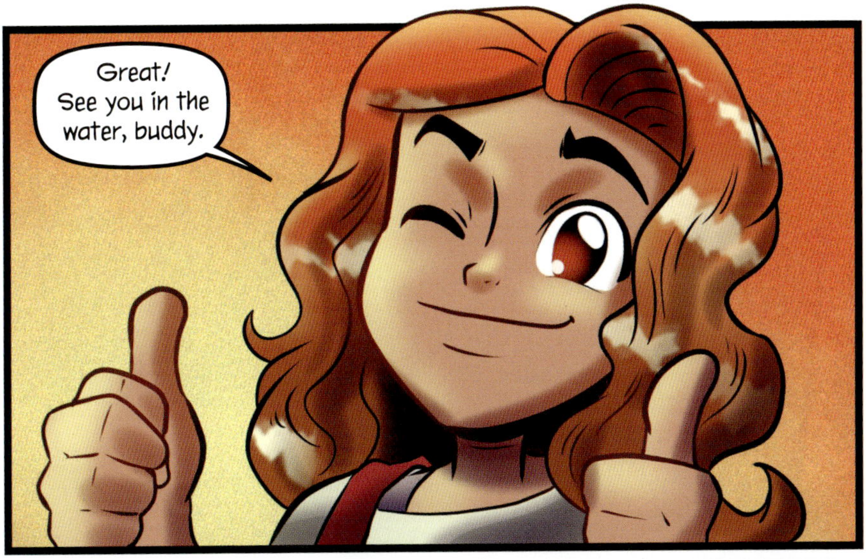
Great! See you in the water, buddy.

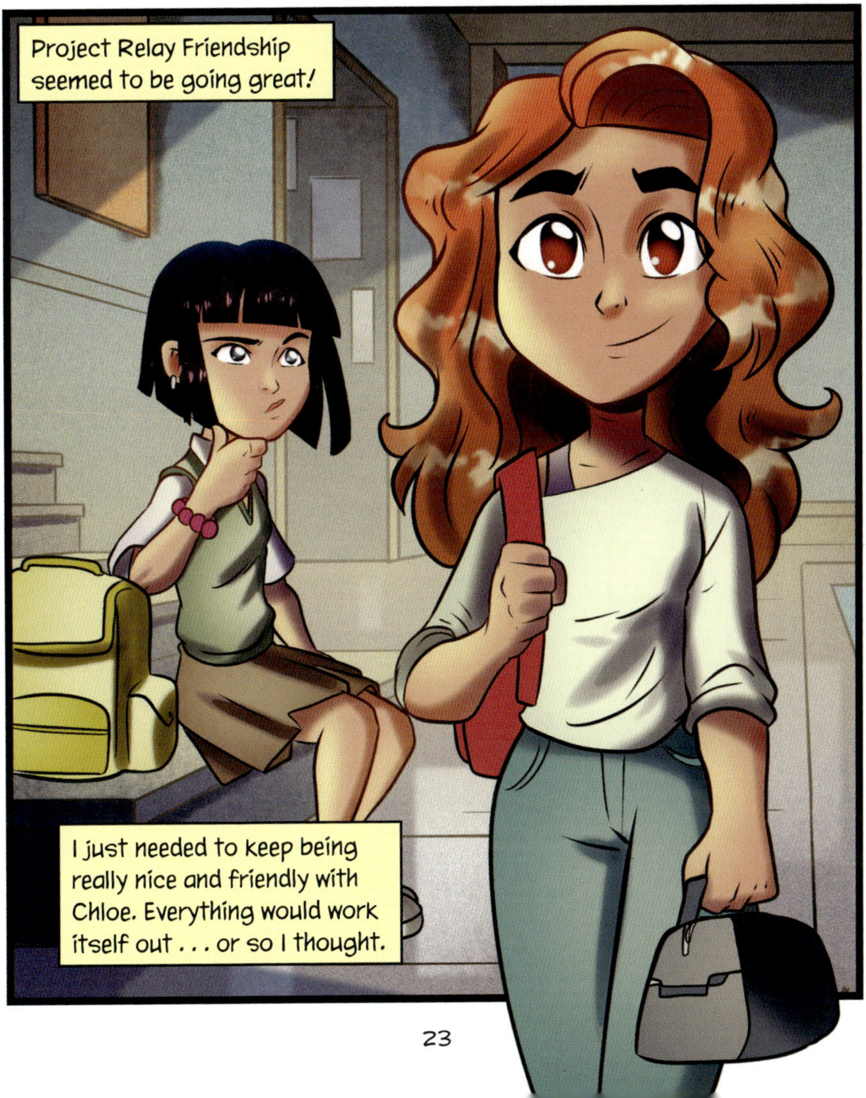
Project Relay Friendship seemed to be going great!
I just needed to keep being really nice and friendly with Chloe. Everything would work itself out . . . or so I thought.

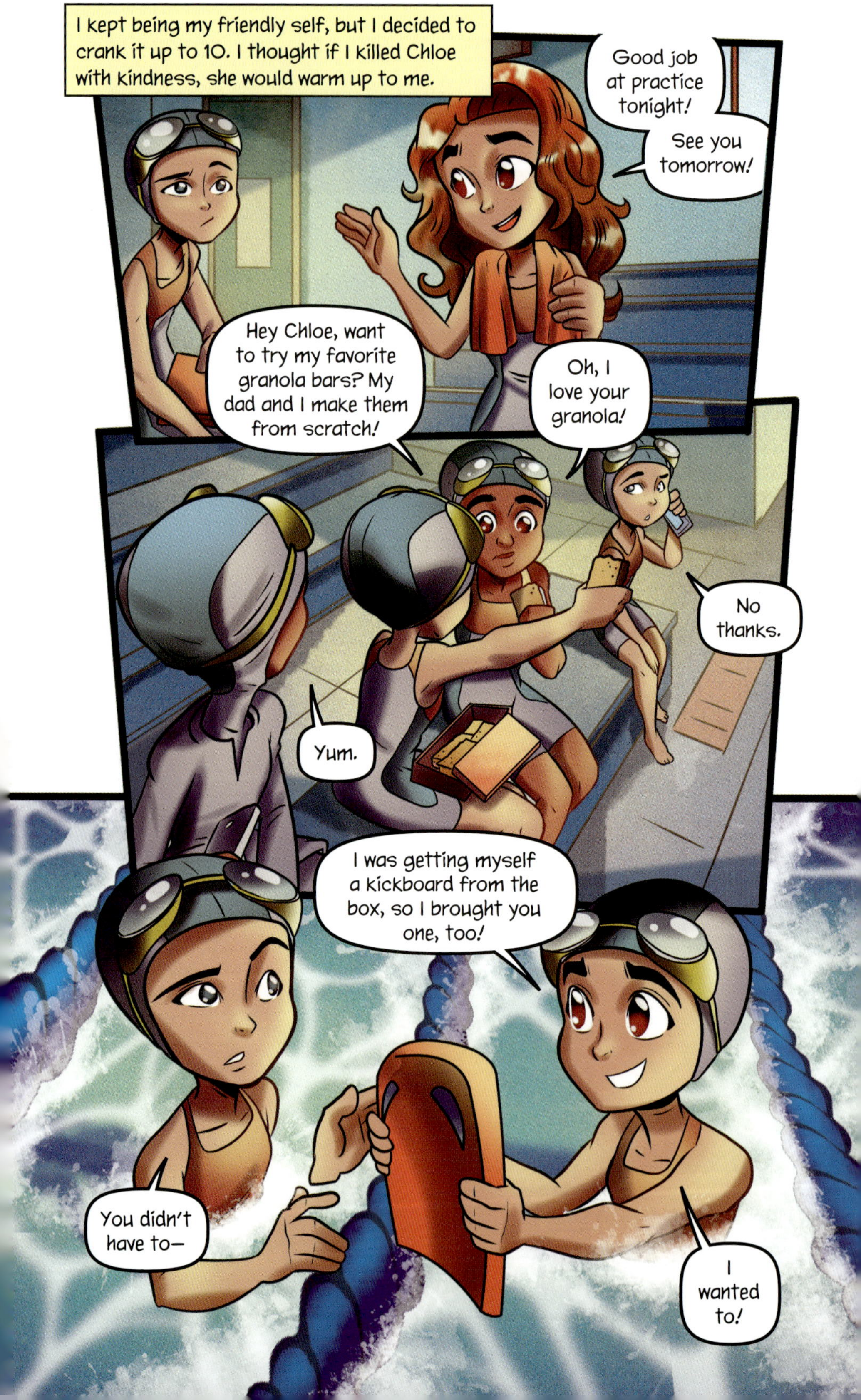
I kept being my friendly self, but I decided to crank it up to 10. I thought if I killed Chloe with kindness, she would warm up to me.
Good job at practice tonight!
See you tomorrow!
Hey Chloe, want to try my favorite granola bars? My dad and I make them from scratch!
Oh, I love your granola!
No thanks.
Yum.
I was getting myself a kickboard from the box, so I brought you one, too!
You didn't have to—
I wanted to!

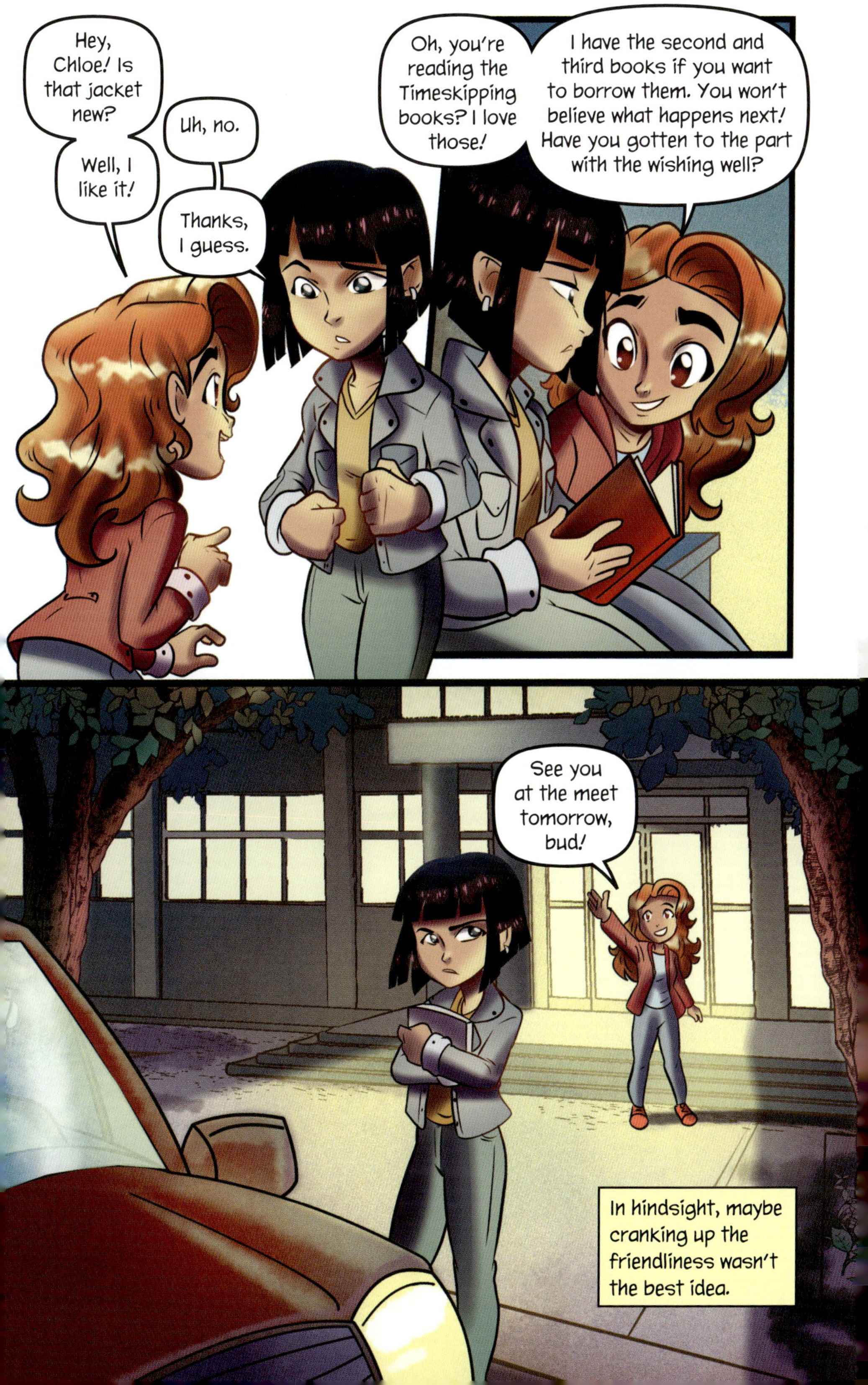

Hey, Chloe! Is that jacket new?
Well, I like it!
Uh, no.
Thanks, I guess.
Oh, you're reading the Timeskipping books? I love those!
I have the second and third books if you want to borrow them. You won't believe what happens next! Have you gotten to the part with the wishing well?
See you at the meet tomorrow, bud!
In hindsight, maybe cranking up the friendliness wasn't the best idea.

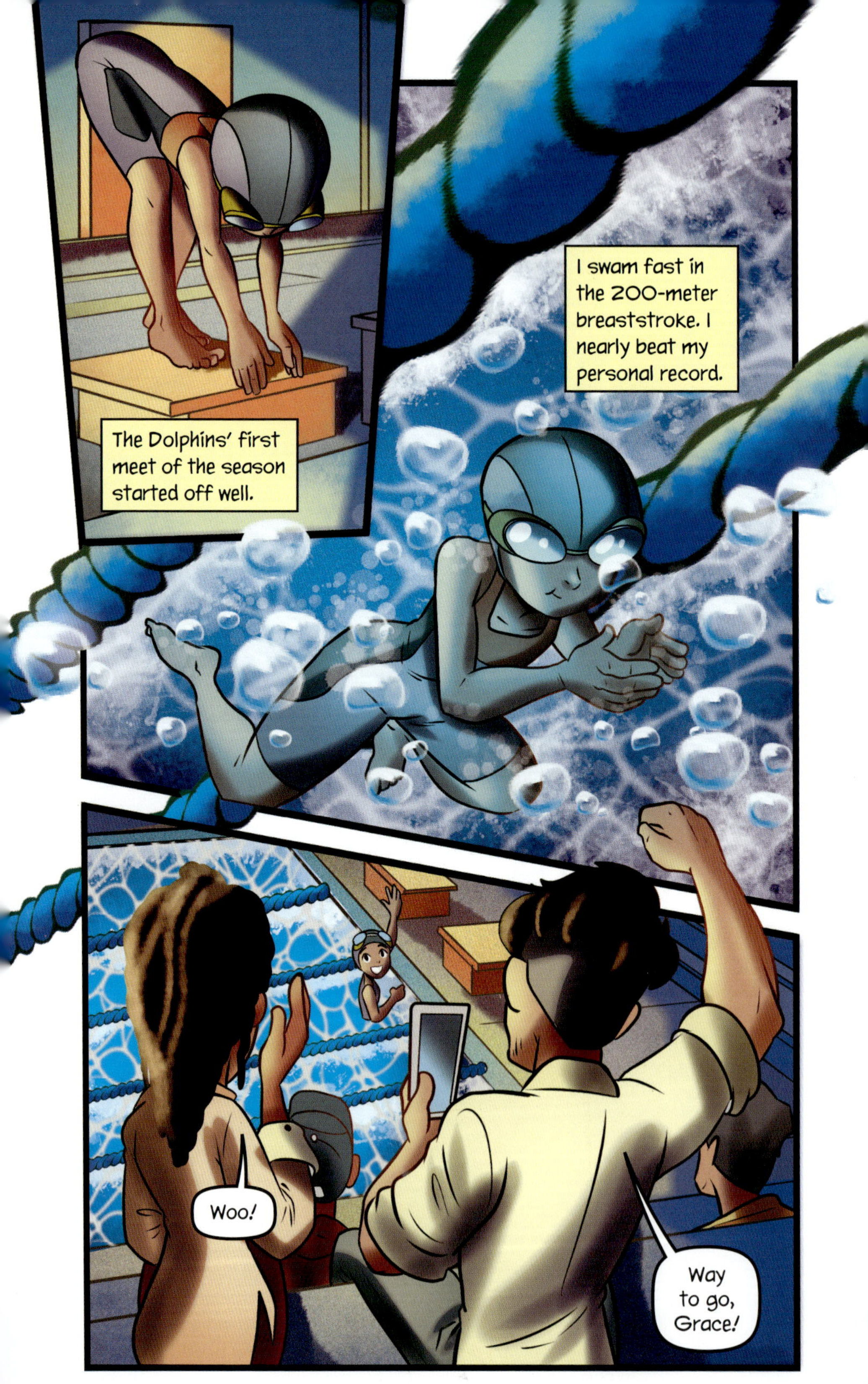
The Dolphins' first meet of the season started off well.
I swam fast in the 200-meter breaststroke. I nearly beat my personal record.
Woo!
Way to go, Grace!

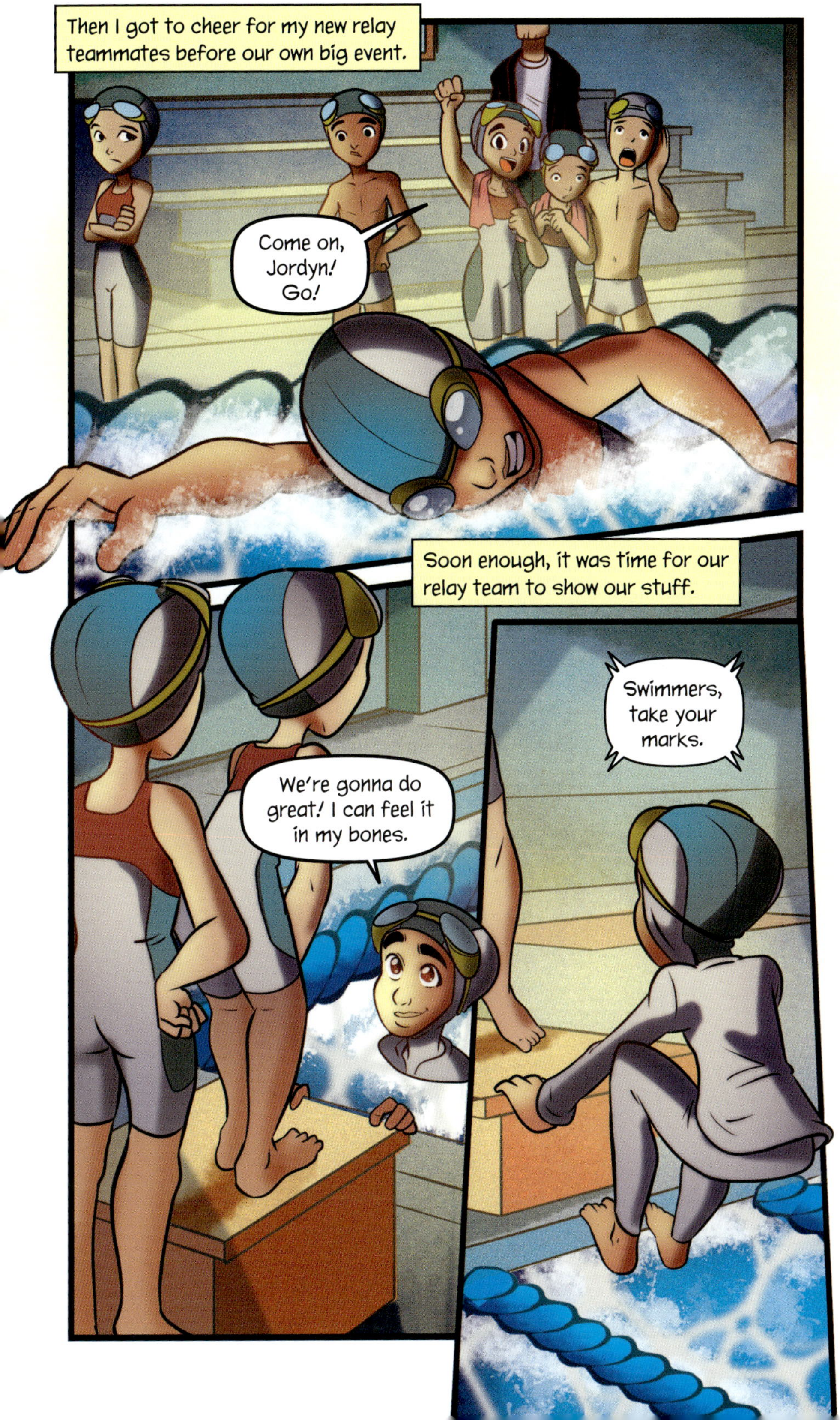
Then I got to cheer for my new relay teammates before our own big event.
Come on, Jordyn! Go!
Soon enough, it was time for our relay team to show our stuff.
We're gonna do great! I can feel it in my bones.
Swimmers, take your marks.

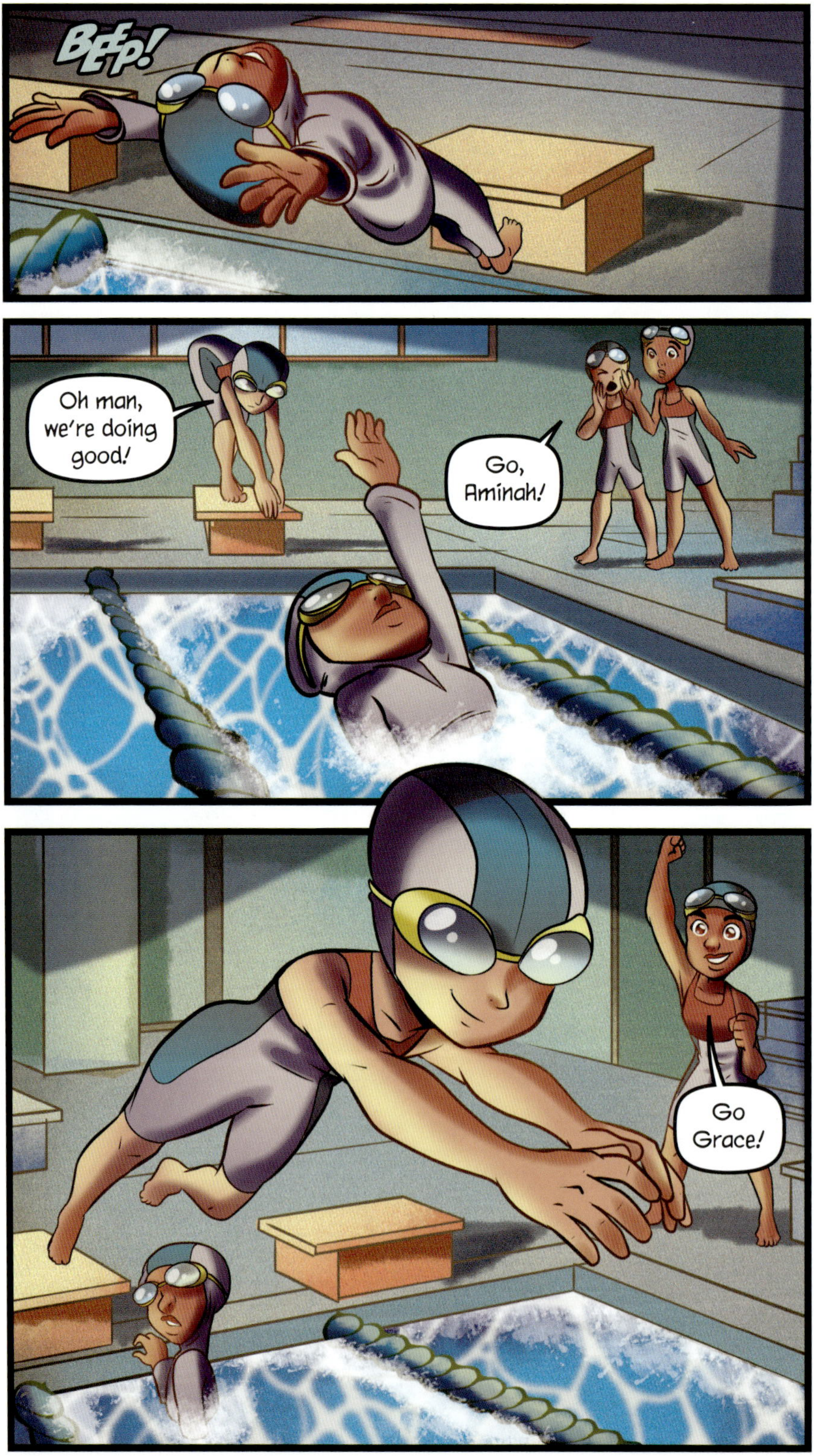
BEEP!
Oh man, we're doing good!
Go, Aminah!
Go Grace!

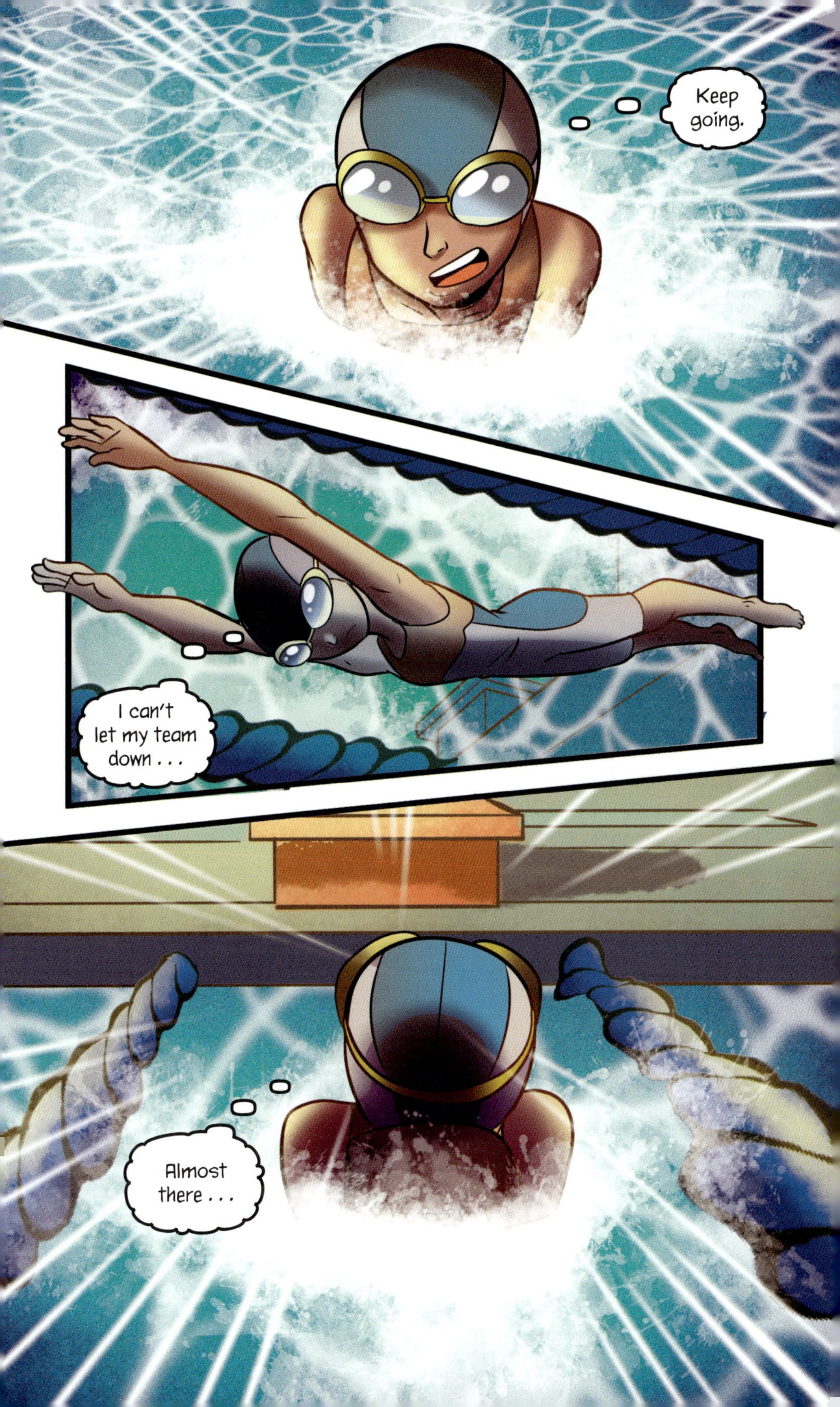
Keep going.
I can't let my team down . . .
Almost there . . .

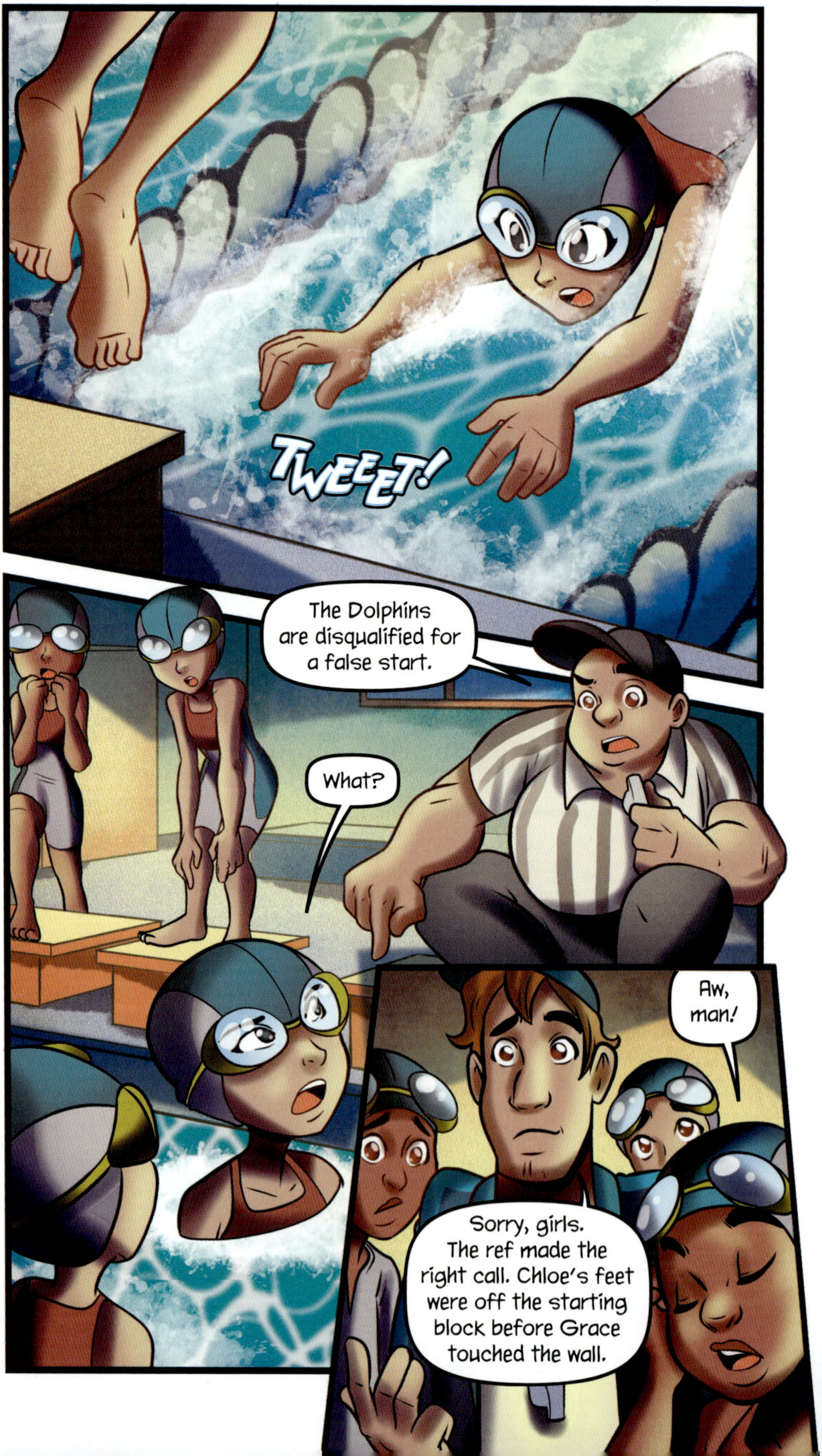
TWEEET!
The Dolphins are disqualified for a false start.
What?
Aw, man!
Sorry, girls. The ref made the right call. Chloe's feet were off the starting block before Grace touched the wall.

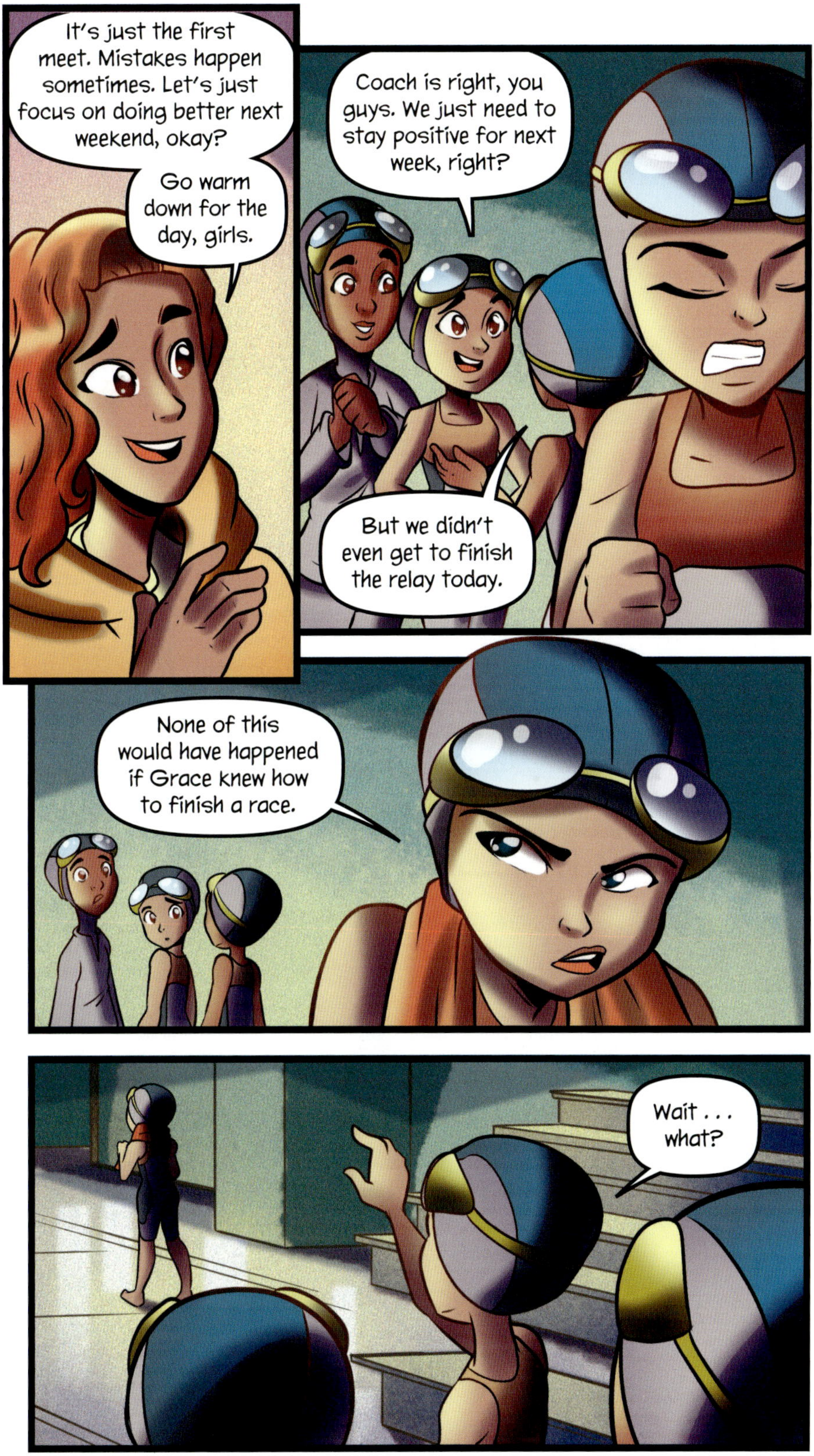
It's just the first meet. Mistakes happen sometimes. Let's just focus on doing better next weekend, okay?
Go warm down for the day, girls.
Coach is right, you guys. We just need to stay positive for next week, right?
But we didn't even get to finish the relay today.
None of this would have happened if Grace knew how to finish a race.
Wait . . . what?

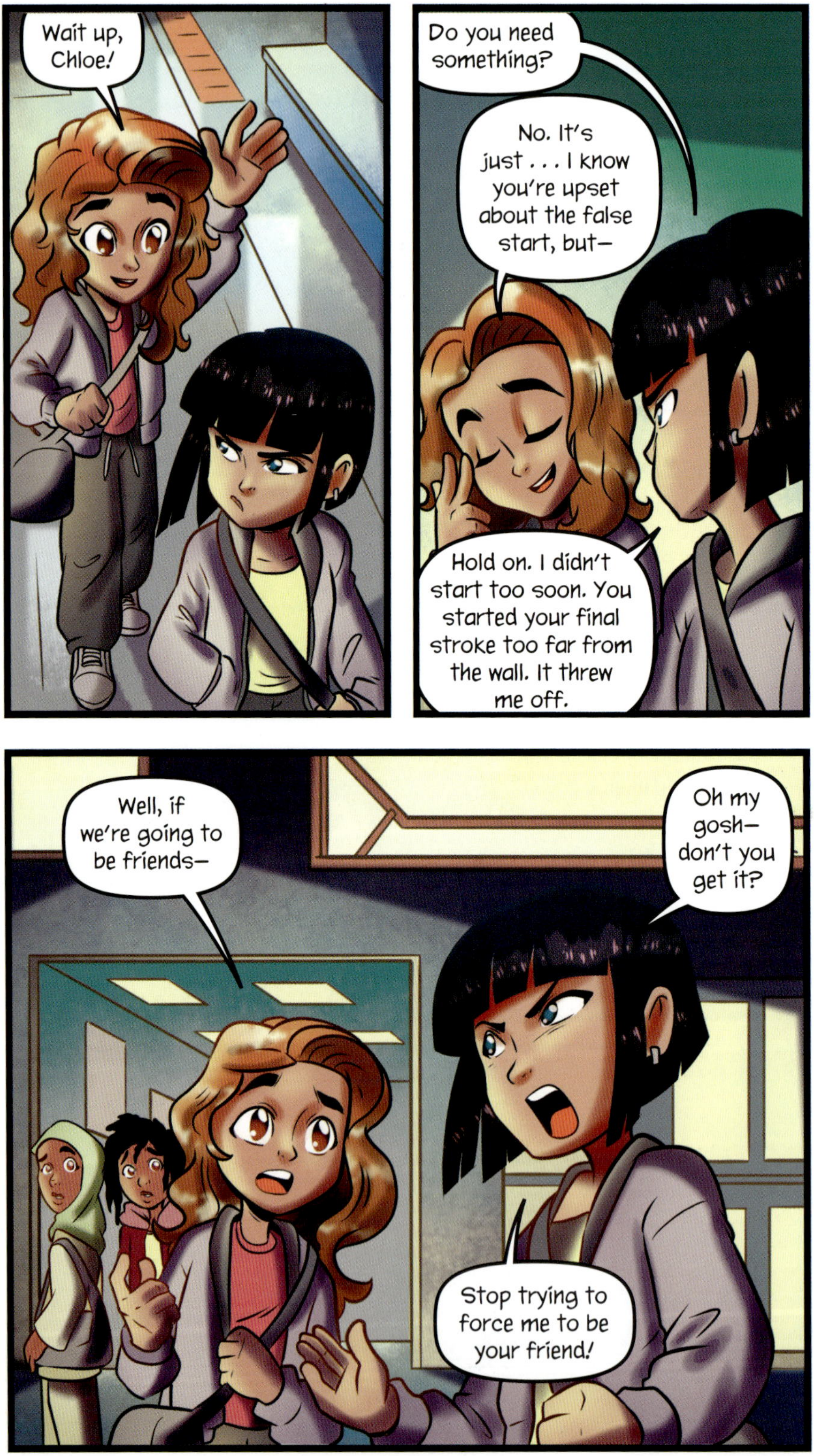
Wait up, Chloe!
Do you need something?
No. It's just . . . I know you're upset about the false start, but—
Hold on. I didn't start too soon. You started your final stroke too far from the wall. It threw me off.
Well, if we're going to be friends—
Oh my gosh—don't you get it?
Stop trying to force me to be your friend!

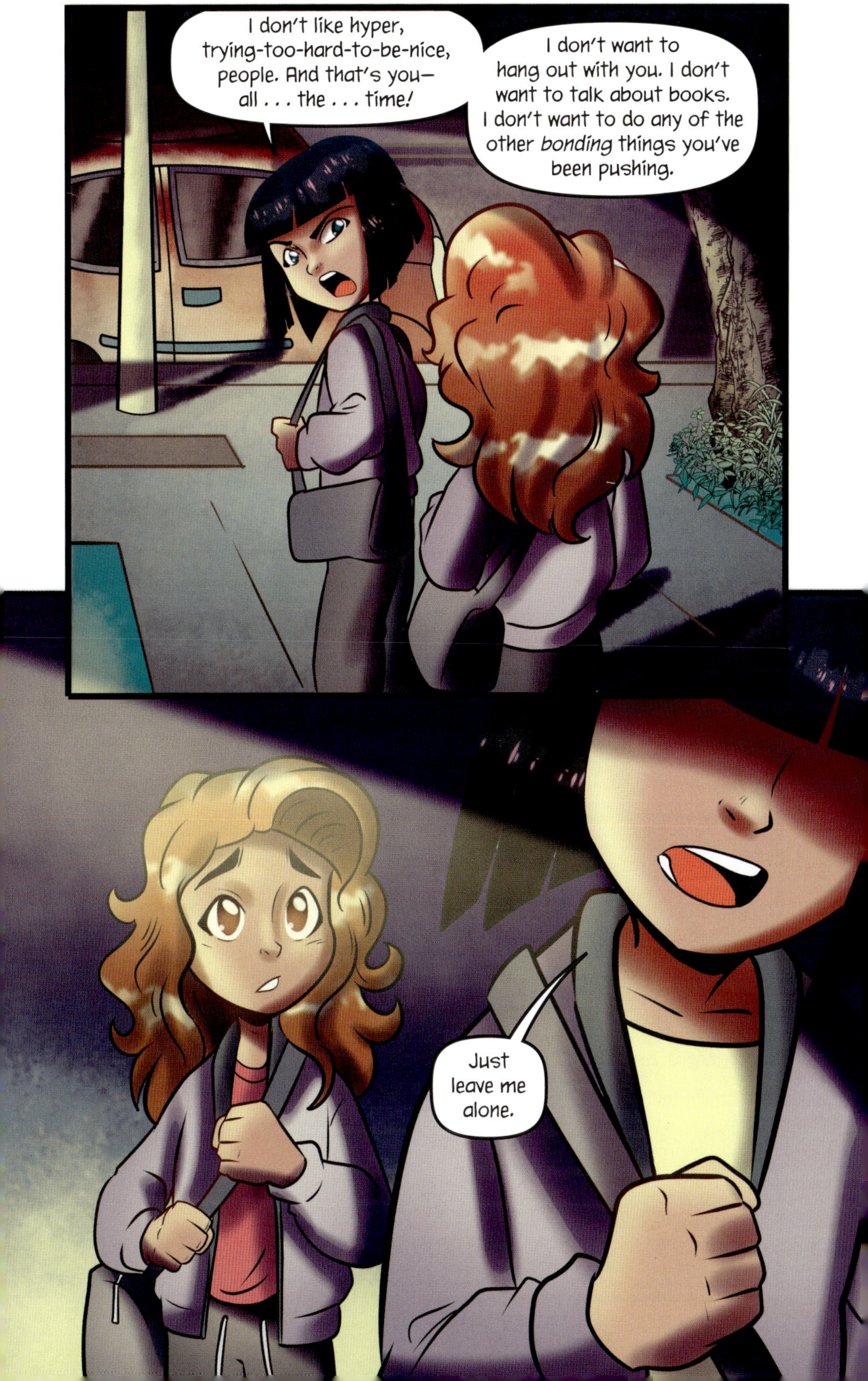
I don't like hyper, trying-too-hard-to-be-nice, people. And that's you—all . . . the . . . time!
I don't want to hang out with you. I don't want to talk about books. I don't want to do any of the other *bonding* things you've been pushing.
Just leave me alone.

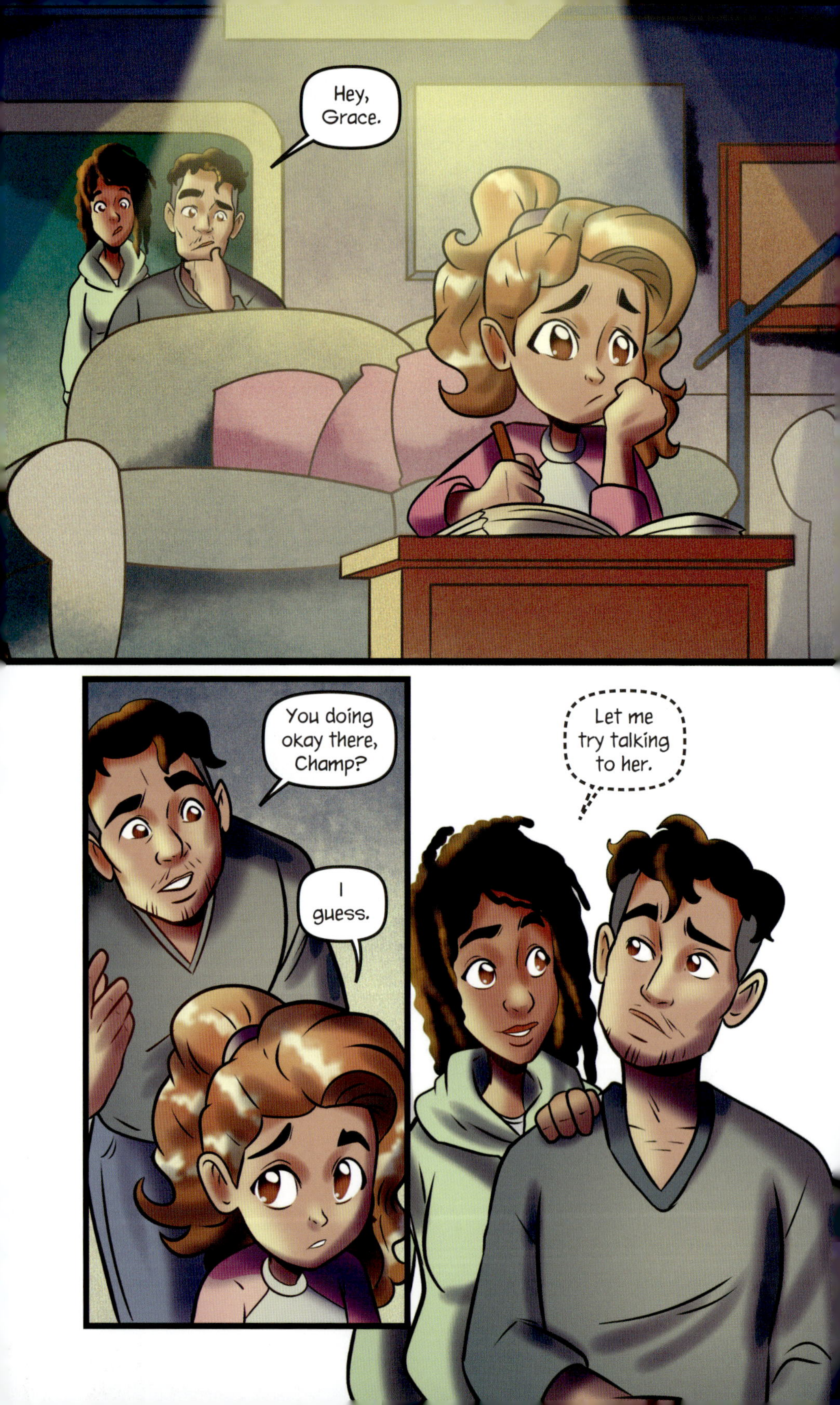
Hey, Grace.
You doing okay there, Champ?
I guess.
Let me try talking to her.

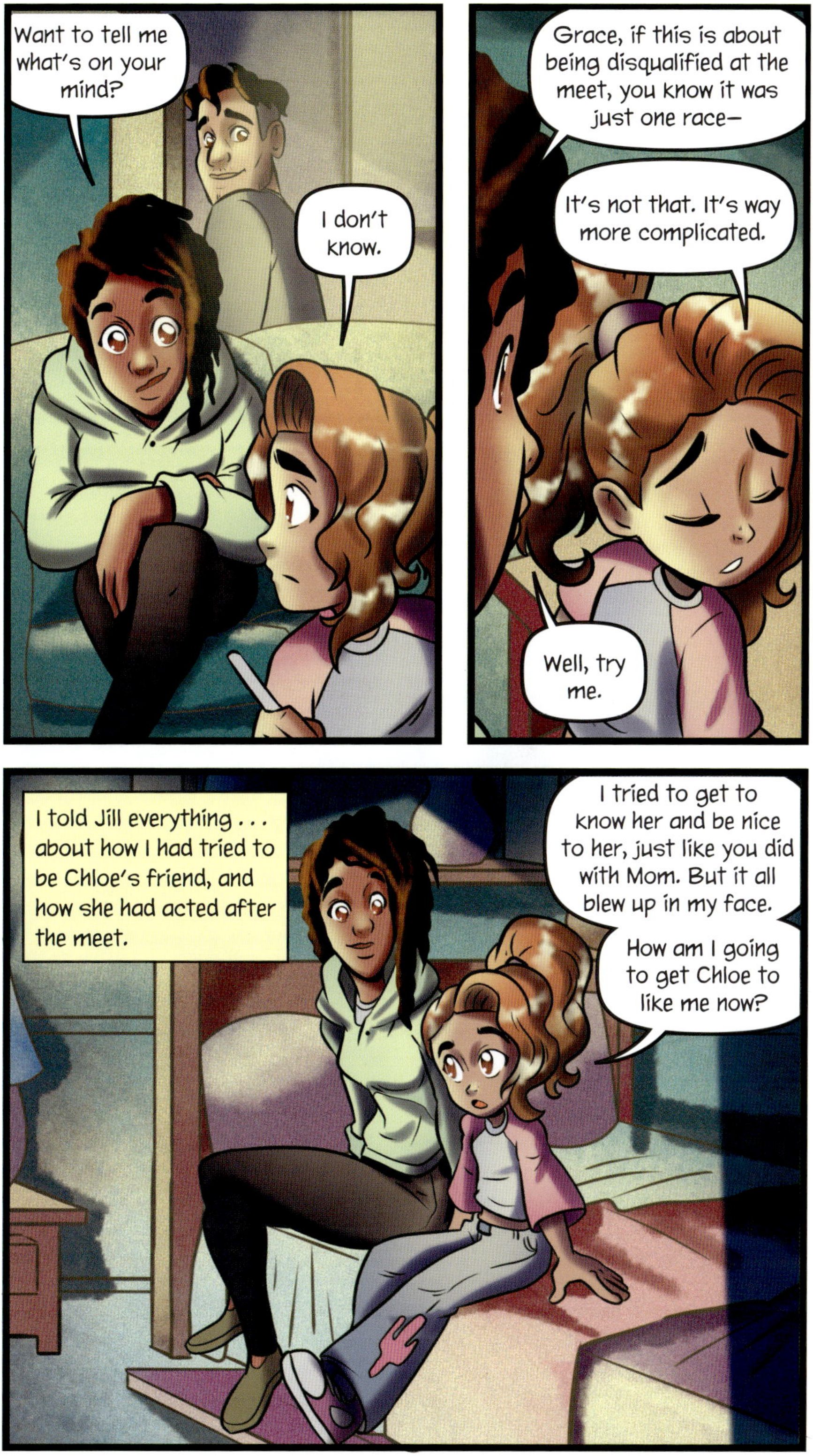
Want to tell me what's on your mind?
I don't know.
Grace, if this is about being disqualified at the meet, you know it was just one race—
It's not that. It's way more complicated.
Well, try me.
I told Jill everything . . . about how I had tried to be Chloe's friend, and how she had acted after the meet.
I tried to get to know her and be nice to her, just like you did with Mom. But it all blew up in my face.
How am I going to get Chloe to like me now?

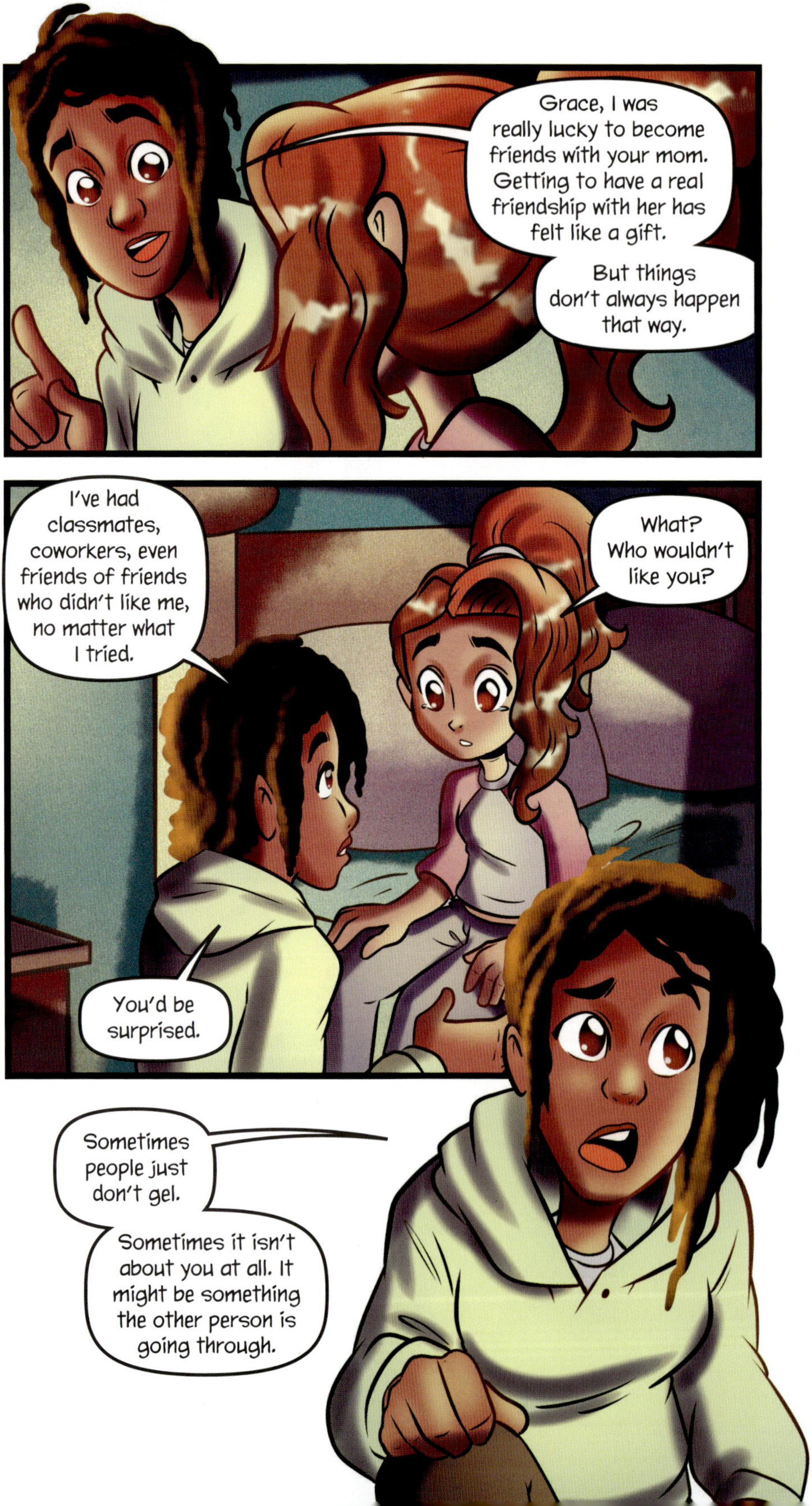
Grace, I was really lucky to become friends with your mom. Getting to have a real friendship with her has felt like a gift.
But things don't always happen that way.
I've had classmates, coworkers, even friends of friends who didn't like me, no matter what I tried.
What? Who wouldn't like you?
You'd be surprised.
Sometimes people just don't gel.
Sometimes it isn't about you at all. It might be something the other person is going through.

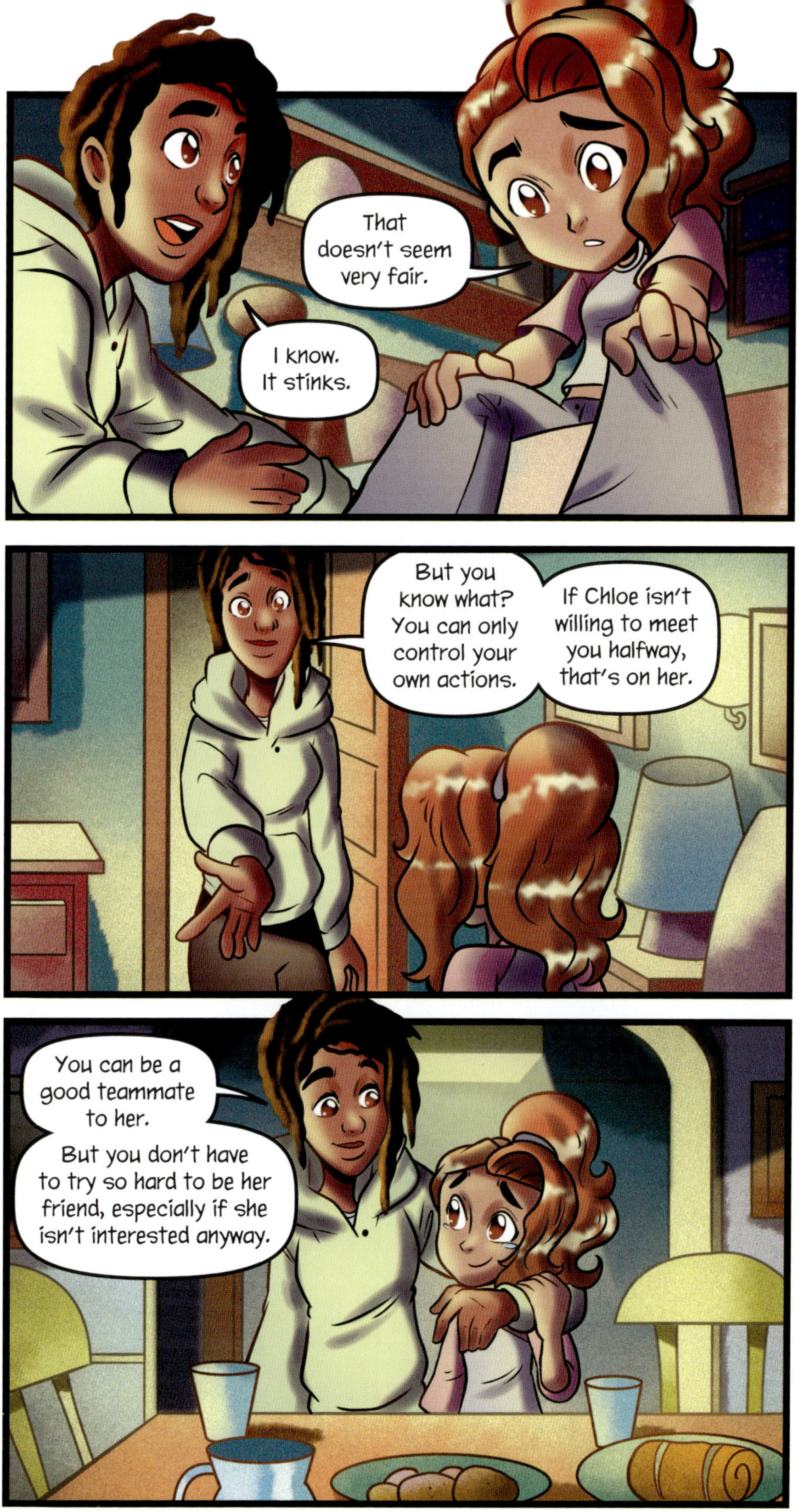

That doesn't seem very fair.
I know. It stinks.
But you know what? You can only control your own actions.
If Chloe isn't willing to meet you halfway, that's on her.
You can be a good teammate to her.
But you don't have to try so hard to be her friend, especially if she isn't interested anyway.

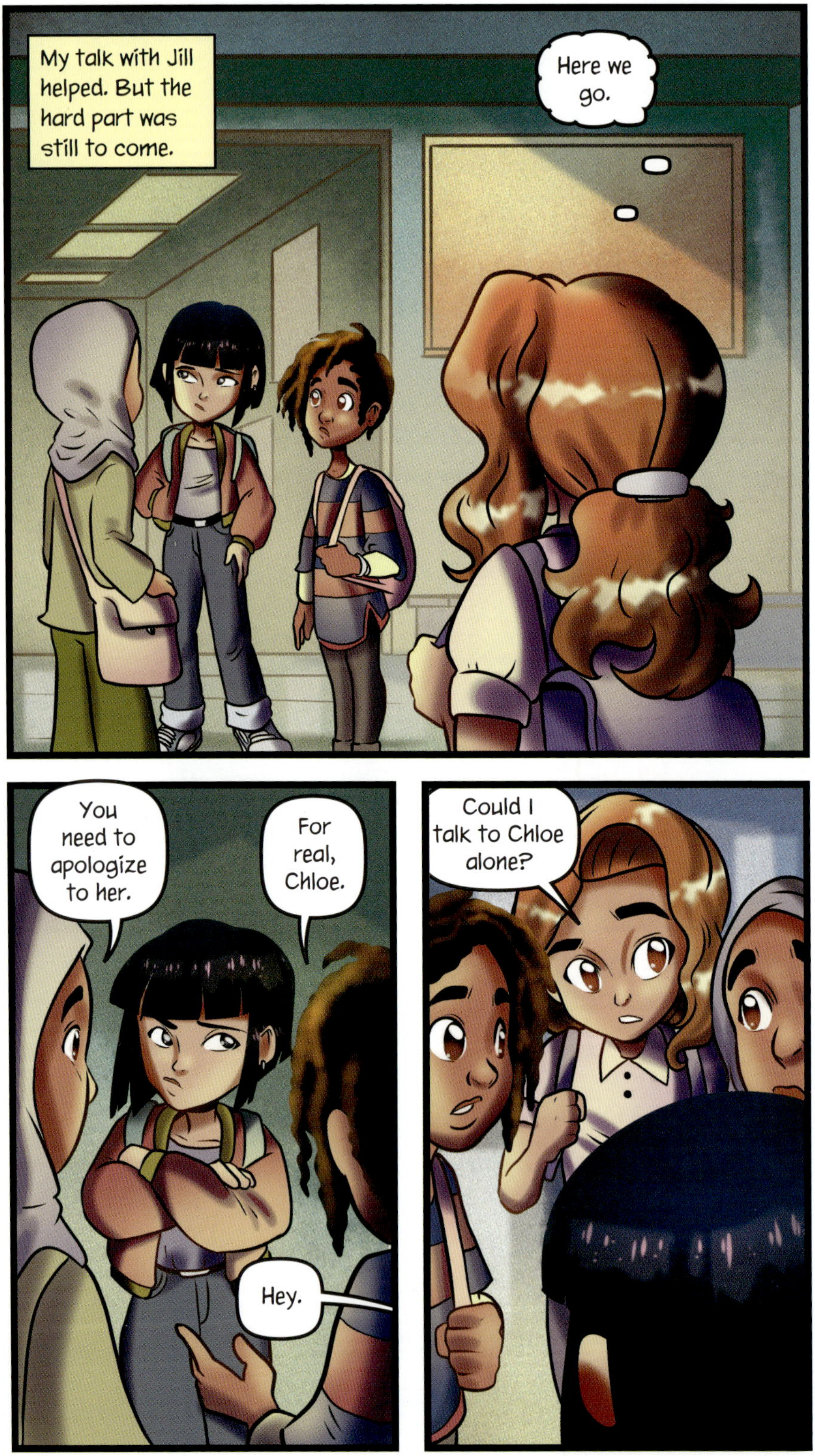
My talk with Jill helped. But the hard part was still to come.
Here we go.
You need to apologize to her.
For real, Chloe.
Hey.
Could I talk to Chloe alone?

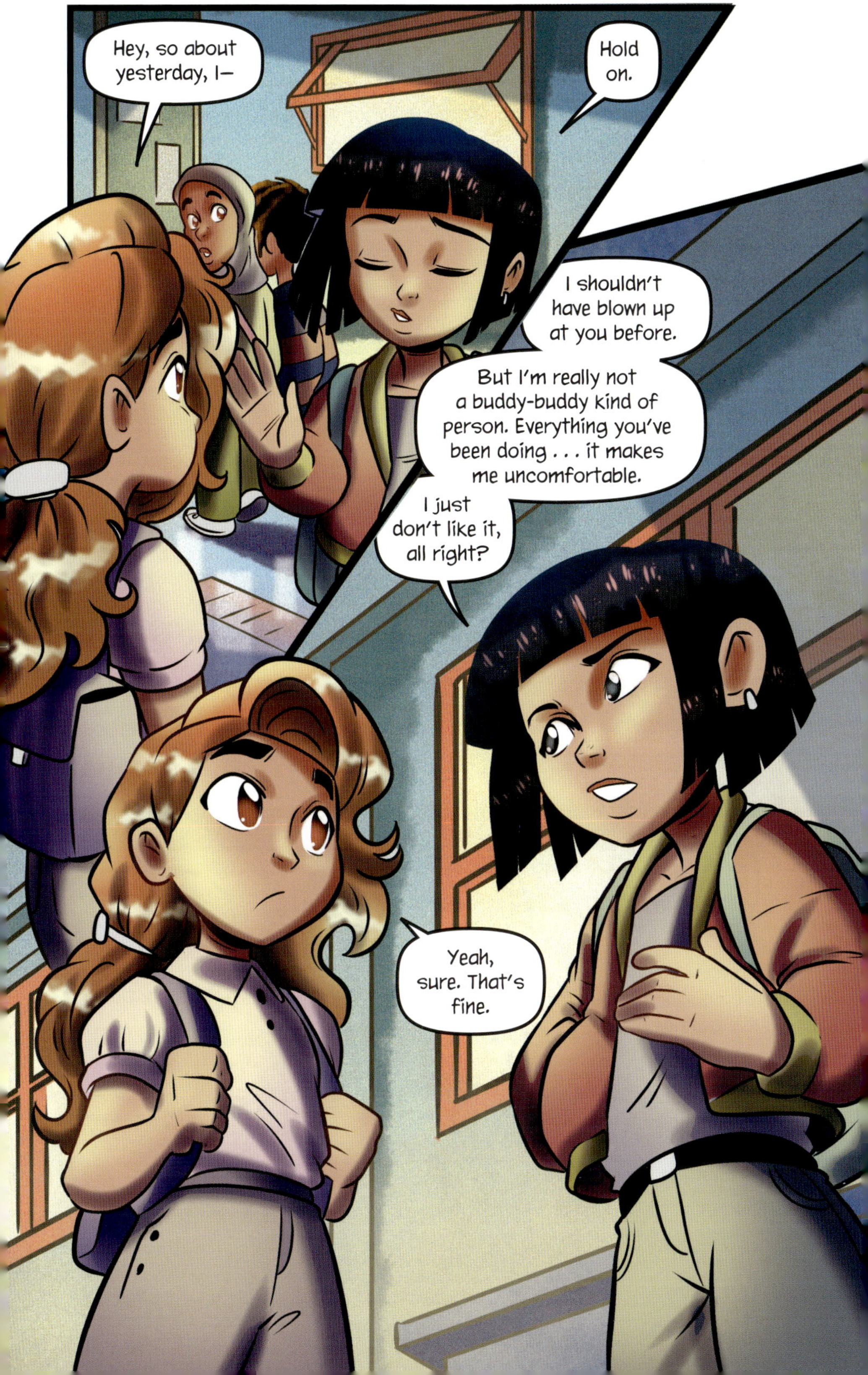
Hey, so about yesterday, I—
Hold on.
I shouldn't have blown up at you before.
But I'm really not a buddy-buddy kind of person. Everything you've been doing . . . it makes me uncomfortable.
I just don't like it, all right?
Yeah, sure. That's fine.

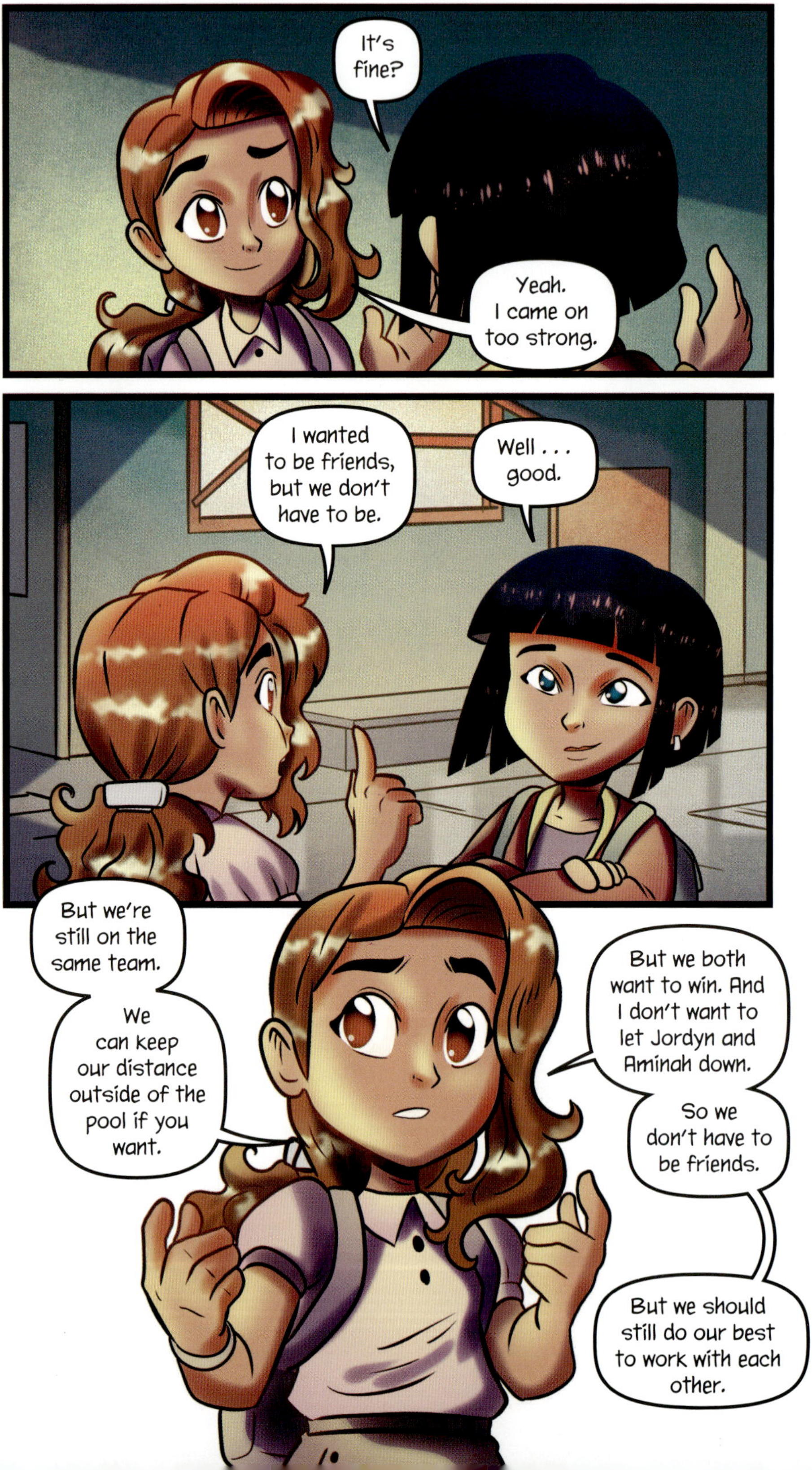
It's fine?
Yeah. I came on too strong.
I wanted to be friends, but we don't have to be.
Well . . . good.
But we're still on the same team.
We can keep our distance outside of the pool if you want.
But we both want to win. And I don't want to let Jordyn and Aminah down.
So we don't have to be friends.
But we should still do our best to work with each other.

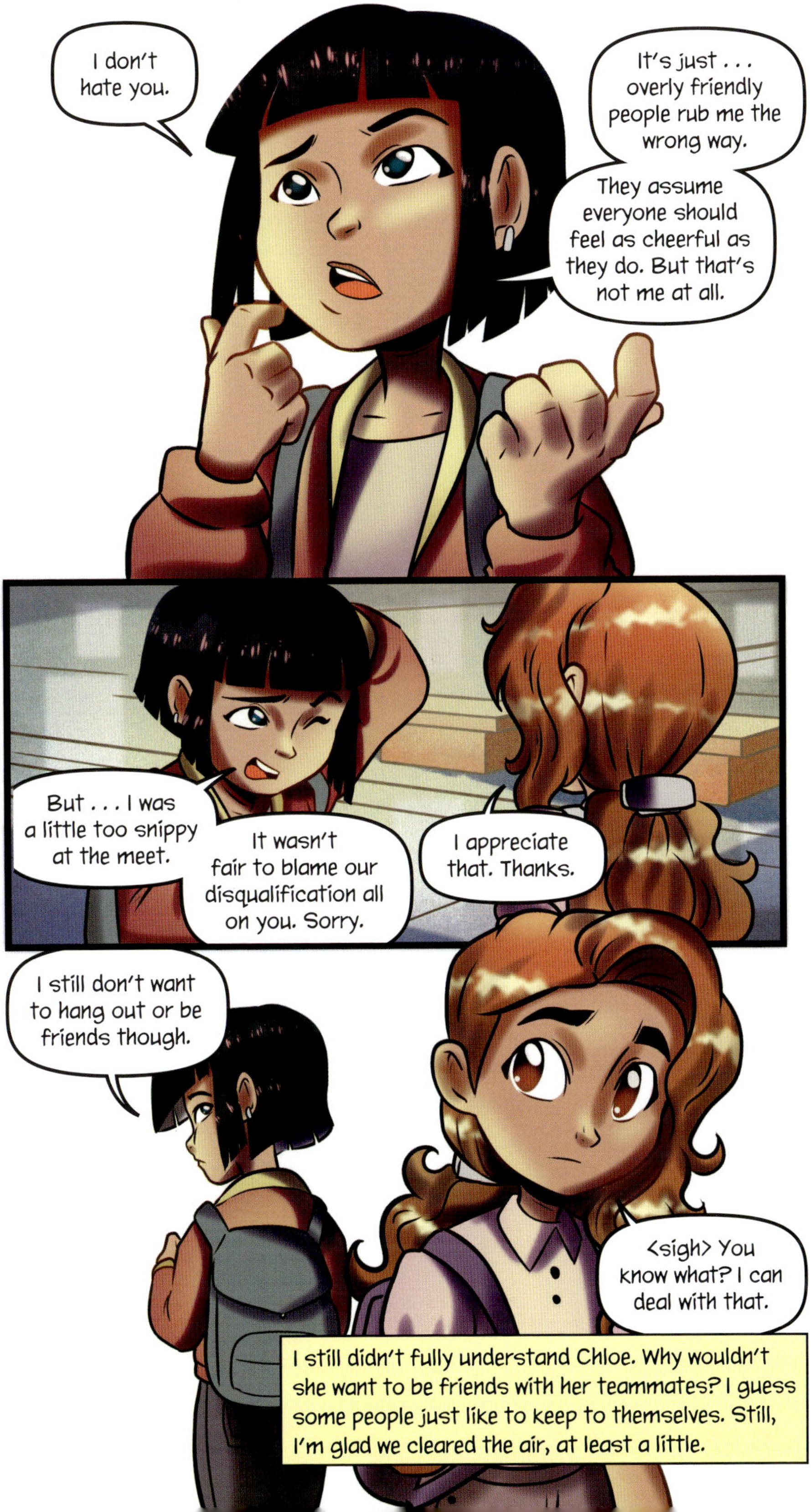
I don't hate you.
It's just . . . overly friendly people rub me the wrong way.
They assume everyone should feel as cheerful as they do. But that's not me at all.
But . . . I was a little too snippy at the meet.
It wasn't fair to blame our disqualification all on you. Sorry.
I appreciate that. Thanks.
I still don't want to hang out or be friends though.
<sigh> You know what? I can deal with that.
I still didn't fully understand Chloe. Why wouldn't she want to be friends with her teammates? I guess some people just like to keep to themselves. Still, I'm glad we cleared the air, at least a little.

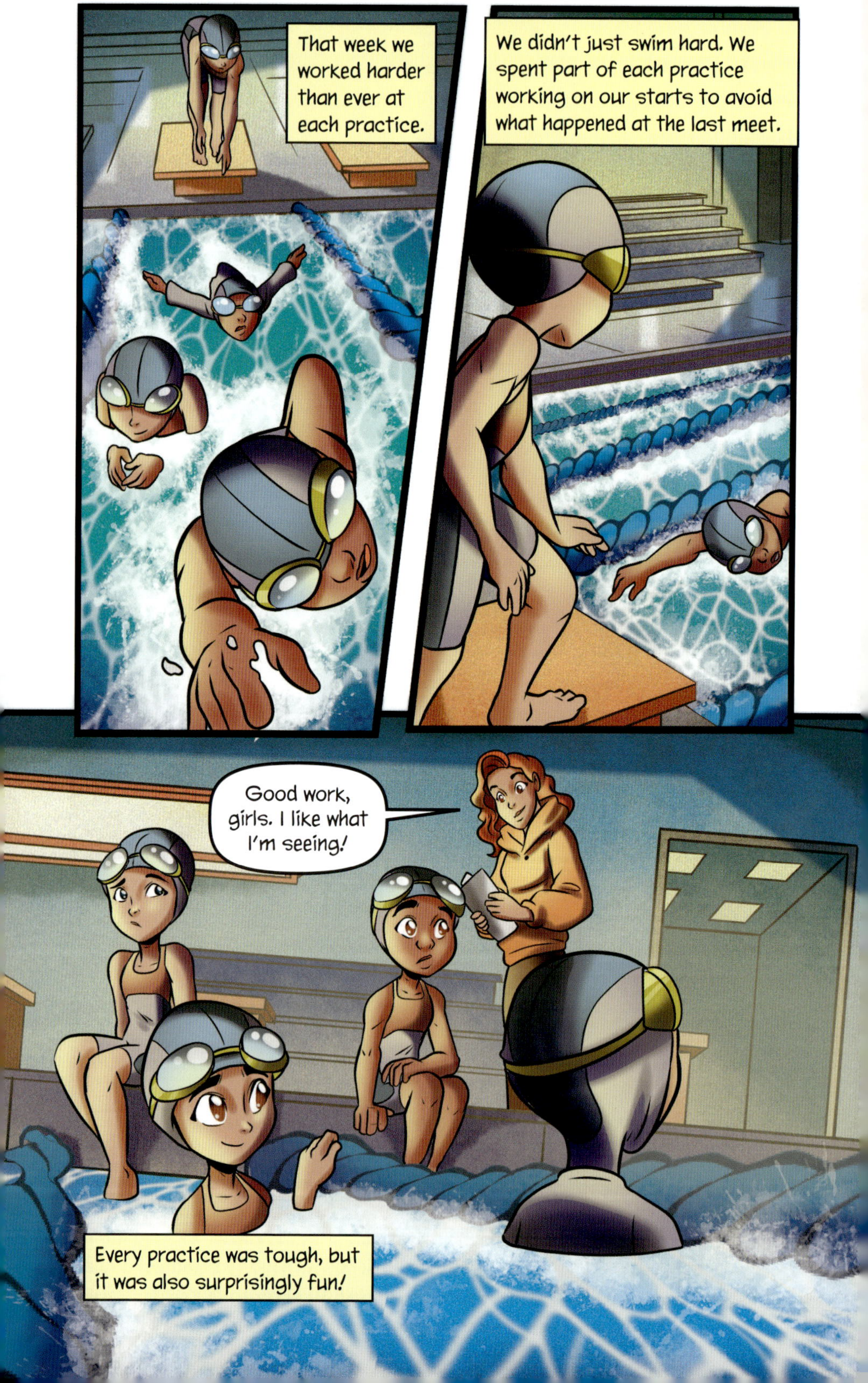
That week we worked harder than ever at each practice.
We didn't just swim hard. We spent part of each practice working on our starts to avoid what happened at the last meet.
Good work, girls. I like what I'm seeing!
Every practice was tough, but it was also surprisingly fun!

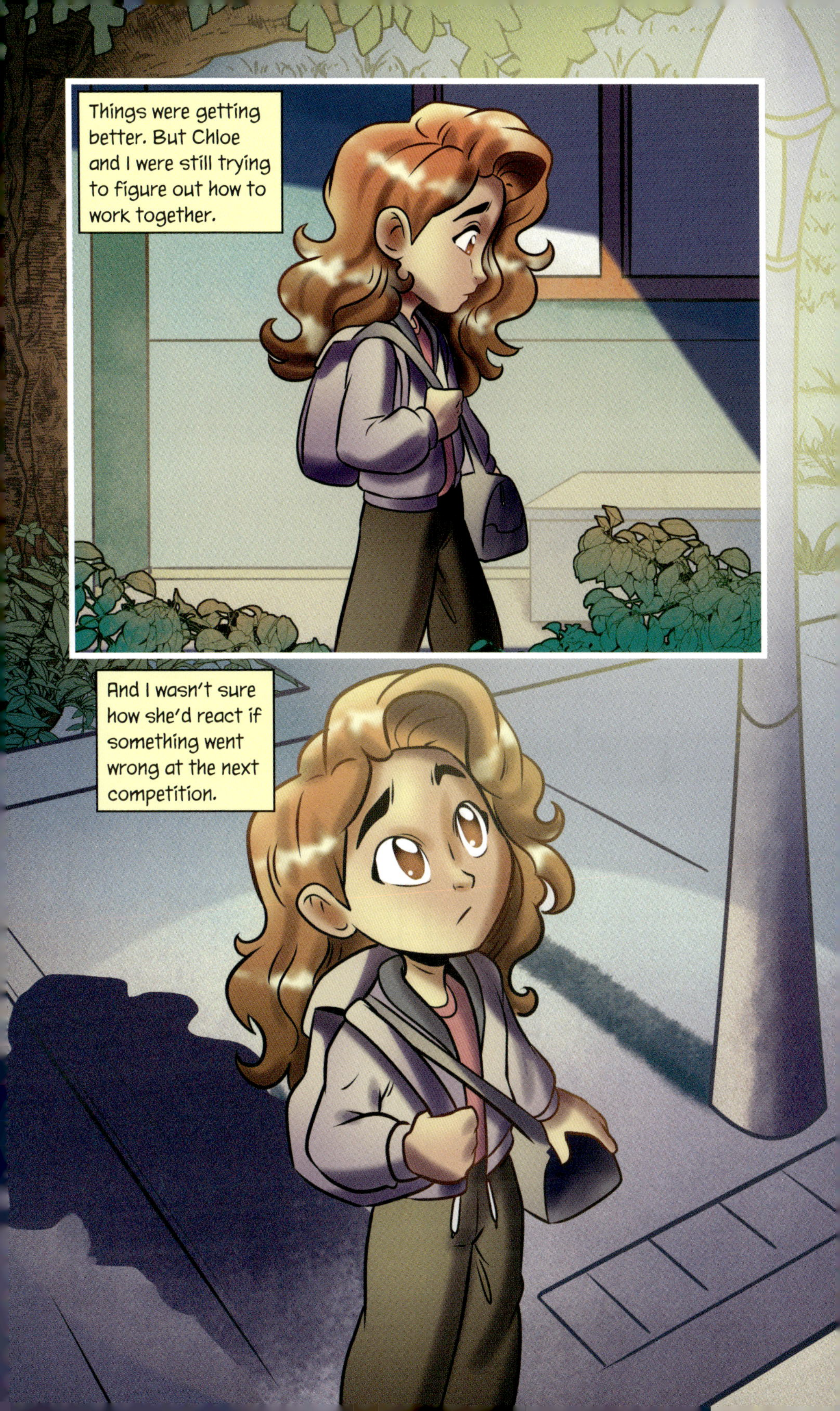
Things were getting better. But Chloe and I were still trying to figure out how to work together.
And I wasn't sure how she'd react if something went wrong at the next competition.

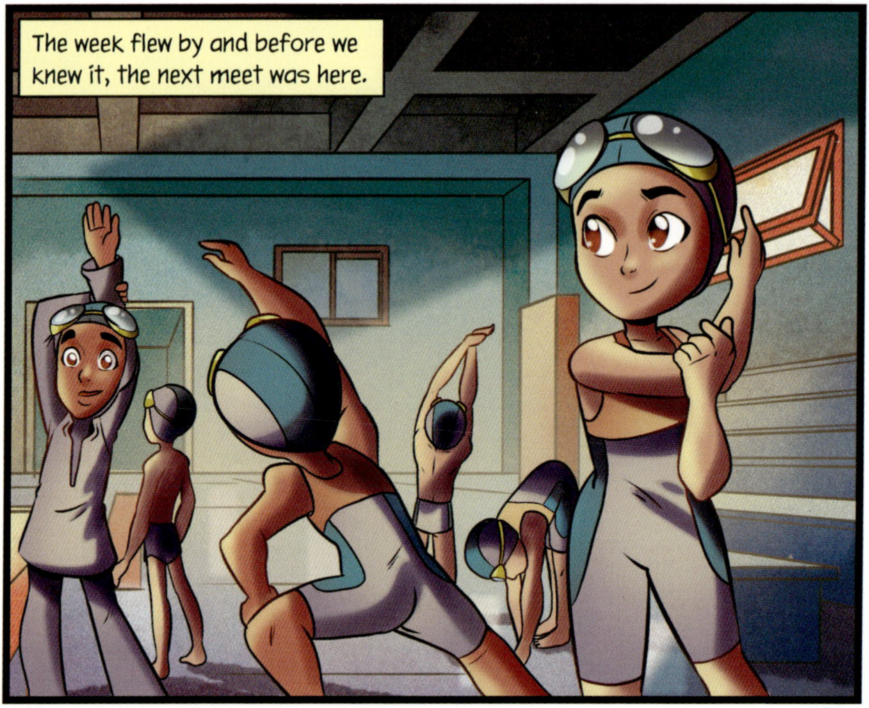
The week flew by and before we knew it, the next meet was here.

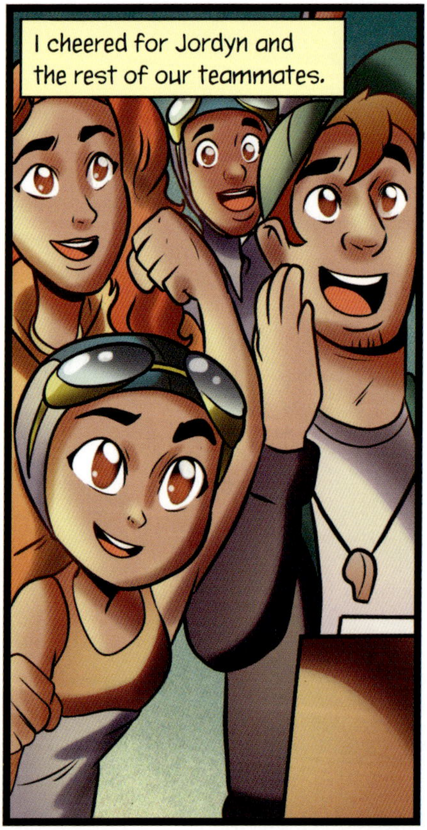
I cheered for Jordyn and the rest of our teammates.

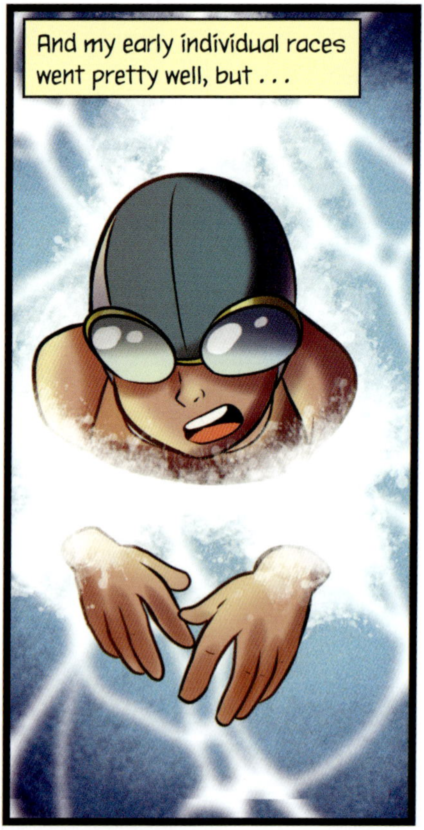
And my early individual races went pretty well, but . . .

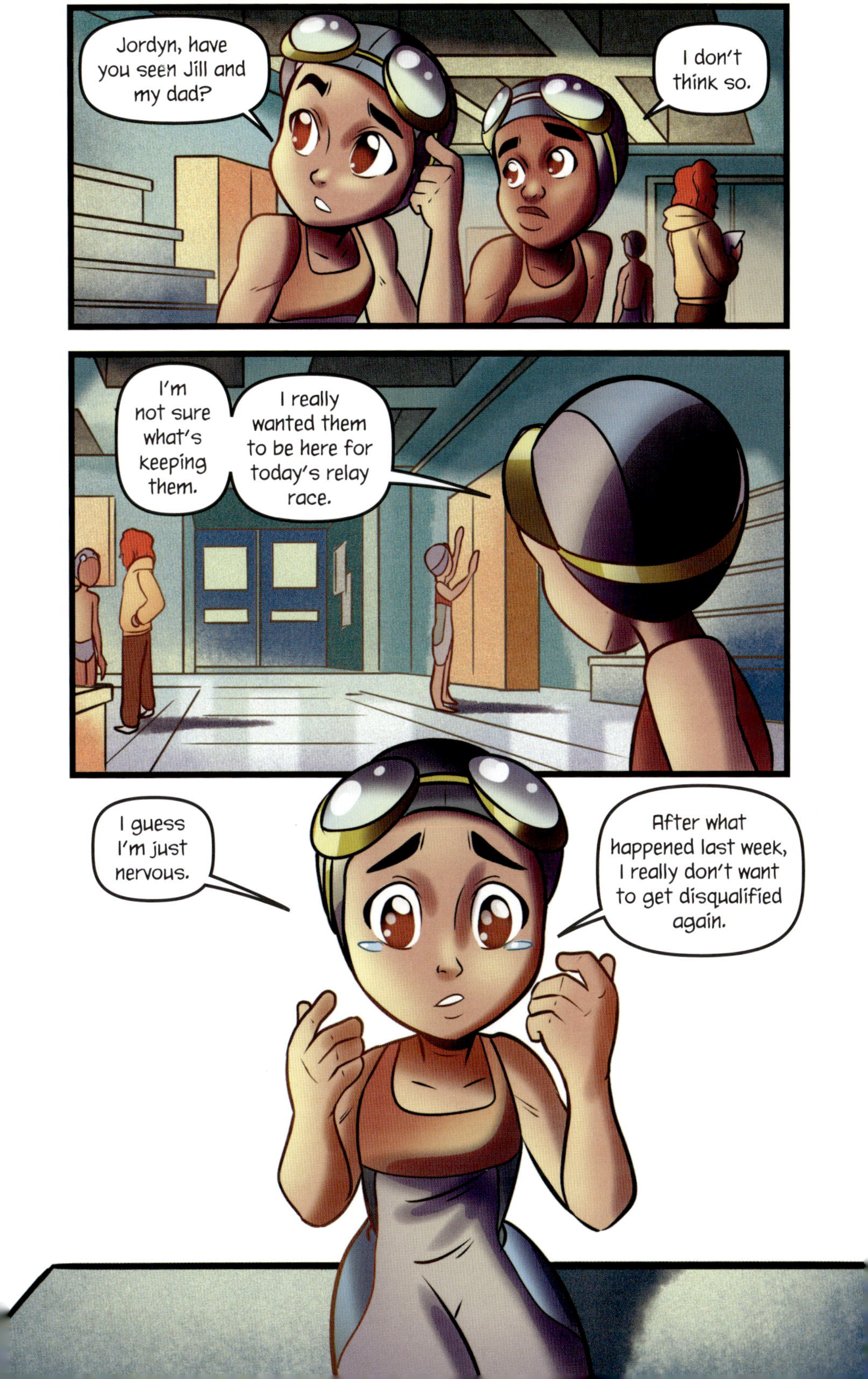
Jordyn, have you seen Jill and my dad?
I don't think so.
I'm not sure what's keeping them.
I really wanted them to be here for today's relay race.
I guess I'm just nervous.
After what happened last week, I really don't want to get disqualified again.

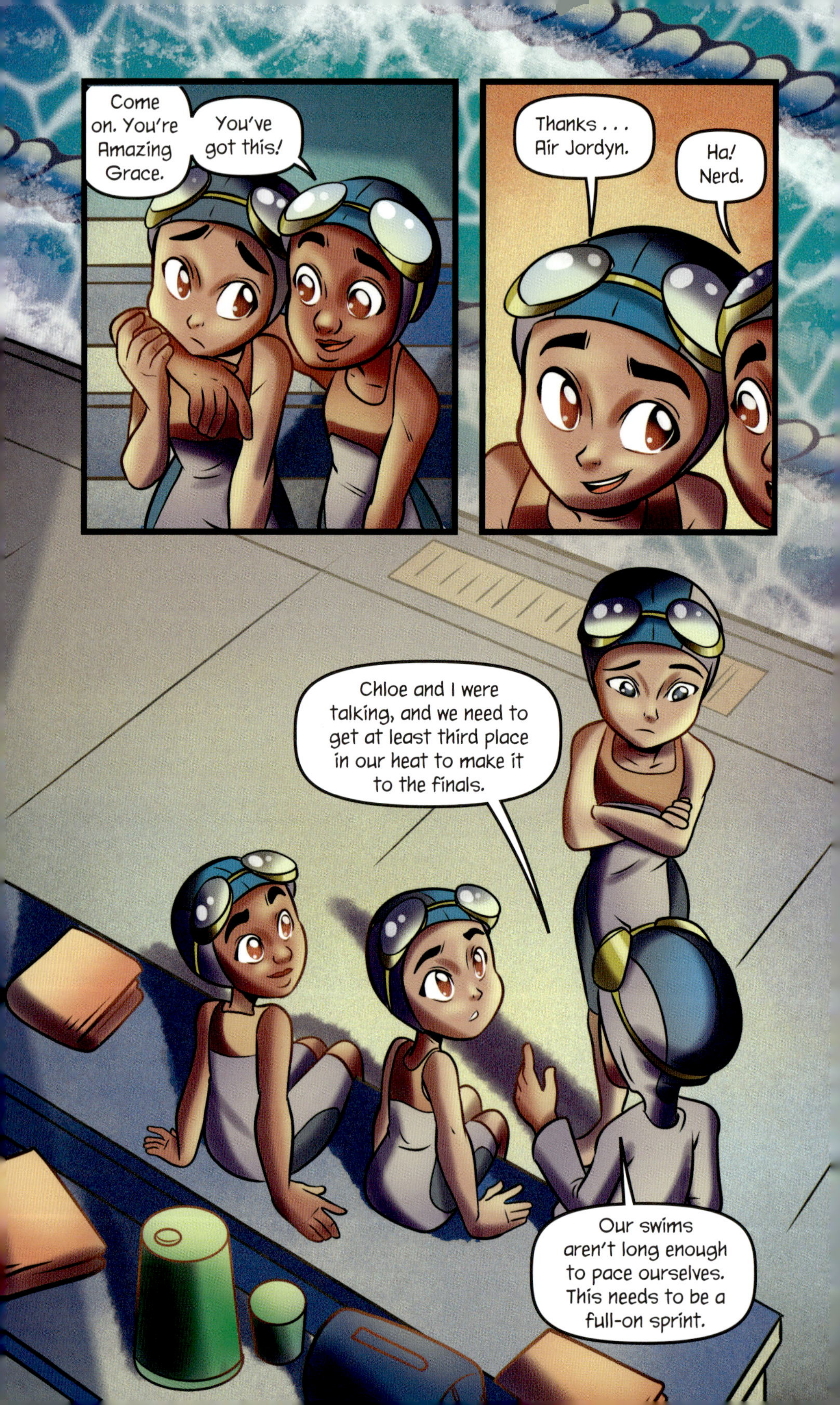
Come on. You're Amazing Grace.
You've got this!
Thanks . . . Air Jordyn.
Ha! Nerd.
Chloe and I were talking, and we need to get at least third place in our heat to make it to the finals.
Our swims aren't long enough to pace ourselves. This needs to be a full-on sprint.

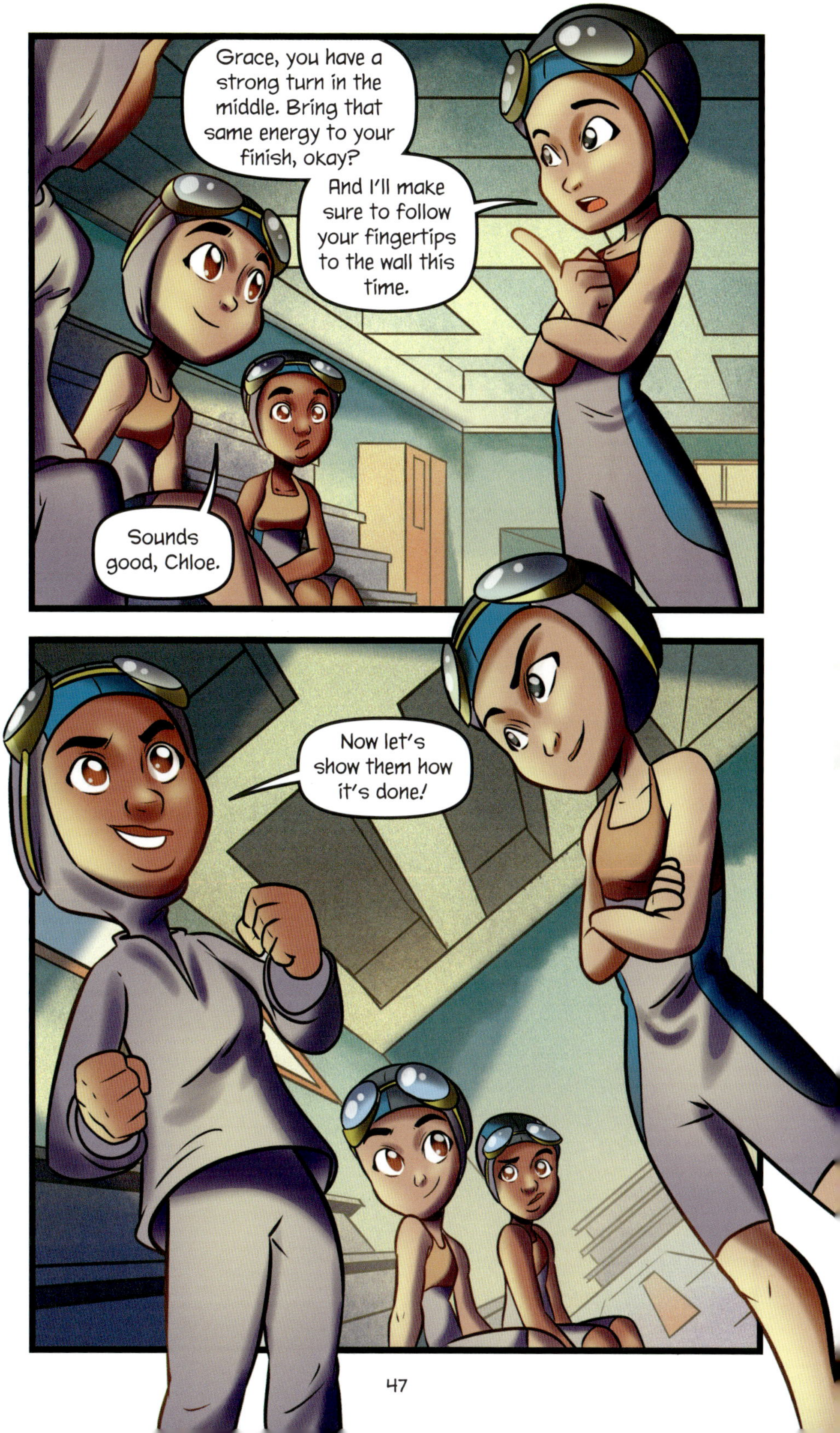
Grace, you have a strong turn in the middle. Bring that same energy to your finish, okay?
And I'll make sure to follow your fingertips to the wall this time.
Sounds good, Chloe.
Now let's show them how it's done!

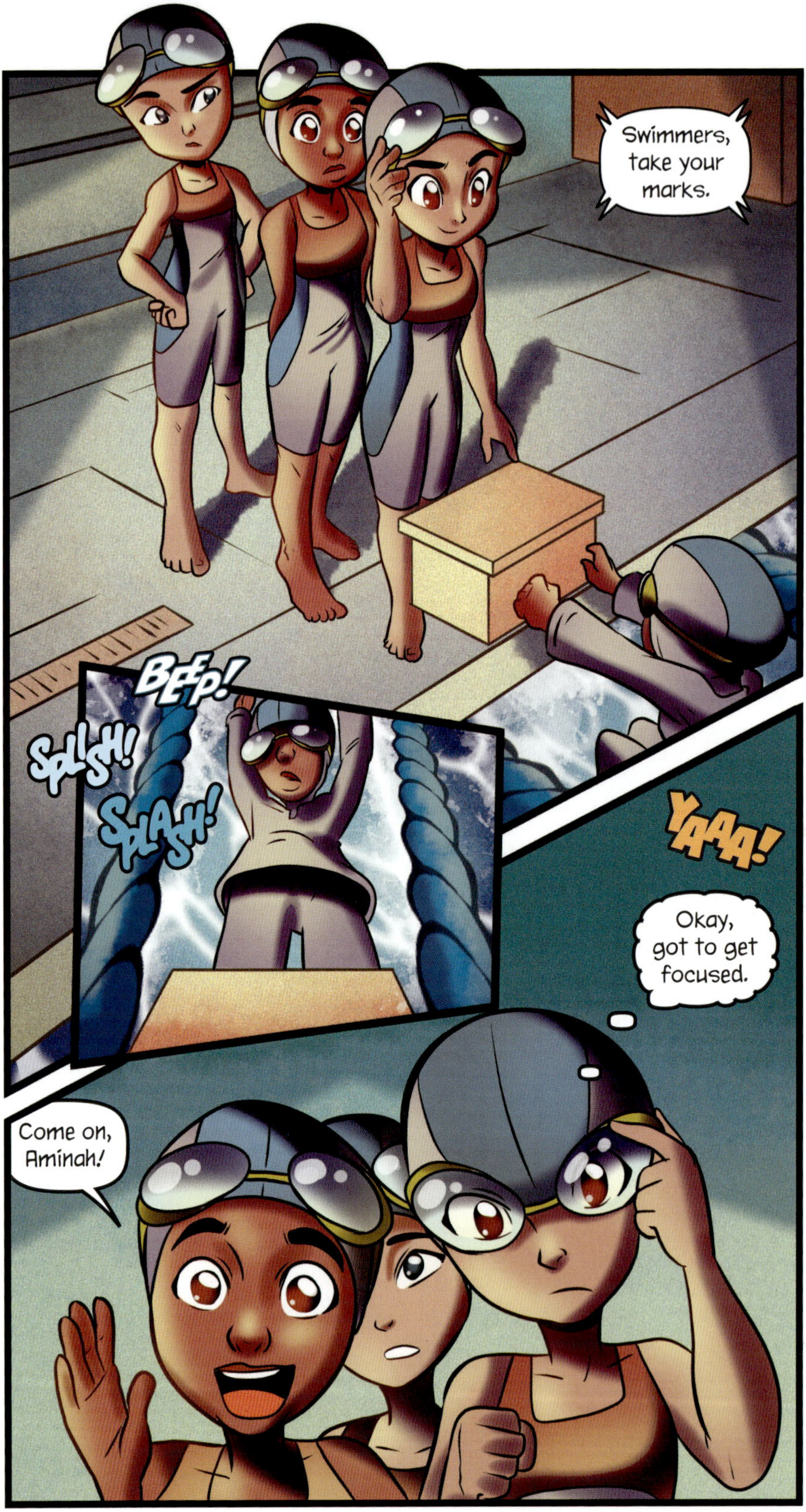
Swimmers, take your marks.
BEEP!
SPLISH!
SPLASH!
YAAA!
Okay, got to get focused.
Come on, Aminah!

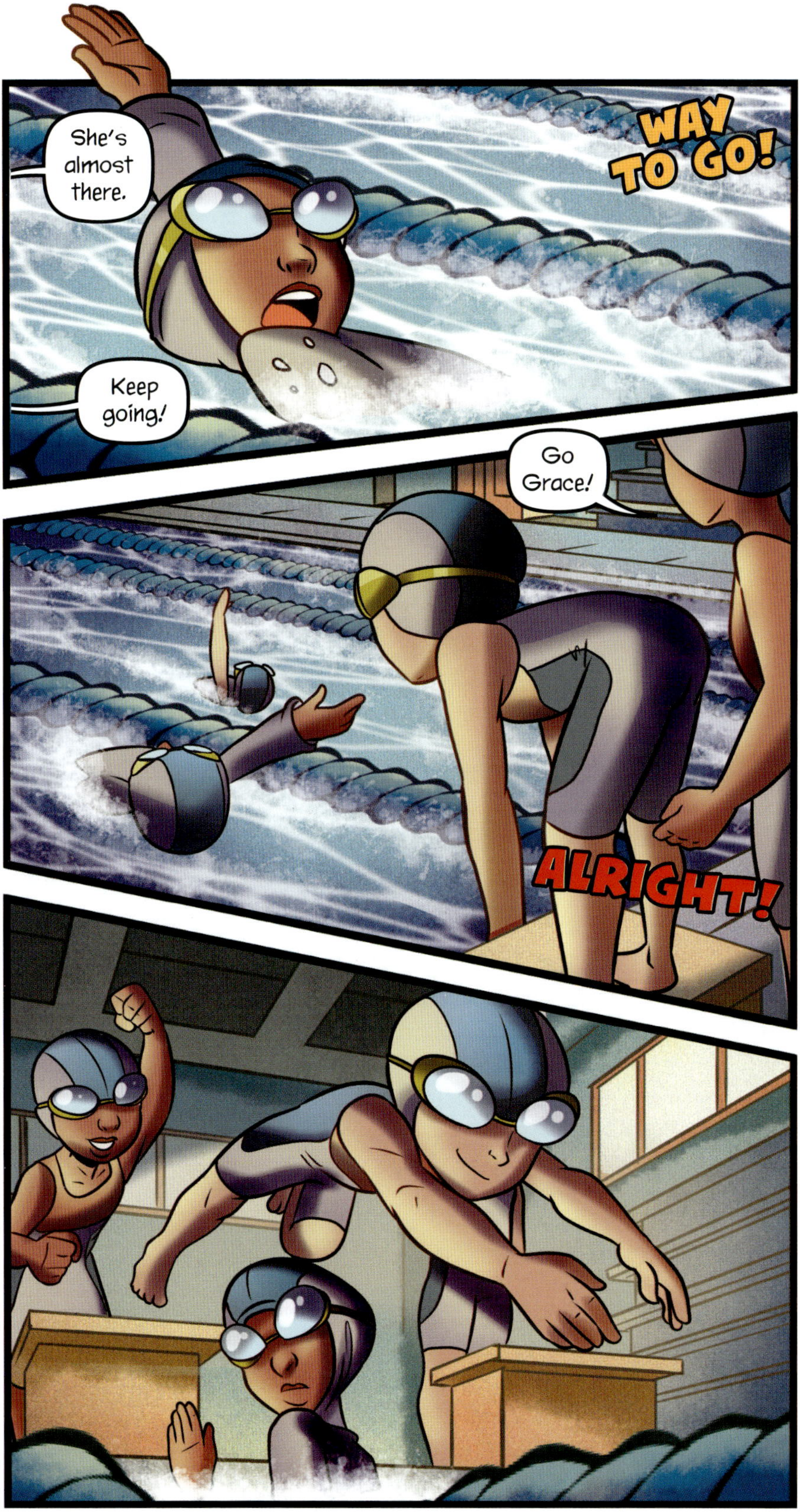

She's almost there.
WAY TO GO!
Keep going!
Go Grace!
ALRIGHT!

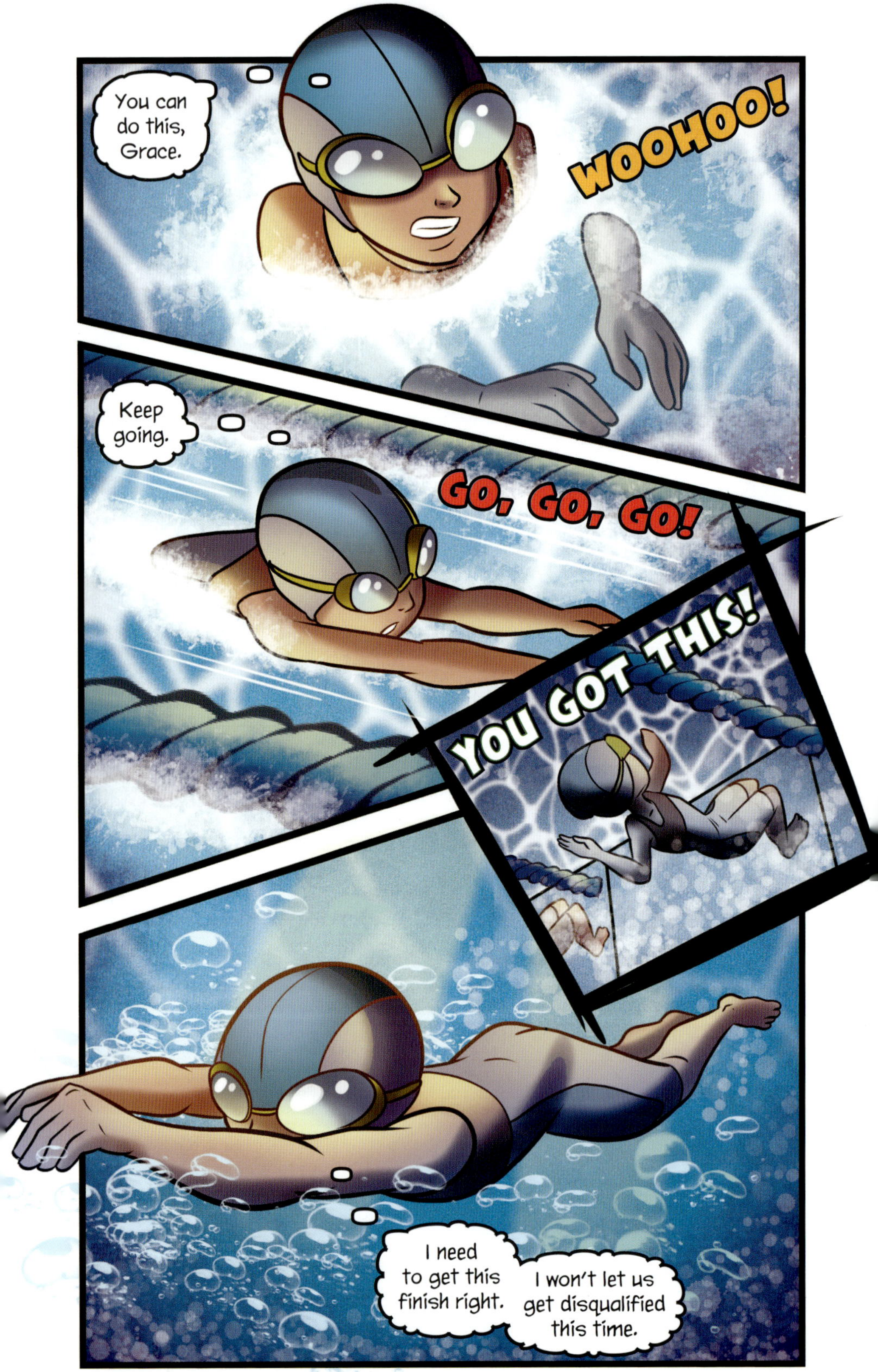
You can do this, Grace.
WOOHOO!
Keep going.
GO, GO, GO!
YOU GOT THIS!
I need to get this finish right.
I won't let us get disqualified this time.

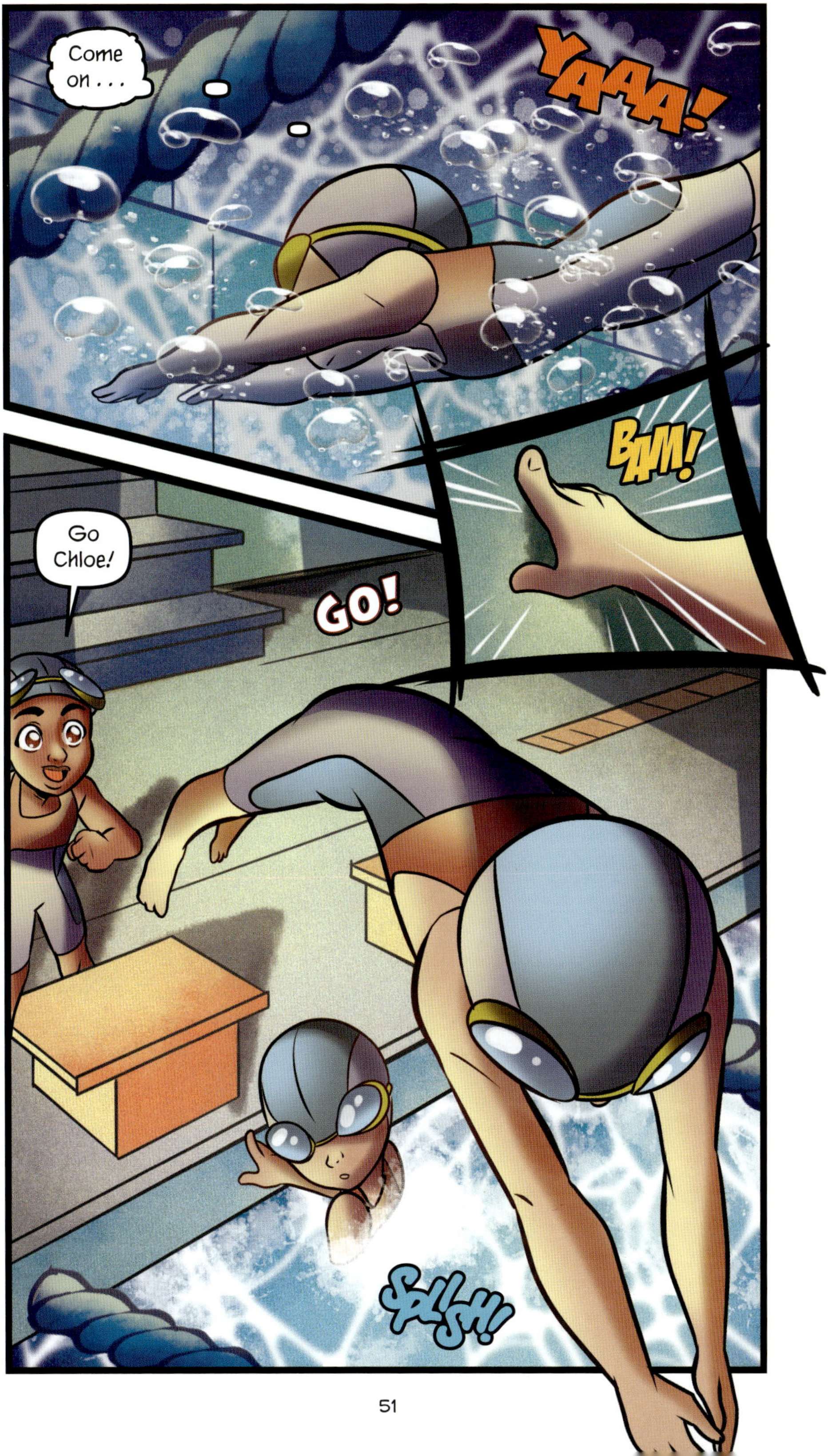
Come on . . .
YAAA!
BAM!
Go Chloe!
GO!
SPLISH!

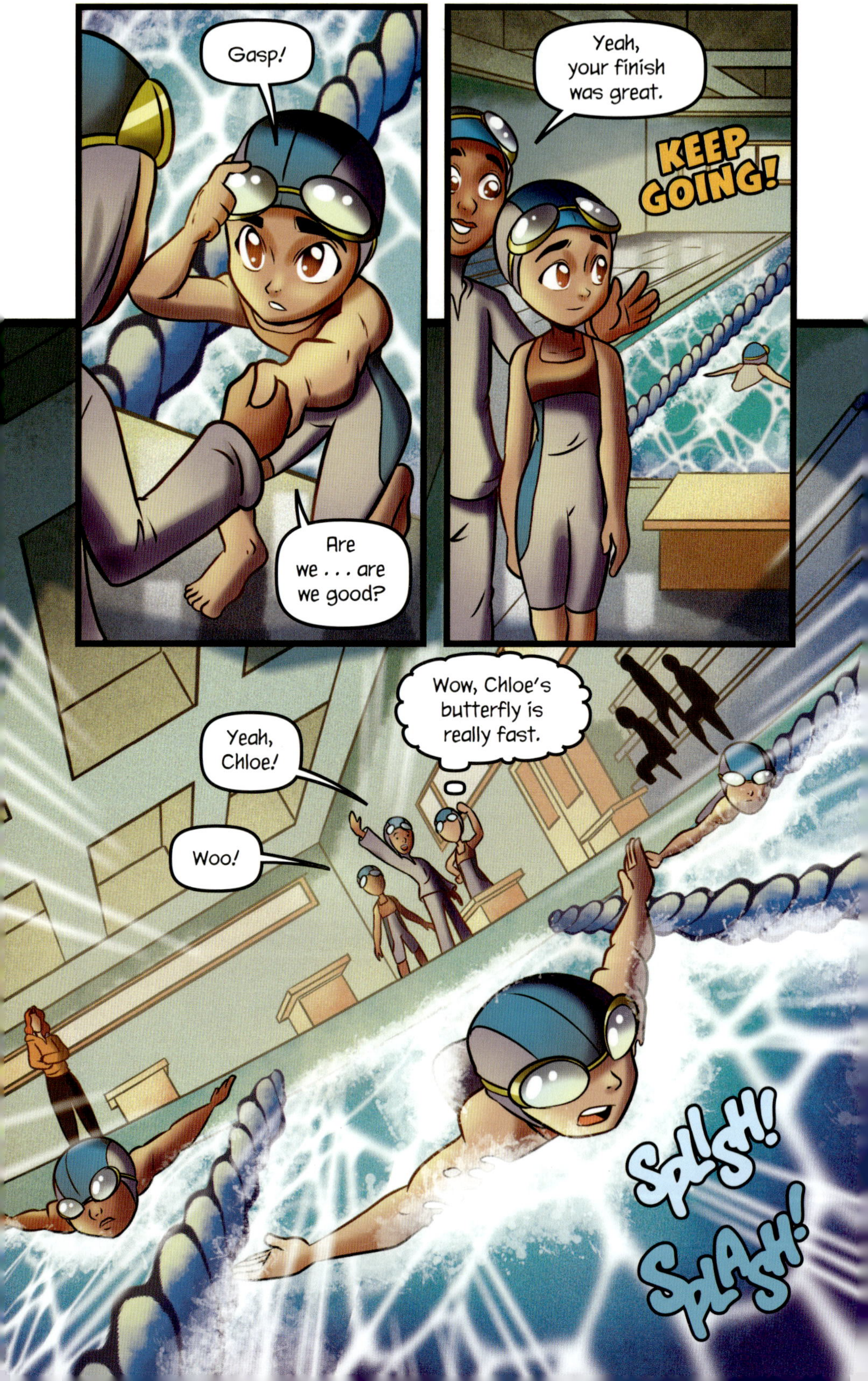
Gasp!
Are we . . . are we good?
Yeah, your finish was great.
KEEP GOING!
Yeah, Chloe!
Woo!
Wow, Chloe's butterfly is really fast.
SPLISH!
SPLASH!

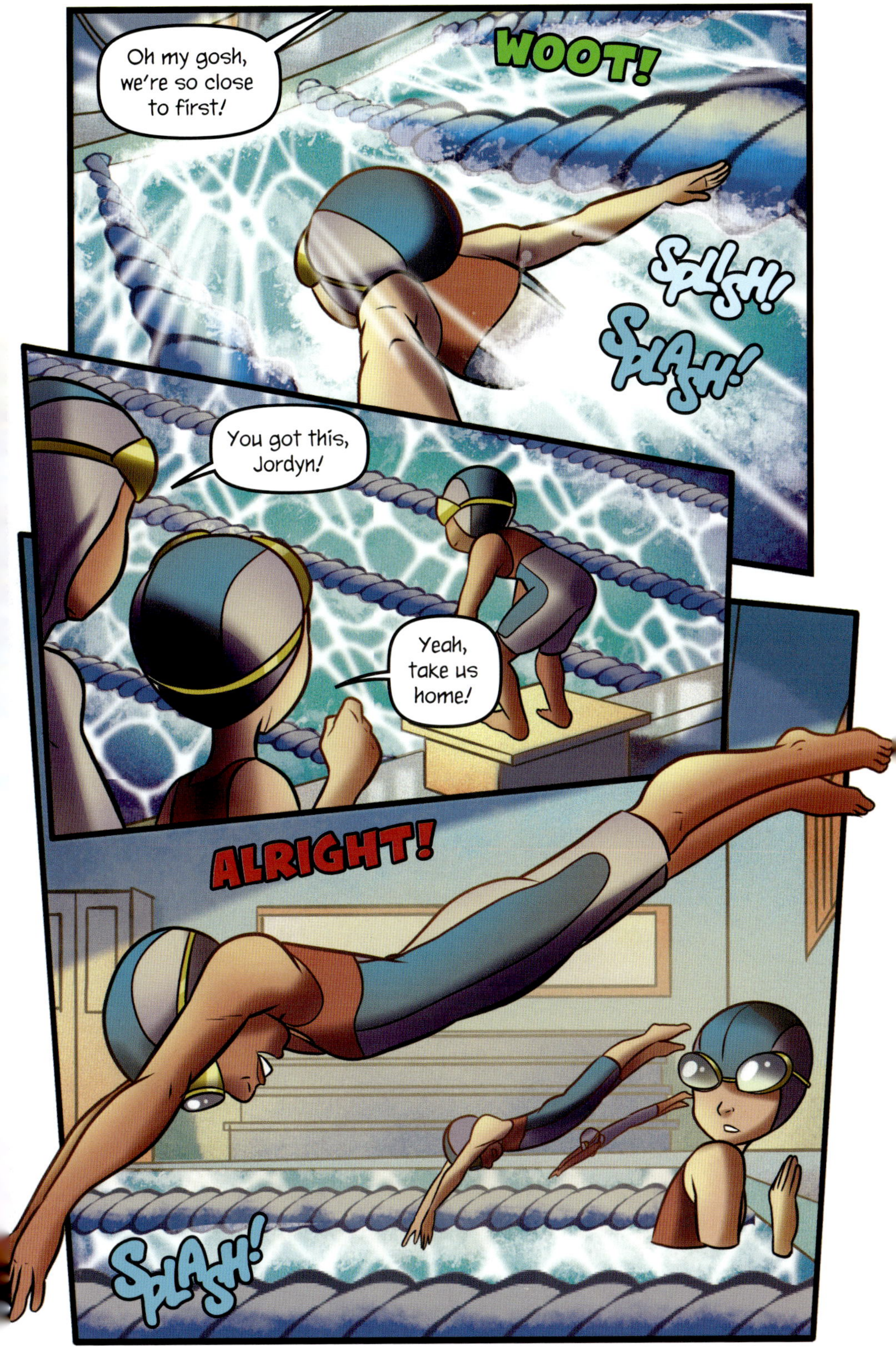
Oh my gosh, we're so close to first!
WOOT!
SPLISH!
SPLASH!
You got this, Jordyn!
Yeah, take us home!
ALRIGHT!
SPLASH!

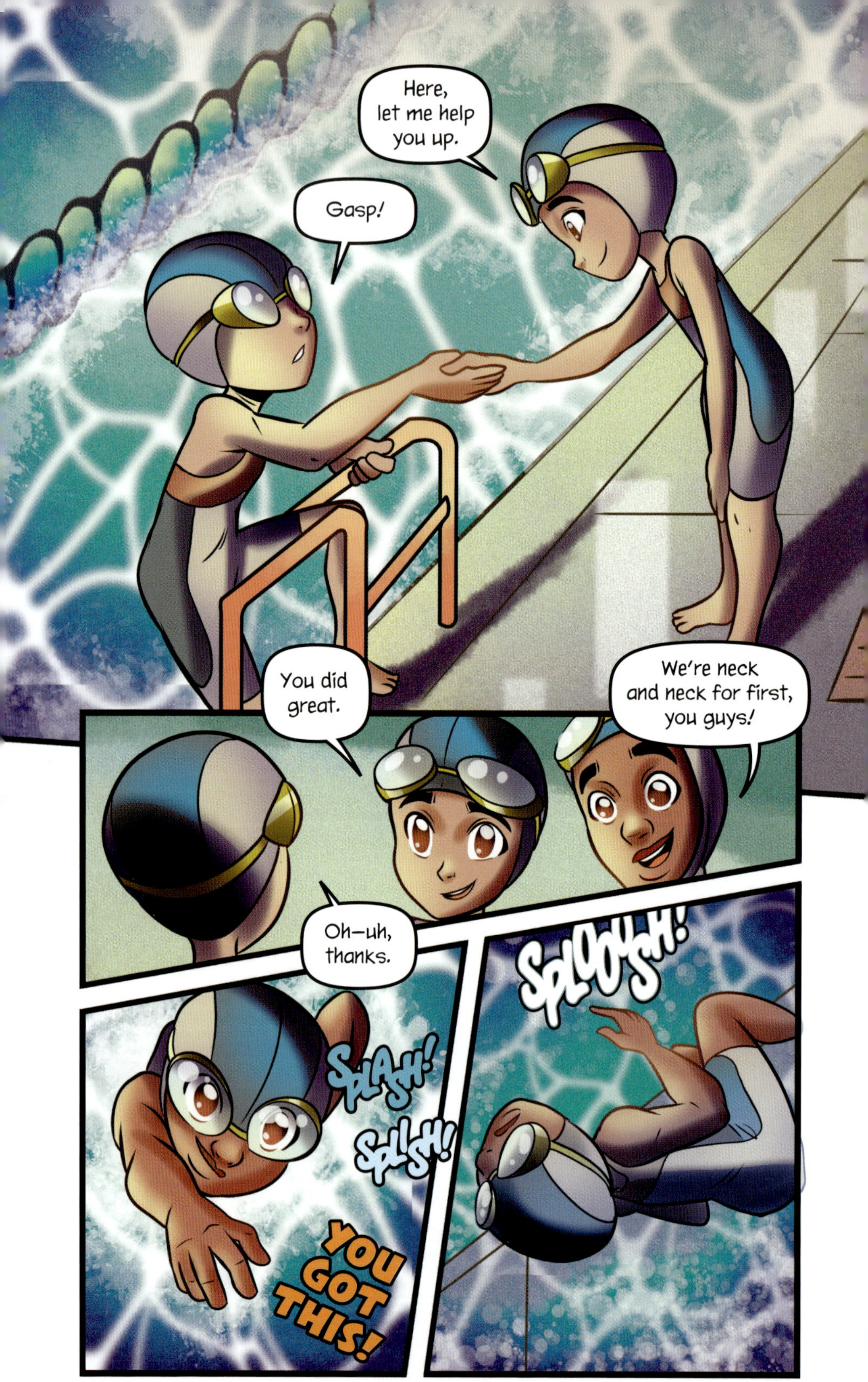
Here, let me help you up.
Gasp!
You did great.
We're neck and neck for first, you guys!
Oh—uh, thanks.
SPLASH!
SPLISH!
YOU GOT THIS!
SPLOOSH!

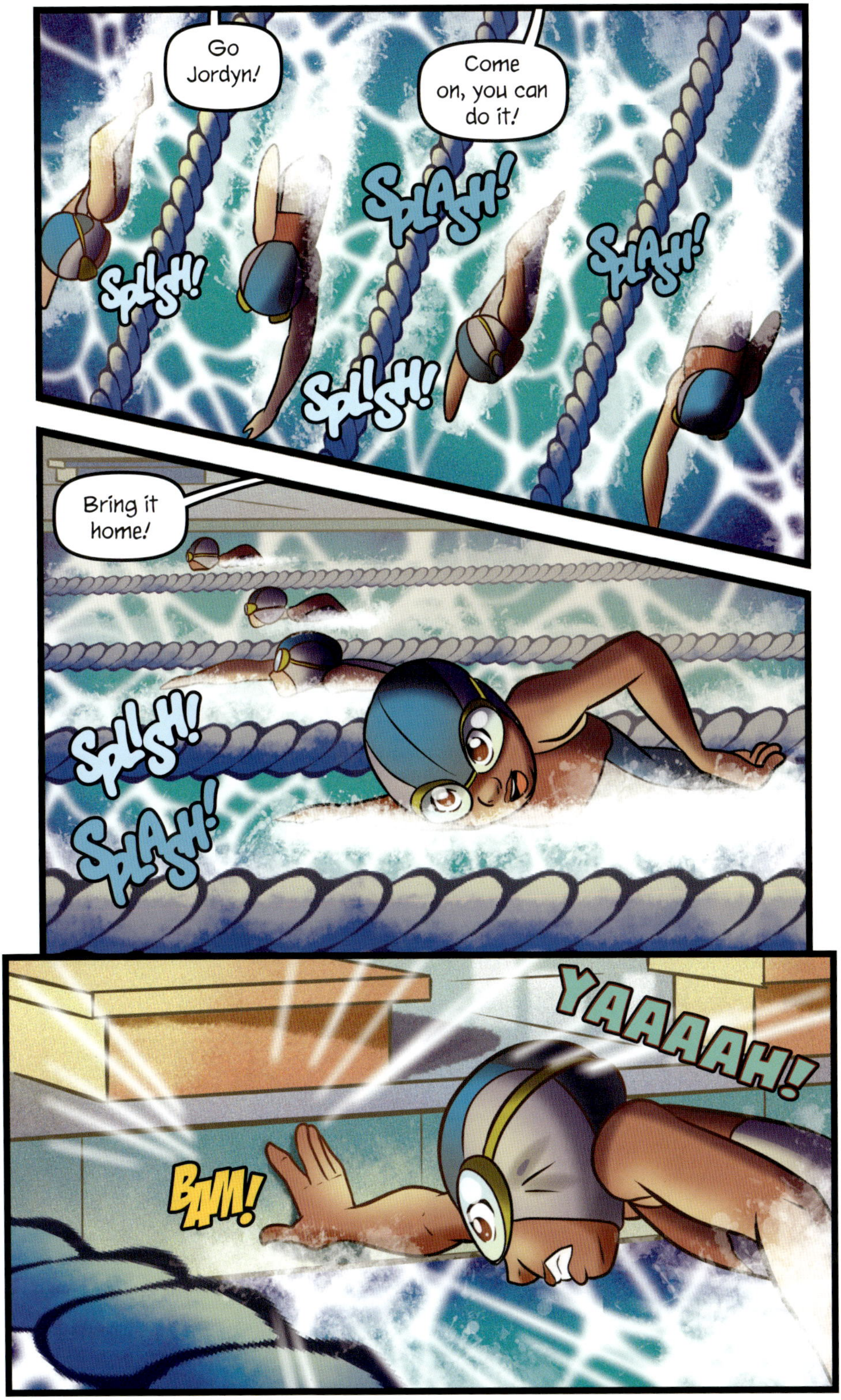
Go Jordyn!
Come on, you can do it!
SPLASH!
SPLISH!
SPLASH!
SPLISH!
Bring it home!
SPLISH!
SPLASH!
YAAAAAH!
BAM!

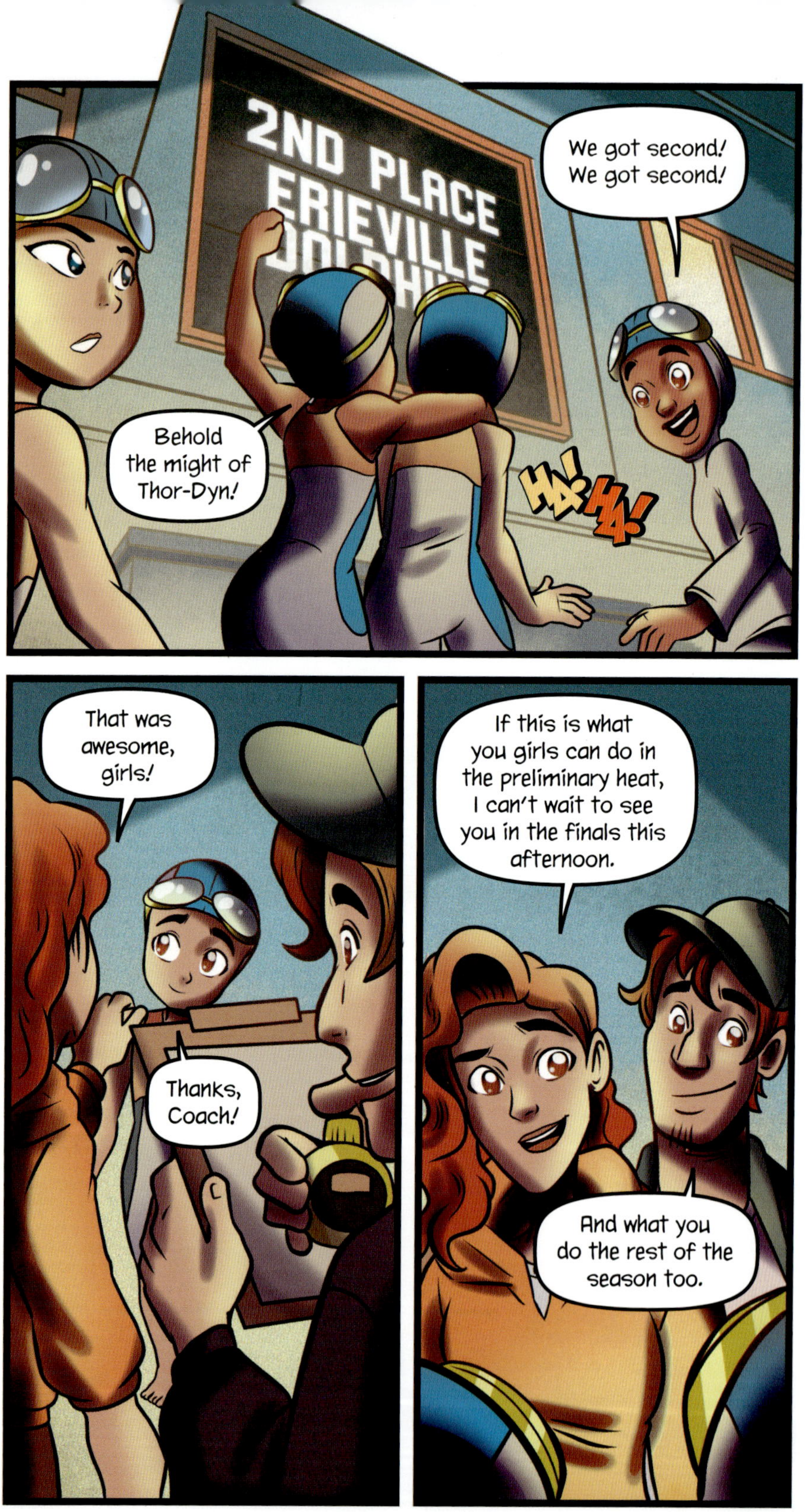
2ND PLACE
ERIEVILLE
We got second! We got second!
Behold the might of Thor-Dyn!
HA! HA!
That was awesome, girls!
Thanks, Coach!
If this is what you girls can do in the preliminary heat, I can't wait to see you in the finals this afternoon.
And what you do the rest of the season too.

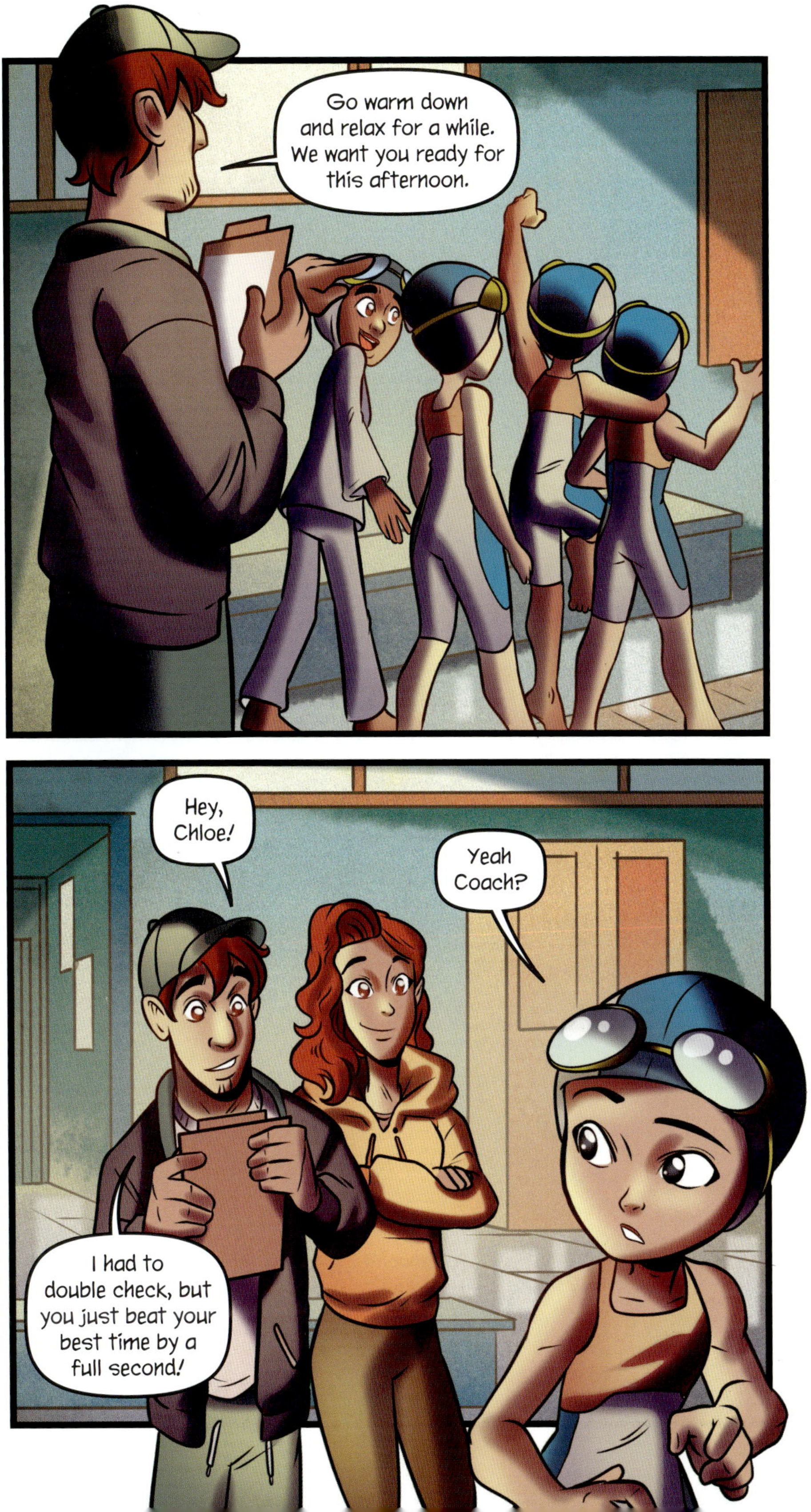
Go warm down and relax for a while. We want you ready for this afternoon.
Hey, Chloe!
Yeah Coach?
I had to double check, but you just beat your best time by a full second!

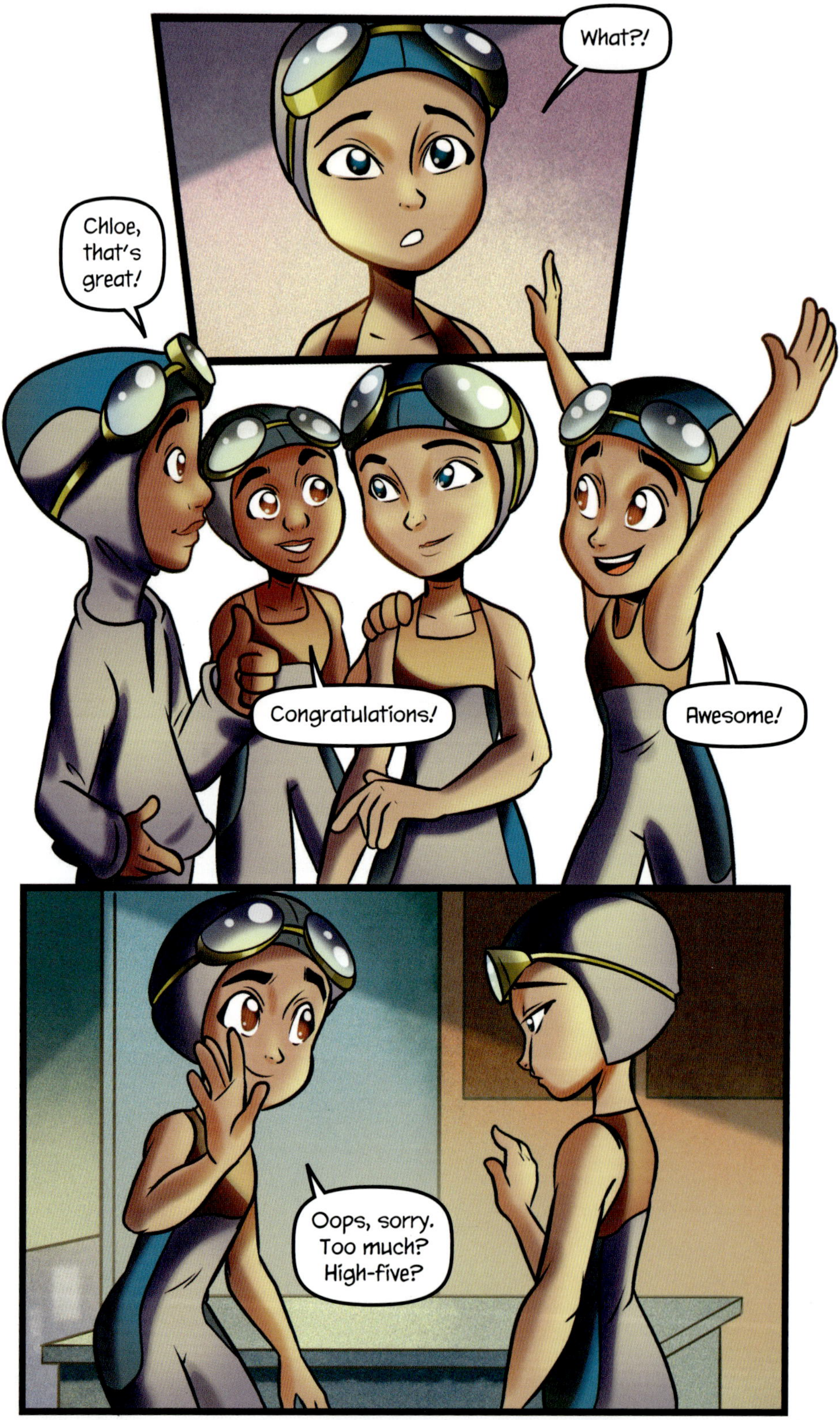
What?!
Chloe, that's great!
Congratulations!
Awesome!
Oops, sorry. Too much? High-five?

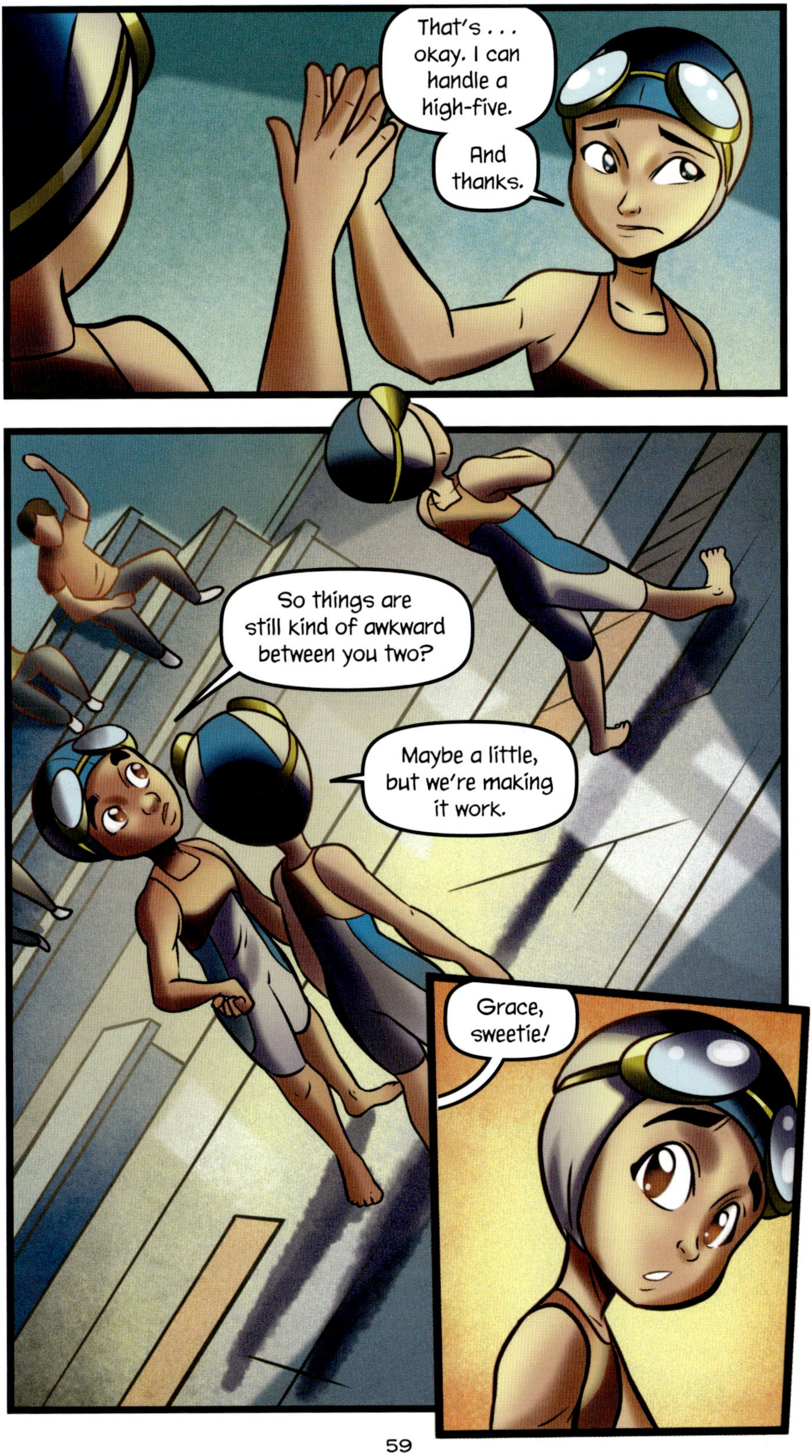
That's . . . okay. I can handle a high-five.
And thanks.
So things are still kind of awkward between you two?
Maybe a little, but we're making it work.
Grace, sweetie!

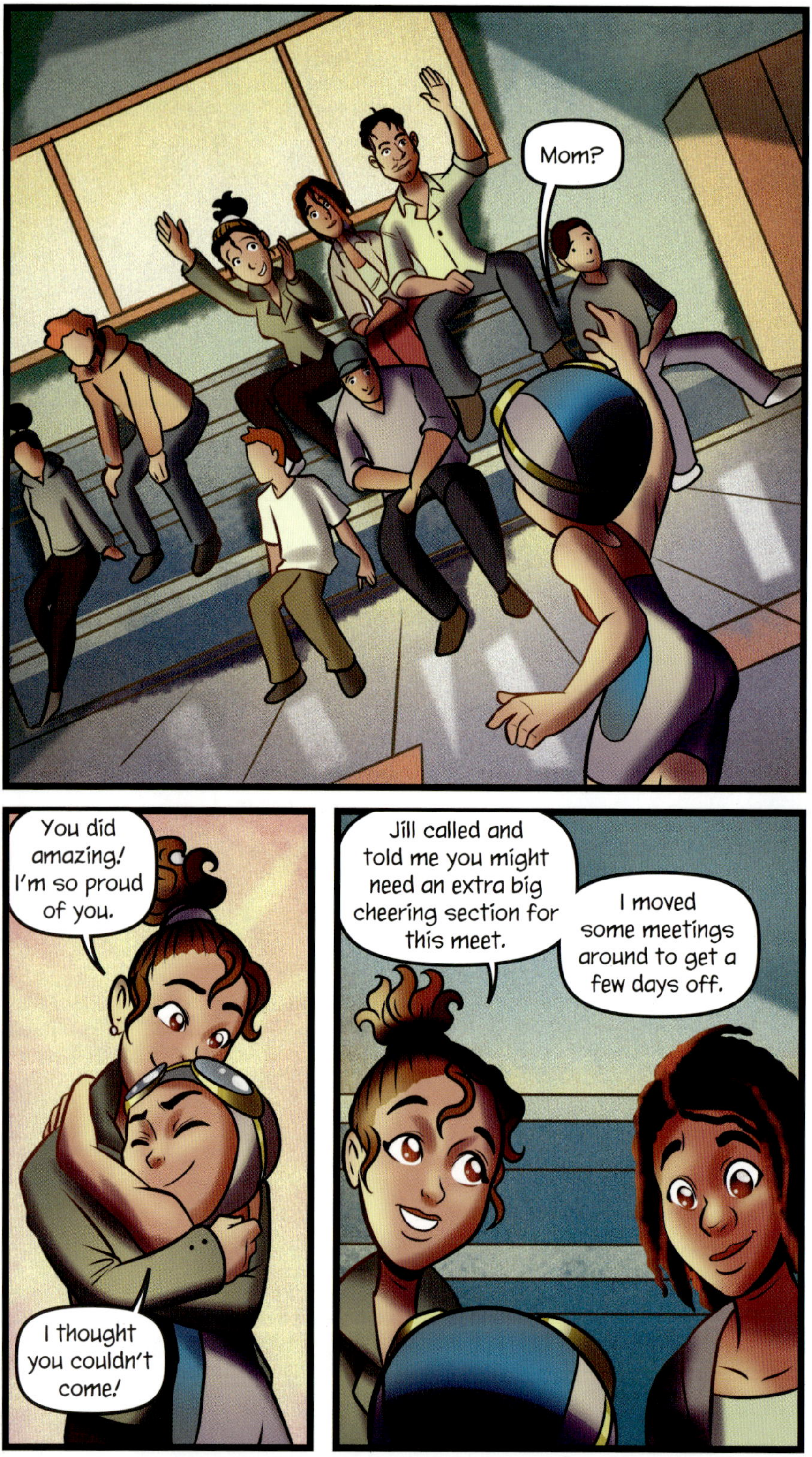
Mom?
You did amazing! I'm so proud of you.
I thought you couldn't come!
Jill called and told me you might need an extra big cheering section for this meet.
I moved some meetings around to get a few days off.

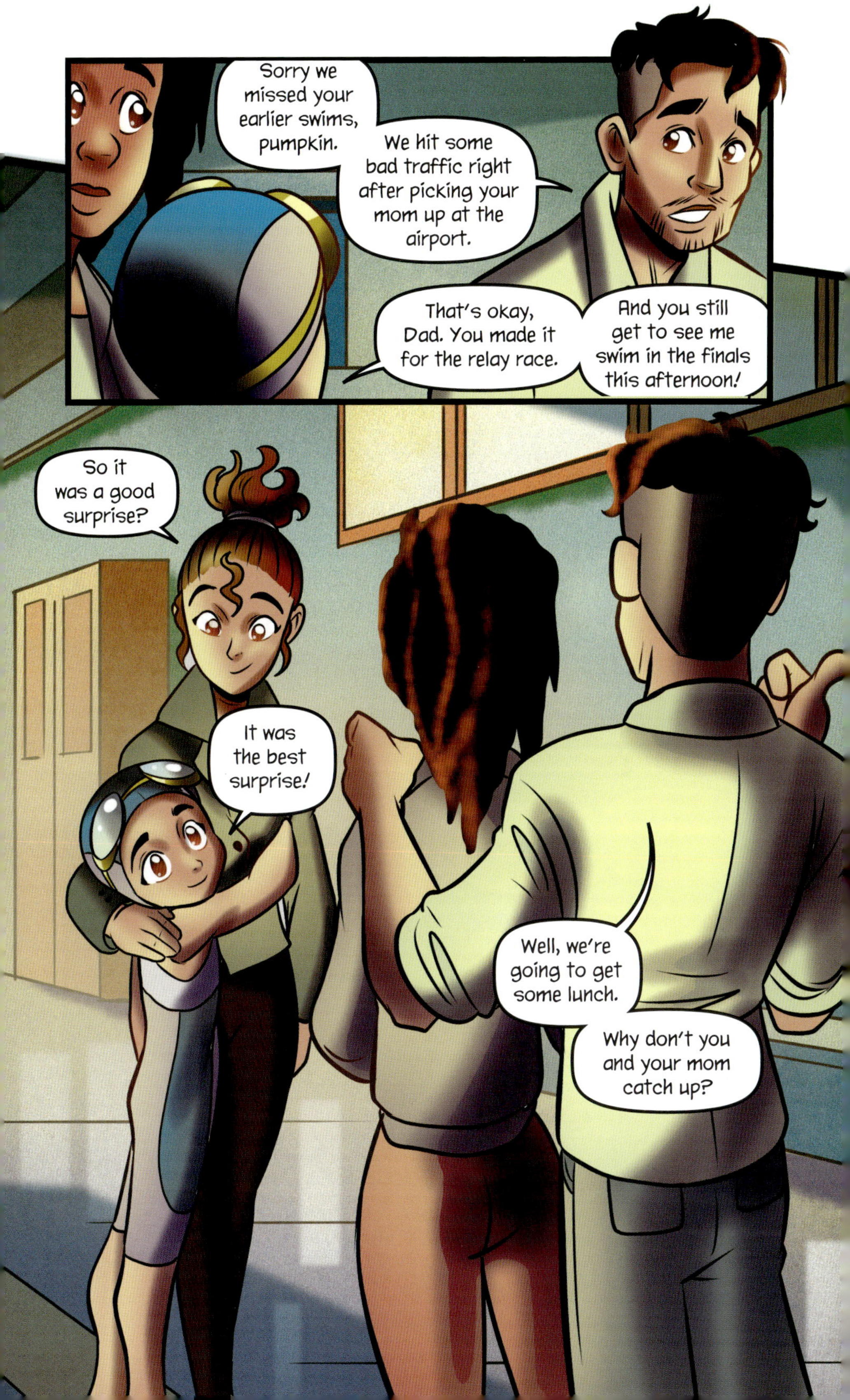
Sorry we missed your earlier swims, pumpkin.
We hit some bad traffic right after picking your mom up at the airport.
That's okay, Dad. You made it for the relay race.
And you still get to see me swim in the finals this afternoon!
So it was a good surprise?
It was the best surprise!
Well, we're going to get some lunch.
Why don't you and your mom catch up?

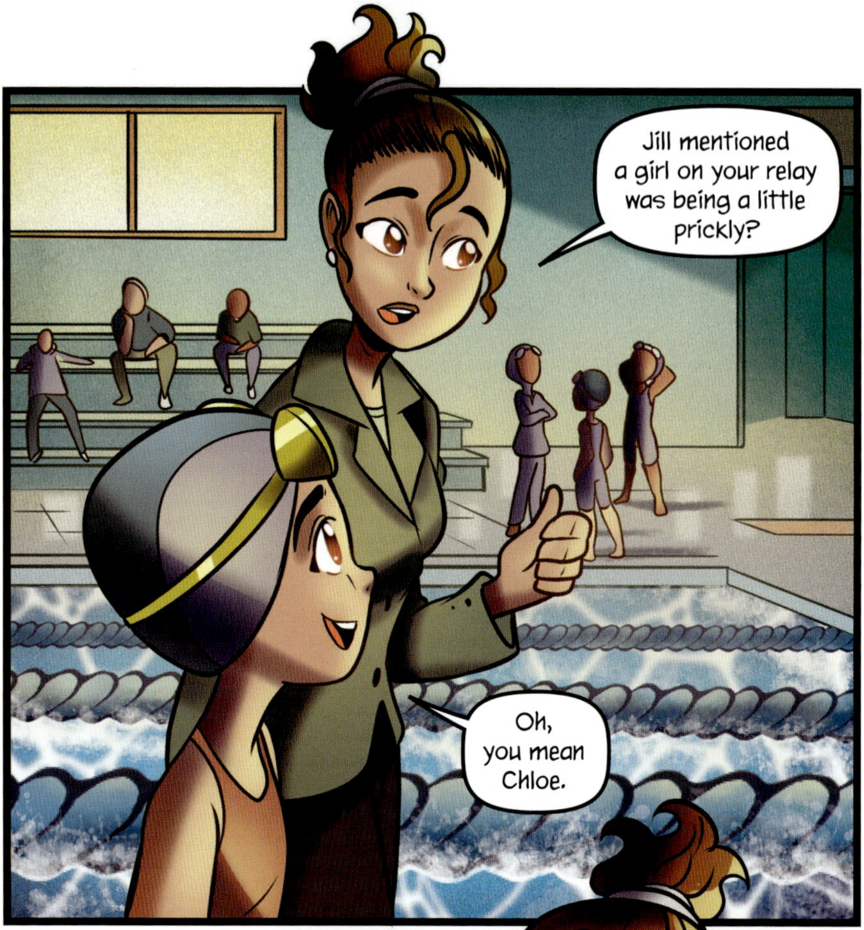
Jill mentioned a girl on your relay was being a little prickly?
Oh, you mean Chloe.

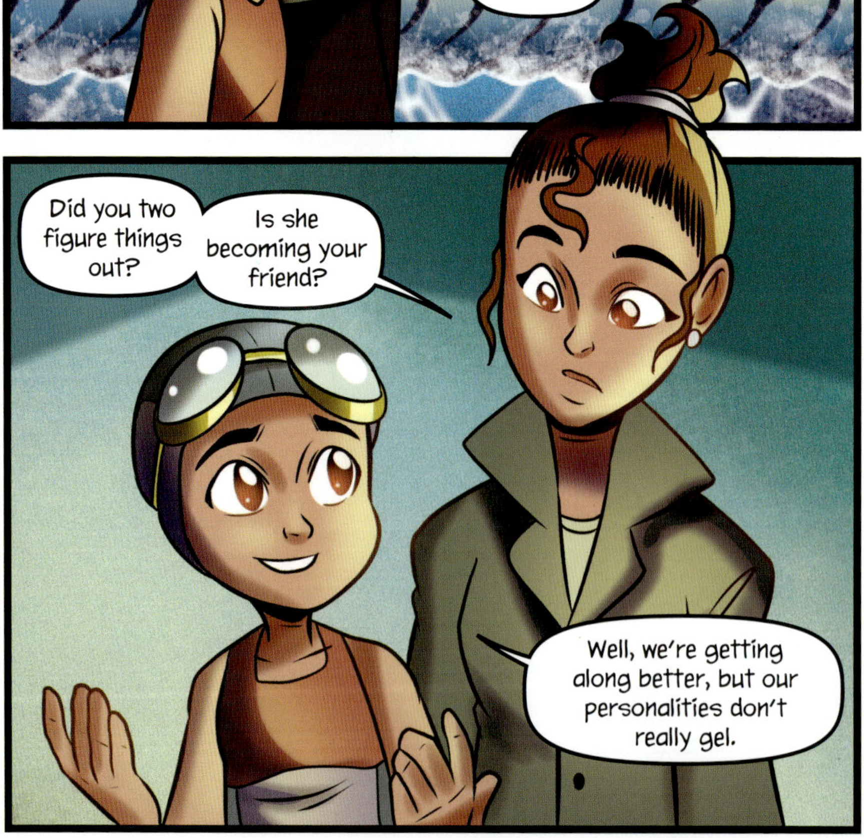
Did you two figure things out?
Is she becoming your friend?
Well, we're getting along better, but our personalities don't really gel.

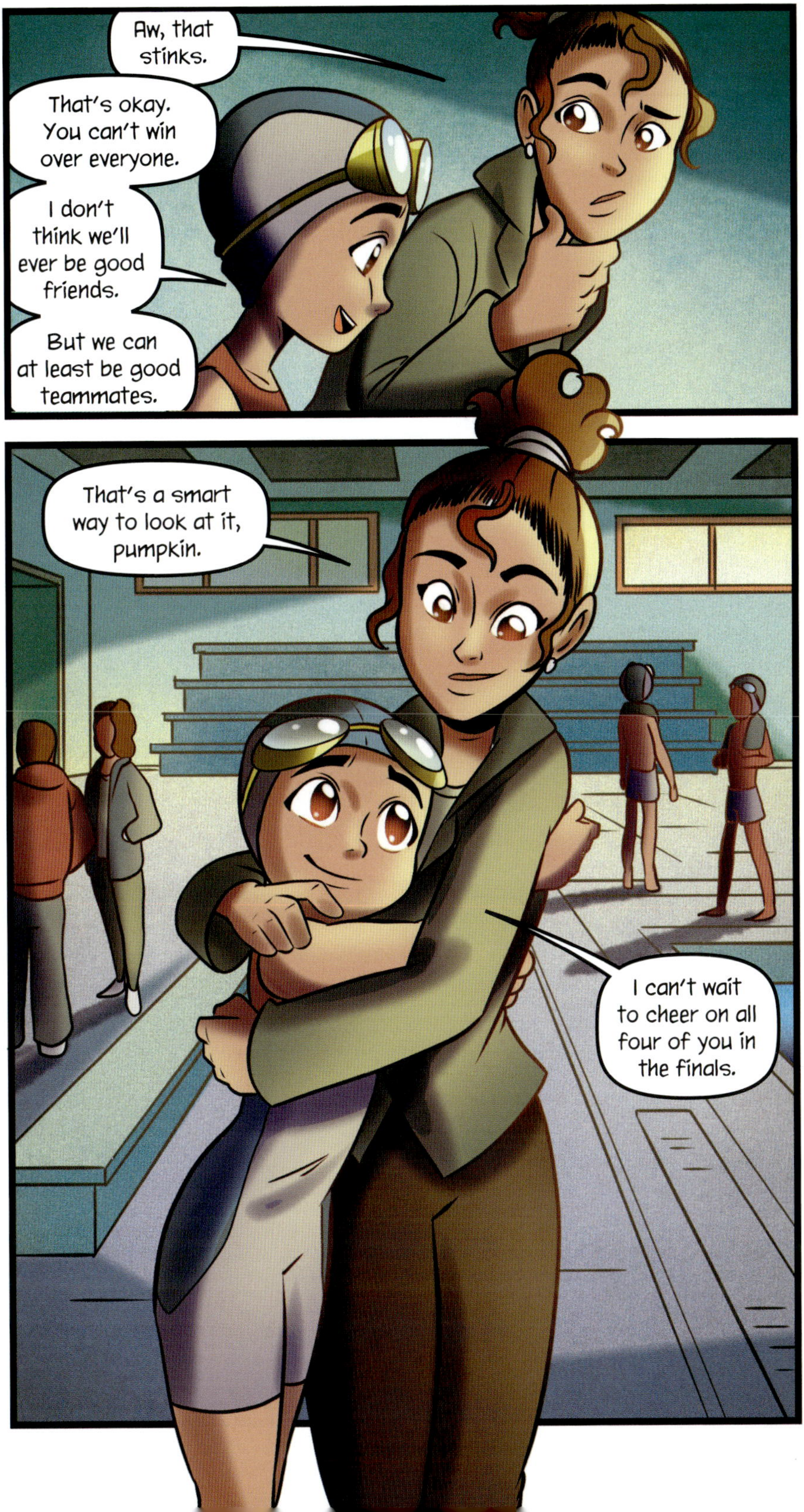
Aw, that stinks.
That's okay. You can't win over everyone.
I don't think we'll ever be good friends.
But we can at least be good teammates.
That's a smart way to look at it, pumpkin.
I can't wait to cheer on all four of you in the finals.

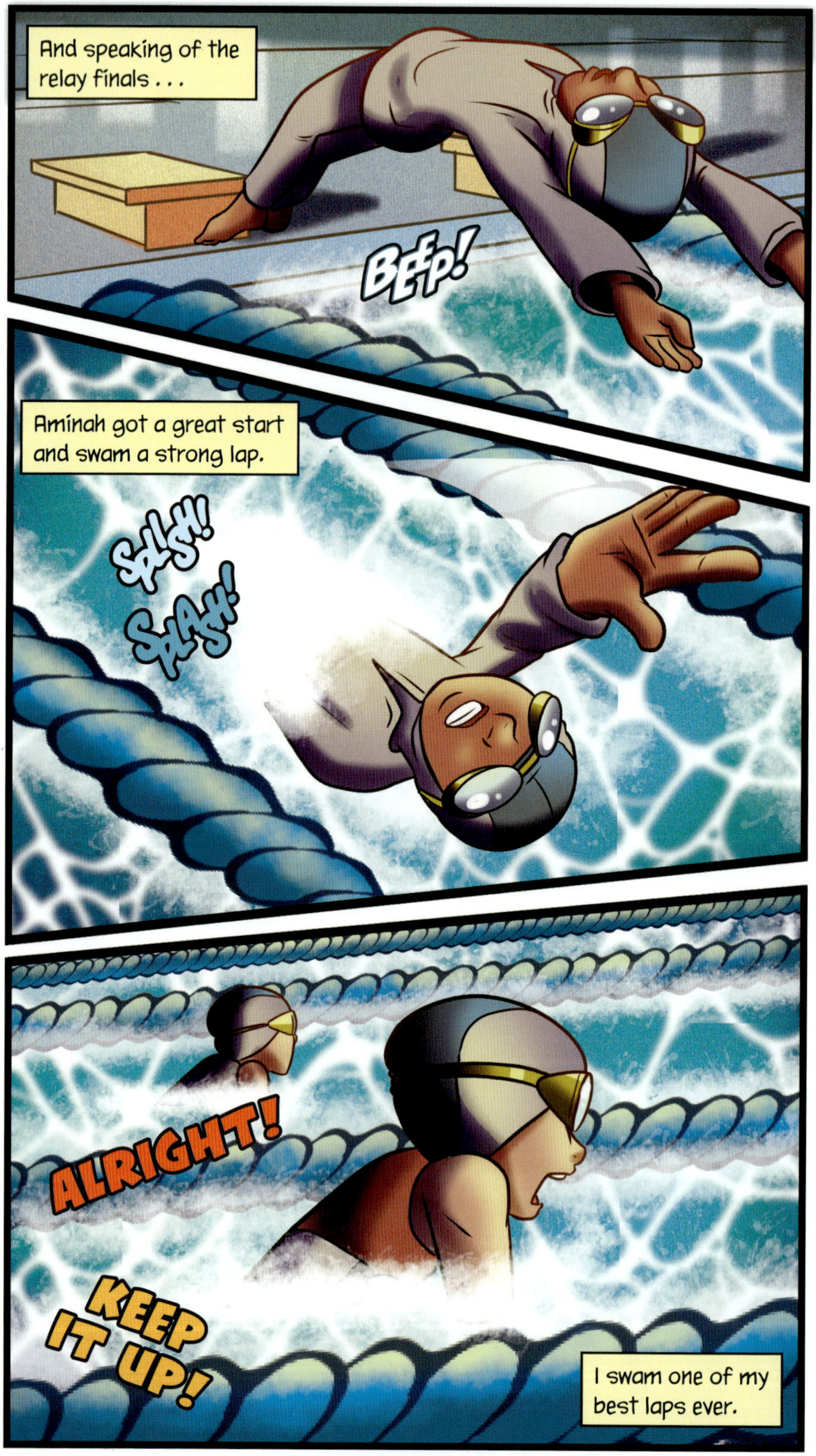

And speaking of the relay finals . . .
BEEP!
Aminah got a great start and swam a strong lap.
SPLISH!
SPLASH!
ALRIGHT!
KEEP IT UP!
I swam one of my best laps ever.

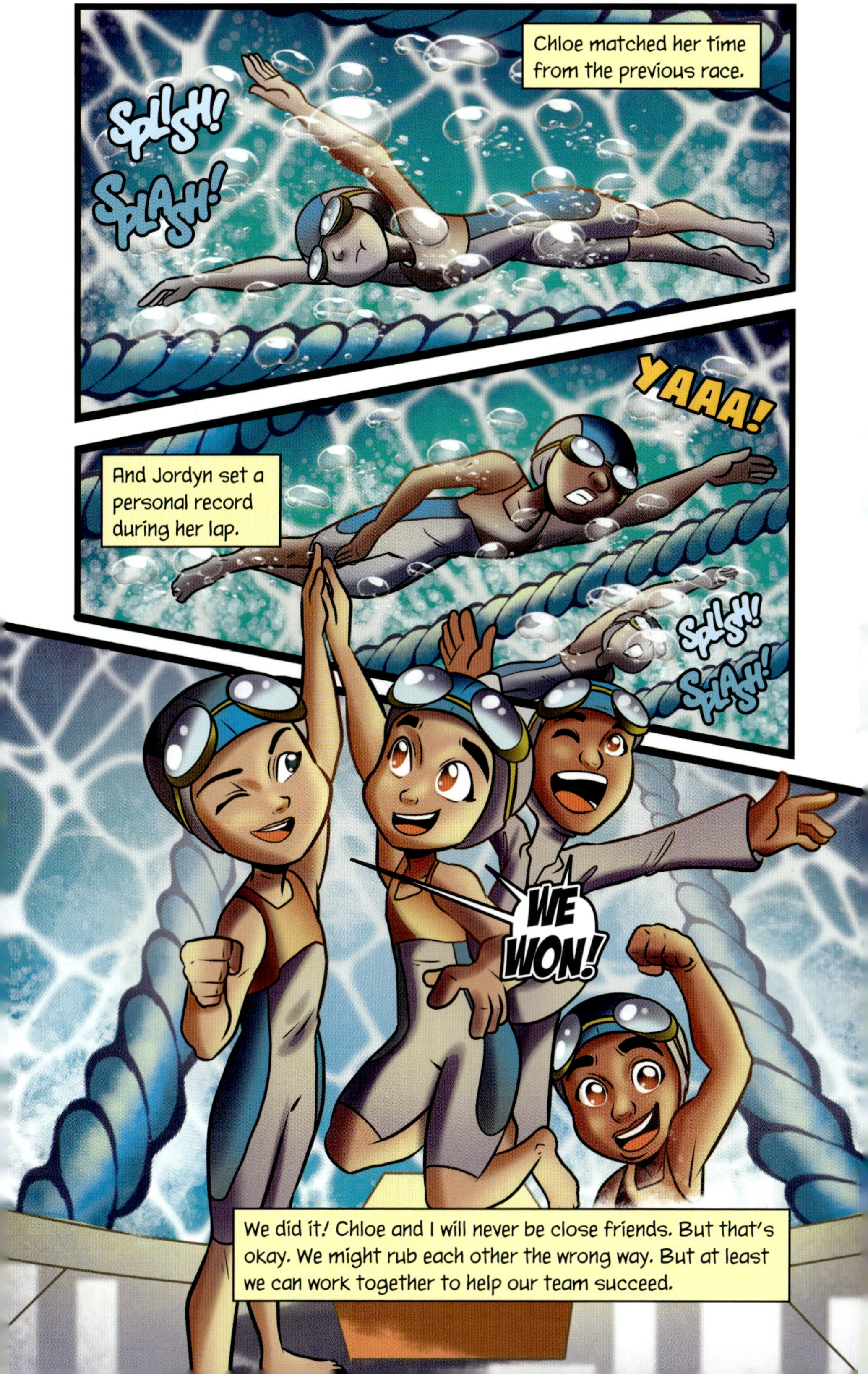
Chloe matched her time from the previous race.
SPLISH!
SPLASH!
YAAAA!
And Jordyn set a personal record during her lap.
SPLISH!
SPLASH!
WE WON!
We did it! Chloe and I will never be close friends. But that's okay. We might rub each other the wrong way. But at least we can work together to help our team succeed.

VISUAL DISCUSSION QUESTIONS

1. Study the image to the left. Why do you think the artist created it this way? Does it help you learn who the different characters are in the story?

2. Artists use lighting to show characters' moods in certain scenes. Can you tell what the characters are feeling based on the lighting in this panel?

3. A character's clothing can tell you a lot about them. Notice how Aminah's swimsuit is different from the other girls' suits. What can you learn about Aminah from her swimsuit and her other clothing in the story?

4. Facial expressions tell us a lot about what a character is thinking or feeling. Can you tell what Chloe is thinking just by looking at this closeup?

5. In graphic novels the art is often as important to the story as the words. Look at the below art panels. Can you tell what's happening, even without any words?

FAMOUS FEMALE SWIMMING TRAILBLAZERS

Gertrude Erdele: Gertrude Erdele was one of the most famous athletes of the early 20th Century. After medaling at the 1924 Olympics, Gertrude was the first woman to swim across the icy cold English Channel in 1926. Not only did she complete the 21 mile (33.8 kilometer) channel, she swam the Channel faster than the men who had done it before her! She came back to America as a national hero.

Dara Torres: Dara Torres was the first U.S. swimmer to compete in five different Olympic games. Starting in 1984, she won 12 medals over the course of 24 years. Dara finished her Olympic career in 2008 at the age of 41!

Simone Manuel: Simone Manuel helped Stanford win the NCAA team championship two years in a row. Simone made waves at the 2016 Olympics in Rio de Janeiro, Brazil, when she won two gold and two silver medals. She made history as the first Black woman to win an Olympic medal in swimming.

SWIMMING TERMS

backstroke—a stroke done on one's back using a flutter kick and alternating overhead arm motions

breaststroke—a front stroke using a knee-bending kick and short, scooping arm motions in front of your chest

butterfly stroke—a front stroke using a dolphin kick and simultaneous overhead arm motions

drills—exercises that make up each swim practice; each day's drills are different depending on what swimmers need to focus on

dryland training—exercises such as stretching, jogging, crunches, and push-ups done on dry land to increase strength, flexibility, and speed

false start—when a swimmer leaves the starting block too early, often resulting in disqualification

freestyle—a front stroke using a flutter kick and alternating overhead arm motions

heat—one of a series of preliminary races to determine who will compete in the final rounds

medley relay—a group event in which four teammates each swim a different stroke in this order: backstroke, breaststroke, butterfly, and freestyle

turn—the way a swimmer pushes off the wall during a race; swimmers use a somersault turn for backstroke and freestyle; in breaststroke and butterfly they grab the wall and push off to turn

warm down—slow-paced swimming done between a race and the end of the meet to help lower heart rate and improve blood flow

GLOSSARY

crunches (KRUHNCH-ez)—exercises performed by repeatedly raising and lowering the upper body while laying back on the floor with your knees bent; crunches help strengthen abdominal muscles

disqualify (dis-KWAHL-uh-fy)—to prevent someone from taking part in or winning an activity; athletes can be disqualified for breaking the rules

granola (gruh-NOH-luh)—a breakfast or snack food made from rolled oats, raisins, nuts, and other healthy ingredients

hyper (HYE-per)—overly excited or stimulated

kickboard (KIK-bohrd)—a rectangular board that floats, often held by a swimmer while practicing kicking movements

meet (MEET)—a sporting event featuring a series of races or contests

personality (pur-suh-NAL-uh-tee)—all of the qualities or traits that make a person unique

About the Author

Katie Schenkel is a comic writer best known for the critically acclaimed, Eisner Award-nominated graphic novel *The Cardboard Kingdom*. She especially loves to write about girls' friendships and their perspectives on the world around them. Katie was a competitive swimmer for many years, so writing *Swim Team Trouble* was very special for her. Midwest to her core, Katie lives in Chicago with her partner, Madison.

About the Artists

Berenice Muñiz is a graphic designer and illustrator from Monterrey, Mexico. She has done work for publicity agencies, art exhibitions, and even created her own webcomic. These days, Berenice is devoted to illustrating comics as part of the Graphikslava crew.

Jaymes Reed has operated the company Digital-CAPS: Comic Book Lettering since 2003. He has done lettering for many publishers, most notably Avatar Press. He's also the only letterer working with Inception Strategies, an Aboriginal-Australian publisher that develops social comics with public service messages for the Australian government. Jaymes is a 2012 and 2013 Shel Dorf Award Nominee.

READ THEM ALL!

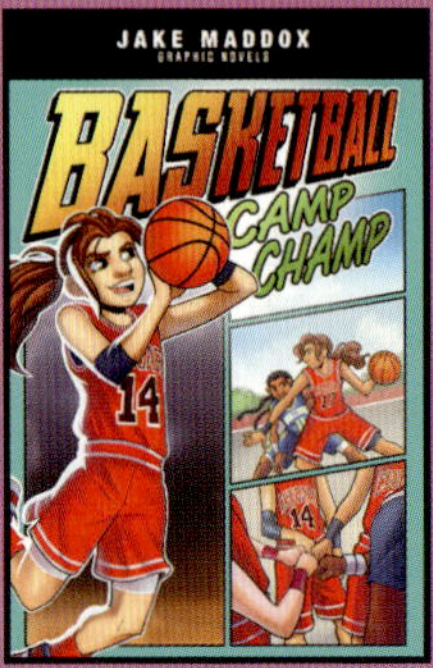
JAKE MADDOX
BASKETBALL CAMP CHAMP

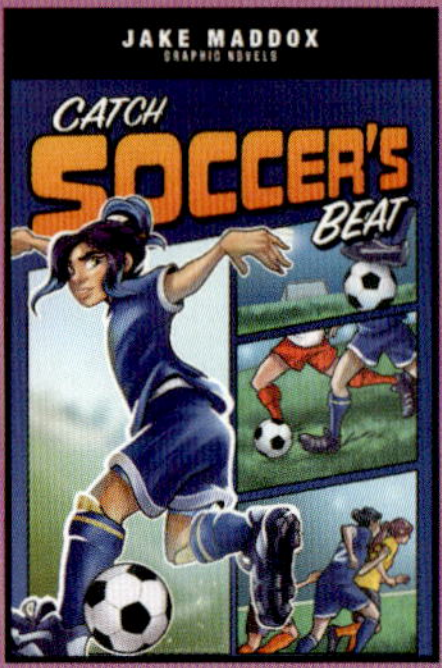
JAKE MADDOX
CATCH SOCCER'S BEAT

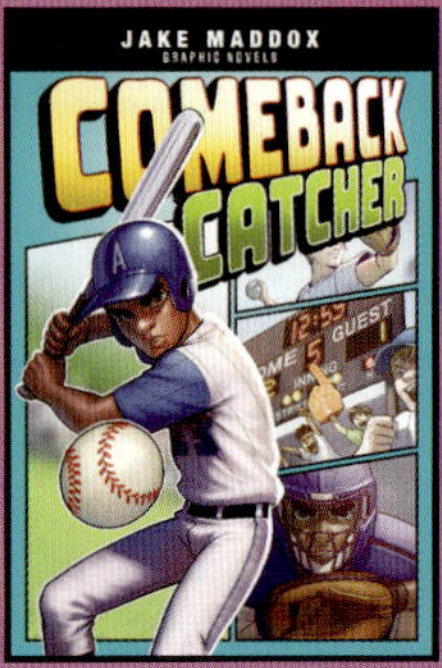
JAKE MADDOX
COMEBACK CATCHER

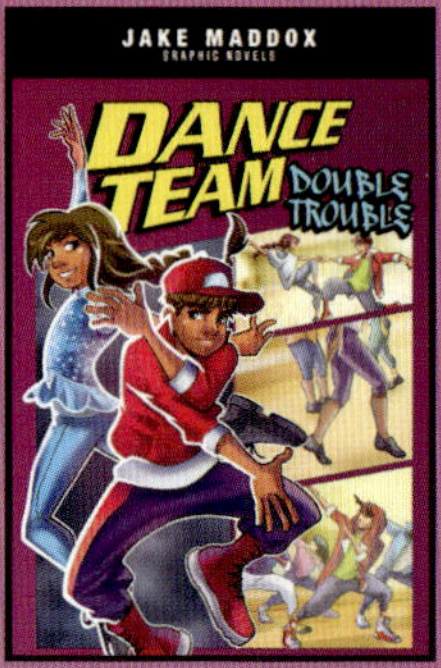
JAKE MADDOX
DANCE TEAM DOUBLE TROUBLE

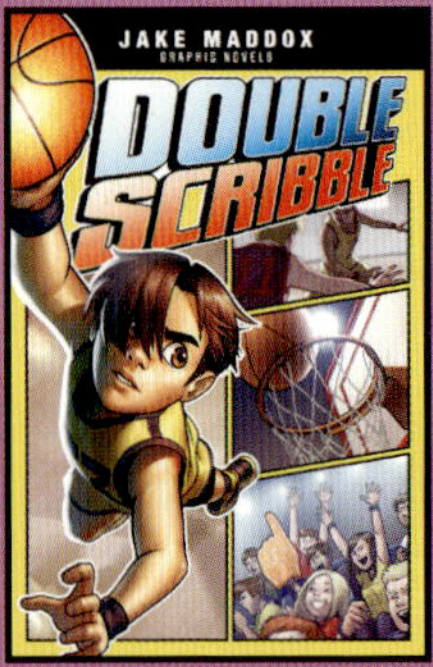
JAKE MADDOX
DOUBLE SCRIBBLE

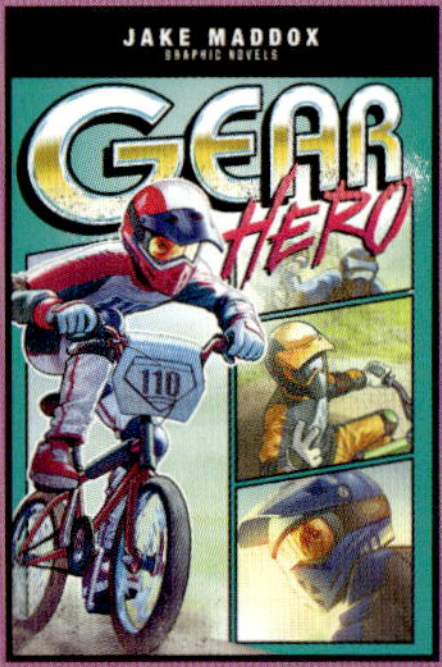
JAKE MADDOX
GEAR HERO

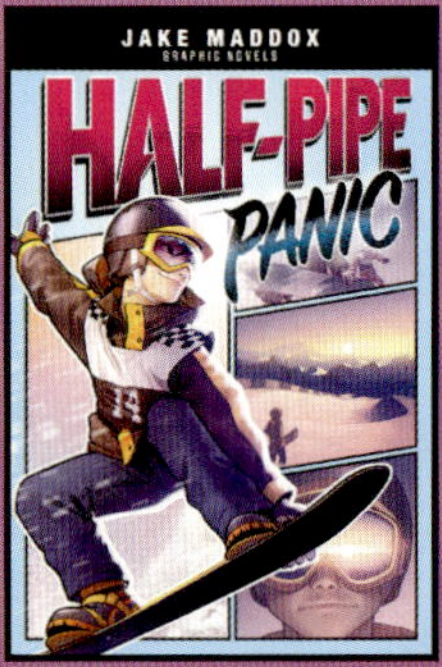
JAKE MADDOX
HALF-PIPE PANIC

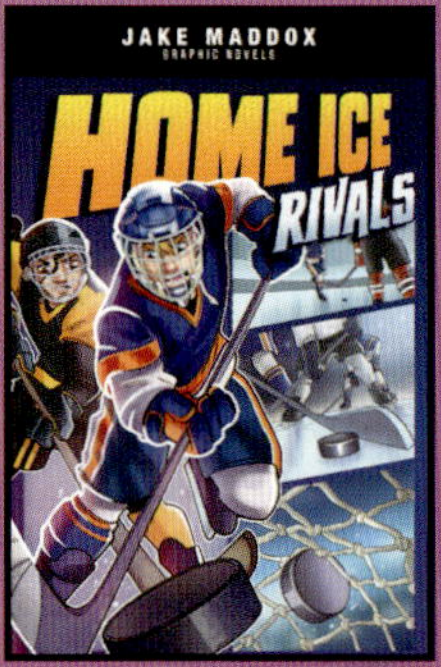
JAKE MADDOX
HOME ICE RIVALS

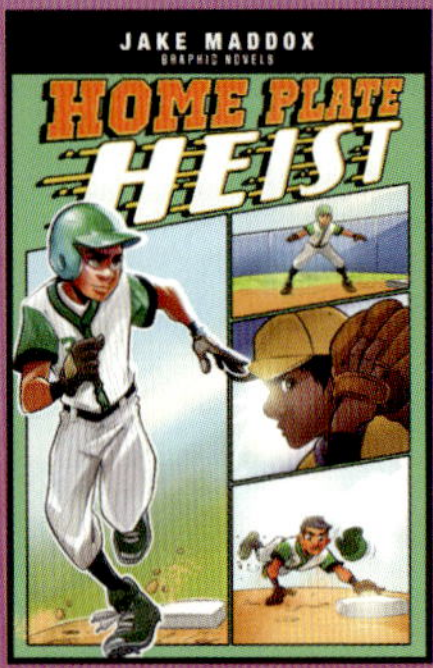
JAKE MADDOX
HOME PLATE HEIST

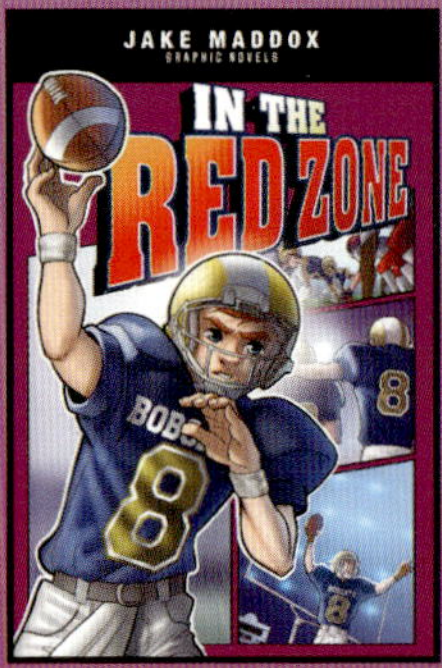
JAKE MADDOX
IN THE RED ZONE

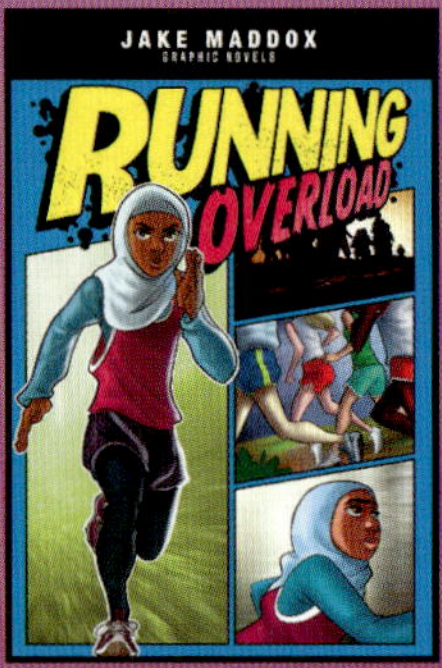
JAKE MADDOX
RUNNING OVERLOAD

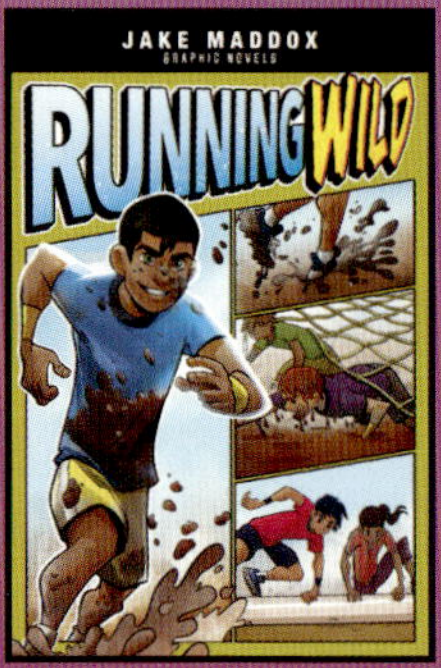
JAKE MADDOX
RUNNING WILD

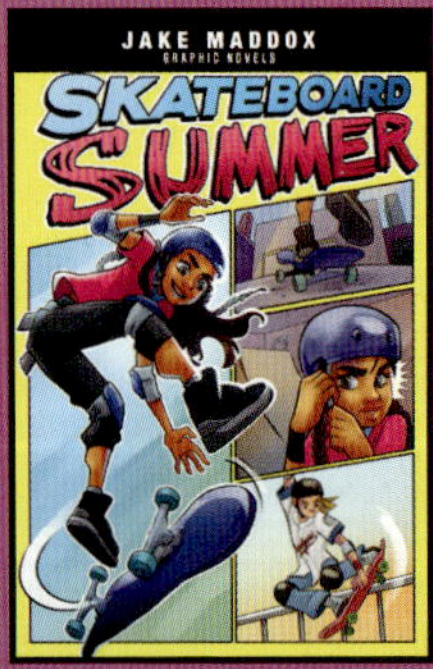
JAKE MADDOX
SKATEBOARD SUMMER

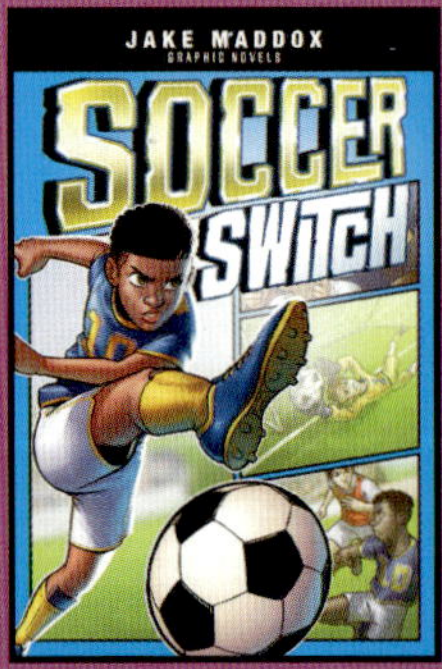
JAKE MADDOX
SOCCER SWITCH

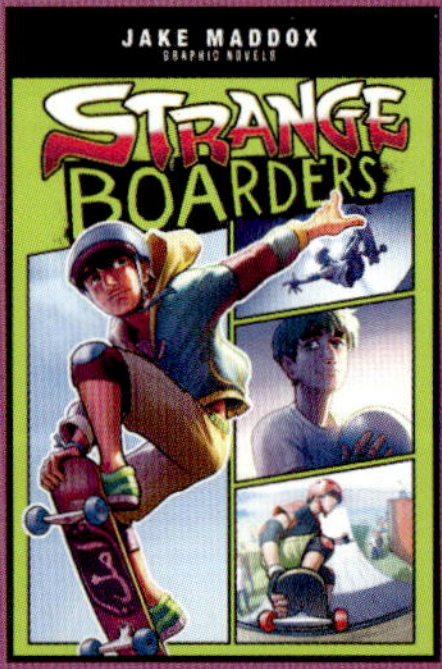
JAKE MADDOX
STRANGE BOARDERS

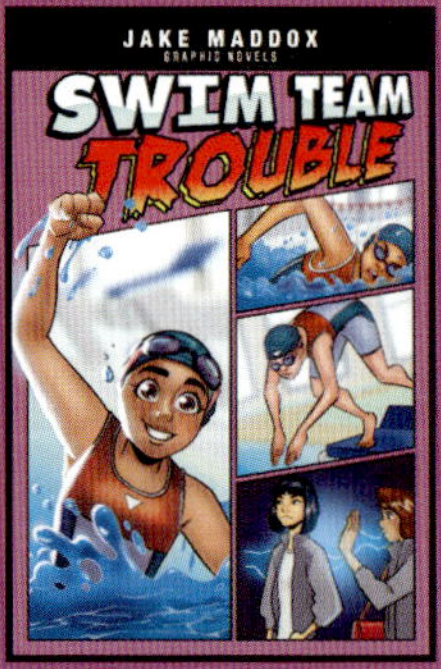
JAKE MADDOX
SWIM TEAM TROUBLE

JAKE MADDOX
GRAPHIC NOVELS

SOCCER SWITCH

STONE ARCH BOOKS
a capstone imprint

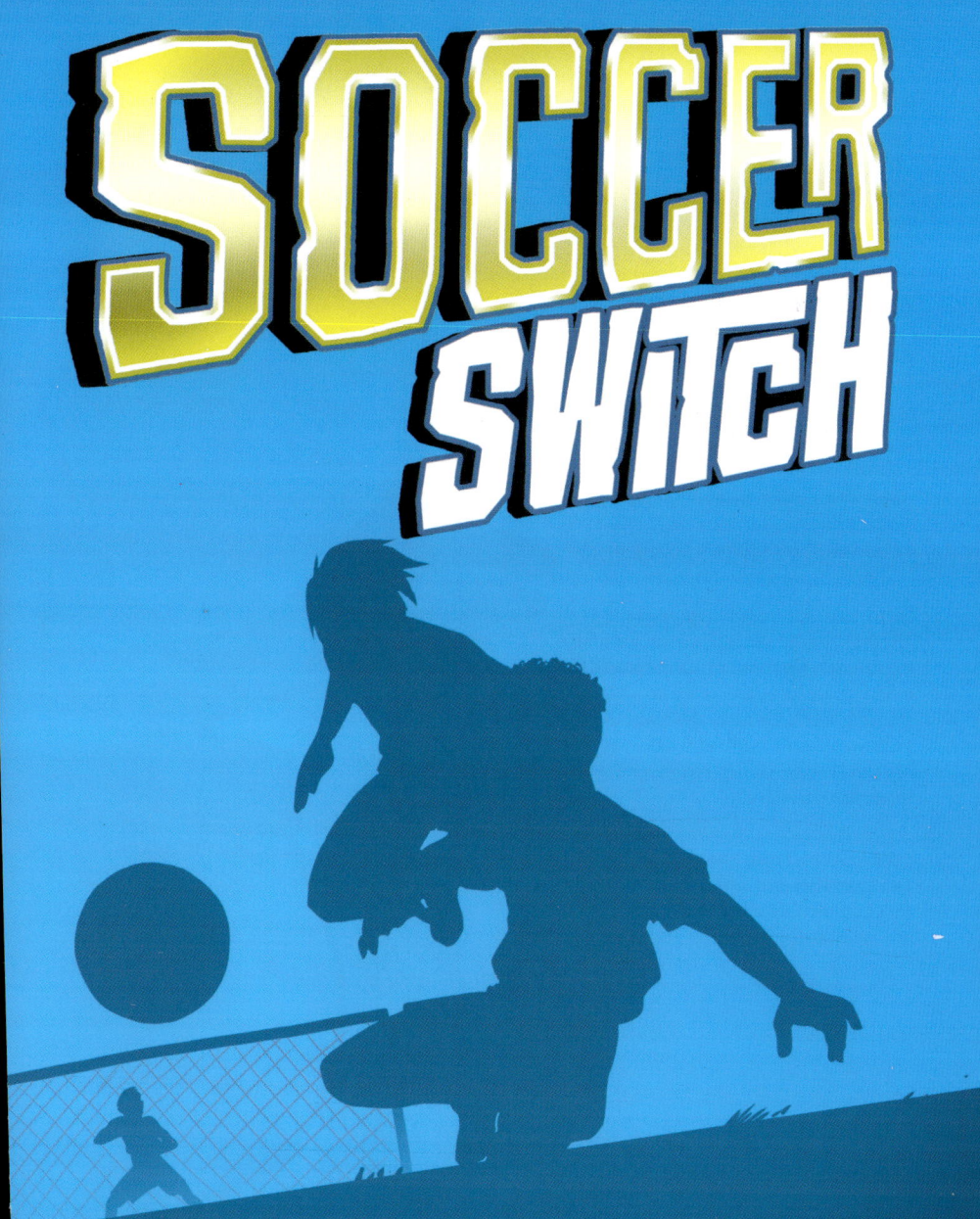

JAKE MADDOX
GRAPHIC NOVELS

Jake Maddox Graphic Novels are published by
Stone Arch Books, a Capstone imprint
1710 Roe Crest Drive
North Mankato, Minnesota 56003

www.mycapstone.com

Copyright © 2017 Stone Arch Books

All rights reserved. No part of this publication may be reproduced in whole or in part, or stored in a retrieval system, or transmitted in any form or by any means, electronic, mechanical, photocopying, recording, or otherwise, without written permission of the publisher.

Library of Congress Cataloging-in-Publication Data is available on the Library of Congress website.

ISBN: 978-1-4965-3699-0 (library binding)
ISBN: 978-1-4965-3703-4 (paperback)
ISBN: 978-1-4965-3719-5 (ebook PDF)

Summary: Andre Makuza is excited for another championship season with his middle school summer soccer team. But a new coach is taking over, and his unusual training methods have the team feeling frustrated. Will the coach's oddball ways ever lead to victory, or is the soccer switch too much for Andre and his teammates to handle?

Editor: Abby Huff
Designer: Brann Garvey
Production: Gene Bentdahl

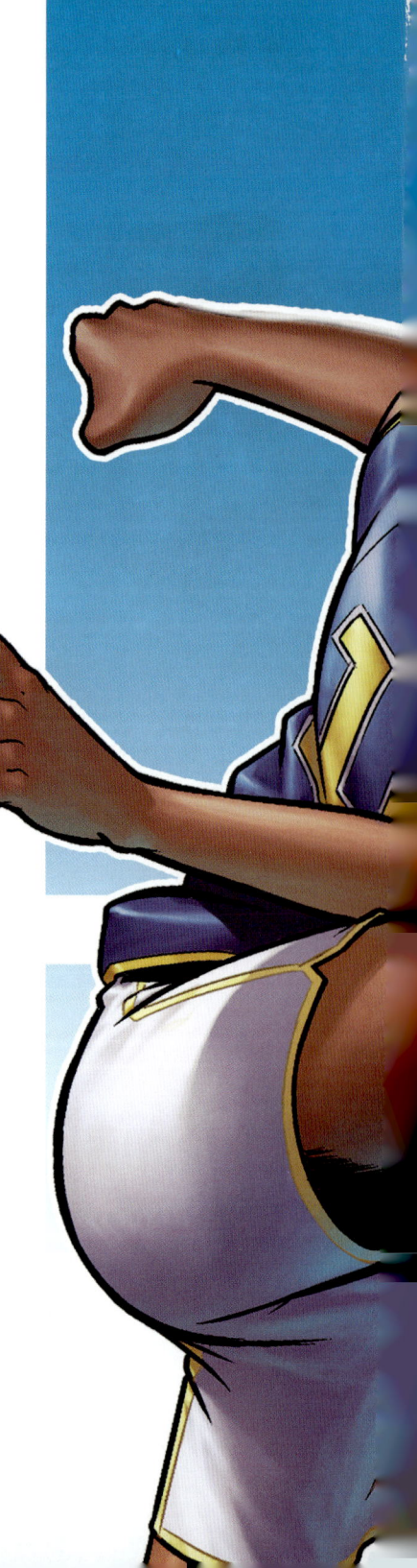

Printed and bound in China. PO 6096

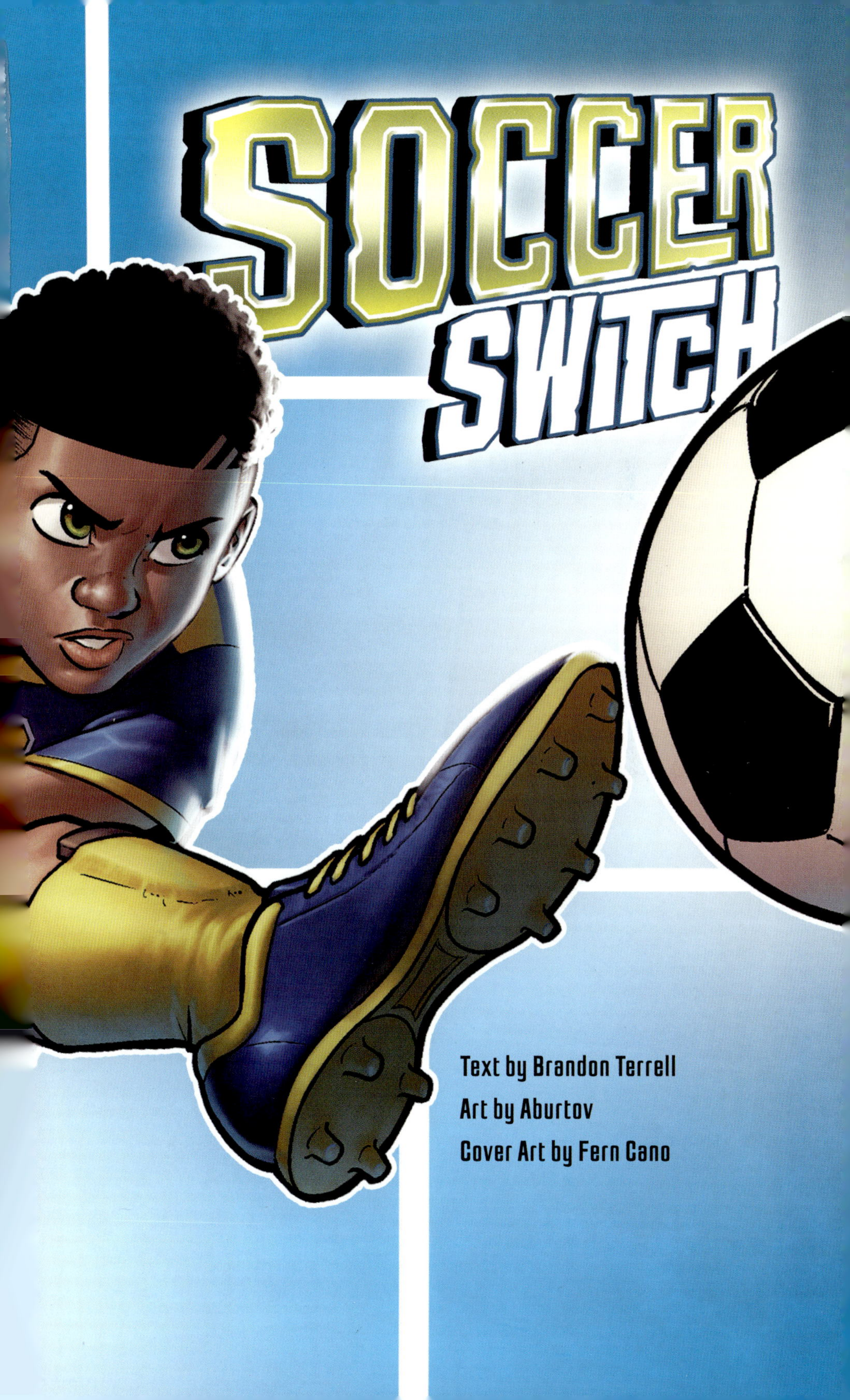
SOCCER
SWITCH
Text by Brandon Terrell
Art by Aburtov
Cover Art by Fern Cano

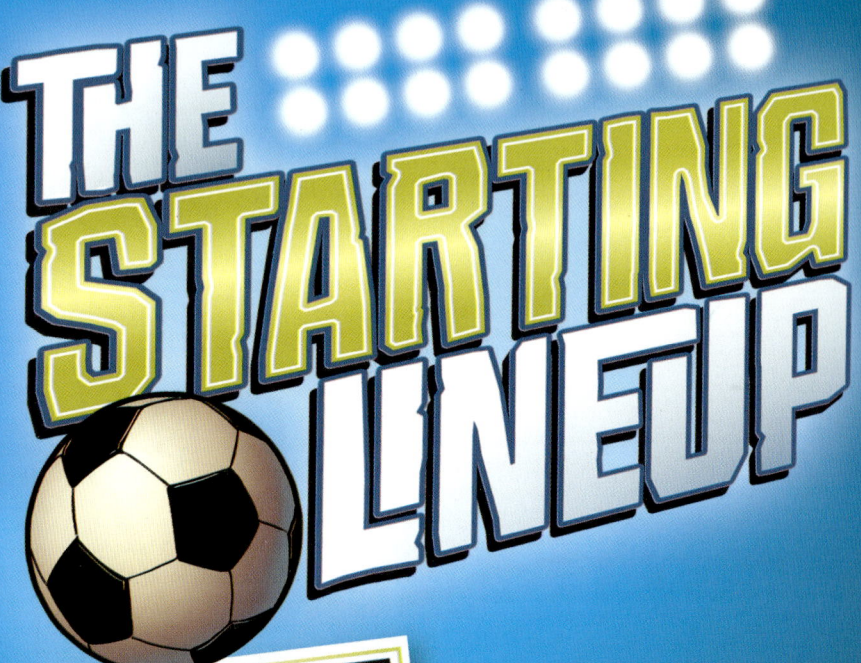

ANDRE MAKUZA

CULLIN HAWKE

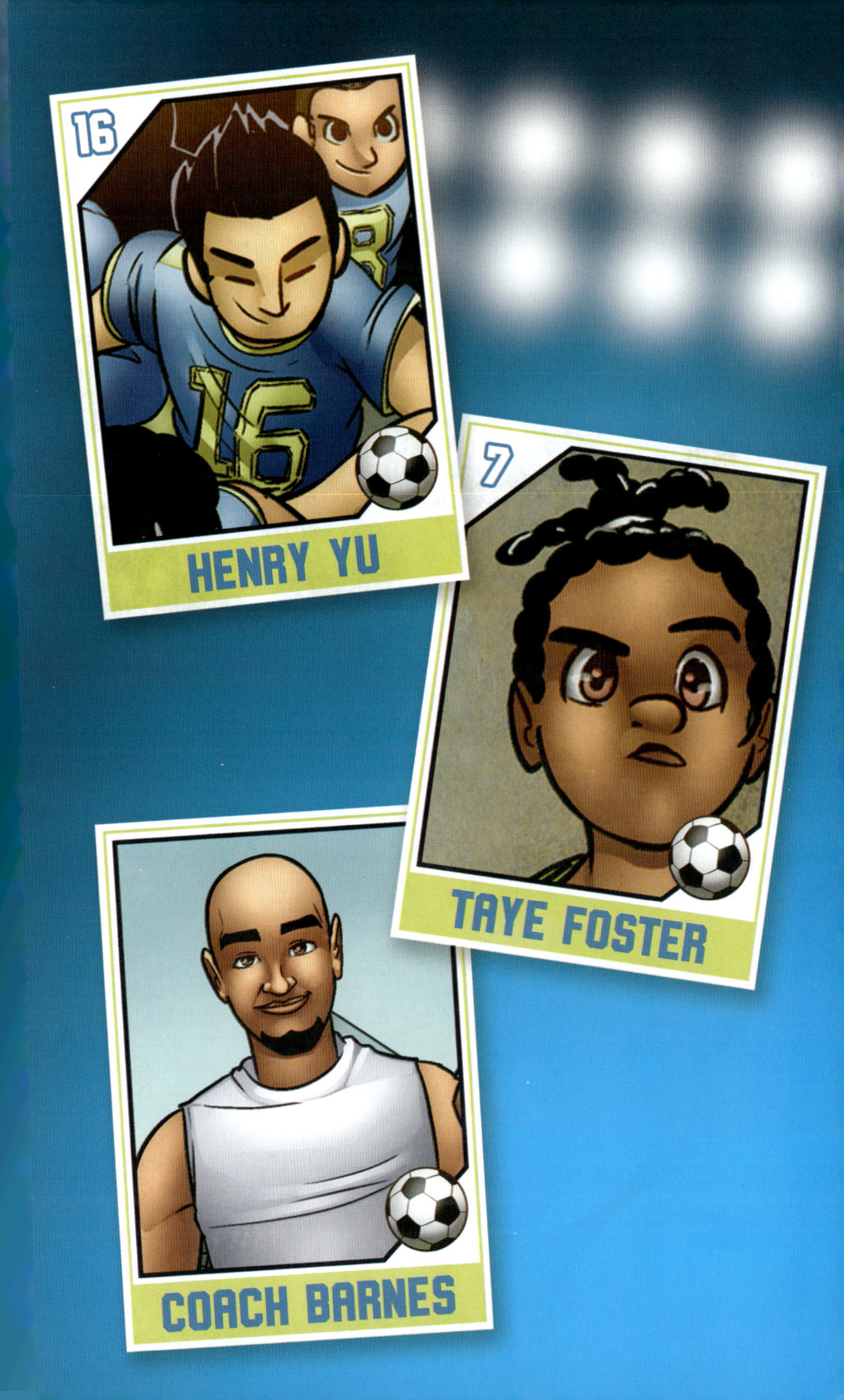
16
HENRY YU
7
TAYE FOSTER
COACH BARNES

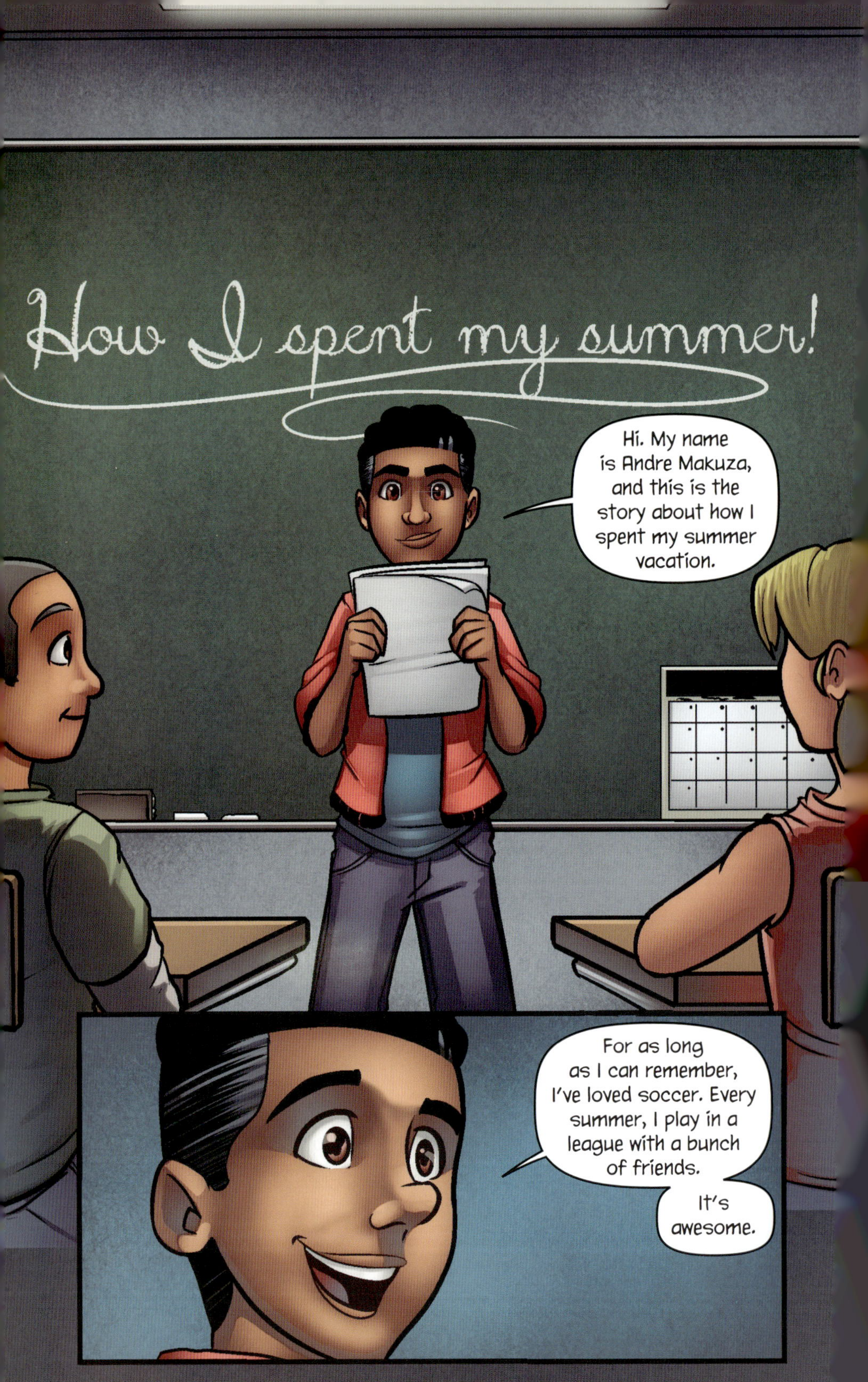
How I spent my summer!
Hi. My name is Andre Makuza, and this is the story about how I spent my summer vacation.
For as long as I can remember, I've loved soccer. Every summer, I play in a league with a bunch of friends.
It's awesome.

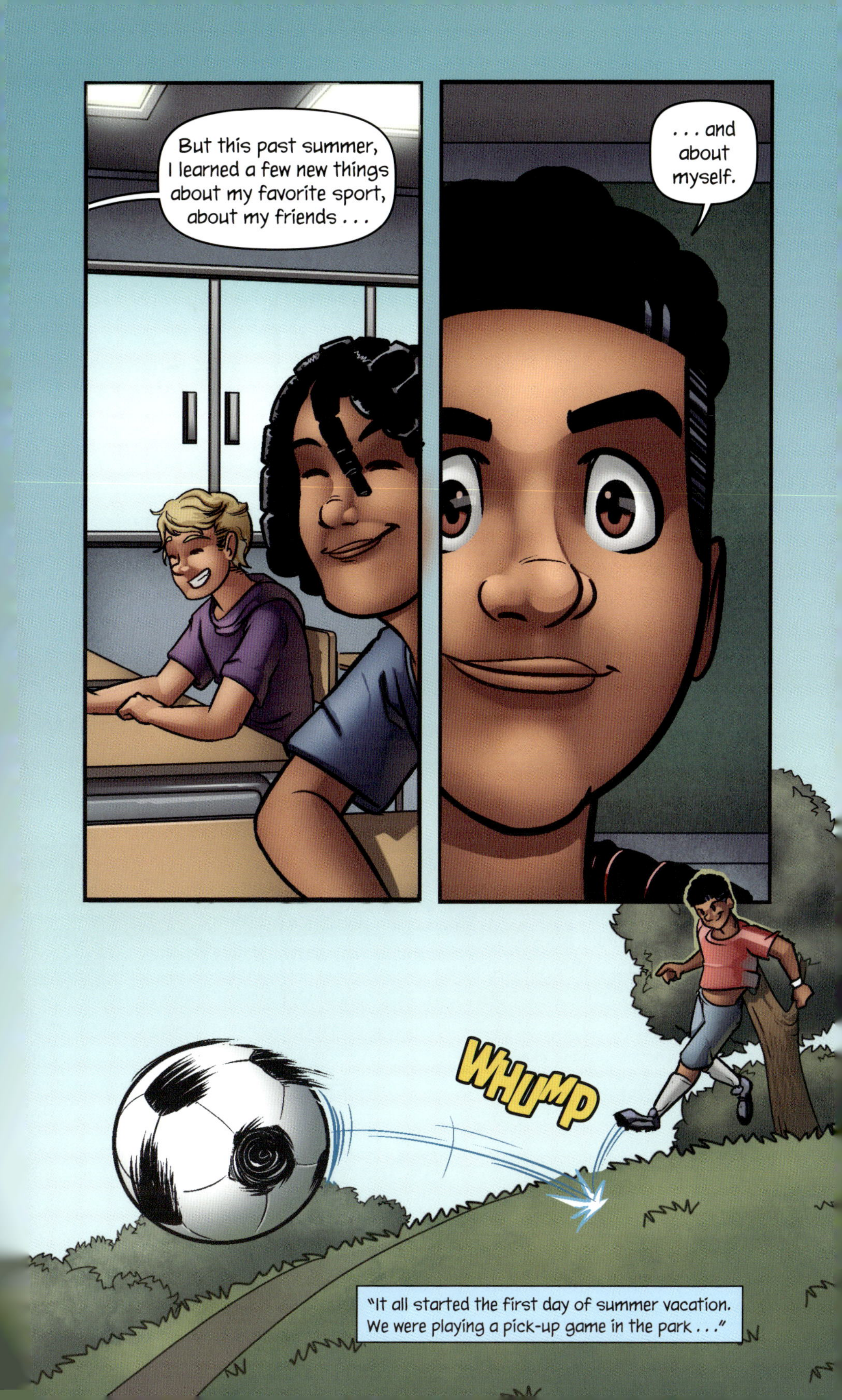
But this past summer, I learned a few new things about my favorite sport, about my friends . . .
. . . and about myself.
WHUMP
"It all started the first day of summer vacation. We were playing a pick-up game in the park . . ."

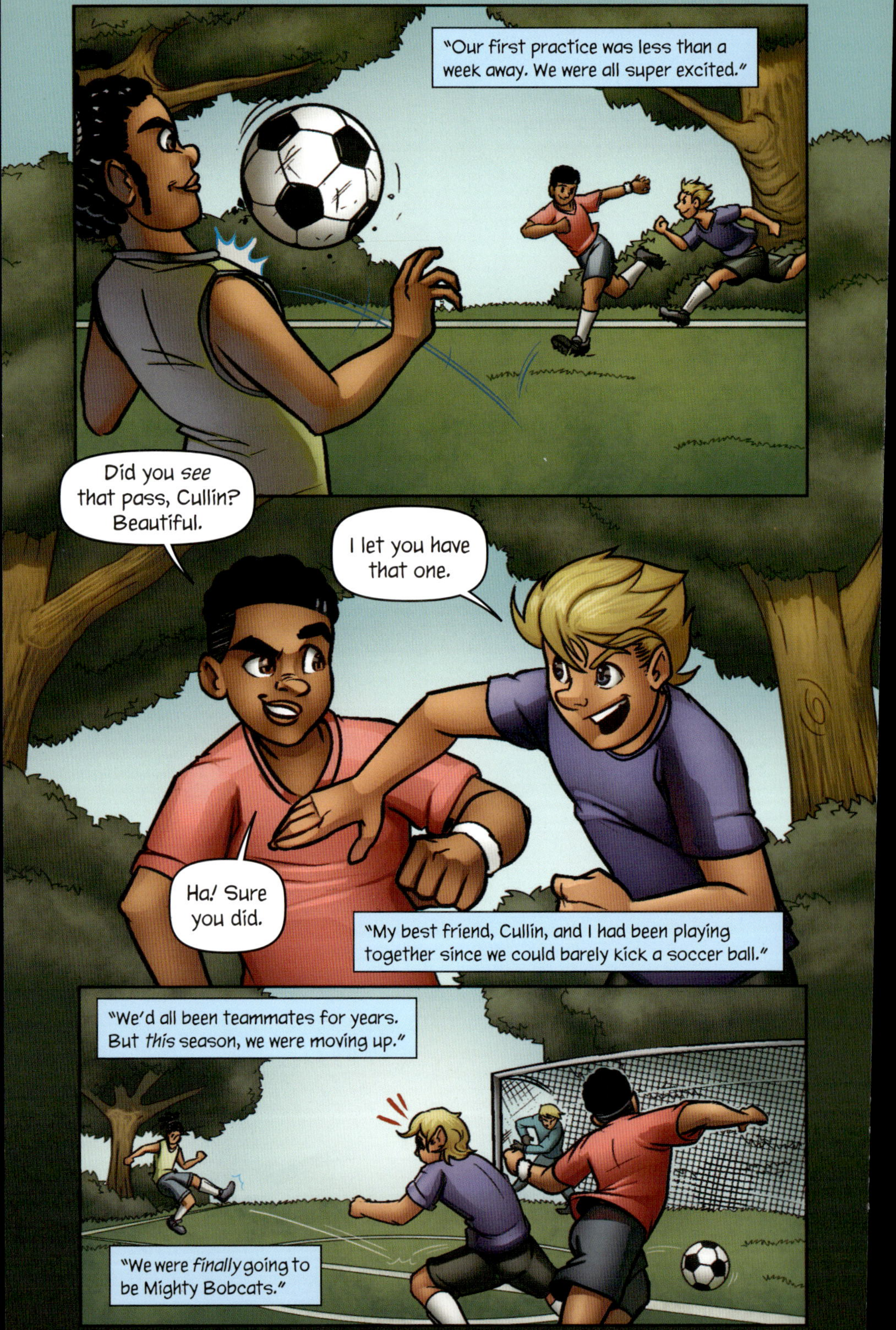
"Our first practice was less than a week away. We were all super excited."
Did you *see* that pass, Cullin? Beautiful.
I let you have that one.
Ha! Sure you did.
"My best friend, Cullin, and I had been playing together since we could barely kick a soccer ball."
"We'd all been teammates for years. But *this* season, we were moving up."
"We were *finally* going to be Mighty Bobcats."

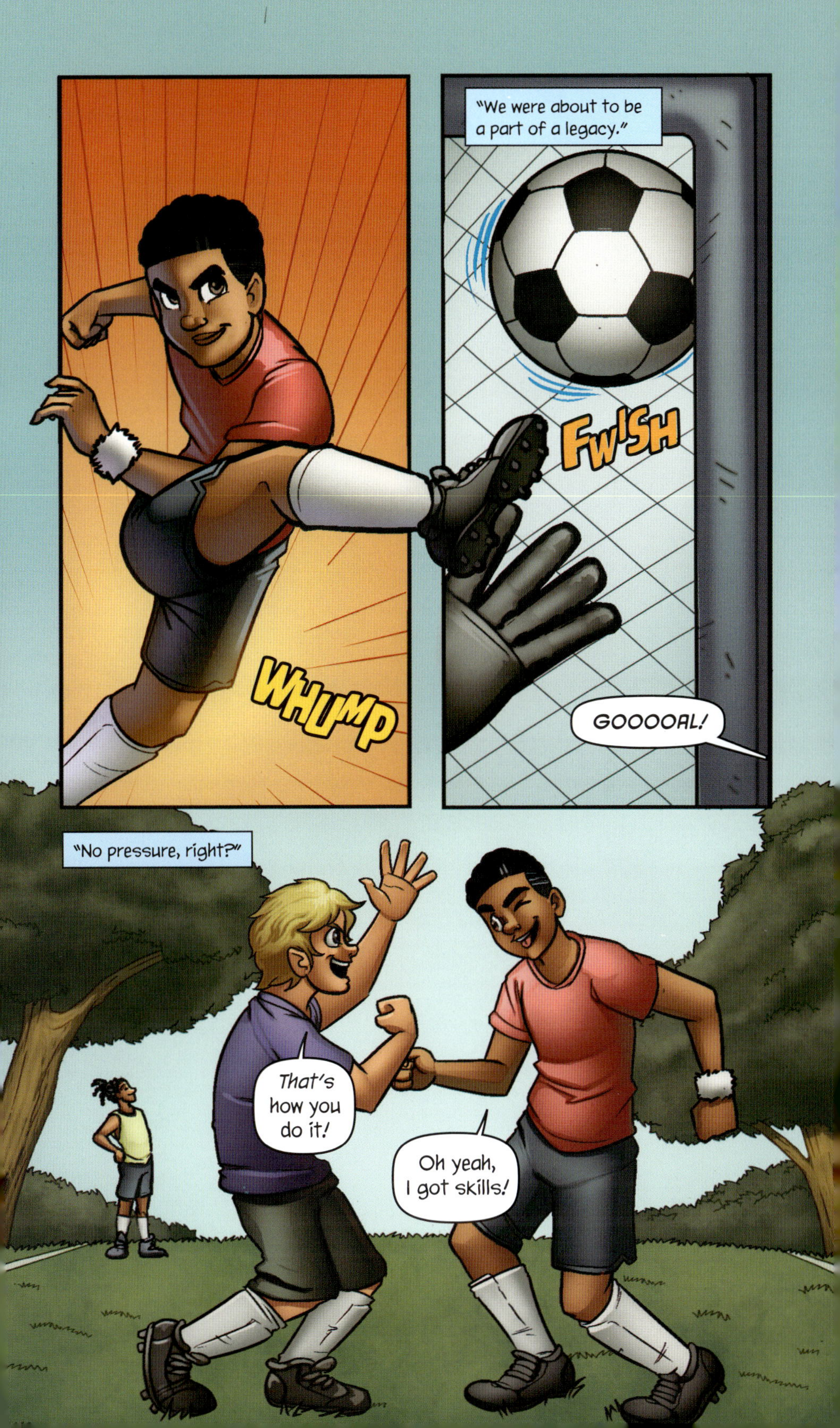
WHUMP
"We were about to be a part of a legacy."
FWISH
GOOOOAL!
"No pressure, right?"
That's how you do it!
Oh yeah, I got skills!

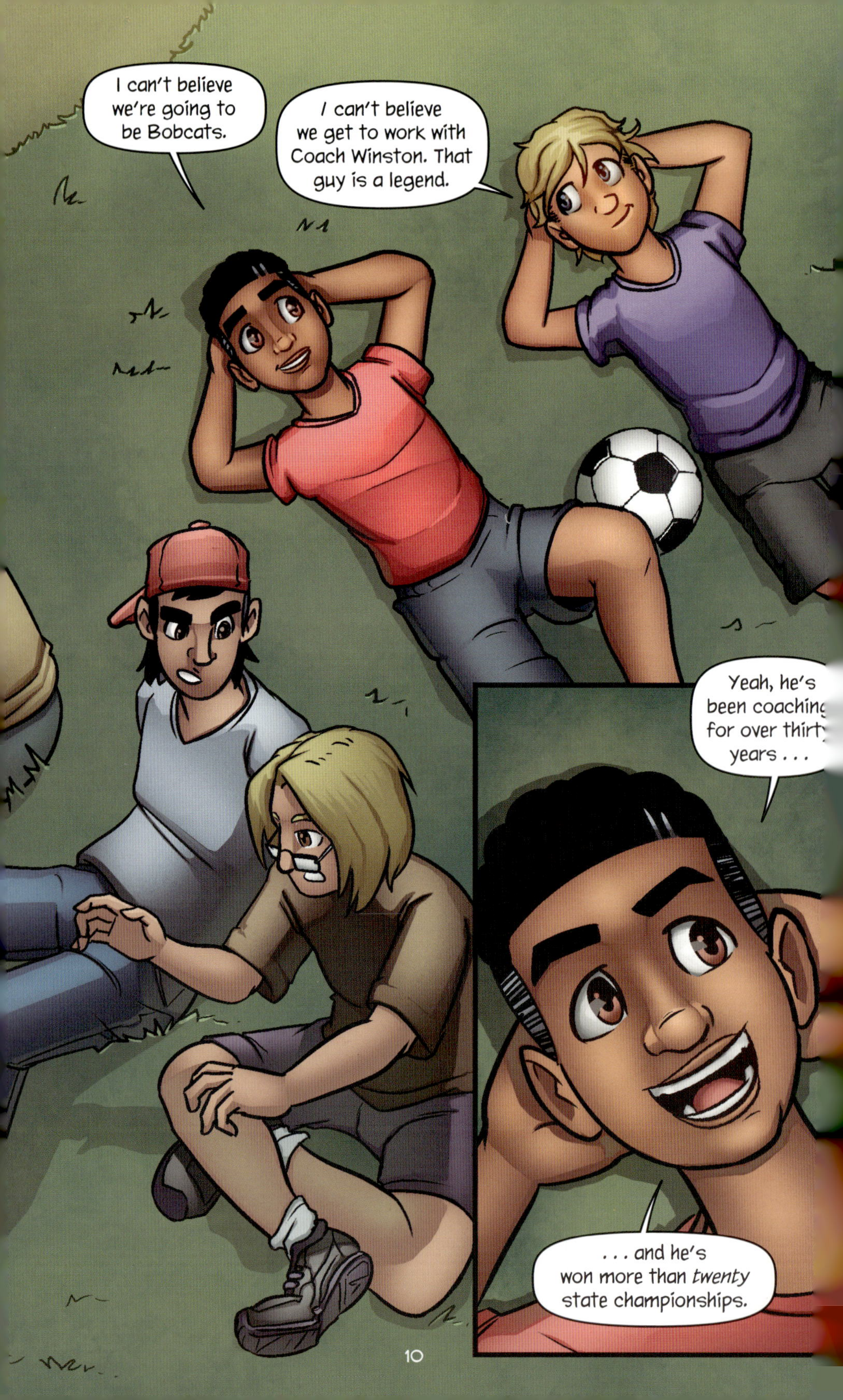
I can't believe we're going to be Bobcats.
I can't believe we get to work with Coach Winston. That guy is a legend.
Yeah, he's been coachin for over thirt years . . .
. . . and he's won more than *twenty* state championships.

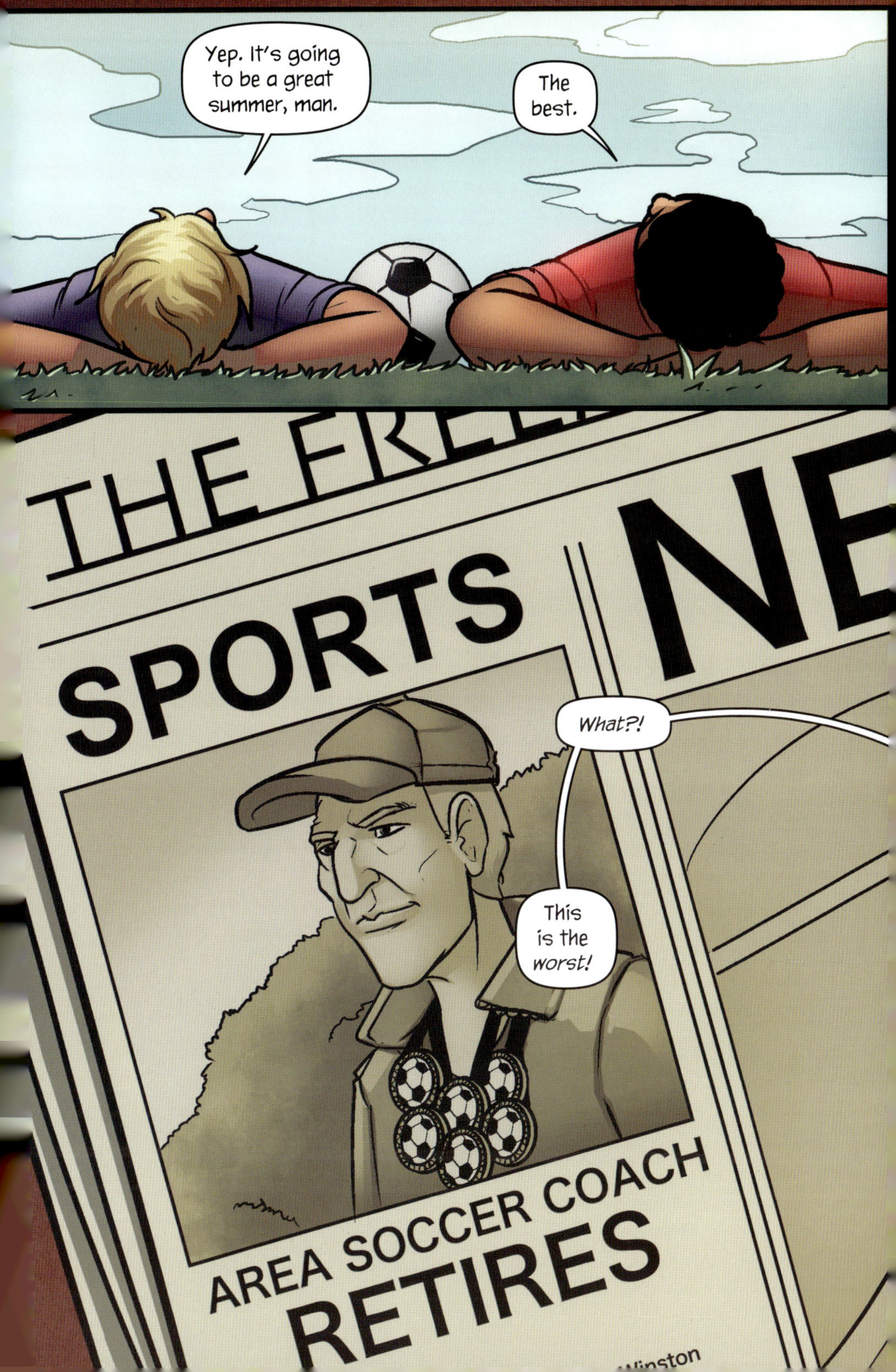
Yep. It's going to be a great summer, man.
The best.
THE FREE
SPORTS
NE
What?!
This is the worst!
AREA SOCCER COACH
RETIRES

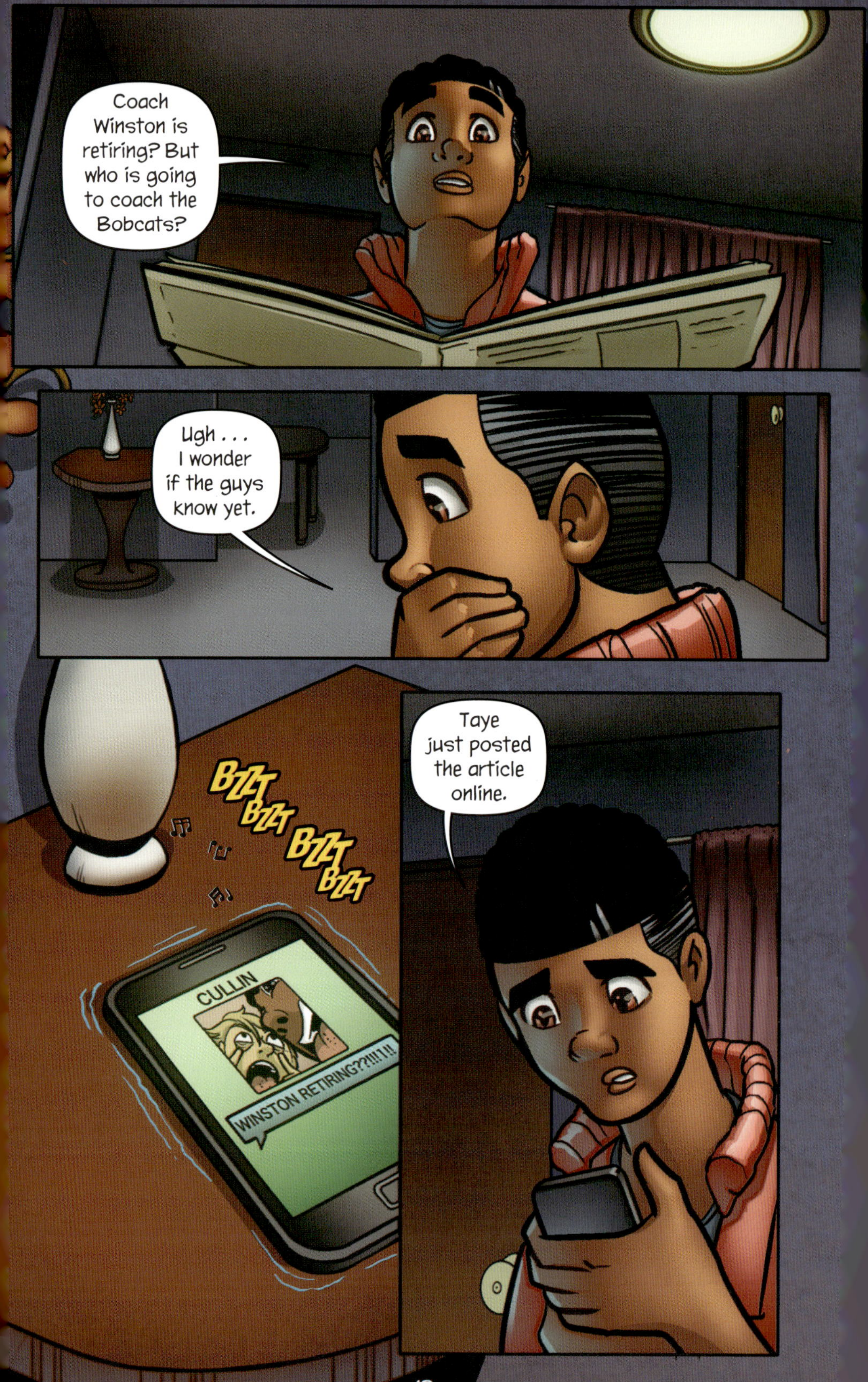
Coach Winston is retiring? But who is going to coach the Bobcats?
Ugh . . . I wonder if the guys know yet.
BZZT BZZT BZZT BZZT
CULLIN
WINSTON RETIRING??!!!1!!
Taye just posted the article online.

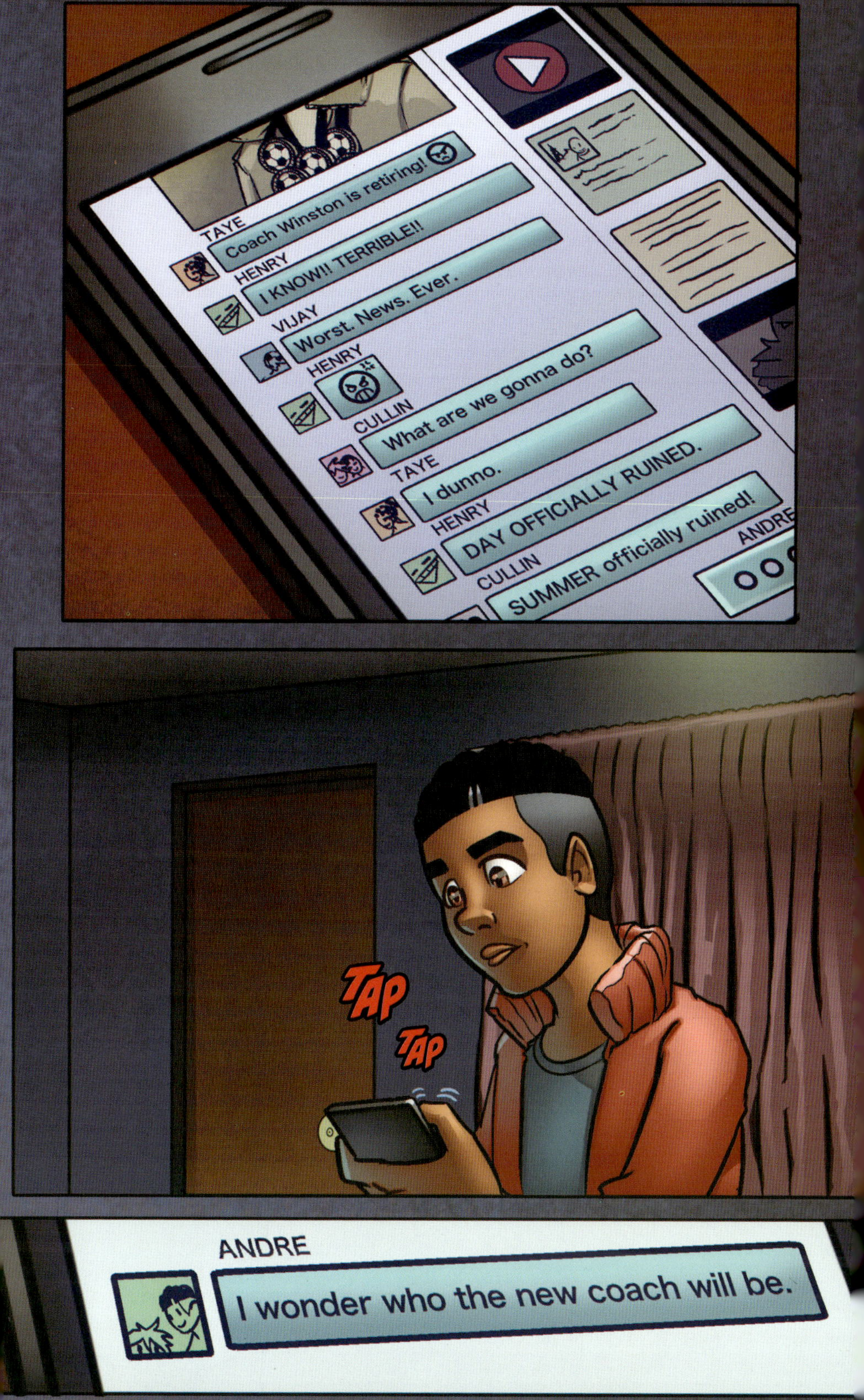
TAYE
Coach Winston is retiring!
HENRY
I KNOW!! TERRIBLE!!
VIJAY
Worst. News. Ever.
HENRY
CULLIN
What are we gonna do?
TAYE
I dunno.
HENRY
DAY OFFICIALLY RUINED.
CULLIN
SUMMER officially ruined!
TAP
TAP
ANDRE
I wonder who the new coach will be.

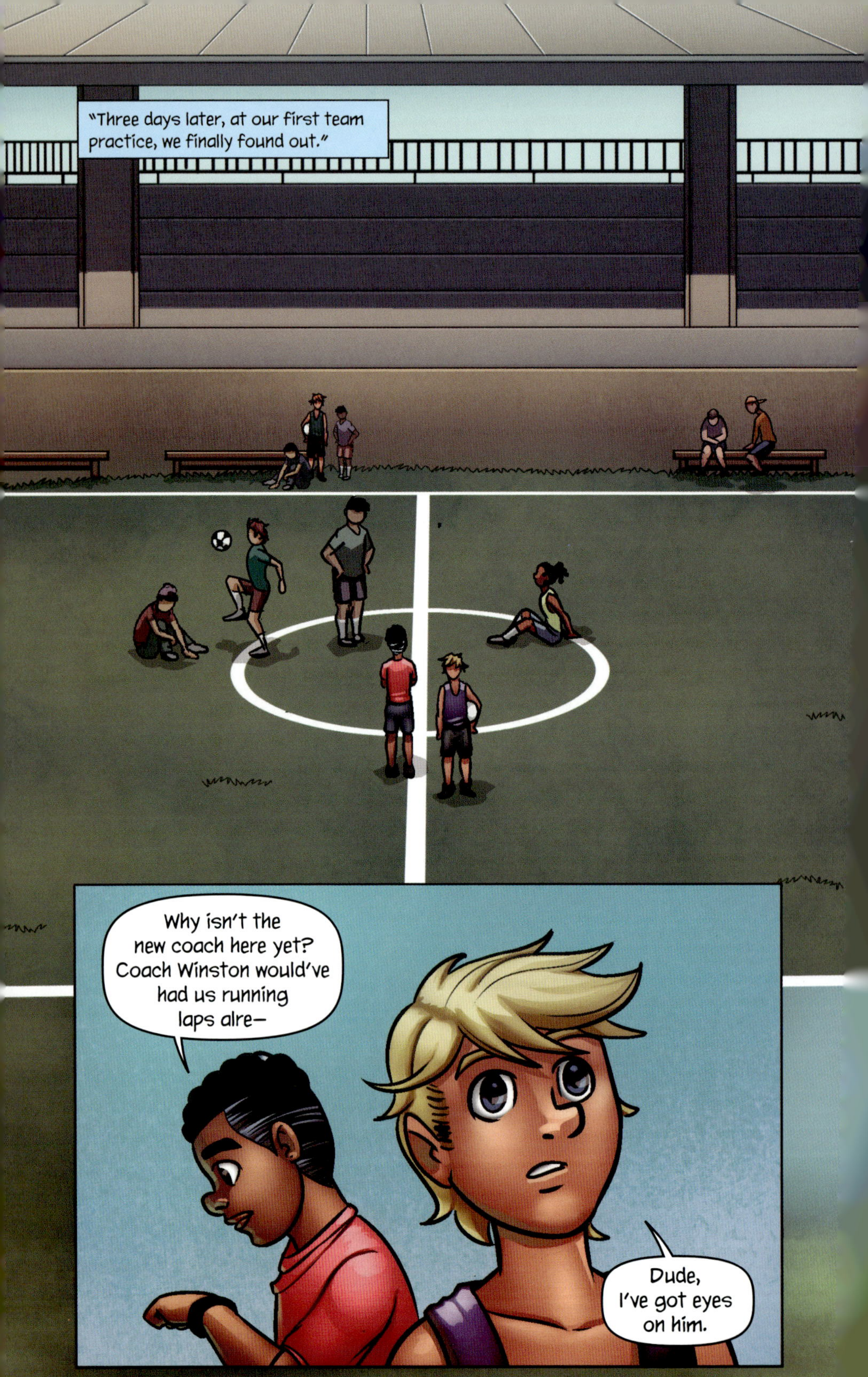
"Three days later, at our first team practice, we finally found out."
Why isn't the new coach here yet? Coach Winston would've had us running laps alre—
Dude, I've got eyes on him.

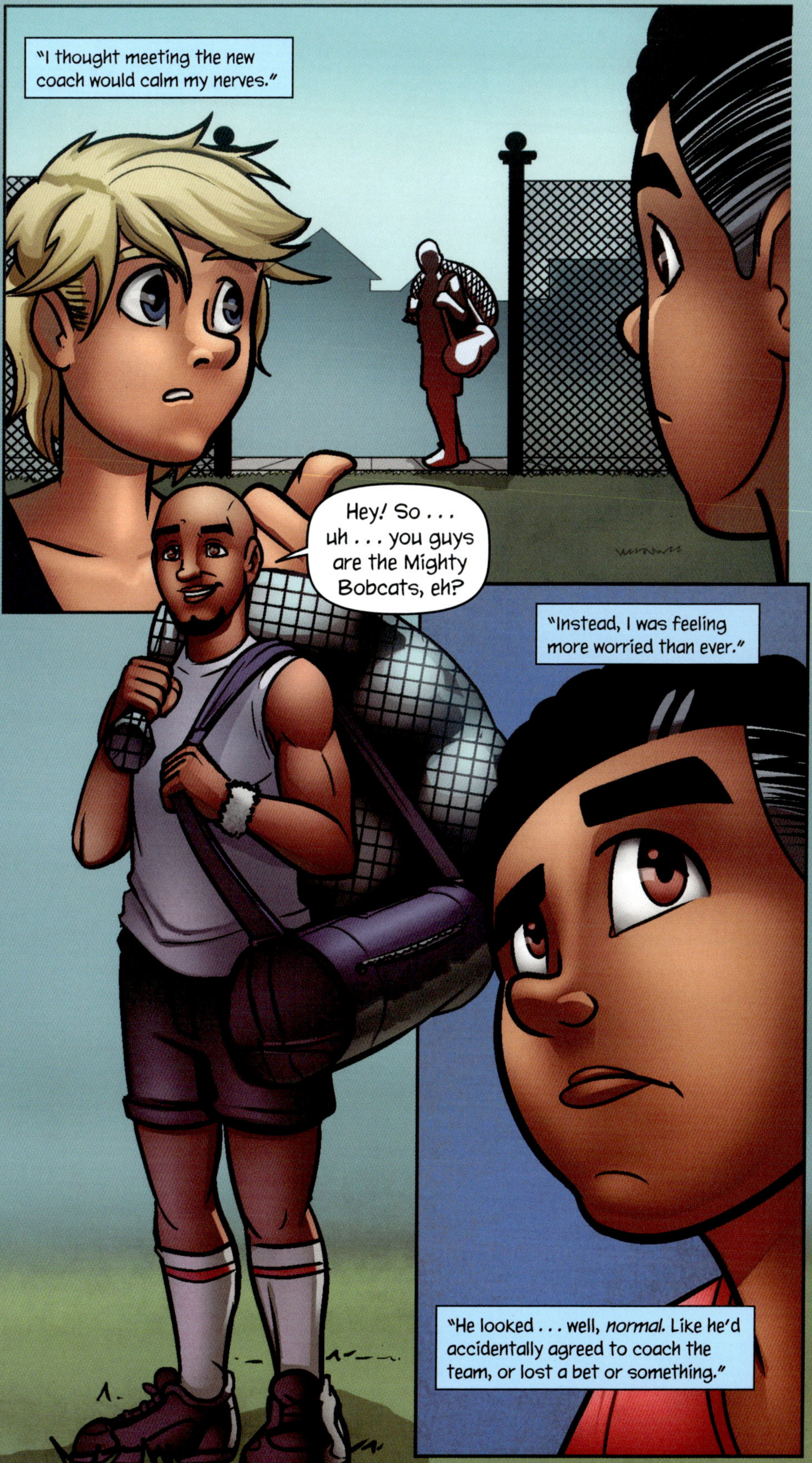
"I thought meeting the new coach would calm my nerves."
Hey! So . . . uh . . . you guys are the Mighty Bobcats, eh?
"Instead, I was feeling more worried than ever."
"He looked . . . well, *normal.* Like he'd accidentally agreed to coach the team, or lost a bet or something."

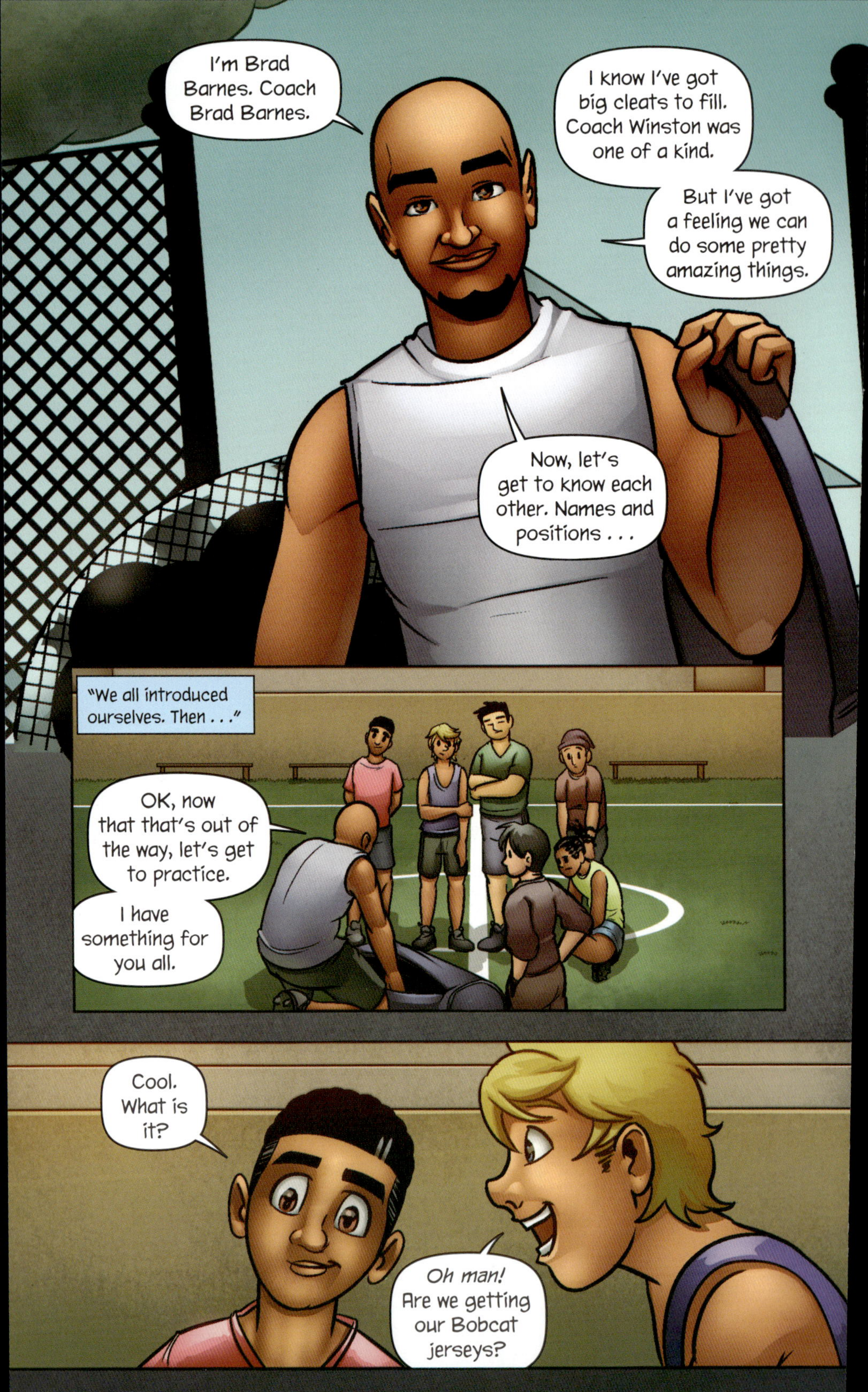
I'm Brad Barnes. Coach Brad Barnes.
I know I've got big cleats to fill. Coach Winston was one of a kind.
But I've got a feeling we can do some pretty amazing things.
Now, let's get to know each other. Names and positions . . .
"We all introduced ourselves. Then . . ."
OK, now that that's out of the way, let's get to practice.
I have something for you all.
Cool. What is it?
Oh man! Are we getting our Bobcat jerseys?

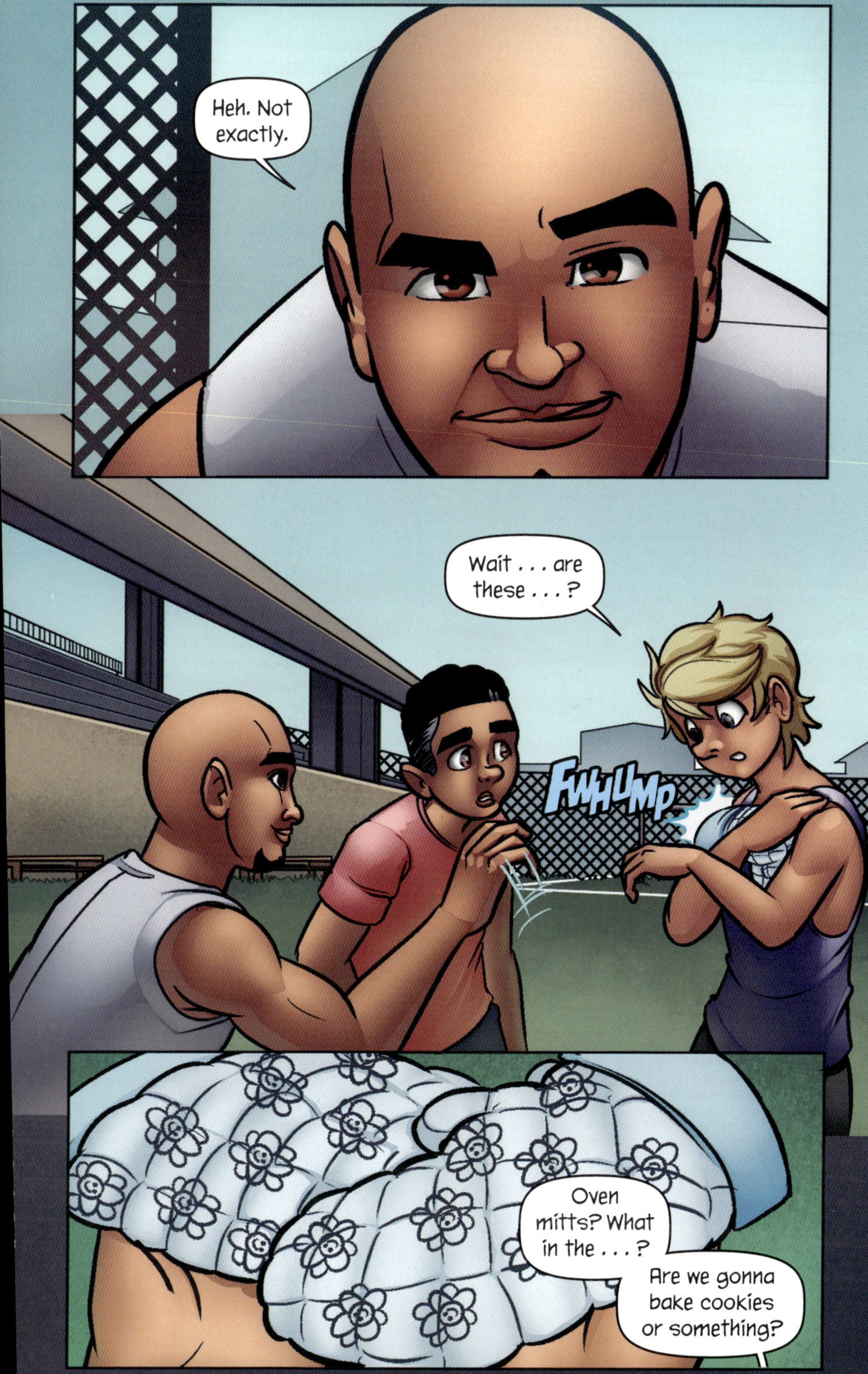
Heh. Not exactly.
Wait . . . are these . . . ?
FWHUMP
Oven mitts? What in the . . . ?
Are we gonna bake cookies or something?

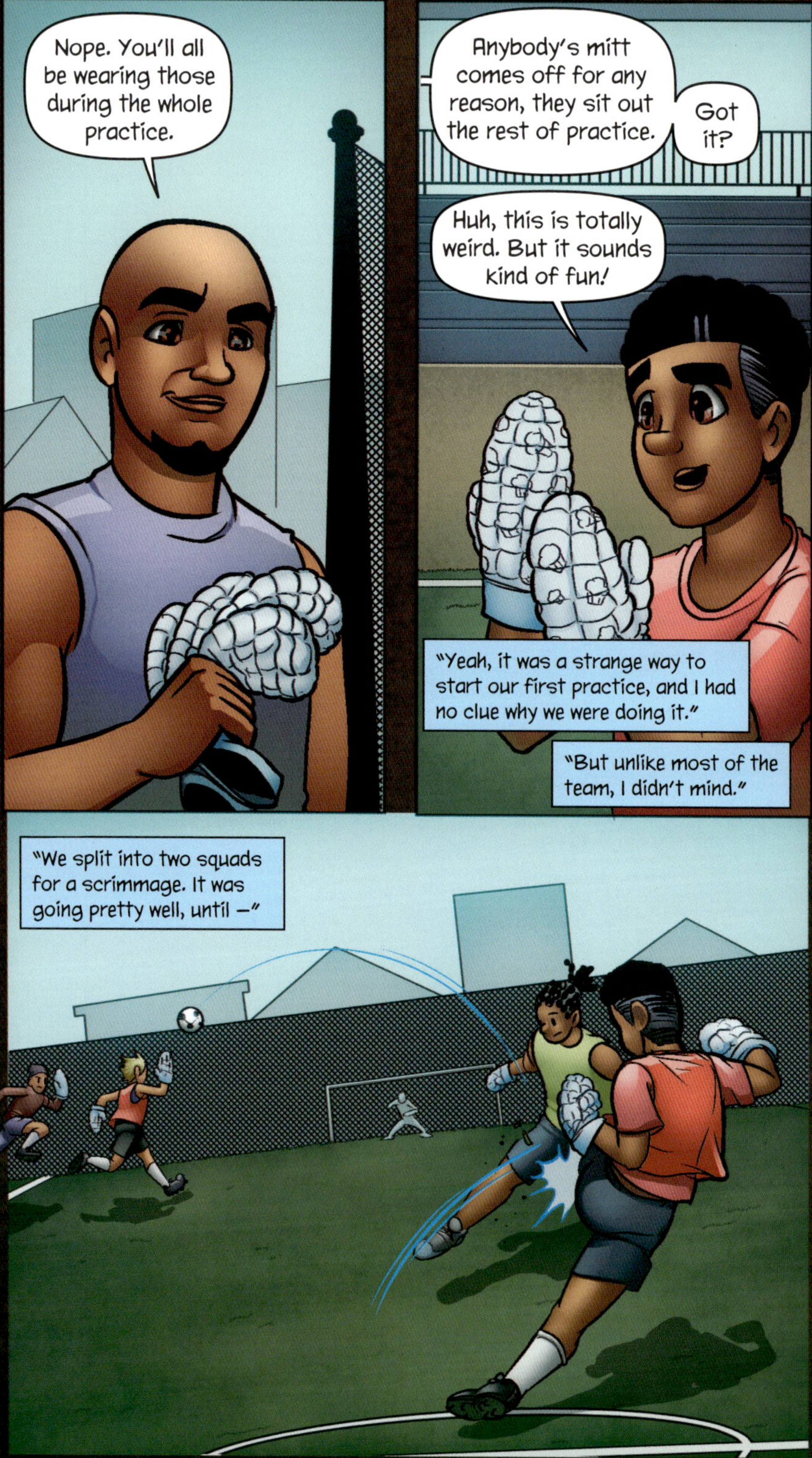
Nope. You'll all be wearing those during the whole practice.
Anybody's mitt comes off for any reason, they sit out the rest of practice.
Got it?
Huh, this is totally weird. But it sounds kind of fun!
"Yeah, it was a strange way to start our first practice, and I had no clue why we were doing it."
"But unlike most of the team, I didn't mind."
"We split into two squads for a scrimmage. It was going pretty well, until –"

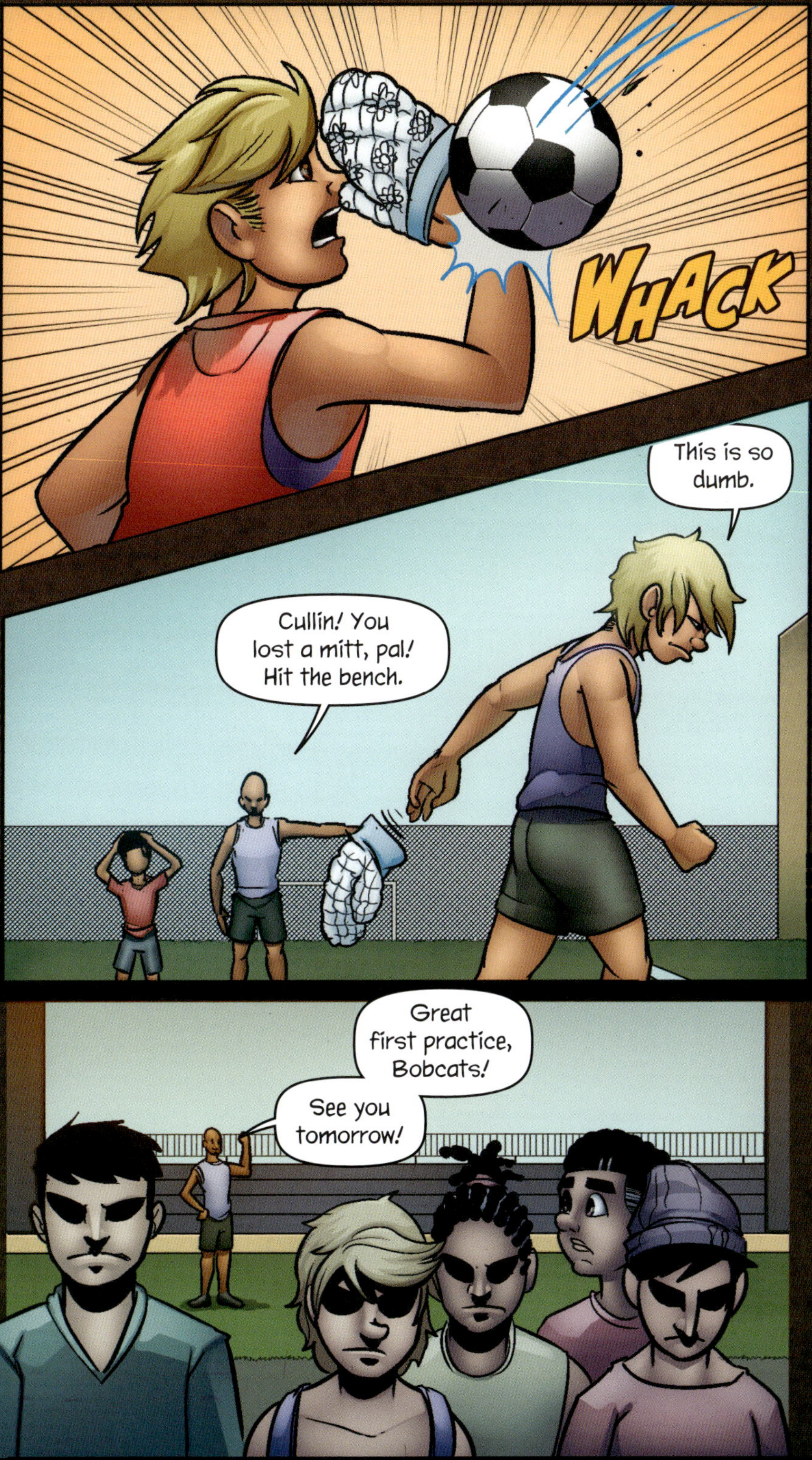
WHACK
This is so dumb.
Cullin! You lost a mitt, pal! Hit the bench.
Great first practice, Bobcats!
See you tomorrow!

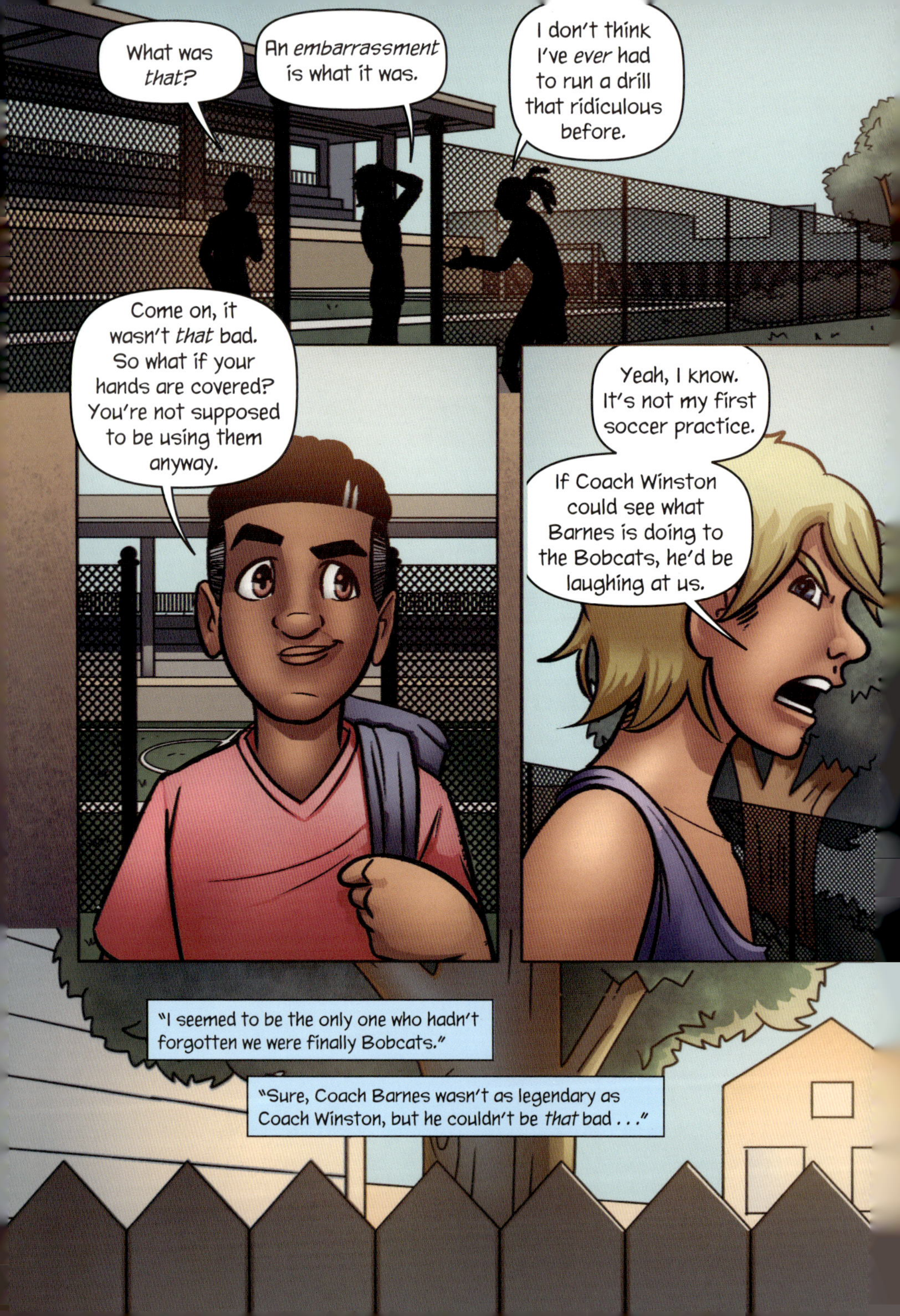
What was *that?*
An *embarrassment* is what it was.
I don't think I've *ever* had to run a drill that ridiculous before.
Come on, it wasn't *that* bad. So what if your hands are covered? You're not supposed to be using them anyway.
Yeah, I know. It's not my first soccer practice.
If Coach Winston could see what Barnes is doing to the Bobcats, he'd be laughing at us.
"I seemed to be the only one who hadn't forgotten we were finally Bobcats."
"Sure, Coach Barnes wasn't as legendary as Coach Winston, but he couldn't be *that* bad . . ."

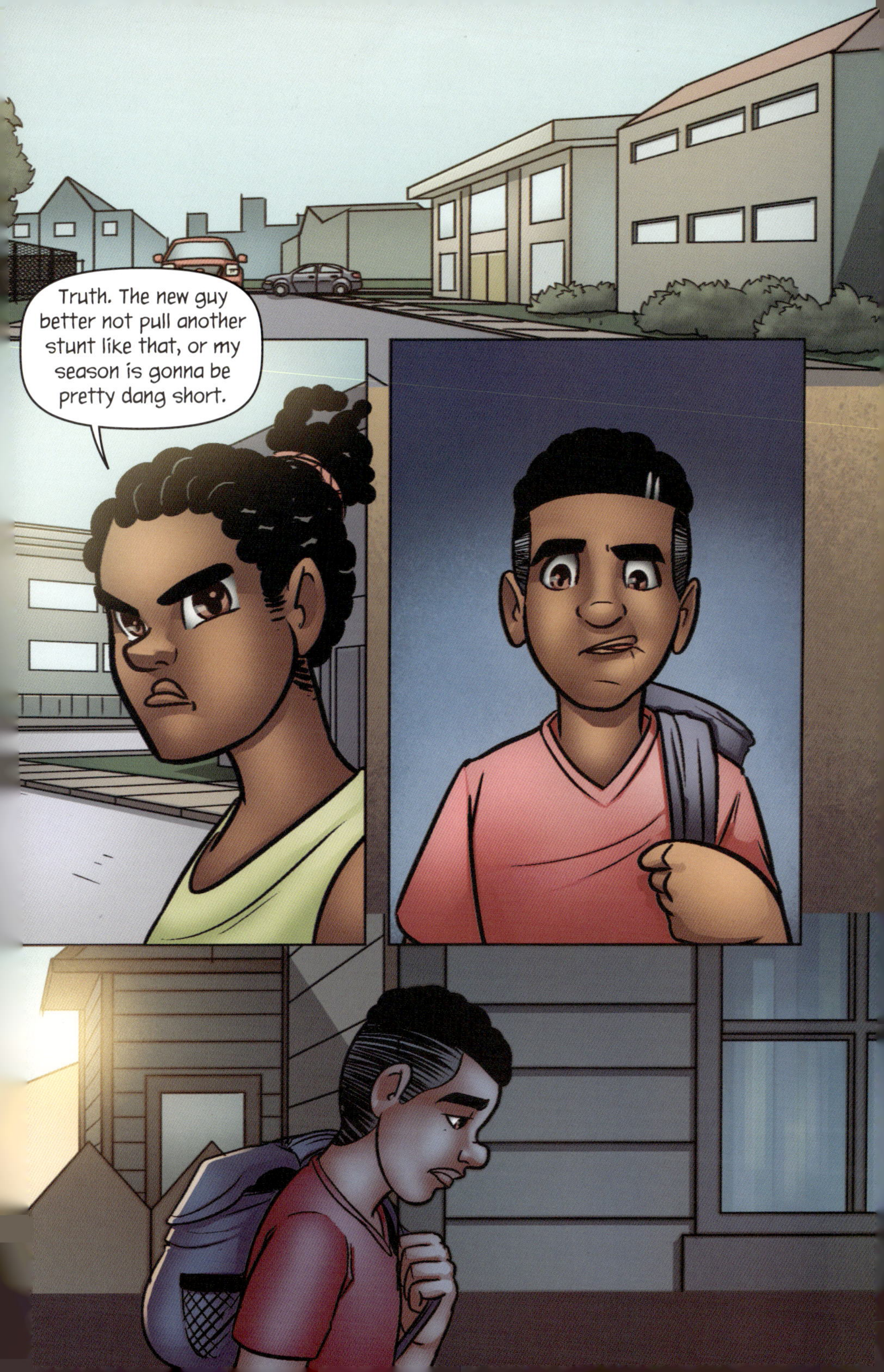
Truth. The new guy better not pull another stunt like that, or my season is gonna be pretty dang short.

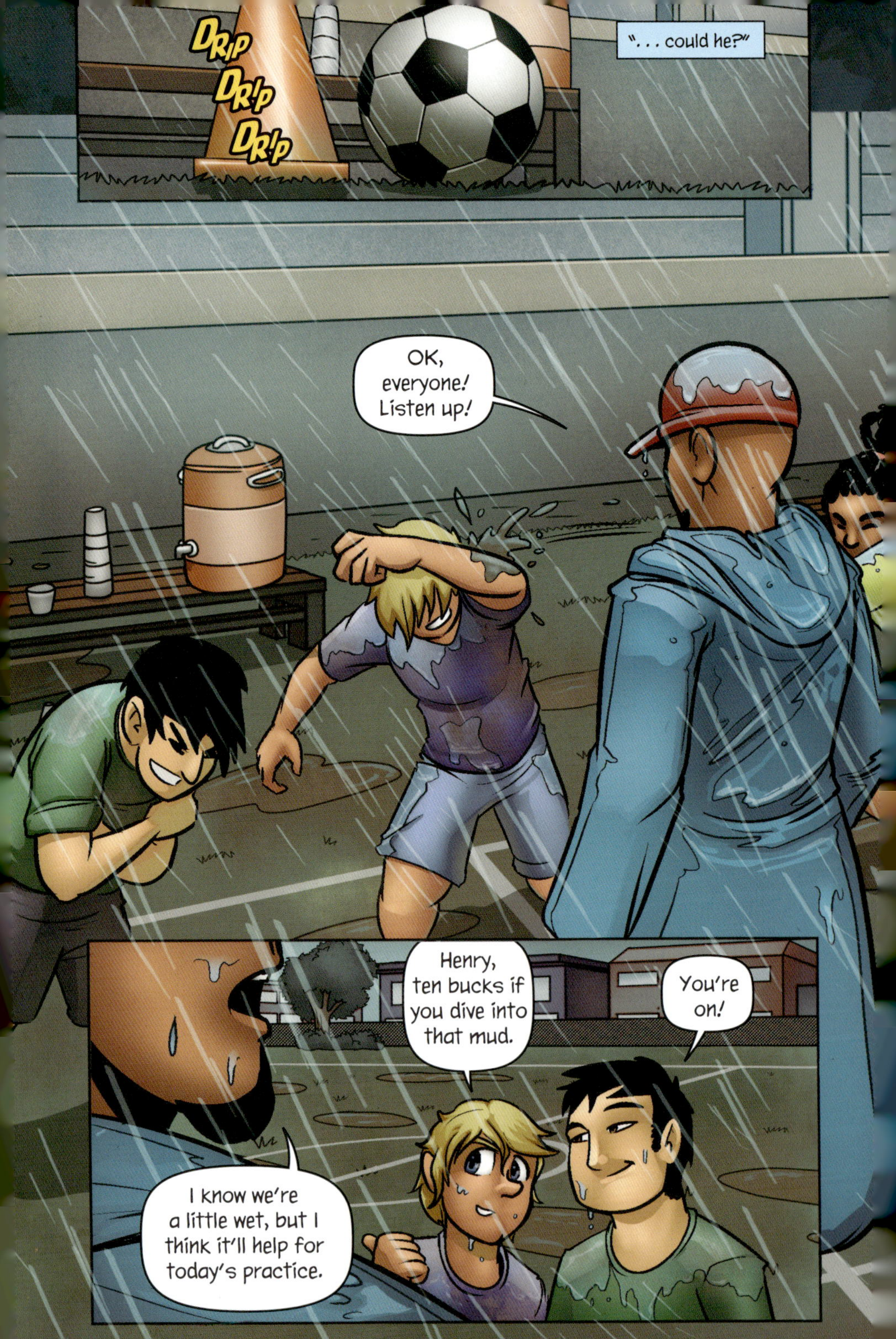
DRIP
DRIP
DRIP
". . . could he?"
OK, everyone! Listen up!
Henry, ten bucks if you dive into that mud.
You're on!
I know we're a little wet, but I think it'll help for today's practice.

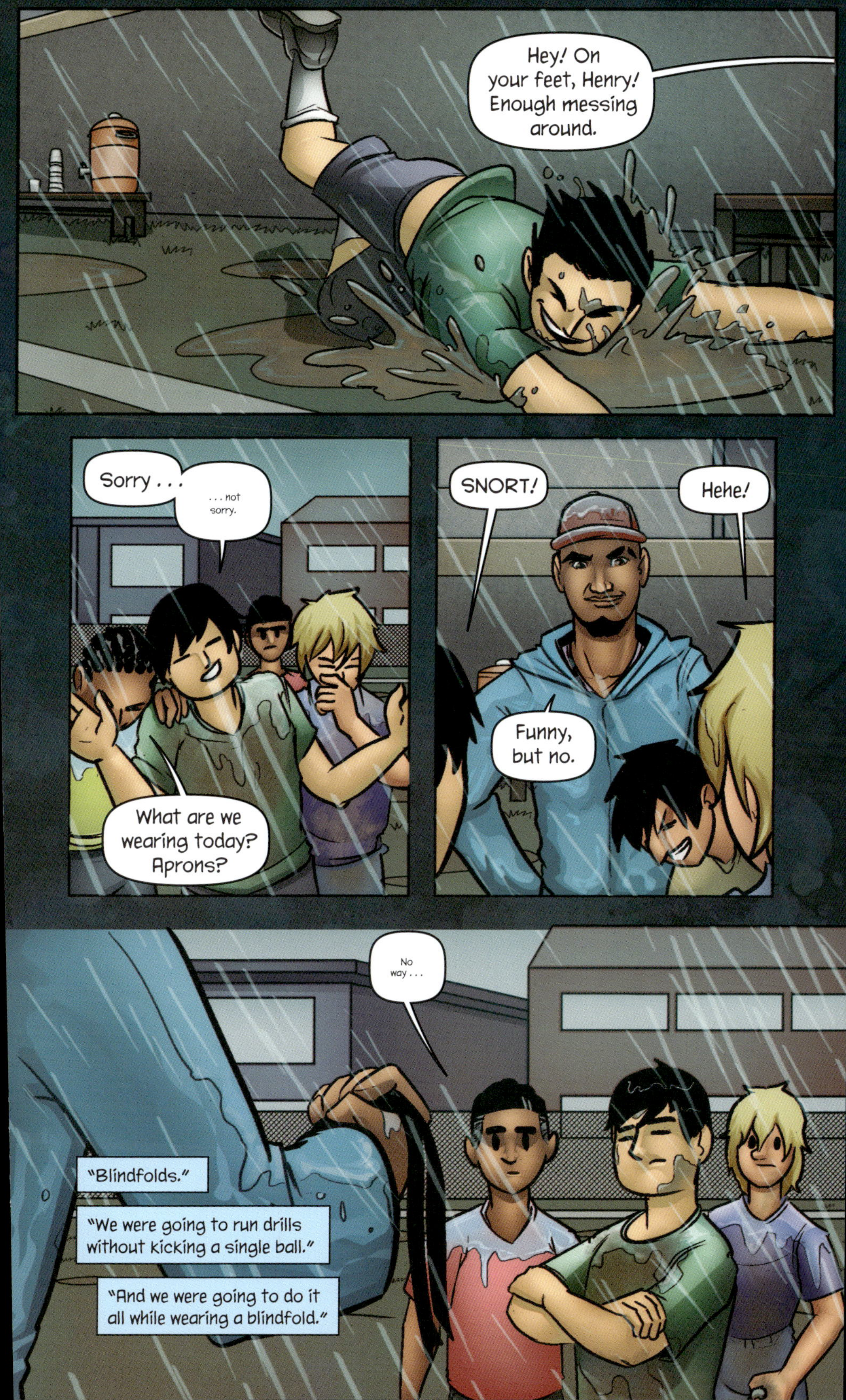
Hey! On your feet, Henry! Enough messing around.
Sorry . . .
. . . not sorry.
What are we wearing today? Aprons?
SNORT!
Hehe!
Funny, but no.
No way . . .
"Blindfolds."
"We were going to run drills without kicking a single ball."
"And we were going to do it all while wearing a blindfold."

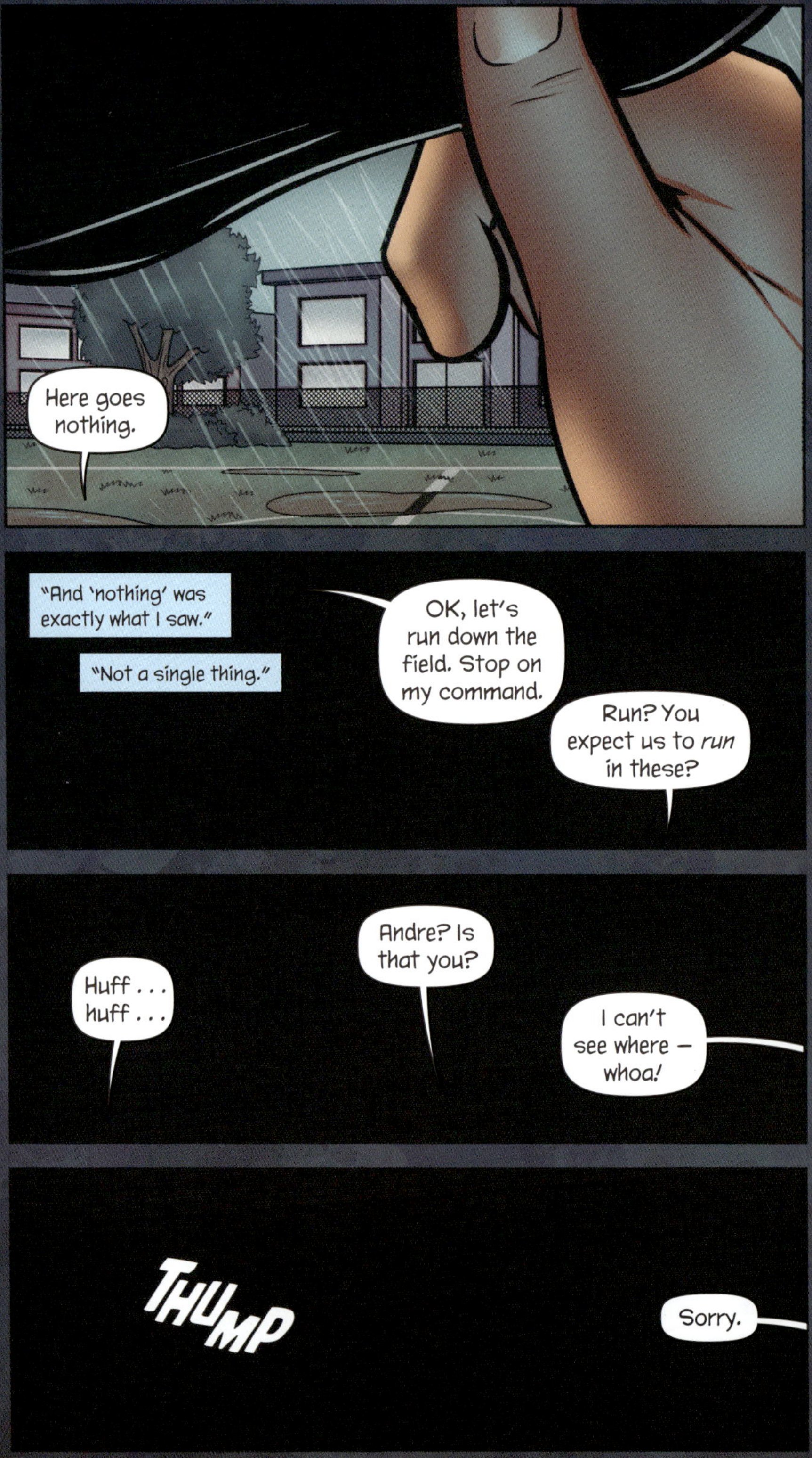
Here goes nothing.
"And 'nothing' was exactly what I saw."
"Not a single thing."
OK, let's run down the field. Stop on my command.
Run? You expect us to *run* in these?
Huff . . . huff . . .
Andre? Is that you?
I can't see where — whoa!
THUMP
Sorry.

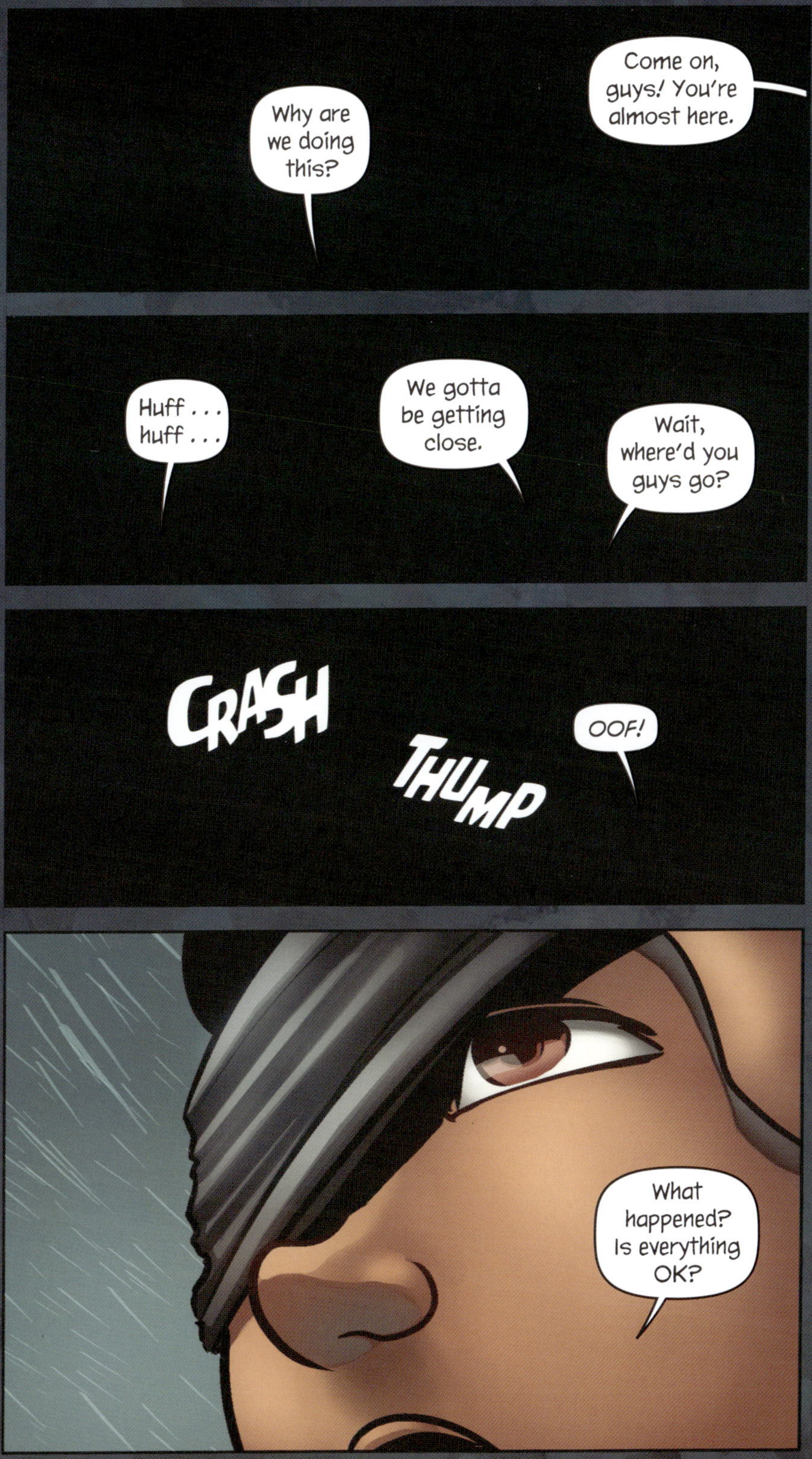
Come on, guys! You're almost here.
Why are we doing this?
Huff . . . huff . . .
We gotta be getting close.
Wait, where'd you guys go?
CRASH
THUMP
OOF!
What happened? Is everything OK?

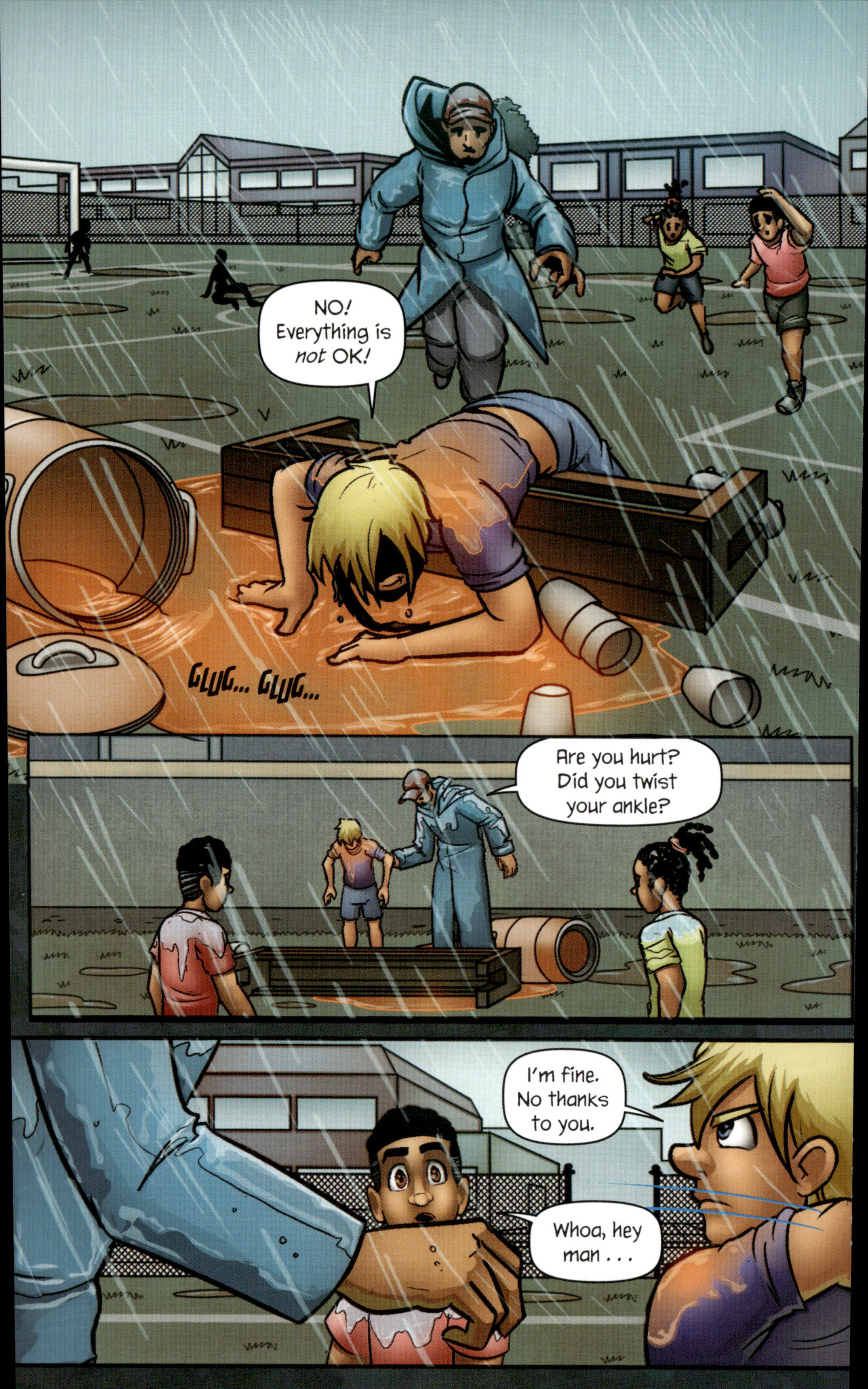
NO! Everything is *not* OK!
GLUG... GLUG...
Are you hurt? Did you twist your ankle?
I'm fine. No thanks to you.
Whoa, hey man . . .

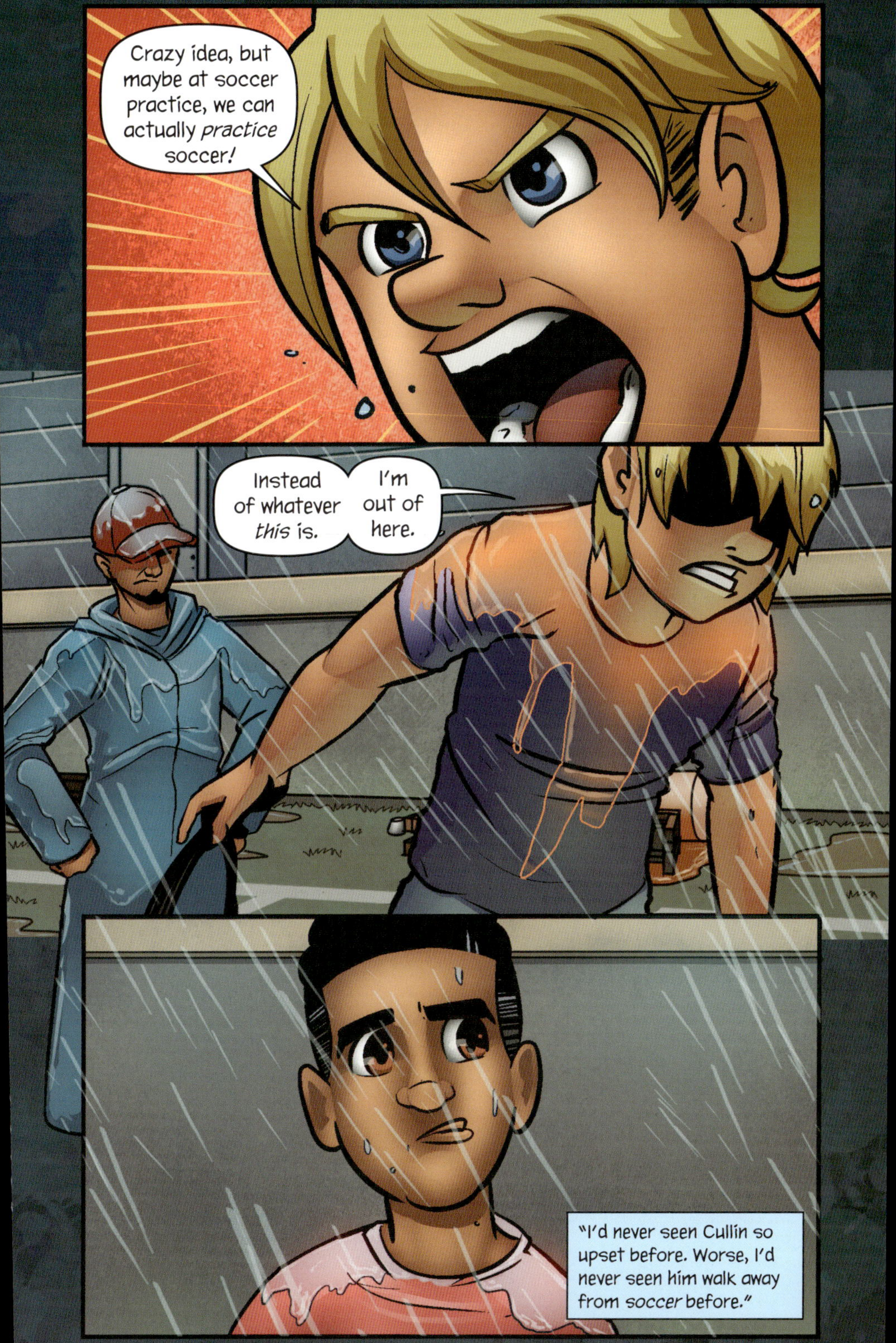
Crazy idea, but maybe at soccer practice, we can actually *practice* soccer!
Instead of whatever *this* is.
I'm out of here.
"I'd never seen Cullin so upset before. Worse, I'd never seen him walk away from *soccer* before."

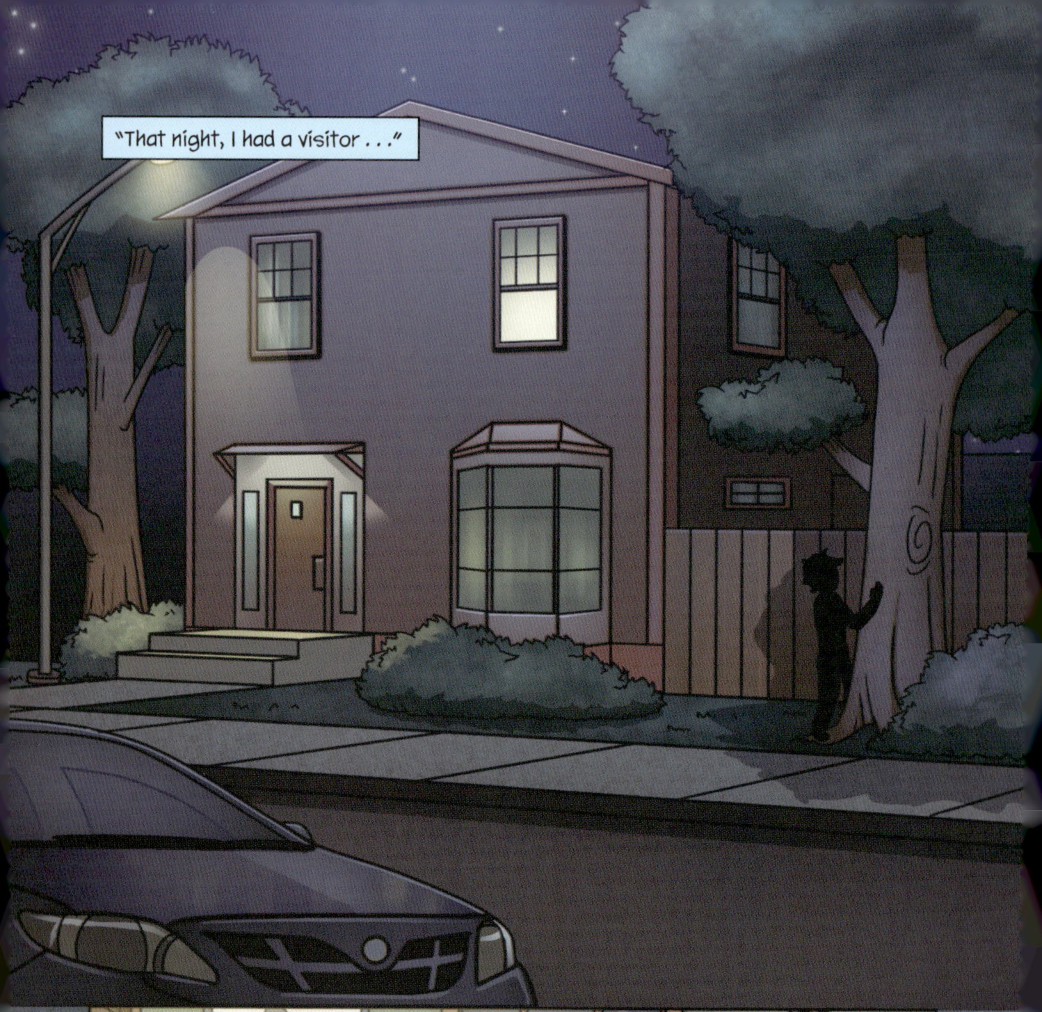
"That night, I had a visitor . . ."

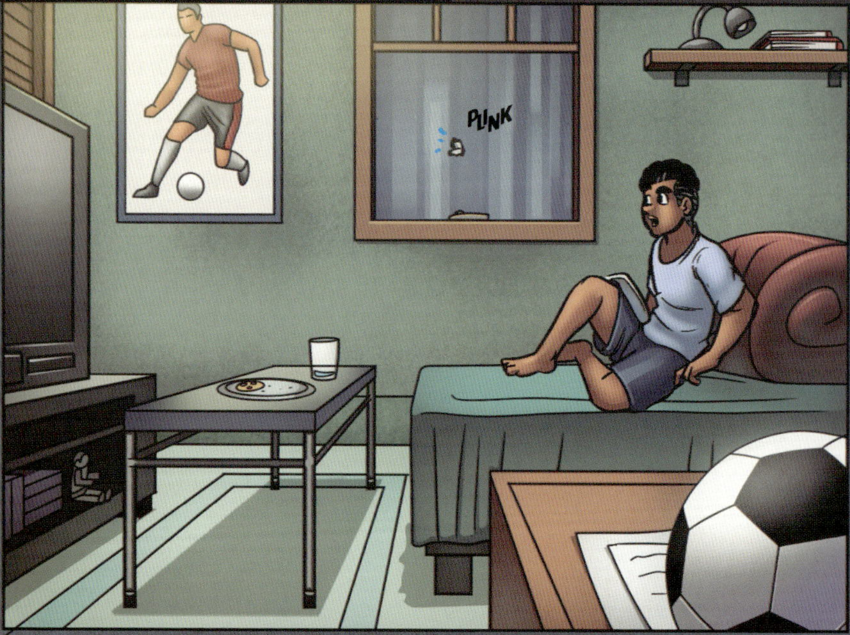
PLINK

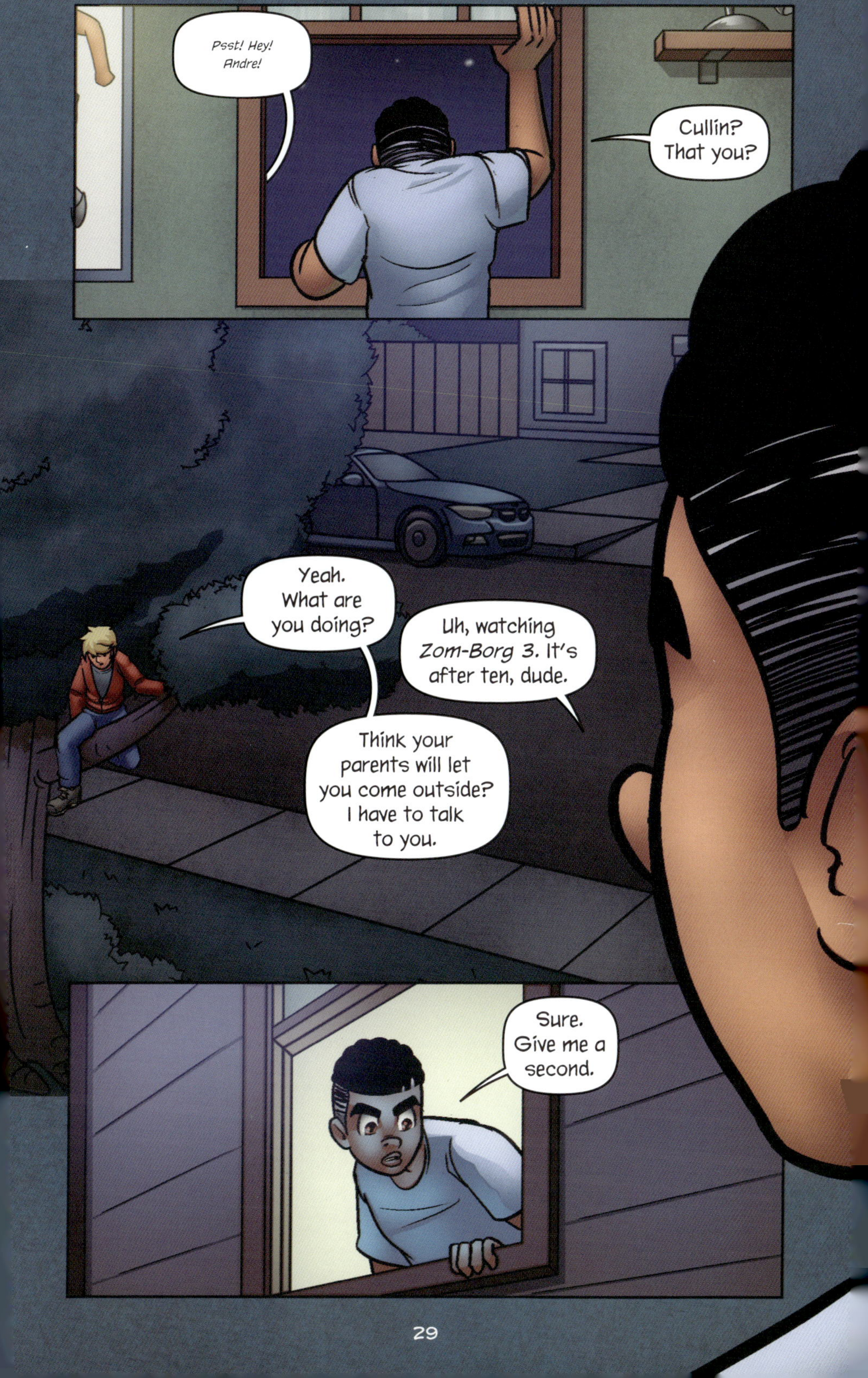
Psst! Hey! Andre!
Cullin? That you?
Yeah. What are you doing?
Uh, watching *Zom-Borg 3.* It's after ten, dude.
Think your parents will let you come outside? I have to talk to you.
Sure. Give me a second.

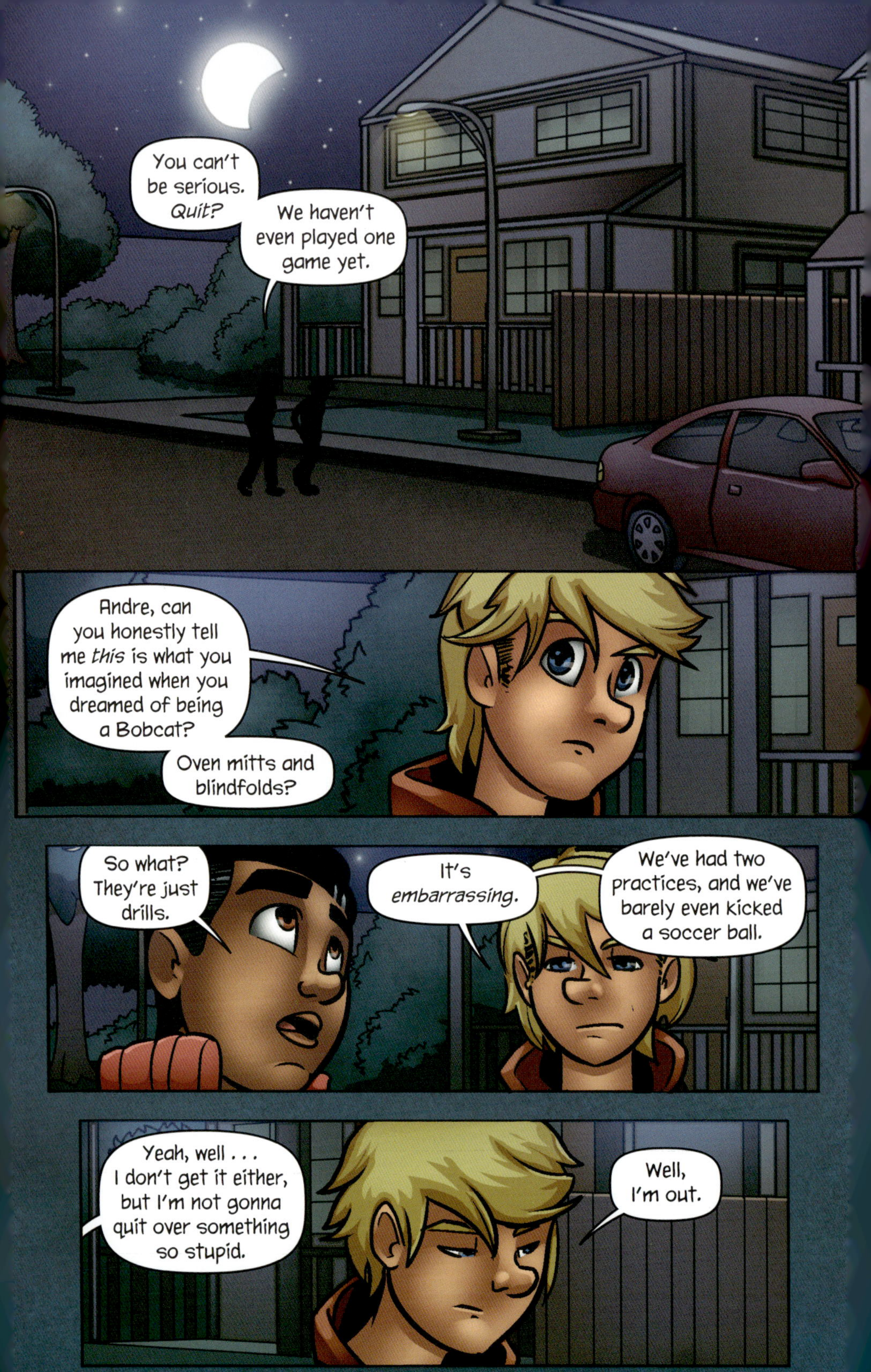
You can't be serious. *Quit?*
We haven't even played one game yet.
Andre, can you honestly tell me *this* is what you imagined when you dreamed of being a Bobcat?
Oven mitts and blindfolds?
So what? They're just drills.
It's *embarrassing*.
We've had two practices, and we've barely even kicked a soccer ball.
Yeah, well . . . I don't get it either, but I'm not gonna quit over something so stupid.
Well, I'm out.

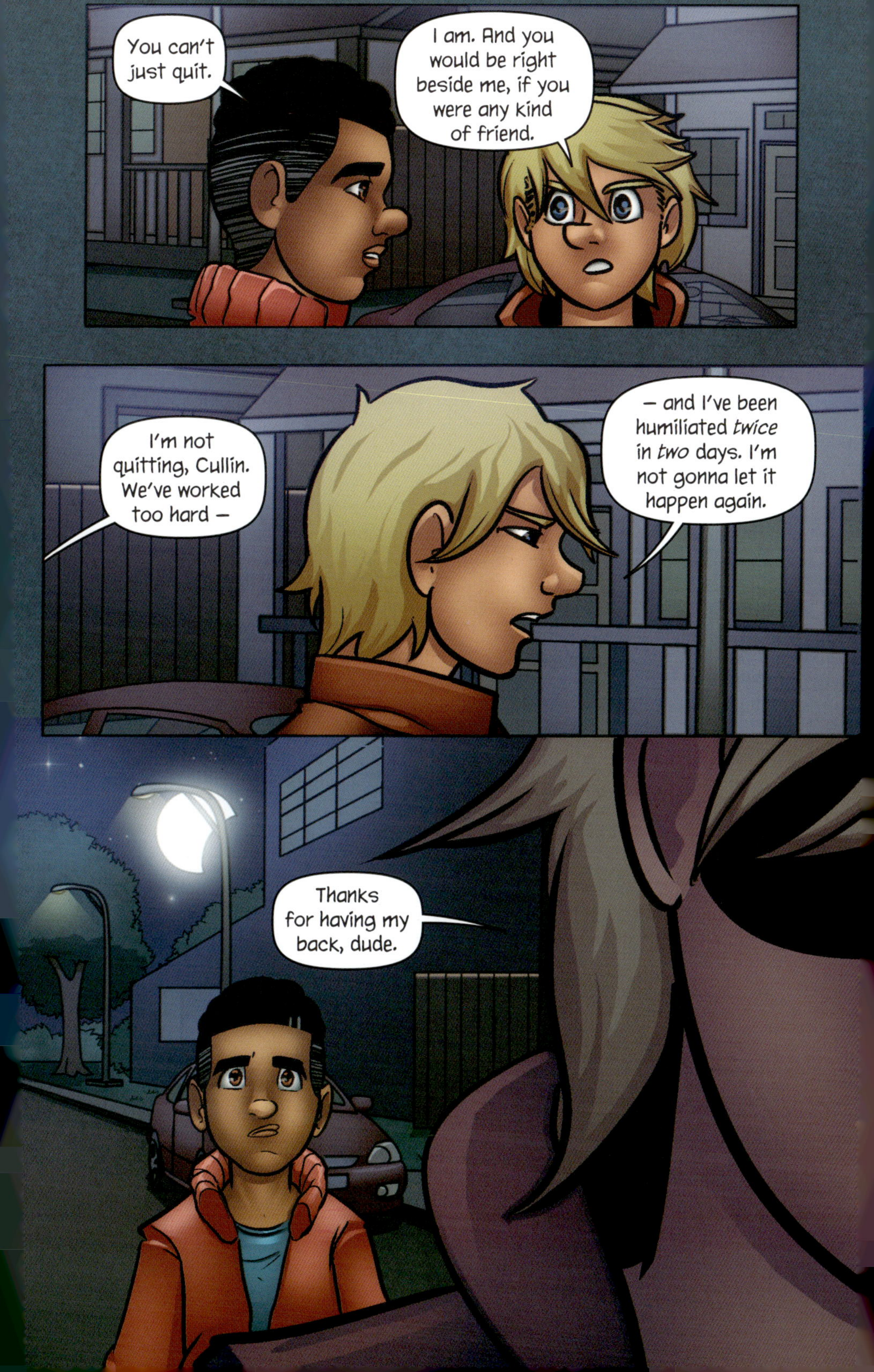
You can't just quit.
I am. And you would be right beside me, if you were any kind of friend.
I'm not quitting, Cullin. We've worked too hard –
– and I've been humiliated *twice* in *two* days. I'm not gonna let it happen again.
Thanks for having my back, dude.

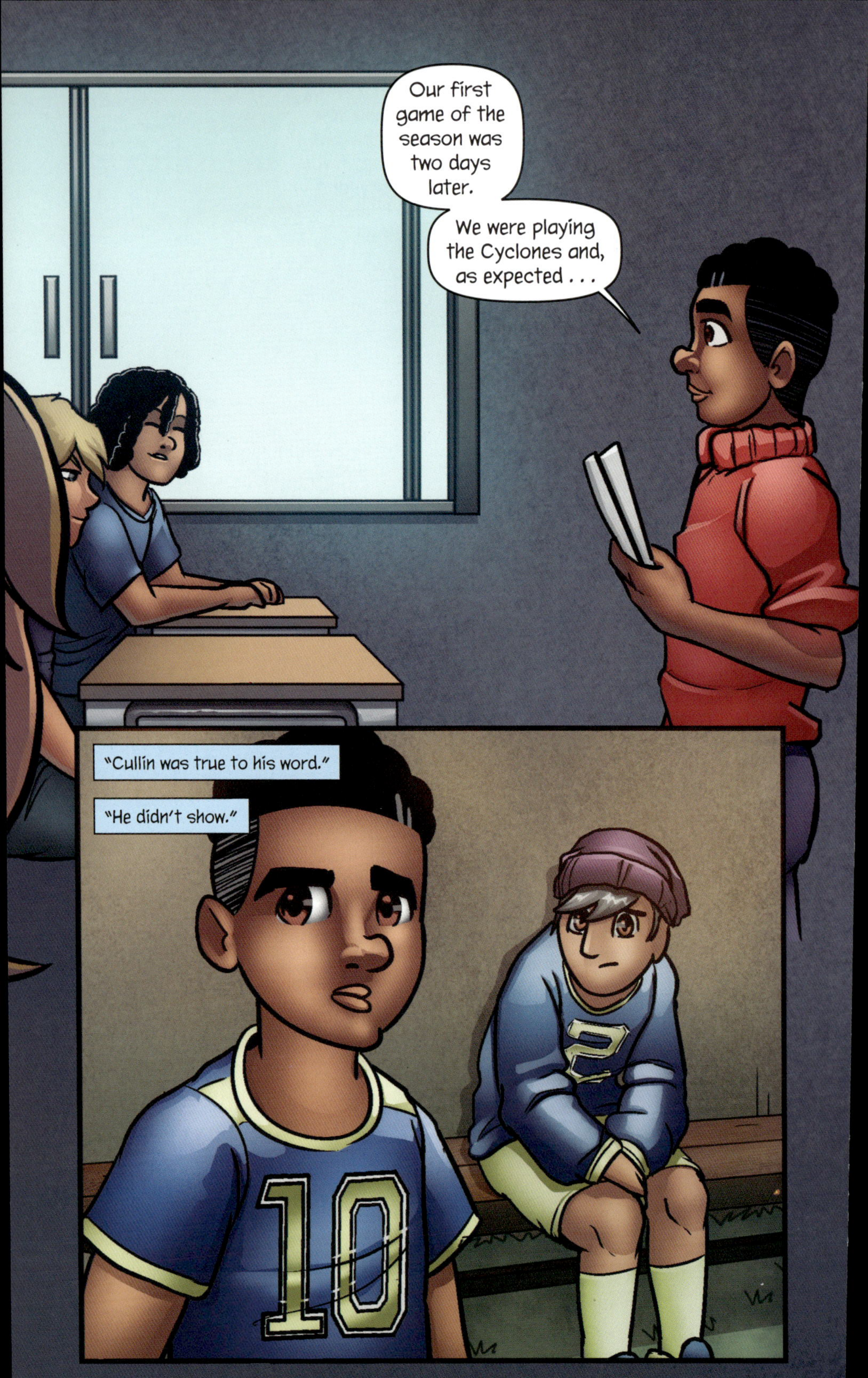
Our first game of the season was two days later.
We were playing the Cyclones and, as expected . . .
"Cullin was true to his word."
"He didn't show."

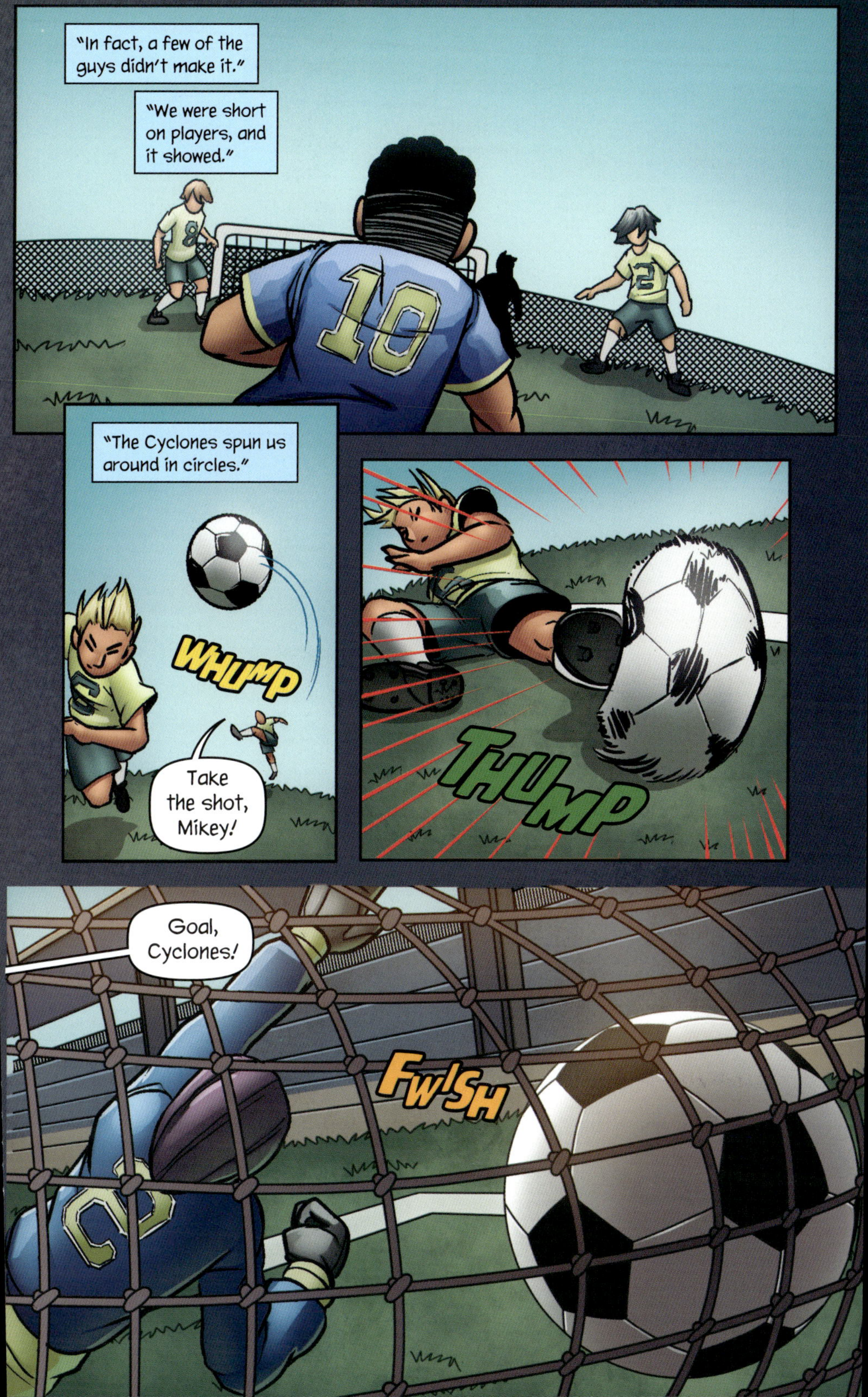
"In fact, a few of the guys didn't make it."
"We were short on players, and it showed."
"The Cyclones spun us around in circles."
WHUMP
Take the shot, Mikey!
THUMP
Goal, Cyclones!
FWISH

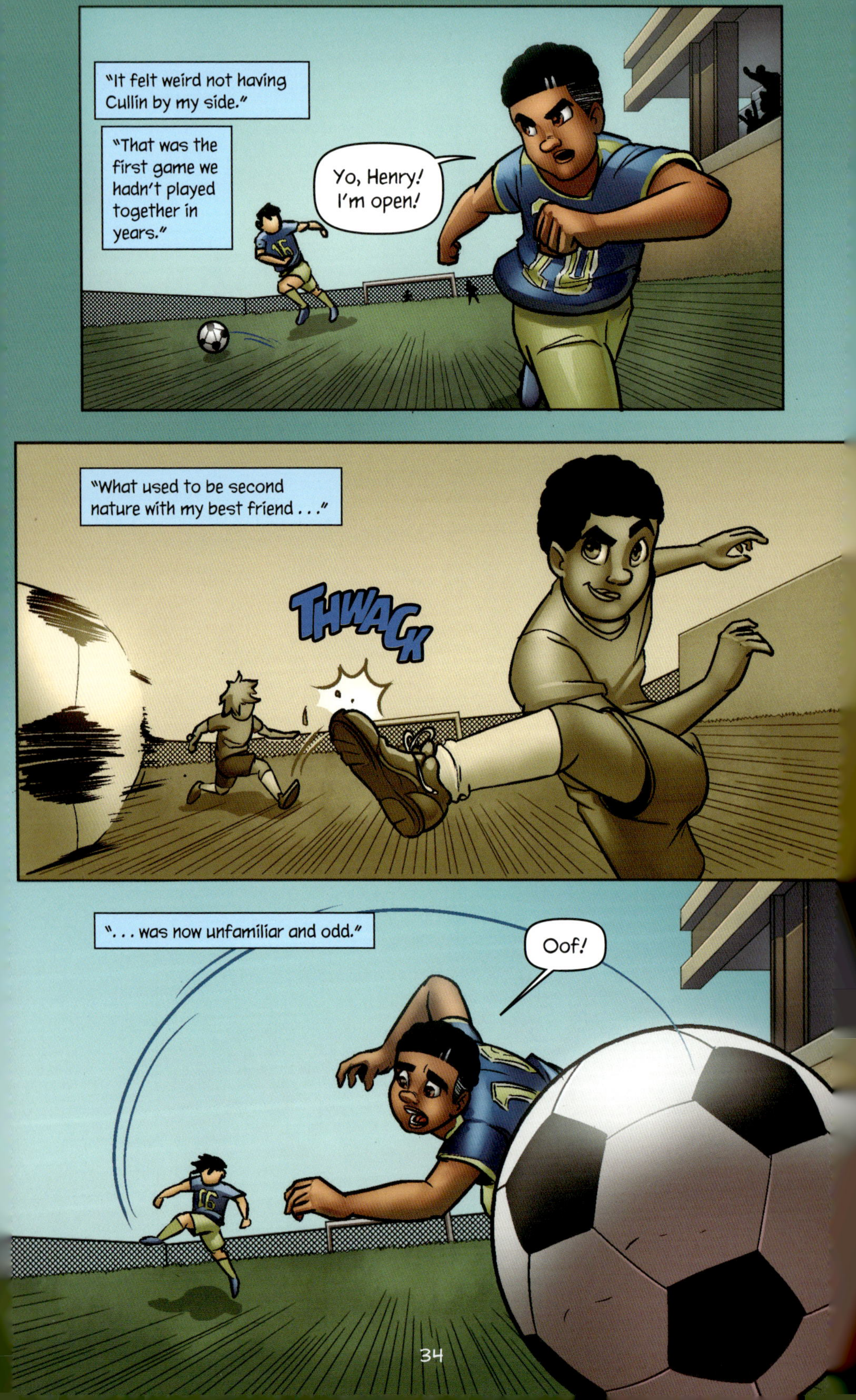
"It felt weird not having Cullin by my side."
"That was the first game we hadn't played together in years."
Yo, Henry! I'm open!
"What used to be second nature with my best friend . . ."
THWACK
". . . was now unfamiliar and odd."
Oof!

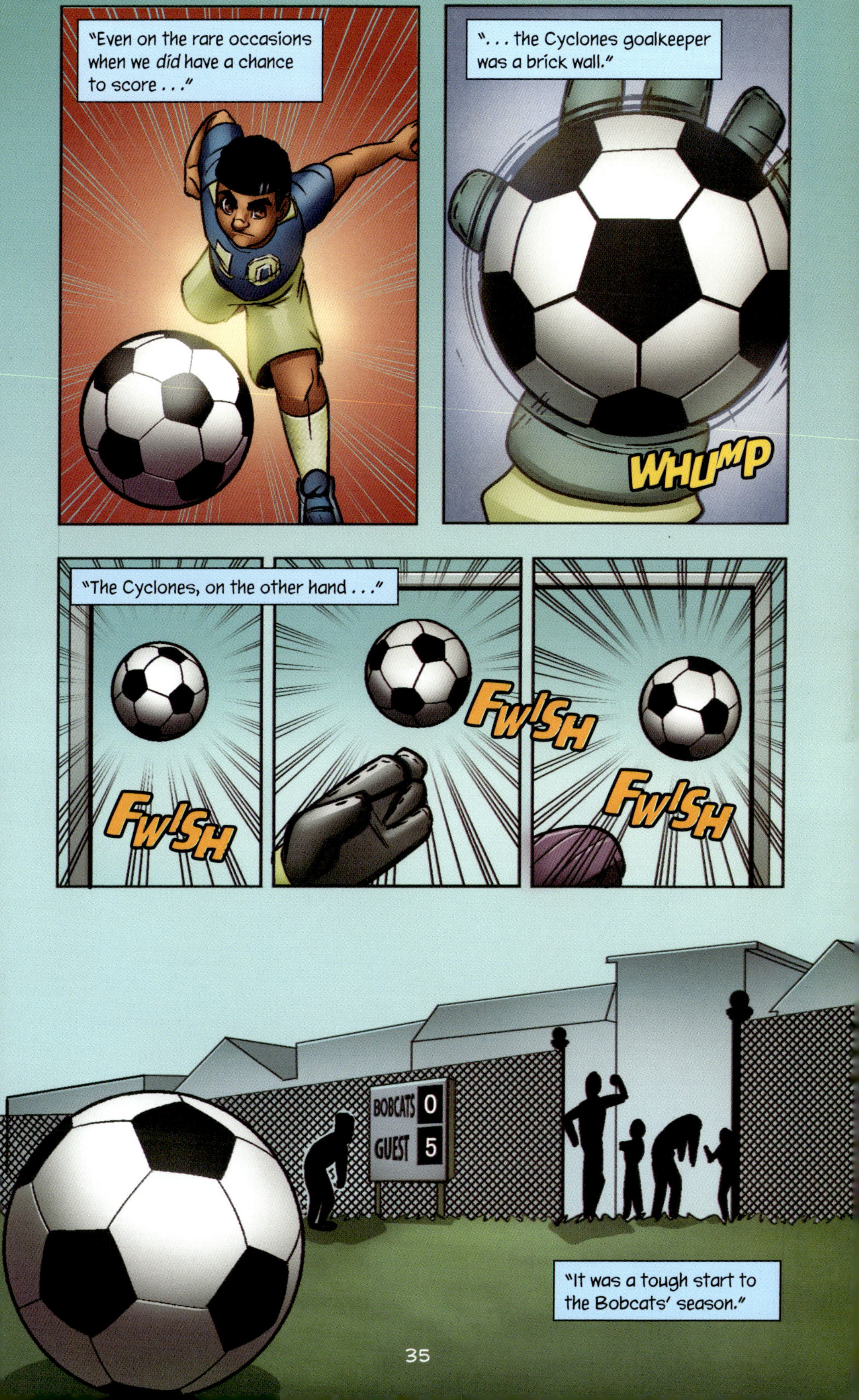
"Even on the rare occasions when we *did* have a chance to score . . ."
". . . the Cyclones goalkeeper was a brick wall."
WHUMP
"The Cyclones, on the other hand . . ."
FWISH
FWISH
FWISH
BOBCATS 0
GUEST 5
"It was a tough start to the Bobcats' season."

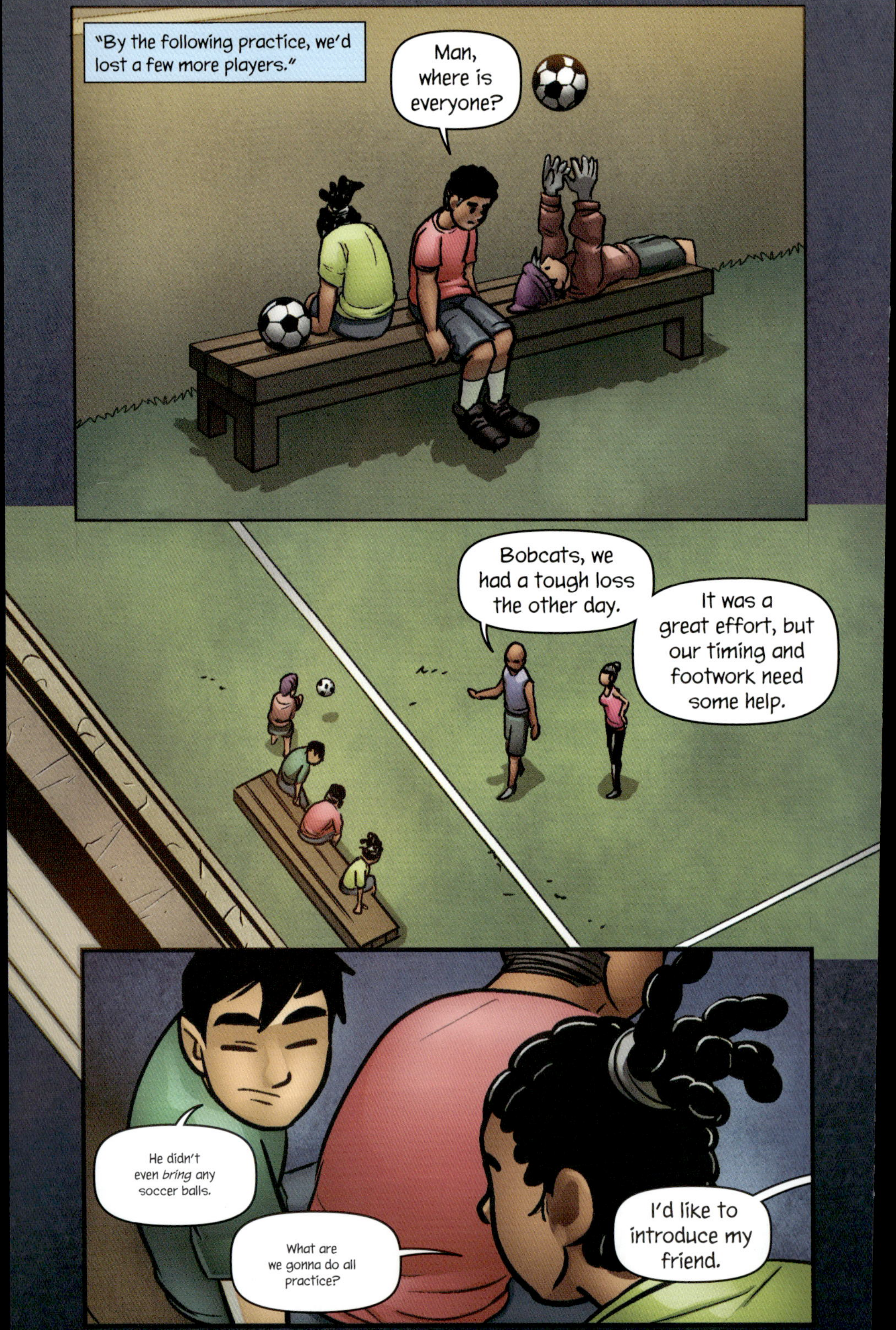
"By the following practice, we'd lost a few more players."
Man, where is everyone?
Bobcats, we had a tough loss the other day.
It was a great effort, but our timing and footwork need some help.
He didn't even *bring* any soccer balls.
What are we gonna do all practice?
I'd like to introduce my friend.

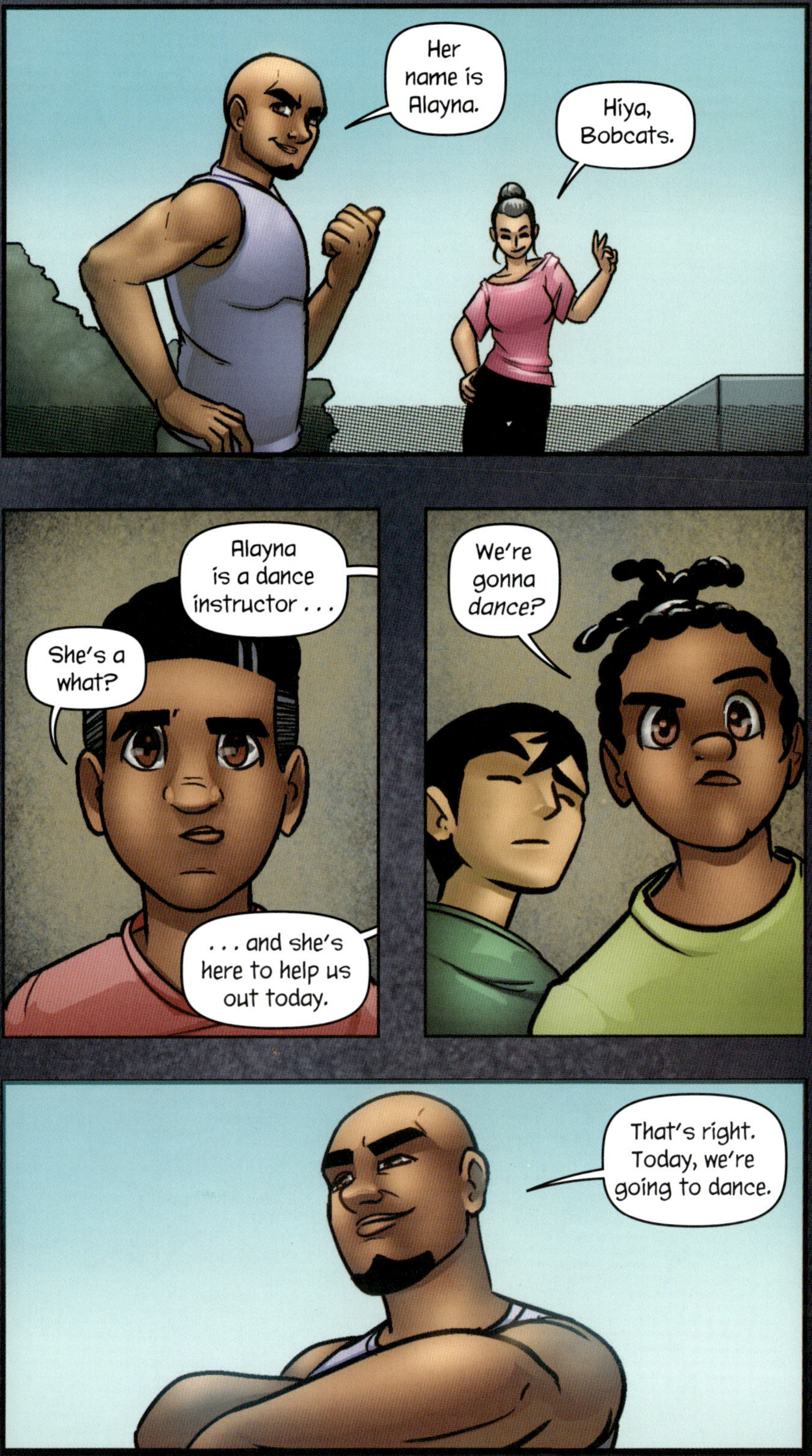
Her name is Alayna.
Hiya, Bobcats.
Alayna is a dance instructor . . .
She's a what?
. . . and she's here to help us out today.
We're gonna dance?
That's right. Today, we're going to dance.

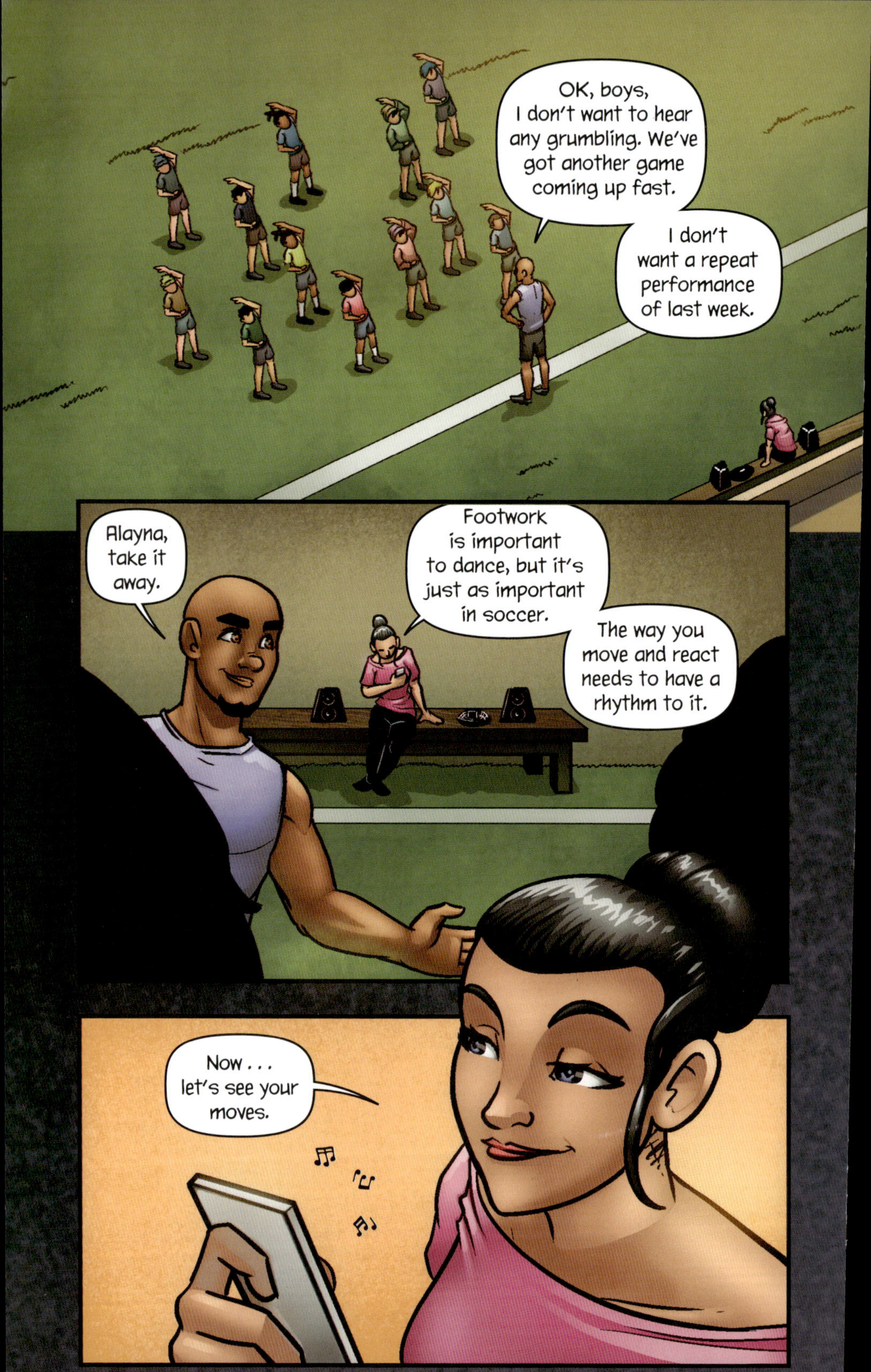
OK, boys, I don't want to hear any grumbling. We've got another game coming up fast.
I don't want a repeat performance of last week.
Alayna, take it away.
Footwork is important to dance, but it's just as important in soccer.
The way you move and react needs to have a rhythm to it.
Now . . . let's see your moves.

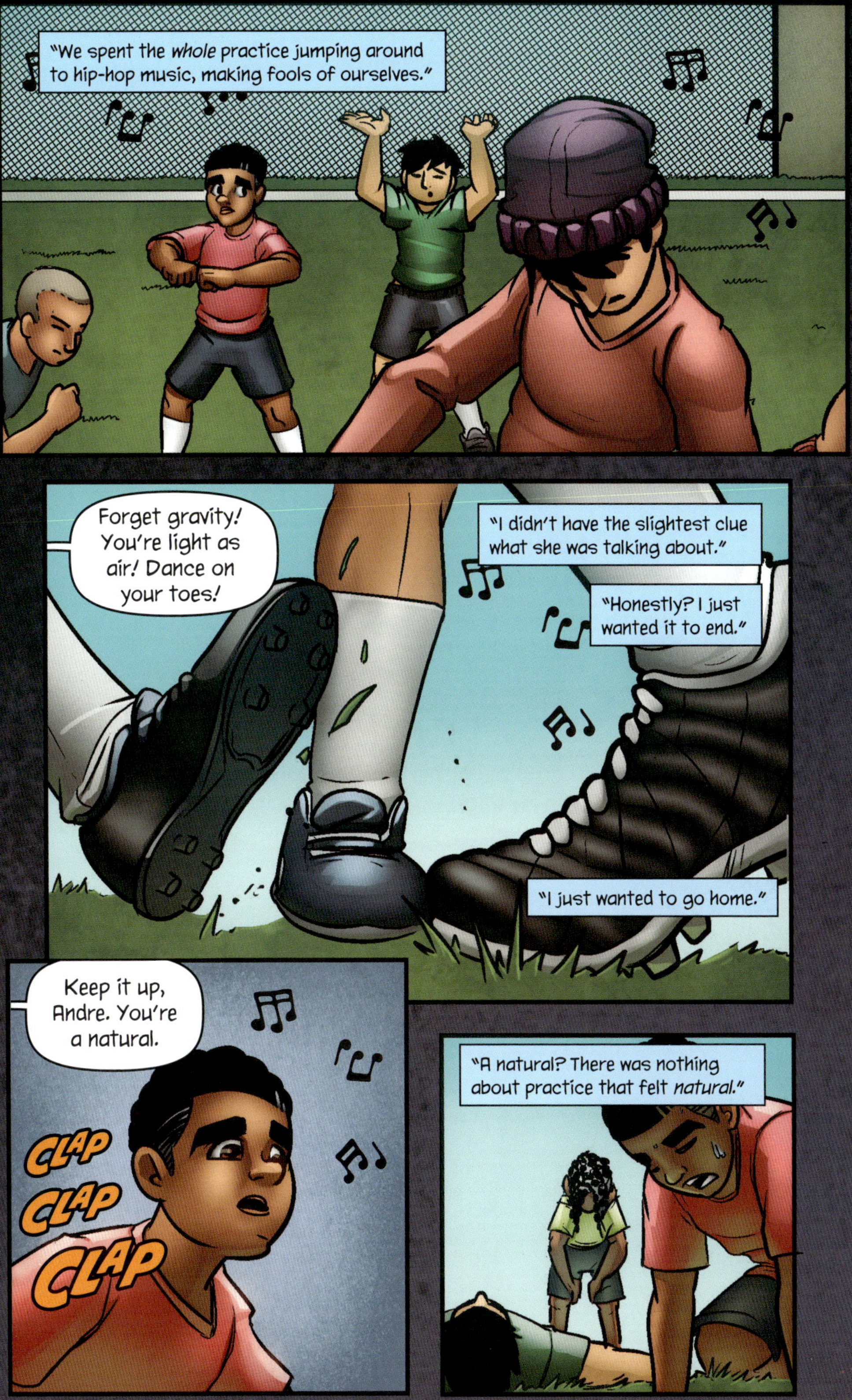
"We spent the *whole* practice jumping around to hip-hop music, making fools of ourselves."
Forget gravity! You're light as air! Dance on your toes!
"I didn't have the slightest clue what she was talking about."
"Honestly? I just wanted it to end."
"I just wanted to go home."
Keep it up, Andre. You're a natural.
CLAP
CLAP
CLAP
"A natural? There was nothing about practice that felt *natural*."

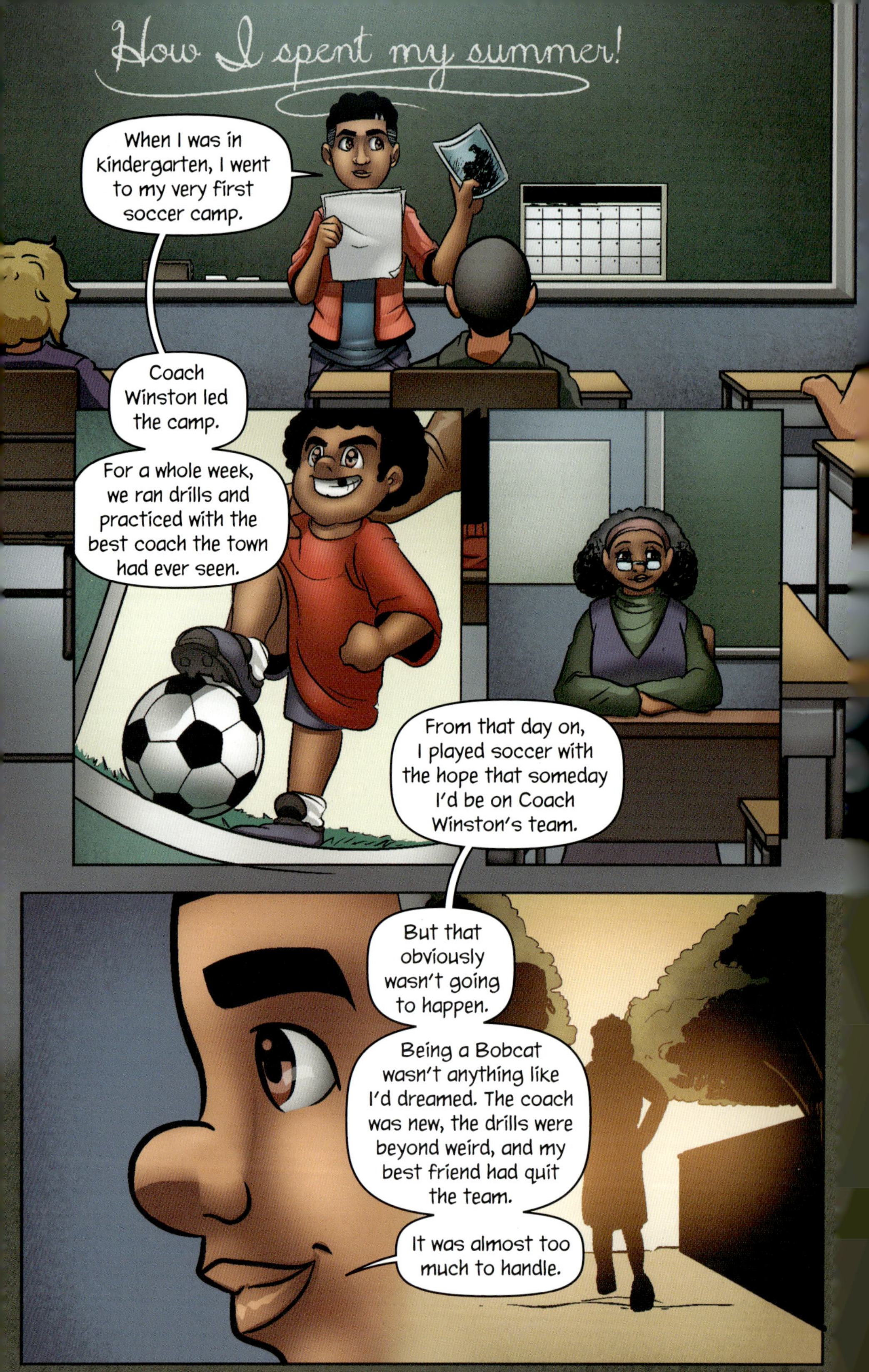
How I spent my summer!
When I was in kindergarten, I went to my very first soccer camp.
Coach Winston led the camp.
For a whole week, we ran drills and practiced with the best coach the town had ever seen.
From that day on, I played soccer with the hope that someday I'd be on Coach Winston's team.
But that obviously wasn't going to happen.
Being a Bobcat wasn't anything like I'd dreamed. The coach was new, the drills were beyond weird, and my best friend had quit the team.
It was almost too much to handle.

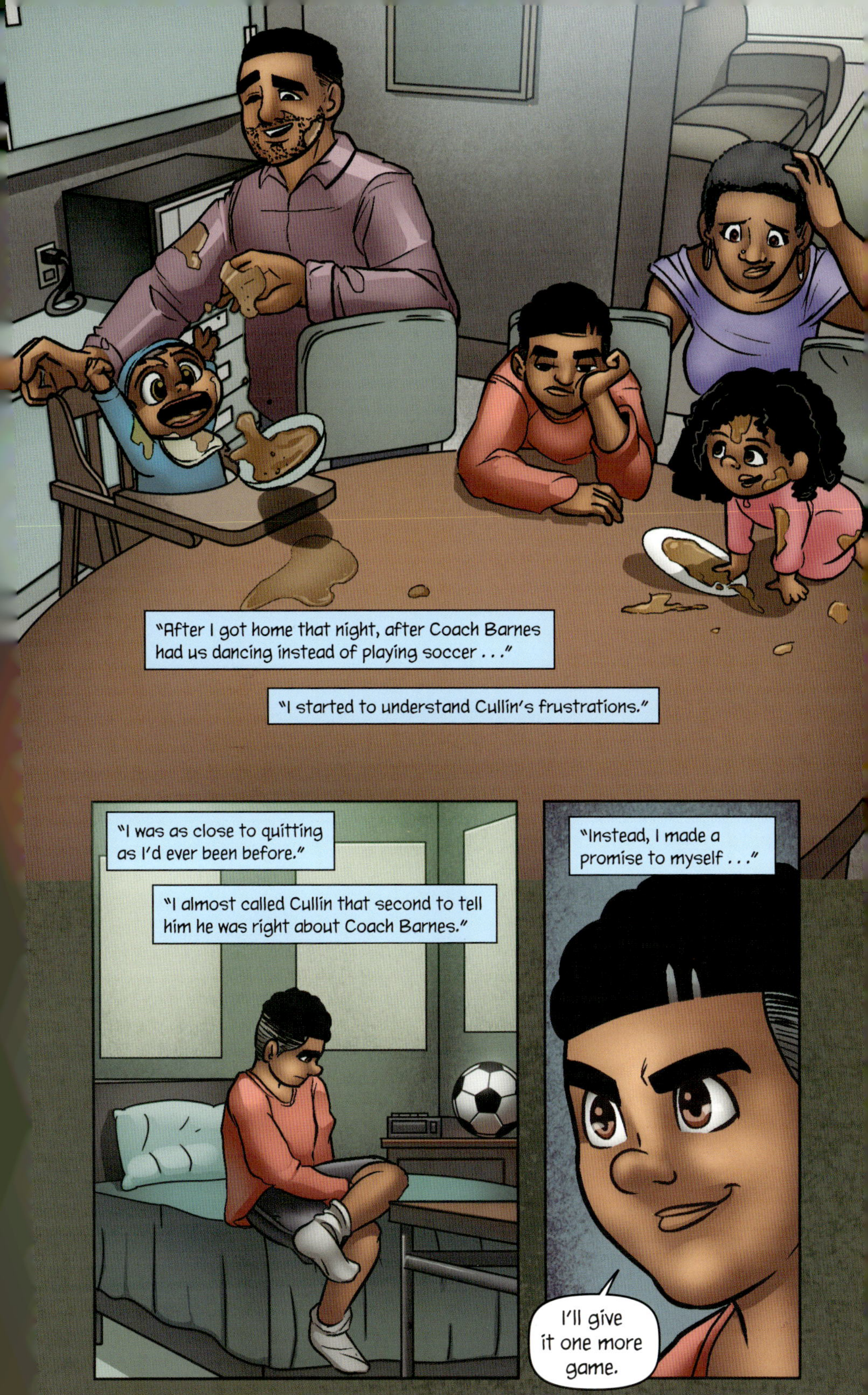
"After I got home that night, after Coach Barnes had us dancing instead of playing soccer . . ."
"I started to understand Cullin's frustrations."
"I was as close to quitting as I'd ever been before."
"I almost called Cullin that second to tell him he was right about Coach Barnes."
"Instead, I made a promise to myself . . ."
I'll give it one more game.

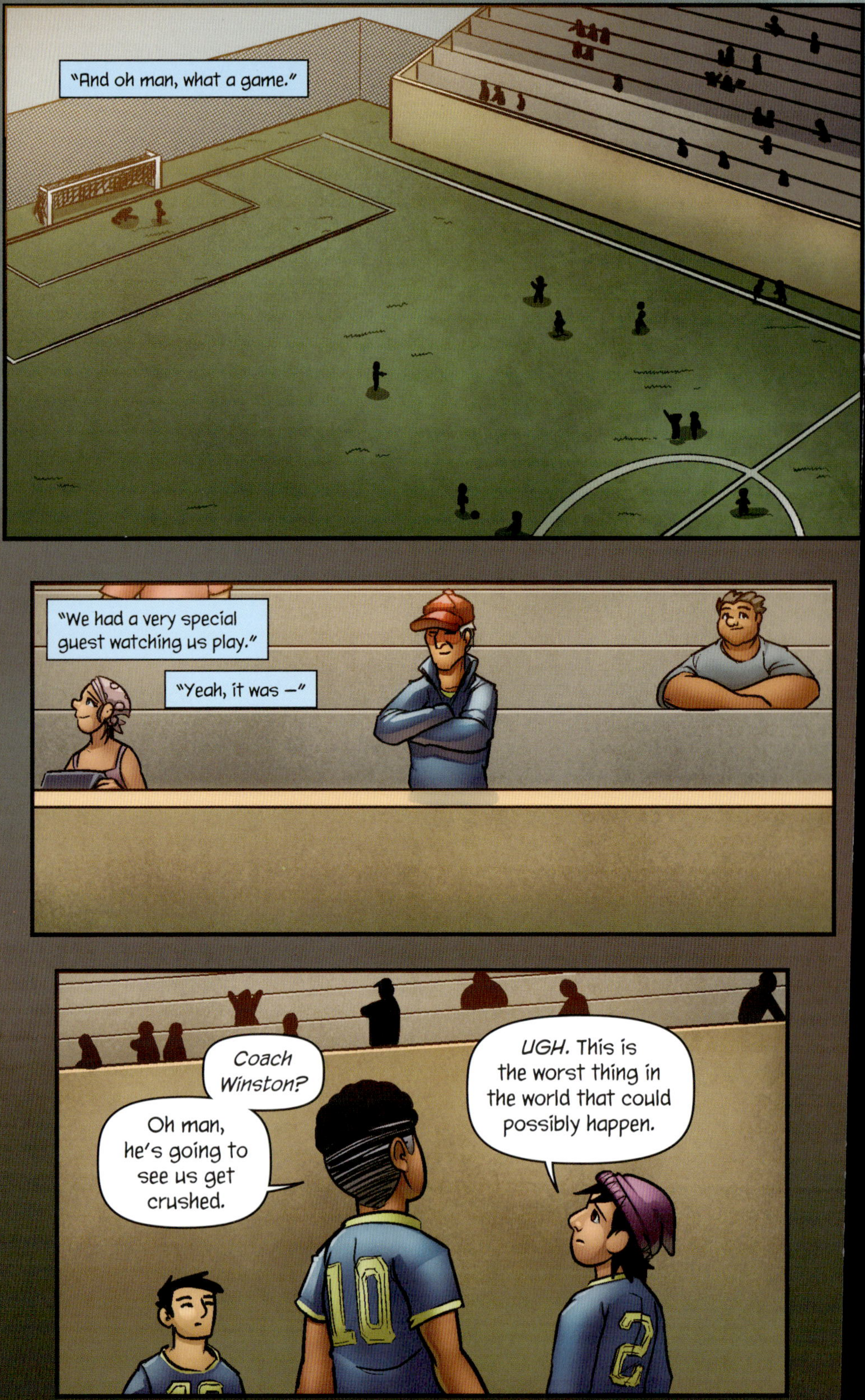
"And oh man, what a game."
"We had a very special guest watching us play."
"Yeah, it was —"
Coach Winston?
Oh man, he's going to see us get crushed.
UGH. This is the worst thing in the world that could possibly happen.
10
2

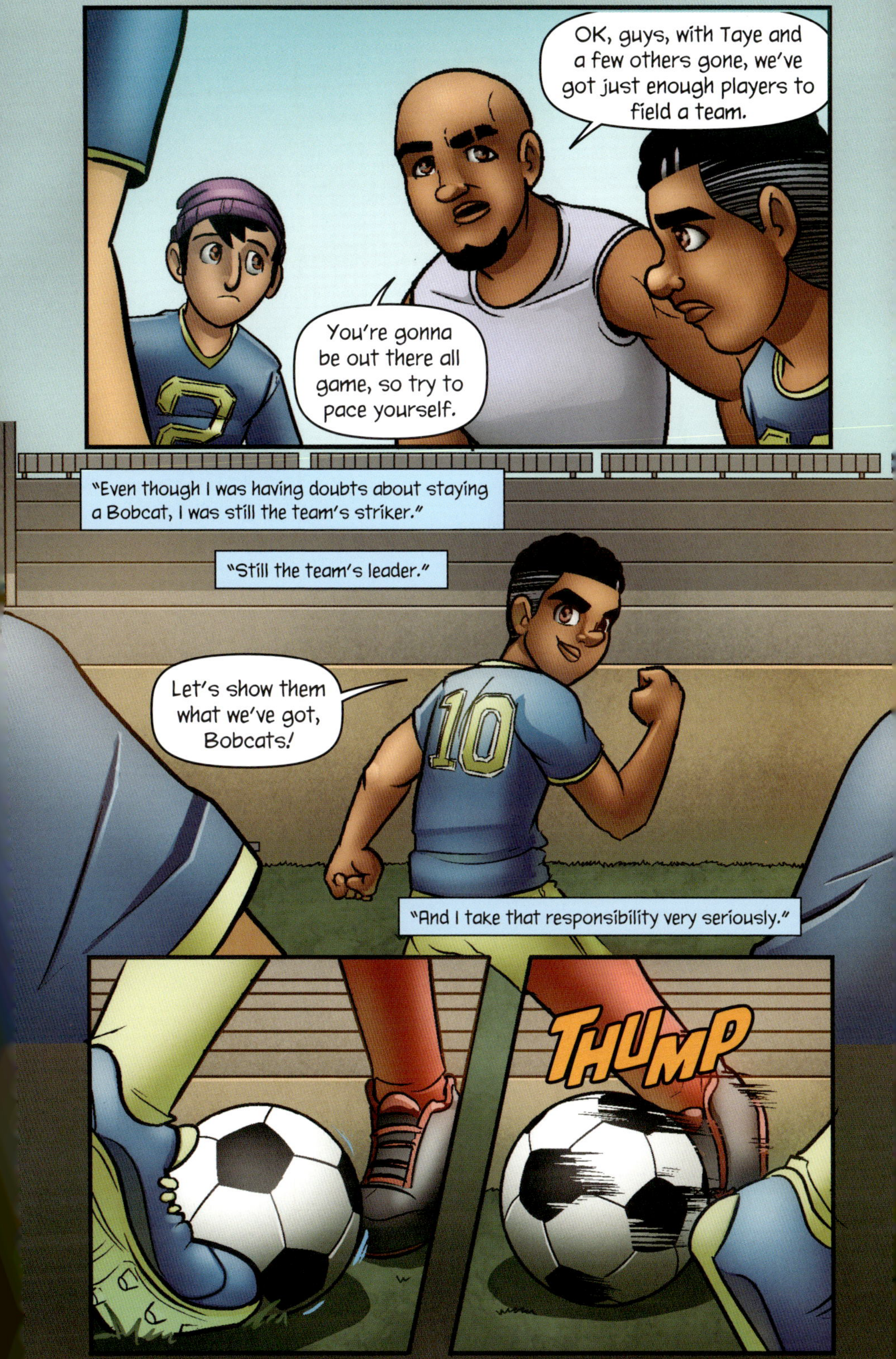
OK, guys, with Taye and a few others gone, we've got just enough players to field a team.
You're gonna be out there all game, so try to pace yourself.
"Even though I was having doubts about staying a Bobcat, I was still the team's striker."
"Still the team's leader."
Let's show them what we've got, Bobcats!
"And I take that responsibility very seriously."
THUMP

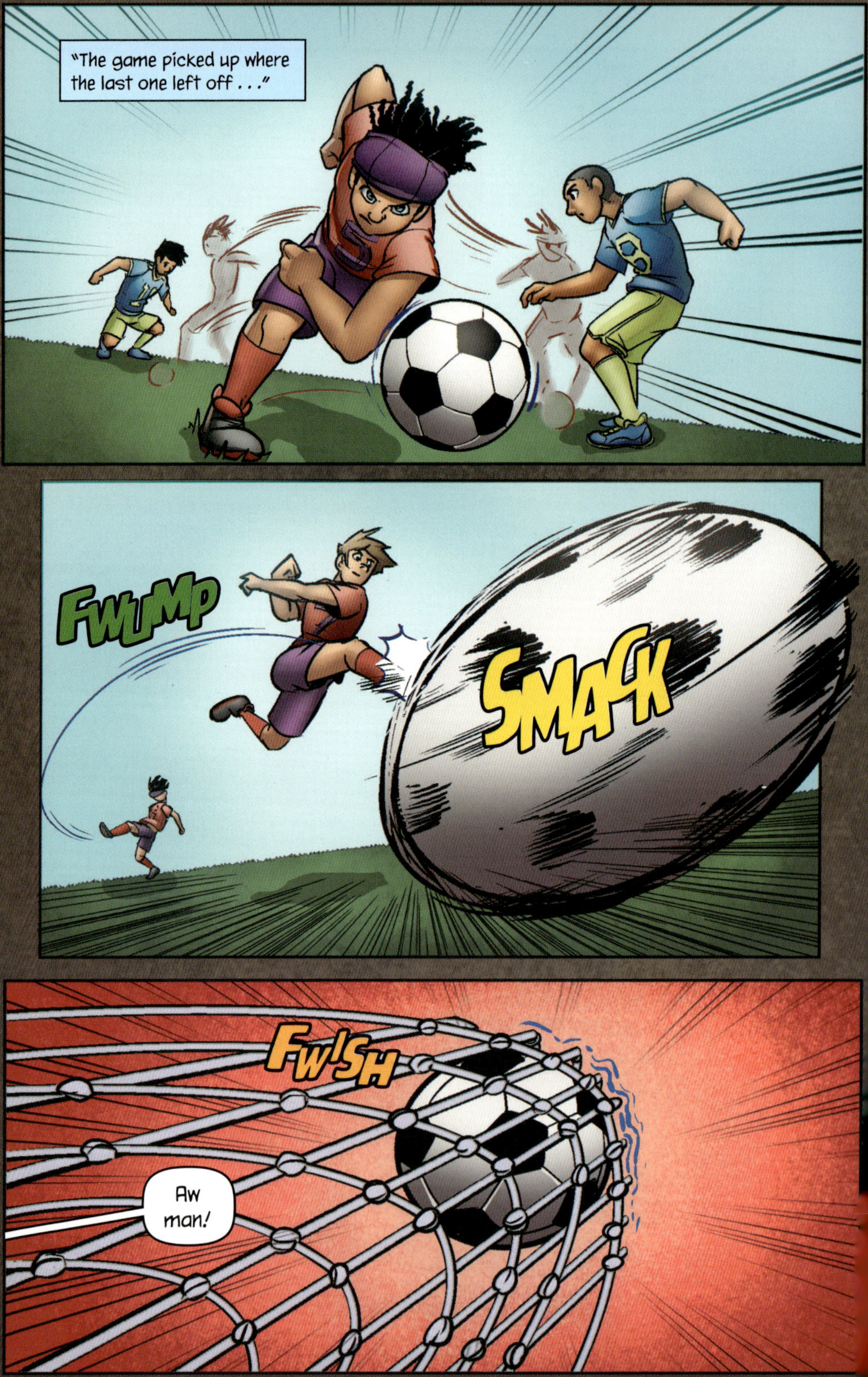
"The game picked up where the last one left off . . ."
FWUMP
SMACK
FWISH
Aw man!

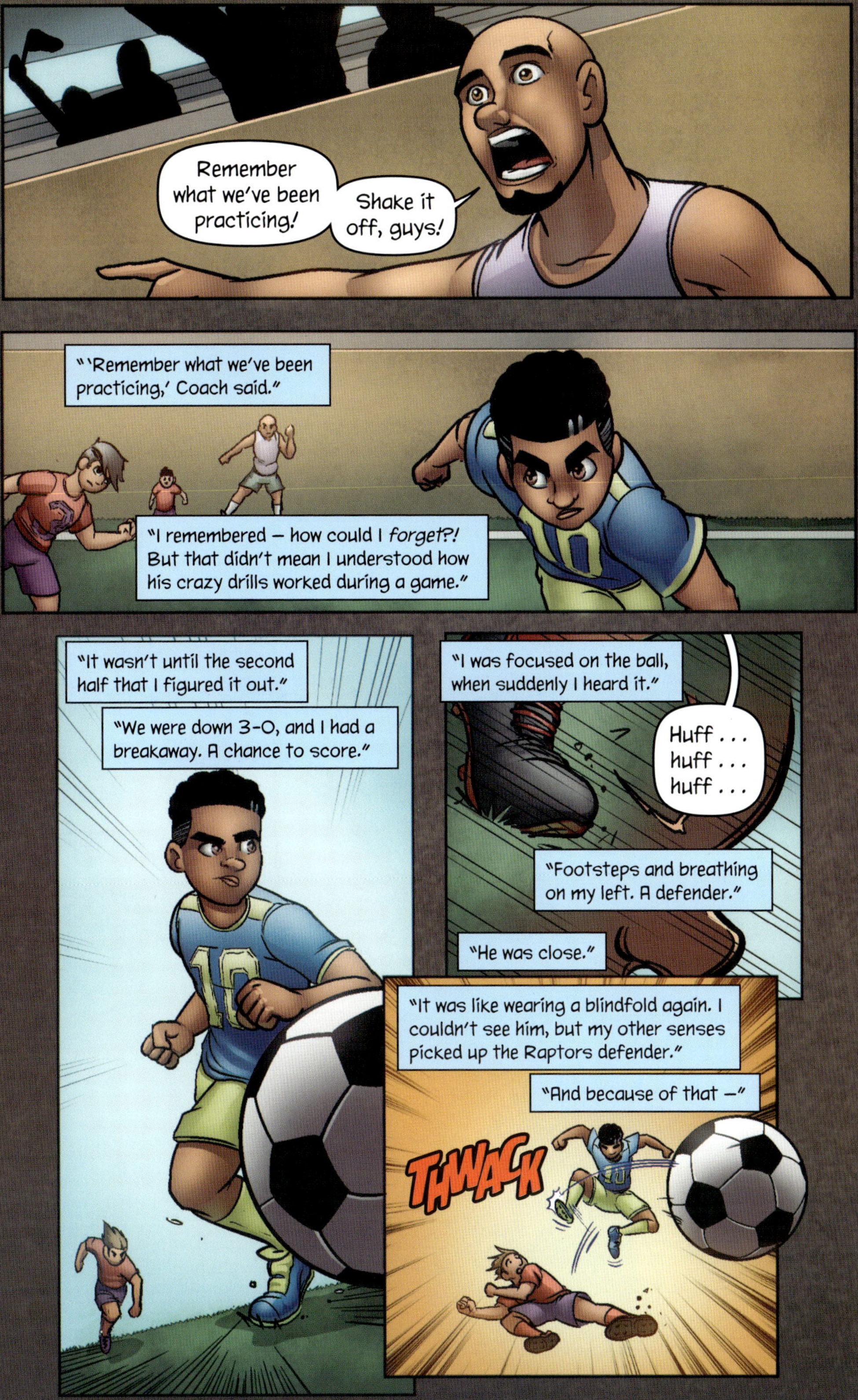
Remember what we've been practicing!
Shake it off, guys!
"'Remember what we've been practicing,' Coach said."
"I remembered — how could I *forget*?! But that didn't mean I understood how his crazy drills worked during a game."
"It wasn't until the second half that I figured it out."
"We were down 3-0, and I had a breakaway. A chance to score."
"I was focused on the ball, when suddenly I heard it."
Huff . . . huff . . . huff . . .
"Footsteps and breathing on my left. A defender."
"He was close."
"It was like wearing a blindfold again. I couldn't see him, but my other senses picked up the Raptors defender."
"And because of that —"
THWACK

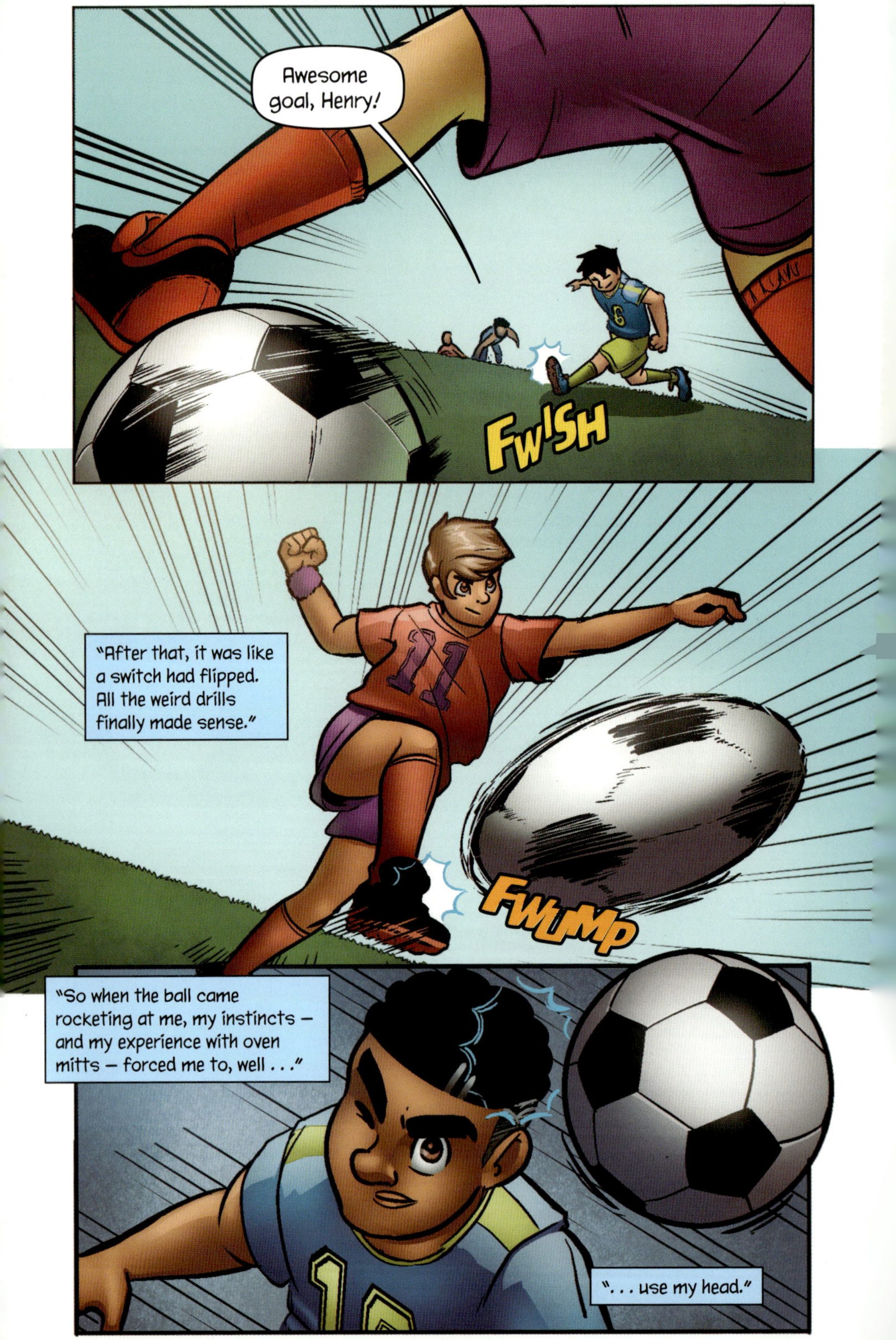
Awesome goal, Henry!
FW'SH
"After that, it was like a switch had flipped. All the weird drills finally made sense."
FWUMP
"So when the ball came rocketing at me, my instincts – and my experience with oven mitts – forced me to, well . . ."
". . . use my head."

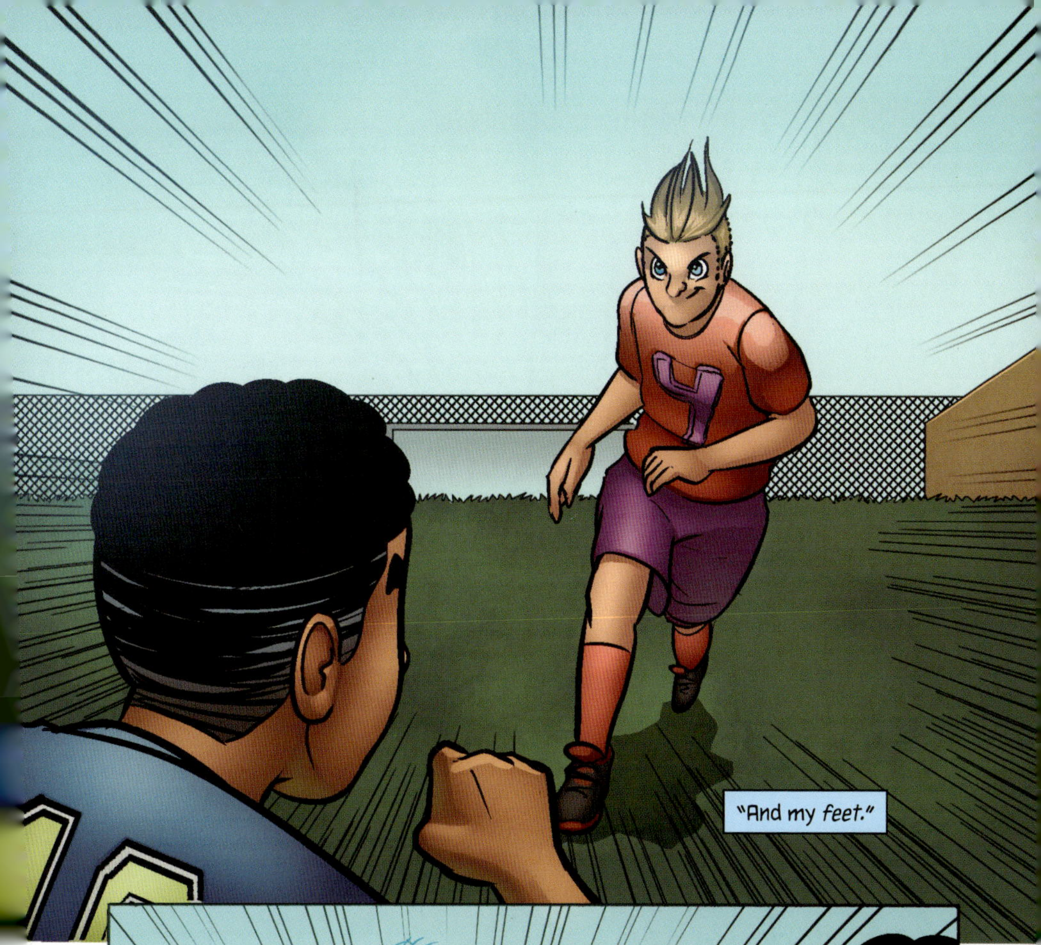
"And my *feet*."

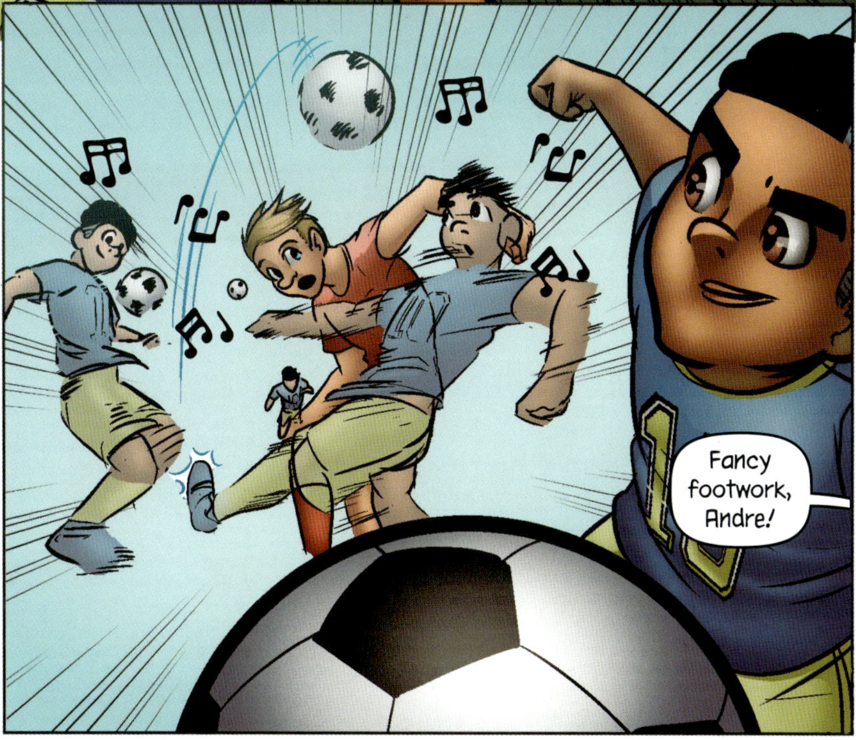
Fancy footwork, Andre!

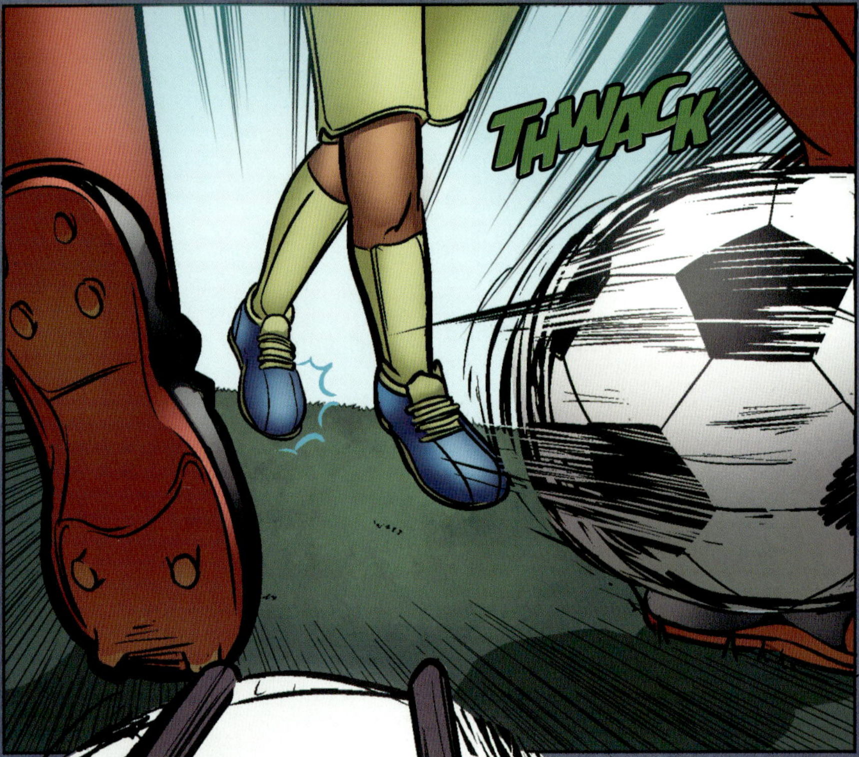
THWACK
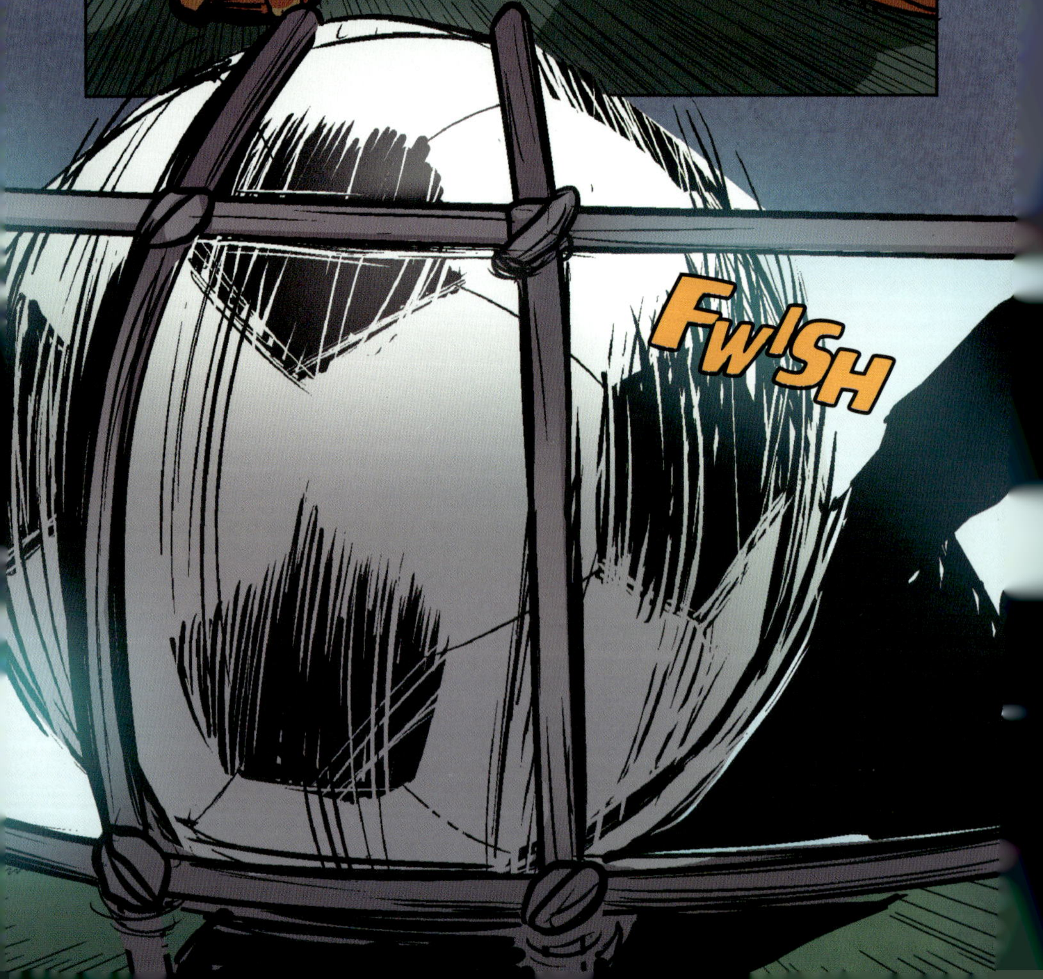
FWISH

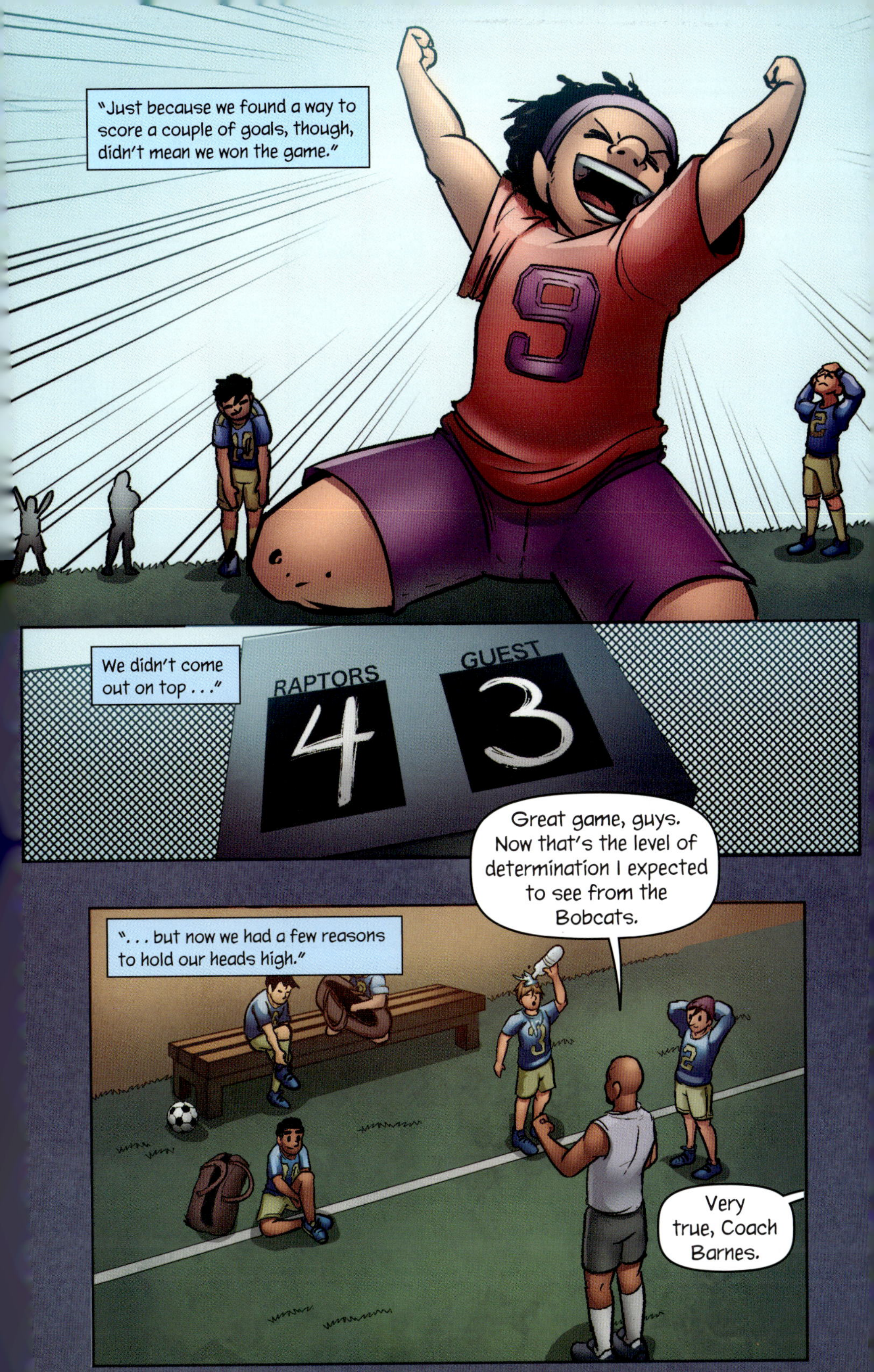
"Just because we found a way to score a couple of goals, though, didn't mean we won the game."
9
We didn't come out on top . . ."
RAPTORS
4
GUEST
3
Great game, guys. Now that's the level of determination I expected to see from the Bobcats.
". . . but now we had a few reasons to hold our heads high."
Very true, Coach Barnes.

Hard work, determination, and loyalty have always been the greatest virtues for a Bobcat.
You all displayed this today. Especially your striker . . .
. . . Andre.
He's a fine example of a team leader.
I *know*. Coach Winston knew who I was.
I was totally geeking out.
I spent my
"But then I spied someone in the crowd, and I wasn't listening to Coach Winston anymore."

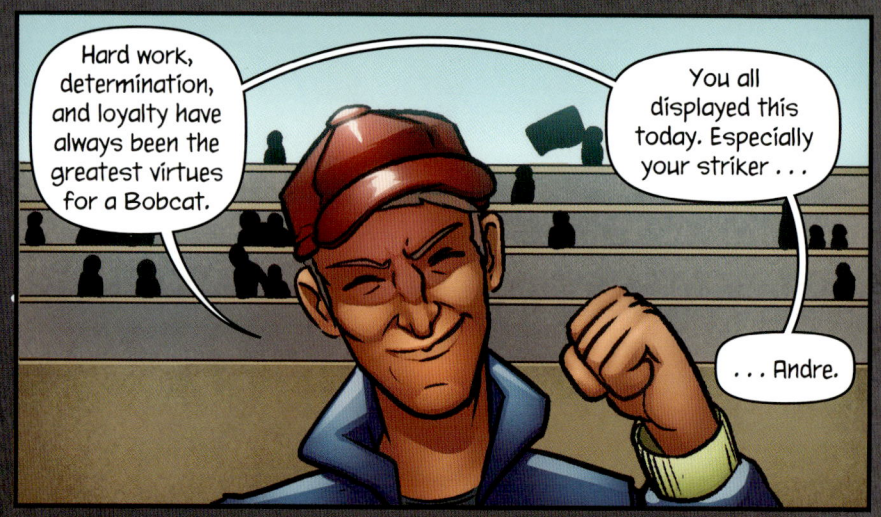

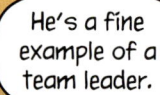

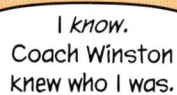

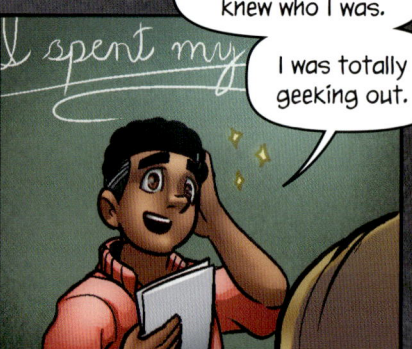

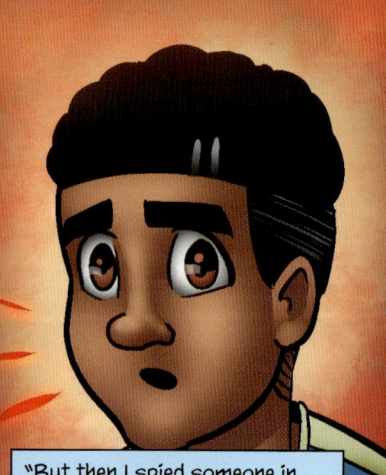

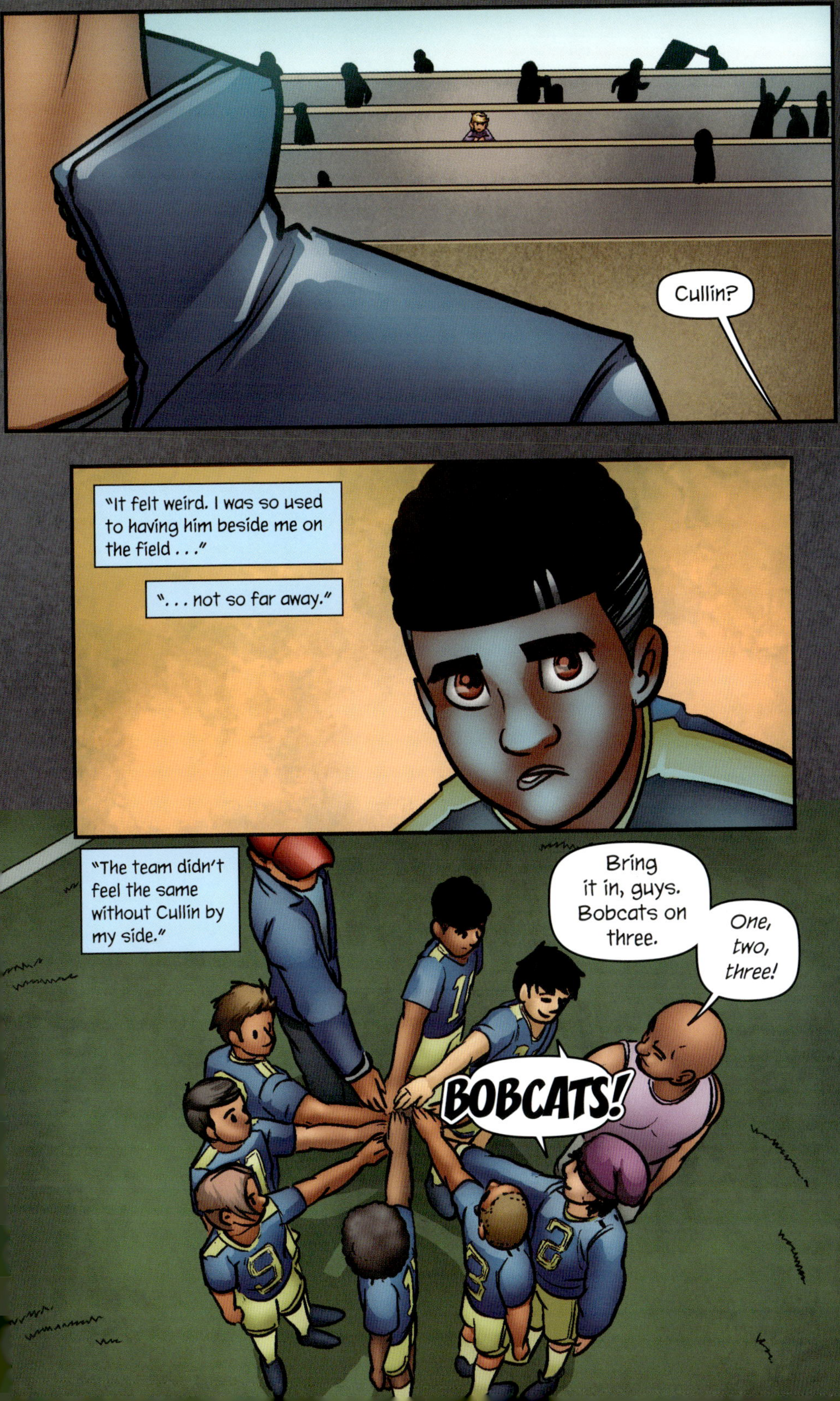
Cullin?
"It felt weird. I was so used to having him beside me on the field . . ."
". . . not so far away."
"The team didn't feel the same without Cullin by my side."
Bring it in, guys. Bobcats on three.
One, two, three!
BOBCATS!

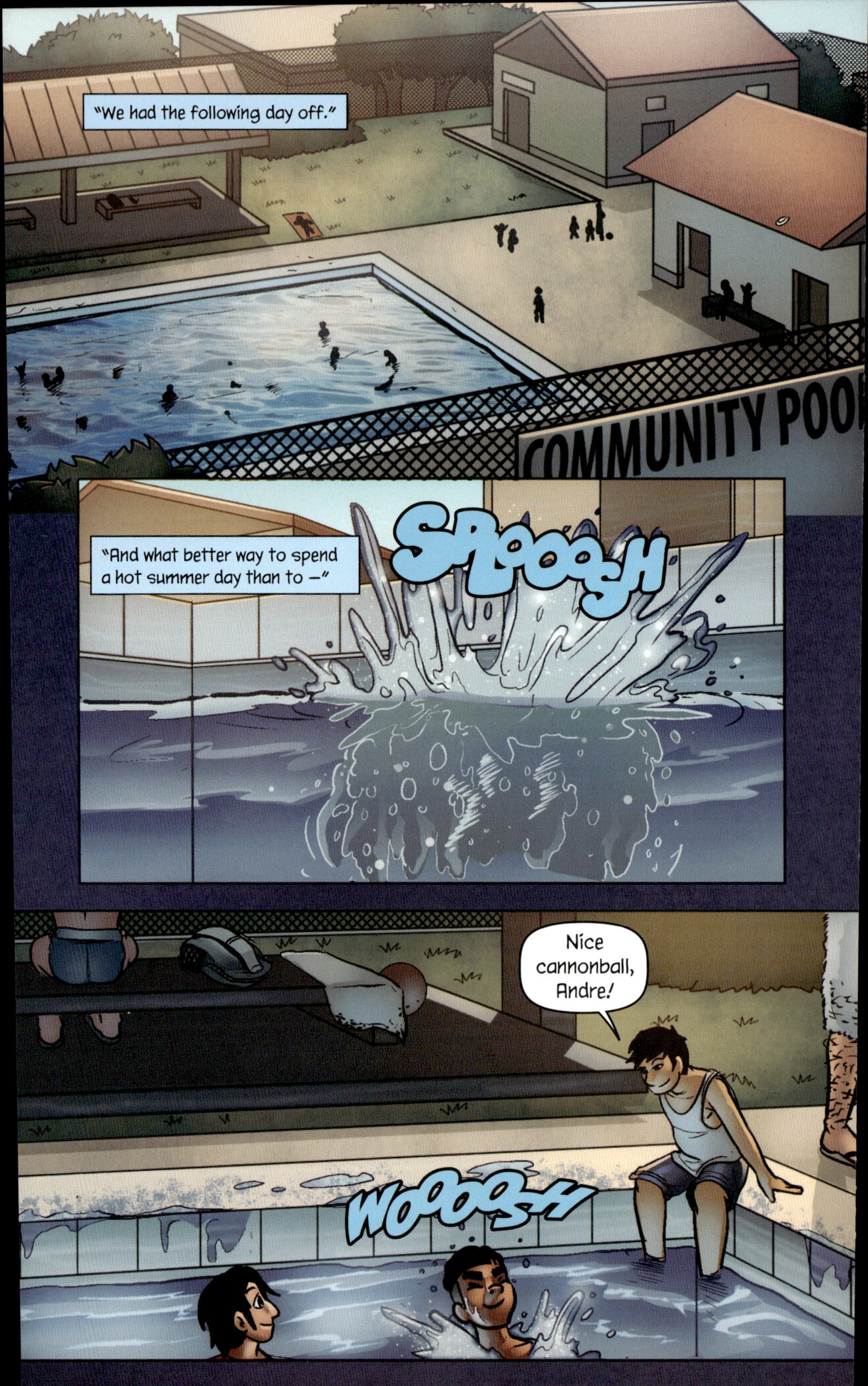
"We had the following day off."
COMMUNITY POO
"And what better way to spend a hot summer day than to —"
SPLOOOSH
Nice cannonball, Andre!
WOOOSH

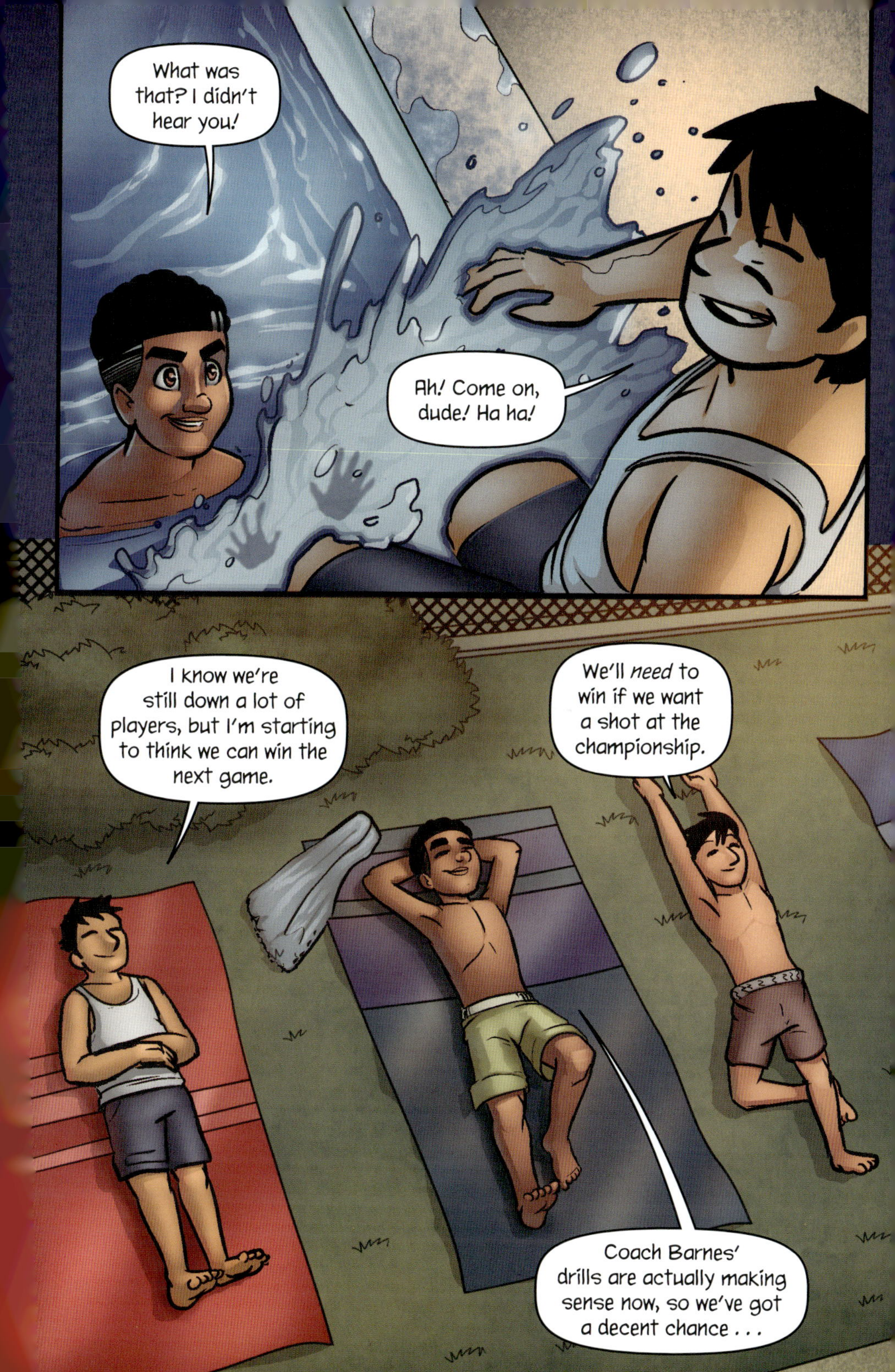
What was that? I didn't hear you!
Ah! Come on, dude! Ha ha!
I know we're still down a lot of players, but I'm starting to think we can win the next game.
We'll *need* to win if we want a shot at the championship.
Coach Barnes' drills are actually making sense now, so we've got a decent chance . . .

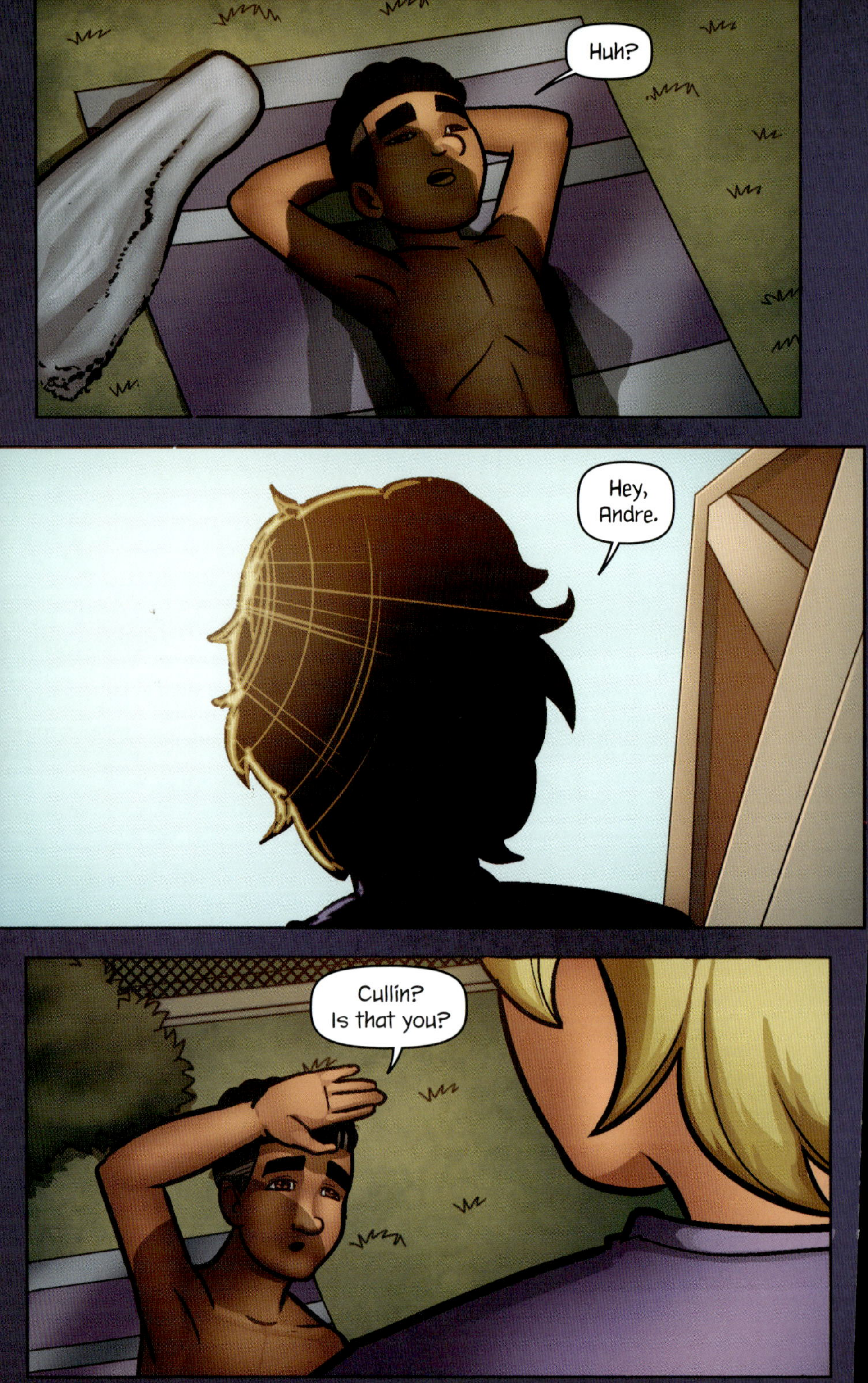
Huh?
Hey, Andre.
Cullin? Is that you?

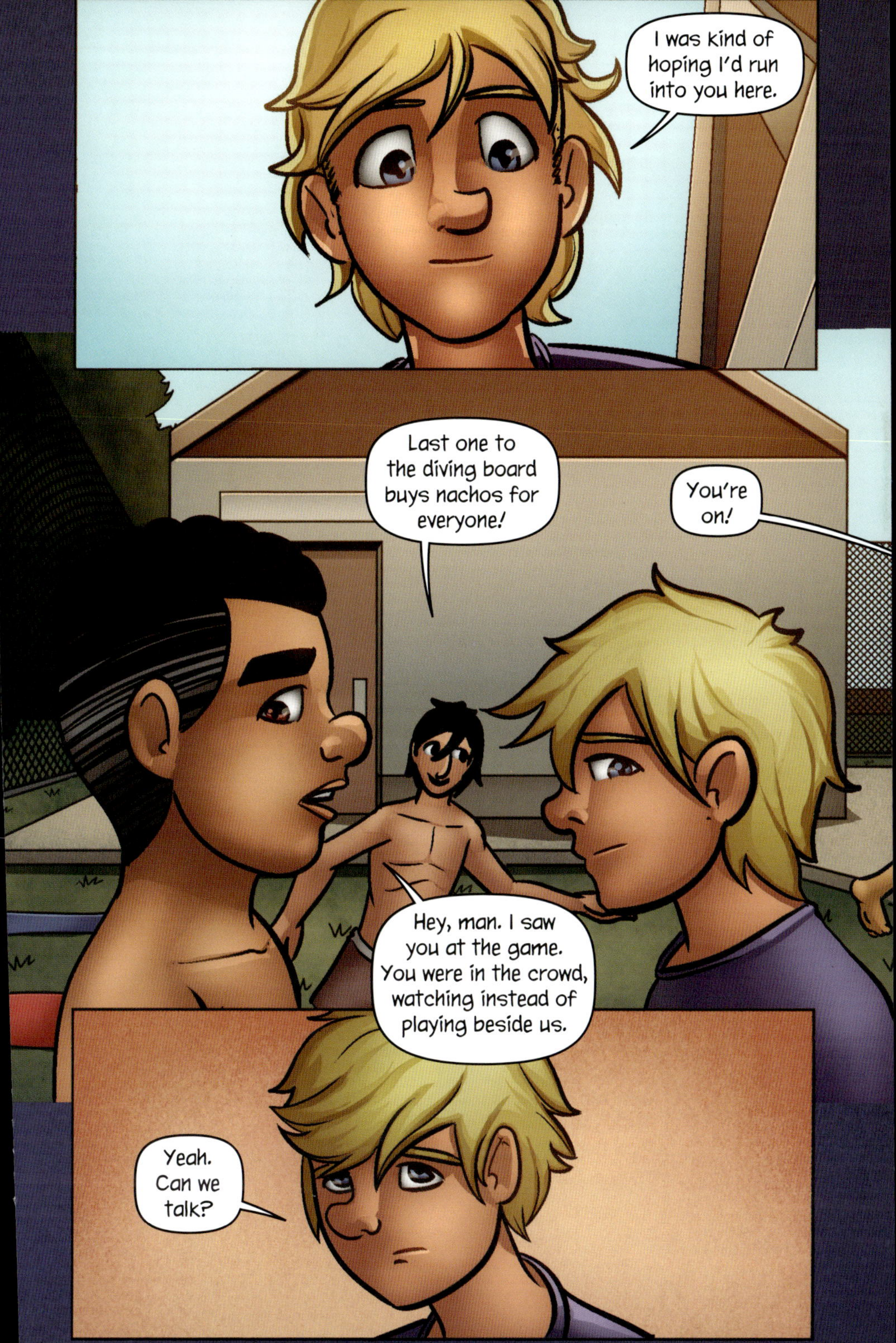
I was kind of hoping I'd run into you here.
Last one to the diving board buys nachos for everyone!
You're on!
Hey, man. I saw you at the game. You were in the crowd, watching instead of playing beside us.
Yeah. Can we talk?

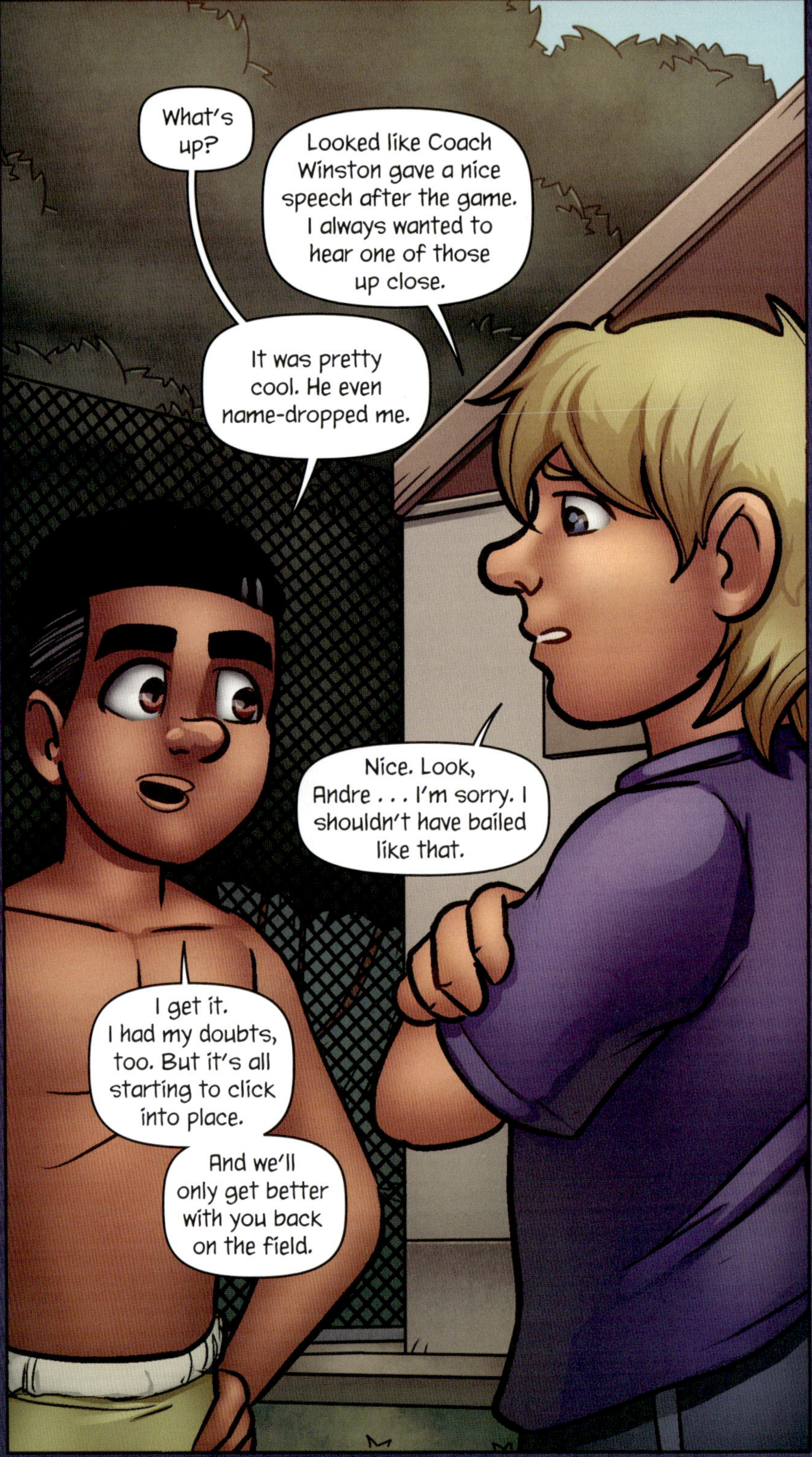
What's up?
Looked like Coach Winston gave a nice speech after the game. I always wanted to hear one of those up close.
It was pretty cool. He even name-dropped me.
Nice. Look, Andre . . . I'm sorry. I shouldn't have bailed like that.
I get it. I had my doubts, too. But it's all starting to click into place.
And we'll only get better with you back on the field.

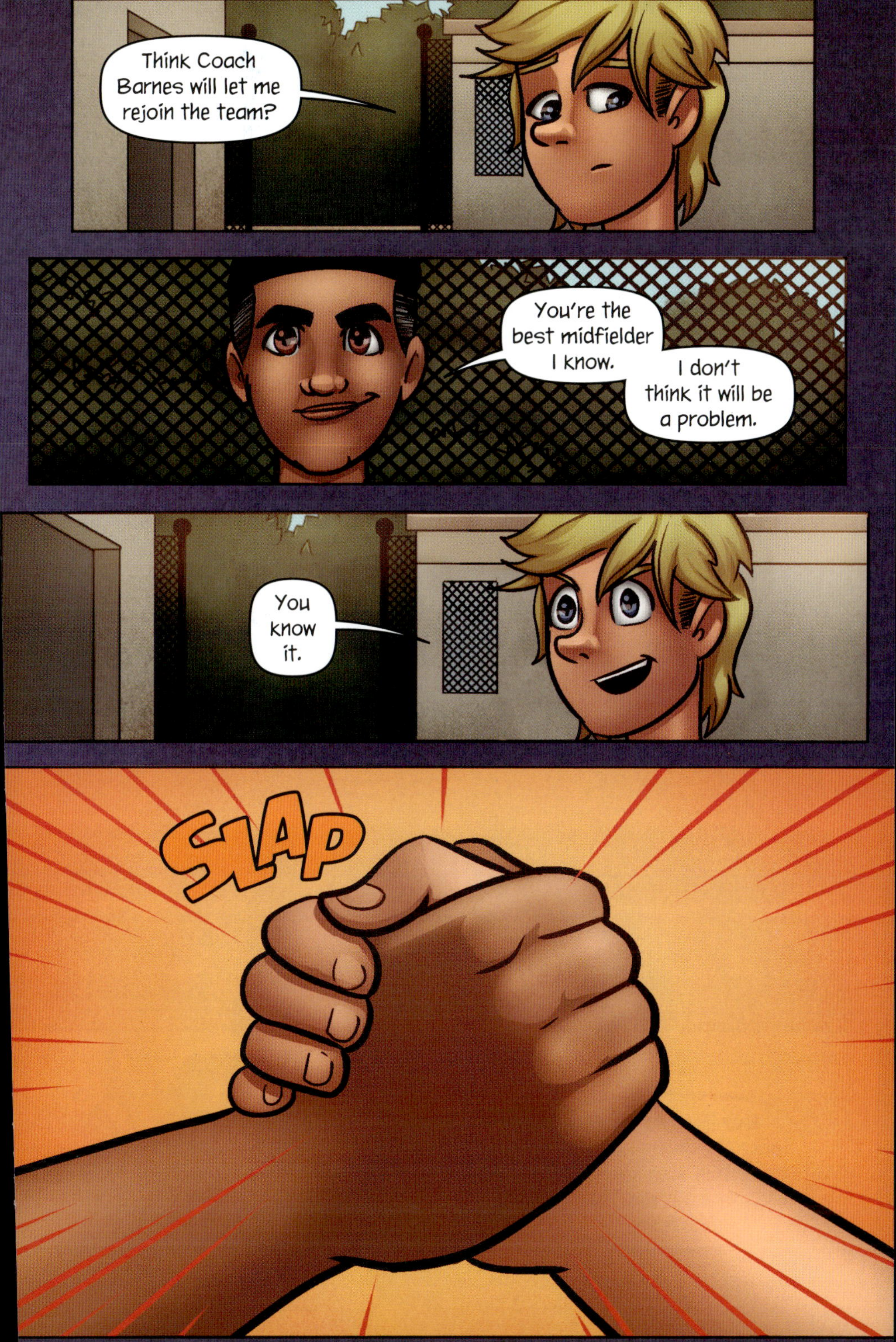
Think Coach Barnes will let me rejoin the team?
You're the best midfielder I know.
I don't think it will be a problem.
You know it.
SLAP

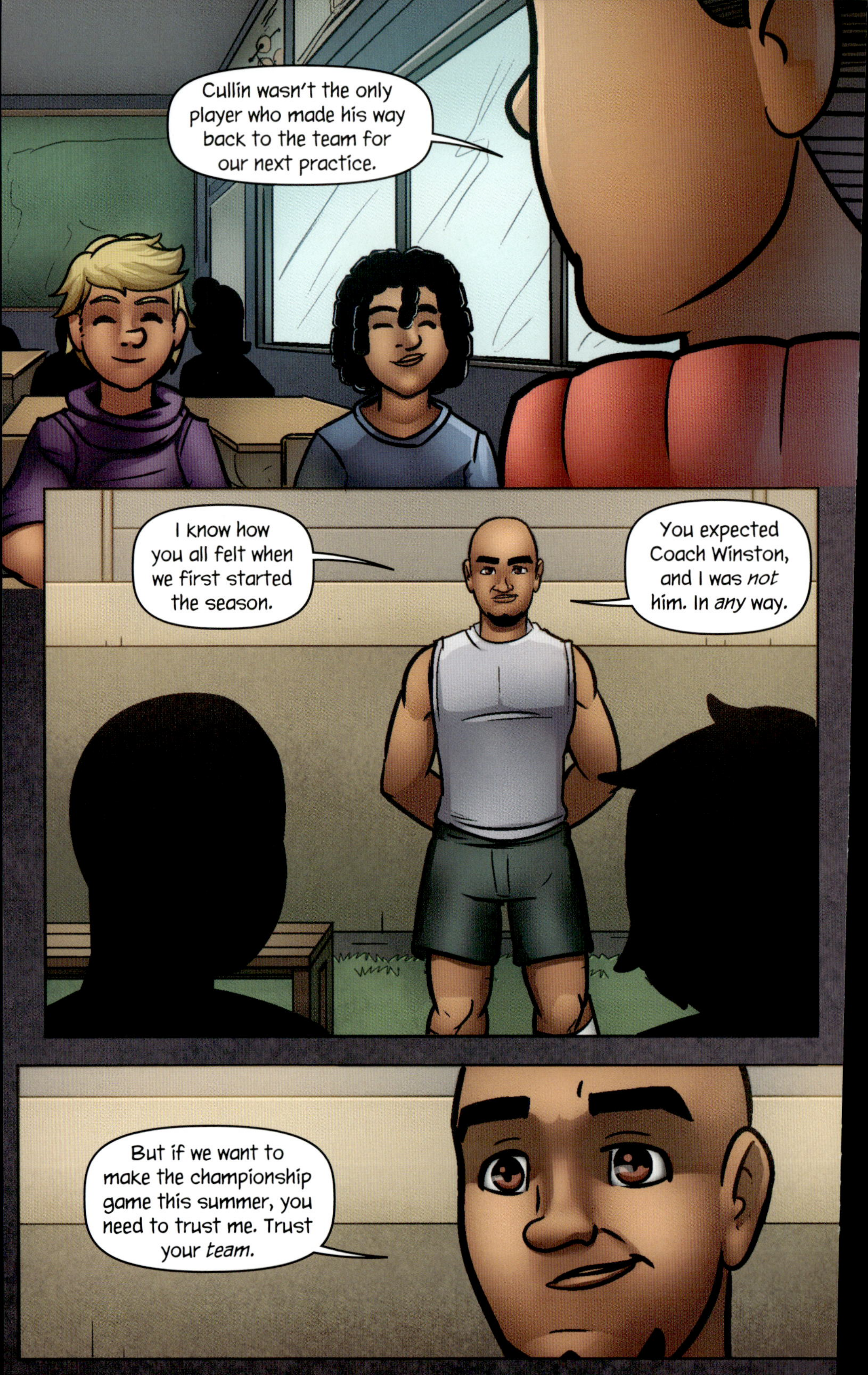
Cullin wasn't the only player who made his way back to the team for our next practice.
I know how you all felt when we first started the season.
You expected Coach Winston, and I was *not* him. In *any* way.
But if we want to make the championship game this summer, you need to trust me. Trust your *team*.

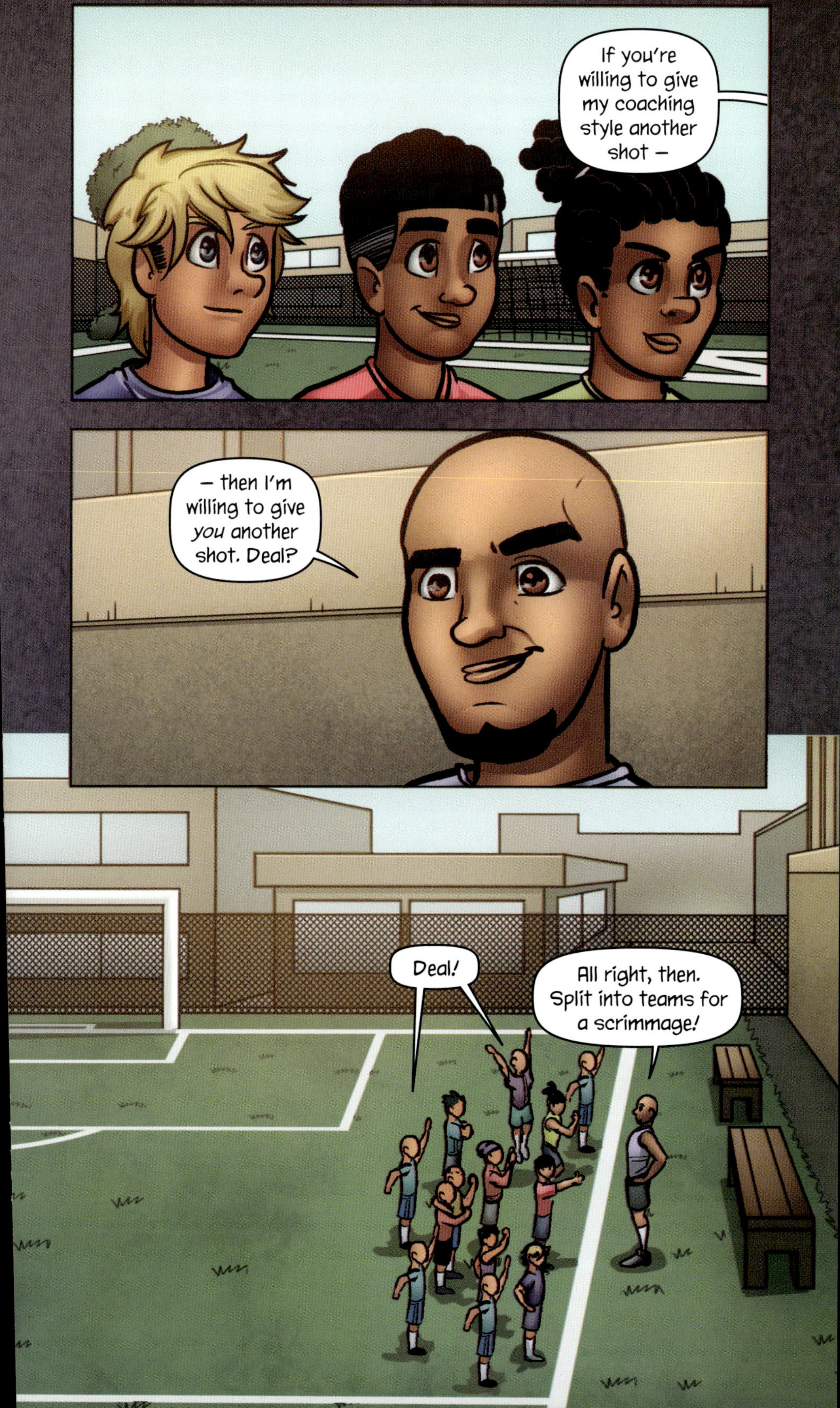
If you're willing to give my coaching style another shot –
– then I'm willing to give *you* another shot. Deal?
Deal!
All right, then. Split into teams for a scrimmage!

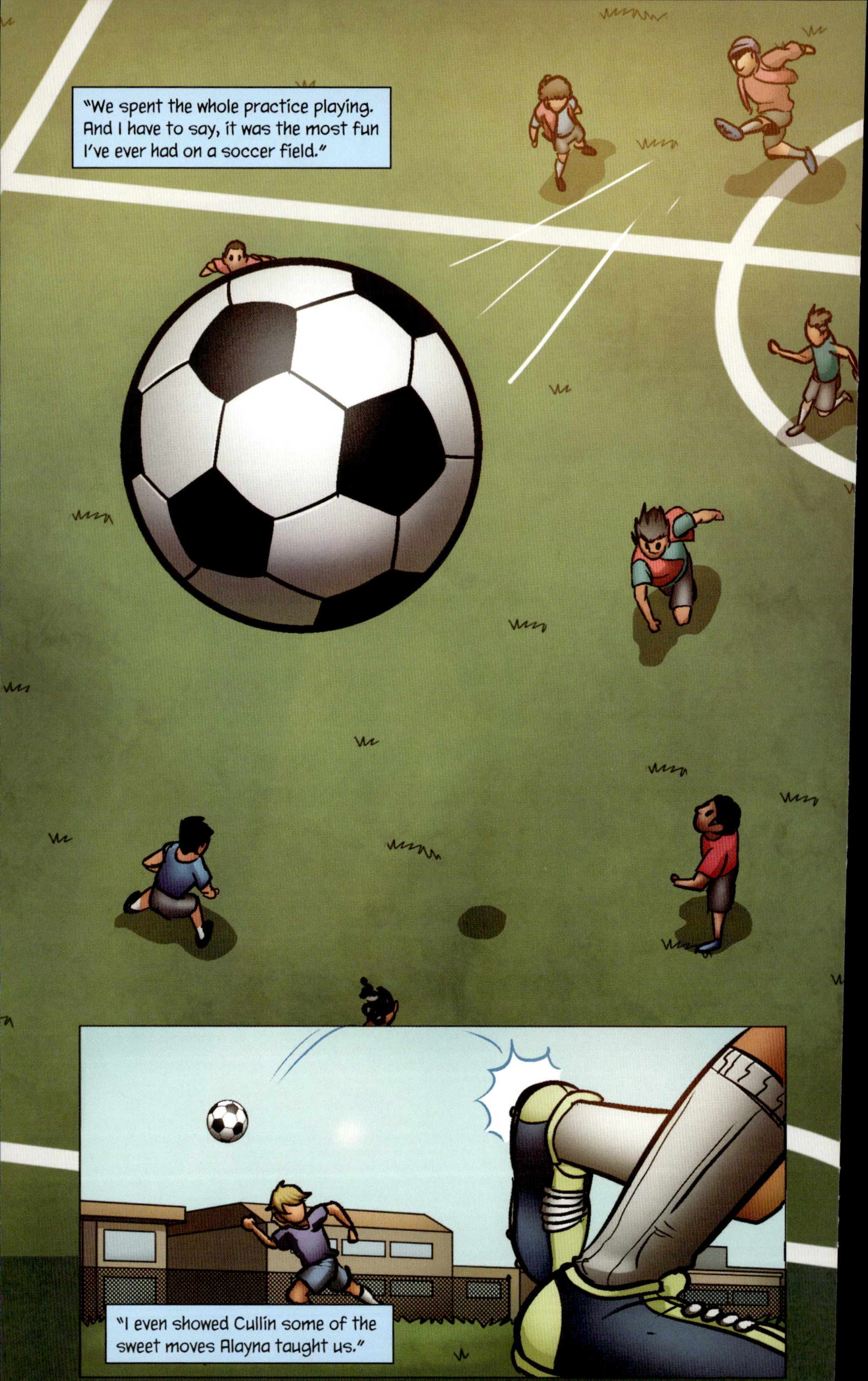
"We spent the whole practice playing. And I have to say, it was the most fun I've ever had on a soccer field."
"I even showed Cullin some of the sweet moves Alayna taught us."

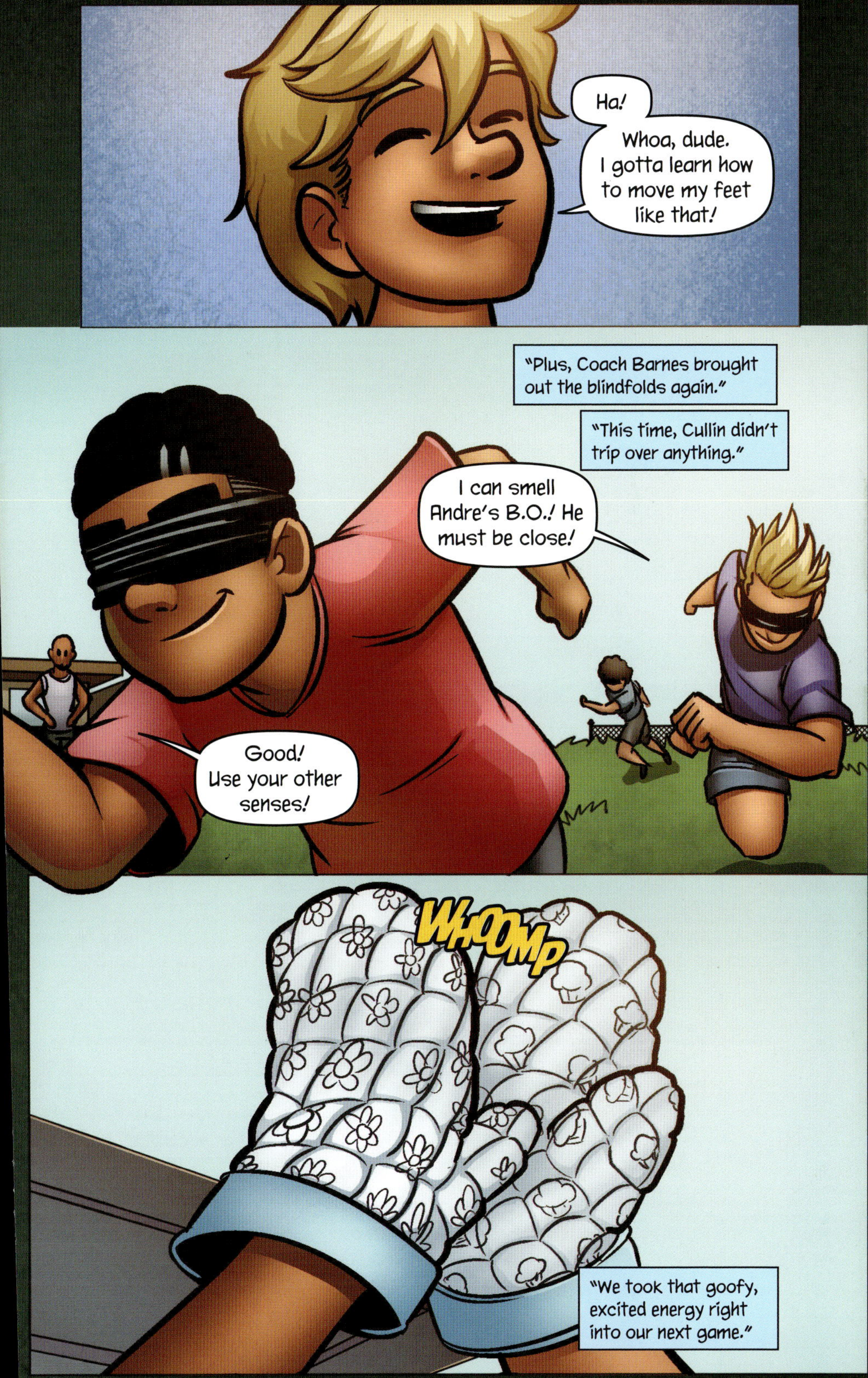
Ha!
Whoa, dude. I gotta learn how to move my feet like that!
"Plus, Coach Barnes brought out the blindfolds again."
"This time, Cullin didn't trip over anything."
I can smell Andre's B.O.! He must be close!
Good! Use your other senses!
WHOOMP
"We took that goofy, excited energy right into our next game."

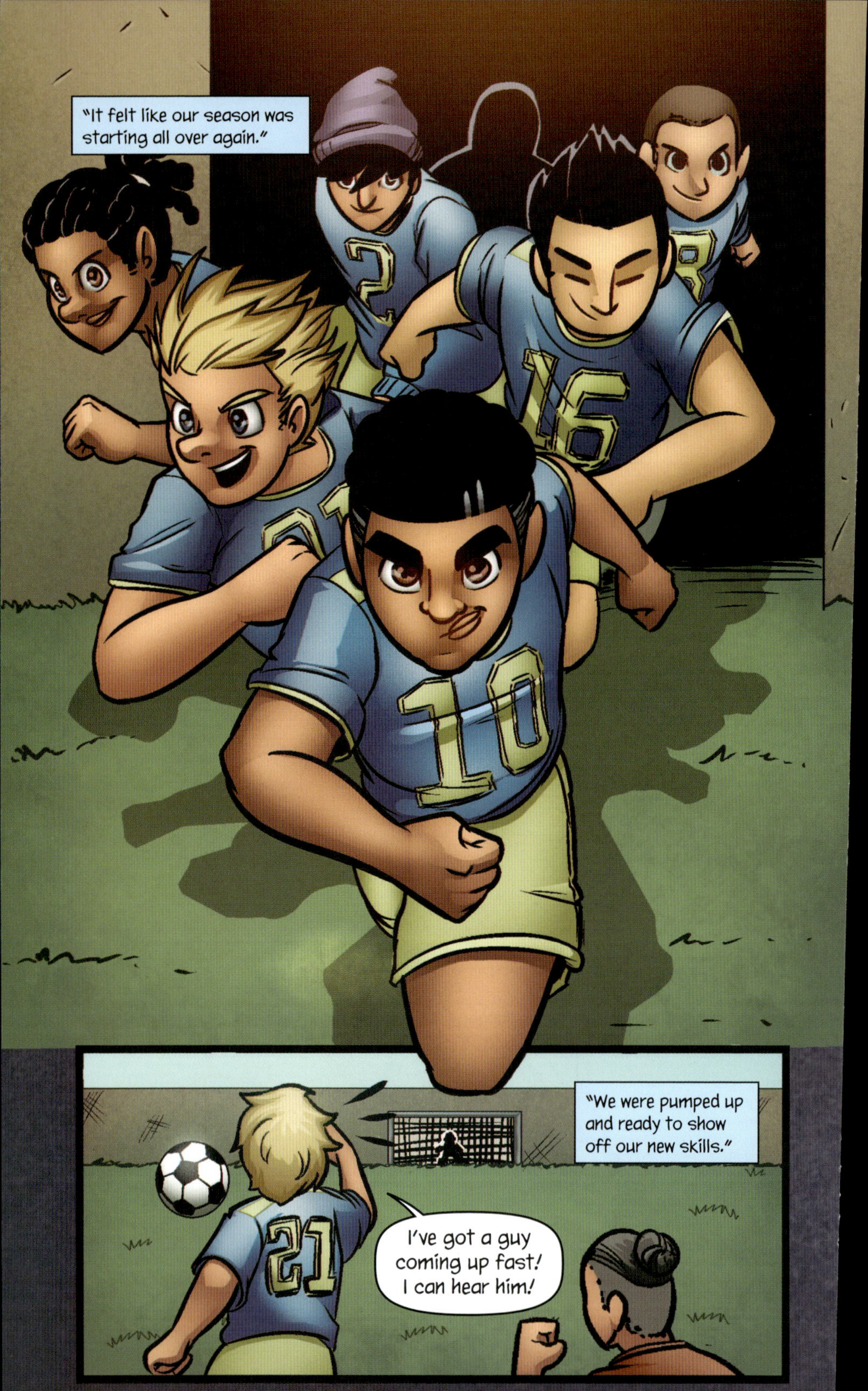
"It felt like our season was starting all over again."
"We were pumped up and ready to show off our new skills."
I've got a guy coming up fast! I can hear him!

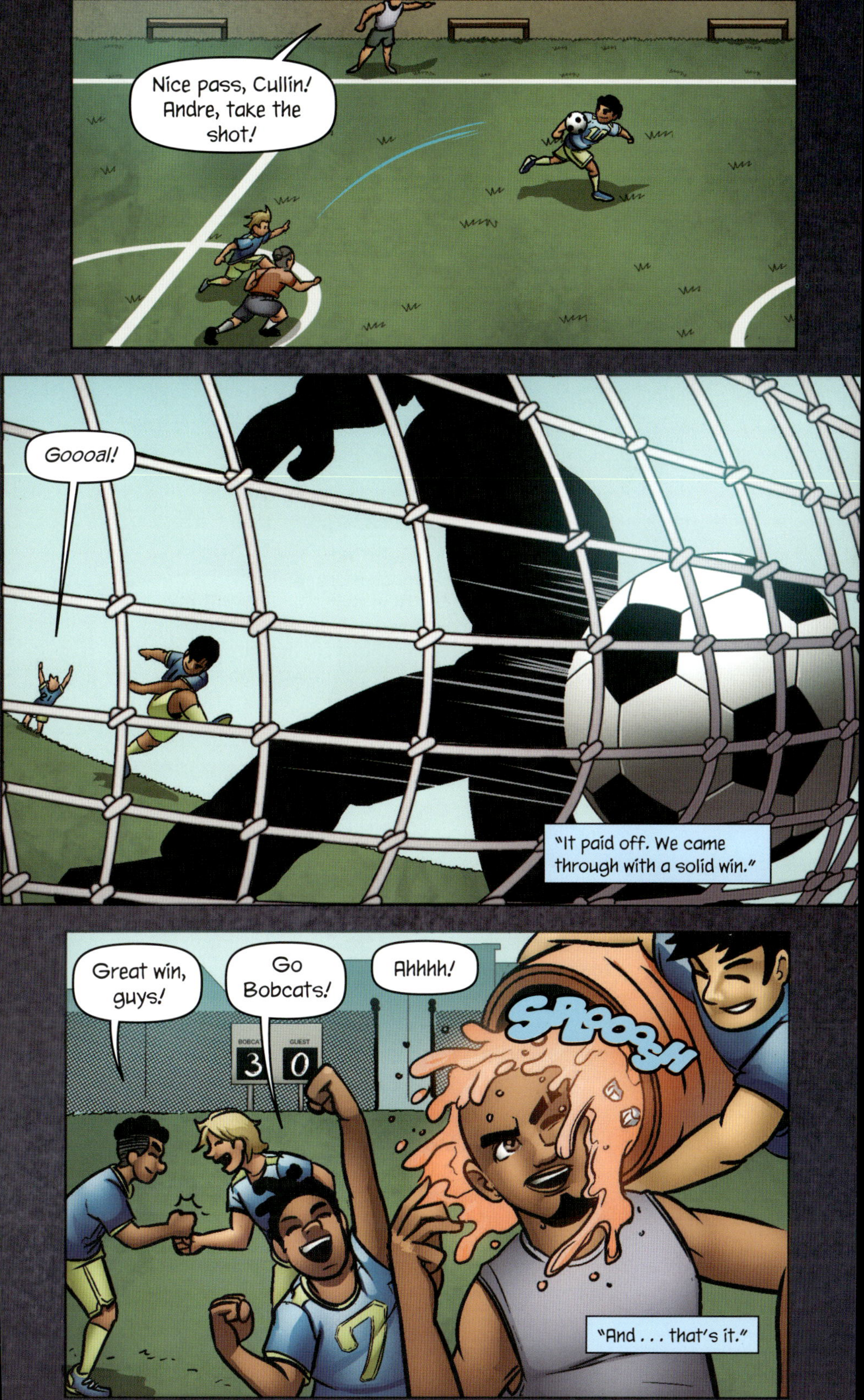
Nice pass, Cullin! Andre, take the shot!
Gooooal!
"It paid off. We came through with a solid win."
Great win, guys!
Go Bobcats!
Ahhhh!
SPLOOOSH
"And . . . that's it."

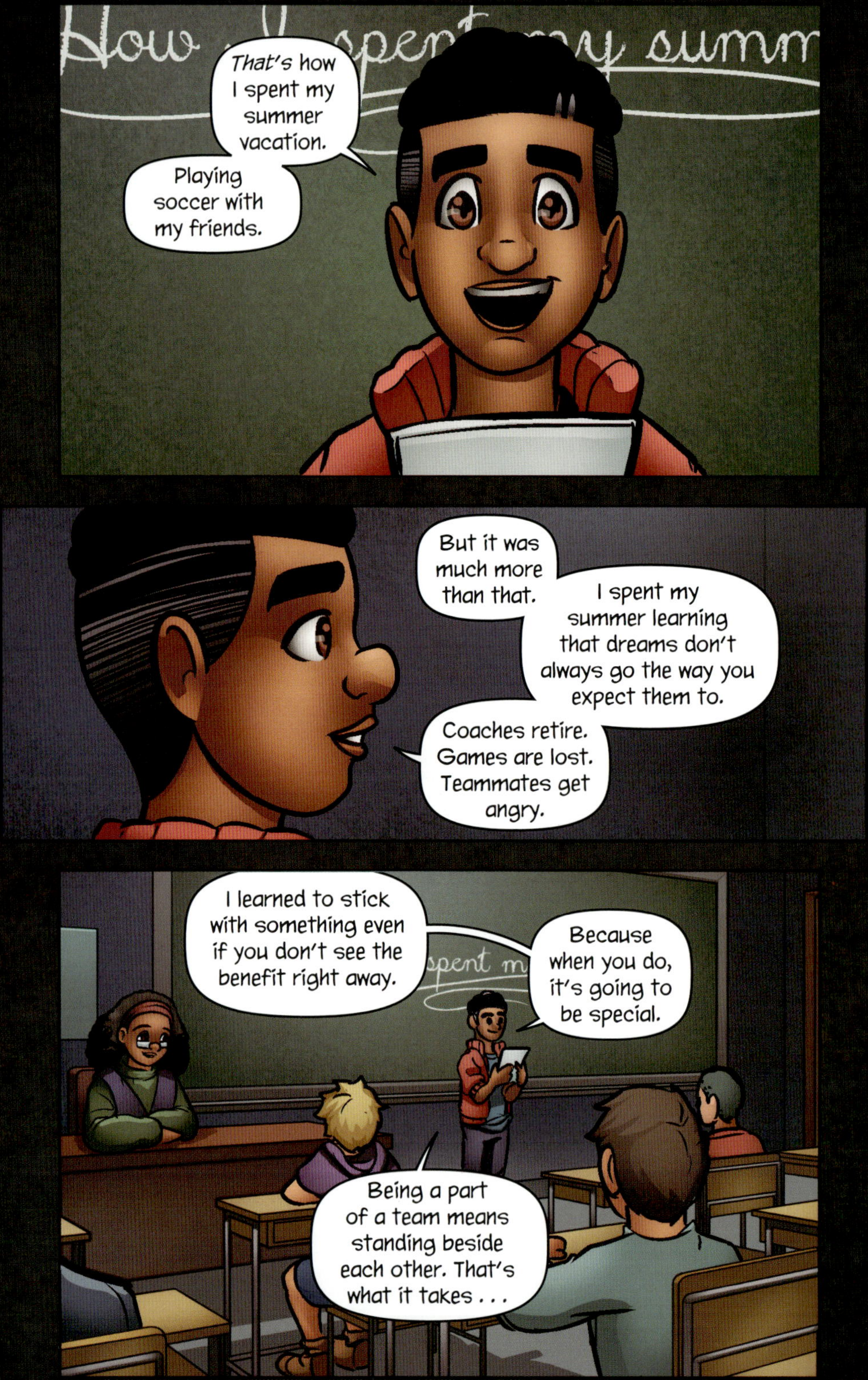
How I spent my summ
That's how I spent my summer vacation.
Playing soccer with my friends.
But it was much more than that.
I spent my summer learning that dreams don't always go the way you expect them to.
Coaches retire. Games are lost. Teammates get angry.
I learned to stick with something even if you don't see the benefit right away.
Because when you do, it's going to be special.
Being a part of a team means standing beside each other. That's what it takes . . .

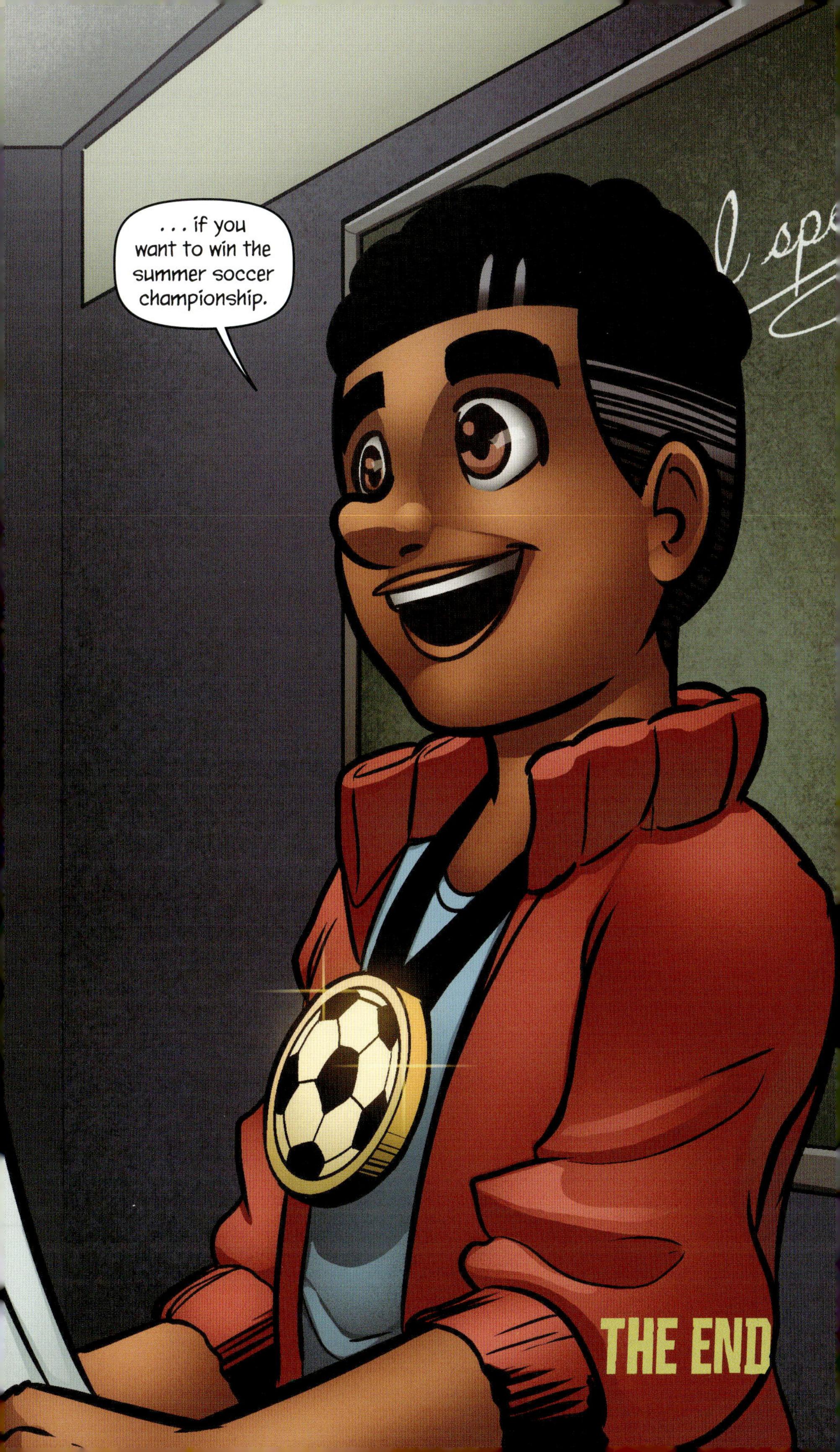
. . . if you want to win the summer soccer championship.
THE END

VISUAL QUESTIONS

Truth. The new guy better not pull another stunt like that, or my season is gonna be pretty dang short.

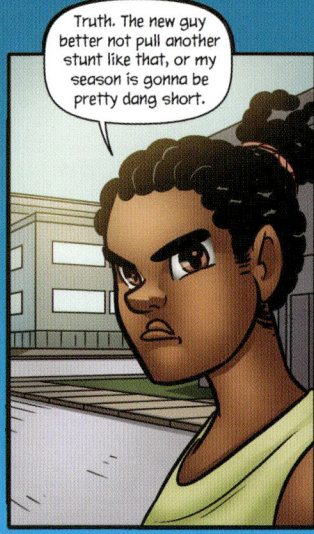

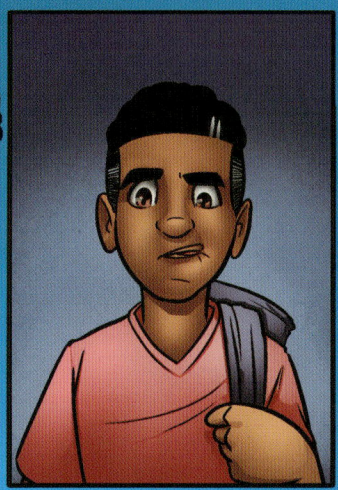

1. Andre doesn't reply after Cullin and Taye say how upset they are about practice and the new coach. But with graphic novels, you can often figure out what a character is thinking through his facial expression. What does Andre's expression tell you? What might he be thinking?

2. Why are some panels completely black during the blindfold drill? How does not seeing anything help you understand what the players are experiencing?

Here goes nothing.
"And 'nothing' was exactly what I saw."
"Not a single thing."
OK, let's run down the field. Stop on my command.
Run? You expect us to *run* in these?

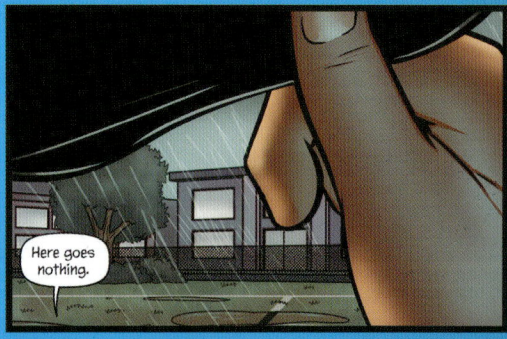

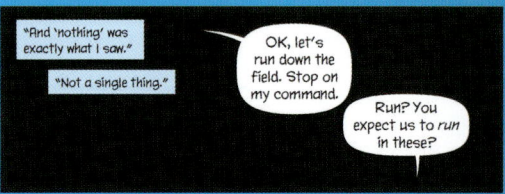

3. Why is Cullin upset? Look back through the story and write down three reasons he's feeling frustrated.

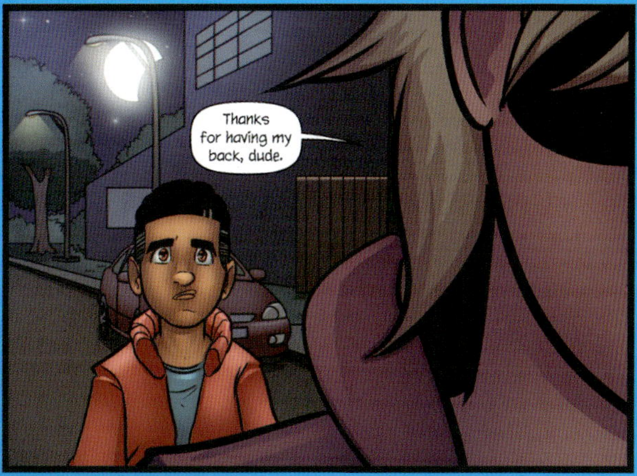
Thanks for having my back, dude.

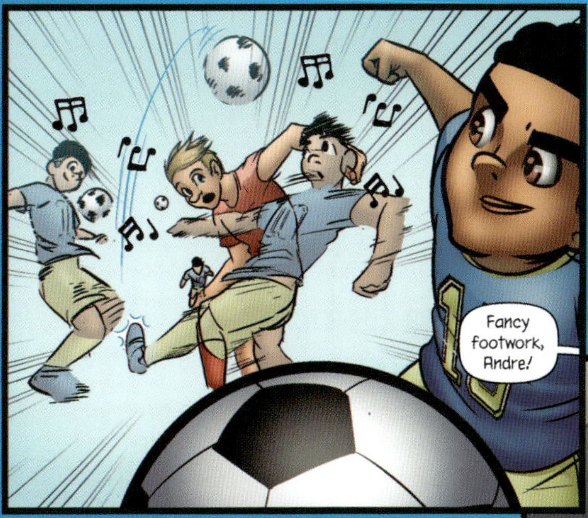
Fancy footwork, Andre!

4. Describe what's happening in this panel. Why is Andre shown four times in one panel? Talk about your answer.

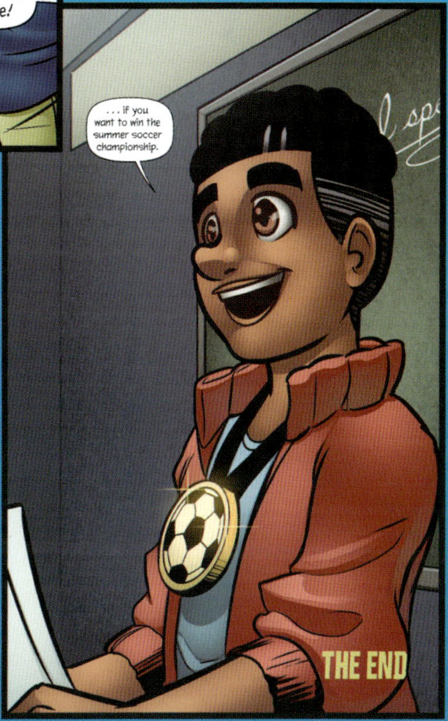
. . . if you want to win the summer soccer championship.
THE END

5. What is Andre wearing around his neck? Were you surprised by the ending? In your own words, write a paragraph about how the team was able to turn their season around and come out champions.

ALL-STAR SOCCER MOVES

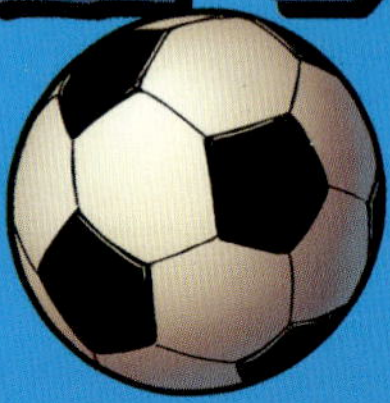

Ready to up your game? Soccer — or football, as it's known to most of the world — requires coordination, control, and speed. Read on to learn about advanced techniques that'll challenge your skills. Remember, practice is key to perfecting any new move!

CRUYFF TURN

Beat a defender with this classic turn. Put one foot to the side of the ball. Reach around the ball with your other foot. Stop the ball briefly with the inside of your foot. Pull the ball back. Turn and start dribbling in the other direction. First used by Dutch soccer player Johan Cruyff in the 1970s, this turn is still a popular dribbling skill.

RONALDO CHOP

Try out a signature move from famous Portuguese soccer pro Cristiano Ronaldo. As you're dribbling, take a small hop over the ball with both feet. Bring one foot down in front of the ball. Use the inside of your other foot to kick the ball as you land. Be sure to angle your foot at 45 degrees so you tap the ball forward. The sudden change in direction is perfect for throwing off a charging defender.

RAINBOW

Send the ball flying in an arc over your opponent. Use your dominant foot to roll the ball up the back of your other leg. Lean forward and quickly flick the ball with your non-dominant heel. At the same time, bring your dominant foot forward to help you land. Do all steps in one quick motion. The ball should pop up over you in a high curve. Keep running forward to recover the ball when it lands.

CHIP

Use this kicking technique to send the ball curving up into the air. As you approach the ball, plant one foot to the side of the ball. Swing your other leg back. A shorter swing will give you more control over the ball. Point your toes and bring your foot under the ball. Scoop the ball up and launch it into the air. The chip is good for passing, getting the ball past opponents, and tricking the goalie.

BENDING KICK

Curve the ball in midair with this expert kick. Approach the ball at an angle. Plant one foot to the side of the ball. Strike the ball with the inside of your other foot. Start at the bottom corner of the ball, and kick up and around it. Be sure to finish with your shoulders pointed in the direction you want the ball to travel. Use the bend to pass around an opponent or for shots on goal.

GLOSSARY

determination (di-tur-muh-NEY-shuhn)—the quality or act of continuing to try do something and not giving up, even though it may be difficult

drill (DRIL)—a repetitive exercise that helps you learn a specific skill

embarrassment (em-BAR-uhss-muhnt)—something or someone that causes you or a group to feel uncomfortable and foolish in front of others

experience (ik-SPIHR-ee-uhnss)—knowledge or skill gained from doing something

frustrations (fruh-STREY-shuhnz)—feelings of anger and annoyance because of something not going as planned or not being able to do something

humiliated (hyoo-MIL-ee-ate-ed)—made to feel ashamed and foolish

instincts (IN-stingktz)—behaviors that you don't have to think about in order to do

legend (LEJ-uhnd)—a person who is famous for doing something very well

retire (ri-TIRE)—to stop doing an activity or working a job, often because of old age

ridiculous (ri-DIK-yuh-luhss)—extremely silly and against common sense

scrimmage (SKRIM-ij)—a practice game between members of the same team

virtues (vir-CHOOZ)—very good qualities or features

READ THEM ALL!

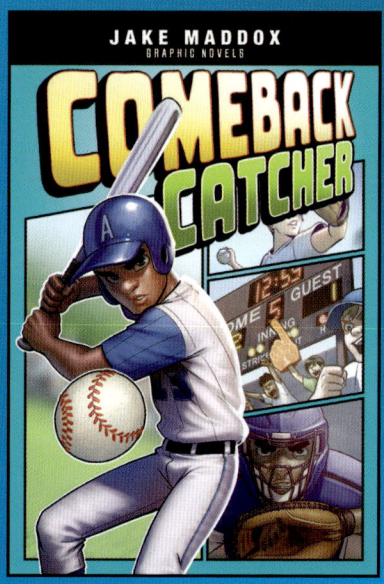
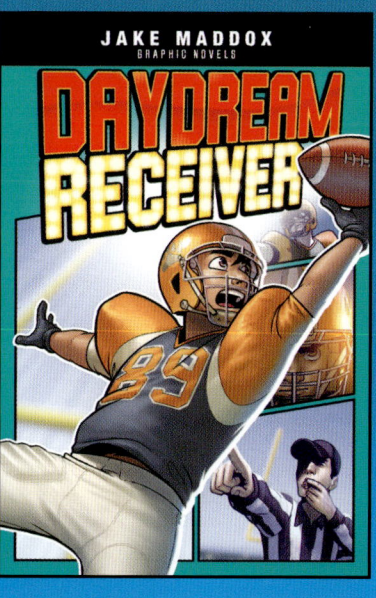
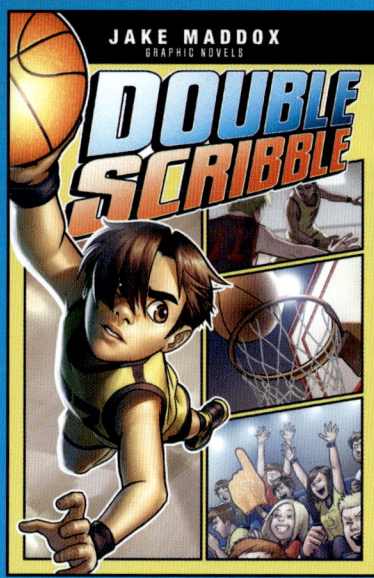
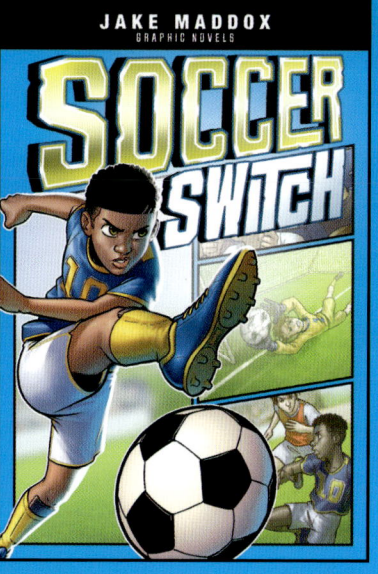

FIND OUT MORE AT
WWW.MYCAPSTONE.COM

ABOUT THE AUTHOR

Brandon Terrell is the author of numerous children's books, including six volumes in the Tony Hawk's 900 Revolution series and several Sports Illustrated Kids Graphic Novels. When not hunched over his laptop writing, Brandon enjoys watching movies, reading, watching and playing baseball, and spending time with his wife and two children in Minnesota.

ABOUT THE ILLUSTRATOR

Aburtov has worked in the comic book industry for more than eleven years. In that time, he has illustrated popular characters such as Wolverine, Iron Man, Blade, and the Punisher. Recently, Aburtov started his own illustration studio called Graphikslava. He lives in Monterrey, Mexico, with his daughter, Ilka, and his beloved wife. Aburtov enjoys spending his spare time with family and friends.

JAKE MADDOX
GRAPHIC NOVELS

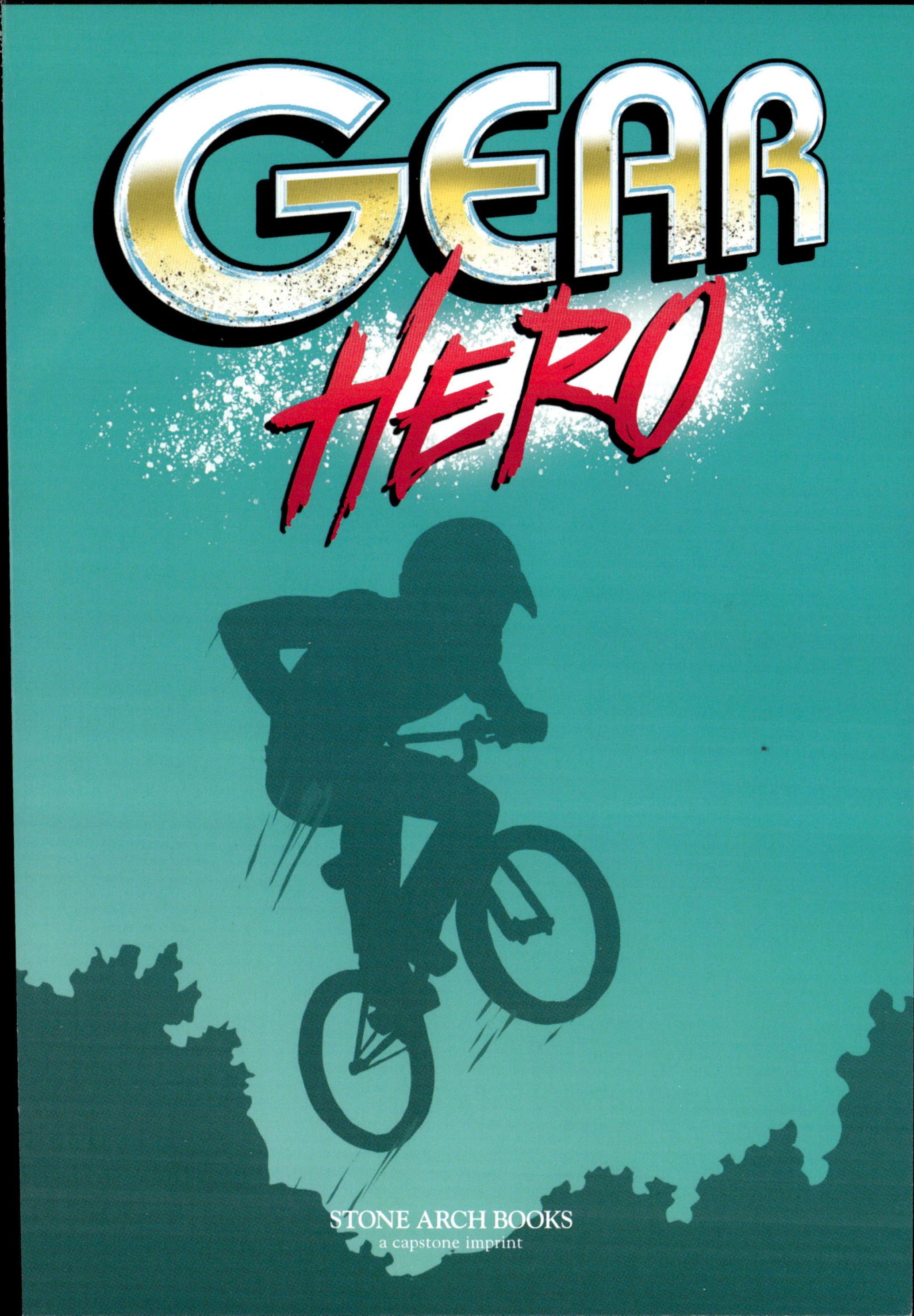
GEAR
HERO
STONE ARCH BOOKS
a capstone imprint

JAKE MADDOX
GRAPHIC NOVELS

Jake Maddox Graphic Novels are published by
Stone Arch Books, a Capstone imprint
1710 Roe Crest Drive
North Mankato, Minnesota 56003

www.mycapstone.com

Copyright © 2019 Stone Arch Books

All rights reserved. No part of this publication may be reproduced in whole or in part, or stored in a retrieval system, or transmitted in any form or by any means, electronic, mechanical, photocopying, recording, or otherwise, without written permission of the publisher.

Library of Congress Cataloging-in-Publication Data is available on the Library of Congress website at https://lccn.loc.gov/2018005697

ISBN: 978-1-4965-6045-2 (library binding)
ISBN: 978-1-4965-6049-0 (paperback)
ISBN: 978-1-4965-6053-7 (ebook PDF)

Summary: Nelson Greenwood loves drawing superheroes, particularly Major Speed—the hero of his own comic book. Nelson modeled Major Speed after his twin brother Nick, a skilled BMX rider. However, when a crash knocks Nick out of a big race, he suggests that Nelson take his place. But Nelson isn't sure he can summon the courage and skill of Major Speed to compete against the best BMX riders, especially Nick's biggest nemesis—Cain Otto.

Editor: Aaron Sautter
Designer: Brann Garvey
Production: Tori Abraham

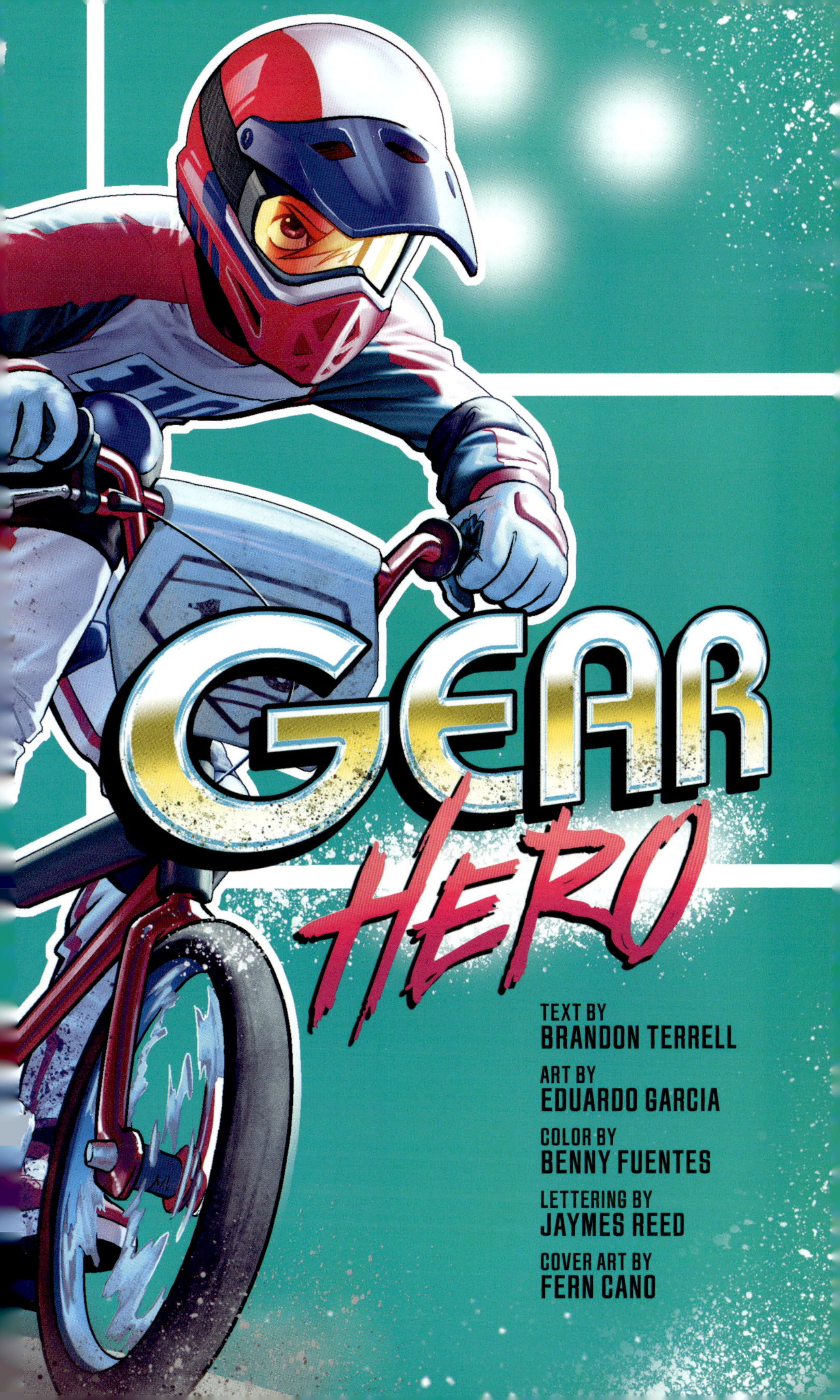
GEAR
HERO
TEXT BY
BRANDON TERRELL
ART BY
EDUARDO GARCIA
COLOR BY
BENNY FUENTES
LETTERING BY
JAYMES REED
COVER ART BY
FERN CANO

CAST OF CHARACTERS

NELSON GREENWOOD

NICK GREENWOOD

CAIN OTTO

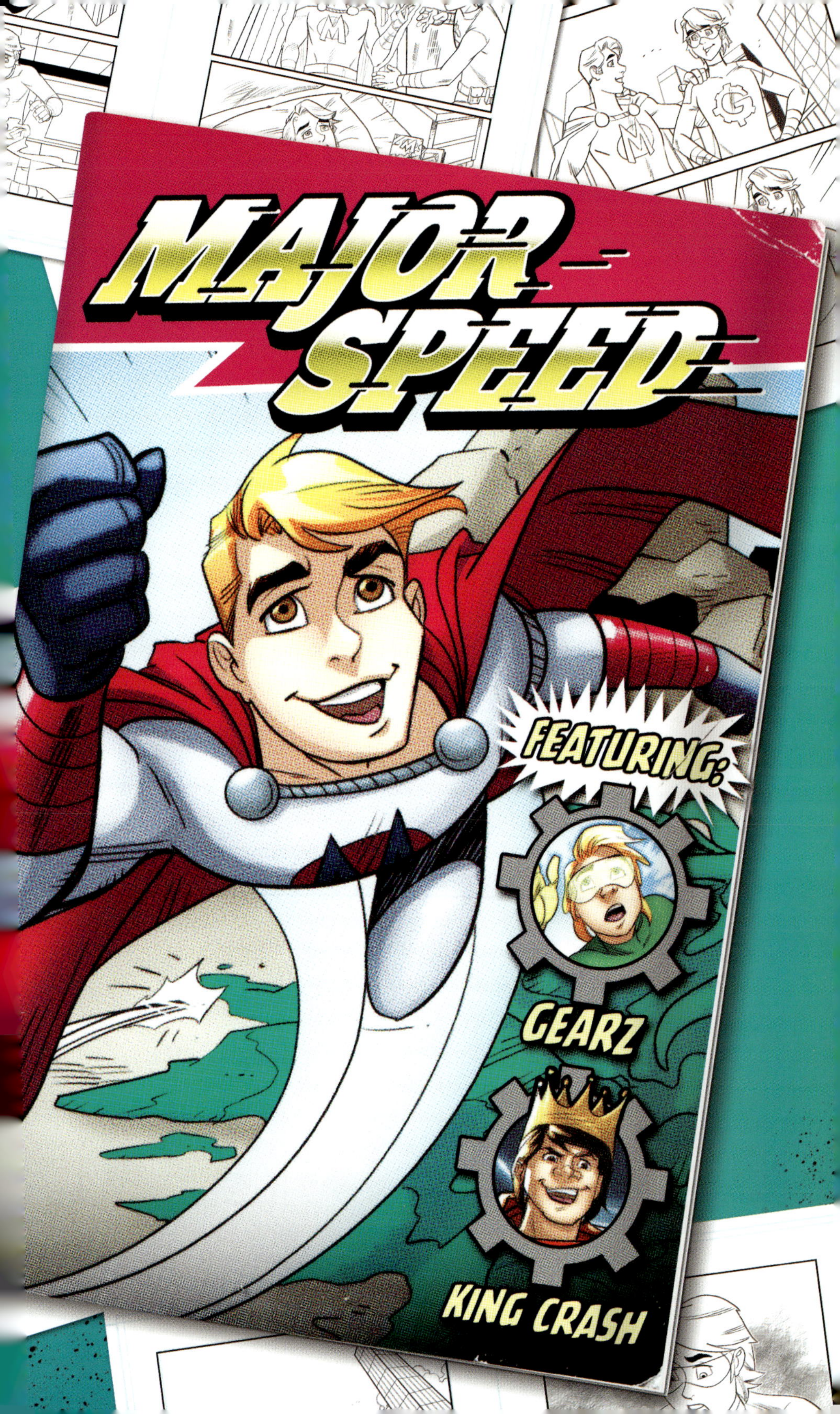
MAJOR SPEED
FEATURING:
GEARZ
KING CRASH

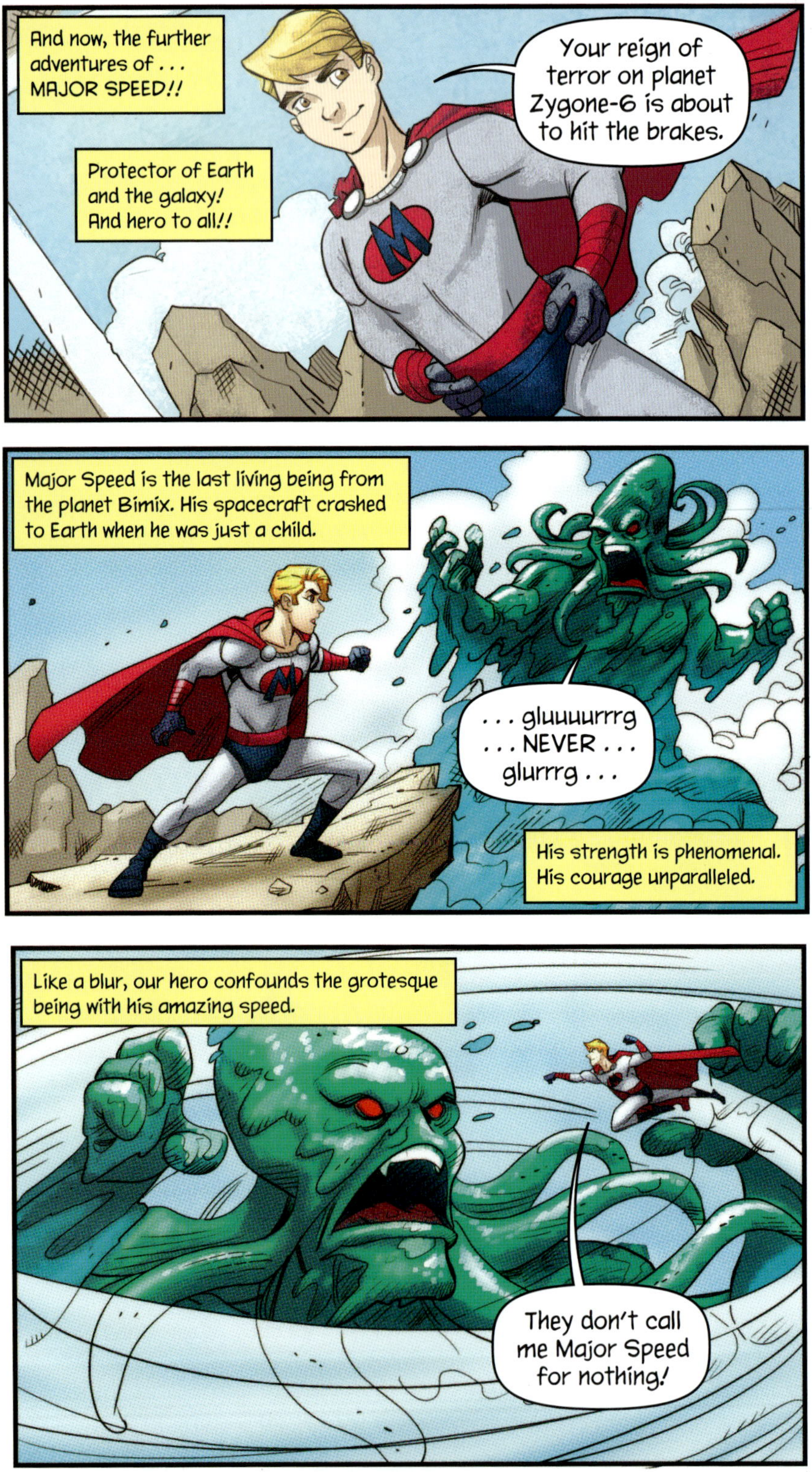

And now, the further adventures of . . . MAJOR SPEED!!
Protector of Earth and the galaxy! And hero to all!!
Your reign of terror on planet Zygone-6 is about to hit the brakes.
Major Speed is the last living being from the planet Bimix. His spacecraft crashed to Earth when he was just a child.
. . . gluuuurrrg . . . NEVER . . . glurrrg . . .
His strength is phenomenal. His courage unparalleled.
Like a blur, our hero confounds the grotesque being with his amazing speed.
They don't call me Major Speed for nothing!

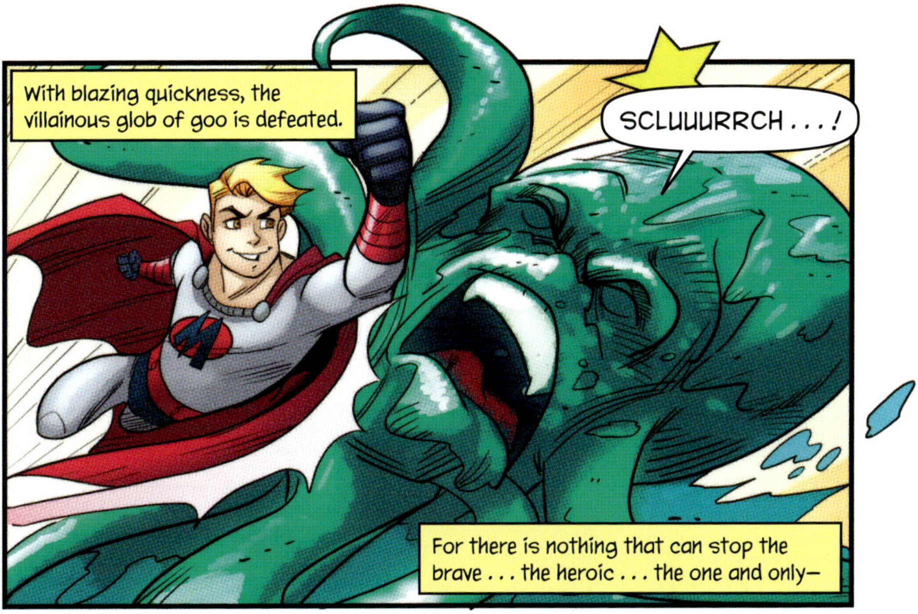
With blazing quickness, the villainous glob of goo is defeated.
SCLUUURRCH . . . !
For there is nothing that can stop the brave . . . the heroic . . . the one and only—

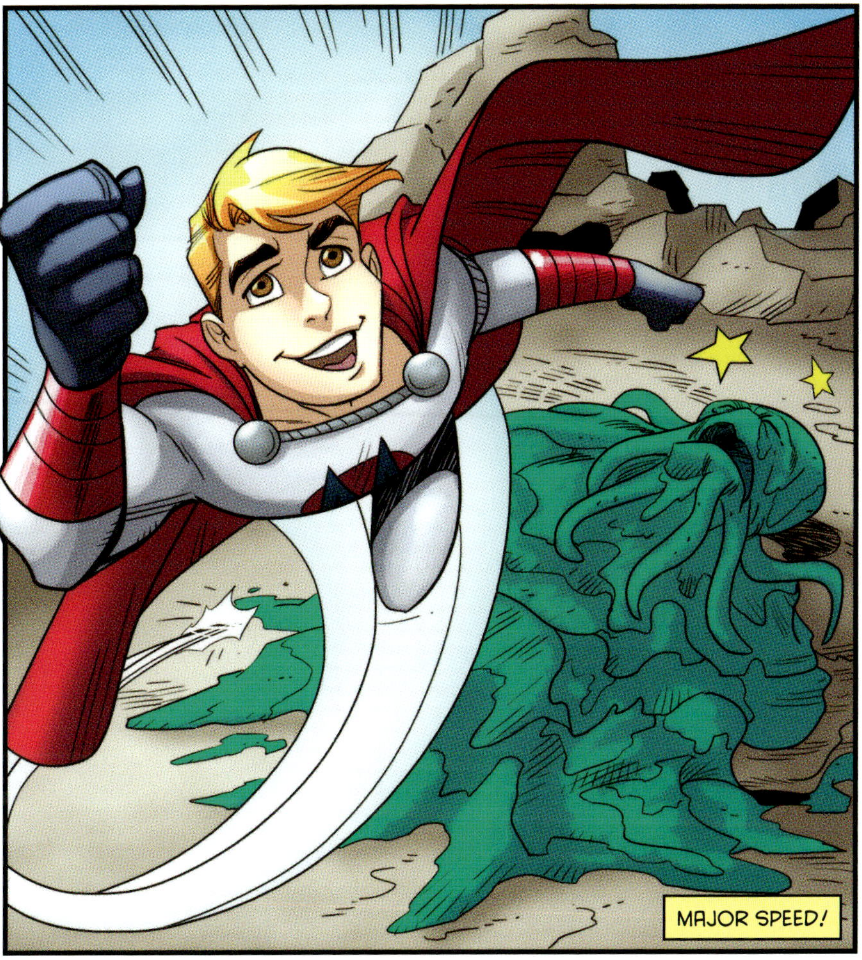
MAJOR SPEED!

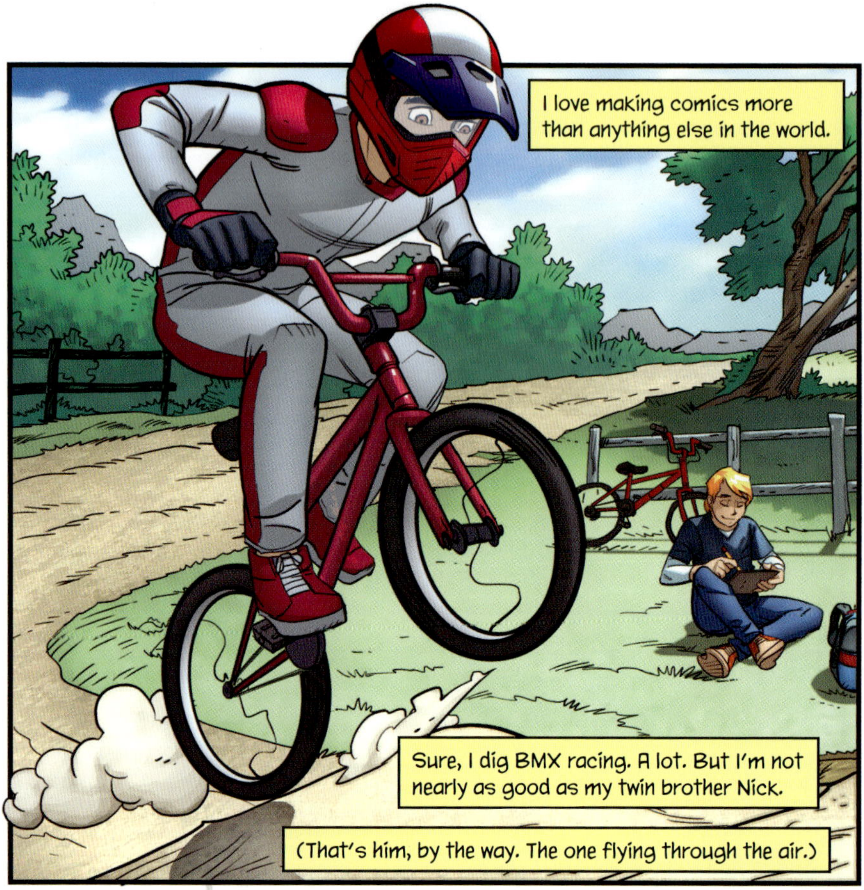
I love making comics more than anything else in the world.
Sure, I dig BMX racing. A lot. But I'm not nearly as good as my twin brother Nick.
(That's him, by the way. The one flying through the air.)

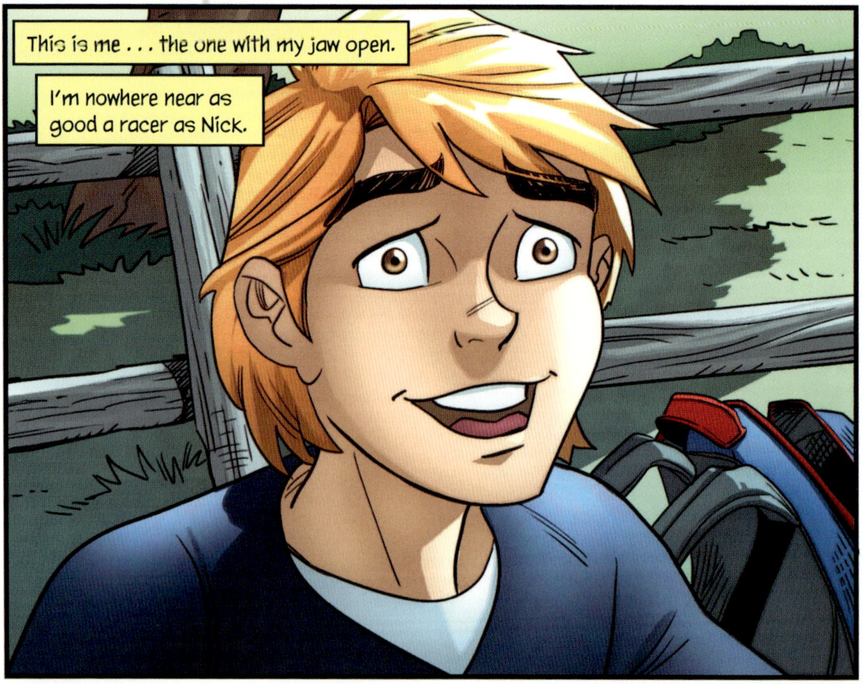
This is me . . . the one with my jaw open.
I'm nowhere near as good a racer as Nick.

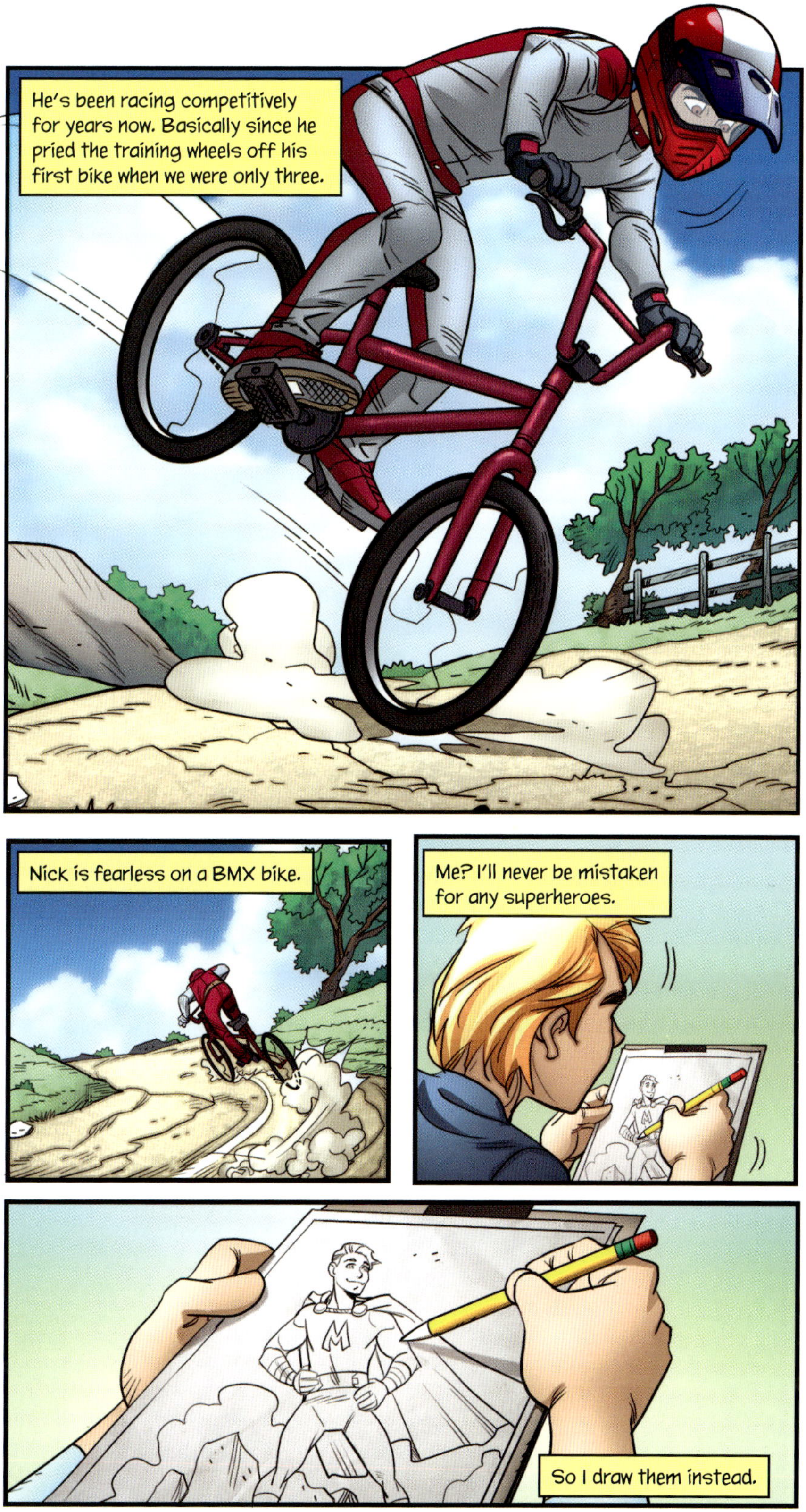
He's been racing competitively for years now. Basically since he pried the training wheels off his first bike when we were only three.
Nick is fearless on a BMX bike.
Me? I'll never be mistaken for any superheroes.
So I draw them instead.

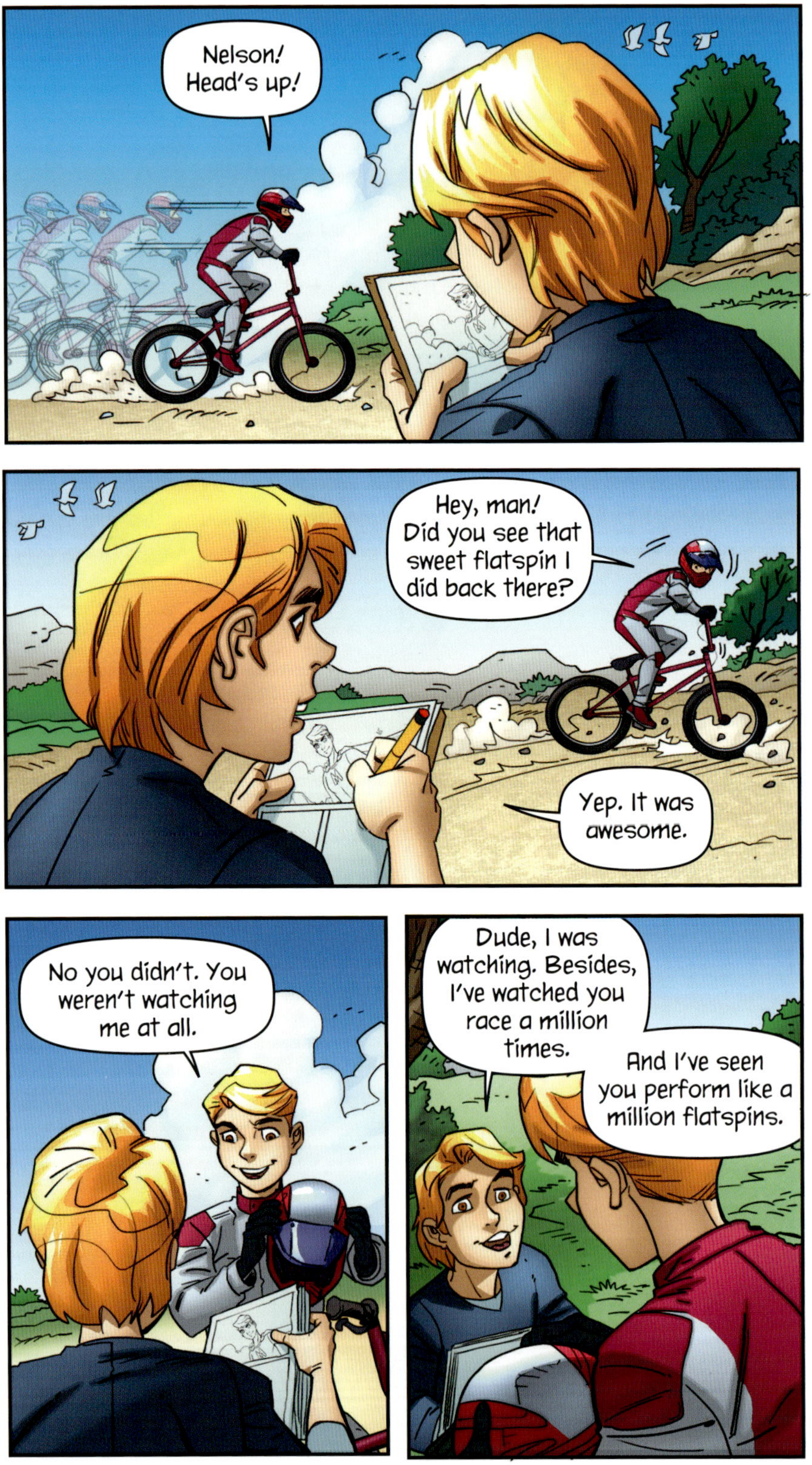
Nelson! Head's up!
Hey, man! Did you see that sweet flatspin I did back there?
Yep. It was awesome.
No you didn't. You weren't watching me at all.
Dude, I was watching. Besides, I've watched you race a million times.
And I've seen you perform like a million flatspins.

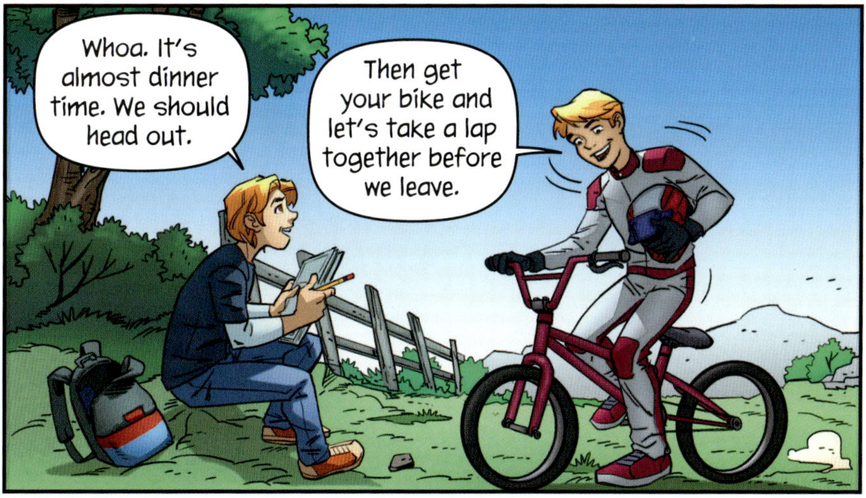
Whoa. It's almost dinner time. We should head out.
Then get your bike and let's take a lap together before we leave.

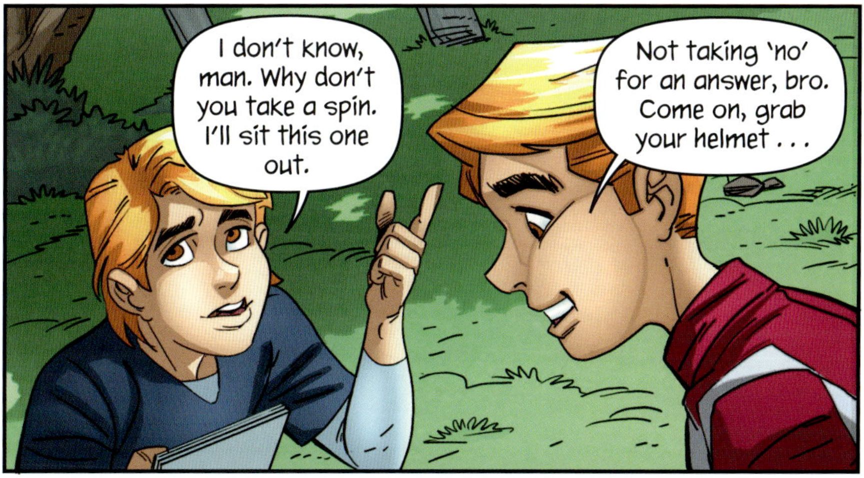
I don't know, man. Why don't you take a spin. I'll sit this one out.
Not taking 'no' for an answer, bro. Come on, grab your helmet . . .

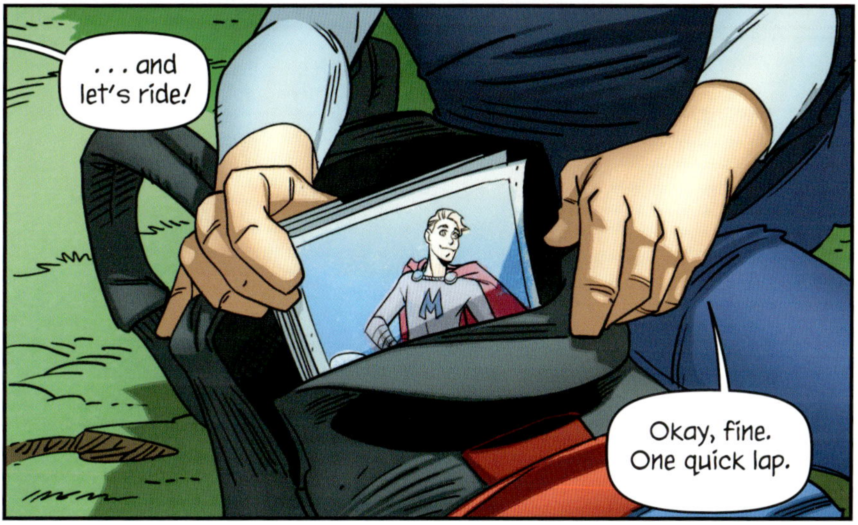
. . . and let's ride!
M
Okay, fine. One quick lap.

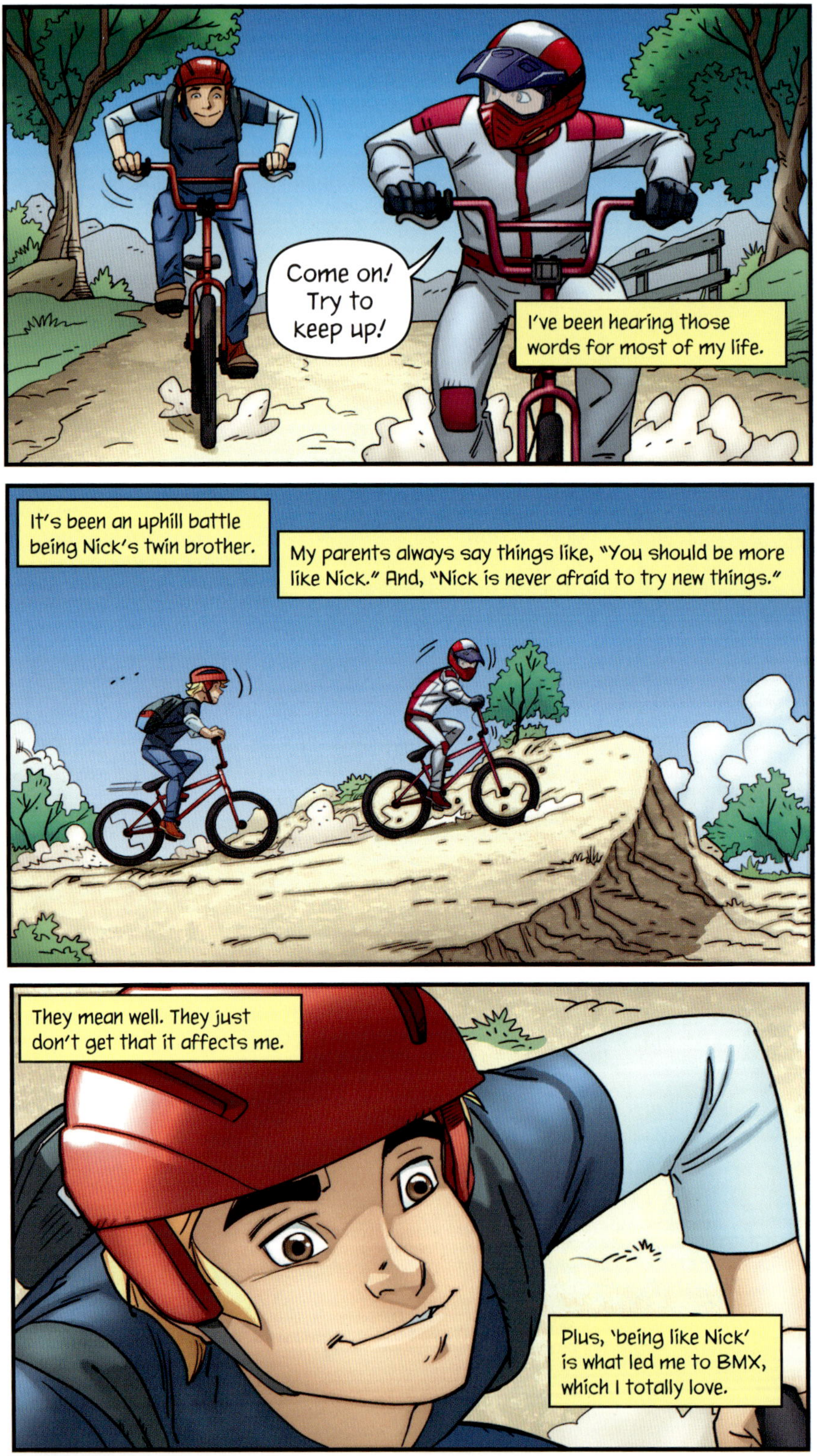
Come on! Try to keep up!
I've been hearing those words for most of my life.
It's been an uphill battle being Nick's twin brother.
My parents always say things like, "You should be more like Nick." And, "Nick is never afraid to try new things."
They mean well. They just don't get that it affects me.
Plus, 'being like Nick' is what led me to BMX, which I totally love.

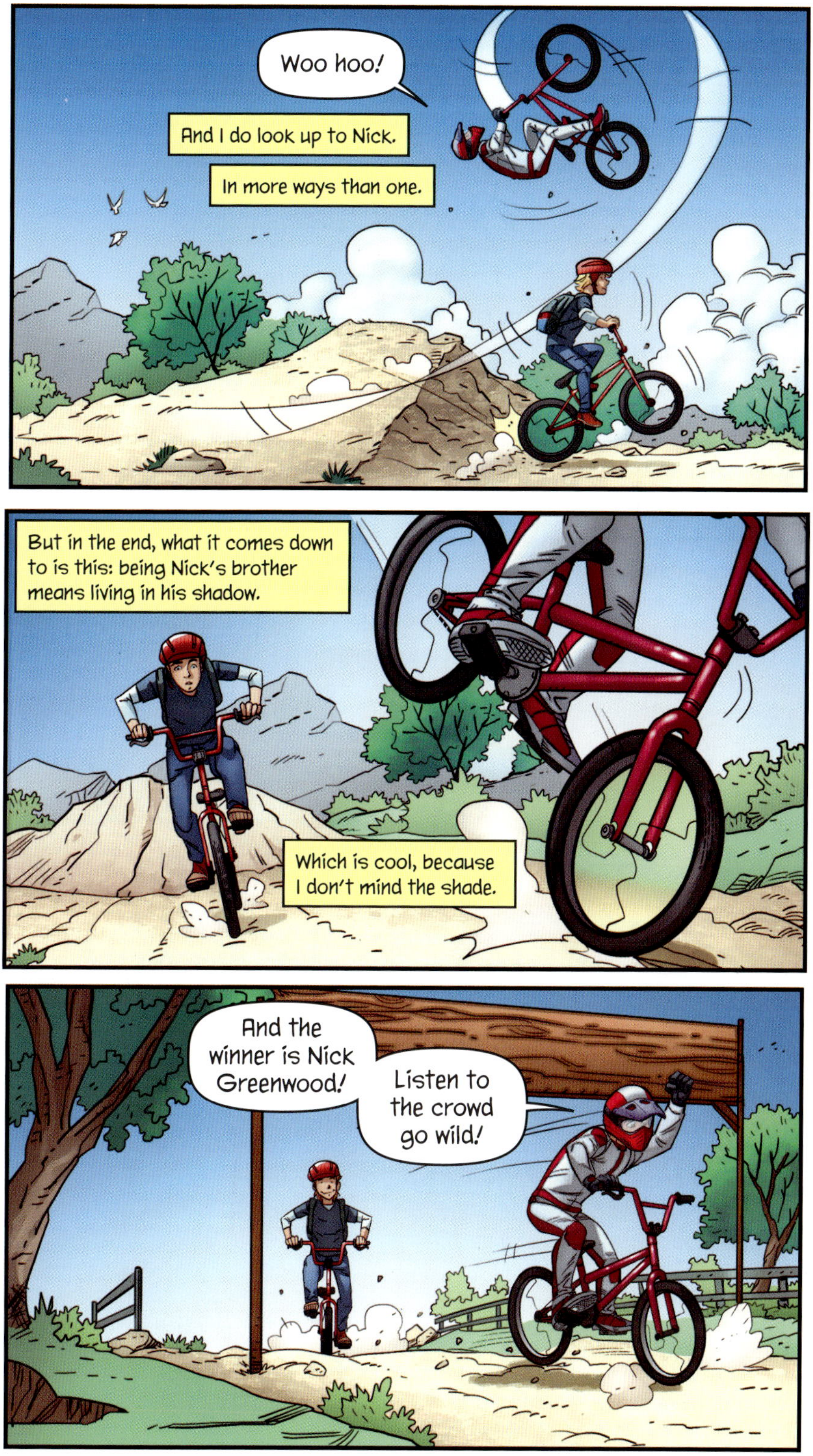
Woo hoo!
And I do look up to Nick.
In more ways than one.
But in the end, what it comes down to is this: being Nick's brother means living in his shadow.
Which is cool, because I don't mind the shade.
And the winner is Nick Greenwood!
Listen to the crowd go wild!

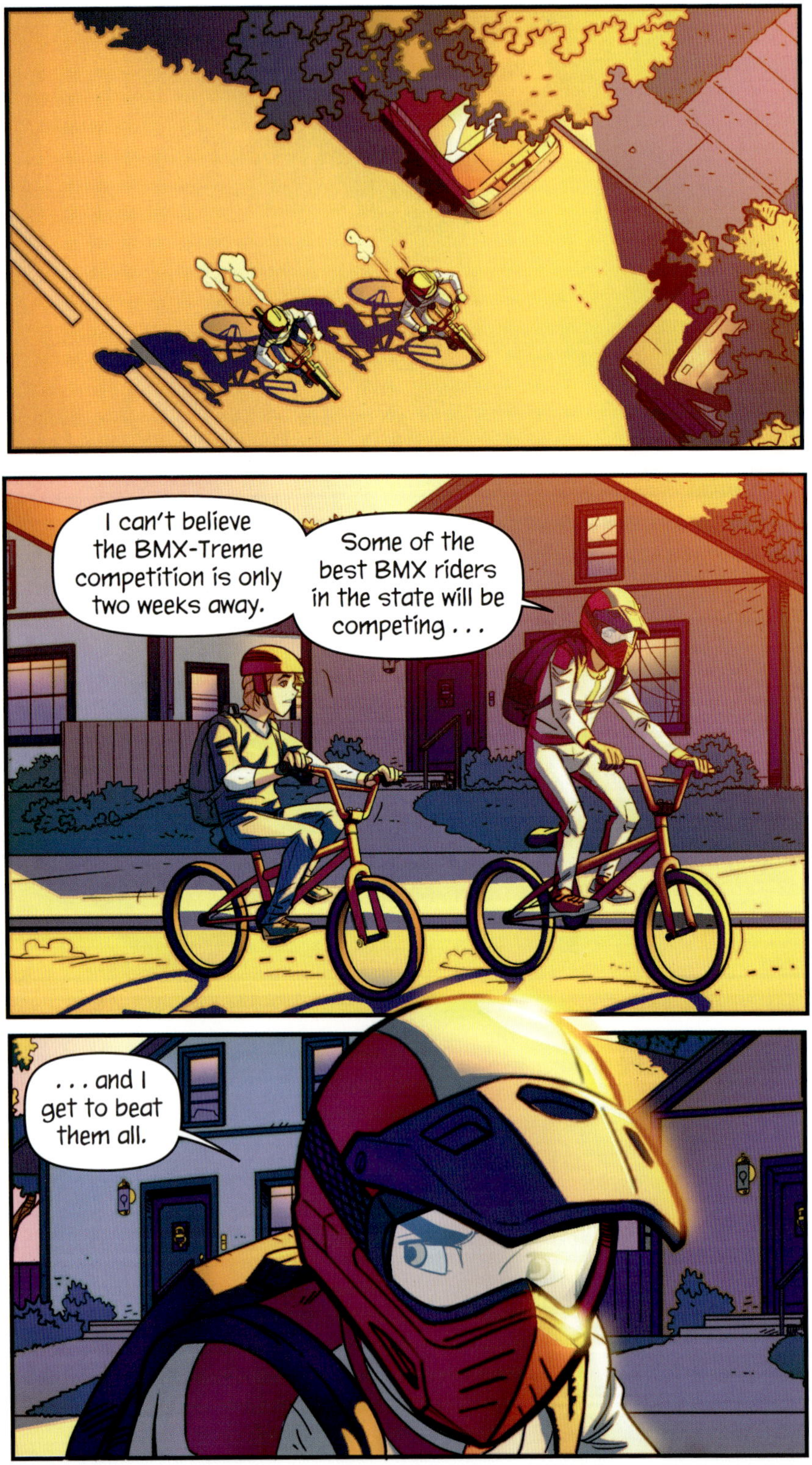
I can't believe the BMX-Treme competition is only two weeks away.
Some of the best BMX riders in the state will be competing . . .
. . . and I get to beat them all.

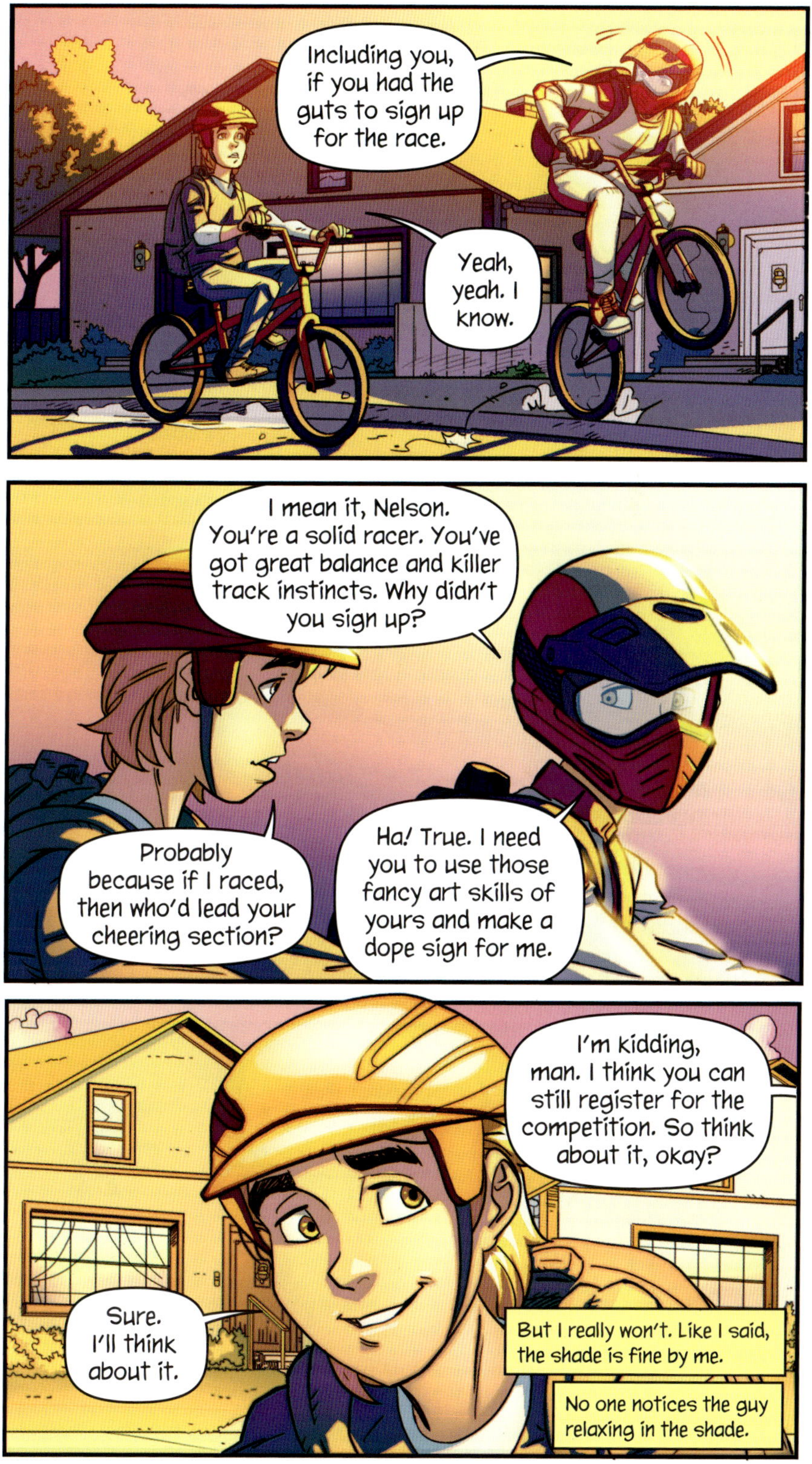
Including you, if you had the guts to sign up for the race.
Yeah, yeah. I know.
I mean it, Nelson. You're a solid racer. You've got great balance and killer track instincts. Why didn't you sign up?
Probably because if I raced, then who'd lead your cheering section?
Ha! True. I need you to use those fancy art skills of yours and make a dope sign for me.
I'm kidding, man. I think you can still register for the competition. So think about it, okay?
Sure. I'll think about it.
But I really won't. Like I said, the shade is fine by me.
No one notices the guy relaxing in the shade.

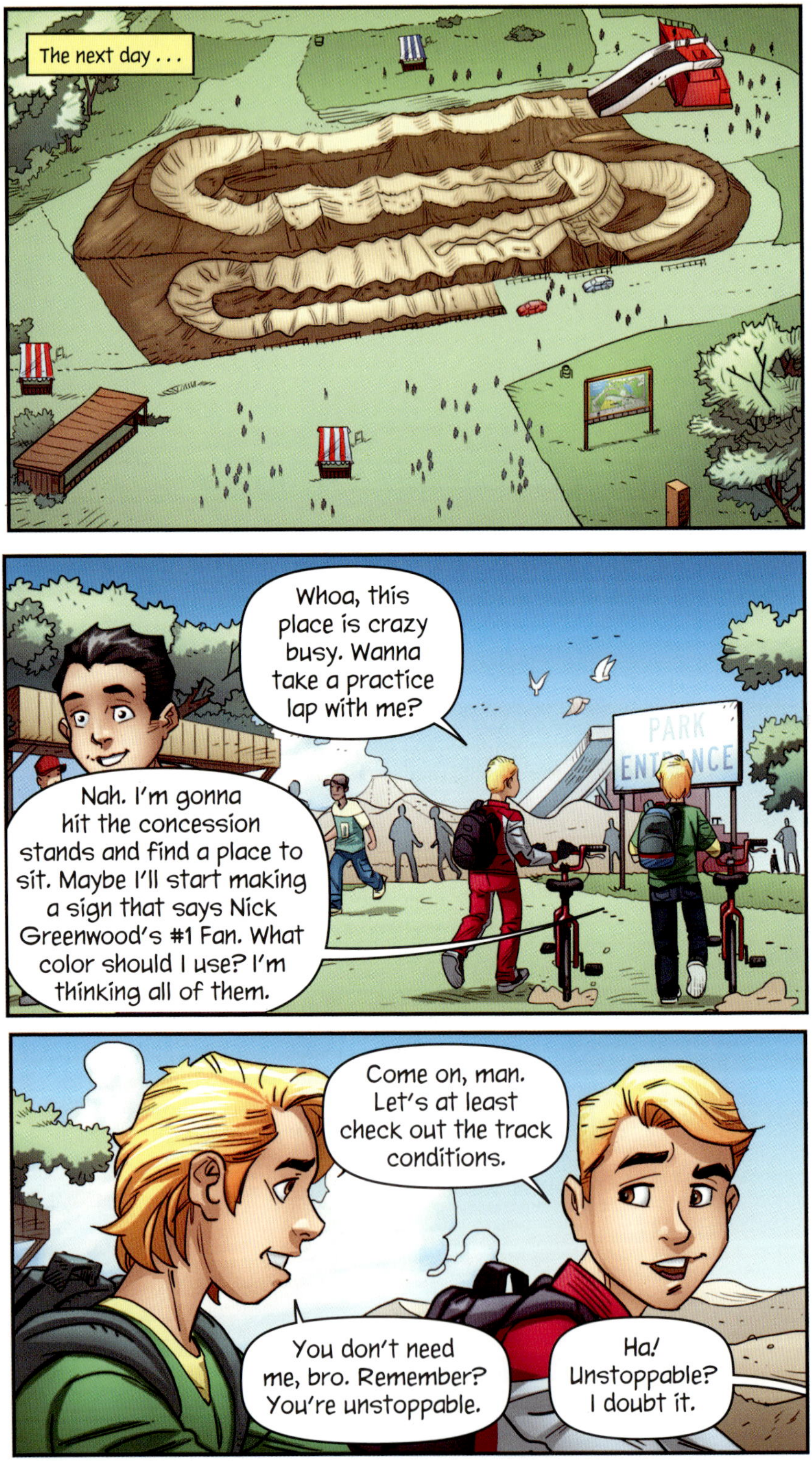
The next day . . .
Whoa, this place is crazy busy. Wanna take a practice lap with me?
Nah. I'm gonna hit the concession stands and find a place to sit. Maybe I'll start making a sign that says Nick Greenwood's #1 Fan. What color should I use? I'm thinking all of them.
Come on, man. Let's at least check out the track conditions.
You don't need me, bro. Remember? You're unstoppable.
Ha! Unstoppable? I doubt it.

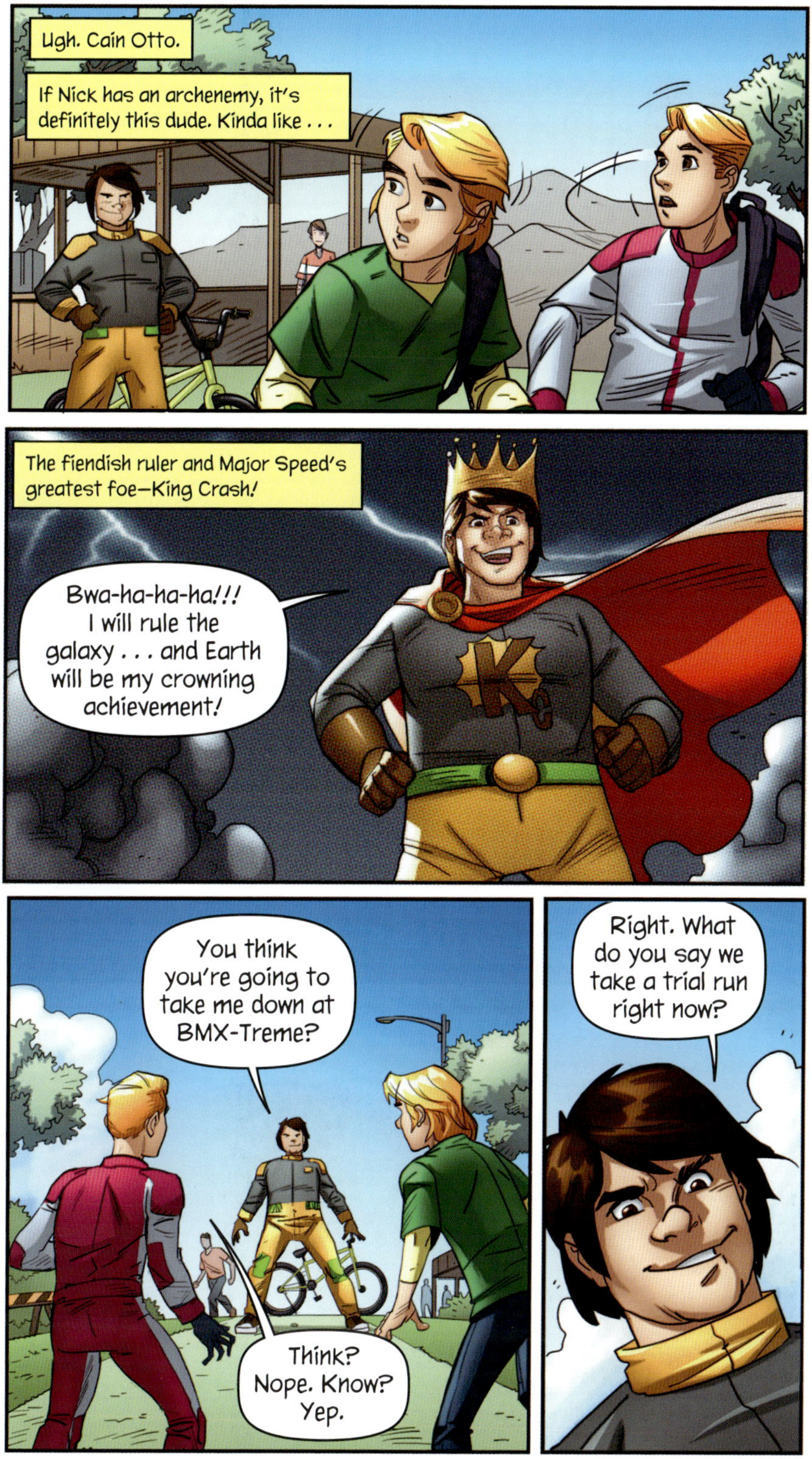
Ugh. Cain Otto.
If Nick has an archenemy, it's definitely this dude. Kinda like . . .
The fiendish ruler and Major Speed's greatest foe—King Crash!
Bwa-ha-ha-ha!!! I will rule the galaxy . . . and Earth will be my crowning achievement!
You think you're going to take me down at BMX-Treme?
Think? Nope. Know? Yep.
Right. What do you say we take a trial run right now?

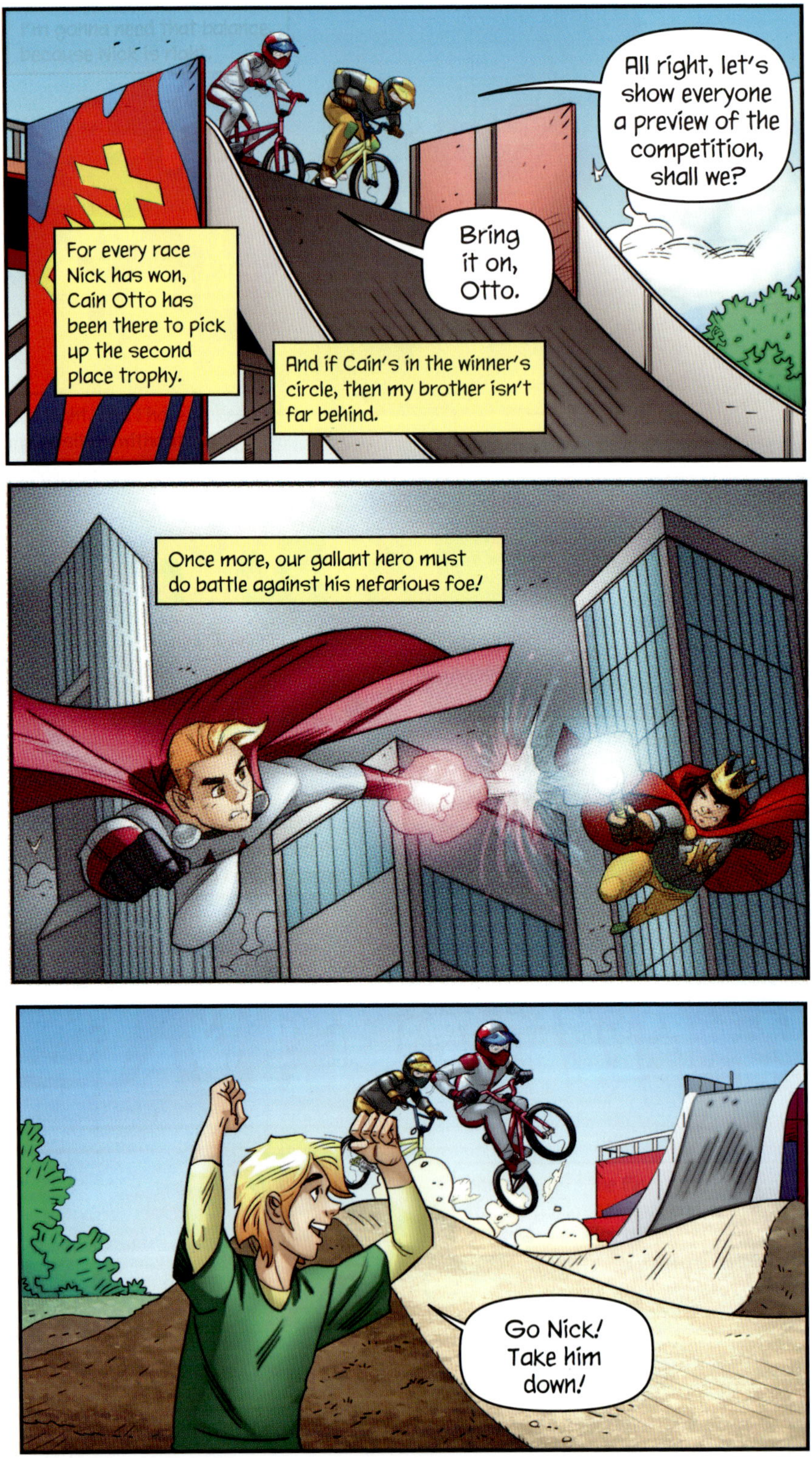

All right, let's show everyone a preview of the competition, shall we?
Bring it on, Otto.
For every race Nick has won, Cain Otto has been there to pick up the second place trophy.
And if Cain's in the winner's circle, then my brother isn't far behind.
Once more, our gallant hero must do battle against his nefarious foe!
Go Nick! Take him down!

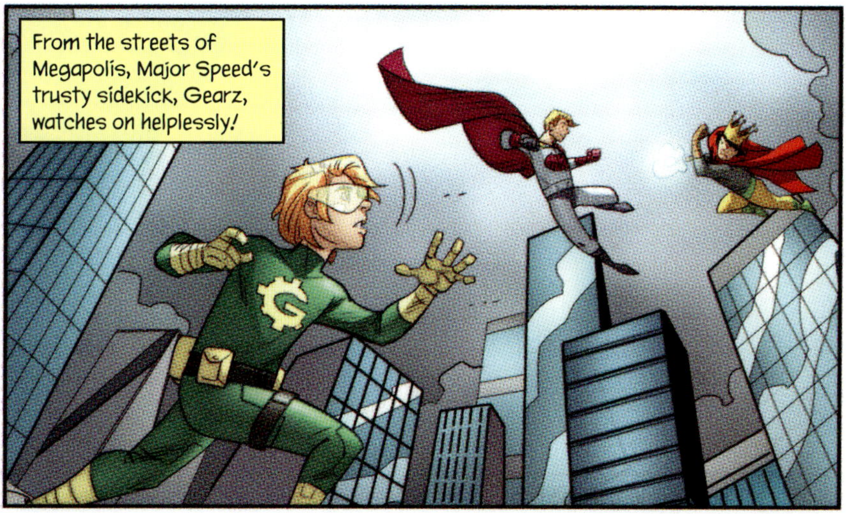
From the streets of Megapolis, Major Speed's trusty sidekick, Gearz, watches on helplessly!

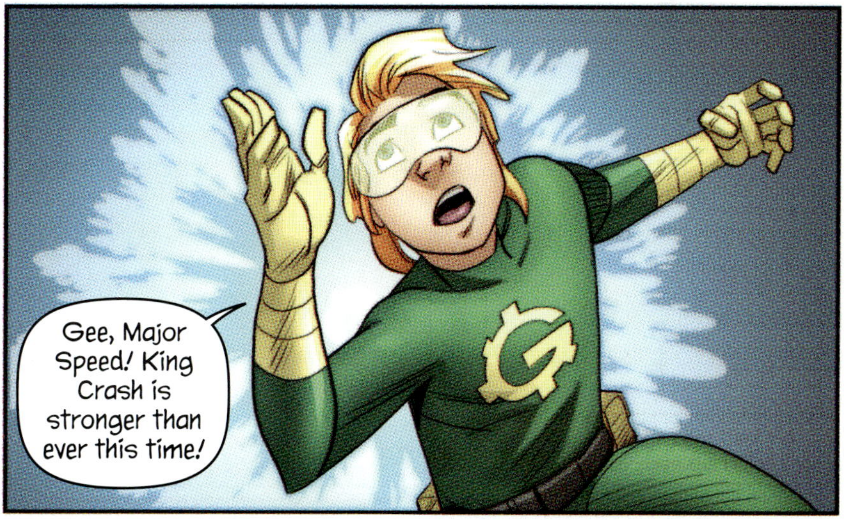
Gee, Major Speed! King Crash is stronger than ever this time!

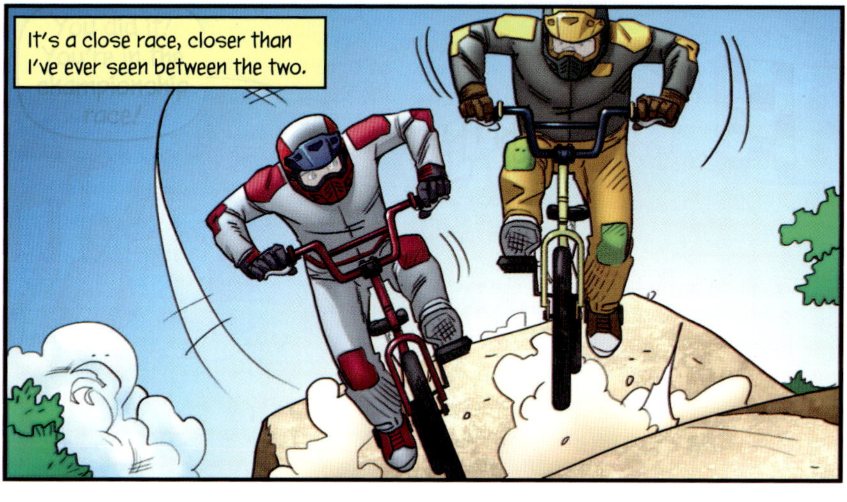
It's a close race, closer than I've ever seen between the two.

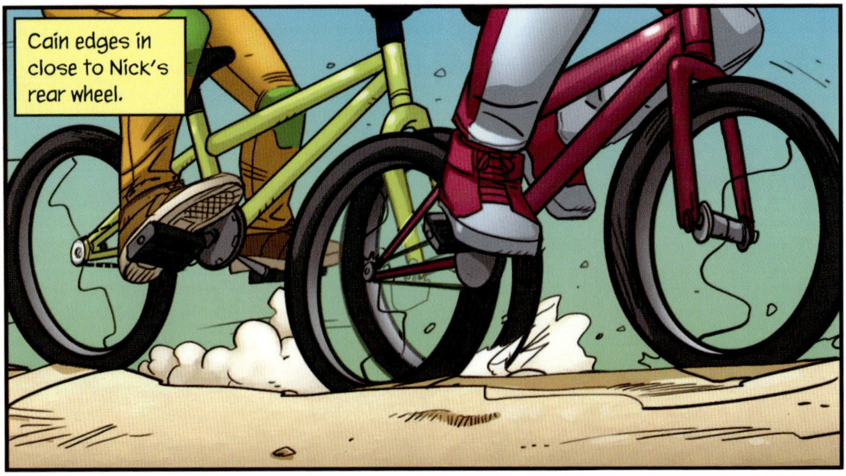
Cain edges in close to Nick's rear wheel.

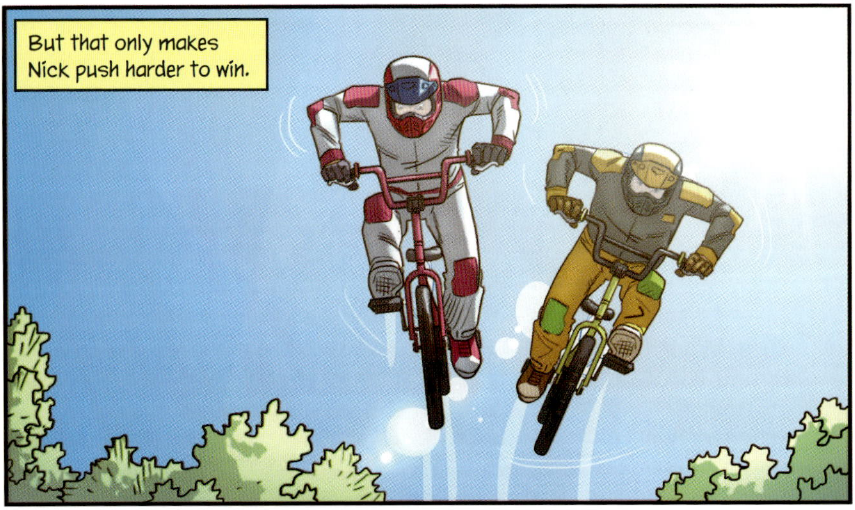
But that only makes Nick push harder to win.

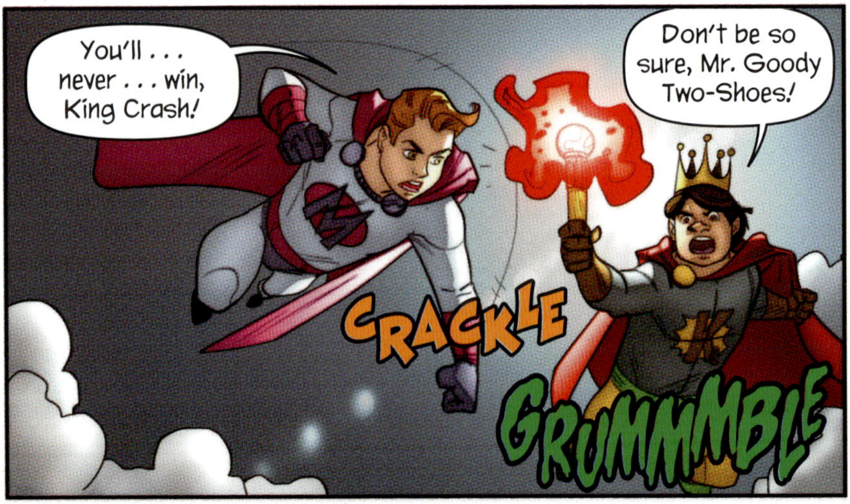
You'll . . . never . . . win, King Crash!
Don't be so sure, Mr. Goody Two-Shoes!
CRACKLE
GRUMMMBLE

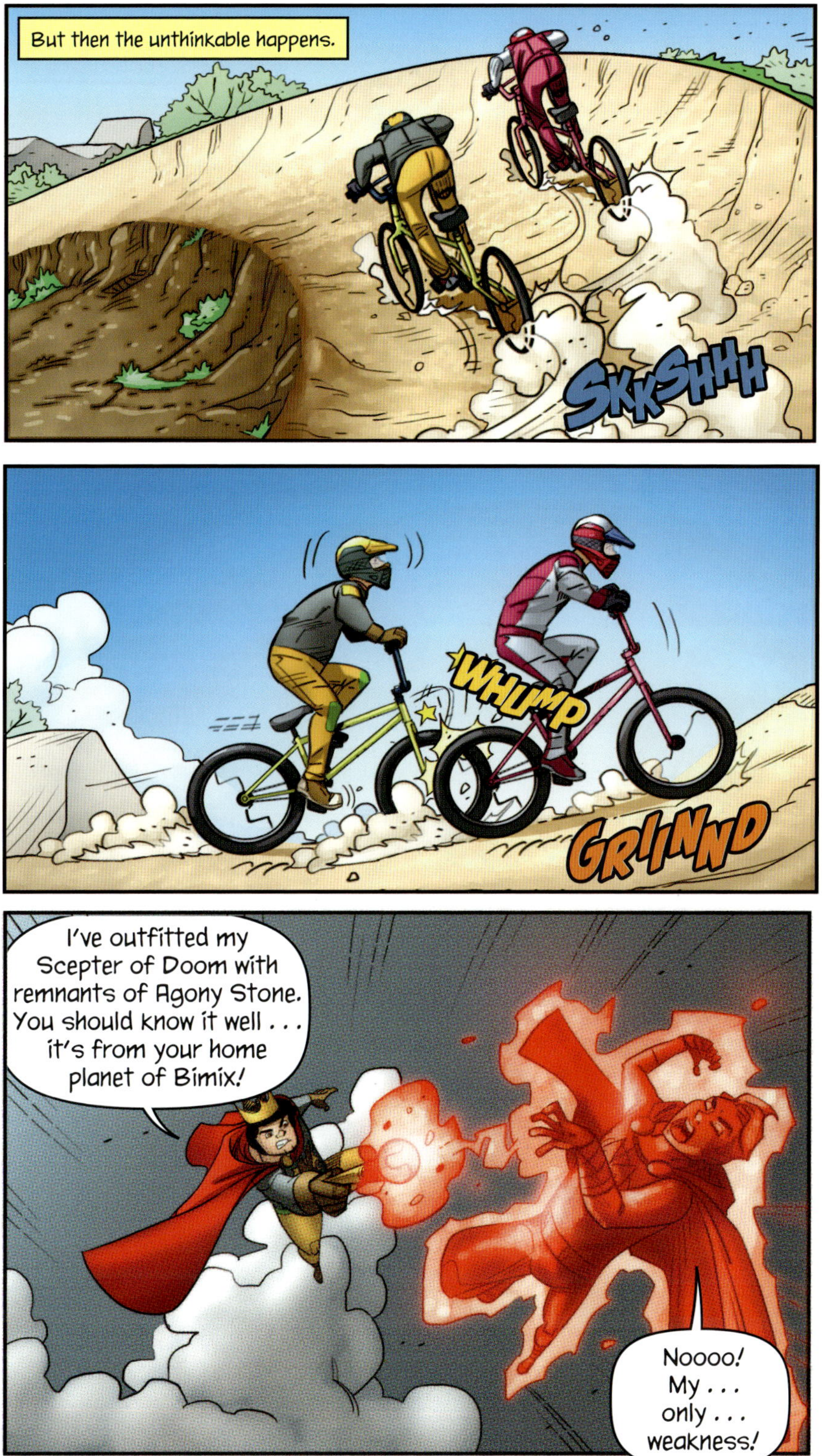
But then the unthinkable happens.
SKKSHHH
WHUMP
GRIINND
I've outfitted my Scepter of Doom with remnants of Agony Stone. You should know it well . . . it's from your home planet of Bimix!
Noooo! My . . . only . . . weakness!

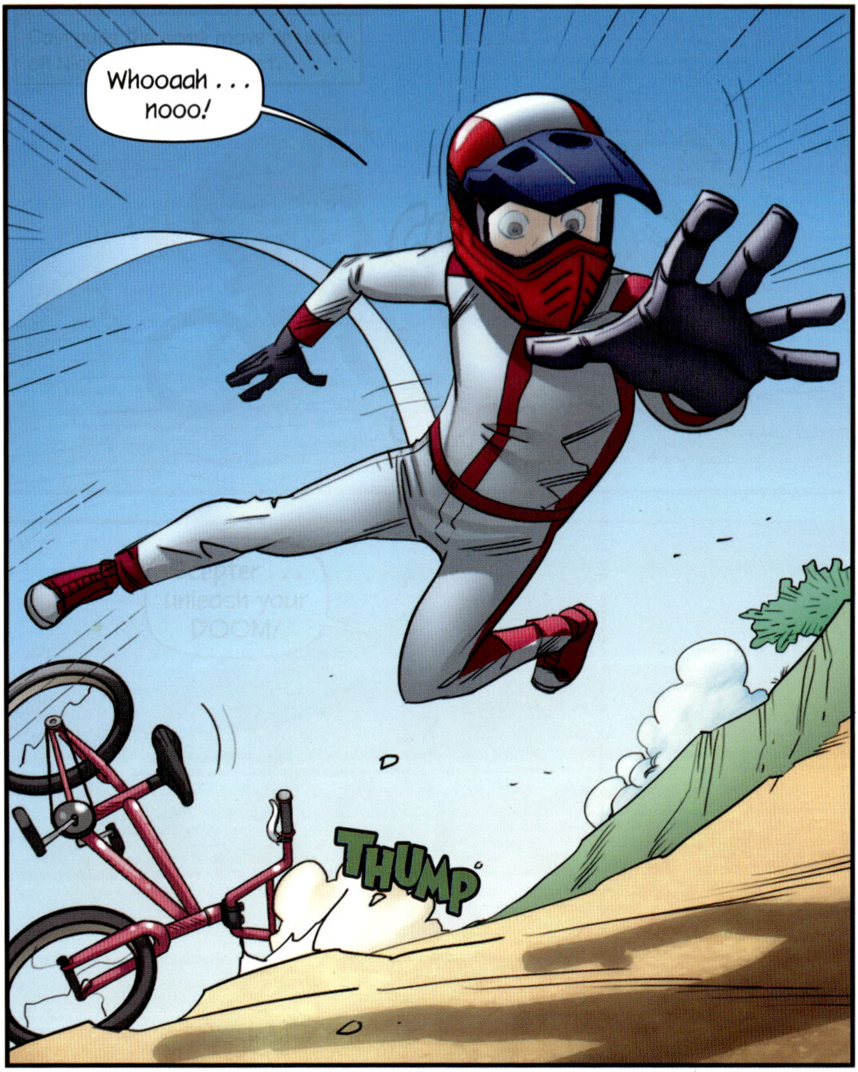
Whooaah . . .
nooo!
THUMP

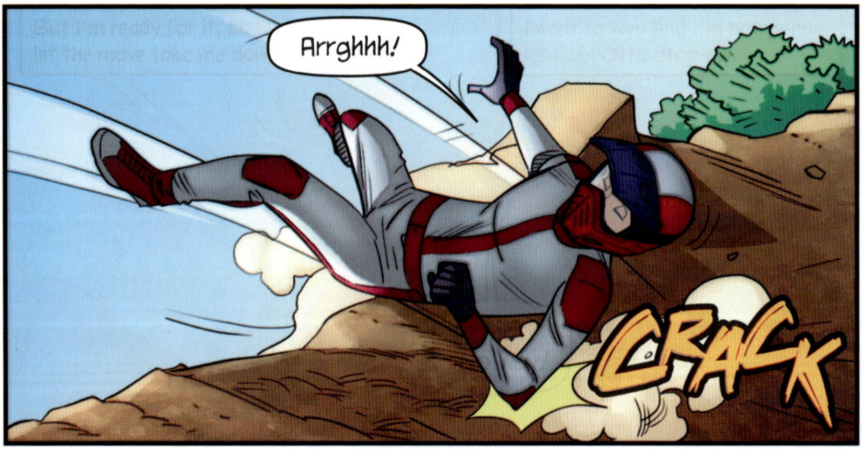
Arrghhh!
CRACK

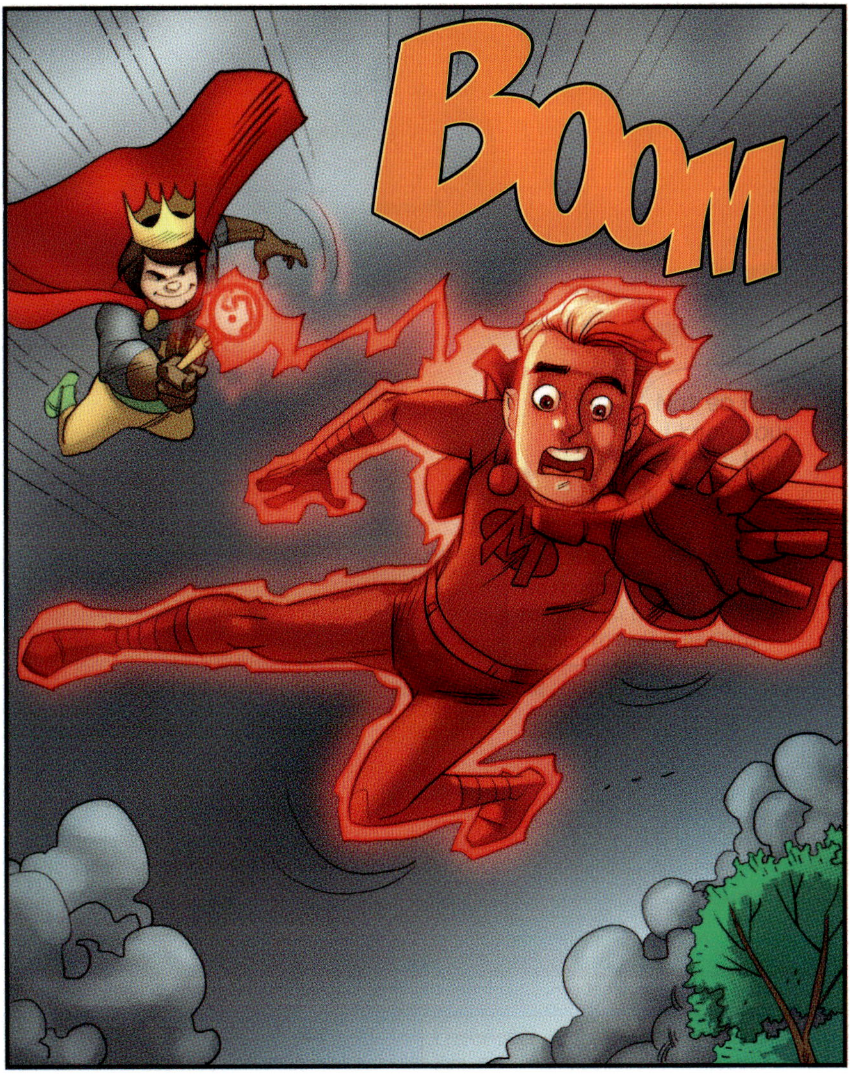
BOOM

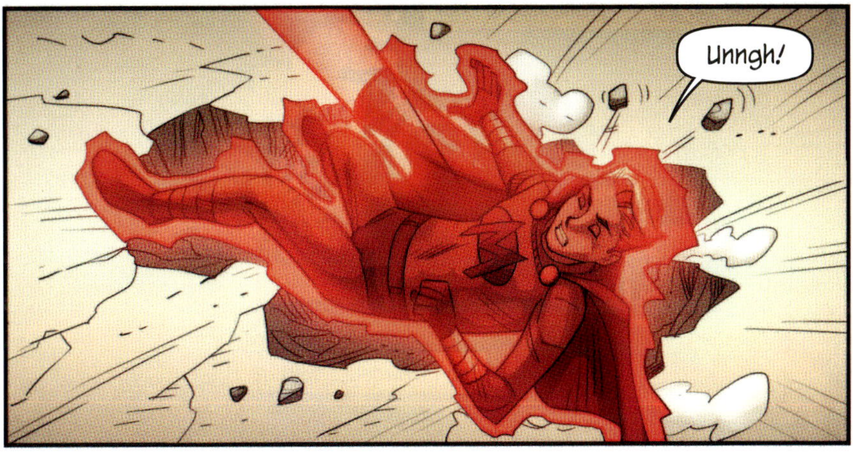
Unngh!

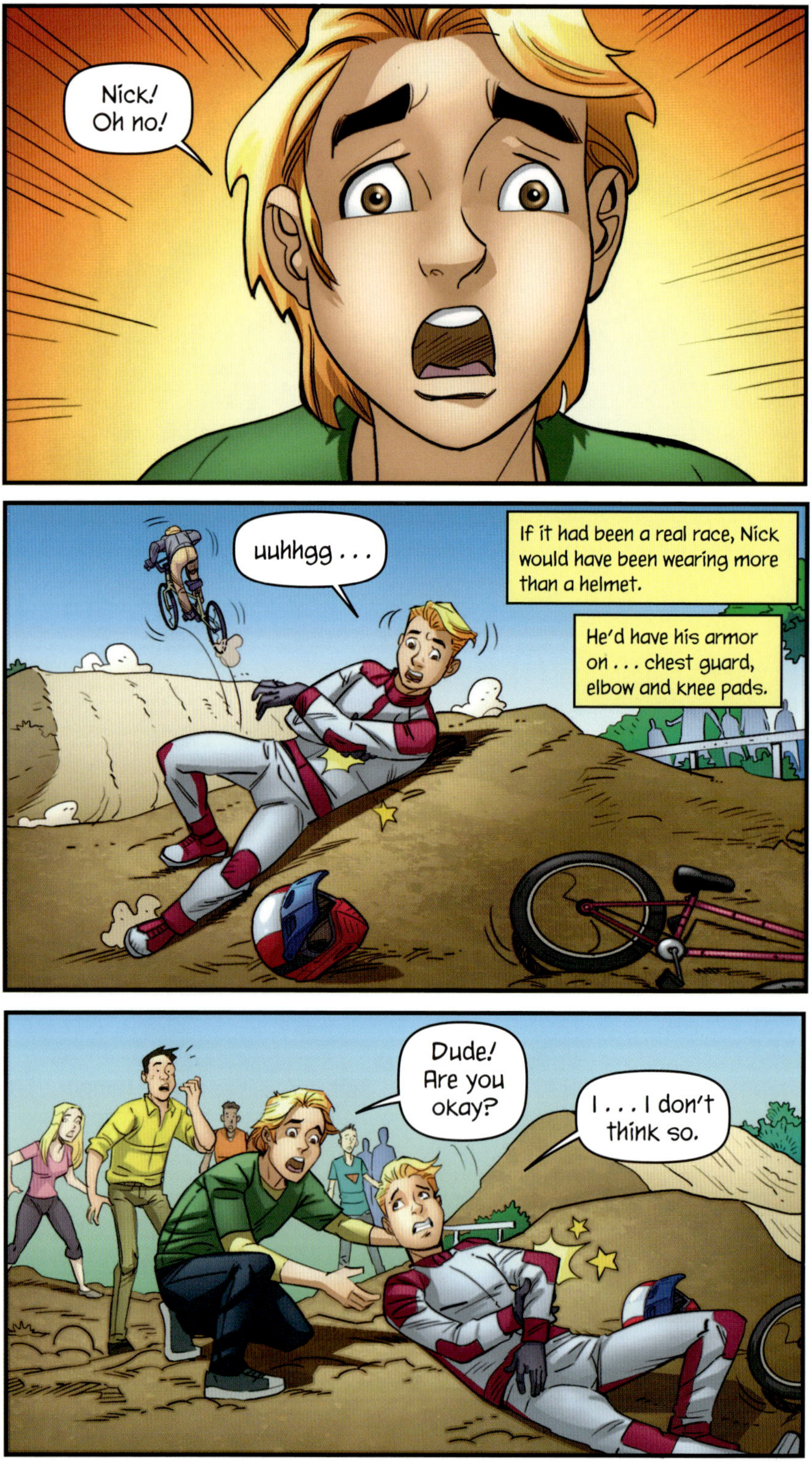
Nick!
Oh no!
uuhhgg . . .
If it had been a real race, Nick would have been wearing more than a helmet.
He'd have his armor on . . . chest guard, elbow and knee pads.
Dude! Are you okay?
I . . . I don't think so.

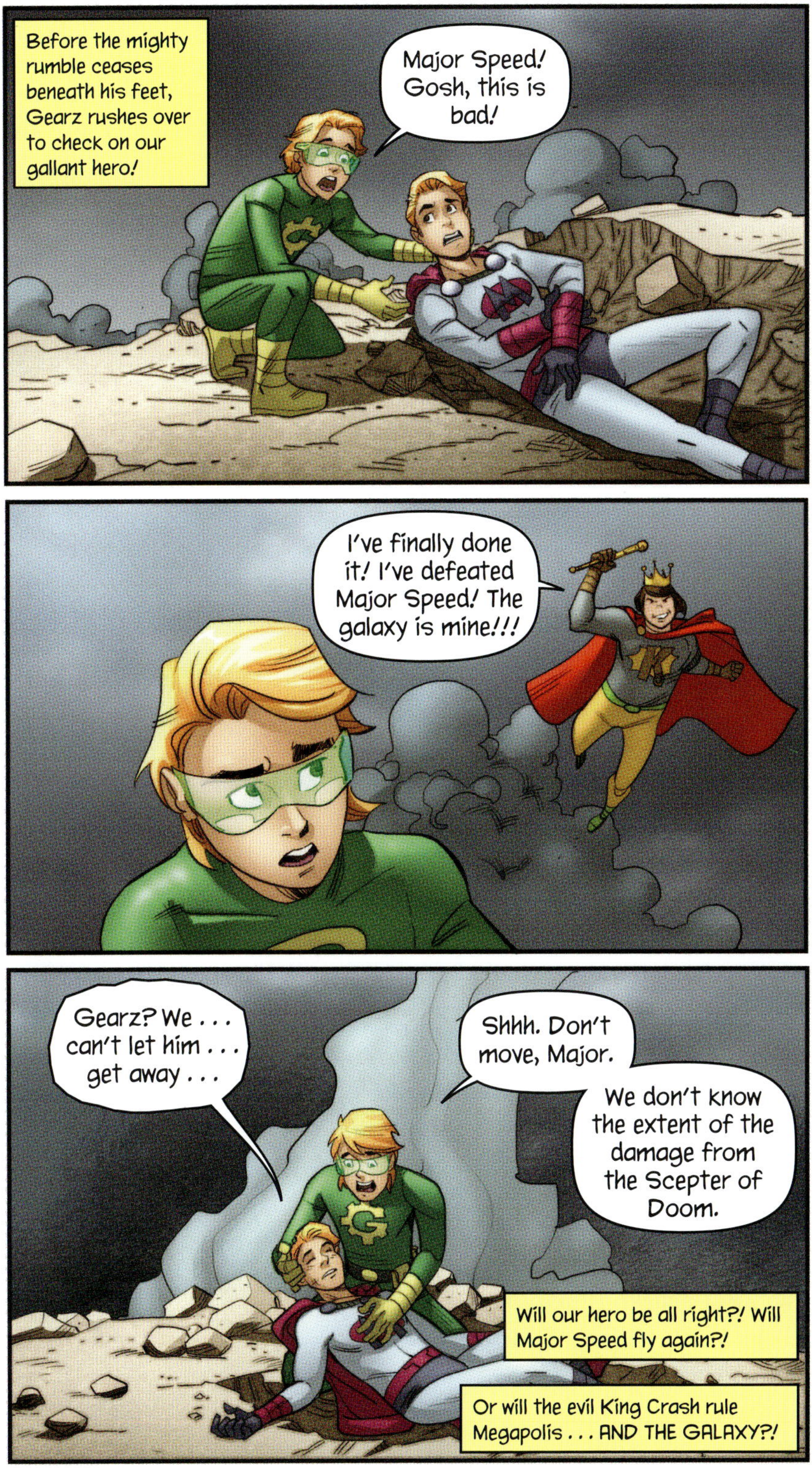
Before the mighty rumble ceases beneath his feet, Gearz rushes over to check on our gallant hero!
Major Speed! Gosh, this is bad!
I've finally done it! I've defeated Major Speed! The galaxy is mine!!!
Gearz? We . . . can't let him . . . get away . . .
Shhh. Don't move, Major.
We don't know the extent of the damage from the Scepter of Doom.
Will our hero be all right?! Will Major Speed fly again?!
Or will the evil King Crash rule Megapolis . . . AND THE GALAXY?!

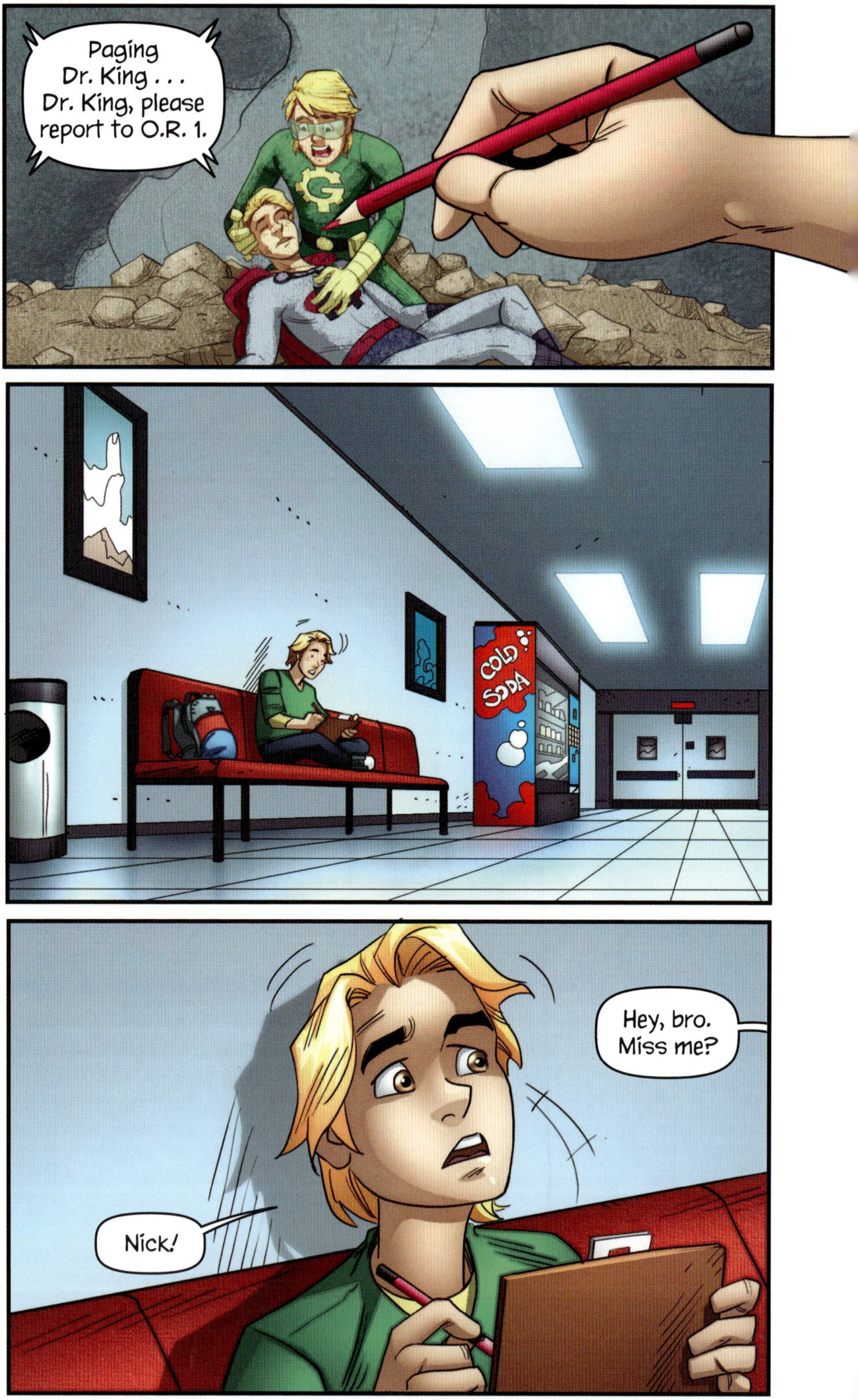
Paging Dr. King . . . Dr. King, please report to O.R. 1.
COLD SODA
Nick!
Hey, bro. Miss me?

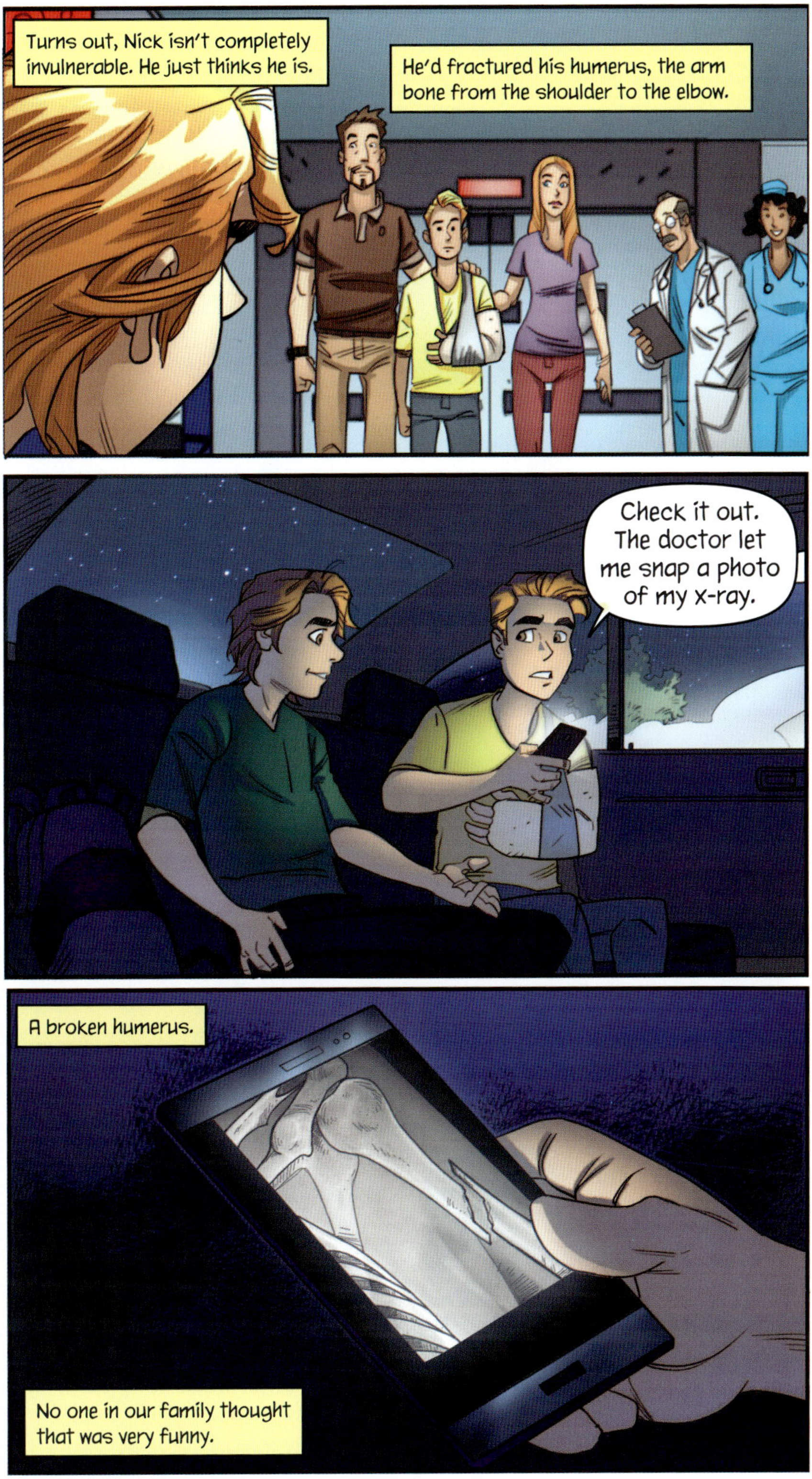
Turns out, Nick isn't completely invulnerable. He just thinks he is.
He'd fractured his humerus, the arm bone from the shoulder to the elbow.
Check it out. The doctor let me snap a photo of my x-ray.
A broken humerus.
No one in our family thought that was very funny.

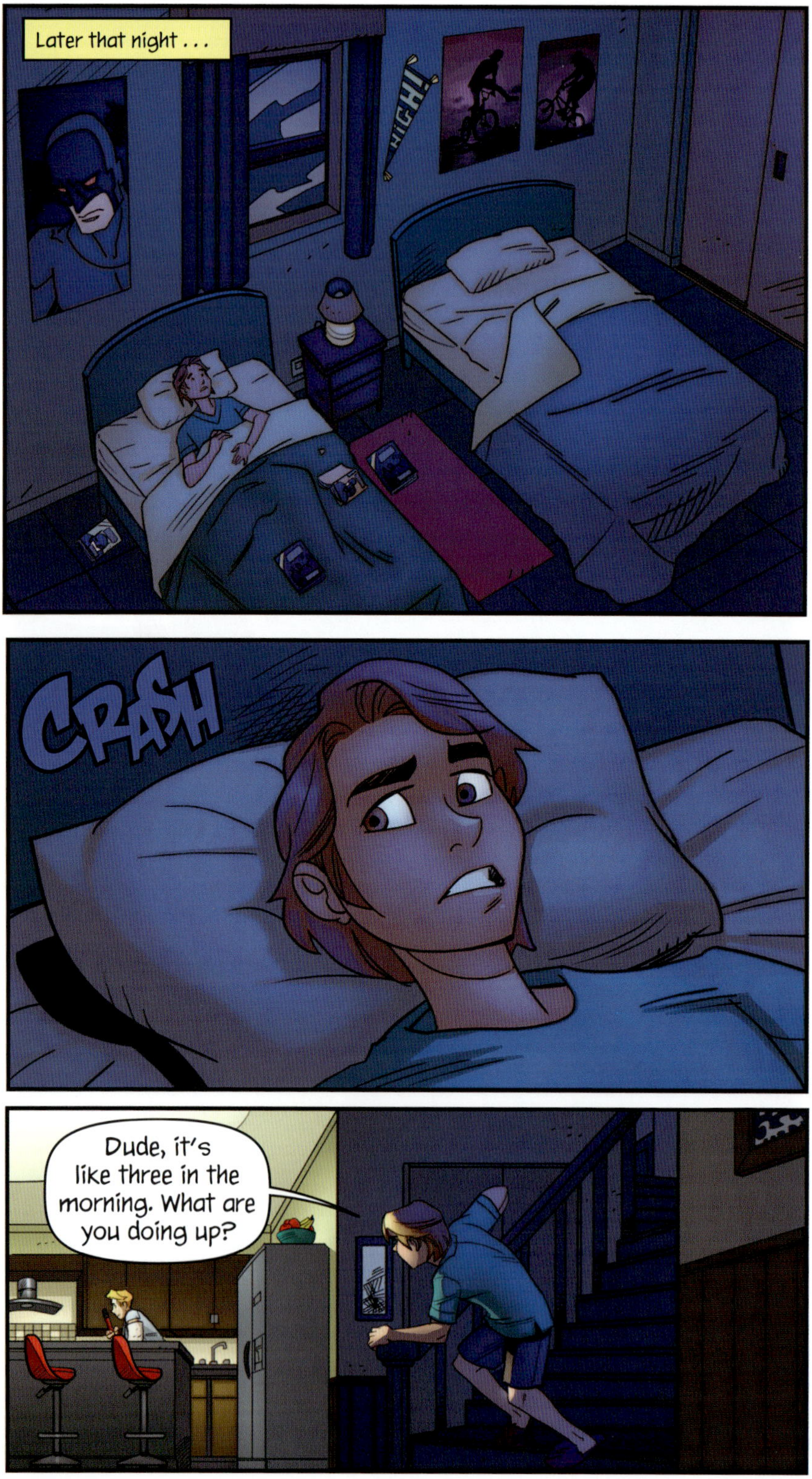
Later that night . . .
HIGH!
CRASH
Dude, it's like three in the morning. What are you doing up?

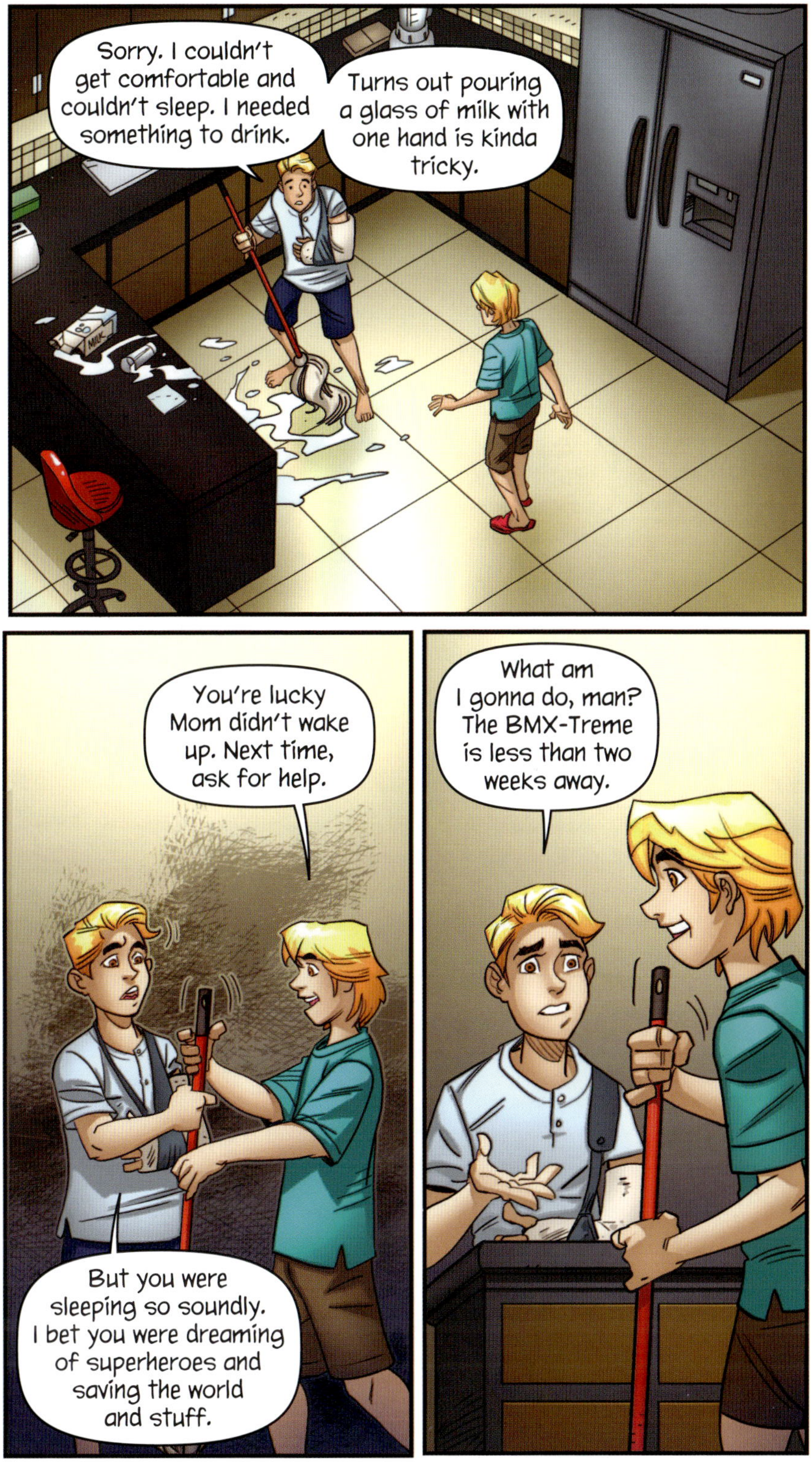

Sorry. I couldn't get comfortable and couldn't sleep. I needed something to drink.
Turns out pouring a glass of milk with one hand is kinda tricky.
MILK
You're lucky Mom didn't wake up. Next time, ask for help.
But you were sleeping so soundly. I bet you were dreaming of superheroes and saving the world and stuff.
What am I gonna do, man? The BMX-Treme is less than two weeks away.

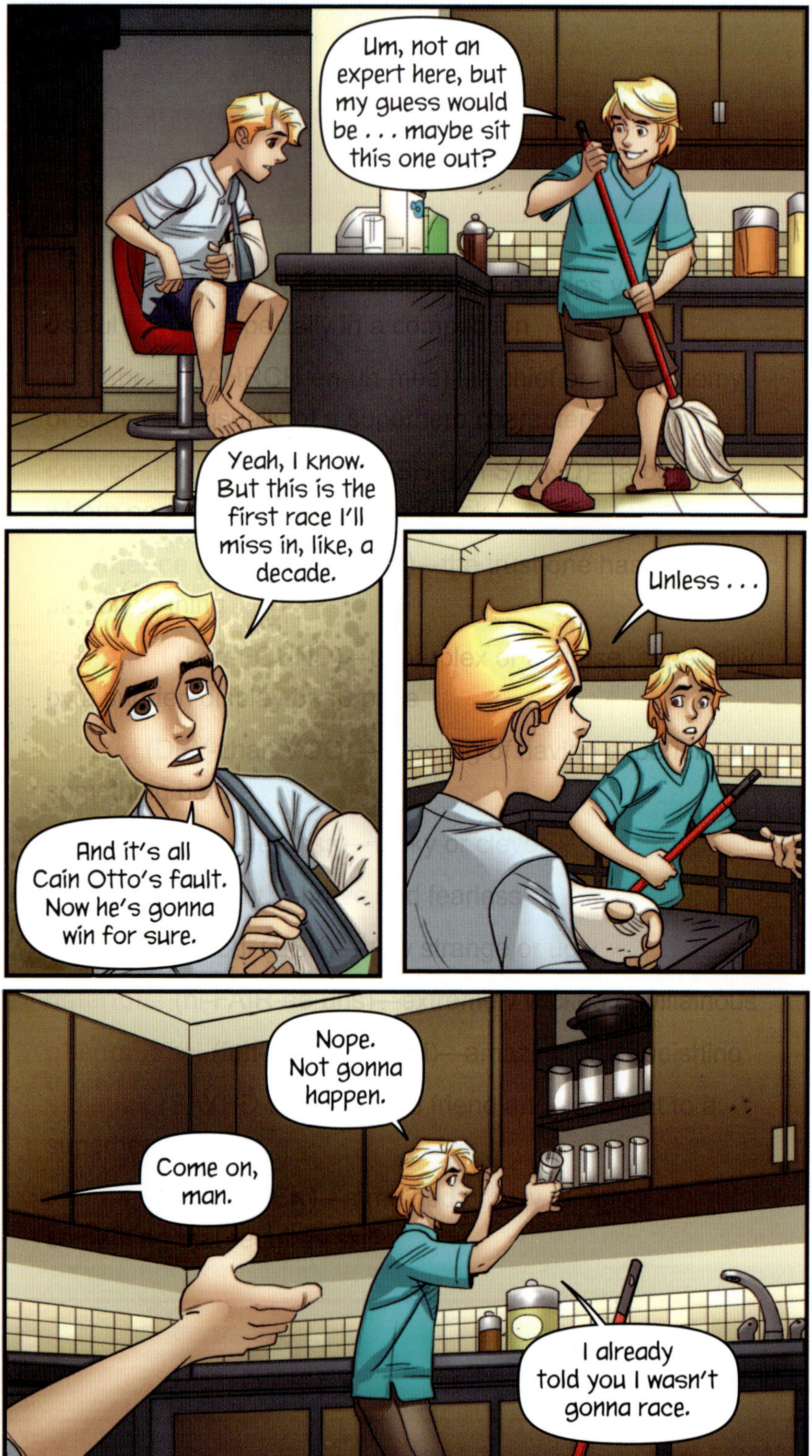
Um, not an expert here, but my guess would be . . . maybe sit this one out?
Yeah, I know. But this is the first race I'll miss in, like, a decade.
And it's all Cain Otto's fault. Now he's gonna win for sure.
Unless . . .
Nope. Not gonna happen.
Come on, man.
I already told you I wasn't gonna race.

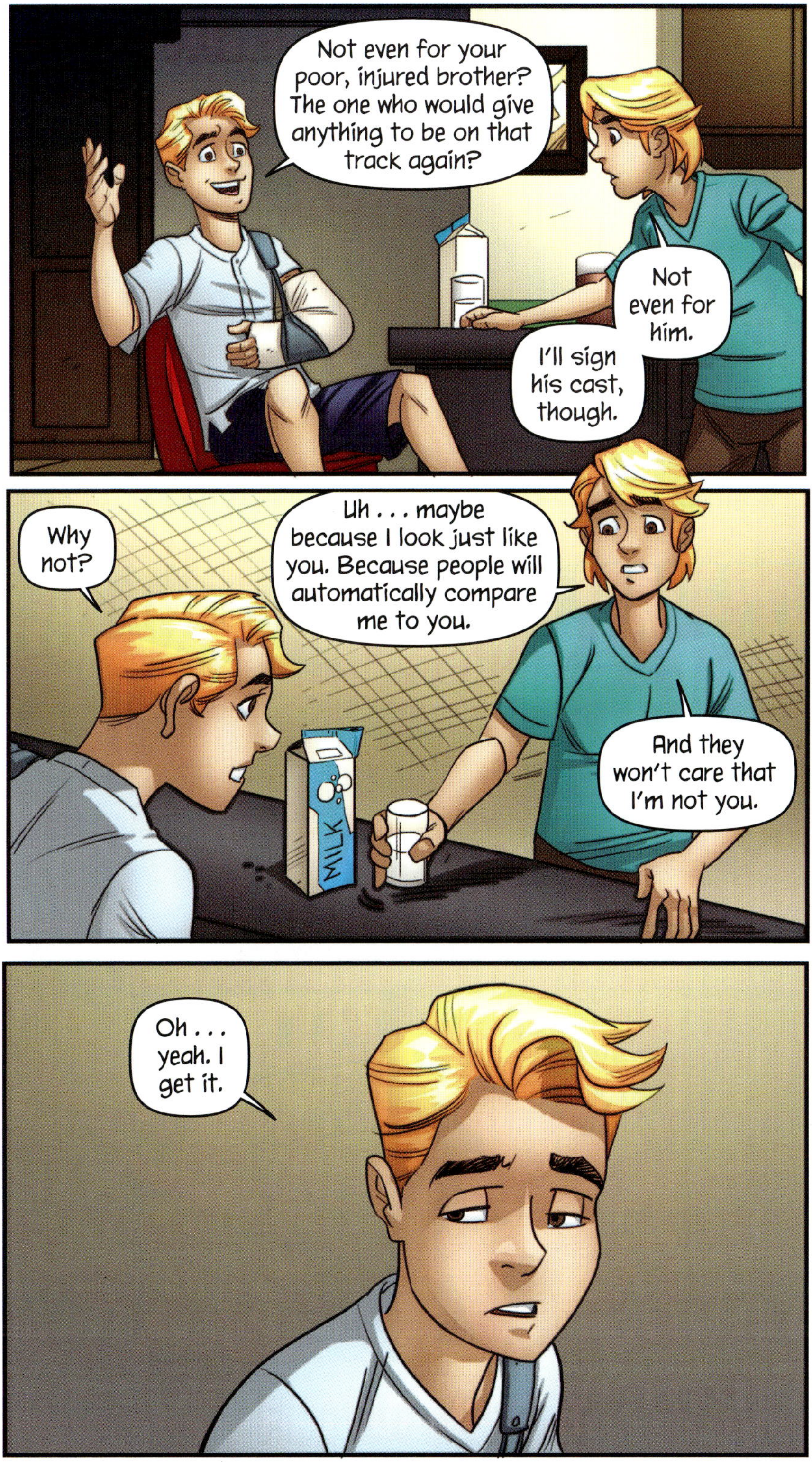
Not even for your poor, injured brother? The one who would give anything to be on that track again?
Not even for him.
I'll sign his cast, though.
Why not?
Uh . . . maybe because I look just like you. Because people will automatically compare me to you.
And they won't care that I'm not you.
MILK
Oh . . . yeah. I get it.

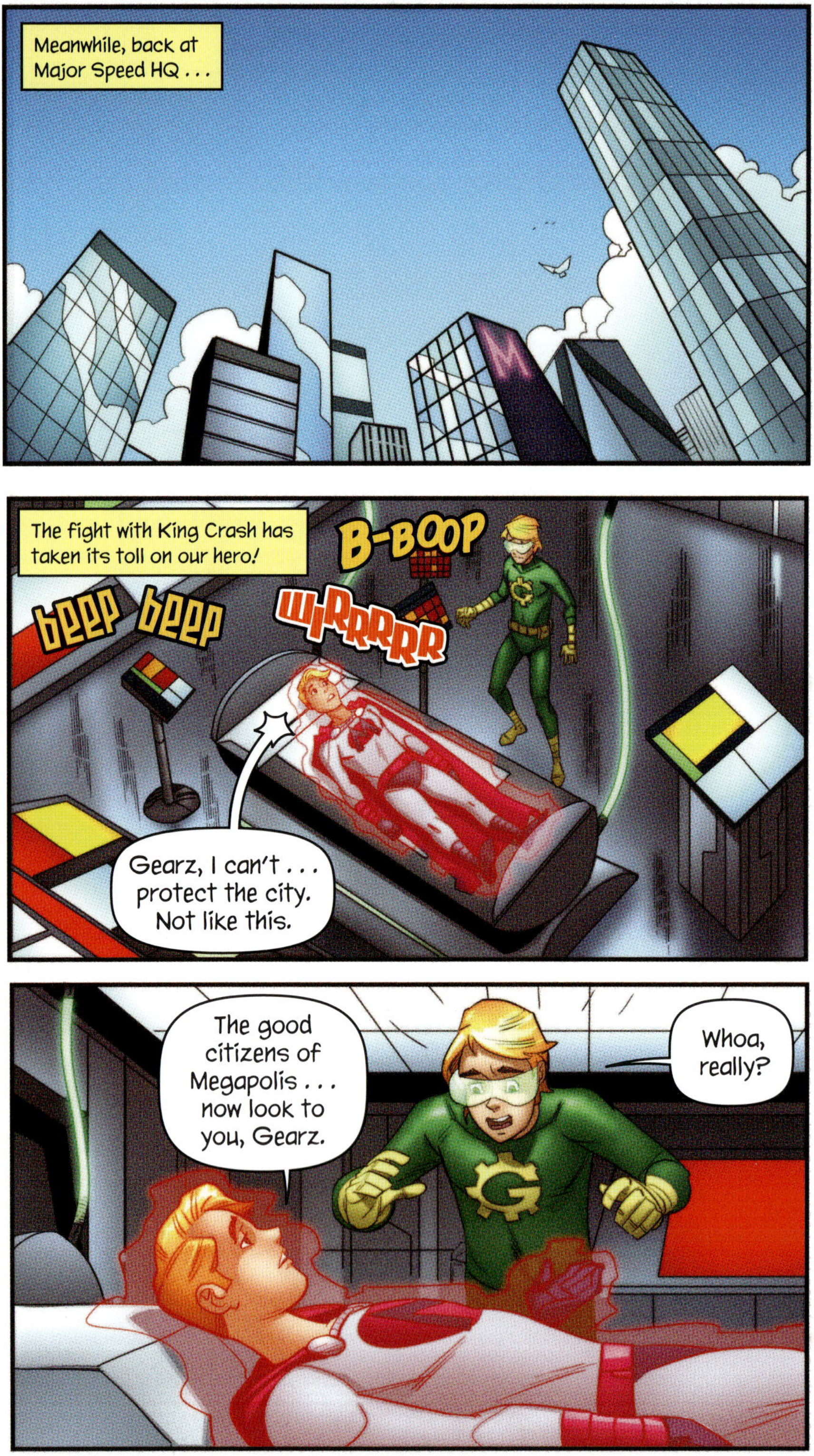

Meanwhile, back at Major Speed HQ . . .
The fight with King Crash has taken its toll on our hero!
beep beep
B-BOOP
WIRRRRR
Gearz, I can't . . . protect the city. Not like this.
The good citizens of Megapolis . . . now look to you, Gearz.
Whoa, really?

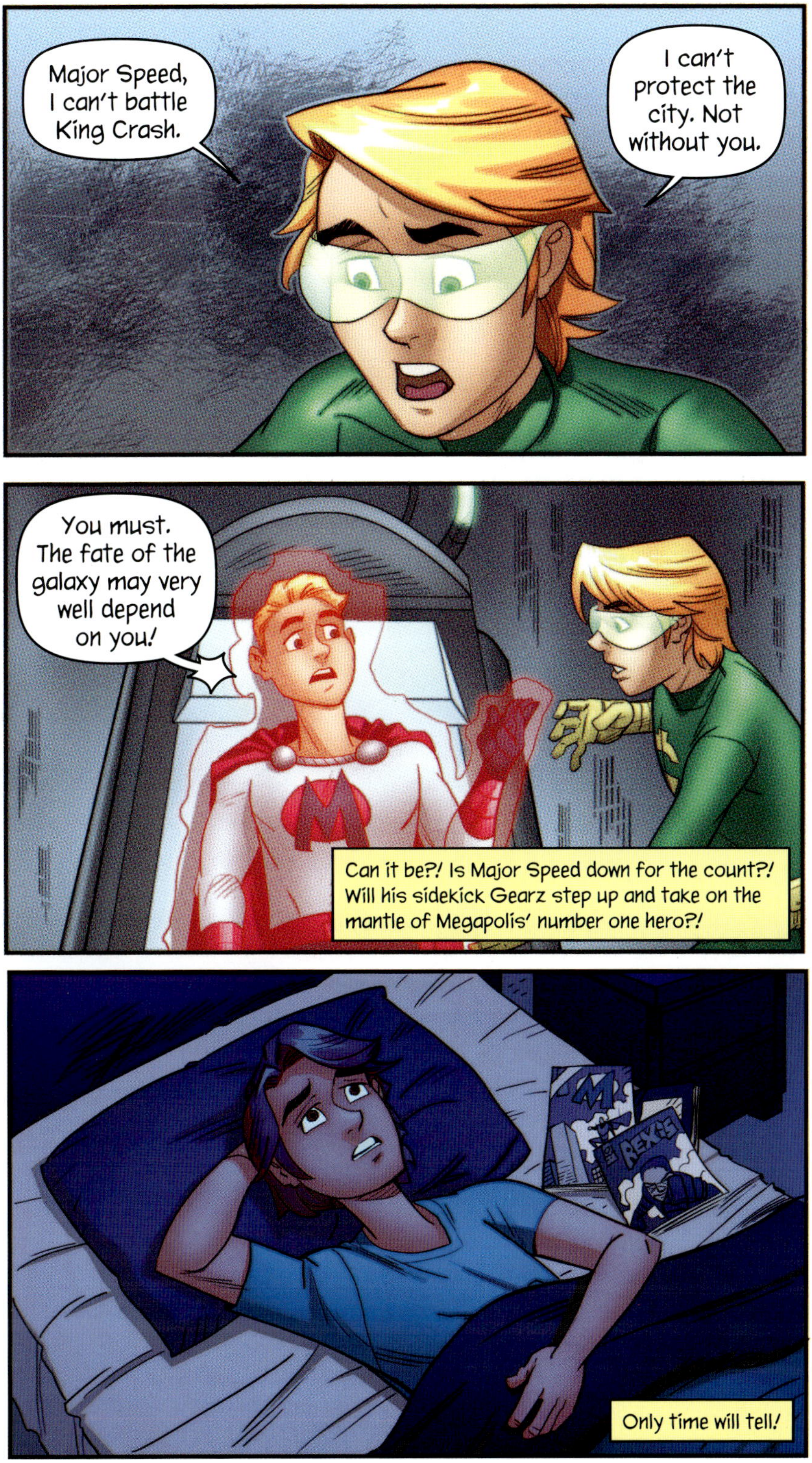
Major Speed, I can't battle King Crash.
I can't protect the city. Not without you.
You must. The fate of the galaxy may very well depend on you!
Can it be?! Is Major Speed down for the count?! Will his sidekick Gearz step up and take on the mantle of Megapolis' number one hero?!
Only time will tell!

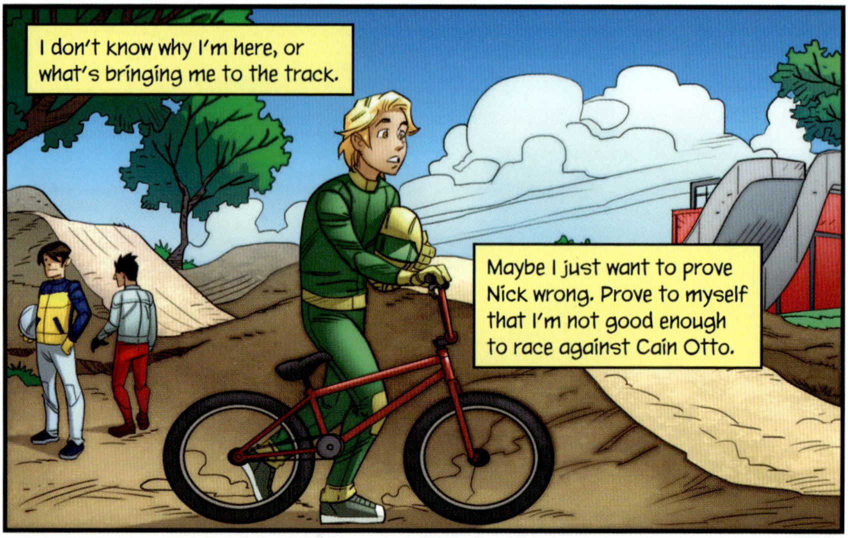
I don't know why I'm here, or what's bringing me to the track.
Maybe I just want to prove Nick wrong. Prove to myself that I'm not good enough to race against Cain Otto.

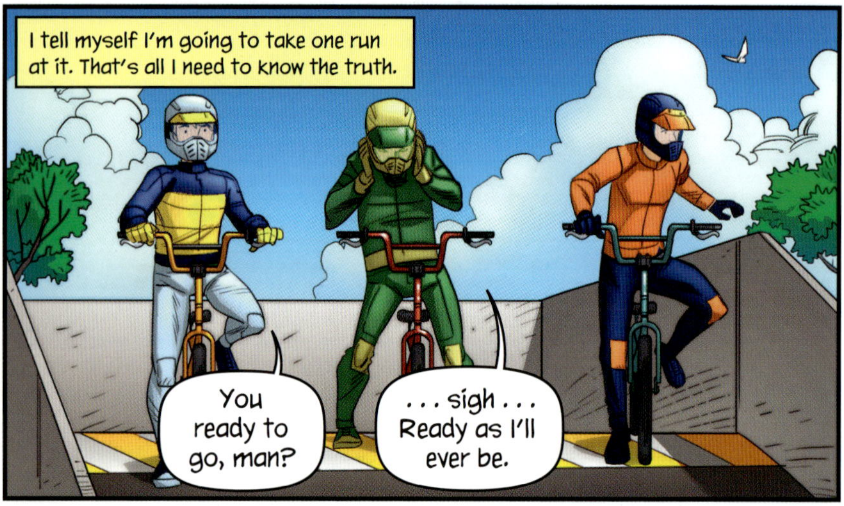
I tell myself I'm going to take one run at it. That's all I need to know the truth.
You ready to go, man?
. . . sigh . . . Ready as I'll ever be.

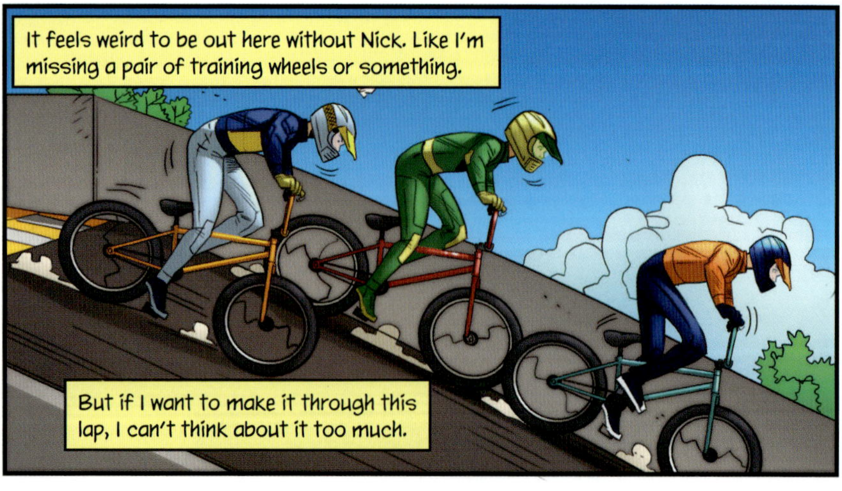
It feels weird to be out here without Nick. Like I'm missing a pair of training wheels or something.
But if I want to make it through this lap, I can't think about it too much.

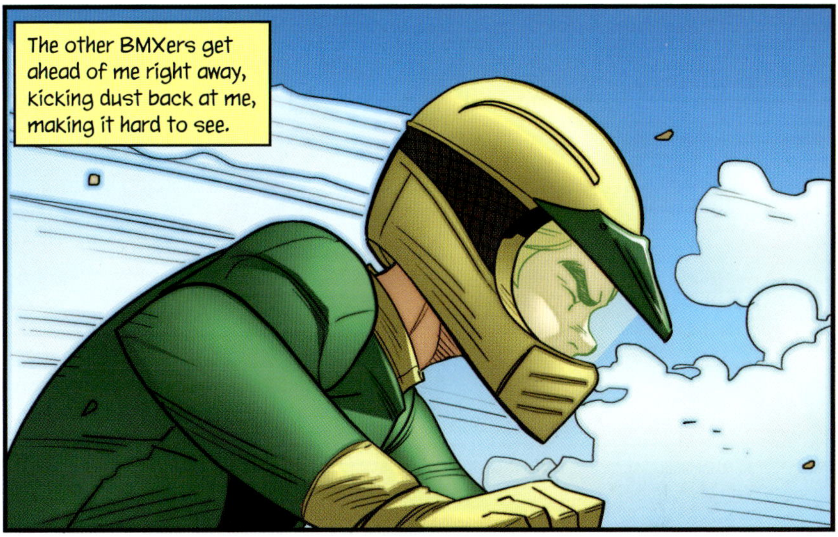
The other BMXers get ahead of me right away, kicking dust back at me, making it hard to see.

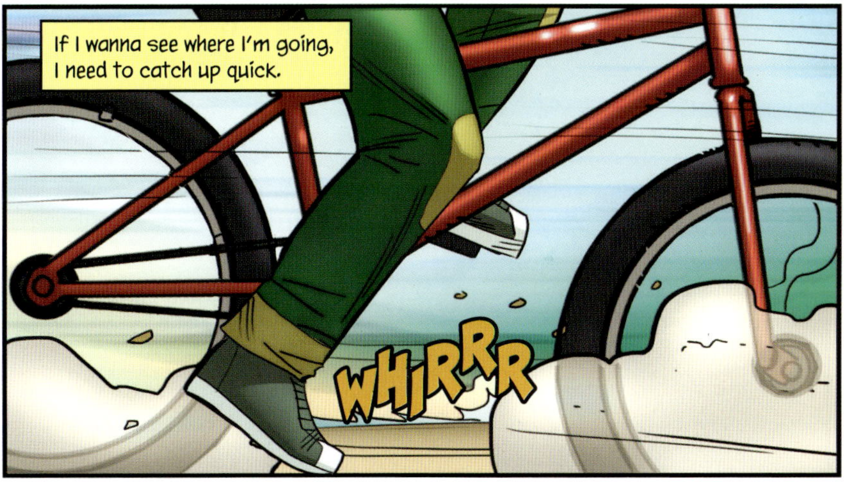
If I wanna see where I'm going, I need to catch up quick.
WHIRRR

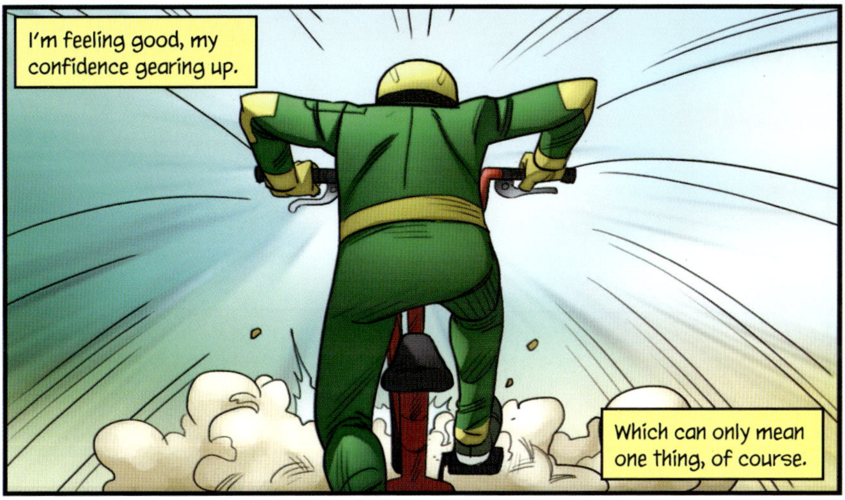
I'm feeling good, my confidence gearing up.
Which can only mean one thing, of course.

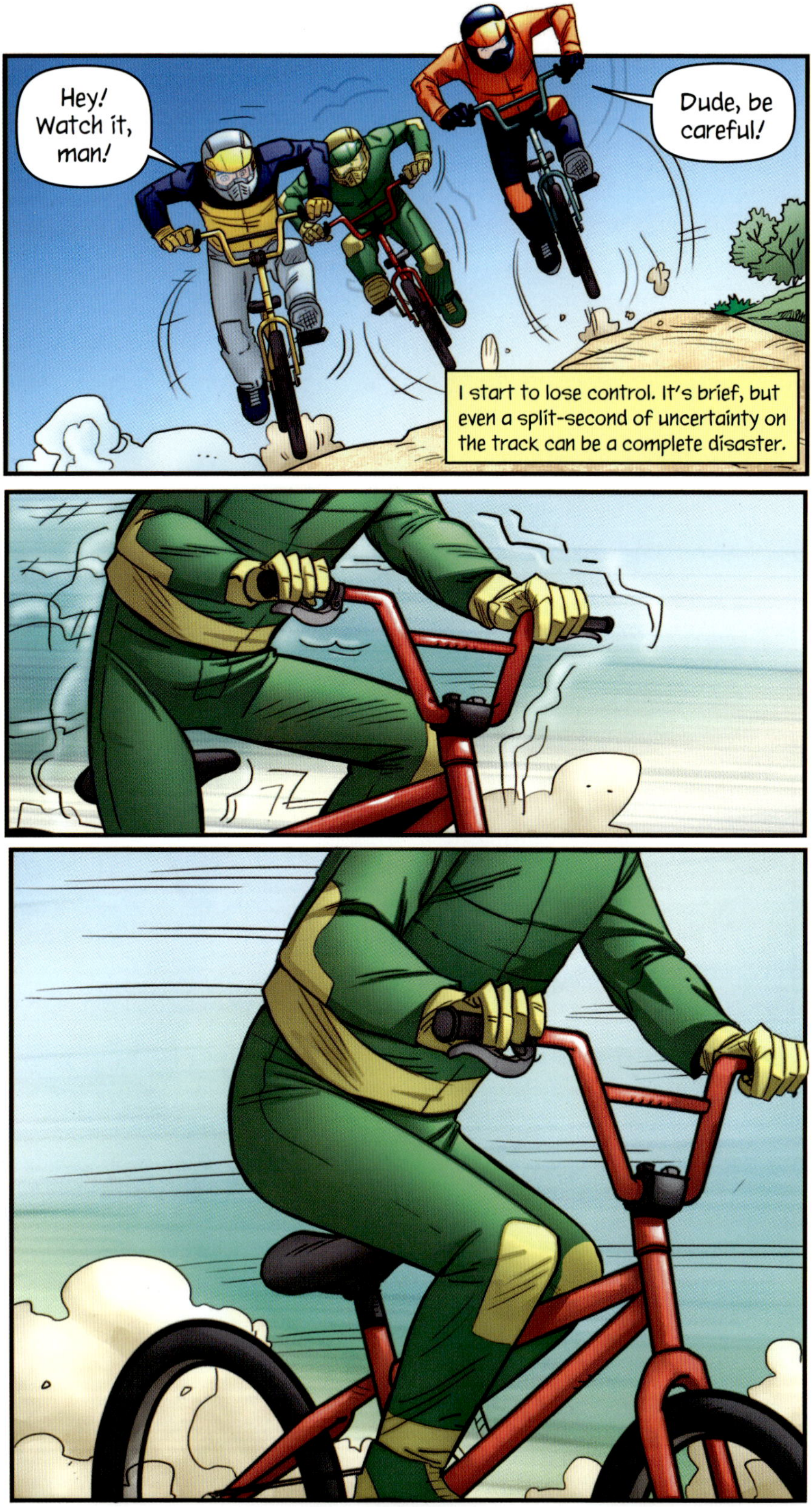
Hey! Watch it, man!
Dude, be careful!
I start to lose control. It's brief, but even a split-second of uncertainty on the track can be a complete disaster.

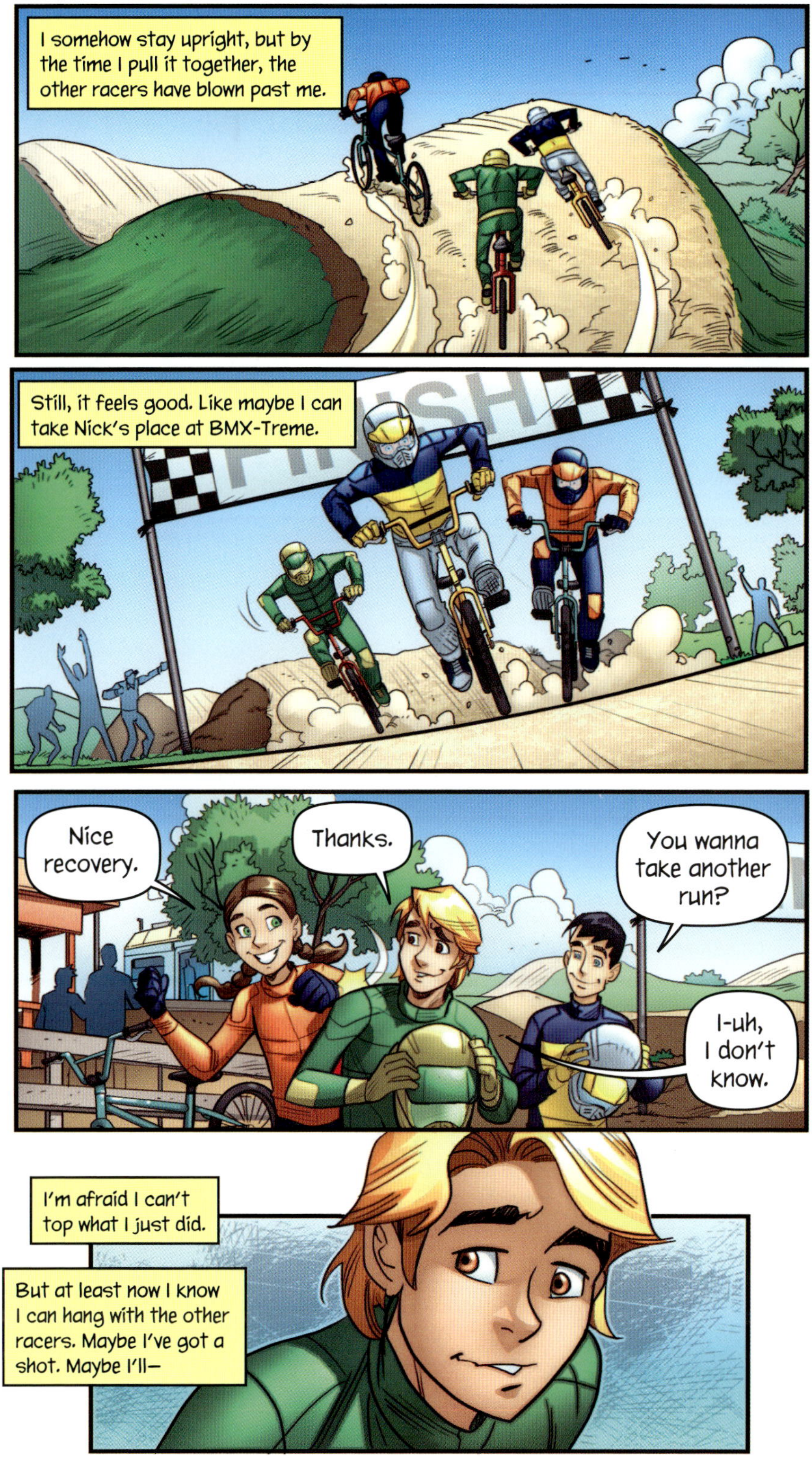
I somehow stay upright, but by the time I pull it together, the other racers have blown past me.
Still, it feels good. Like maybe I can take Nick's place at BMX-Treme.
FINISH
Nice recovery.
Thanks.
You wanna take another run?
I-uh, I don't know.
I'm afraid I can't top what I just did.
But at least now I know I can hang with the other racers. Maybe I've got a shot. Maybe I'll–

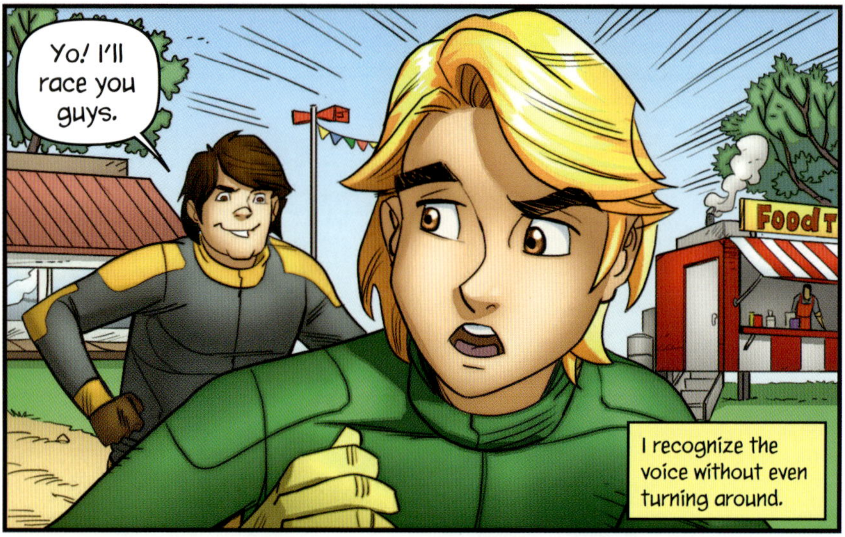
Yo! I'll race you guys.
I recognize the voice without even turning around.
Food

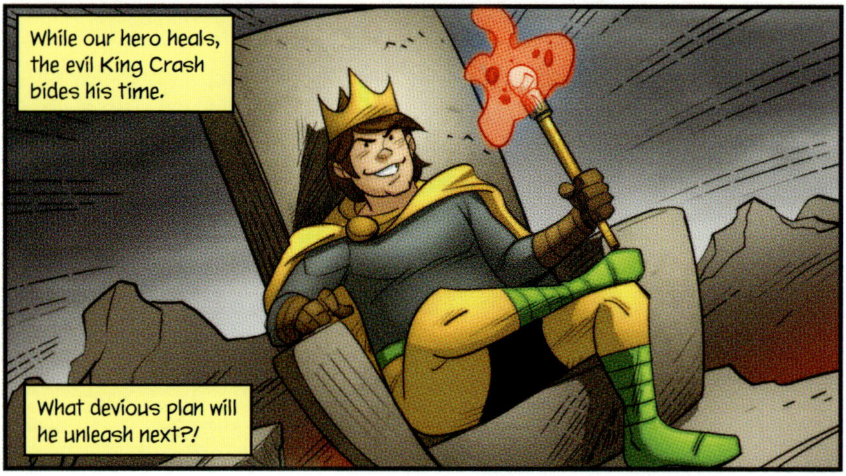
While our hero heals, the evil King Crash bides his time.
What devious plan will he unleash next?!

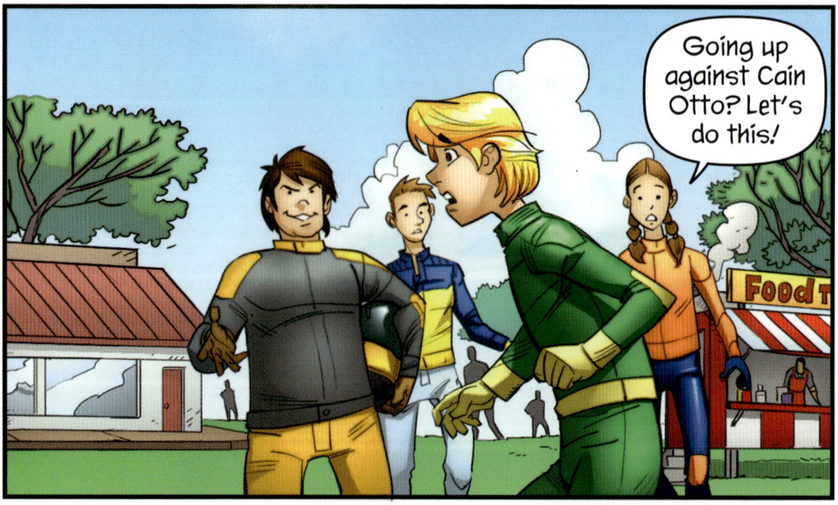
Going up against Cain Otto? Let's do this!
Food

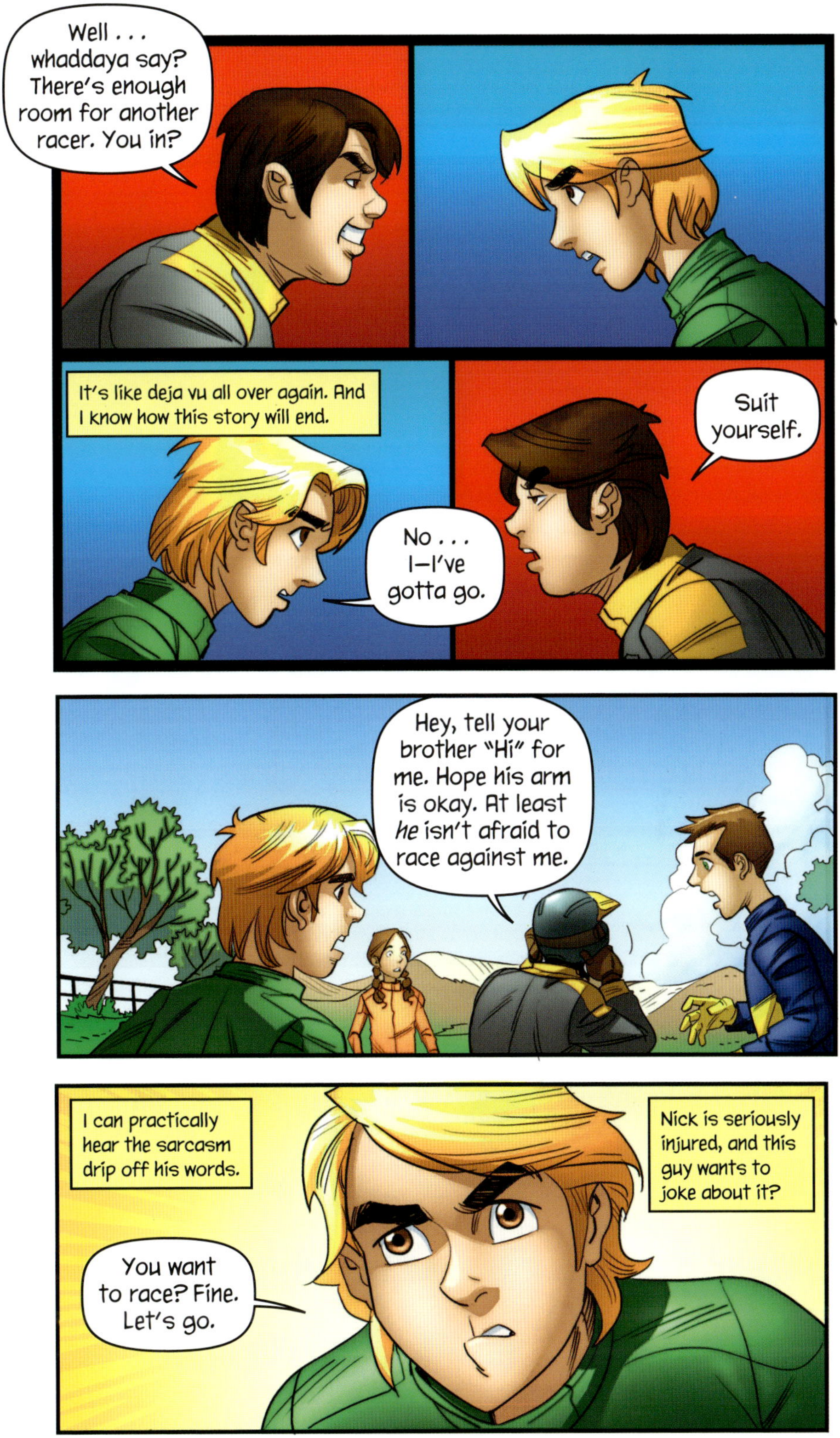
Well . . . whaddaya say? There's enough room for another racer. You in?
It's like deja vu all over again. And I know how this story will end.
No . . . I—I've gotta go.
Suit yourself.
Hey, tell your brother "Hi" for me. Hope his arm is okay. At least *he* isn't afraid to race against me.
I can practically hear the sarcasm drip off his words.
Nick is seriously injured, and this guy wants to joke about it?
You want to race? Fine. Let's go.

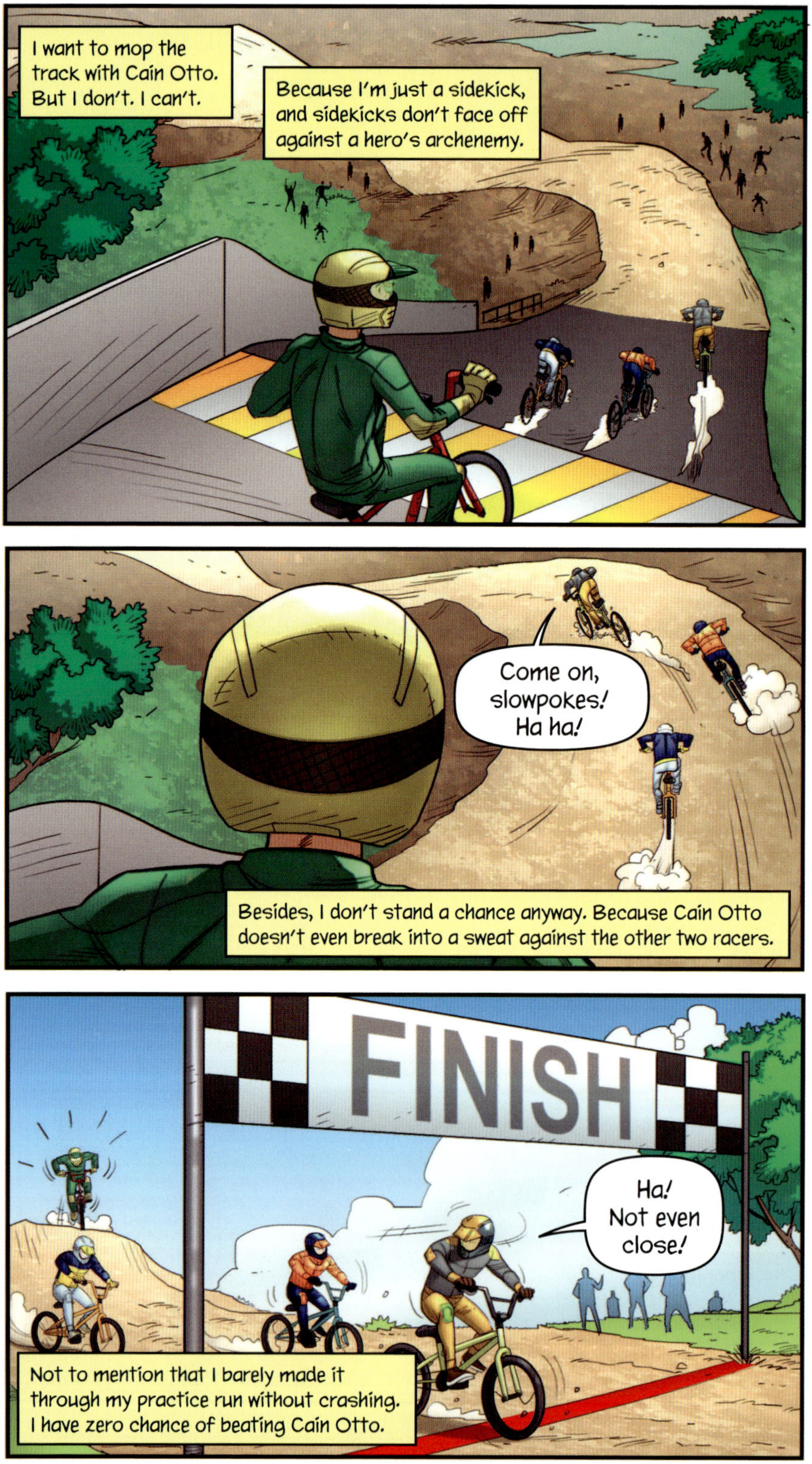
I want to mop the track with Cain Otto. But I don't. I can't.
Because I'm just a sidekick, and sidekicks don't face off against a hero's archenemy.
Come on, slowpokes! Ha ha!
Besides, I don't stand a chance anyway. Because Cain Otto doesn't even break into a sweat against the other two racers.
FINISH
Ha! Not even close!
Not to mention that I barely made it through my practice run without crashing. I have zero chance of beating Cain Otto.

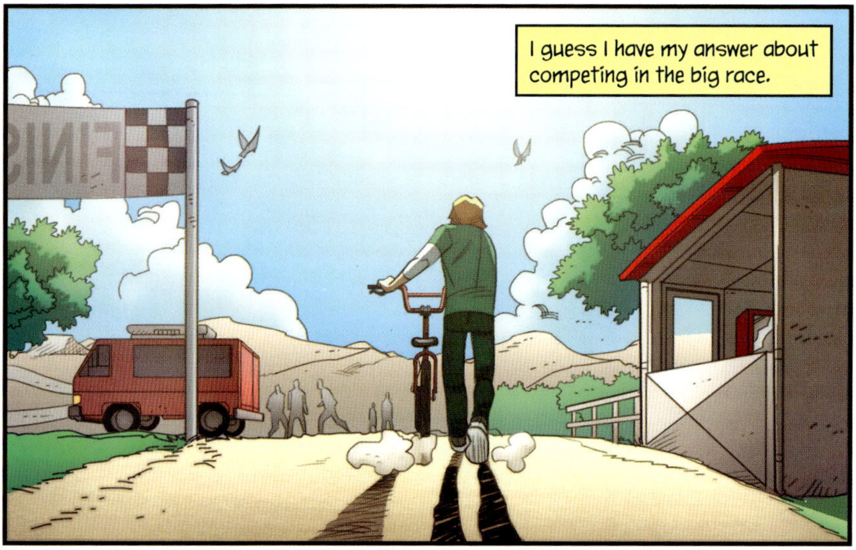
I guess I have my answer about competing in the big race.
FINIS

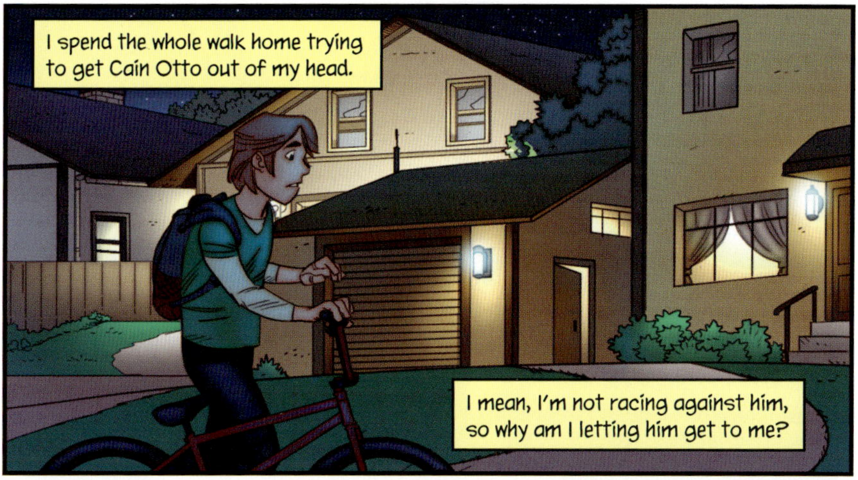
I spend the whole walk home trying to get Cain Otto out of my head.
I mean, I'm not racing against him, so why am I letting him get to me?

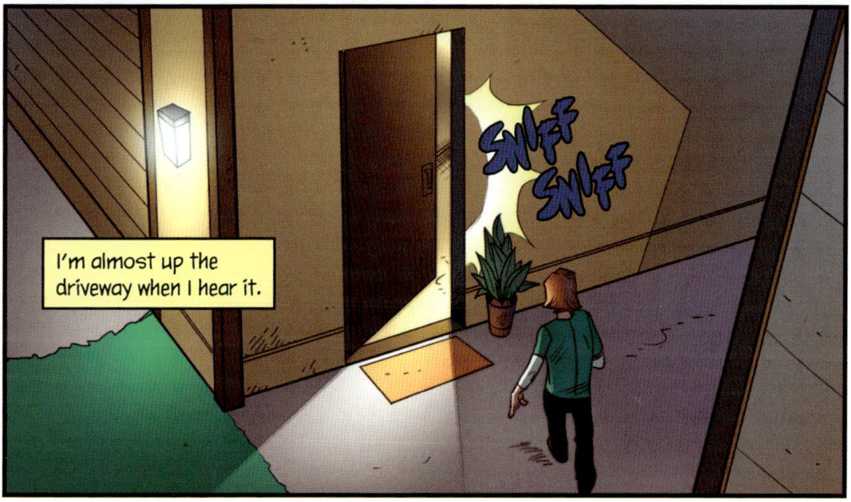
SNIFF
SNIFF
I'm almost up the driveway when I hear it.

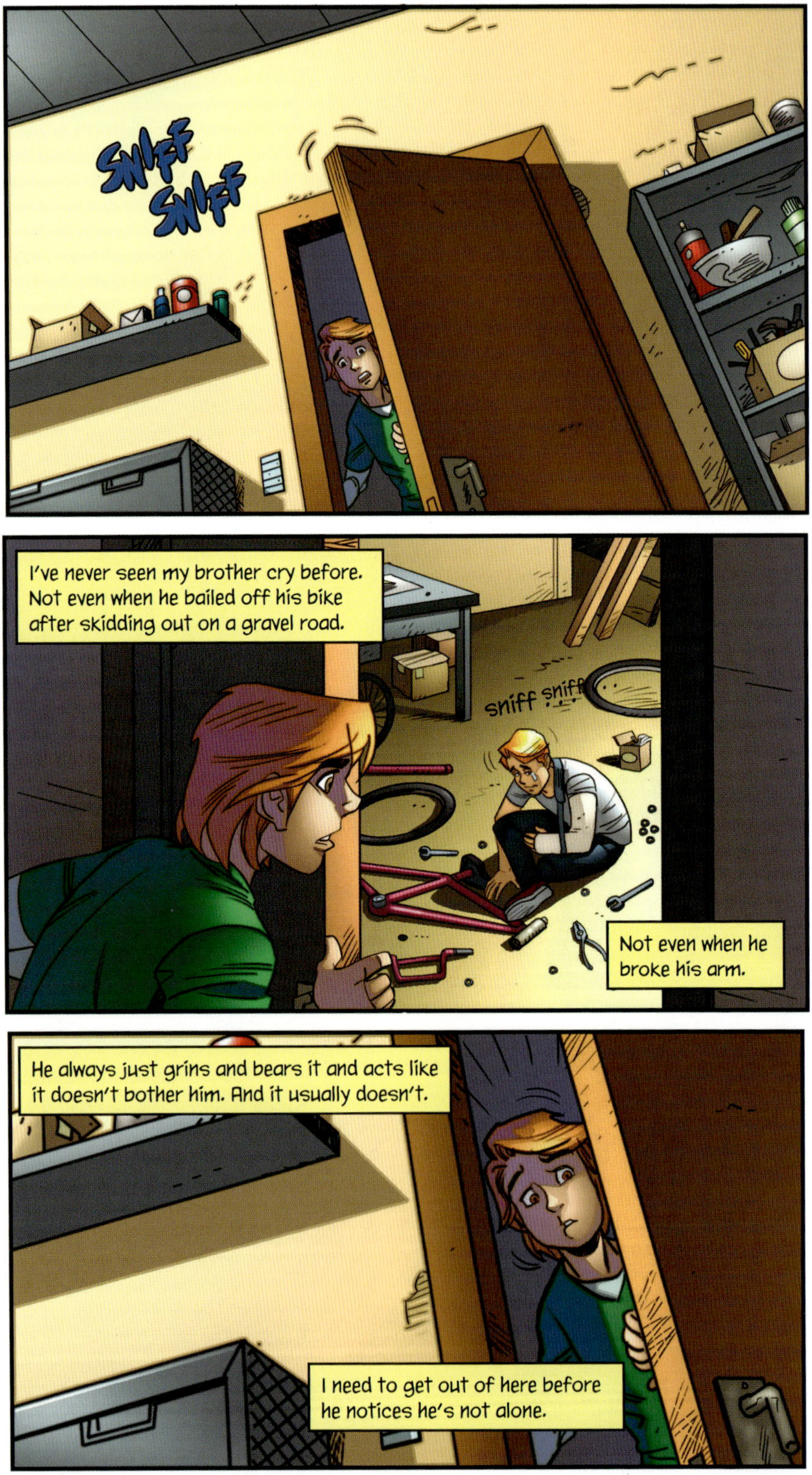
SNIFF SNIFF
I've never seen my brother cry before. Not even when he bailed off his bike after skidding out on a gravel road.
sniff sniff
Not even when he broke his arm.
He always just grins and bears it and acts like it doesn't bother him. And it usually doesn't.
I need to get out of here before he notices he's not alone.

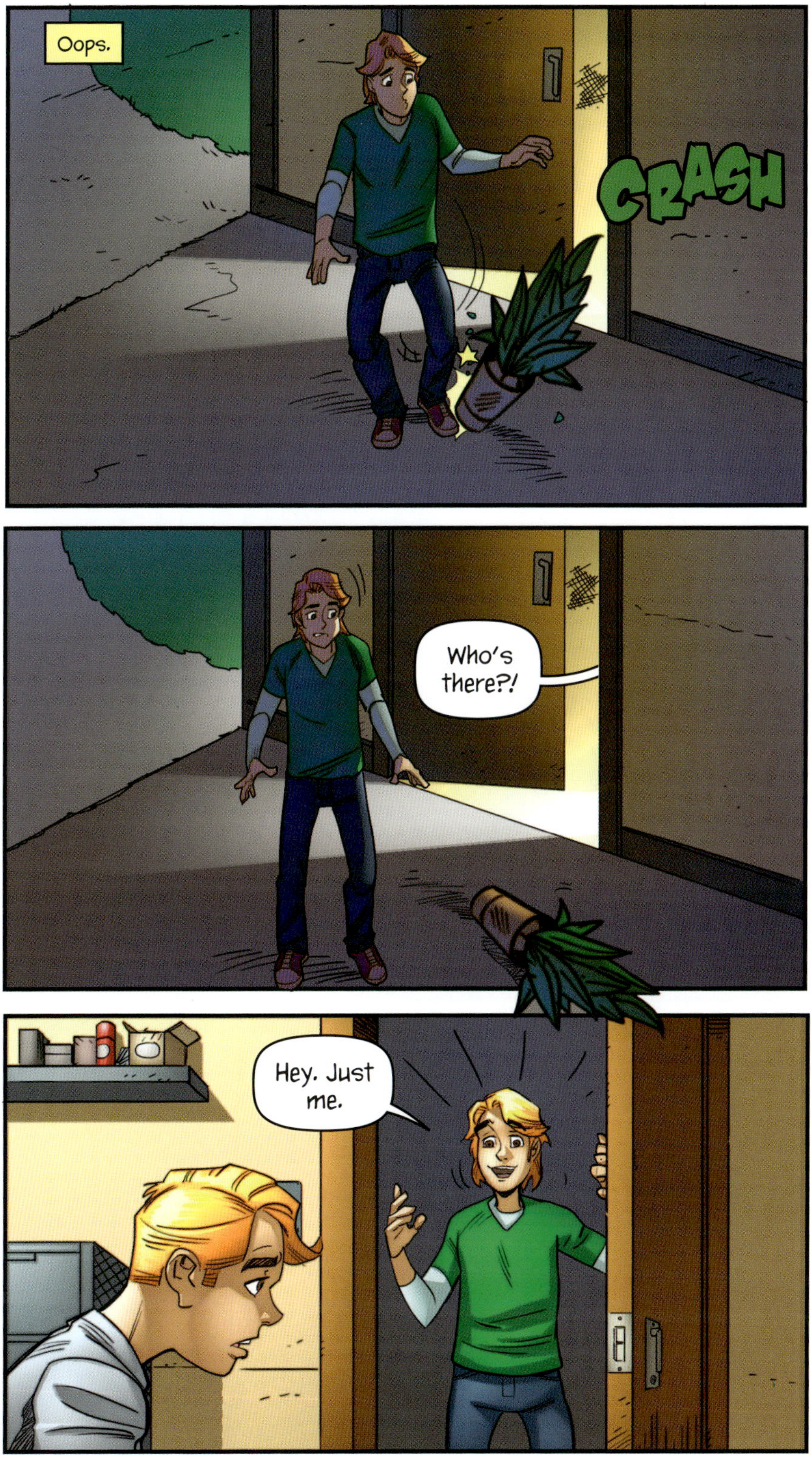
Oops.
CRASH
Who's there?!
Hey. Just me.

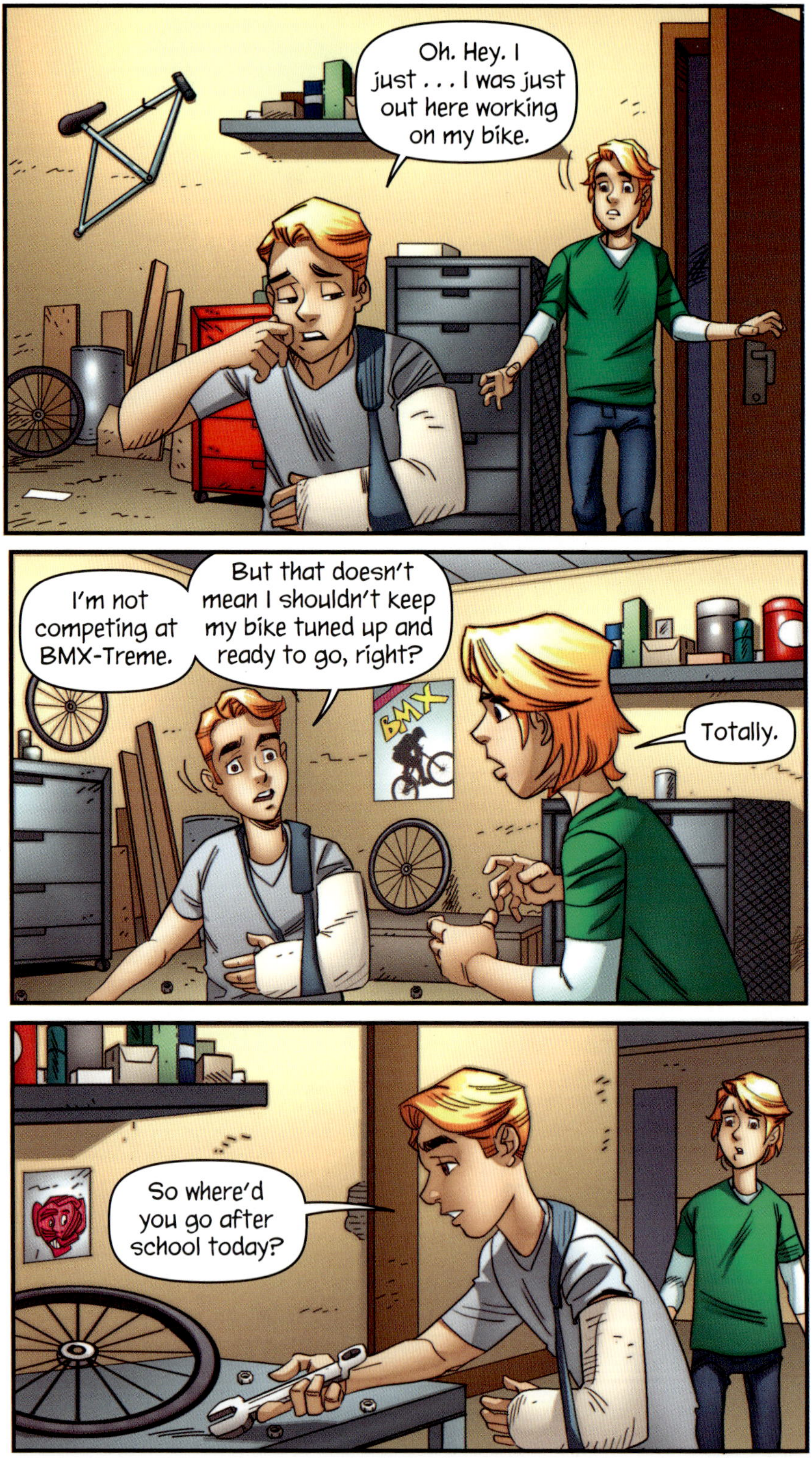

Oh. Hey. I just . . . I was just out here working on my bike.
I'm not competing at BMX-Treme.
But that doesn't mean I shouldn't keep my bike tuned up and ready to go, right?
BMX
Totally.
So where'd you go after school today?

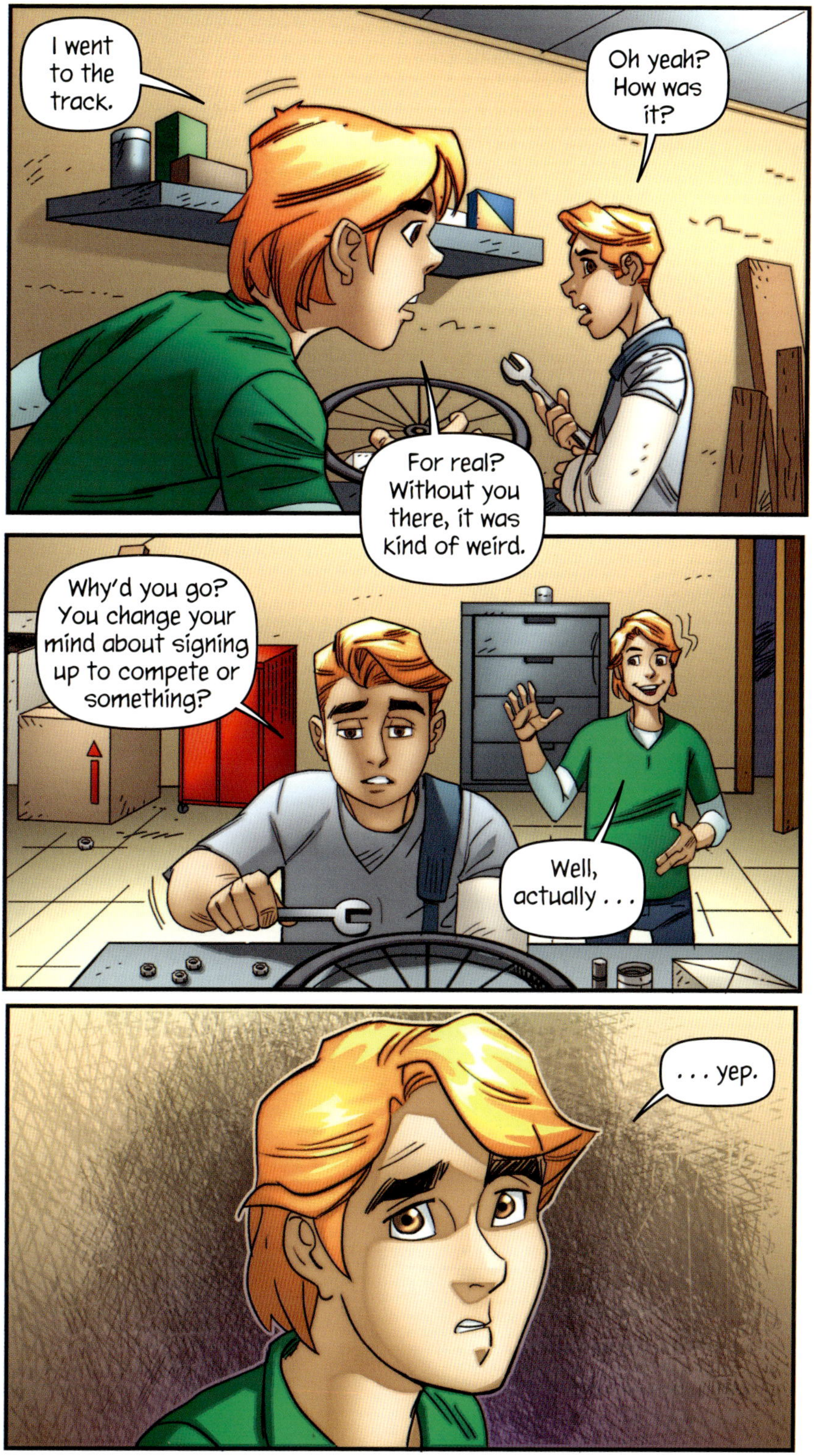
I went to the track.
Oh yeah? How was it?
For real? Without you there, it was kind of weird.
Why'd you go? You change your mind about signing up to compete or something?
Well, actually . . .
. . . yep.

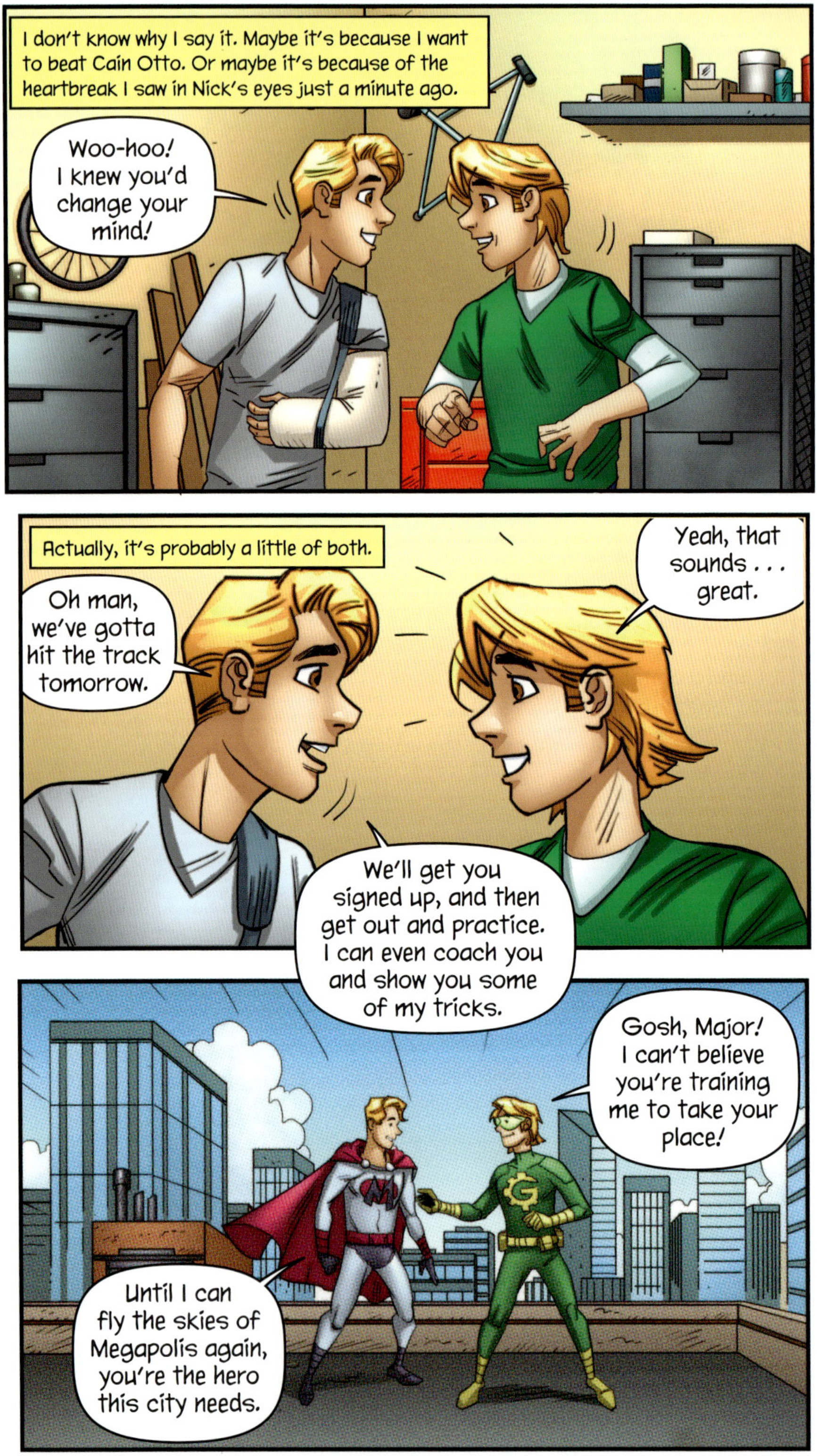
I don't know why I say it. Maybe it's because I want to beat Cain Otto. Or maybe it's because of the heartbreak I saw in Nick's eyes just a minute ago.
Woo-hoo! I knew you'd change your mind!
Actually, it's probably a little of both.
Oh man, we've gotta hit the track tomorrow.
Yeah, that sounds . . . great.
We'll get you signed up, and then get out and practice. I can even coach you and show you some of my tricks.
Gosh, Major! I can't believe you're training me to take your place!
Until I can fly the skies of Megapolis again, you're the hero this city needs.

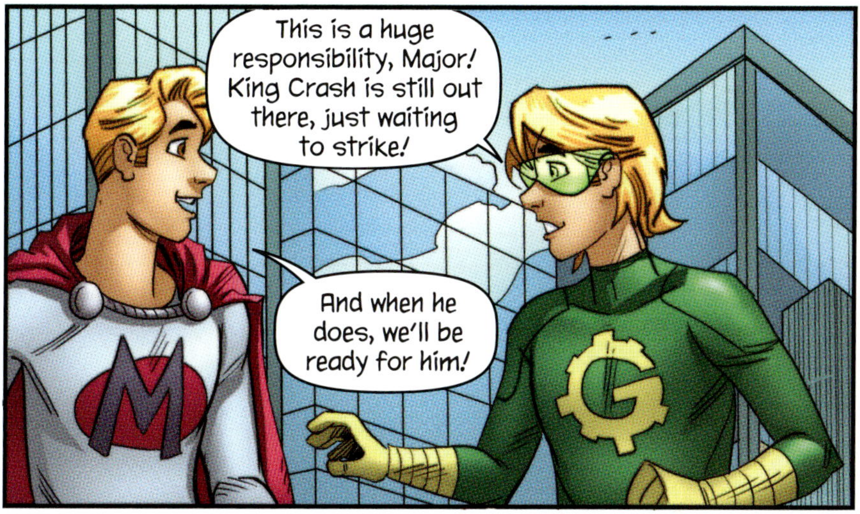
This is a huge responsibility, Major! King Crash is still out there, just waiting to strike!
And when he does, we'll be ready for him!

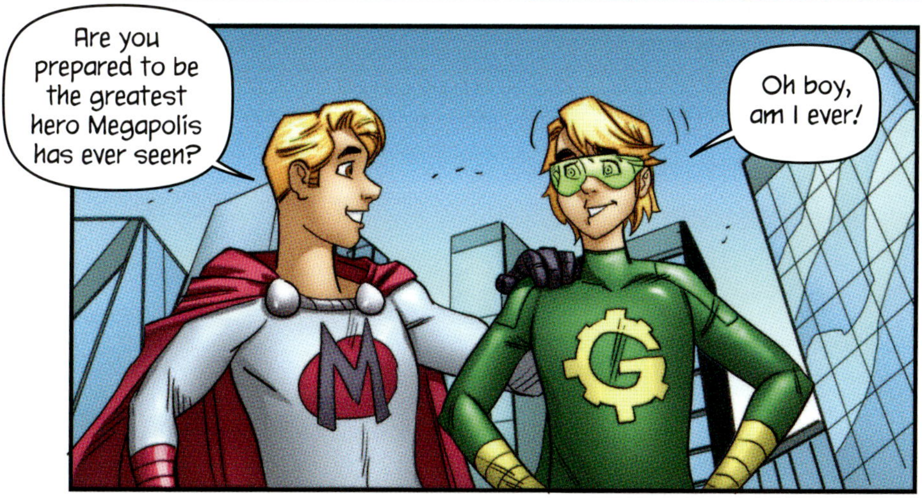
Are you prepared to be the greatest hero Megapolis has ever seen?
Oh boy, am I ever!

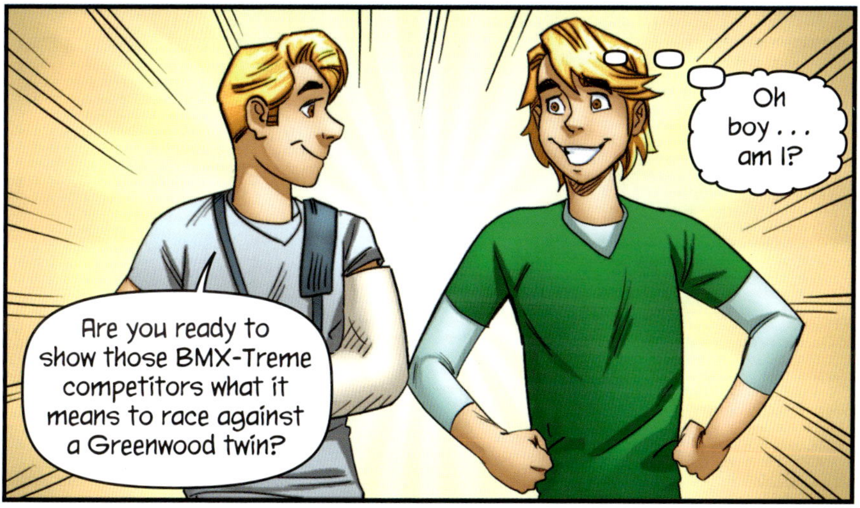
Oh boy . . . am I?
Are you ready to show those BMX-Treme competitors what it means to race against a Greenwood twin?

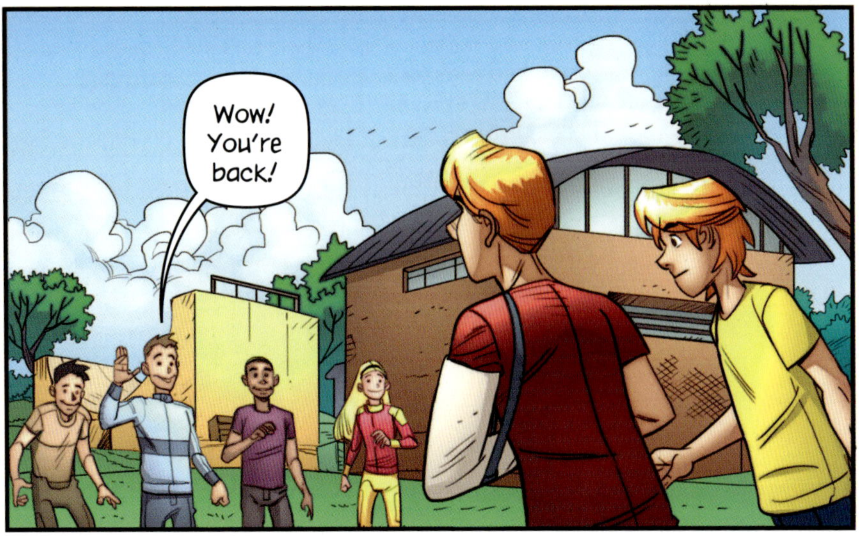
Wow! You're back!

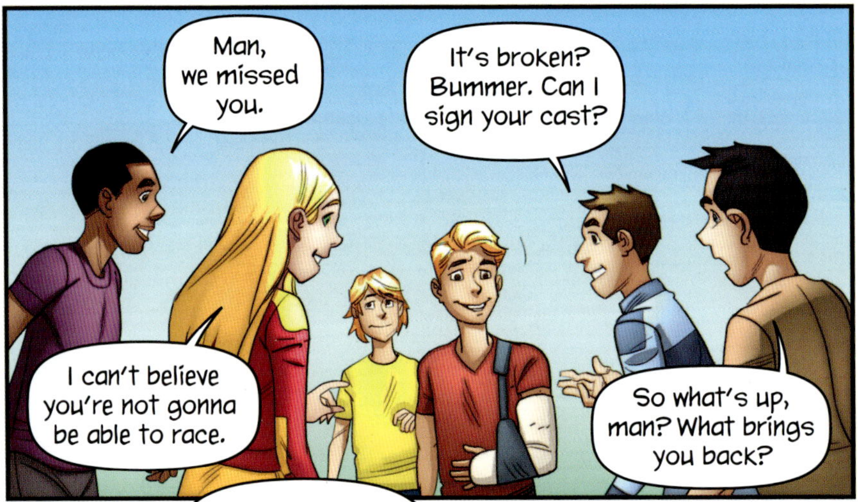
Man, we missed you.
It's broken? Bummer. Can I sign your cast?
I can't believe you're not gonna be able to race.
So what's up, man? What brings you back?

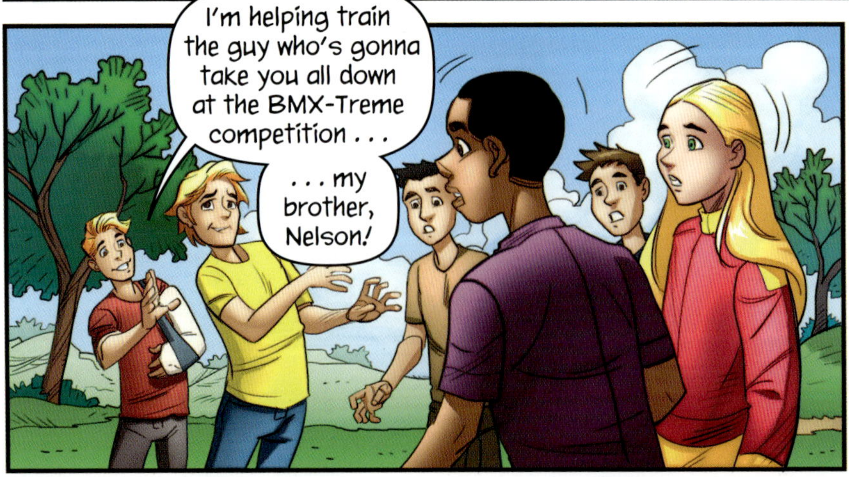
I'm helping train the guy who's gonna take you all down at the BMX-Treme competition . . .
. . . my brother, Nelson!

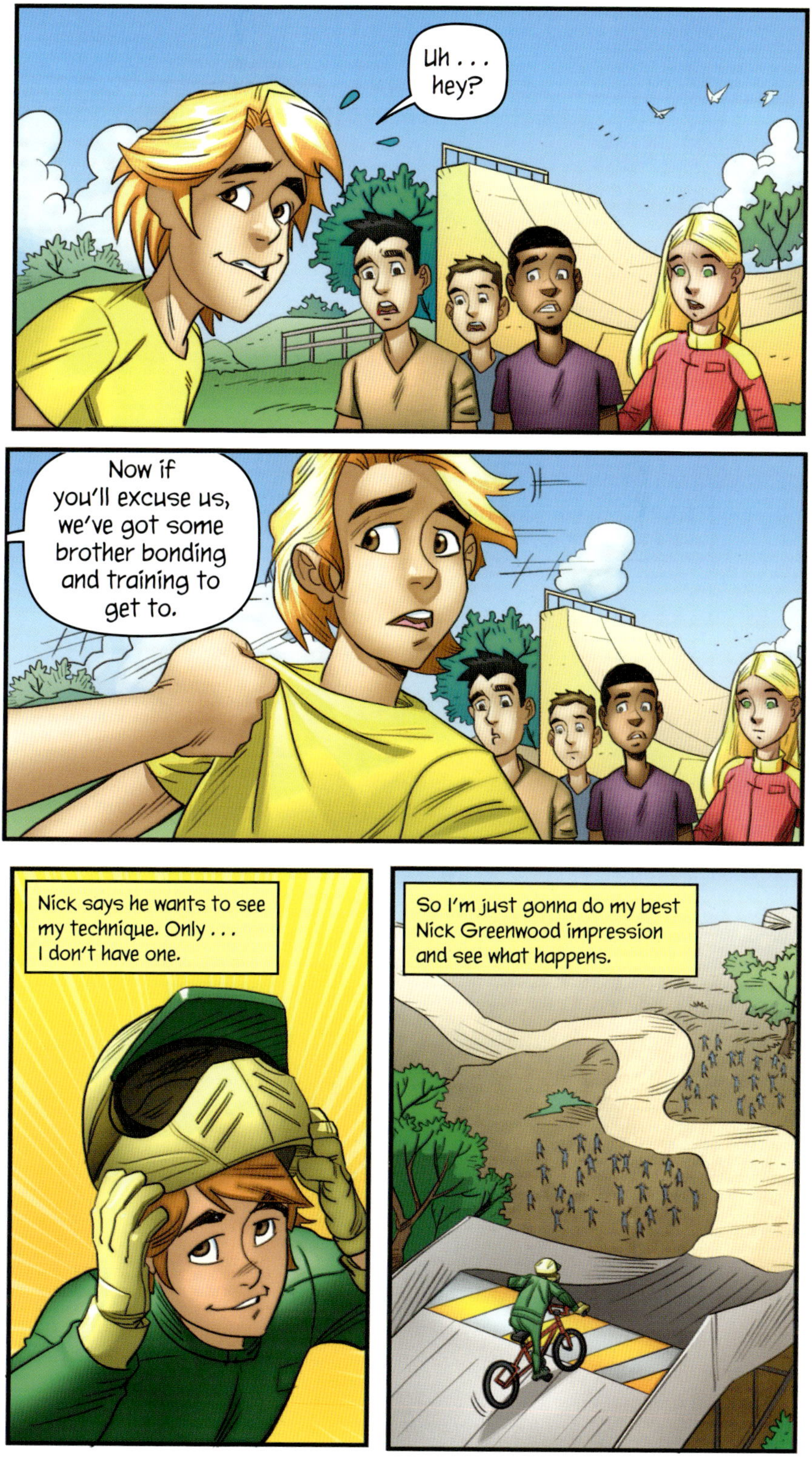
Uh . . . hey?
Now if you'll excuse us, we've got some brother bonding and training to get to.
Nick says he wants to see my technique. Only . . . I don't have one.
So I'm just gonna do my best Nick Greenwood impression and see what happens.

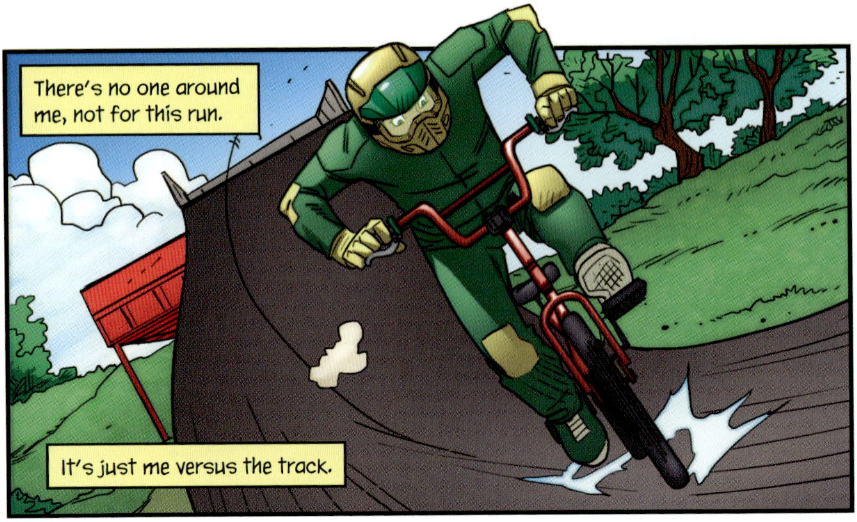
There's no one around me, not for this run.
It's just me versus the track.

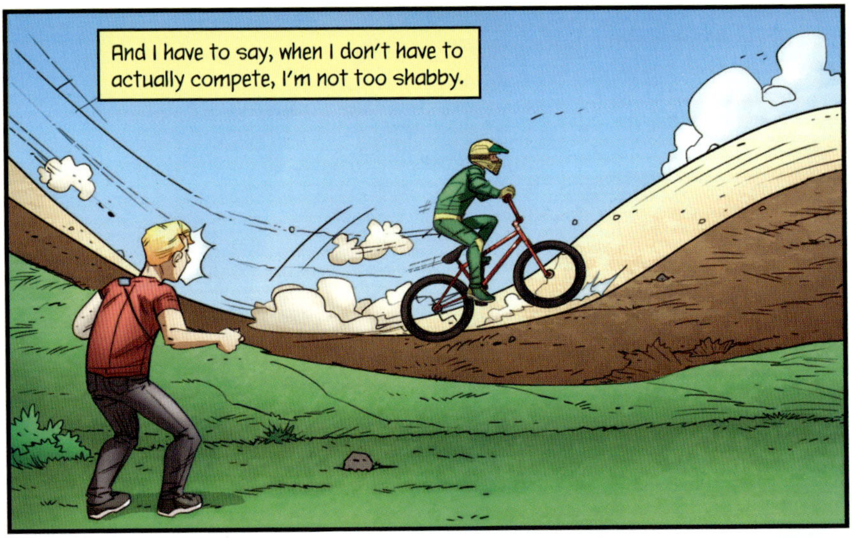
And I have to say, when I don't have to actually compete, I'm not too shabby.

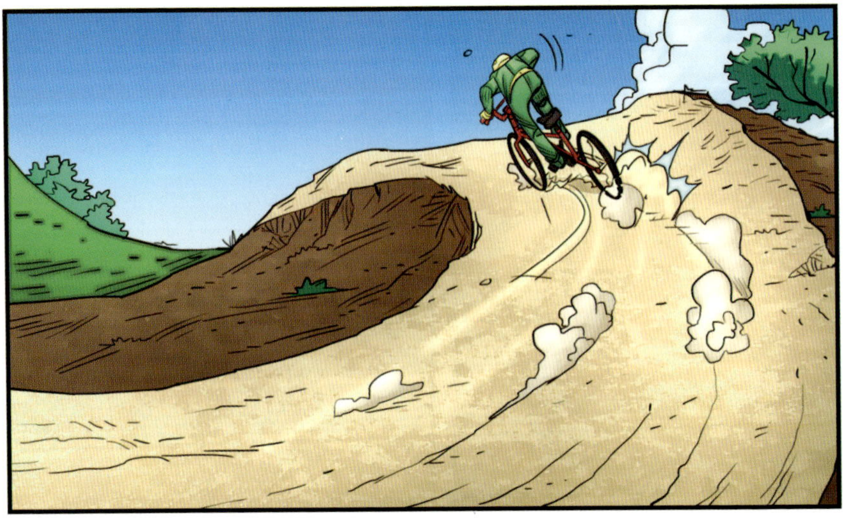

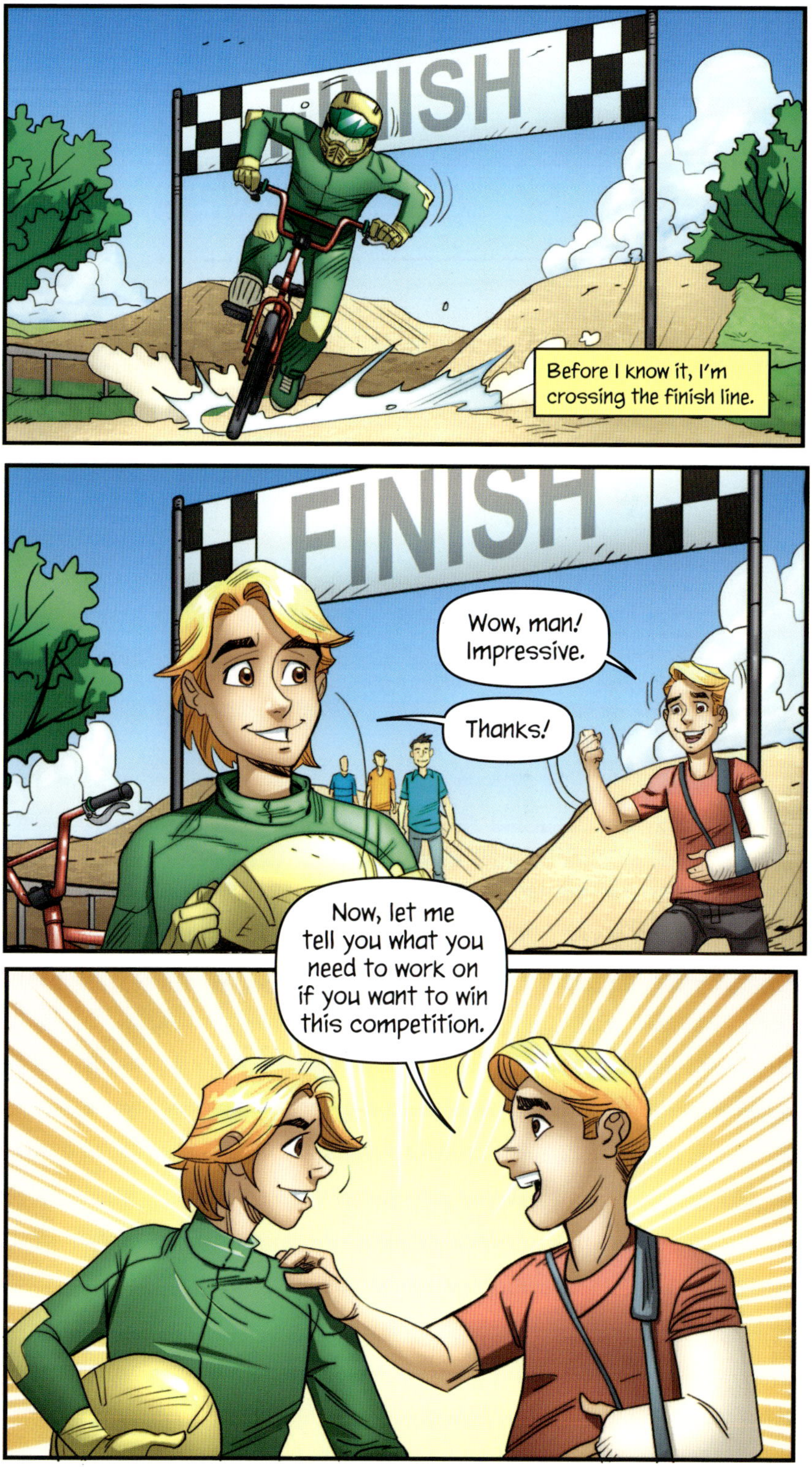
FINISH
Before I know it, I'm crossing the finish line.
FINISH
Wow, man! Impressive.
Thanks!
Now, let me tell you what you need to work on if you want to win this competition.

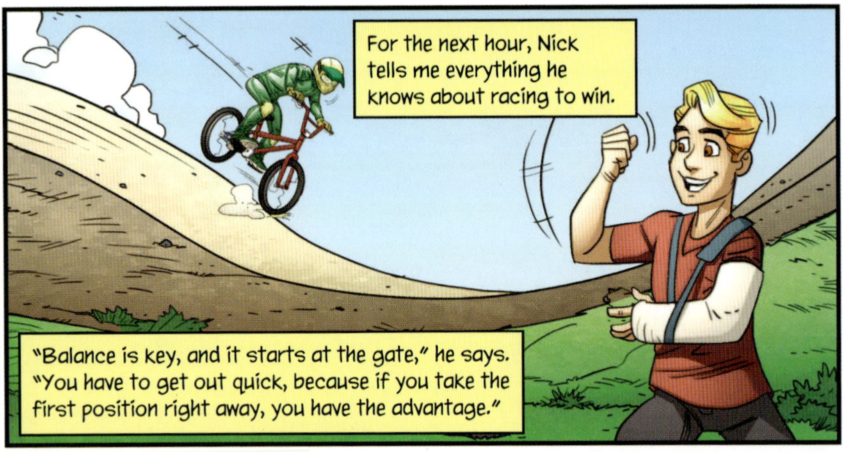
For the next hour, Nick tells me everything he knows about racing to win.
"Balance is key, and it starts at the gate," he says. "You have to get out quick, because if you take the first position right away, you have the advantage."

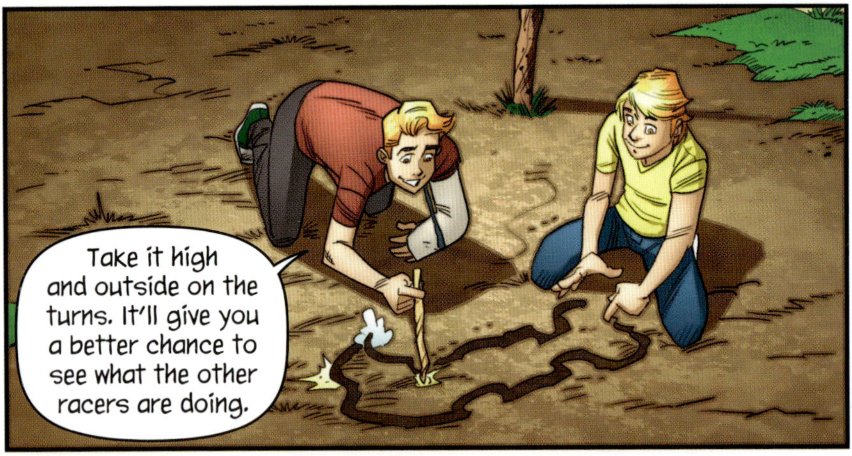
Take it high and outside on the turns. It'll give you a better chance to see what the other racers are doing.

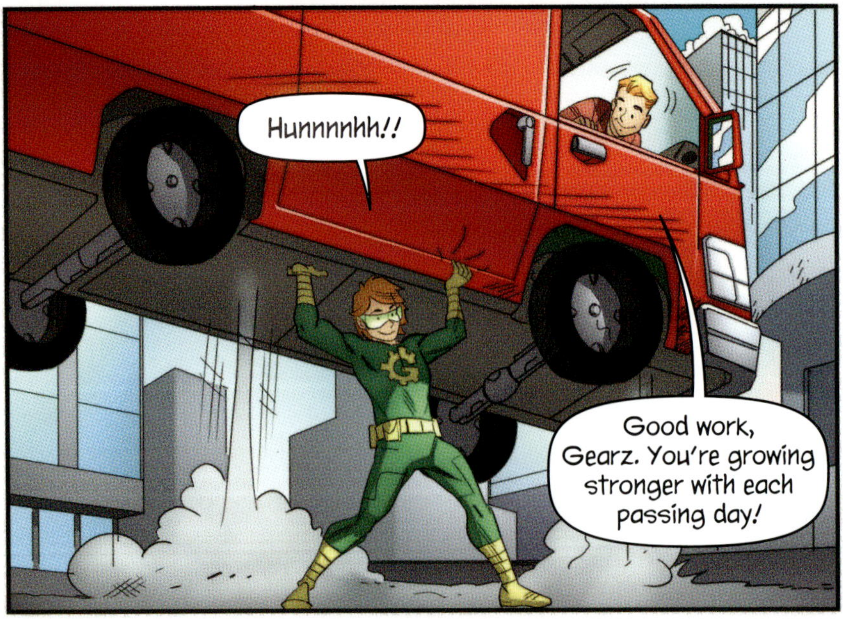
Hunnnnhh!!
Good work, Gearz. You're growing stronger with each passing day!

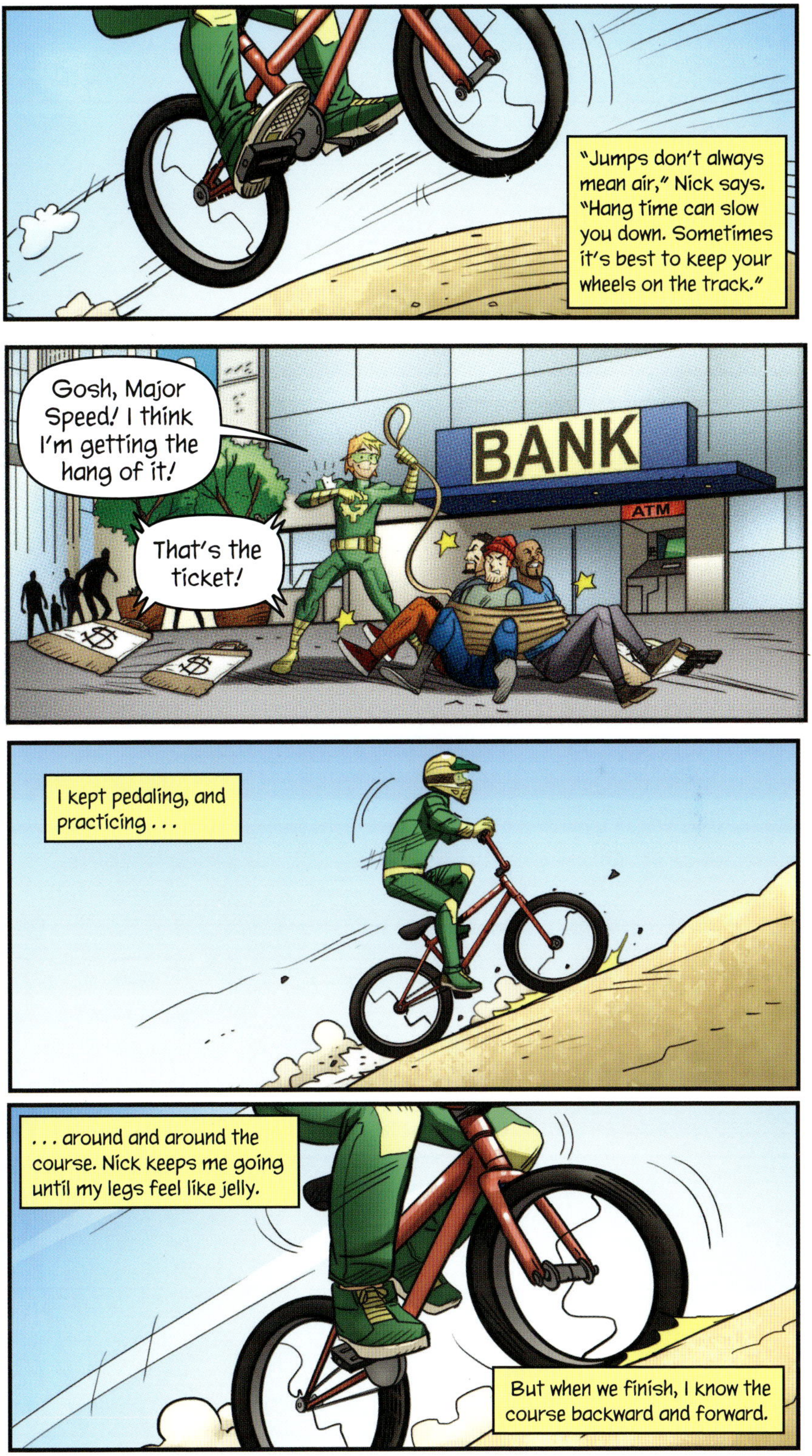
"Jumps don't always mean air," Nick says. "Hang time can slow you down. Sometimes it's best to keep your wheels on the track."
Gosh, Major Speed! I think I'm getting the hang of it!
That's the ticket!
BANK
ATM
I kept pedaling, and practicing . . .
. . . around and around the course. Nick keeps me going until my legs feel like jelly.
But when we finish, I know the course backward and forward.

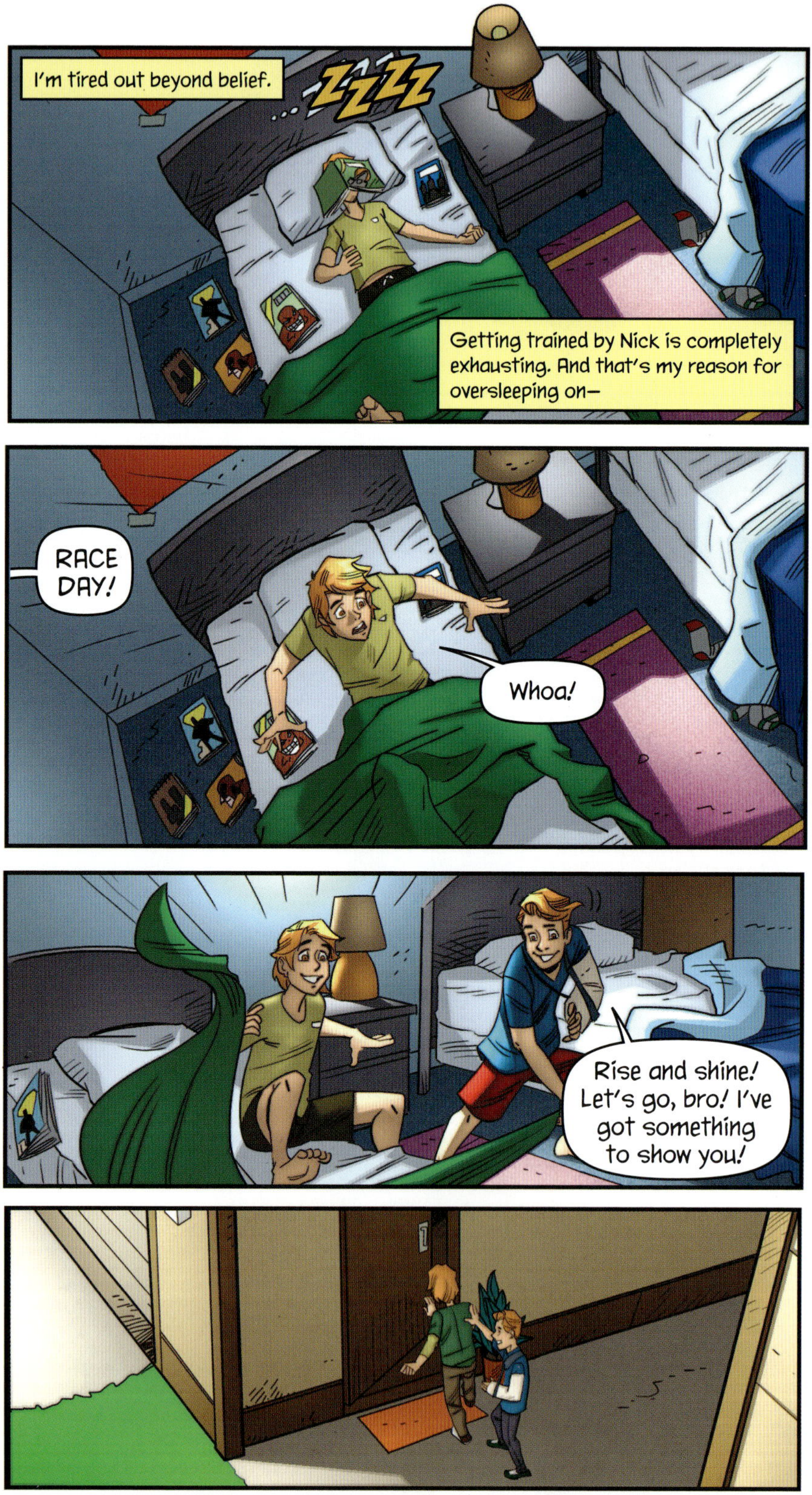
I'm tired out beyond belief.
...ZZZZ
Getting trained by Nick is completely exhausting. And that's my reason for oversleeping on–
RACE DAY!
Whoa!
Rise and shine! Let's go, bro! I've got something to show you!

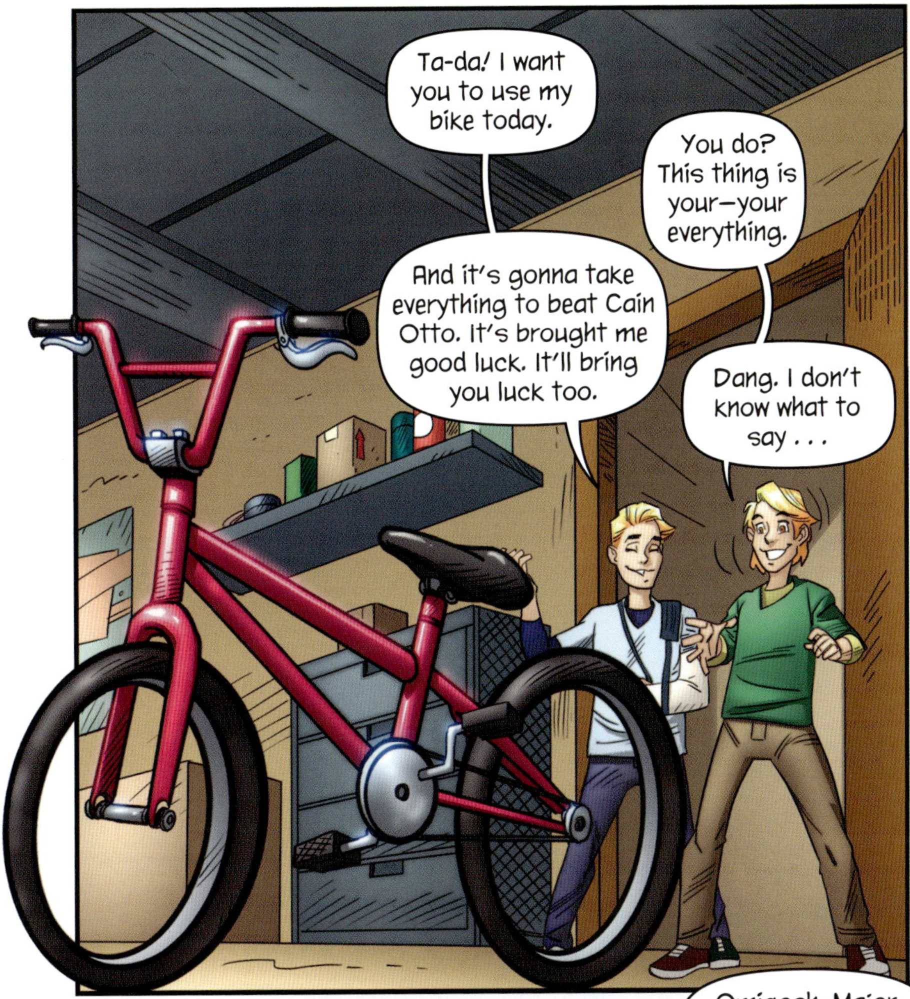
Ta-da! I want you to use my bike today.
You do? This thing is your—your everything.
And it's gonna take everything to beat Cain Otto. It's brought me good luck. It'll bring you luck too.
Dang. I don't know what to say . . .

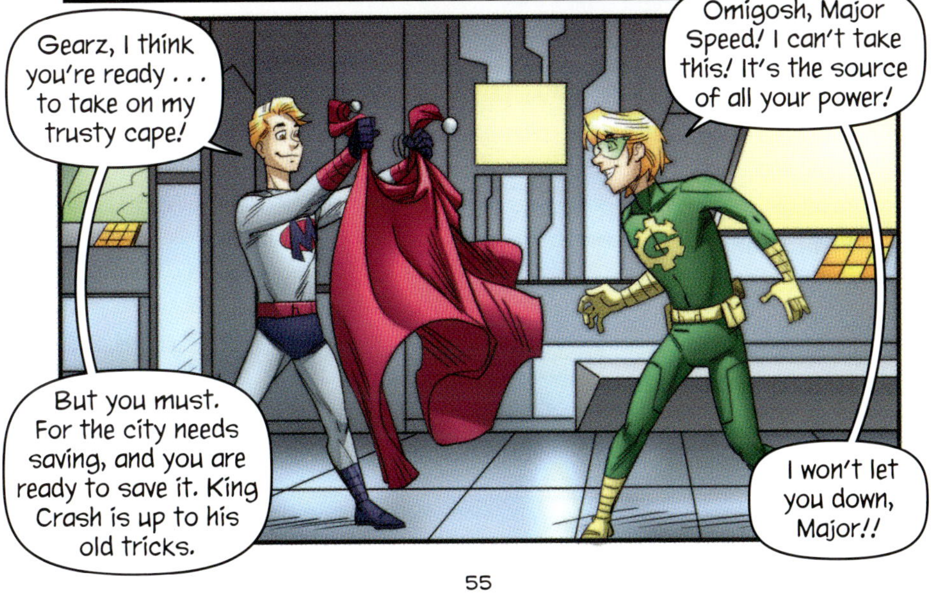
Gearz, I think you're ready . . . to take on my trusty cape!
Omigosh, Major Speed! I can't take this! It's the source of all your power!
But you must. For the city needs saving, and you are ready to save it. King Crash is up to his old tricks.
I won't let you down, Major!!

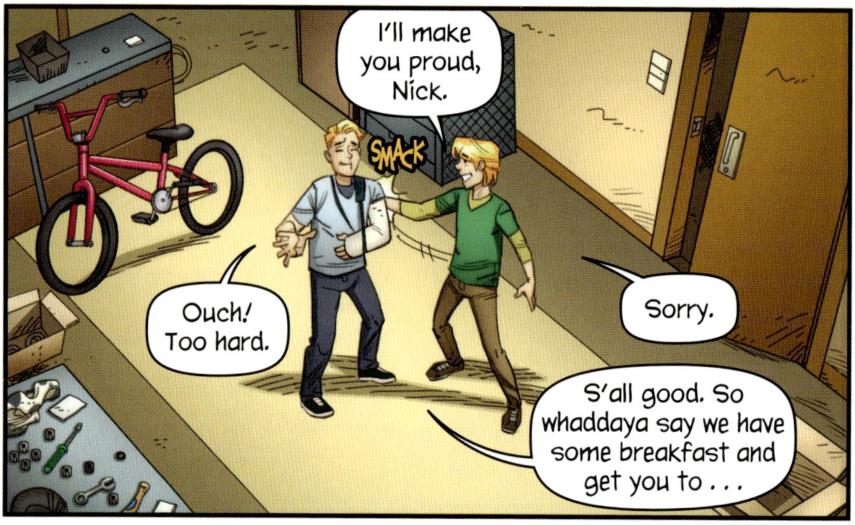
I'll make you proud, Nick.
SMACK
Ouch! Too hard.
Sorry.
S'all good. So whaddaya say we have some breakfast and get you to . . .

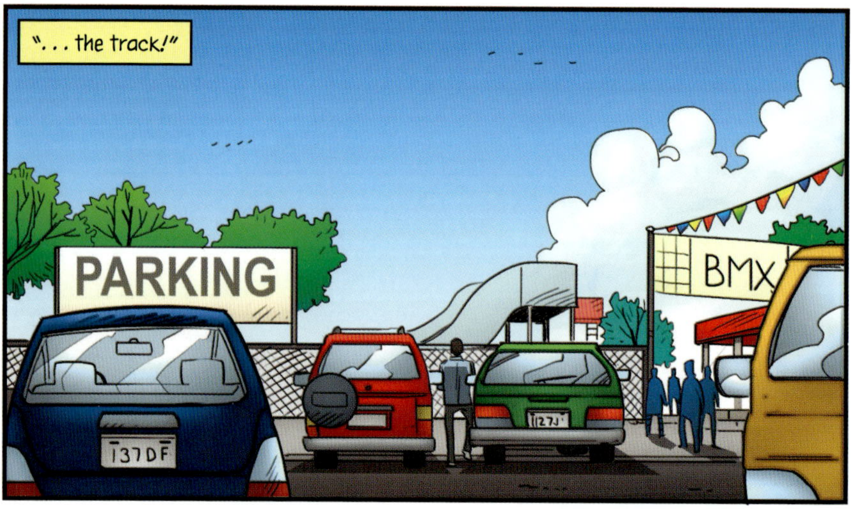
". . . the track!"
PARKING
BMX
137DF

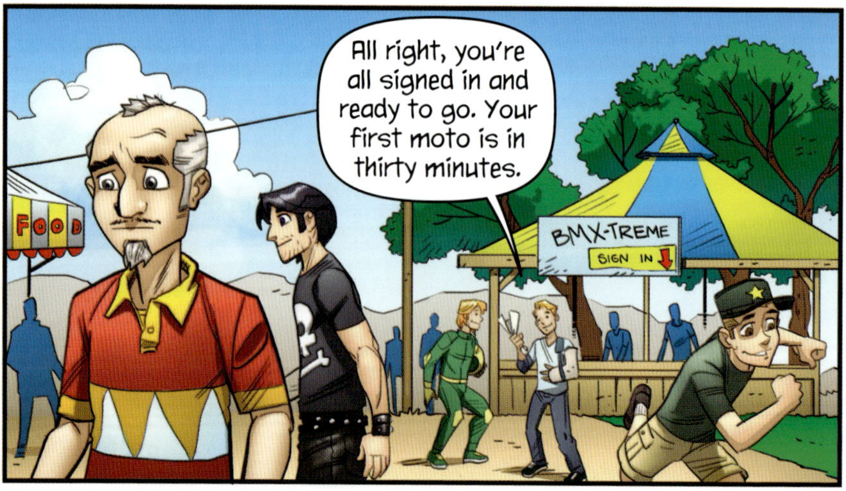
All right, you're all signed in and ready to go. Your first moto is in thirty minutes.
FOOD
BMX-TREME
SIGN IN

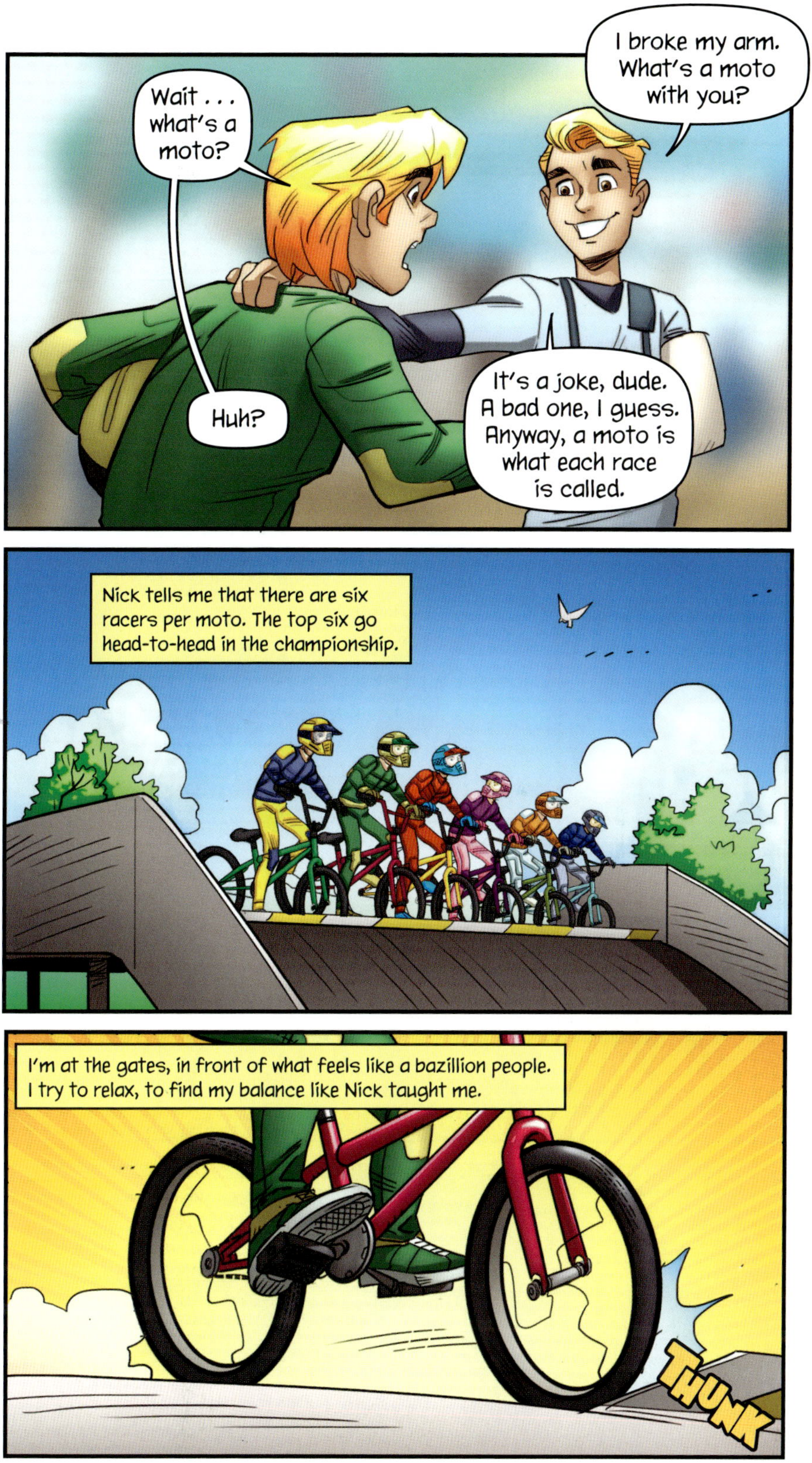
Wait . . . what's a moto?
I broke my arm. What's a moto with you?
Huh?
It's a joke, dude. A bad one, I guess. Anyway, a moto is what each race is called.
Nick tells me that there are six racers per moto. The top six go head-to-head in the championship.
I'm at the gates, in front of what feels like a bazillion people. I try to relax, to find my balance like Nick taught me.
THUNK

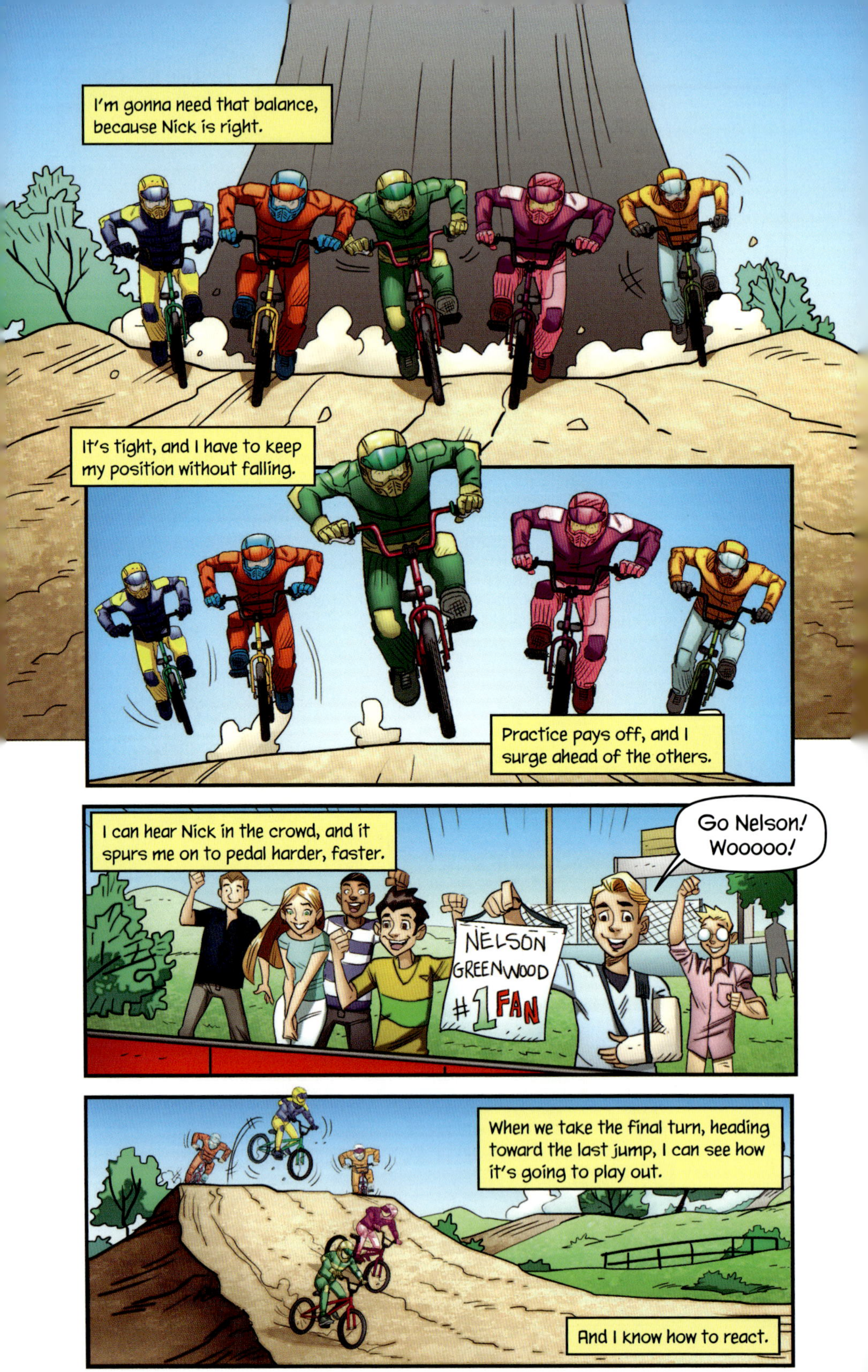
I'm gonna need that balance, because Nick is right.
It's tight, and I have to keep my position without falling.
Practice pays off, and I surge ahead of the others.
I can hear Nick in the crowd, and it spurs me on to pedal harder, faster.
Go Nelson! Wooooo!
NELSON GREENWOOD #1 FAN
When we take the final turn, heading toward the last jump, I can see how it's going to play out.
And I know how to react.

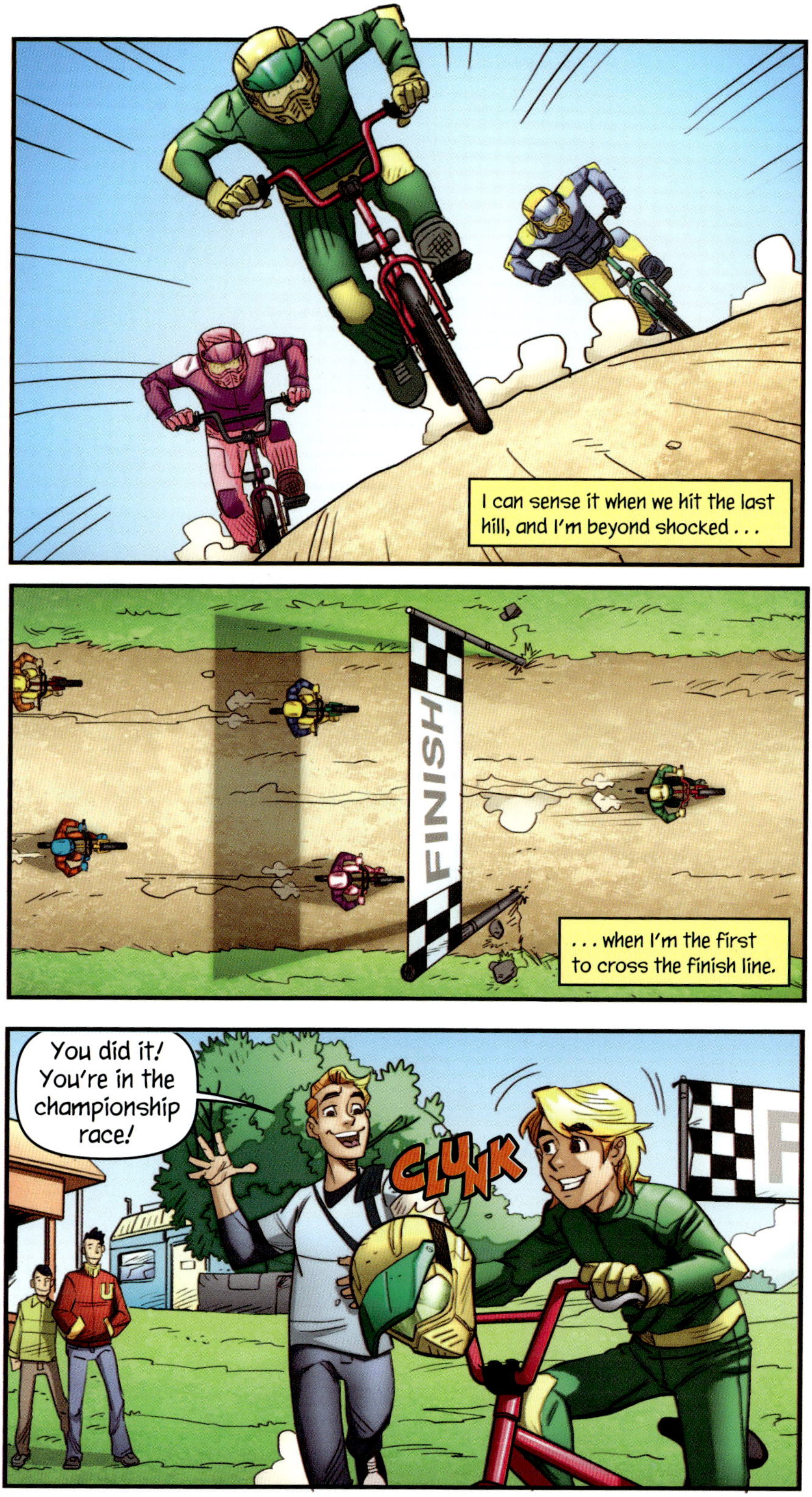

I can sense it when we hit the last hill, and I'm beyond shocked . . .
FINISH
. . . when I'm the first to cross the finish line.
You did it! You're in the championship race!
CLUNK

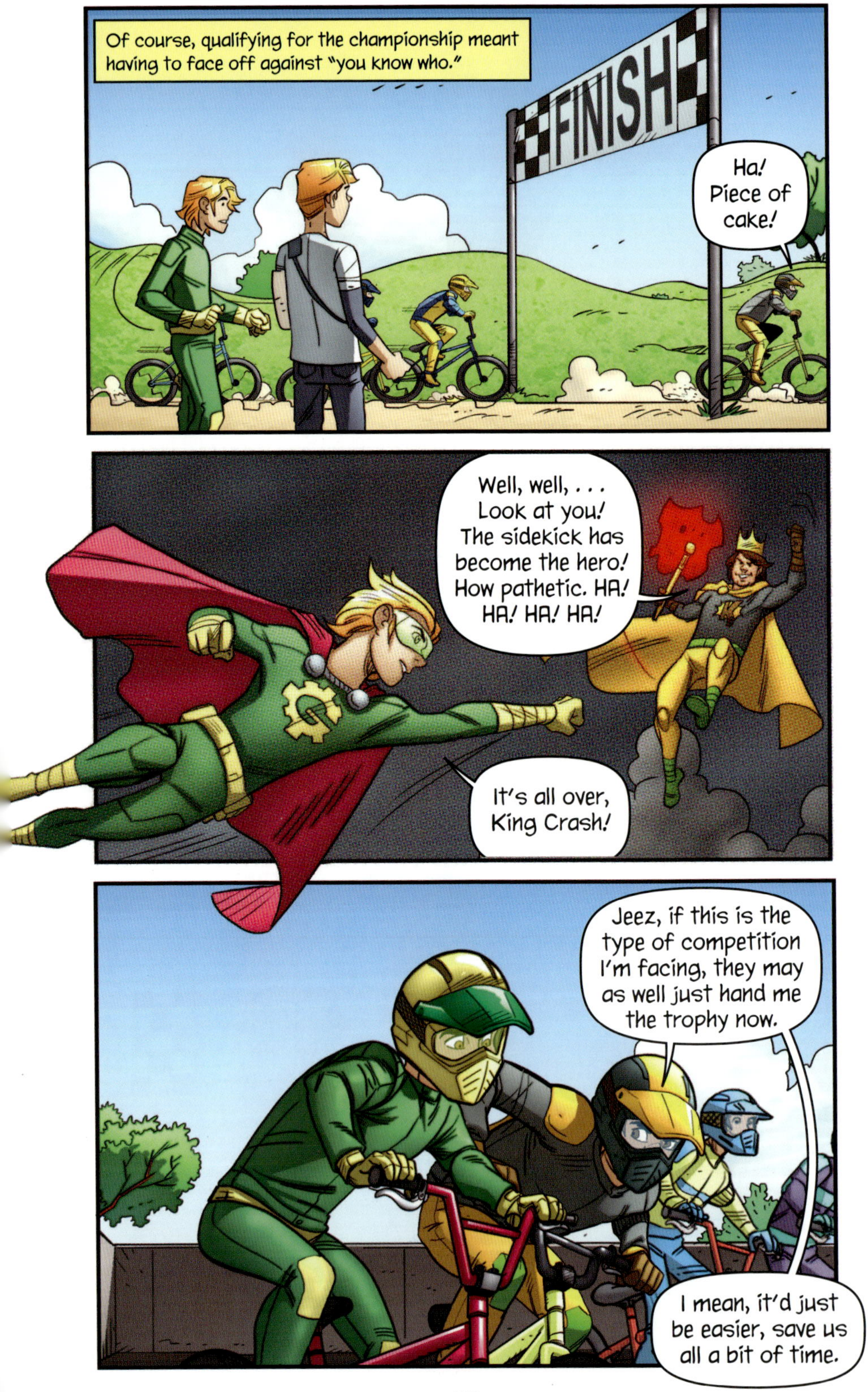
Of course, qualifying for the championship meant having to face off against "you know who."
FINISH
Ha! Piece of cake!
Well, well, . . . Look at you! The sidekick has become the hero! How pathetic. HA! HA! HA! HA!
It's all over, King Crash!
Jeez, if this is the type of competition I'm facing, they may as well just hand me the trophy now.
I mean, it'd just be easier, save us all a bit of time.

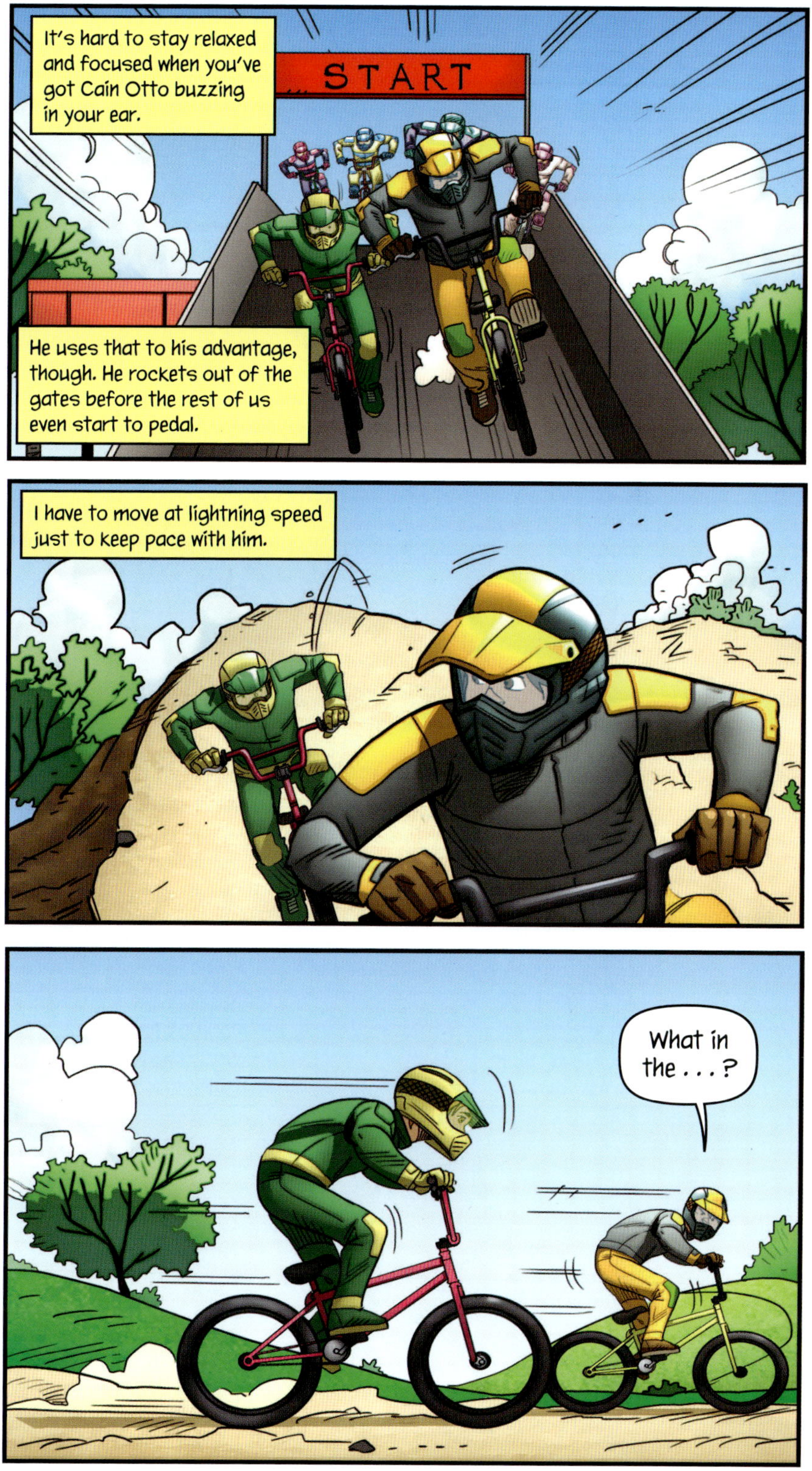
It's hard to stay relaxed and focused when you've got Cain Otto buzzing in your ear.
START
He uses that to his advantage, though. He rockets out of the gates before the rest of us even start to pedal.
I have to move at lightning speed just to keep pace with him.
What in the . . . ?

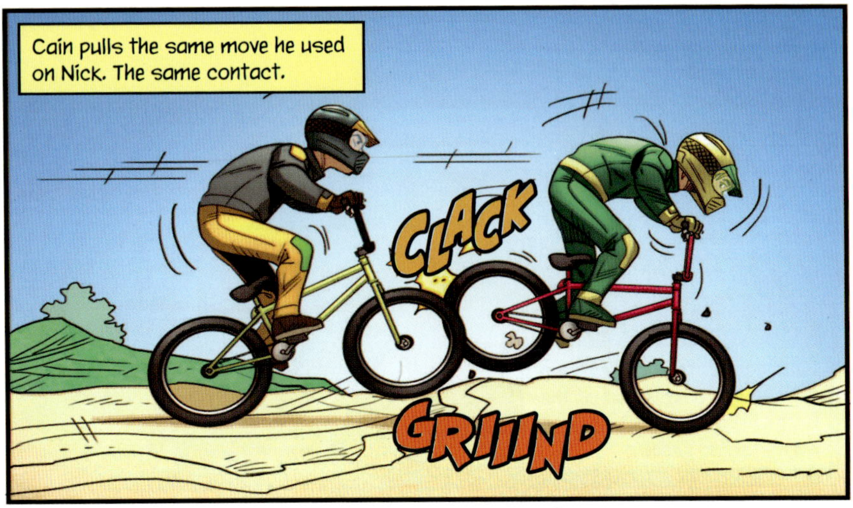
Cain pulls the same move he used on Nick. The same contact.
CLACK
GRIIIND

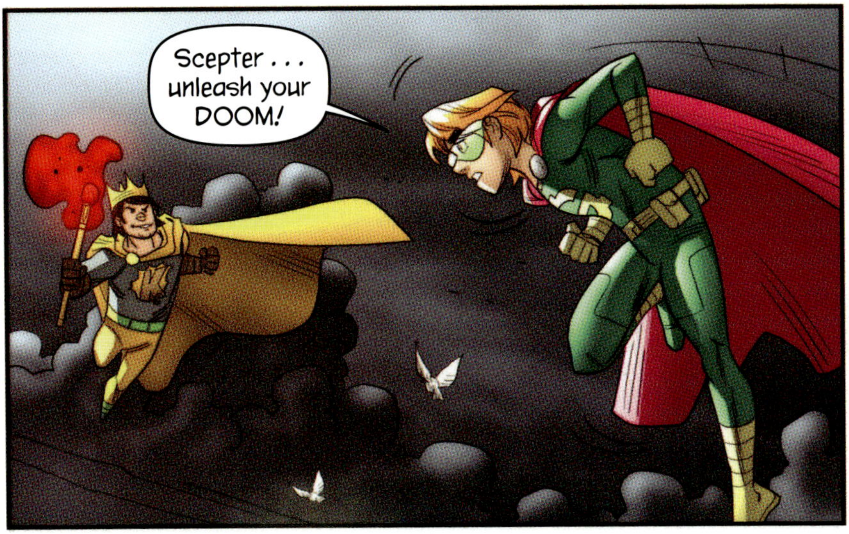
Scepter . . . unleash your DOOM!

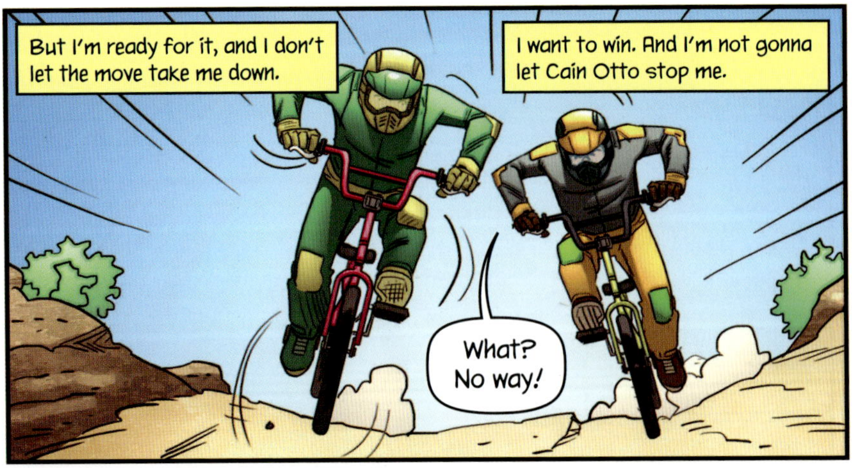
But I'm ready for it, and I don't let the move take me down.
I want to win. And I'm not gonna let Cain Otto stop me.
What? No way!

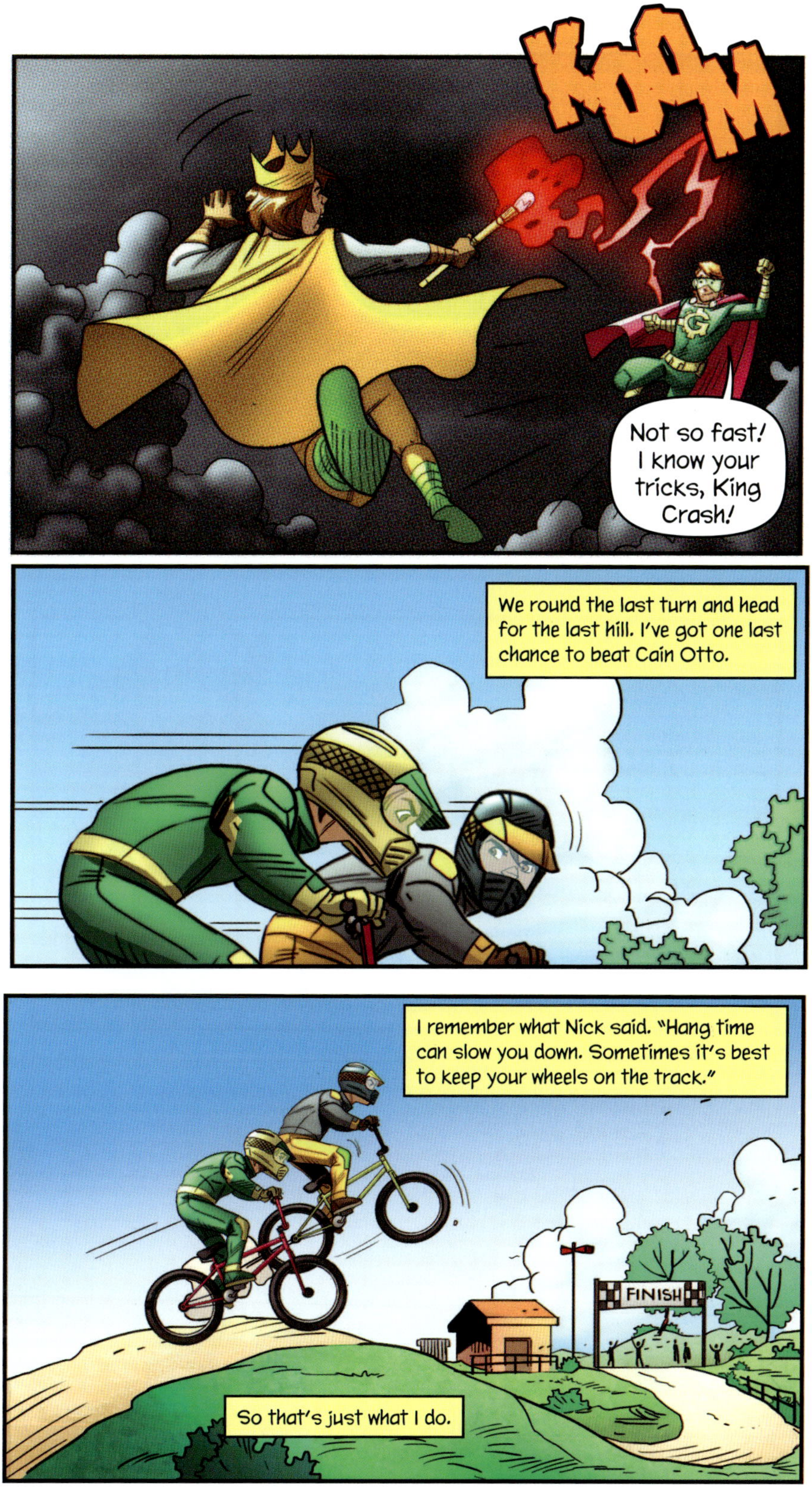
KOOM
Not so fast! I know your tricks, King Crash!
We round the last turn and head for the last hill. I've got one last chance to beat Cain Otto.
I remember what Nick said. "Hang time can slow you down. Sometimes it's best to keep your wheels on the track."
FINISH
So that's just what I do.

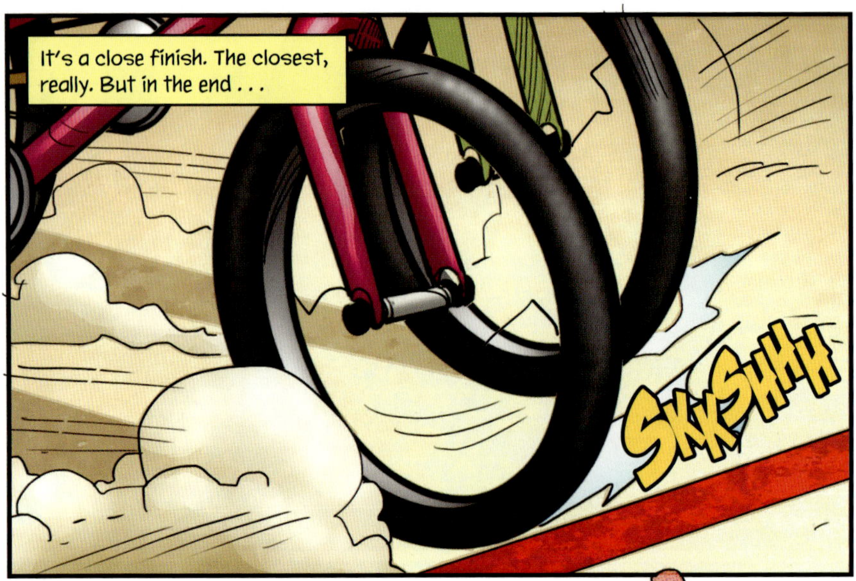
It's a close finish. The closest, really. But in the end . . .
SKKSHHH

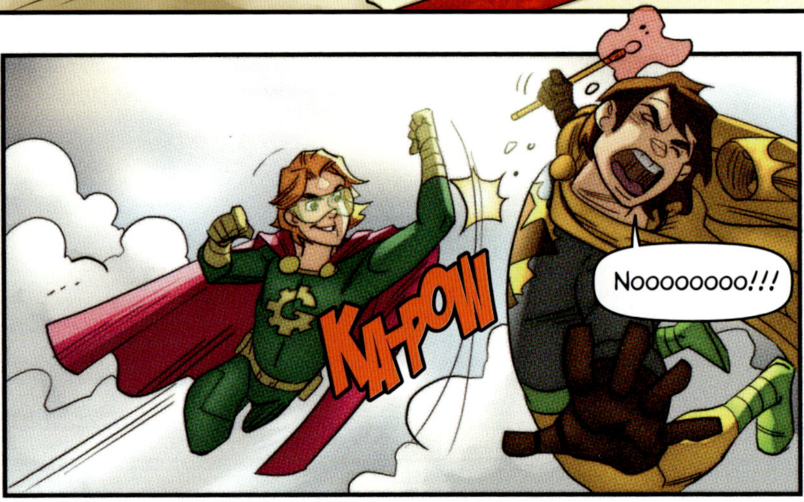
KA-POW
Noooooooo!!!

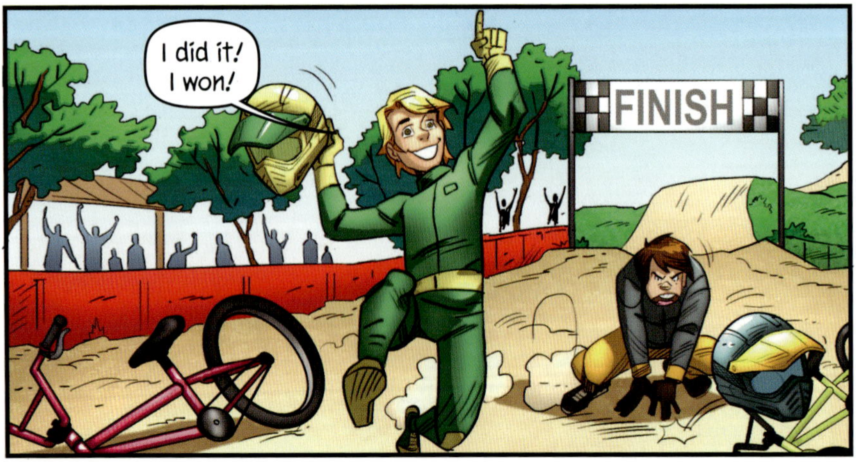
I did it! I won!
FINISH

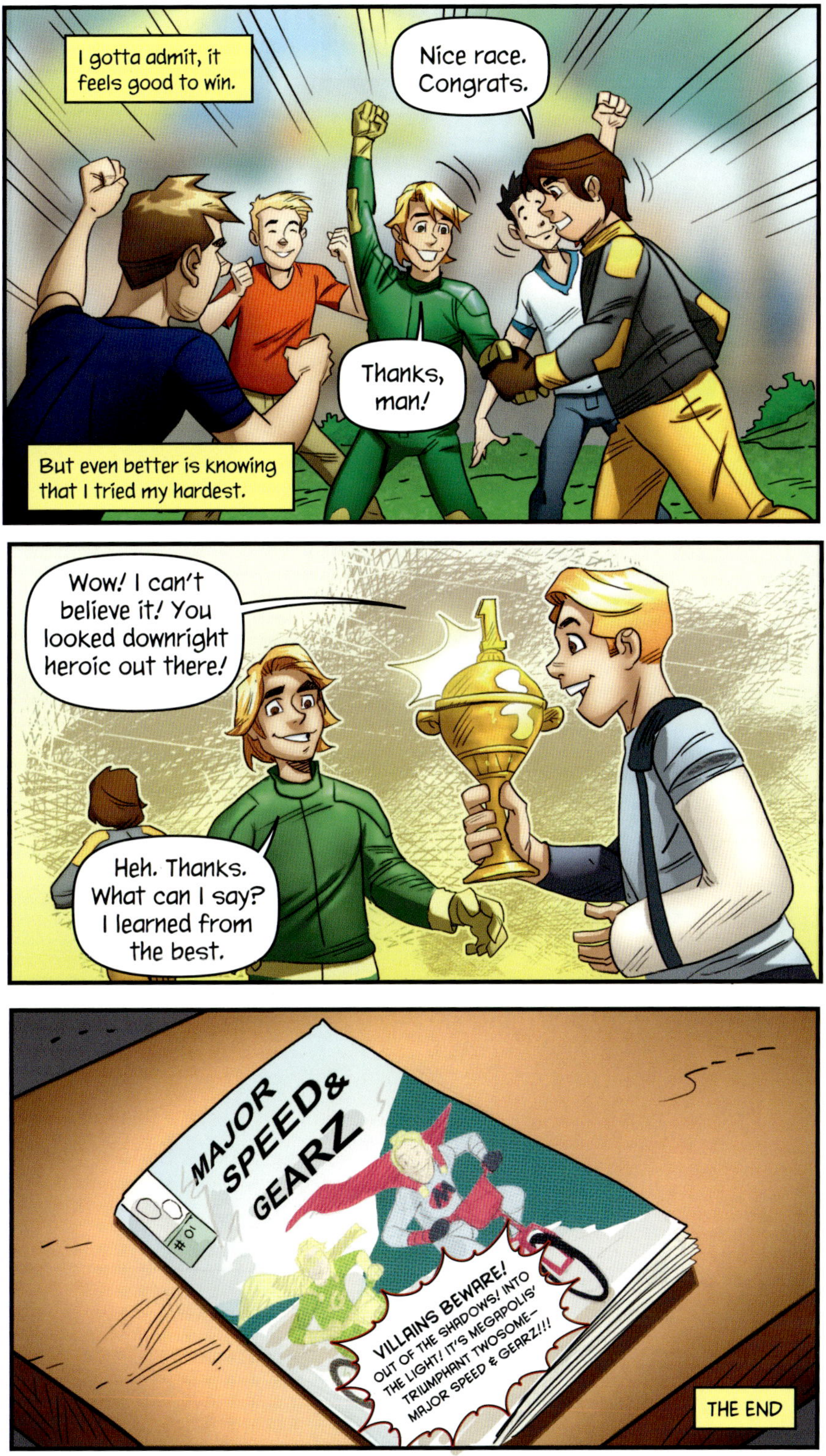
I gotta admit, it feels good to win.
Nice race. Congrats.
Thanks, man!
But even better is knowing that I tried my hardest.
Wow! I can't believe it! You looked downright heroic out there!
Heh. Thanks. What can I say? I learned from the best.
MAJOR SPEED & GEARZ
#01
VILLAINS BEWARE! OUT OF THE SHADOWS! INTO THE LIGHT! IT'S MEGAPOLIS' TRIUMPHANT TWOSOME— MAJOR SPEED & GEARZ!!!
THE END

VISUAL QUESTIONS

1. The characters in Nelson's comic book, Major Speed and Gearz, strongly resemble himself and his twin brother Nick. From the above panel, how do you think Nelson feels about his relationship to his brother? Explain your answer.

2. Graphic artists often use dramatic angles to help show what a character is feeling. Look at the above panel. What do you think Nelson is thinking or feeling in this scene?

3. Graphic art can often show what's happening in a scene without needing any words. Look at the panels to the right. Describe what you think is happening. What has changed between the panels, and why has the change occurred?

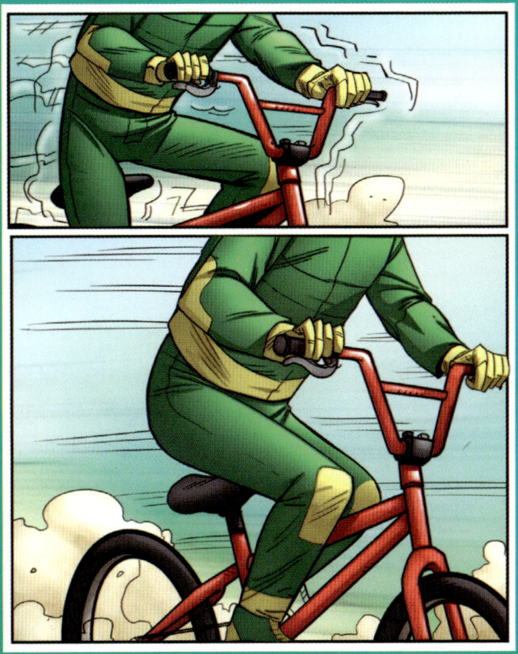

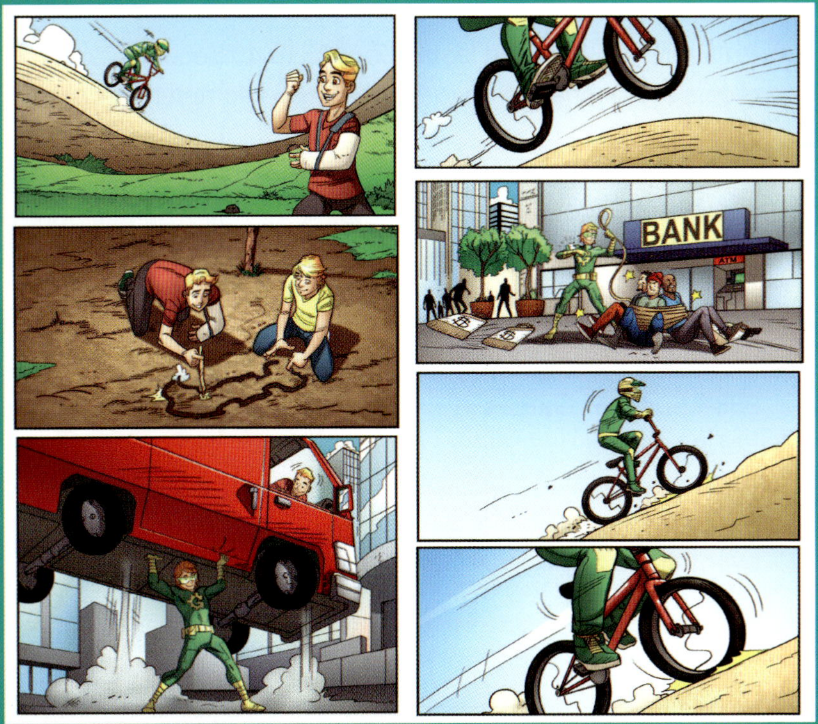
BANK
ATM

4. Sometimes a series of panels is used to show the passage of time in the story. Look at the series of panels above. Can you describe how Nelson's character grows and changes based on what the panels show?

MORE ABOUT BMX

- BMX is a cycling sport made up of extreme, motocross-style racing on tracks with incline starts and several obstacles on the course. BMX stands for Bicycle Moto Cross.

- BMX was invented in the late 1960s in Southern California. It was created because of the popularity of motocross, or off-road motorcycle racing.

- A standard BMX bike is smaller than an average road bike and has a fixed frame. It also has only one gear, which makes racing easier. There are three specific bike models: traditional, freestyle, and jump.

- An average BMX race lasts about 25 to 40 seconds, and racers reach speeds up to 35 miles (56 kilometers) per hour!

- Dirt racetracks usually measure about 1,000 feet (305 meters) in length.

- BMX is also an Olympic sport. It became a medal sport in the 2008 Summer Games in Beijing, China.

- Today, freestyle BMX is a major event at the Summer X Games.

AWESOME BMX MOVES

BARSPIN — To complete a barspin, hop your BMX into the air. Throw your handlebars so they spin while you're in mid-jump, and catch them before you land.

BUNNY-HOP — A bunny-hop is when both the front and back wheels of your BMX jump off the ground at the same time. It's used to jump over small obstacles.

FLATSPIN — While in the air during a high jump, do a complete horizontal spin on your BMX before landing.

FRONT POGO — A 'pogo' can be done on either your front or back wheel. For a front pogo, apply your front and rear brakes until the back wheel comes off the ground. Then hop on the front wheel like you would on a pogo stick.

MANUAL — A manual is basically riding your BMX on the back wheel, with the front wheel up in the air for a long period of time. Use your arms and legs to maintain your balance.

TAIL WHIP — To perform a tail whip, catch air and rotate your BMX frame once around the handlebars, which remain stationary.

X-UP — After going off a jump, spin your BMX's handlebars 180 degrees, so that your arms form the letter X. Quickly rotate them back before landing.

GLOSSARY

advantage (ad-VAN-tij)—something that helps you or is useful to you, especially in a competition

archenemy (AHRCH-en-uh-mee)—a chief or main enemy of someone, usually of a superhero character

concession stand (kuhn-SESH-uhn STAND)—a booth where people can buy food and drink

confidence (KON-fuh-duhnss)—the trust one has in a person or thing

confound (kon-FOUND)—to perplex or confuse, especially by a sudden display or surprise

deja vu (DEY-zhah VOO)—a feeling of having experienced something before

devious (DEE-vee-uhss)—tricky or clever

gallant (GAL-uhnt)—brave and fearless

grotesque (groh-TESK)—very strange or ugly

nefarious (ni-FAIR-ee-uhs)—extremely wicked or villainous

phenomenal (fuh-NOM-uh-nuhl)—amazing or astonishing

sidekick (SAYHD-kik)—a close friend and assistant to a superhero

technique (tek-NEEK)—a method or way of doing something that requires skill

READ THEM ALL!

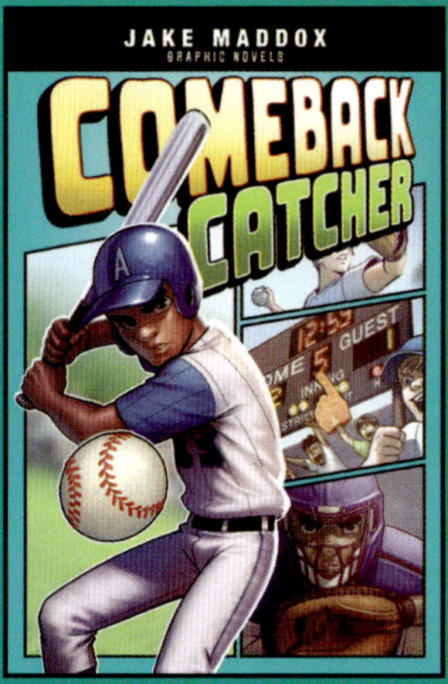

JAKE MADDOX
GRAPHIC NOVELS
COMEBACK CATCHER

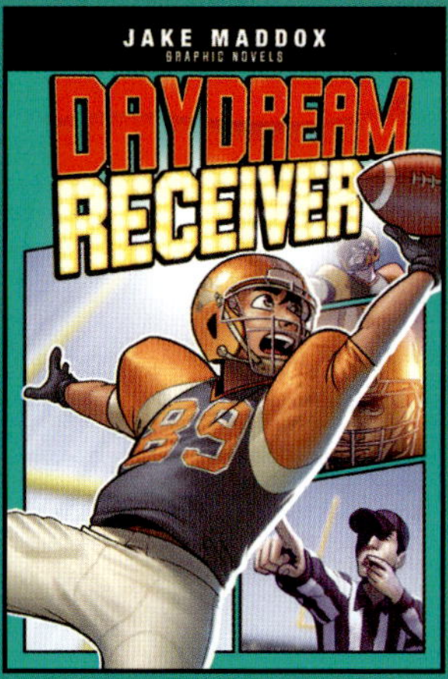

JAKE MADDOX
GRAPHIC NOVELS
DAYDREAM RECEIVER

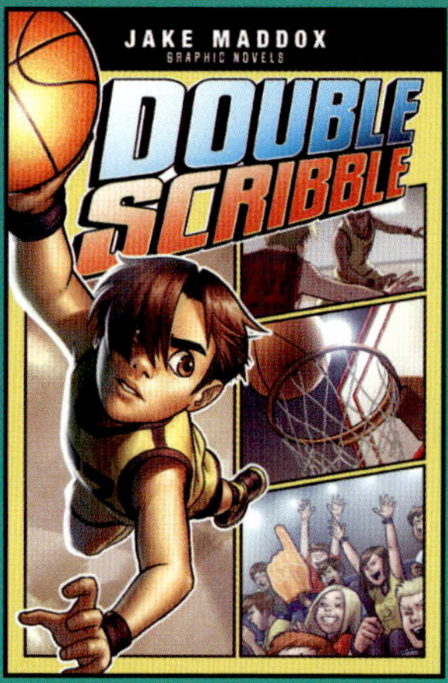

JAKE MADDOX
GRAPHIC NOVELS
DOUBLE SCRIBBLE

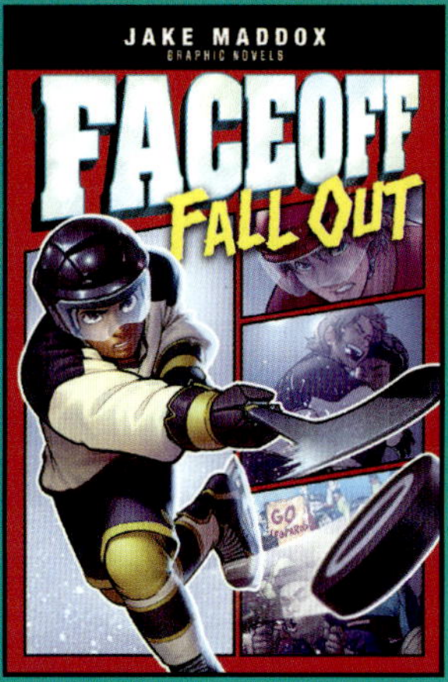

JAKE MADDOX
GRAPHIC NOVELS
FACEOFF FALL OUT

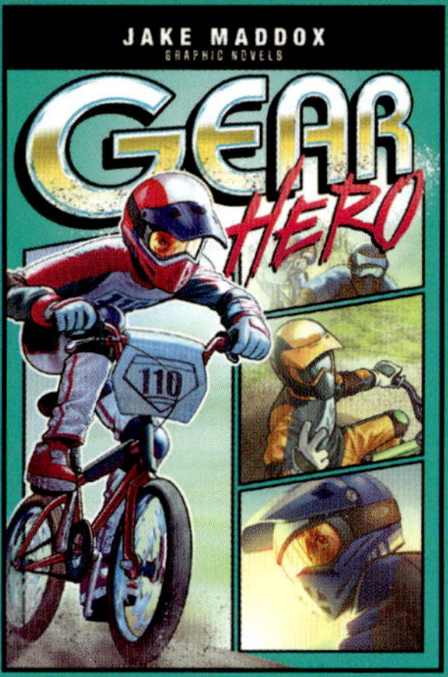

JAKE MADDOX
GRAPHIC NOVELS
GEAR HERO

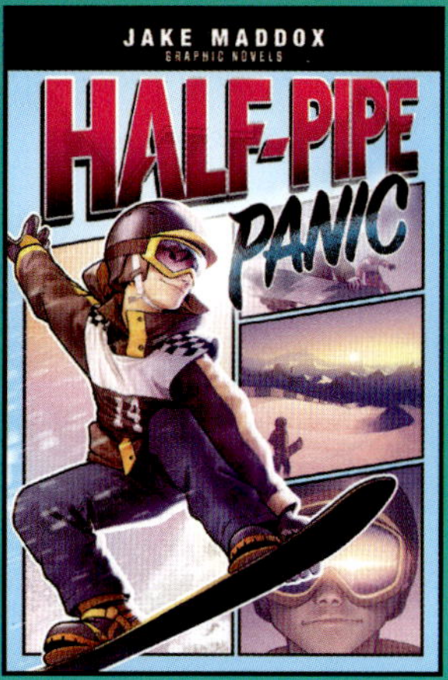

JAKE MADDOX
GRAPHIC NOVELS
HALF-PIPE PANIC

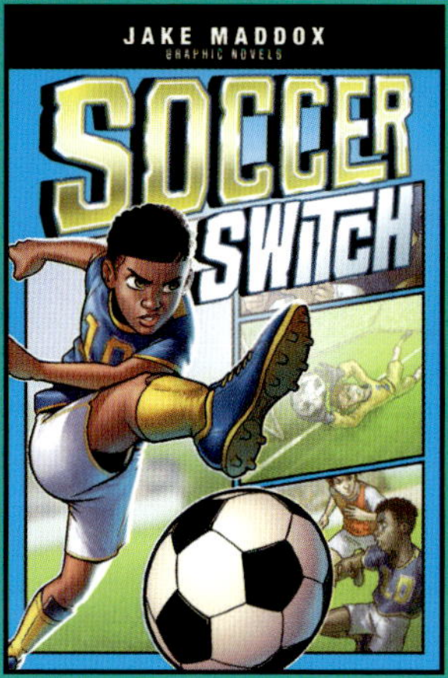

JAKE MADDOX
GRAPHIC NOVELS
SOCCER SWITCH

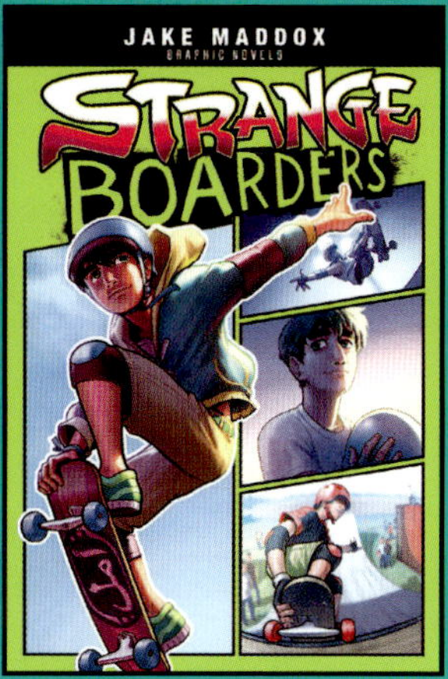

JAKE MADDOX
GRAPHIC NOVELS
STRANGE BOARDERS

FIND OUT MORE AT
WWW.MYCAPSTONE.COM

ABOUT THE AUTHOR

Brandon Terrell is the author of numerous children's books, including several volumes in both the Tony Hawk 900 Revolution series and the Tony Hawk Live2Skate series. He has also written several Spine Shivers titles, and is the author of the Sports Illustrated Kids: Time Machine Magazine series. When not hunched over his laptop, Brandon enjoys watching movies and TV, reading, watching and playing baseball, and spending time with his wife and two children at his home in Minnesota.

ABOUT THE ARTISTS

Eduardo Garcia works out of Mexico City. He has lent his illustration talents to such varied projects as the Spider-Man Family, Flash Gordon, and Speed Racer. He's currently working on a series of illustrations for an educational publisher while his wife and children look over his shoulder!

Benny Fuentes is a Mexican-based digital illustrator who has worked on several books for companies such as Marvel, DC, Image Comics, and of course, Capstone Publishers. He also works as a volunteer at a local animal shelter during his free time.

Jaymes Reed has operated the company Digital-CAPS: Comic Book Lettering since 2003. He has done lettering for many publishers, most notably and recently Avatar Press. He's also the only letterer working with Inception Strategies, an Aboriginal-Australian publisher that develops social comics with public service messages for the Australian government. Jaymes is also a 2012 and 2013 Shel Dorf Award Nominee.